CW00407810

HAUNT

A NOVEL

CHRISTINA MARAZIOTIS

HAUNT

LOVELETTING BOOK I

EXISTENTIAL
PUBLISHING
HOT SPRINGS

H[A]UNT

LOVELETTING BOOK I

Copyright © 2022 by Christina Maraziotis

The trademark LOVELETTING™ is pending registration
with the U.S. Patent and Trademark Office.

First published by Existential Publishing: October 2022

eBook, $9.99............ISBN-13: 978-1-959776-00-0, ASIN: B0BKY7ZH23
Paperback, $29.99......ISBN-13: 978-1-959776-01-7, ISBN-10: 1959776010
Hardcover, $39.99.....ISBN-13: 978-1-959776-02-4, ISBN-10: 1959776029
Audiobook, $39.99.....ISBN-13: 978-1-959776-03-1, ISBN-10: 1959776037

Library of Congress Control Number: 2022920302

This is a work of fiction. References to real people, events, establishments, organizations, or locales are intended only to provide a sense of authenticity, and are used fictitiously. All other characters, and all incidents and dialogue, are drawn from the author's imagination and are not to be construed as real.

All rights reserved. No part of this book may be used or reproduced in any manner whatsoever without written permission except in the case of brief quotations embodied in critical articles and reviews.

For more information about the author's work, or for permission to reproduce selections from this book, please contact her directly:
christina@christinamaraziotis.com | www.christinamaraziotis.com

Cover Photograph by Lee Browning Ezell & Christina Maraziotis
Editing, design, and typography by Lee Browning Ezell
Frontispiece art of Mac Kinnon by Hanna Spindel

10 9 8 7 6 5 4 3 2 1

TRIGGER WARNING

This series is a work of fiction, but it also touches upon some extremely difficult topics within its pages. It is not intended to be politically correct, but rather an examination of the very imperfect human condition. The characters are inherently morally grey, and the philosophies implied by their situations are intended to challenge the reader. So, please, continue with an open mind.

Difficult situations are often described in graphic detail. Spanning the entire series, this includes (but is not limited to) the subjects of sex, lust, vulgarity, sexual assault, child abuse, animal abuse, hunting, molestation, incest, violence, firearms, gore, torture, necrophilia, vodou, cannibalism, ritual practice, hematophagy, necromancy, self-harm, disability, post traumatic stress disorder, mental illness, schizophrenia, death, grief, suffering, infant mortality, cultic worship, possession, blasphemy, and religion.

These subjects are, at best, controversial. They are not written to be politically correct. They may also be triggering to a traumatised or otherwise sensitive reader. Being explicit in the description of these subjects is vital to the story being told, and always in a tasteful manner…but please heed this warning, before continuing at your own discretion.

"Stories you read when you're the right age never quite leave you. You may forget who wrote them or what the story was called. Sometimes you'll forget precisely what happened. But if a story touches you, it will stay with you, haunting the places in your mind that you rarely ever visit."

NEIL GAIMAN

Fear is a choice you embrace
Your only truth
Tribal poetry
Witchcraft filling your void
Lust for fantasy
Male necrocracy
Every child worthy of a better tale

WEAK FANTASY | NIGHTWISH

Somewhere in time I will find you and haunt you again
Like the wind sweeps the earth
Somewhere in time when no virtues are left to defend
You've fallen deep
I was a liar in every debate
I rule the forces that fuelled your hate
When the cold in my heart leaves it comes to an end
Quietly I'll go to sleep

THE HAUNTING | KAMELOT

Sweet is the curse of hearts entwined but lost
Detached but bound
Sad is their fate without relief
Cruel is the curse of love
So luscious yet so dangerous
Sweet curse, our hell

SWEET CURSE | REVAMP

For Lee, who wanted me to *feel.*

C. M.

PROLOGUE

"I CATCH MYSELF WONDERING, IF I'M STILL HERE — *still present. A speck of matter in this world's fickle maze, one of no particular importance. For I have already forgotten it, or perhaps it never existed.*

"The weakening of my hands' grip does not scare me no longer, for my heart has long skipped its beat, ever so often, ever so slightly. And the foreboding warning, I laugh caustically at.

"For I know as much, one day, there is no beat left, no heart to constrict a pulse, no veins to pump blood within me. One day, there will be black liquid ash, splattered across the white-washed walls; another painting of my 'solemn' being, yet this time, I'll be the one to paint it.

"Meanwhile, while I grieve in my pitiful nook of odious nothingness, I'll be holding breaths in my chest not knowing when or how to release them — for the memory fails me. A lot of memories fail me. I failed them, too.

"What have I become in those years of torment; a body with no soul, limp with no feeling; all but numbness, and you? You are still the same…A man of substance, a ghost in flesh and bone, sinews and scars to prove you're real. And yet, do you still bleed the same as I remember?

"Or, was I the only who did…"

She sighed, fiddling her turquoise stone loosely still attached to her ring. Black hat heavily shadowed her hazel eyes, its veil softly laying on her long brown braided hair. Her skin, pale against her tightly tied corset, the same old black one, now stained with muck and sin; gaze empty, directed to the wall. Bleak, beneath the frames.

The photographs, a loss to never find.

CHAPTER 1

The Desert

I

SHE FLED. IN THE MIDST OF A BRAWLING THUNDERSTORM, sweeping through Nephilim Cove, running off to the unknown void of the West. For weeks, riding on deserted roads. Lost, petrified, tracing circles around herself, riding through sand dunes, and canyons, beneath the cloud, and scorching sun, as sandstorms covered the road signs just outside of Rocky Spine Ridge, bewildering her in trickery furthermore. Crinkled map clutched in her grip, struggling to read it, comprehend it, in failed attempts to orient herself in all her inexperience, she rode further towards the nearest town.

Her face still lingered within her mind, unable to forgive herself for letting it come to that. Eyes of menace and aversion that haunted her all her life, suddenly turned pale, glazed with serenity she perhaps longed to feel in all her weary demise, cloaked in ominous grace she never had.

Death; its face revealed to her at last, not in an expectant gaseous instant form, yet in an unflattering brutality, oddly leaving her with an eerie coldness in her heart, as though the loss of her mother was but a relief, as though death was meant to not stir any emotions, as though her heart wasn't taught how to break for someone yet.

There was an odd relief to not have to endure the years of psychological turmoil, nor to witness her mother's decline, as if death was something she carried within her all along, creeping up in her soul, in the sin and the filth she clung onto. Tangled, stubbornly, bound to rot in it.

She was young. Yet twenty-six years too old. A blend between inexperienced naïvety and acquired wisdom. It took that long to suck in one final courageous breath to make a life-altering decision; to free herself. From her. Her words. Scared, yet brave enough — or perhaps stubborn enough, at best, to travel through unknown terrain — begging to sink into a trap within Great Desert Basin's vast potential for an untimely demise.

Her mother warned her about the West, enforcing the idea that nowhere was safe enough for her to escape to — imprisoning her furthermore, for her own needs. Her own selfish motives. She'd always crack a grin on her face, one of dark amusement and satisfaction, watching her daughter crawl back into that hollow room with the packed saddlebags over her shoulders. Crushed.

Yet since her death, there was nothing more tying her to her hometown, for her mother was the sole reason she had remained; petrified to disappoint her furthermore, and yet disturbed to leave her alone, knowing her mind had deranged, clasping the edge of Hell, or rather Hell clasped her all along.

She kept her hand hovering over her dirty old revolver — one she barely knew how to even use, let alone disassemble to clean. Scanning around herself frantically, barely shutting an eye every night, she crossed vast stretches of cacti and sweltering sand, rotten brush and drought cracked rivers, traveling beneath star stricken skies with gloomy clouds swallowing her shadow whole. Names of gunslingers echoed in her head, for she'd seen them back in that mucky hometown of hers. She'd seen what they had done to women and children. The romantic notion of riding out west, and settling down, was long gone, she thought, riding further, halting at a sign; it too was covered — a thick layer of sand, dried up in sparkling specks.

Head bowed back down.

Cougar's Tooth, it read on her map.

A town of chaos, its only force keeping it together was its marshal, Patrick Tilghman — the one respected marshal in the entire state; feared by outlaws and gangs, as he was well known for his cold-heartedness to uphold order in this town. Deadly efficient in his use of power; were someone to disobey him, chances are they'd disappear too in a blink of an eye. Ruthless, yet awfully charming. So her mother always said.

II

"WE ARE ALMOST THERE, BOY." SHE SIGHED OUT LOUD, gently patting the horse's burgundy neck that was dripping down with white foamy streaks of perspire. "I can already see the windmill...so I believe, the town will be right after this hill, and then, we'll be able to rest some without having to worry about anyone killing us in our sleep..." She snorted sardonically. "Well, perhaps not you, for you're too pretty to be killed, my love." Her hands lowered the reins, letting them rest on the saddle horn; her braided ponytail swinging back and forth, following the movement of the horse's hindquarters climbing up the hill. Back arched, stretching for some comfort, neck tilting left and right, feet hanging loosely beside the stirrups, trying to regain some feeling in her benumbed legs.

It was a strenuous journey, riding through the desert under the hot beaming sun. A desperate fool would only attempt this, her mother always forewarned — and yet, perhaps she was right for once.

Trotting into town with great anticipation, envisioning a soft tidy bed, and a dark room to provide some shade and escape from the scorching heat — for the sun was burning down their necks for far too long, and the thirst had been building up for the last hours — they both sighed in great relief. They licked their lips simultaneously, trying to hydrate any cracks, only to make them worse.

Cougar's Tooth was a good place to restock on canned supplies and have a refreshing drink at the saloon. If you were a man, that was. It was peaceful, yet lively, considering how desolated it appeared — nothing compared to the desert's silence, traveling with no sign of life around. The general store offered a wide variety of dehydrated foods, such as meat jerky or even fruit, as well as handmade ponchos to help stay cool under the sun — albeit, none of that she could afford.

"Here, sir." she said to the stable boy, clinging onto her horse's reins until she felt comfortable enough to entrust him with it. "He'll need a good brushing and some fresh hay; land's been too dry to graze on, and...well, he has a long journey ahead of him. Please, do offer him a few carrots, and you can

3

add that to the bill as well, sir." she ordered the stable boy, now allowed to grip the reins and lead the big chestnut stallion into the barn.

She always felt uneasy trusting her horse to others; horses were considered livestock, a mere form of transportation — not a lifelong partner you trusted all your belongings and life to, as they carried you through rocky terrains and steep cliff sides, battling ambushes and predators with their shield of a body.

Finn was different to her; he was all she had.

"Where ya headed, miss?" A robust voice startled her. None other than Marshal Tilghman's, as he shouted at her from the inside of his building, rocking on his chair with a polished star shining bright on his modishly tight vest. Eyebrows cocked with judgment, studying her clumsy movements as her exhausted legs struggled to walk. It was unusual to have travelers come through, let alone a young woman with a piece of metal on her hip.

"Traveling north." She sighed sheepishly, with a tremble in her voice that betrayed a white lie.

Tilghman was a giant of a man; brawny, well-muscled, equipped with all sorts of silvery bling-blings she could not identify, intimidating in every aspect, and every word someone spoke could be held against them if possible. He was smart as a whip, and wasn't fond of strangers, or people in general for that matter. Luckily he did have a soft spot for helpless women, or anything pretty-looking, really. This alone would fool the smartest of men, it seemed.

"I have…family expecting me near Birdsboro, sir." she added, after taking a sip of water from her refilled canteen, swallowing down her lie with ease.

"Mhm…family, is that so?" He smirked, amused, as somehow he didn't believe her.

"Yup…family, indeed…" She bobbed her head, slowly tearing her gaze away from him. He was charming, she briefly noticed, from all she could see in shadow.

"Mhm…good for ya then, ma'am." He smiled with a shiny golden tooth — placed two teeth to the right of his front — unable to not fixate his gaze on her body as he did. "Stayin' here for the night?" he then asked, and she swallowed down a knot.

"Yes, sir…but I will be heading out at dawn." she said, and he nodded.

"Alright then…keep your eyes peeled; there's lots of evil, and it don't show no mercy to no one." He pointed with his silver Lemat revolver to a prisoner in his jail, who was barely hanging onto the cell's iron bars as the flies devoured his sunburnt skin. "Have a good day, miss, and a safe trip." He winked at her and proceeded to light up a cigar, his eyes still nailed on her, somehow more polite and intrigued than usual.

"Thank you, sir." She tipped her hat to him, gifting him a smile, and walked hastily towards the wooden shack she'd rented for the night.

I I I

FINN WAS RESTED; HE GREETED HER WITH A PLAYFUL NEIGH as she walked into the barn, flapping his velvety lips at her as he did. She wrapped her arms around his strong muscular neck, letting her fingers rake through his mahogany mane, while his soft muzzle was nibbling ever so gently at her long wavy ponytail. The stable boy had him already saddled up, tethered to a post, and thoroughly brushed from head to toe; he even sneaked some fresh carrots into the saddlebag, as he took quite a liking on Finn — after all, he was a very respectful stallion, who always sought attention with his loving and comical personality.

Leading him out of the barn, she halted briefly beneath a lantern, still dimly illuminating the world around her, for sun hadn't risen yet. "Alright… so…Boomtown is further that way…" she muttered to herself, letting her finger slide across the map.

"Marshal! I saw the coyotes!! Got ma chickens!!" A man's shrill voice hit her ears, followed by another one, a lot deeper and robust.

"Yes, Earl…What else is new? Every goddamn night there's a damn coyote at your place! And I don't even need to know 'bout it!" the marshal fussed to him and she blinked awkwardly at them, able to see one large silhouette and one more of a midget in comparison, slowly advance towards her.

"But Marshal! I always have to alert the authorities of the town!!" the man spoke again and she suppressed a chuckle; somehow it appeared comical to her.

"Goddammit, Earl…don't ya have church to go to so early this mornin'??" he grumbled, and tore his gaze away, absently locking eyes with her. She froze, petrified, yet was unable to pull her glare away, and neither was he, until Earl tugged on his shirt to her rescue.

They left Cougar's Tooth in haste, at dawn to avoid the sun for a few hours. Galloping across the desert, through brush and cacti. Roads were empty, and the whole world was at their feet. Finn wasn't fond of the desert reptiles they would come across; known to spook at the smallest of threats, yet would have no issues trampling over an entire pack of wolves if he needed — to which she prayed, it wouldn't come down to that.

Covered in a dusting of fine desert sand, they finally arrived in Boomtown. A graveyard would appear more inviting than this illness-infested town. People laid there, unresponsive outside the buildings — someone would have to poke them with the rifle to see if they were still moving, yet nobody dared, nor cared to. They were just a number for the coroner to write down in the books, just another rotten body to dispose of. Some were grunting in harrowing pain, others were emptying their guts in the alleyways. Corpses were laying in freshly dug-out holes just outside of the town; not bothered to be covered or properly buried. There, death ruled more than life; even the air was ominous and vile.

Finn, who was studying the people as they passed them carefully, would flare his nostrils, pin his ears, and paw at the ground as if to warn her. A snort with every stride, as the fragrance of a death rattle stirred the arid air.

"Easy, boy…" She soughed, brushing a hand across his neck. "We won't be stopping here…just passing thr…" A loud crash interrupted her; shards of glass spread throughout the air in front of them as time froze still before her gaze. The sound of a deep, blood-curdling growl alerted her, as a large mass, draped within a dark cloak followed right after through the saloon's now shattered window. Upon closer inspection, it was a man that slammed against the ground.

Finn reared up, frightened, for the man landed right in front of him — creating a whirlwind of a blinding sandstorm around them. His eyes dilated, aghast, ears set forward, neck arched curiously as he reached to sniff the man's body lying before his feet, covered by the thick air as the dust had yet to settle.

The man, upon lifting his head, locked eyes with Finn and startled at his significant presence hovering right over him — for his intoxicated mind made

Finn appear horrendously distorted, he stumbled over his leg, failing to get up, landing back on the ground again. The man, flustered, dug his hands in the grimy soil, lifted his body up, and the snapping sound of his knee forced him to let out a hesitating groan, making her jolt and clench her teeth in compassion. He brushed off his duster coat, picked up his leather hat off the ground — brushed it off as well against his chest. A black leather hat, with two loops of dark brown rope coiled around it.

She cleared her throat nervously, and his gaze nailed at hers, locking eyes through the golden haze and the sudden eerie silence that engulfed them.

"What yer lookin' at?" He scowled, clasping his hand on his knee.

"I said, what yer lookin' at, lass?!" he growled, now in embarrassment, pointing his finger at her with a faint threat. A thick irish accent escaped him, and all she could do was blink, for now she realized the furious man was referring to her, since she was staring at his bloody face, busted lip, and torn-up vest.

"My apologies sir, I was just…passing by." she mumbled worriedly, eyes dropping at the double holsters attached to his belt. His fists were clenched tight, and lips quivered in rage. He bowed his head, feeling his breath suddenly come in shallow gulps. Then turned to face her with a frown, in bewilderment. His brows snapped together in fury, and his mouth cracked open to scowl again.

"Good. Now, git!" he gruffly said, turned his back away, and limped towards his horse that was hitched in front of the saloon.

Finn pinned his ears and snorted at him.

Rude, Finn must have thought.

"Don't ever come back here, ya son of a bitch!" A throttling voice followed right after, with a balled fist shaking frantically through the window; a face busted open, drooling of blood, as the saloon owner hid behind him, shaking irrationally, wilted into a ball of fear.

The man shoved his boot into the stirrup, hopped a couple times, and mounted his black, blue-eyed steed. Spitting out some blood to the side, he squinted his eyes in great discomfort — feeling the sudden pain shoot right through his leg, he collected the reins in a hand as his other held onto his knee cap steadily. He pressed his spurs into the animal's sides, and not long after, they galloped away — leaving nothing but a storm of dust behind.

Who knows what went on in the saloon; usually, Boomtown is sluggish and hauntingly tranquil. You couldn't pay someone to even consider staying there for longer than it took a drink to gulp down. The curiosity was nagging her, but even more so, she was appalled by this man's ill-mannered demeanor. After all, it wasn't her fault he made Finn spook like that.

CHAPTER 2

Controlling Fear

I

THE DESOLATED DESERT WAS LONG BEHIND THEM, NOW. Riding into the wilderness of Kitunaha, she could finally embrace the freshness of the gnarled trees — tall and primeval, reminding just how much wiser they were than herself. Richly colored leaves brushed against her face as she weaved her way through. Lithe branches whip-lashed against them, almost in a foreboding manner, for the woods of Kitunaha bore secrets of their own.

The subtle sweetness of the wildflowers — a burst of colors, yellow and purple, gently luring them out of the woods — and as they pranced through them, a wave of prickling wind crystallized all the blooms in front of her eyes. And there, through the empty gap between two ironwood trees, the sinuous, fertile meadows of Caledonia Territory laid out in the near distance. She smiled in a sigh of relief.

Finally, you could walk through the spring-grown grass, which was utterly irresistible to Finn. He proved to be a handful to ride that morning; for the relentless gush of chilled wind encouraged him to feel frisky and trot a buoyant stride, lope all his pent-up bucks out, and behave like the stubborn yearling he still was in his mind — and yet she couldn't blame him, for alone the sugared grass he nibbled on was as if he had forgotten what it tasted like after so many days in the desert.

They had reached Caledonia Territory, and were headed to a town called Bisonhorn, named after the spiritual belief in the animal symbolizing both survival and safety — as the town was inhabited by both the elite and common settlers from the West, both starting new beginnings in a fresh land of opportunity.

Finn's saddle cinch had worn out, it was essential to replace it to continue the journey, and this town carried the finest selection of handmade saddles, and other useful tack this side of the Mississippi River.

"This cinch is woven from the finest mohair; it's durable, lightweight, and flexible — it will take you aaaaanywhere you please, and will give your horse the comfort it deserves. Four bucks and you got ya self a deal, lady!" the man said, excitingly offering her with a steady wink upon his lazy eye, and waved the cinch before her own eyes enticingly.

You didn't have to do a lot of convincing, as she would give any money in the world for this horse — if she had it, that was. She was a smart woman, but when it came down to Finn, she would lose her sense real quick.

The town lit up its lanterns as evening approached. From townsfolk walking on the sidewalks, couples visiting the inviting looking theatre, or the weary retired photographer still busy across the street — it was alive at night. A nostalgic feeling overcame the excitement of the new cinch, as her eyes wandered around her.

"We don't have time for this now, do we, Finny boy?" She patted his neck and continued leading him around town. Trying to suppress any wishful thoughts that may have arisen, suddenly she noticed some posters hanging on the walls, with a very familiar face printed on them. She rode closer towards them.

WANTED

FOR MURDER, ESCAPE, ROBBERY

MYRIAD ATROCITIES AGAINST MAN

SACRILEGE IN THE EYES OF GOD

OFFERING $25,000 CASH REWARD

FOR CAPTURE OF MAC KINNON

VALID BOTH DEAD OR ALIVE

LAST SEEN IN SPANISH PEAKS

She looked at the man's eyes and recalled the same hollowed eyes looking back at her. With the chiseled jawline, the cleft chin, and the stubble beard — even covered in blood, you could not mistake this admittedly attractive face.

"That rude, rude man!" she yelled loudly in disbelief. "I told you, Finn, he was an odd stick!" She pointed at the poster, as if Finn would be able to read it.

She hitched her horse and marched to the sheriff's office with the poster clasped within her fist, ready for her vengeance. Knocking frantically on the door, a man showered with gray hair and wrinkles cocked his brow at her upon snarling the door open.

"Sheriff, this man! This man right here was last seen in Boomtown! Last seen by Finn and I! I mean...by me, in the very front of the saloon! Covered in blood and dirt and sand and had a limp and..."

"Slow down, miss! Slow down! Ya mean to tell me, ya captured *the* Mac Kinnon?" He chuckled derisively, glancing over at her womanly frame, with the holster wrongly attached around her belt. "Is he...tied up on your horse, madam? Or perhaps...kept at Boomtown, at the sheriff's jail?" He grinned tauntingly, spotting Finn munching on the wooden facade of his office building.

"Yes, sir! I mean, no sir." she stammered awkwardly, as she realized she seemed, and sounded, like an utter fool to him.

He looked at her confused, puffing on his cigar — blowing the earthy scented smoke at her face through his crinkled nose.

"Which one is it, miss?" he asked, irritatedly.

"I saw this man...Mac, right in front of me in Boomtown. He was in a bar fight, I assume, or perhaps drunk? I ain't sure...but he was thrown through the window right in front of my horse. He made my horse spook, this rude man, he did! Ugh." She paused to take a deep breath, as the frustration made her forget what actually happened; meanwhile, his eyes widened in shock, and his lips shook with an eerie thrill of excitement. "I did not realize he was a wanted man, so I let him go, or rather said, he...well, he made the decision for me..." She bowed her head and shrugged her shoulders in exasperation, then noticed the sheriff twitch his mustache nervously upon lifting her uncertain gaze up to him.

"Kinnon...out in civilization..." He snorted. "Can't be possible, lady...

the man's been in hidin', for too long now…" he muttered to her, as the cigar sat loosely between his lips.

"Sheriff, this was the man I speak of!" She shook the poster before his eyes. "I ain't gone crazy yet…" She noted, almost doubting herself, as perhaps the desert had messed with her mind.

"Alright…let's assume so then! Which way did he go, ma'am?" He started walking towards the deputies, slinging his rifle around his back in haste.

"Ehm, I think…" her writhing arm lifted north.

"This way, boys! We got a hint for our dear boy, Mac! Buckle up! We're gonna have a hog-killin' time!" he ordered them excitedly as he swung his leg over the saddle. "Ma'am, I'd lay low, was I you — this man ain't to be meddled with. If ya really was the last person he seen, he'll make sure to drop ya out of sight." He warned her earnestly, as he realized she was indeed rather young and innocently ignorant.

"Oh, I ain't afraid of no man, especially him." She hinted briefly at her holster, pretending to be stronger than she felt. The deputies burst out in laughter, and rode past her — demeaning her without a spoken word needed.

"What's your name, ma'am?" The sheriff chuckled at her frown, as he adjusted his necktie, now trotting on his way out.

"Charlotte."

I I

BISONHORN'S DOCKS WERE OCCUPIED BY FISHERMEN early in the morning. The butcher was skinning carcass after carcass, and deputies would make the rounds in town after the news of the outlaws' appearance had spread like a wildfire. Charlotte couldn't help herself but think about Mac Kinnon, and how he got away so effortlessly — twenty-five thousand dollars would have changed her life situation quite a bit; if she could've caught him alive, that is. Mac wasn't a man of puny size; his broad shoulders, large wide chest, and arms that could wrestle anyone, somehow stuck within her memory, as faint as it was. She reminisced how his duster coat shaped against his small waist and how his muscular back eyed her menacingly, as he walked away from her.

"No question about it, I could have shot him right then and there…darn me." she fussed through clenched teeth — realizing she had never shot a man before, thinking it surely wouldn't have been so hard to do.

Living on the road was no easy life for a woman; besides all the dangers, she dreamed of a better life for herself and Finn — and money; money simply seemed to change everything. She sighed, looking at the townsfolk dressed in pretty long dresses, matching their elegant teardrop hats. Flourishing skirts of all colors, corsets that accentuated the women's shapes, and dainty heels that echoed all across town as they walked so eloquently through it.

*No telling how much they paid for this…*she wondered, as she looked down at her torn-up pants, hiding the tear with the palm of her hand — in shame, as if anyone could see it.

III

THE SHERIFF AND HIS DEPUTIES HAD ARRIVED IN BOOMTOWN late the night before; interrogating the whole town of "walking dead" regarding the where-abouts of Mac Kinnon. "Tell us about that varmint Kinnon, from the day before." The sheriff leaned over the bar, staring right at the saloon owner's face — following the quivering of his mouth, demanding a swift answer out of it.

"He…he…was having a couple sh…sh…shots, a…a…and…he…he…" A deputy banged the owner's head with his revolver before he could finish his sentence.

"Boss, we ain't got time for that! Speak loud and clear, you peasant!"

"He dr…drunk and and B-Big E recognized him, he started to br-brawl, but w…was too…drunk to…" the man stuttered in immense fright, protect-ing his face with his shaking hands, as he kneeled down before them, begging to not get hit.

"This ain't helpin' us any! That much is obvious! Where did he head to??" the sheriff angrily demanded, grabbing the man from his shirtfront.

"N…n…n…north!" he exhaled with every fiber of his being, keeping his eyes shut, his teeth clenched, and his head tilted away from them as his sweat dripped down his chin.

IV

STILL DEJECTED FROM THE ORDEAL WITH THE SHERIFF and his deputies after they had moved on, the saloon owner looked over at the corner of the bar. Big E was leaning forward on his elbows behind the old poker table, creating the illusion of a small breakfast nook due to his sheer hulking mass; though there was space for twelve grown men to play around the circle.

All the owner wanted to do was put this mess behind him as much as he could, while still holding a cold slab of meat against his head to combat the repeated offenses of gunmetal striking his head, time after time at the hands of the law.

He was still in far better shape than Big E, though; he had been sitting at that table, ever since the night before on a record binge of utter depression — even by his standards of "days off".

Every Friday for the last decade, Big E was the undisputed champion of the saloon's illegal bare-knuckle boxing ring, as he'd never lost a single match. The bets against him never printed, but he was certainly a draw for aspiring fighters and gamblers to bring at least some money into the long-forgotten town.

He knew the story he told the sheriff wasn't true, as Big E was even meaner drunk than he was sober; in fact he'd never fought without being at least three sheets to the wind anyway. So even the owner couldn't understand what happened that night, and curiosity got the best of him.

"What *really* happened, E?" the owner asked, as he finally sat down next to the champion. Big E looked up at him with bloodshot eyes and let out a groan as he laid his throbbing head back down on the table.

"Saw a 'legend'…felt like stompin' a mudhole in his ass." He sighed with a gurgle, and a burp for good measure. "Couldn' touch 'em. Little bitch shoulda' been cake. Couldn't land nothin', Hell…he knew what I'd do before I did." He actually started to tear up, amazing the owner even more than the fight itself. "He was gonna *kill me*, bud. Nothin' I could do but push him off me…lucky I did…sorry 'bout your winder, but I don' care ta fight no more. I'm done."

The owner swallowed down the lump in his throat in greater dismay than

the brush with the law could ever have caused, because his entire family's live-
lihood in Boomtown was already hanging on by a thread — and that thread
was called Big E.

V

FINN WAS PRANCING IN THE PADDOCK BESIDE THE BARN, where he was stalled
for the day — utterly excited to be, for there were mares in the distance. Big,
stout, well-bred, Thoroughbred mares, grazing in the wide open, so he would
neigh and paw, and throw his head around, arching his muscular neck and
look back at them to capture their reaction. A reaction of nothing more than
pinned ears and squeals, which only upset him further more.

"Silly boy, it will take a lot more than that to get a lady's attention." She
chuckled with his silliness, and climbed up on the fence, mucky boots shoved
within the gaps.

"He is a *fine* specimen…" A man strode towards Charlotte, while his
eyes examined Finn's vibrant mahogany color, his asymmetrical yet perfectly
placed white stockings sinking deeper into the mud the harder he pranced
around. His toned muscles and swollen veins illuminated by the harsh sun,
emphasized all the more by his long smooth strides.

Charlotte, startled, looked at the man standing suddenly behind her —
almost slipping off the wooden board, by the swift way she turned towards
him. "Thank you, uhm, sir…" She halted her breath, when she noticed his
dignified and fancy attire — making her wish he was blind, so as not to see
her pitiful condition. "He is…my pride." she added, embarrassed, tucking
her loose shirt within her roughened pants. She wasn't used to talking to
strangers; and certainly not to the elite of high society, as he appeared to be.
Bisonhorn seemed a busy town, too hectic for what she was accustomed to.

"William Griffiths." He bowed his head, reached his hand to her with
an endearing smile on his face, as his pocket watch that hung from his vest,
swung towards her as well. "But, if I may, and it is not too bold of me to ask,
please, do call me, Will, my lady." he said and she blinked, almost terrified.

"Charlotte…" she mumbled faintly, and reached for his hand tentatively.

He clasped her palm gently and raised her hand up to his lips to kiss. Her face fell, and her hair stood erect — shone by the early sun's light, for a man's lips had never touched her skin before, and it rather prickled and goosed it.

The dark-haired man with the sharpest pencil mustache, tidy, taut across his upper lip — and with no hint of alcohol or food remains atop it she was more accustomed to seeing, stared at her in awkward silence, as if shy himself. She tore her gaze away from his, aiming it right back at Finn, as if Finn would come rescue her from the elitist creature she didn't know what to do with.

"Miss Charlotte…" The creature spoke again, and she almost choked. "May I ask, what brings you here in Bisonhorn? For I suppose, if it is not too rude of me to declare, I would have noticed you before." He smirked kindly, still clasping her intense hazel eyes within his mind.

"Oh, you would've, huh?" She cocked a brow, the snide words spurting out of her mouth involuntarily, for sarcasm was all she knew. His brown doe eyes blinked at her in response, and swiftly, a lump of embarrassment clogged her throat. "I'm just passing by…I'm leaving the town this evening — headed north to find some work…hopefully, that is." She cleared her throat, meanwhile thinking of all the work she wouldn't qualify to do — besides riding and talking to ponies.

"Already, miss? That is certainly a shame…" He folded his arms, disappointed, as ideas stormed in his mind.

"Yes…yes, indeed. Well…I uhm…"

"I am familiar with a place of utmost decency, that is seeking for a hired hand if you were so interested, Miss Charlotte…For I can't ignore the vigorous character you so elegantly portray, for you appear like the kind of lady that might enjoy the art of 'wrangling', for better words, horses, if I may assume such." He smiled again, that rare smile of kindness that perplexed her, noticing his eyes glance down to her riding boots — weathered, with a loosened heel shifting off its place as she walked. "It would be such a delicious scheme; and I dare say you would find yourself greatly accommodated at the ranch." he said and she suppressed a laughter.

"…delicious?" She gaped at him, and he bobbed his head in earnest.

There was a sudden breeze that interrupted them; picking up leaves off the ground, whirling them in the air. Some elderly wanderers were setting up camp nearby, with a warm stew already brewing — herbs of thyme and oregano were tingling their noses, and the tastes of flavors suddenly flooded in their mouths. A flock of ravens flew over them, stretching their enchanting onyx wings, as if they'd encourage them to fly with them.

"I truly apologize, kind sir…I have to saddle him up and get to it. Albeit, I will consider the offer…" she said, trying to find the words to meet his level of speech, and before he could form a sentence, she spoke again. "It was a pleasure meeting you, Tim!" She then rushed to the stable, with the bridle in her hand — shutting the heavy gate behind her, disappearing into the barn.

"Entirely mine…and, it's Will…"

V I

THE WATER FELT SO SATISFYINGLY COLD AGAINST HER MUDDY SKIN; after weeks of traveling, Charlotte could not afford a luxurious bath in town and the constant itching of dirt feasting at her flesh had gotten unbearable. The river was every bit as pleasant, though, and the strong currents would wash away every stain on her body. She un-braided her long hair and scrubbed it between the rosy palms of her hands, laying on her back, spreading her arms wide open, and floating on the surface as she watched the hawks fly over her — blocking the sun for a split second to gift her some shade. Armies of bluebirds and cardinals flying in from the south danced around her, and she observed their vibrant feathers in awe.

Sweetwater river was crossing the Kitunaha territory, Caledonia, and the Freelands region. It was a popular fishing spot for bluegill and trout, and any fisherman's wildest fantasy.

Charlotte didn't have the best experience with fishing, but she did carry a bamboo fishing pole with her — just in case anything was dumb enough to bite all her insufficient bait. She didn't grow up around a father figure to teach her how to hunt or fish, not even how to shoot a gun to defend herself. Her father was just a client; a client with no name or face known to her, as her mother was a working lady in the alleyways of Nephilim Cove. Eventually, succumbing to her fate. Shot, dismembered, and discarded in the woods of

Red Giants, found dead by her very own daughter.

Charlotte would cast the line, and untangle it from branches of trees behind her; she would twist her body, hold the line with her trigger finger, and release it while she cast again. She would wait a while and pull when she felt the line resist, only to drag up a bunch of seaweed and startle Finn as she did.

"You're one scaredy-pony, Finn!" She laughed as he snorted once again, bending his body away from an intimidating slimy yellow monster.

"Oh, how I wish this would go faster…" She sighed disappointedly as she absently flicked the pole, watching the fishermen up ahead, catching fish after fish and hanging them on their line.

"Canned beans it is, then!" She impatiently collected her line, and secured the pole on her saddle with a loose strap of leather, her gaze drifting off to the pebbled sand. Dreading to feel her stomach rumble for the rest of the evening, starved.

"Miss Charlotte!" A familiar voice emerged behind her, and she gasped with a startle.

Charlotte turned after looping the leather piece through the buckle of the saddlebag and faced him, baffled. "Sheriff?"

"How are the fish treating ya this fine morning?" he questioned her, as he noticed the piles of seaweed lying pitifully around her.

"Can't complain…" She forced a kind smile, hating to admit any failure; particularly to him, after his deputies were mocking her the other evening.

"Terrific. So tell me, miss…" He sniffed and twitched his grey mustache. Dismounting his horse, the whole saddle shifted, and the bay-colored steed re-adjusted to catch its balance. The sheriff was rather frail; much worn down by this line of work. He had a steady limp, but carried himself proudly — he should have been retired by now, but seemed to enjoy chasing after outlaws instead.

Charlotte was leaning against Finn's saddle, interested to hear his words further.

"…they said Kinnon was headed north, same direction ya was headed to." He cocked a brow, and her jaw slacked.

"Oh — you do not think I have anything to do with this scamp, sir?" She interrupted him in great annoyance, raising her voice respectfully.

"Whoa, ma'am!" He motioned with his hands, confused with her defensiveness. "Quite the opposite; we was thinking of some way to…" He paused, glancing over at the fishermen luring in their fish. "…to lure him in."

Charlotte was quiet, confused, and her mouth could not make a sound. Even fishing suddenly made more sense than this.

"Ya see, ma'am, Kinnon is a smart fella…he ain't foolin' round leaving no trace behind. There are no campfires, no remains we can track; he is changing clothes, perhaps cutting his hair every time he crosses a border to a new state. He's been a wanted man for over a decade and has changed many faces and personas. A new identity every time, and our trail goes stone-cold…if ya could even say we had one to start with." He patted Finn on his cheek, and turned his head to face Charlotte. "We need your help, madam." he hummed urgently, as her eyes dilated in shock.

"Wh…what do you…"

"Twenty-five thousand dollar reward; all yours, if ya can lure him in for us — ya won't have to waste a bullet on him, ya won't have to do nothin'." he promised, as he wanted to be the one to capture him alive in blood and flesh. Charlotte's head spun around, her gaze trailing off to the woods behind them, feeling so lightheaded she almost could see a face imprinted on the bark. "He's headed north…been old scuttlebutt for a decade now, that he's been seen in that ol' two-horse town called Marysville — drinkin' with a chap of his. Quite risky, if ya ask me…yet, we've never been able to catch him, and ol' Mickey disputes the accusations…naturally." He brushed his mustache with a gaze of sudden hatred, the more he thought about it. "There's a high chance that he'll pay him a visit again. He hasn't been 'round these parts of the country in many a year…and he'll know if we're 'round, but he won't suspect ya." He kicked the seaweed back into the river, as he drew in another breath. "Ya can visit the saloon owner — don't care how ya do it, but keep a low profile." He looked her in the eyes, expecting her to shake his hand to seal the agreement. "Question the chap…find out what ya can, and if *he* steps inside…just leave from the back door, and notify the town's sheriff."

"What's the catch?" She shifted her weight on her leg, pressed her fingers against her head, and exhaled a deep worried breath held in for too long.

"The catch is…controlling your fear."

CHAPTER 3

The Glove

I

CAN YOU BELIEVE THIS NONSENSE? Why, oh why, did I ever agree to this! I'm not even capable of shooting a rabbit properly, and now I'm supposed to go on a wild goose chase to locate a gunslinger, a…wanted murderer, so he can eventually be shot dead, or captured alive?" She paused, stealing a quick look at her surroundings, making sure no one heard her. She leaned over Finn, and stroked his neck nervously. He let out a deep breath, and kept on trudging lazily through the thick woods of the Pine Hill Forest. "Oh Finn, I should've just gone with that weird, fancy fella's offer…how was he called again?" She titled her head back with a frowned brow, trying to recall his name. "Wrangling horses don't seem so risky now, compared to dealing with… outlaws — however, I could never dream of making that amount of money as a ranch hand… probably get kicked in the head while trying." She reminisced that one time Finn kicked at her when he was just a naughty young colt, as they both learned the language between horse and man.

She snatched the hat off her head, and waved it in front of her face anxiously. She slammed her eyes shut, and gave the reins to her trusty steed to take her to the town of Marysville. There was just one road leading there, night's ebony cloak had draped the whole world around her, and she was mentally exhausted with worry spiraling within her before her "assignment" had even begun.

II

"TWENTY-FIVE THOUSAND BUCKS FOR OUR DEAR GRINGO…" The man grinned, as he passed the poster to his gang members. "Headin' north, he is…" He stroked his goatee, intrigued, after hearing the rumors from the gossiping almost dead, almost alive townsfolk of Boomtown.

"Winter'th thuppothed to be bad, both…" His man warned him, as they were riding towards the Rockies West mountains — hoping to stay ahead of Mac Kinnon, for they were certain he had the same idea of laying low in the most secluded area known to man. "Hunterth died rethently from avalan-theth!" he added with great worry.

Now the man paused in his tracks, sending a menacing glare of immense irritation. "An avalanche won't be the thing killin' ya, amigo, if ya don't shut your goddamn toothless mouth right now!" he leered and pointed his dual revolvers at his head, while his sharp eyes evaporated the misty chilled air before them. "Now, let's get…the gringo won't be expectin' us in them mountains…" he chuckled eerily, as he imagined the sweet smell of freedom sure to be handed over to him by the government, with immense gratitude to have the elusive Mac Kinnon hang in exchange. "After-all…I do want that Winchester 1887 back again." He smirked playfully, urging his mule to climb up a snow-capped rock wall, as his men steadily followed right after into the treacherous path before them.

III

MARYSVILLE WAS OTHERWISE KNOWN AS MUDTOWN, since the streets, buildings and residents were seldom clean — even the tick-infested dogs tried hard to avoid walking in the soupy roads. Nevertheless, it was a hard-working town, where cowboys and herders would bid at horse and cattle auctions, often resulting in a shootout with the slightest disagreement. It was certainly a good place to start snooping around regarding Mac; at least, that's what the sheriff intended.

"Did you have a good night, miss?" the hotel owner spoke, as he heard Charlotte's boots trudging down the squeaky stairs.

"Oh yes, I slept like a rock! Thank you, sir. I really needed a soft bed to rest my worries for once." She chuckled awkwardly, suddenly feeling herself get anxious all over again by the thought of her assignment.

"Oh, how wonderful I could help! Hope you'll enjoy your stay in Marysville, ma'am!" He put his glasses back on, after cleaning them with a piece of cloth.

Although Marysville was quite the muddy mess, it had lots of unhurried and tranquil life to it. Carriages, wagons, and riders on pack horses passing through, elders entertaining themselves around a poker table in the saloon, simple townsfolk shopping at the general store or having a jabbering talk along the sidewalks. Young men working in construction, with a cigarette in one hand and a hammer on the other. Everything felt real, it felt genuine, and it was the closest thing that could make Charlotte feel like home, for Bisonhorn, albeit enchanting in its own way, was a town where a lady with no means could not survive for long.

She was once again running low on supplies, so she visited the general store to restock on some canned food after counting the coins in her tiny leather pouch, nervously, over and over again.

"Howdy, ma'am!" the store owner greeted her with the biggest smile on his face, as he leaned over his desk — waiting patiently to assist her.

"Howdy!" She smiled back, matching his level of speech — a lot simpler than the elite creature's. Fiddling the coins within her sweaty hands, she sheepishly advanced to him.

"Anything I can help you with, miss, you just let me know. We have a great selection of clothing that you can try in our changing room." He pointed to a wooden door right next to some hanging wolf pelts that served as decoration.

"Oh, thank you, but I'm…I'm just here for some canned beans and salted meat…if I can afford so, that is." she murmured, casting a swift glimpse at the brand new pants. "Do you…do you happen to have these? My apologies, I'm new to this town." she then asked.

Charlotte could not afford any new clothing, as she counted every penny to make ends meet for survival. Her mother had kept a hidden stash of money in the attic, she later discovered while looking for a gun before starting her journey — perhaps neither of which combined would be enough to pay for a pair of trousers, were she to sell it.

"Sure, sure we do." The man reassured her, jolted in excitement from his seat, and walked towards the shelves with the canned food — proudly showing her his wide variety. He loved taking care of his customers, let alone travelers, and he made sure to leave a good impression of his store, and while he talked a lot to newcomers, he was a kind man that lived vicariously through their stories.

Charlotte was grabbing can after can, when accidentally she dropped one on the ground, missing her boot by an inch. The man, without giving her a chance to apologize, reached down to pick it up. He noticed her torn up pants right above her knees, that seemed to have been patched a multiple times already. His gentle heart sunk, and his smile slipped within his thick, disheveled beard.

He supported his weight with his hand on his leg, and stood up slowly in awkward silence. "Ma'am, I would like to offer you a welcome gift — it's a... it's customary of my store to do so, with new visitors — yes, it is." he spoke to convince himself, and walked past her to the corner of his shop where all sorts of pants were hanging. A selection of saddle pants, made with a rugged denim cloth to last for an eternity and withstand any hard work.

"Levi's jeans! All the way from Mon Louis's renowned tailor! These are a new addition to our shop, and our customers have been quite pleased with their quality! Made for men; but in secret, adventurous women such as you if I'm allowed to say, find equal utility in them, of course!" His big smile returned to his aged lips.

"Sir, I cannot possibly accept this gift; I could never afford this..."

"Shh shh, miss, I insist. Pick one you like, and I will give you some privacy to try it on. But I'd recommend the smallest size, for these are...well, for men." He led her proudly to the changing room, handing her a bundle of jeans. You could hardly see Charlotte's head while she was carrying them to the room — in subtle but great excitement as she went.

After a while of him waiting in great anticipation to see Charlotte's reaction, she walked out, shutting the door behind her as she did, with her new pair of jeans on — embracing her fine waist and accentuating her curvy hips.

"That looks excellent on you!!" he exclaimed enthusiastically, trying to lift her spirits, and her cheeks crimsoned.

"Thank you…so very much, sir." She grabbed his hand and squeezed it in hers, trying to hold back any emotions, as she was left in awe with the unexpected kindness she received from a mere stranger.

IV

THE WAVES WERE KISSING THE ROCKS HARSHLY, and the moon was lighting the narrow hidden pathway of the cliff as the wind blew through the pine trees that were guarding it along the way. The sparks of the campfire were brushing against his worn-down leather boots, the orange light reflecting on his gently spinning spurs.

He was wiping his hunting knife clean that still had bloodstains from his recent skinning — a whitetail buck carcass strapped onto his horse, that would feed him for the upcoming weeks. He tilted his hat over his face, took a last sip of whiskey, and squeezed his body between the cliff's boulders. Trying to rest for a few hours, with his cocked and loaded rifle entwined within his arms.

V

"AARGH!" HE GRUNTED, AS THE KNIFE CUT THROUGH HIS FINGER.

"Haha! What's wrong, Tommy? Are ya losing your fingers over there?" The bartender mocked the man, trying his luck at five finger fillet on a rusty scarred table in the corner of the room. The man grumbled and ignored the remark, resuming back to his game.

"What can I do for ya, miss? Which poison are we havin' tonight?" He leaned over the bar with his fingers tangled; a cloth over his shoulder, ready to prepare Charlotte a drink.

"I would like a whiskey, please." she ordered, still distracted by the man's self-destructive knife skills — as well as impressed that he would serve her.

"What brings a pretty lady 'round these parts? I'm surprised you'd want to visit a town full of dumb, drunk, stinkin' cowboys." He laughed while wiping down the counter, and then handed over her drink.

"I actually quite like it here, I must admit…" She smirked, causing a subtle dimple next to her full lips. "I'm surprised you allow women to enter here, let alone order a drink; I hate to complain, but the other saloon forbade me to enter, so… that's why I'm here, bothering you now." she added, twisting her glass of whisky on the counter, taking a quick sip — exhaling the burn she was quite accustomed to, for besides a stash of money and a gun, she also found an old bottle of whiskey in the attic that nurtured her along the journey by making her forget the feeling of starvation.

"Oh well, ya know, bunch of backwards milksops over there — no offense, but unless you're a working lady…chances are you're stayin' outta there." He glanced over at Tommy, who had fallen asleep on the table with the knife comfortably stuck in between his fingers.

"None taken, sir?" She tilted her head, waiting for him to reveal his name.

"Mickey!" He pressed a hand against his chest, bowing his head before her.

"Mickey…" She cracked a smile on her lips, for his kindness radiated across the whole saloon. "I rarely have a drink, but today…oh God, today I really felt like I needed one." She sighed upon an eye-roll, insinuating she was troubled.

"Sorry to hear! That surely will take care of it!" He grinned as he happily poured some more poison into her glass. Charlotte giggled, feeling herself strangely comfortable around him, as his infectious smile and undemanding aura warmed her up instantly. "You're travelin' alone?" he questioned her, watching her swirl the liquid in the glass.

"Y…yes…" she hummed tentatively, as she suddenly remembered why she was in the saloon to begin with — supposedly to rob this man's kindness and hospitality. She cleared her throat. "You see… I'm being followed by a wanted man…" She leaned over the bar counter, locking her hazels with his. They flickered with the candle light beside them, and all he could do was get lost within them. "…and I'm so afraid…traveling, all on my own…" she soughed to him, trying to entice him, hoping for him to betray some information.

The man couldn't help but lower his gaze at her lustful lips, wetted from the drink he just served her, and felt instantly hypnotized by her almond-shaped eyes looking directly at him. He wilted — slowly, steadily, like the delicate new branch of a tree gently bending.

"I wish someone could let me know if this man is roaming this town… as I can't keep an eye shut at night…" She looked around and back at the man, sliding the wanted poster across the counter towards him — her mouth remaining slightly open after it posed the question.

Knowing how to act seductive was the only thing she learned from her mother while she had to watch her "work" up her clients as a young child, and the alcohol surely accomplished its own evil, as it worked well to loosen her up and rid her from the embarrassment that otherwise would hinder such an act.

In total confusion from the sudden change of Charlotte's tone and gesture, the man swallowed nervously and looked down at the poster — pouring himself a drink, as well. "… Ma'am, I…"

"I know I'm probably…asking the wrong man; I just don't know who to trust around here" She crinkled the corner of her mouth into a pout, disappointed, and locked eyes with him again. "…and so far you seem the most intelligent out of those…milksops…" she whispered, noticing him stare at the poster with a troubled face; a face that could hide a raveled story.

"Listen, miss. I'd advise ya to…"

The door slammed wide open behind them; Tommy woke up in startled panic, almost falling off his chair, as a gang of five cowboys stormed inside, bringing the chilled wind with them.

"Mickey! Mickey, my boy! Would ya please pour us some whiskey, will ya!" A man with half a tooth still attached in his mouth instructed orders to the bartender, while reserving a table for his fellows.

"Sure thing, Butch, but I don't need no trouble here again, got it?" Mickey warned him, pushing the poster — suspiciously, protectively, back to Charlotte's hands.

"Oh, but we would never…" The sarcasm brightened up Butch's greasy face as he kicked a chair away from the table and flopped himself into it.

Charlotte quickly hid the poster underneath her coat. Frustrated at the loss of opportunity, she grabbed her drink and chugged it down.

"Sir, I have a pony waiting to be fed at the stables, I'll be back another day…perhaps…we can talk then?" She gave a hopeful look, gently tucking a loose strand of hair behind her ear.

"You're welcome anytime…" he mumbled, concentrating on the following thoughts as they escaped his mouth. "Ma'am, please don't…"

"I'll be back…" she interjected abruptly, forcefully winked at him, trying to still remain in character, then rushed on her way out of there, as she could smell the dangerous fumes of intoxication already lurking in the room — fumes that were all too familiar.

While she was shutting the door behind her, Charlotte caught one of the men's eyes. There was a sudden grin scarring his face, a sick grin of dark amusement, and after patting Butch's shoulder, he stood up swiftly. Already drunk, bumping into the chairs, he shuffled on his way out to follow after her.

He belonged to the O'Donnell's Gang — with Butch being the notorious founder and leader. They were outlaws, mostly of Irish descent. Ruthless, filthy, and never hesitating when it came down to murdering innocent men, women, and children — yet the gang's founder was closely related to the town's sheriff — therefore, his crimes always found a serendipitous reason to be swept underneath the rug.

"Madam! Oh, maaaadam!" he called after her with a sickly flirtatious tone in his voice, as he sped up his stride obsessively.

Charlotte felt a knot in her throat, her chest rose, her pulse thudded at the crease of her neck and her breath cut within her lungs. She immediately reached for her gun, and paced faster away from him. The town had gone quiet, apart from the pianist in the more popular saloon, and the drunk gamblers singing along the tune as they raised their stakes on the table.

"C'mere ye pretty thing; if you're woman enough to drink, you're woman enough for more…" He laughed caustically, a distant, vile laughter, and started running after her, sinking in the mud and stumbling over his own legs, while the squeaking of his leather holster was the only sound that prevailed the closer he advanced to her.

The images of drunk men forcing her mother into despicable acts came flashing through her mind. Tears started coursing down her face, for suddenly, nothing mattered anymore. She felt disgusted with herself for fooling around with the bartender over a damn poster, and now this — running from a filthy cowboy in the middle of the night with her brand new Levi's jeans that were covered in mud. Already knowing and fearing what was bound to happen to her, feeling her stomach twist in woeful agony.

Making a sharp turn into an alleyway in hopes of reaching the back of the hotel, the entrance to her safety, for him to lose sight of her, for this vile man to disappear once and for all — sadly she realized, she found herself in a maze of darkness and trash scattered around. After twirling around herself in a desperate hunt for a door, she lifted her gaze and the man surprised her, waiting lecherously at the end of the alley.

As her legs wilted beneath her, cramping and paralyzing into a state of freezing panic, the man launched to her, and tackled her to the ground. He grabbed her hands in his fists, covered her mouth with his greasy elbow, pressing her head against the muddy ground with a vicious force. Charlotte started screaming and kicking the sides of his body — yet he was too drunk to feel, too strong and heavy to move.

"Feisty thing, are ya? Let's see what ya have hiding here…"

He climbed atop her and pressed his body against hers, freeing his hands and coiling them around her tender neck. She could not move, could not make a sound, slowly choking by his menacing grip.

"Come on! Give it a lash!" he nagged, enjoying the sensation of her squirming body underneath him, in utter helplessness.

Trying to reach for the cold metal on her hip with the last ounce of vigor within her, while he was unbuttoning his foul-smelling pants after tearing her shirt apart — she started getting weaker; her body was giving up the fight, her eyes barely able to stay open, tilting her head away as if this was her last way to fight — her last symbol of resistance.

Then suddenly, she felt the air shift. She heard a wing-clopping of a large bird shoot out from above them, smelled a strong fragrance of smoke, and felt drops of a scarlet liquid showering her like rain.

"Arghh!! Sssonn offf, aaaarllllhh!"

The man's grip slowly loosened around her neck, his voice, now a groan of agonizing harrow, his speech a slurred, unfathomable buzzing in her ear — spit and blood came flushing out of his mouth, dripping on top of her bareness. Charlotte felt the shock slither through her, as she dared to look back at him only to notice a thin rope looped around his neck, digging deeper and further into his flesh.

She did not realize yet the turn of events, thus was trembling still in panic, wishing she had never gone to the bar, wishing she had never agreed to such a hideous assignment, wishing for the suffocating air to swallow her whole and end her suffering already, as a wave of woeful regret washed over her, while the rope tightened ever deeper.

A covered face appeared behind the man's strangled neck, briefly halting his lethal grip on the bloody rope to examine Charlotte's condition. Her eyes flared, aghast, slowly realizing why she was still able to breathe.

Swiftly covering her exposed body in shame, while he tossed the dead man to the side effortlessly, he reached for her hand with his — all but a single finger dressed in a black leather glove. She dithered for a moment, for all she could see was a black bandana wrapped around his face, and a faded raven duster coat buttoned up until his neck.

"Th...thank you..." she stammered, barely audible, as his sharp eyes paralyzed her even further. He remained hidden in the darkness, still and collected into place, as his eerie silence surrounded her — his hand still held out firm for her to reach.

"Bill!! Where the damn hell are ya!" The Irish accents emerged from a distance. Now Butch and his boys were wandering around suspiciously, yet annoyed, for their fellow gunslinger to have disappeared so suddenly. "Bill, ya damn bastard!" Butch yelled, inspecting every alleyway they passed.

Charlotte's fleeting breath increased rapidly, for their voices now thudded in her head, advancing to them by the minute. She started to shake, eyes hunting around herself frantically — watching out for their silhouettes painted distortedly on the walls.

"Shh..." The man placed his finger on her lips, and motioned with his hand for her to follow him. She swallowed dryly and nodded to him, now in compliance for he had saved her life after all. They sneaked together through the alleys with muffled movements; him jumping swiftly over broken-down fences and helping her climb over them, keeping his eyes away from her bareness as he did. Hiking up the stairs to the barn's loft, they crouched in slyness and waited in the shadows.

Charlotte, unable to grasp her own condition, let alone the man's strange attire that obscured his identity, nervously she slashed the silence with a question,"Wh…what are we doing now, sir?" She sucked in a stutter, noticing the fresh bloodstains on his coat.

"Shh!" He muted her swiftly, still crouched by the window.

Charlotte hid behind some moldy hay bales, adjusting her torn-up shirt in the attempts to cover herself up more modestly, for no man had ever seen an inch of her skin before, and even though she was almost choked to death, she felt ashamed to appear this way before his eyes.

The man was quiet. She could barely hear him breathe. Even the rattling of rowdy rats and the snores of sleeping pigs beneath the loft were louder than him. He moved like a shadow, as if able to take the shape of any object beside him and morph into it, in utter stillness.

She watched him, dumbfounded, observing the stranger as he slung his rifle around his shoulder to his chest, getting into position to look through what seemed to be a half-damaged scope. The swell of his arm flexed the moment he lifted the heavy gun, and as he looked through it, he slowly exhaled and locked his breath within himself.

He was following the men with it, like an eagle eyeing its prey from a distance, observing every step they took, when suddenly Charlotte reached for his rifle and lowered it with her hand.

"Just…just because he hurt me, we should not kill any more…sir." she suggested kindly, while her eyes traveled to his finger slightly touching the trigger.

The man looked at her with his thick dark blond brows raised in confusion, as if he had never heard a dumber thing before. Suppressing a derogatory snort, he lifted his rifle back into position, completely disregarding her wishes, until her quivering voice interrupted him yet again.

"No! Stop! Please!" she shouted a little bit too loud for the delicate situation they were in, all the while pulling on his coat frantically — waving the barrel in all the wrong directions.

He rushed to her, covering her mouth with a large gloved hand, throwing a sharp glance back at Butch to see if he noticed, as his face halted inches away from hers — with his gun pointed as far from her as possible.

"I'm sorry…" she whispered worriedly behind his strong hand, feeling his warm breath escape through the cotton wild rag. She was emotionally drained and unable to make sense of anything. She sat back in promised silence and unbearable shame — exhausted, cold, and staring at the stranger who was not flinching, not leaving from his vantage point of the men.

"The boy probably got lucky tonight, for once! Let's head to camp." Butch shouted, spat on the ground and mounted his chunky horse — which raised its head up, startled by his brutal landing on the saddle. He never much cared about his men; quantity over quality was his preference, and his men were always replaceable. They loped off.

Her head nodded against the bale, as her eyes started to shut unwillingly — she tilted her head back to him, stealing one last glance at the man in black, hiding in the darkness before her. Slowly dissolving, within the misty veil of the ebony night.

V I

THE SUDDEN SOUNDS OF SQUEALING PIGS and wing-fluttering chickens flooded the barn. Charlotte woke up, startled, with her head itching from all the hay she had slept in the night before — a blanket covering her body, that smelled of cigarette smoke and burning logs of wood. Prying her eyes open, and immediately getting blinded by the sun's rays that pierced through the loft, she peeked outside and spotted herders dividing their sheep into the pens with the help of their heeler dogs. They were pushing the sheep forward while staying behind them, sometimes nipping at their legs if they didn't move fast enough.

"Finn! I gotta feed Finn!" She panicked, scanning around the barn once more, not realizing yet where she had fallen asleep, not even remembering the reason why. "What in the… where am I!" Her eyes flared, as she saw a red-feathered rooster make the rounds some feet before her — giving her a threatening leer, as if she was intruding upon his kingdom of chicks. She rushed down the ladder, almost trampling over the rest of the chickens that were picking away at corn and insects on the ground. "Finn! Where is my horse?!" she shouted frantically at the stable boy. "Where is the chestnut stallion!" she persisted, without giving the boy a chance to answer.

"He's here, ma'am! Horses grazin' on the west paddock this mornin'." he answered, irritated with her disturbance, for he was oiling a saddle — fortunately too occupied to notice her half-braided hair covered in hay, her brand new jeans stained with blood, and the torn up shirt clinging onto life by a mighty strong button.

Charlotte rushed to her horse, picking the itchy pieces of hay from her hair as she did. A sigh of relief escaped her chest the moment she spotted him — resting underneath an oak tree, contentedly overlooking the mares in the next paddock. "Finn!" She shinnied over the fence, running up to him and embracing his neck tightly — breaking down into a well of pent-up tears. Finn stood still like a statue; his shoulder was the only one she could ever cry on all those years, the only shoulder she could ever rely on.

"My dear boy. Never. Ever. Again." she promised in earnest, as he lowered his head for the bridle, and was swiftly kissed by her on his muscular cheek. He wrapped his neck around her and snorted softly, playfully nibbling on her coat. She saddled him up, and the stable boy watched her lead him out of the barn.

"Leavin' so soon already, ma'am?" he questioned her with a cocked brow, for she mounted with suspicious haste, and a soft plop as she hit the saddle.

"Yes. Indeed, we are." she said decisively, as she held the reins as tight as her trembling hands could. "Thank you…for the care." she spoke her thoughts; a twisted bundle of confusion, within her traumatized head. They loped their way out of Marysville — hoping never to return.

CHAPTER 4

Distraction

I

A STORM WAS ROLLING IN FROM THE WEST; heavy rain bombarded Pine Hill Forest as autumn introduced itself with pride, unapologetically blowing the bright, colorful leaves off the muted gray branches; a mundane lattice of emptiness bound to prevail.

Red foxes were hopping into their caves hurriedly, shaking their wet coat in the process. Chirping black squirrels were climbing up birch trees, and wrapping their bushy tails around them to shelter themselves from the rain. A herd of mustangs was nuzzling each other underneath a tall pine tree, keeping warm, staying together in a circle ready to fend themselves from predators — timber wolves being the most common in Pine Hill. It was a peaceful forest for travelers to set up camp and plan their next route. Their horses had plenty of land to graze on, fresh creeks that slashed through the lower meadows, and a vast variety of wild game to hunt.

II

BANG! "DAMN IT!" CHARLOTTE YELLED, FLUSTERED, as the bullet passed right between the rabbit's tall furnished ears. "I cannot do this, Finn! I just cannot! I have, maybe, ten cartridges left here…" she said, sorting through her ammo nervously, dropping most of them onto the wet soil. "All wasted, because I'm useless; I'm useless to fish, I'm useless to hunt, I'm useless to shoot this slimy bastard the other night; I'm useless to find information about a wanted man — I can barely get a fire going!" She threw her weathered rifle on the ground, and muddy water splashed back on her face in wry response. "Gah!!" she hissed in fury, then glanced over at her stallion peacefully munching on the luscious grass that shined from the rain for a fleeting moment before his lips would wrap around it and make it disappear. "They were all right, Finn — they were all right…" She sobbed into her hands, recalling harsh words of discouragement leaving her mother's mouth.

> *"You ain't worth a dime, Charlotte! It's all your fault! I never wanted to carry a child, nor raise one! You needy brat! Ya can't do anything right!"*

Finn neighed sweetly and nudged her head, as if he could sense the rampant beating of her heart. The rain poured down savagely — urging Charlotte to crawl back inside her tent, which miraculously was still standing strong against the violent wind. With a pout and a frown of self-loathing, she drew in a deep breath and laid back into her bedroll.

She would fall asleep and wake up in great distress, breaking a sweat in a chilled fall evening — as the exposed raw flesh from the man's neck, pressed out from around the cutting rope, would emerge before her eyes. She had never seen someone be murdered, let alone be the reason for it. She could not escape this image, no matter how much she drank from the musty old bourbon bottle she'd been carrying around with her.

Her thoughts would wander back to the man behind the black cotton wild rag, almost magically, lulling her eyes to shut again. Sudden bursts of thoughts tormented her restless mind, however. *How did he even find me in this dark alleyway,* she wondered, as she reminisced his almost dreamlike being before her that night.

He appeared way too smart, dressed in a peculiar way; so calm and calculated in every move he made — so quiet, yet so strangely comforting. How she wished she had asked for his name, as no one had ever saved her life before — no one would ever have cared to either. No one had ever showed her that she mattered back in her hometown, besides the bartender — he appeared to care sometimes in his own way of serving her the cloggiest coffee you could find. He worried, for he knew what her mother was.

Slamming her eyes back shut, she fell asleep, imagining the stranger's strong arms wrapped around her; not in a romantic sense, but a longing for a man's protection she never had.

The evening dusk filled up her tent; the bird's cheerful chirps left but a hollow echo in the ear. The steady rain was moving away; giving a chance for the nocturnal wildlife to go on with their routine. A couple of curious, plump raccoons came to visit Charlotte's pitiful camp; searching through the saddlebags with their tiny furry hands, finding some oatcakes to steal. Finn snorted and approached them with pinned ears and yet a curious eye. He towered over them, and after they turned to face the giant steed with flared eyes of mischief, they swiftly rushed through the gap of his legs, darting like bullets beneath his body, carrying their oatcakes in their mouths. Hopping away now on their back legs, they disappeared into the darkness, and Finn laid down again in triumph for protecting the camp.

III

"HE'S BEEN DEAD FOR QUITE A LITTLE WHILE, SHERIFF" the deputy said as he lifted the man's head by his muddy hair, presenting the corpse to him.

"Ugh. That ain't pretty." Sheriff Dorman gagged in repulsion, as he kneeled down to take a closer look at the partially decapitated head.

The naked body was found dumped in a pig stall; half-eaten by the Marysville swine, *which seemed fitting in a darkly comical way.* The man's intestines were hanging out from a large jagged hole, his eyes torn from their sockets — there was barely anything left to identify the corpse just hours later. *Who would do such a barbaric thing?* Gossip had spread around, townsfolk now locked their doors earlier the evenings; fear and suspicion ruled.

HOLLENBERG GAZETTE

NUMBER 27

"MANSLAUGHTER IN MARYSVILLE"

MAN FOUND DECAPITATED. DEPUTIES ARE IN THE EARLY STAGES OF INVESTIGATION, AFTER A MAN WAS FOUND MURDERED IN A HORRIFIC WAY.

THE VICTIM WAS NOT ABLE TO BE IDENTIFIED YET; FURTHER INSPECTION WILL BE UNDERWAY. THE ENTIRE TOWN HAS BEEN ALERTED, AND SELECT CITIZENS WILL BE INTERROGATED TO COLLECT CRITICAL INFORMATION.

THE CURRENT SUSPECT IS WANTED MAN, MAC KINNON, KNOWN FOR HIS ATROCIOUS CRIMES IN MULTIPLE STATES OVER MANY YEARS. HE IS BELIEVED TO BE SIX FEET TALL, WITH SHORT TO MEDIUM LENGTH DARK BLONDE HAIR, AND BLUE EYES. HE CARRIES A SCAR ON THE LEFT SIDE OF HIS TEMPLE.

THE SHERIFF'S DEPARTMENT OF MARYSVILLE IS HANDING OUT POSTERS WITH HIS PICTURE, SHOULD ANYONE NEED ONE. THEY ARE SENDING OUT PATROLS TO SURROUND THE AREAS OF HOLLENBERG AND CALEDONIA.

IMMEDIATELY NOTIFY THE SHERIFF'S DEPARTMENT IF YOU COME ACROSS MAC KINNON, BUT KEEP YOUR DISTANCE. HE IS A MASTER OF HIS CRAFT.

IV

HE FOLDED THE NEWSPAPER IN ONE SWIFT GESTURE, and tossed it into the fire. He lit up a cigarette and watched the paper burn down to ash. There was sort of an unjust feeling, yet also oddly satisfying, to be immediately held accountable for a crime — with not an ounce of evidence pointing towards him. He flipped his stolen silver pocket watch open and checked the time in deep thoughts. He knew it would be difficult, nearly impossible, to ride past the patrols whether it was night or day.

Fort Pipkin — a military fort in the northern part of Pine Hill Forest, was also preparing to send out armies of deputies around this region, for he watched them get their steeds ready through his binoculars. He needed to come up with a big distraction, as the woodlands were dense but small — he knew he couldn't hide any longer here; he knew they would search every inch of it with nowhere for him to escape. He stared at the fire, a hand raking through his brittle hair, watching the sparks land on the dry ground before him. He nodded.

V

"GOOD EVENING! MICKEY, RIGHT?" the sheriff questioned Mickey, walking into the bar, puffing on his Cuban cigar with a condescending glare on his face.

"Yes sir, would ya like a shot of whiskey?" he asked, sealing his lips right after, as he dried the glasses with his cloth, avoiding any eye contact — for he had read the papers.

"No, son. I'm here to ask you a few questions, if ya ain't too occupied that is." He snorted, then leaned on the bar counter, dropping the cigar's ash atop it. "Have you seen this man, Mickey?" He held Mac Kinnon's poster before his eyes — a wave of smoke circled around it, his friendly tone turned cold.

"No, sir. Most definitely not." he defended with a straight face, his fingers drumming on the counter in an undulating motion.

"Hm. Is that so? I could have sworn a fella called Tommy said the other day that a man looking just like this one right here…" He shook the poster aggressively. "…was having a little drinkie with ya. Is he mistaken, Mickey?" He cocked his brow, waiting for a confession.

"Yes sir, he is mistaken. I have many drunkards come in here, Sheriff. I do not know this fecker." he persisted firmly.

"I won't ask one more time, Mickey. I have a whole state depending on me, and YOU WON'T BE THE REASON WHY FOLKS NEED TO BE LOCKED UP IN FEAR!" he shouted, and a gray lock escaped his head of hair covered in pomade.

"Boss!! Boss!!" A deputy flung the door wide open while his hand was clasped on his rising chest, trying desperately to catch his breath.

"WHAT?!!" The sheriff leered, and slammed his fist on the counter — a vein striking across his flushed forehead.

The deputy held his quivering hand out, pointing at the horizon behind him. His eyes, dilated — speechless himself, almost fearing to capture the sheriff's reaction.

Sheriff Dorman turned around in an eerie, slow manner — he looked up, and his dark brown eyes turned scarlet. His face fell. His jaw hit the ground. The poster slipped through his loosened grip, and drifted down to the freshly swept ground.

VI

"FINN?" CHARLOTTE, WOKEN BY THE SQUEALING SOUND of her horse and a thick cloud of smoke choking her, crawled towards the opening of her tent, and looked out, only to find her chestnut horse rearing in anguish. His eyes were big and encircled in white, his nostrils flared — his whole body covered in perspire of panic. Around him, a sea of flames, hissing menacingly and building up by the second. Bare branches now burning and falling beside him, whole trees landing and crashing against others.

Charlotte didn't have to blink twice before she rushed to calm Finn down — and yet sadly, he was rattled beyond comprehension. He had never seen a wildfire before; he had never been faced with such an urge to follow his instinct — to run away from a threat, when every sinew in his body and being ordered him to do so — yet he loyally stood by her side instead. Picking up the saddle and bridle, she started sprinting towards him, but the saddle was too heavy, the reins too long; trapping her legs in them, as she hustled with a benumbed and quivering being to reach him. Then it dawned on her, in the midst of the sparks, the suffocating smoke, and the burst of lethal colors in front of her eyes, merging with the hazel tint within them — she knew she was too slow to escape the fire that chased after her.

"Finn!! Run!!! Git!!" She smacked him on his butt, making him rear and yield his hind away from her, only for him to face back to her respectfully. "No, Finn!! RUN!! RUN!!!" she yelled with all her strength from the top of her lungs, smacking him again, now running next to him — with him, as the tent collapsed in flames behind them.

Finn was trotting next to her, loyally following her pace, thus not being able to go any faster — but they were too slow and soon would be surrounded by flames, not being able to outrun them. She grabbed a handful of his long mahogany mane, now blending in with the horrifying colors around them; she took a giant leap and landed on his bare sweaty back, holding herself up as much as she still could, digging her fingers into his side to pull her body up, trying not to slip off. She swung her leg around him, and kicked his flank to urge him to go faster.

Finn extended his stride like he had never done before; galloping as his and her life depended on it. With his front legs stretched as far as they would go, Charlotte tried to hold on, as she had never ridden a gallop this way. It felt like riding a mass of wind, slashing through a smudged canvas of forestry around her. She had no idea where to lead him to; she had no idea if she even could without the piece of metal in his mouth.

"Take us to safety, Finn!" She loosened her heels, and let him take over. Embracing his mane with her fingers and engulfing his body with her legs. The roads were on fire; packs of coyotes were running together with a herd of deer, jumping through the flaming bushes in complete, harmonic cooperation. Others laying beneath fallen trees, trapped, silencing their whimpers as they burned to their death. Pine Hill Forest was burning; the smoke was blocking every way out you could take.

Clip-clop, clip-clop…

Finn's hooves barely touching the ground; his tail lifted up, his head stretched with his ears darting forward — his mind focused. Charlotte could barely breathe; her lungs filled up with smoke, eyes squinting through the fogged-up air — trying to spot a clear path. Finn had started to wheeze and rasp, yet he wouldn't slow down.

"Finn! Jump!! JUMP!!" she screamed urgently, as a tall birch tree was starting to fall right before them. She coiled around his neck with her arms, shut her eyes, and wrapped her legs tightly around him as they leaped through the scorching wreath of branches of the fallen tree. For a split moment, she felt the ground vanish underneath her, her heart halt its beating, her breath cut in her lungs, her skin prickle and her body feel weightless — a moment of eerie silence, until Finn landed on the other side, pulled by the force of gravity, and continued galloping, as the sparks brushed against his tail.

"Wow!" she exclaimed, in a heavy sigh, petting his neck with such gratitude and amazement, then took a dreadful glance back at the giant tree burning on the ground. "Good boy!!!!" she praised him. A glimmer of hope slithered within her — making her smile widely, when a clear path emerged through the heavy smoke, leading up to the snowy mountains.

Finn did it. He took his rider to safety, as she laid her trust blindly in him. Charlotte looked back to see the woodland covered in a blanket of lethal red. The realization kicked in that she had lost everything. Her mother's saddle — the only valuable thing that was left of her, that held some sentiment. All her supplies, and her hunting rifle, now lost. She looked down on Finn and smiled tenderly — in the end, nothing mattered more than him. After all, they were both lucky to come out of there alive. A sudden rain drop brushed against her cheek; not long after, countless more followed.

VII

THE ROAD AHEAD WAS DENSELY SNOWED IN; the temperature was lower — the air felt crisp and yet searingly dry to breathe. Rockies West was the most dangerous region, right at the perimeters of Kitunaha. Untamed, unexplored, with no inhabitants; as no one could survive a long time in those mountains, let alone an inexperienced traveler. Treacherous iced lakes and glaciers were hidden under a pelt of snow — even the smallest misstep could result in big trouble. However, it was also the most appropriate place for someone to hide from the law…deep into the rugged, snow-laden mountains.

VIII

THERE WAS A RANCH JUST OUTSIDE OF ROCKIES WEST. It seemed empty, quiet, with no sign of inhabitants when Charlotte approached it. There was a well-built baronial barn, a simple shack, and a rather all-encompassing house next to it — hidden at the end of the road Finn led them to.

"What a smart pony you are!" She smiled big, glancing back at what appeared to be a desolated homestead, praying there would be some supplies left behind.

She approached the ranch carefully, sneaking behind the fence and buildings, ensuring she couldn't hear any voices or noise. *The last thing she needed now was for someone to shoot her for trespassing, after everything they survived already,* she rolled her eyes with the thought. Peeking through the fogged up windows, she realized it was indeed, deserted.

"The air seems clear, Finn!" she whistled at him, and he came trotting to her. The joy she felt was indescribable; she couldn't believe how lucky they were, yet again, to find a ranch in the middle of nowhere.

First things first, she led Finn by his mane to the barn — impressed she could even do so. Upon approaching inside, she spotted some fresh hay, carefully sheltered from the weather outside. She also noticed the well cared, freshly oiled saddles, and a numerous selection of bridles, all hanging on the wall next to the stall. This was more than she had hoped for, the moment she eyed the grand barn. *Someone that lived here clearly knew about horses — and well-made equipment,* she thought to herself, briefly second-guessing if it was indeed abandoned. She brushed the gray ashes off his chestnut coat, gave him a bucket of water, and locked him inside the stable. Finn laid down, rolled in the straw, and let out a big deep breath — he was exhausted, and needed some well-earned rest.

"You did so good tonight, boy. I am so proud of you…" she hummed lovingly, and walked out of the barn with her eyes flickering in immense joy and pride to be Finn's devoted rider.

In the house, there was a plethora of canned food, bread, cheese, fruit, and meat. There were letters stacked upon another, and piles of books everywhere she looked. A scent of an expensive cologne lingered in the air, overpowering her ashy clothes in an instant. Charlotte then realized that someone must be living here still, and that the ranch was not deserted after all. Her throat choked by the realization, and guilt swallowed her whole.

Surrounded by the delicious temptations, she hesitated bravely, but her hunger was too strong to resist. She grabbed the piece of bread, the creamy rich cheese, the salted venison, and gorged herself on all of it. She'd been living off of canned beans for far too long — some days even skipping meals, although this wasn't unusual for her growing up either. She hungered for a change of flavor, for something substantial to ease the pain of her stomach.

She bit through a ripe pear, and all the juices started dripping down her chin. The sweetness of its flesh evoking innocent and sacred childhood memories in her — memories she had long forgotten. The fruit was so refreshing; she couldn't believe how dehydrated she was, just from the few hours of fighting their way out of the forest. She took a piece of salty cheese to go with it, and the taste exploded in her mouth. A sensation she would never forget. Bursting, erupting atop her tongue, quenching a thirst she didn't know she had. "Forgive me, Lord." she expressed, as she felt sinful for stealing the family's meals.

> "Sweet Charlotte, you do realize your mama is going to burn in Hell for her sins. God is watching all of us, you know, and there's torment in Hell; unimaginable torture — pain, and nowhere to escape from it. Hell's fire is eternal — and your mommy is gonna burn in it. We, sinners…we all will."

So the client repeated to young Charlotte, as he was preparing his morphine injection in anticipation of his service from her mother.

IX

CIGAR ASHES WERE LANDING ON THE MAP AS SHERIFF DORMAN was plotting his next region of investigation. The lantern on his desk was glowing in the dark room, highlighting the Kitunaha area and the Rockies right beside it. There were many wanted men, but Mac Kinnon seemed to really get under his skin — something about his brilliant shenanigans, his silent moves that would cause havoc everywhere he went, just enough to disappear into thin air again. That's how he had done it for so many years, but he simply could not understand it being possible time after time again.

"Sir, the fire has been extinguished by the storm." a deputy pleasantly informed him, as he strode through his office.

"Have you found a trace?" he forcefully asked, while picking on his cracked lips.

"…no, sir. We searched the whole forest and was not able to find nothin' but a burnt saddle." he mumbled sheepishly, leaning his back against the cell.

"A burnt saddle…" He snorted caustically. "That is…a TRACE, you FOOLS!!" He tossed the end of the cigar on the ground and turned his head abruptly to him.

"Sheriff…the saddle has been identified by our stable owner already. It belonged to a…Miss Charlotte, that left town the other day." The deputy looked at the cigar, as the sheriff was smashing it with his boot.

"Charlotte…" He raised his head, appearing to be in deep thoughts. "This sneaky little…" He stood up and marched to Mac Kinnon's poster, hanging next to the cell.

"Sheriff?" The deputy waited patiently for an explanation.

"They was both headed north…" He paced back and forth in the room; his spurs jingling as he walked and talked to himself. "She left Marysville in a rush after the man was murdered."

His suspicion raised, his paranoia grew.

The deputy remained in silence; he knew better than to interrupt his boss, known for his short temper and outbursts of rageful emotions.

"Our boy, Mac, has been usin' this gal as a distraction all along." he grimly murmured as he glanced at the deputy beside him. "She came right to me in Bisonhorn, claiming to have seen the bastard." he added aggravatedly. "The dead body…a distraction, to buy them time." he whispered, throwing a haunting glimpse at the pig stall through his window. "The saddle was left behind, again, to mislead us — to slow us down." His eyes lit up, as he felt a big mystery was being solved.

He leaned over the widespread map; his two fingers walked across it, measuring, and calculating until they landed over Rockies West. "That's where they're hidin'." he proudly said, pointing around the area.

"Sheriff, if I may, wasn't the gal…the one supposed to snoop around 'bout Kinnon?" the deputy posed the question, as he recalled him talking about the whole plan.

"This don't matter no more!" the sheriff yelled, completely disregarding the fact that he was the one that begged Charlotte to help him. "Prepare the draft horses, you're ridin' up the mountains." he ordered as he tore Mac's poster in half. "Oh, and…if you find her first, bring her directly to me."

CHAPTER 5

Brown Doe Eyes

I

THE DOOR CRACKED SLIGHTLY OPEN, and a barrel of a rifle emerged through.

"Who's there?!" A stern, yet soft voice startled Charlotte, who had fallen asleep on the table with a piece of bread still clasped in her fist.

"I…I, please! Don't shoot! I, I can explain, sir!" she begged, frightened, grabbing the butter-knife and hiding it underneath the table.

The man noticed the feminine voice and lowered his weapon swiftly — cracking the door further to take a glimpse of her. When he found Charlotte before him, he couldn't believe his eyes — nor his sudden stroke of luck.

"Miss Charlotte?" he exclaimed, a smile revealed across his lips.

"Tim! Oh my goodness!" Her shocked eyes softened by his presence. "I…I am genuinely…I sincerely apologize for…" Her lips struggled to speak, for his brown eyes suddenly captivated her, as if she saw them in a different light, or perhaps, it was the heartwarming relief that painted them in a different light.

"I beg you, my lady." He motioned with a calm hand, brushing off the wrong name she used again. "It is not compulsory of you to explain yourself to me. Your countenance appears…exhausted, my lady." he said, and she blinked, trying to find what part of her he even meant. "I suppose it's no misapprehension of mine that you may have a story to tell?" he asked with the most comforting voice, as he placed his rifle in the corner.

"Where to even start, hah." She chuckled, a chuckle of both relief and contentment. Relief to see a familiar face; one that strangely felt like a compassionate friend she never had.

A clean-burning fire sparked in the stone chimney, illuminating their tranquil faces as they sat together before it to warm up their chilled bodies, for the house had turned stone cold. The temperatures towards the east of Kitunaha reached as low as fifteen degrees Fahrenheit year-round, and much lower than that in the extreme north.

"Here, miss Charlotte. Do be careful, for it is burning hot." He warned her gently, and handed her a cup of freshly brewed coffee.

"Burning hot seems fitting!" she said and they laughed together, as she grabbed the cup from his neat, supple hands — the nutty, smoky scent hitting her face as she breathed it in.

Charlotte didn't really trust people, never opened up to them either, for how could she, when her whole hometown was ruled by filth and insincerity. However, Will appeared at the right place, at the right time — or rather, she did. In a state of serenity, she chose to unleash all her troubles on him; escaping from Nephilim Cove right after her mother's death, the wildfire, losing everything she owned — the drunk, slimy O'Donnell tackling her in the muddy alley of Marysville. However, she refrained from mentioning her secret knight in black armor who rescued her that night; as she recalled it, she just magically ran away.

"I cannot fathom how someone could do such a horrible thing…" he said as he carefully placed his hand on hers, "But it does not fail to surprise me; these men are known for such atrocities." He looked at the fire, slowly dancing before them, illuminating Charlotte's serene face in the most woefully poetic manner.

"Perhaps, to not talk about it any further, Tim…they don't deserve such recognition." she said, convincing herself as she looked back at him. His hand, now caressing hers.

"You are absolutely correct. They deserve no such attention." he agreed, swallowing down his last sip of coffee. "It is 'Will', by the way…" He chuckled, and her eyes flared in shame.

"Oh my God…I am so…so very sorry, Will…" she bit her lip, wishing for the whole room to swallow her whole, and yet, he smiled gently at her — the kind of smile that would reassure any woman.

"You are most certainly, fine, my lady…dare I say." he said shyly, and her cheeks flushed redder than the flames that scorched the wood. "In contrast to my fear of stepping out of line, Miss Charlotte. I would like to declare that I am quite impressed and astonished with your bravery, for I expected to find a young lady of less courage than my character alone can offer." he said humbly, glancing over at her, fiddling nervously with the rings between his fingers.

Charlotte remained in awkward silence, as she wasn't used to such kind, generous statements, nor having a deeper conversation with someone in the higher echelons of society. All she was ever surrounded by was the lowlifes of Nephilim Cove, and they certainly couldn't put two words together that weren't interrupted by drunken slurs. But right now, she was talking to a man — a living, breathing creature of a man, and a handsome one at that, she didn't fail to notice a multiple times. And even-though she could barely keep up with his phrases, his voice alone would spark a warm, sweltering flame within her chest.

"Miss Charlotte…of course I know that your journey is a matter of necessity, as you so clearly stated, but that does not ease my concern. May I be so bold as to offer you an accommodation, for a few days — or as long as you might require to get back on your feet. For I am certain your fine stallion, Finn, would greatly benefit from a warm stable after the myriad unfortunate events he endured as well." he looked down at his empty metal cup, worried for rejection.

"That is so very generous of you, Will. I would never want to be a bother to you, but I honestly don't know where to go right now. I don't even have a saddle…it's a wonder I stayed on bareback for so long." She chuckled, reminiscing a few close calls during Finn's gallop.

"I cannot restrain myself from hoping that you will allow me to take care of you." he said in earnest and then swiftly reheard his words in his head, realizing how forward they sounded, and his sharp palid cheeks crimsoned. "I have a handsome collection of some fine saddles we can try on Finn, if you would enjoy…" he attempted a correction of subject.

"I'm afraid I cannot turn down your offer in my current condition; but I promise you, I will make it up to you." she said, then coughed and bowed her head in embarrassment, as she accidentally tasted the coffee grounds in the bottom of her cup. "I owe you, Will, after everything you've done for me." she locked eyes with him, and searched his face — now able to notice in greater detail, his jet-black pencil mustache slightly covering what appeared to be the softest lips on a man she'd ever laid eyes on.

"You owe me, naught…Miss Charlotte." He clasped her hand, his thumb caressing tenderly across it for a few polite strides.

"Please, do call me Charlotte…" She chuckled, unable to blanch her cheeks, unable to grasp how a man could be anything other than an intoxicated, loud-mouth, degenerate, for Will — he was everything but that. Her thoughts briefly wandered back to the encounter with the wanted man, and she rolled her eyes internally.

"I shall obey to any injunction you lay upon me, my lady." He smiled and she blinked blankly. "Charlotte it shall be, forthwith." he added and she chuckled nervously.

"Right…" she muttered beneath her breath, and glanced back at the feral fire — its rowdy language of a hiss, oddly feeling more familiar to her than creatures of the pencil-mustached variety.

"I have a couple of handsome horses I need to sell; they're boarded at a ranch out in Mustang Valley. Dare I say, I could make use of a woman's touch with a stubborn mare I just fail to get through to." He inclined his head to her, with a pearly white smile.

"Well, I ain't no expert, but I would love to have a look at your mare — us women can be a mystery sometimes." Her eyes wandered down to his hollow dimples that dared to emerge the moment he threw a smile at her, flinching, as his big brown eyes softened every time he noticed her smile in response. His wavy raven hair kissing his shoulders, highlighting his pale defined face. He was certainly sculpted to fit the idea of beauty, almost ominously in perfection.

He took her hand, and kissed it tenderly in greeting.

"My lady…" he excused himself, stood up, and went on his way to the shack where he kept a spare bed for the occasional work-hand, wishing to leave her the whole homestead for her privacy and comfort.

Charlotte had never experienced such a tingly feeling in her stomach before; she did not know how to handle this odd and foreign emotion, as if a hand reached within her chest, clasped her heart, and forced it to constrict with the most tender grip — for he had the most tender grip.

She couldn't stop grinning that night. His sweet-scented, woodsy cologne still lingered in the unencumbered and most comfortable room she had ever laid within. *He was so kind and gentle, so handsome, so picture-perfect and polite…* her mind rambled to her — a train of thoughts tormenting her sweetly, thoughts of his lips brushing a kiss upon her hand, his mustache that tingled every inch of her skin — forbidden thoughts of the way his lips would feel against hers, thoughts she never dared to let arise before, and yet something within herself suddenly changed and forced her drowned imagination to resurface and go wild.

II

HIS BROAD SHOULDERS SWAYED CONFIDENTLY with every swing of his stride, kicking open the wooden hut with an already cocked shotgun. Eyes of woeful terror launched at the gaping mouth of the barrel. *Bam!* There was no breath to be exhaled, no word to be spurted. No action to be taken, for his was already steps ahead. He shot the hunter in his head, as he was hurrying up off his bed — his raccoon hat hitting the ground before his corpulent body did. Bright blood soaked in his bear coat, that swaddled his layers of fat and grossness.

He picked up the dead-weight body and dragged it to a frozen lake the hut was built next to, overlooking the bed of crystal ice. Taking out his knife, he broke the ice into large pieces, fumbling some out and watching the rest spread apart. He threw the man inside, and as his head was still floating on the surface, eyes glaring back at him with the expression of haunting dismay, he slit his throat wide open and kicked it down, watching it slip unseen underneath a thick layer of ice.

III

"HERE YOU GO, FINNY BOY!" SHE GAVE HIM A FRESH CARROT, which he gobbled down in one bite, skimming her hand with his velvety lips for any juicy remains. "You're not supposed to devour it, you silly boy!" She chuckled, as

Will's footsteps hit her ears.

"Might you have a favorable impression of this one, my lady?" Will strode to them excitedly, with a shiny brown saddle over his shoulder, and Charlotte's face fell upon locking eyes with it. "I acquired it from the handsome stables in Mon Louis — cost me a fore and hind limb, but its comfort is incomparable. I think a skilled rider such as yourself would find great pleasure in the use of it." He swung it over Finn's body, before Charlotte had a chance to answer, or rather a chance to pick up her jaw from the oaken ground.

"It is absolutely beautiful, but…I really don't need anything fancy or expensive, Will…" she said to him, gently touching his arm, signaling to take the saddle off.

"I feel no hesitation in avowing that you deserve to be spoiled a little bit; why do I surmise that no one ever has done so?" he asked her in earnest, as he was adjusting the saddle on his withers. There was a sudden silence from her; realizing how truthful his statement actually was. She was never spoiled by someone, aside from the bartender again, gifting her a free cup of coffee every so often. One, perhaps, that was too dreadful to serve anyway.

"My apologies, Miss." He bowed his head in shame, feeling unable to control his thoughts beside her, as if this young, adventurous, beautiful woman stirred something different within him as well "I must express it to be my utmost desire, if you might permit me the honor of knowing more about yourself?" He inclined his head to her for a split second, and jerked away again, puzzled. Her eyes blinked again, they would do so often around him. There was always a pause in her brain, just to rehearse his sentence well enough to answer.

"I understand… there's just not that much to say. Why don't you…start first, about yourself?" she frowned, her eyes searching for his expression, making sure she didn't upset him in any way, for somehow he appeared a sensitive creature after all — beneath all the layers of fanciness and wealth.

"You amuse me, my lady." He smiled, and fastened the cinch. "To expound upon my position in life…the patriarch of my family, my father, was an oil magnate who operated companies all across California. That responsibility was later on passed down to me, when tuberculosis…sadly took him." He paused, as he walked to his bridle selection to figure out which would compliment Finn the most. "Which…eventually, I gave leave to myself to sell my interest as primary shareholder." His gaze turned eerily hollow, as if he saw a ghost before him. "I decided to re-invest in ranches and stables across the country, instead. Importing sought out horses of ancient breeds, like the Andalusian, or even Arabian." he muttered, walking back to them with a fancy-looking brown leather bridle in his hand.

Charlotte froze still, as she couldn't believe that Will was involved so much with equestrian matters — the only thing she really cared about or understood, besides a woman's attempt to appear seductive — which did not identify with her shy, cocooned personality after all. She stared at his hands, measuring the bridle next to her pony's face, lowering his head with the softest touch, gently opening his mouth to put the bit in it — every move he made was so smooth and tender, as if his fingers were feathers of velvet, almost floating atop any surface they glided along.

"I also own a few…homes, across the country, but seldom find myself there anymore." He sniffed, twitching his perfectly trimmed mustache. "Charlotte?" He frowned, bewildered, when he noticed her, wide-eyed staring back at him.

"I'm…I'm just amazed at everything you've achieved in your life; I guess I've never come across someone like you before." She lowered her head, wondering if this gave away her lowly upbringing; surrounded by drug-loving drunks, and woman beaters. Suddenly, she felt inadequate for him. Suddenly, she felt the warmth in her chest turn eerily cold. Suddenly her heart dropped to the pit of her stomach. She tore her gaze away discreetly, pretending to be admiring the bridle that fit like a glove on Finn, as the woeful realization hit her like a brick.

"My lady, I must beg to differ as sometimes I wish I led a life of simpler character; that of one with no responsibilities to suffocate every fiber of one's being. The dreadful result of a long life, lived ostentatiously. For it is not always delightful to keep a high profile, and that is precisely why I acquired this house. Here, in the middle of nowhere." He chuckled and caressed her back with his hand, noticing her tension from the previous conversation slowly release and wilt with every stroke.

Charlotte joined him with a shy grin, as his distracting caress suddenly sent shivers down her spine. Her heart skipped a beat and her breath labored for a fleeting moment. *Is this how it feels like? Did my mother feel this way with every client?* she wondered.

"Which I'm quite thankful for, as you would have never found me again otherwise." he added, blushing yet again as he bit his lip. "Now, let us make haste, as I wish to introduce you to someone rather special." He held Finn's reins for her, and helped to lift her up as she mounted.

IV

DISMOUNTING HIS HORSE, THE DEPUTY LANDED on the fresh carpet of snow upon a steep cliff deep in Rockies West. Suddenly the weather had deteriorated, and they were hit by a white-out blizzard, unable to find a single pinprick of clear view.

"John! This is impossible to navigate through! We need to return! The horses can't go any further!" he shouted to his fellow deputy, who was only a few feet behind him.

"We can't be turnin' back! Dorman's gonna hang us if we return without him!" he yelled loudly, unable to even hear himself through the gale of wind that was flinging snow all over them.

"What you say?!" he shouted over at John, losing complete sight of him. "Jooohn!?! Where'd you go!!" he strode towards him, backing up his horse along the narrow pathway.

WHUMPH

A harsh thudding noise — louder than the wind that pierced their ears, fuller than the snow that cocooned their feet — pulled their gaze to the top of the cliff. All at once, the snow sheared off the lip of the mountain, shattered into a single hard slab, now falling straight down.

The deputies did not have a chance to move an inch further before they were thrown off the cliff, catapulted like weightless rocks, still hanging on to the reins of their horses as if clinging to the only sign of life; eventually getting buried in the embrace of a lethal avalanche.

V

"PHHHR!" A SNORT ESCAPED THE FLEA-BITTEN GRAY MARE, the moment Will approached her stall.

"Delighted to see you too, madam!" He frowned, swiftly taking a step back when he noticed she was about to strike him with her powerful legs of fury.

"Wow, so that's the mare you were talking about?" Charlotte stared at the proud animal in awe; enormous, elegant, and strong-spirited, and certainly with a bite of spiciness.

"That is all her, indeed!" He snorted with sarcasm. "A Lady Waberton offered me an exquisite deal on her. She resides east of the White Elk River and I hardly paid the cost of an apple — nothing but a gesture to make it official — apparently, for a good reason." he added as the horse was eyeing him from the corner of the stable, with ears pinned, almost glued to the back of its head. "She is a lot of horse for someone who has never trained one; she is rideable, but it is impossible to get to her without being bitten or kicked in the process...just a fair warning."

The mare cut her eyes at him with a grimace of rage, the same pinned ears almost unable to be pulled forward, as he described her in full transparency.

"I can see that...she is a beauty, though." Charlotte pointed out for her flea-bitten coat appeared silky-soft, and her eyes, albeit squinted menacingly, seemed molded from the kindest of shapes.

"Certainly, that she is." he huffed, and bobbed his head. "Can you recall that time in Bisonhorn, when I made you an offer regarding a business opportunity? Well, permit me to reveal it to you, for this is that opportunity." He twisted his lips to the side, hoping she wouldn't decline, or at the very least, lend him some advice. "You see, my lady, I have an important auction arranged at the end of this month down in Mon Louis, and this delightful lady here is to be sold there. She is a full-blooded Arabian / Thoroughbred cross, so I expect a windfall return on my investment when she sells — if we can entice her to behave properly, that is." he huffed, and searched for Charlotte's expression.

Charlotte looked the horse in the eyes, and felt a sudden sadness wash over her. While she seemed awfully aggressive, dreadfully reserved, and almost broken-spirited, something traumatized her to react this way. She could tell as much. She couldn't comprehend *why* he had to sell her — she could never sell Finn, no matter how much someone would offer her. Then again, horses were considered just plain soulless livestock to most. *Why did it have to be Will, as well?* she thought, disappointed.

"Will, you are aware I'm not a horse wrangler, right?" She shook her head with a frown, and wondered why he would put her in such a risky situation, realizing that he himself didn't actually know about the actual minds and wellbeing of horses after all.

"Yes, of that I am aware, but it was undeniable the bond you had with Finn when I first saw you in Bisonhorn; and this mare needs someone to trust — someone to bond with. Also, she harbors the deepest loathing of men, right to the very core..." He tried to convince her, knowing she had chased away a bunch of cowboys who already tried their luck with her to no success.

"So you will sell her to someone unknown at the auction, who might end up mistreating her?" she interrupted him, feeling oddly protective of her, as an uneasy feeling ruled her stomach.

"No, my lady. I beg to clarify." He cleared his throat, and she folded her arms before her heated chest. "There is to be a lot of money involved in this sale...why would anyone pay a small fortune for a horse, only to mistreat it? I haven't the smallest doubt that they would not." He defended his shady business, knowing very well Charlotte was right to question the dangerous uncertainty of the mare's future.

"But how would you know...never mind. My apologies, Will...in the end, this does not concern me. And yes, I do owe you for the saddle and your generosity, so I will do my best with her — if I can, that is." She promised, casting a hopeful glance over at the horse, immediately regretting her decision as she stomped on the ground and squealed at the broom that was left a just little too close against her stall window.

"Lovely! I am delighted to hear that. We may start tomorrow, if you don't mind." he excitedly said, and she nodded in absence. "There's a quaint guest house here, in which you can find accommodations for yourself..." He pointed to a compact ranch house with a couple of wooden hitching posts

before it, and a homegrown garden beside it. It was charming, though —
better than anything Charlotte had ever lived in. "I have organized everything
for you already, my lady." he said and daringly caressed her back. Charlotte
pulled away instinctively, as if the flame he had ignited within her extinguished in the helpless eyes of the animal.

VI

"SHERIFF DORMAN…" HE SAID SHEEPISHLY, and with a gesticulating nod of the
sheriff's head, he proceeded. "We received word that we lost a group of men
in an avalanche in Rockies West. The army is returning back to Caledonia
Territory. We still have our men trapped up there, trying to find a way to
Hope, but the blizzard makes it impossible, sir." the deputy reported to the
sheriff, who was shaving his beard with a straight razor.

"Such a shame…" He dipped the blade in the water.

"Sir…we don't have the people or the supplies to sustain ourselves there
for a very long time…we…can't imagine how Mac Kinnon could have ridden
through the snow, sir. Let alone live, or survive, under such brutal weather
conditions." he stammered, in fear of his reaction.

He stroked his sharp blade over his Adam's apple, shaving the last patch
of hair, pressing slightly harder than needed — then his eyes cut through the
mirror, darting to the deputy's direction. "If you…think…for a moment,
that Mac darn Kinnon cannot ride through a darn blizzard…then he already
outsmarted you YOKELS!" He leered, his blade quivering against his skin.
"I'M GIVING THE ORDERS HERE. NO. ONE. IS. LEAVING. THAT.
GODDARN. MOUNTAIN!!!" he yelled, and a drop of blood coursed down
his neck.

CHAPTER 6

Flea Bitten Gray

I

HOPE — A DESERTED SETTLEMENT THAT WAS ABANDONED during a heavy blizzard in eighteen eighty-four. There lay numerous buildings that served as accommodation for miners, as well as a stable to the south of them to keep their horses warm and rested between work. A small derelict church of a domed architecture lies north of the ghost town, with a graveyard right beside it, filled with numerous tombstones cocooned in the veil of snow. Although most of the buildings are ruined, with sunken and decayed roofs, timbered walls with missing planks of wood, some more windowless than others — it still offers a peaceful place to take shelter from the extreme weather and be able to lay low, for those who are able to trudge so deep into the mountains.

II

"WHOA! EASY, GIRL." SHE SOUGHED SOFTLY, as she was nearing the mare with gentle movements, eyes avoiding hers, approaching her shoulder with the rope in her hands. The horse would pin its ears, blow scorching gales of air through its nostrils, stomp, rear, and threaten to charge at Charlotte; yet she stood unfazed before her, as much as her bravery could encourage her to do so.

"I have never in my life seen such a poor yet magnificent animal in this type of distress…" she noted, shaking her head with a pout, as Will watched from outside the corral. His polished boot shoved between the wooden boards, his arms crossed, and his judgmental stare — one of bewilderment and disappointment, locked on them. His mustache would twitch every time the mare would take two steps towards Charlotte, concerned for her safety.

"She merely attempts to intimidate you, is all, my lady! Don't relinquish your progress just yet!" He tried to encourage her, for words were easier than actions.

"Really? So how come you're not here instead?" she nagged, silencing him swiftly. She advanced to the mare again, and as she reached her hand to her muzzle, she jerked her head back and snarled her teeth like a wolf. Charlotte shooed her away with the rope and turned around to face Will, whose face had blanched.

"Will, this won't work. If I push her any further, she will pin me to the ground! She ain't bluffing!" she exclaimed in defeat, putting down her rope and leaving the pen with a bowed head in thought. Meanwhile, the mare was kicking up her heels in the air in frustration and slight satisfaction as she managed yet again to get rid of someone — proudly prancing around the corral, side-eyeing everyone to ensure they witnessed her majesty.

"This horse needs freedom; she has been locked up in the stall for God knows how long — no wonder she is going crazy! She needs to be a horse first, before anyone's mount!" She searched Will's face that was deep in thought, as he carefully considered her remarks. "Will, some things just can not be rushed; I never rushed things with Finn, I always took my time to show him the ropes." she mumbled, briefly reminiscing the mistakes she made with him when she first adopted him, and how he protested before she understood to read him better.

Will glimpsed at Charlotte, trying to make sense of why she was the one deciding or giving instructions now; confused as he never had someone dictate how things should be done, even within his powerful circle of acquaintances. He remained silent, yet Charlotte's sudden change of authority intrigued him.

"You said she can be haltered within the stable?" she asked.

"Indeed, my lady…" He nodded.

"So, let's take her on a hack together. I will pony her off Finn, and you will follow next to us on your horse in case something were to happen." she offered as she took her yellow leather gloves off, shoving them into the back pocket of her jeans. "This will 'force' her in a kinder way to trust us — I cannot do anything faster until the end of the month. After that, I will be able to work with her in the round pen, once her mind is more freed. Besides, Finn will be more than happy to show this pretty mare around." She chuckled, as she glanced over at Finn who was still shocked with the mare's squealing sounds and bucking fits, lowering his head down and peeking through the fence at her in slyness.

"What do you think, Finn? Are you ready to show her around?" she shouted at him, and he raised up his head with flared eyes.

He neighed to Charlotte as if to say, *No way!*

"Charlotte, you just continue to amaze me." Will suddenly exclaimed in a soothing warm tone, and walked towards her. Now, his face towering over hers. "If I may…" he hummed, and wrapped his arms around her waist, pulling her close to him. "Thank you for attempting to help me. This has been such a stressful situation for me…my whole life…has been upside down, as of late." His sharp jaw clenched, as if he recalled something awful. "You're simply wonderful, my lady…and you came at the right time in my life." he said, his tender fingers caressing her rosy cheek that turned all the more vibrantly scarlet.

Charlotte was mesmerized by his chivalrous behavior; washing away all her worries about him prior. She had an unhealthy relationship with men; not familiar with anything else but the dishonest, filthy and abusive kind — thinking all this time, that was the norm. Her mother never taught her otherwise; she could only understand the way they would make her feel — equally filthy, equally worthless. Will, however — he made her feel appreciated, and that slight prickling feeling arose every time he came close — too uncomfortably close.

III

HIS HANDS QUIVERED UPON SKINNING THE MASSIVE ELK; his fingers frozen together with the knife, yet determined to finish the job — as they always tended to do. He tied the animal's limp feet, and wrapped the end of the rope around his saddle horn, dragging it up to the stables of Hope, and continued butchering it there.

He laid out the elk hide on a piece of wood that was braced against his leg, and started fleshing it out carefully with his sharp knife. The pelt would help him stay warmer than his regular duster coat, and the meat would keep him fed for a good month or two. Living away from any trace of society, distancing himself from the noose of its arms — this wasn't something new to him, for he had been surviving in this way for two decades. A harrowing, harsh journey that had started from youth.

His desperate but loving family immigrated from Ireland to the United States; they took on dangerous jobs to support and raise him, however were murdered in the process — which sadly made him end up a guttersnipe for several years on the streets of Mon Louis. He was later found as an intoxicated eight year old, who would steal items and trade them with rum dealers in exchange for liquor. A Protestant charity corralled orphaned kids by searching all over the city to locate them.

One of them, was Mac Kinnon. He was transported with the "orphan train" from Mon Louis to the Holy Ranch in Hollenberg, where he was auctioned to the highest bidder. A well-respected farmer, who lived strictly by the word of God.

IV

"ARE YOU, ARE YOU SURE ABOUT THIS, MY LADY?" There was a tremble in Will's voice; a faint, or rather not so faint trace of fear at the tip of his tongue, as Charlotte handed him the mare for a split second so she could mount up on Finn. He wasn't very comfortable around horses to begin with, even if he acted like he was. He knew all about expensive breeds and equipment, and that aspect was all he cared about too. Charlotte was determined to change his mind, however, for if their crossed paths were meant to continue along in harmony, he *needed* to be a horseman.

"Haha! Don't be afraid…silly man! She can sense that immediately." Suddenly, she spoke confidently about her, as she'd spent the last hour trying to halter her — breaking the ice between them, with a few carrots that proved to be an excellent currency.

"Well…if you deduce as much, Charlotte. So, where are we headed to again?" Will asked her, glancing at the mare every second he could, making sure she wouldn't bite his head off the moment he looked away.

"I'm thinking of going down to White Elk River. I studied the map last night, and it seems like the perfect place to let her be a horse for once." she declared with blithe amusement, and took the rope from his grip — already drenched in sweat from it.

"You mustn't be suggesting…to let her loose??" His eyes flared, his brows snapped together in shock, and upon her nod, his jaw slacked and hit the ground, for it confirmed to him, she wasn't kidding.

"Trust me, she won't go far from Finn; she already took a liking on him — he is awfully charming, after all." She winked at Will, hinting that she found him awfully charming as well.

She wrapped the lead rope loosely around the saddle horn and trotted their way out to White Elk River. The embarrassed, self-conscious girl that almost burned to ashes in a wildfire, was now leading the way with a big grin plastered on her face; a straightened back screaming confidence, and an unmeasured joy in her puffed-out chest doing what she loved most. Horses.

V

"TOMMY, YA BASTARD, WHY WOULD YA SNITCH ON ME LIKE THAT?" the bar owner leaned over Tommy, who was practicing his knife skills once again — a dozen knife cuts added to his collection.

"Ah, just eff off, will ya?! The fecker was here drinkin' with ya, and besides, I was absolutely fluthered when the sheriff questioned me." Tommy defended himself, proceeding to tap a blade between his fingers.

"This ain't right boy, and you know it. Mac ain't all that they claim him to be." His eyes, irritatedly following Tommy's still-tapping knife.

Right - left, right - left, right - left, at a steady tempo.

"Yeah well, I'd stay away from this dosser, was I you, or ya mind end up hanged next to 'im." he said, now his knife tapped faster.

Tap-tap-tap-tap-tap

Mickey grabbed the knife from his hand and pressed it against Tommy's throat. "Watch out, boy, what ya say or what ya wish for; I'd be more than obliged to grant your wish, only under my terms." he whispered in his ear with a threat, and Tommy turned his glance towards him in complete shock to see his old-time friend threaten him.

"Mickey, the more ya spend time with 'im, the more ya turn like 'im." he said, and there was a moment of silence between them, a silence long enough to reflect upon his behavior.

Mickey then lowered the knife, and nailed it on the table. He looked around to notice the people had stopped chugging down their drinks; a few had their hands over their holsters in case things turned south and others had a taunting grin taut across their faces. "I must crack on; lots to do." He walked away in defeated silence, recognizing he was out of character.

CHAPTER 7

White Elk River

I

"FINN, HAVE FUN SWEETIE!" SHE TOOK HIS BRIDLE OFF and left a halter on him with a lead rope tied around his neck. Smacking him softly on the hind, she encouraged him to gallop away with the spicy and yet most exquisite Arabian-Thoroughbred mare. He didn't dither anymore to do so, for in fact, he was quite infatuated by her and her feral attitude; vigorous enough to correct him, were he to get out of line.

"Is he not going to…*you know*…with him, uhm, being a stallion…" Will blushed, as he saw Finn's ornaments jiggle from behind as he shot off like a bullet across the lavender decorated meadow.

"No…he is not." she chuckled. "He is…well, he is a very respectful boy, and she is not showing any signs of…well…" She snorted shyly, then broke into laughter, losing all her train of thought as she noticed his endearingly crimsoned cheeks, almost the color of the blooms around them.

"A true gentleman, I suppose?" He threw a blanket over the tall grass, and reached for her hand. "If I may, my lady…"

"I suppose so…" She blushed and sat down with him, with the help of his grip. Her heart suddenly started to beat faster, vibrating before her chest, thudding like the sound of the horses' hoof-clops that slammed against the ground. There was a flare of joy within her, making her light-headed with excitement. This was the first time a man ever took her out — even if it was a picnic of strictly business matters, *or was it?* She quizzically wondered, unable to bury her smile beneath her lips.

He wrapped his arm around her daringly, and grabbed her softly from her razor-edged jaw, gently turning her face towards his. She could feel his fingers quiver upon her skin, and yet she couldn't tell if it was her whole face that writhed instead.

"You're so enchantingly lovely, Charlotte, if you might be so kind as to accept my saying so." He locked eyes with hers, not letting them go. "I simply did not possess the willpower nor vigor to pull my gaze from you, from ever I first became aware of you…it was as if an ethereal beauty, far beyond our mortal realm, had graced my presence." he whispered, making her melt within his arms, almost breaking into a sob for such words were otherworldly, so far-fetched from her brittle imagination and mundane reality. He had such a fluent way with words; so intellectual, so articulate, so sensual, and she — she simply blinked, in dull response. "You possess such a compelling, carefree grace about yourself; so different than anyone I've yet to encounter. You just make me feel…alive; I am able to relax my very soul around you, to just…'be', in all the simple pleasure that entails. The delightful hours I have passed in your society have left an impression on my mind and heart, one that is alto-gether indelible, and cannot be effaced even by time itself…" he continued burning her up inside with his endearing words, and yet all she could do was nod blankly, and force her brain to come up with an answer, for his sealed mouth appeared to expect one.

"I…I…certainly, haven't encountered…such a…a…man like you, before." She sucked in a stutter, instantly realizing how terribly dull and dreadfully awful this sounded compared to his flawlessly eloquent speech. For knowing how to be seductive to entice a man, if need be — like at that bar down in Marysville — was no effort to her. *But this kind of romantic talk? What was this even, and how do you deal with this?* She asked herself, with a knot in her throat. She'd been only talking to a chestnut stallion for the last several years — she was surprised she didn't just neigh at him in response.

Will leaned towards her, and her breath immediately caught in her lungs. Daringly, he caressed her soft rosy cheek, letting his tender fingers explore her lips, feeling of their shape in great infatuation.

"There's just something about you, miss…I can't quite put my finger on it, but it bewitches me to my very core." he said and a gasp escaped her, one that was not intended to be heard, and yet that lured him in even further. He closed his eyes, his lips now started nearing hers, with nothing but a breath between them. Charlotte's heart labored in the sweetest form of panic, and almost instinctually, she shut her eyes as well. He got closer, her fingers pressing on his chest — for the first time, feeling a man's pectoral muscles beneath the palm of her hand. His mustache tickled her nose, and as he inclined his head to her, it roared.

"*Rrroaaaar!!*"

Both startled to the pit of their core, they snapped their eyes open swiftly to spot, just a few yards away, a massive grizzly bear launching full force towards them.

"Shoot!!" Charlotte shouted, stood up, and rushed to Will's horse to grab the rifle; her survival instinct kicking in faster than Will's sense to even get up. Will, stumbling over himself, sprinted after her. Before he could adjust his balance, she threw the rifle to him and he cocked it as fast as he could. He turned around to face the charging beast, and started shooting repeatedly — completely missing it, barely brushing against the waving topaz coat.

Bang! Bang-bang!

He was in such a state of shock, having never seen such a massive predator, he could not aim properly at the bear no matter how hard he tried. Charlotte noticed the panic scarred across his face, and rushed to mount his horse. "Will! Mount up!" she cried to get his attention.

He ran towards her, throwing the rifle on the ground as he jumped on top of his horse behind her, clinging on the saddle with his every being. The horse took off at full gallop, with the bear charging right behind it.

"Come on, faster! Hiya!" Kicking the horse across the fields of lavender and fruitful creeks, she spotted Finn in the distance, rearing in distress himself. She slammed the reins on the horse's withers and encouraged it to gallop faster towards him.

"Your horse cannot support both of us for long; I will have to jump on Finn!" she shouted at Will, declaring her odd departure, getting herself ready for a leap as Will's color drained from his face.

Steering the horse beside Finn, as he had picked up a gallop himself, she tied the split reins around the cantle with quivering hands, and before Will could mutter anything, she stood on the saddle, clasping Will's shoulder, and jumped on top of Finn with a force she didn't know she possessed. Holding on to the saddle horn until she untied the lead rope around his neck to use as reins, she glanced back to check on Will who was completely benumbed from fear and shock — after seeing this frail woman who wandered into his house for shelter, now perform such impressive moves and acts of bravery. He was left speechless.

"Char…Charlotte, are you alright??" he yelled out for her.

"Yes!" she exclaimed, a spike of adrenaline burning within her veins. She knew Will was incapable of handling a bear, more incapable than her, as it were. She knew she needed to be the one to drive it away from them, and her heart sunk as she advanced to the bear. "We need to separate. You take care of the mare, and I will try to confuse the bear! Lead it away from you!" she yelled upon a command, now loping and circling around the bear; putting into test Finn's loyalty at the same time, albeit unwillingly — and challenging her own heart's grit, smothering her fright in this moment of trance. Once the bear focused on her, she kicked Finn on his sides, urging him to go faster — heading north.

"Wh…what???" Dumbfounded, he cowardly chose to do as she instructed, turning his horse west, and galloping successfully away from the bear which was now but a brown speck on the horizon — a shadow, that blended within the deep woods they slashed through.

The grizzly was still running after Finn, through berries, brush, and gnarled trees; trampling all the lavender flowers — grunting and roaring from the core of its chest. *To be that aggressive,* she thought to herself, *it must have been starving or have cubs nearby. Perhaps it was simply and utterly annoyed by Will's elite poetry — or the lack of her own.*

Finn was fearless around large predators; he felt too proud of a stallion to portray any fear — this, of course, didn't apply to small critters or seaweed monsters. Like a soldier, he was listening to Charlotte's leg and vocal cues, navigating through hills, and rocky terrain filled with trees and an uneven ground, bound to trip over boulders and break a leg.

This area was completely foreign to her; she contemplated if getting up high would be best to lose the bear — however the bear kept on chasing after them, no matter where they went or turned to. Riding further deep into the somber woods, and higher up the menacing mountains, they finally cut on a road leading to Rockies West and galloped through the thin dusty layers of snow — only for them to become deeper, heavier...darker.

Every time he lifted his legs upon a gallop, the trapped snow in his hooves was cast out in a thousand pieces and his leaden breath would subtly paint the air for a brief moment, and freeze into icicles, evaporating right after in an almost magical manner. It was one road, and the bear kept charging after them. There was nowhere to turn, but only to go further.

The snow got heavier, the altitude higher. Suddenly the wildfire felt like a feeble breeze to escape from — Charlotte realized their situation was critical, even in her inexperience and the rush of adrenaline pumping blood of confidence within her, she was alarmed.

Fear slowly creeped in.

A whole different planet suddenly emerged before their eyes, one built upon boulders of snow. Tall, horridly black and beetling cliffs draped in a cloak of whiteness, almost able to hear them roar an echo of a foreboding greeting as they passed them. A ruthless gush of glacial wind hitting against their faces, as big flakes fell like petals, only this time they felt like needles in her benumbed skin.

Finn was a tough steed, but the sudden icy blast and the quicksand of frost beneath his feet was too much for him to bear. His quivering legs kept on pushing further, and yet they were starting to give out — sinking deeper into the holes he carved.

He started losing his balance.

He was slowing down.

"Finn, please! We gotta push!" she cried, fearing for the worst, her life flashing before her eyes, haunting scenes of getting mauled to death by the claws of the bear, the dreading squealing of Finn rang in her ears, and somehow she didn't know if it was her imagination or the keening winds that slashed through her lungs. She didn't even have to look back; she could hear the threatening roars still advancing to them from behind.

"Come on, Finn!!!" she yelled, begging him, her voice coarse and fragile. It was cold. It was so cold, her lungs ached — they burned and her soul rummaged desperately for warm shelter. Her view was engulfed with fog, barely able to see through it, and yet the shadow behind her kept on pushing them forward.

Finn snorted in determination, and lifted his legs higher, trying to hop through the snow at a faster pace. Leaping up high, his front legs caught against a rugged texture, now stumbling over a gigantic rock that was hidden underneath the snow. Right in front, a small cliff overlooking the frozen Lake of the Grizzlies. They plunged.

Flipping in the air, descending by gravity's vigorous grip, they landed on top of the frozen lake. Finn's legs gave out upon a last breath of trying — he could not keep his balance, so they slid across the sheet of ice together.

Charlotte's leg, still attached to the stirrup, benumbed in shock, her breath caught in her throat, her ears deafening by the second, her eyes scorched by the crystallized frost around her — she watched her brave steed slide in an eerily poetic motion, as the skin-crawling noise of ice breaking hit her ears — cracking, in every direction around them.

"No!!! Help!!!" she instinctively screamed as loud as her wheezing voice still allowed — not realizing that she was in the middle of the most dangerous terrain possible, with no one to hear them but the growling bear behind them.

They slid right towards an ebony hole, pulling them in into the ice-cold waters — in such freezing temperatures, they wouldn't last more than a few minutes. A wave of penetrating cold twirled them a few feet deep, and Charlotte found herself stuck underneath Finn's body; his legs struggling to move, trying not to hurt her, for he was well aware his lady was beneath him, squirming for a lungful of air. He froze his legs into place as to not trample her further, yet she was sinking rapidly into a dark void with him.

Instinctively with the last spark of adrenaline still pulsating within herself, Charlotte grabbed the stirrup, climbing up the saddle, emerging back to the surface with a loud gasp escaping her bluish lips. Finn swam closely next to her, helping her brace herself against him, now paddling together to the block of ice that was strong enough to withhold the impact. In a fleeting moment of triumph and relief, she hooked her nails into the sheet of frost and climbed out, shaking, plopping herself on her back to inhale the arctic air — her hands, unable to move nor feel, her ears, swollen and stuffed with water, her mouth, quivering and numb, her jaw clenched and aching. She gathered up her grit, and twisted around to pull out Finn, yet it was too late. Finn could not reach the ice, and had started to sink back into the deadly water.

"FINN!!!!!!! NOOOOO!!!" she screamed — a caterwaul of emotions burst louder than before, louder than she knew she was able to. "HELP!!! SOMEONE!!"

Her nails clasped the iced surface, numbing them even further, sliding across as she crawled on her knees to the far end of the block, trying desperately to reach for his halter — mane, rope, anything she could get her hands on without falling back in.

And then it emerged, like an ominous reverberation from the outer world; Finn's squeal she had envisioned, now rumbling loud and clear — the anguish and distress painting the ebony air with further more cold brutality — his echo shaking the sharp mountains around them. Eyes flared in horror, nostrils inflating to catch a breath, front legs frantically slamming against the ice, hooves reaching over it, without hope of purchase, only for them to slip off every single time he tried — he sunk again.

The grizzly paced frustratedly back and forth right behind Charlotte. The only thing preventing its urge to charge and demolish her was the layer of ice between them — and its layer of instinct warning it to not cross. However, all Charlotte cared about — perhaps naïvely so, was getting Finn out of the iced lagoon. Bursting into tears as the adrenaline succumbed to her fear and desperation, she couldn't help but think this would be the last moment they would ever have together. Her defeated face fell into the mirrored ice, for she simply could not reach him.

Grunting, rearing, growling, sweeping its long, sharp claws against the ground, and upon a grimace of snarled teeth, the bear finally leaped over the ice, bracing itself for support, now sprinting straight to her.

Feeling the ice suddenly shift underneath her, the water splash beneath her knees, the sudden cracking sound sending chills down her spine, and Finn's wheezing turn into another forewarning squeal; she tensed, turned her head back swiftly, pulling herself back into a state of alertness and froze within its menacing gaze — the grizzly standing tall on its back feet, ready to attack with its humongous paw lifted right above her. She embraced herself and buried her head within the noose of her arms, praying, begging, quivering beneath the lethal beast.

POW!

A clap of thunder slashed through the leaden air, smothering any sound around her. There was a moment of stillness, as if her heart halted its beating, as if her shut eyes envisioned a dark hollow void, almost wondering if she had already died and passed through another dimension. There was a sound of gravity, grappling onto a mass and jerking it downwards. The peaceful stillness turned into an incessant collision, and frozen time burst through the ice.

Charlotte, startled, snapped her eyes wide open to witness the animal drop dead on the spot mere inches before her, whiplashing her face with a forceful wind as it did. Now realizing, the rattling of thunder was but a violent gunshot, still ringing in her ears, and she was still alive enough to notice. The powerful impact created ripples in the water, splashing against Finn's saddle — covering him freshly in a blanket of ice as he kept on floating, nearly breathless. Jerking her head back to Finn, she gasped in horror and crawled a few feet towards him.

The sounds of echoing, galloping hooves followed right after and her chest rose in hope at the familiar sound.

"Will?!!" she yelled, extended arms trying desperately to get ahold of Finn, rapidly losing the will to fight. "Will!! I need help!! Finn is in the water!! Quick!!!" her voice, that of a distressed animal, screaming in harrowing anguish. Her eyes darted back to the shadow that was approaching faster and faster through the fog. Suddenly, a long, stiff rope was slung over her head, slashing through the hoarfrost, slashing through the punishing cold, slashing through her breath and gaze, landing atop Finn, hugging the saddle horn in a tight embrace.

"Stay back." A low, steady voice filled the void, as heavy footsteps glided effortlessly over the ice. Now the shadow taking a form through the enveloping mist — a form that was definitely not Will's.

"Roy…" His black steed, with white stockings and a white bald face, came striding slowly on the ice towards him as if he had done it a thousand times before. Eyes of crystal blue, reflecting sharply against the glassy surface. Ears contentedly snapped forward, and neck arched in alertness.

Charlotte, whose jaw had clenched, aghast, stared at the man rushing back to the steed, without a word able to be muttered. The man tied the rope around his saddle horn and whistled twice, and the black stallion started pulling in an instant — while the man was pulling on the rope behind, as well. Finn's breathing was labored more and more; his squeals had vanished somewhere deep within his collapsed lungs, and his movements were but faint flinches of his limbs.

"Finn!! Hang on, boy!! Please!!" Charlotte wriggled on her knees and elbows towards him, trying to reach for the rope with her quivering self.

"I said, stay back!" The man scowled, concerned she would fall into the water. Charlotte retrieved her hand, dithering.

He whistled loudly again, and the steed halted. He took out another lasso from his saddle bag and threw it over Finn's hind, coiling it around it. He tied it to the saddle horn, casting a discreet glimpse at Charlotte whose face was covered in absolute horror.

She was in tears, sobbing in eerie loneliness, dreading to hear that her best friend drowned within the ice. Dreading to look at him; dreading to see him lifeless — frozen to death. For all those years, Finn had been the healthiest horse she could have wished for, and this has been the first time to see her "little" boy in such life-threatening danger. *Please, save him…*she whispered within herself, and dared to look at him again.

After the man's steed started pulling again, Finn managed to be pulled over the ice, but his weight was too heavy, as if he had soaked up the entire lake within his coat — and the ice broke further. He slid back into the water, causing another huge impact underneath the glaze.

"No!!! Please, do something!!!! Please! He is all I have!!" she cried, and yelled, and panicked, rushing to get up, now trying to help pull on the rope with her frozen hands.

"I said stay back, woman!!" He grabbed her from her tensed shoulders and pushed her away, making her land abruptly on her bottom.

"Roy. Pull." he commanded eerily calm again, and his horse lowered his head, an arch of muscle stirring the fog around it, and with huge, muscular shoulders straining harder than ever, pulling Finn up and over the ice little by little.

Charlotte rushed to him adamantly again, grabbed Finn's lead rope, and started to pull at it too. The man noted her sheer stubbornness as he tugged behind her and his brow cocked. She squeaked with every tug, and yet her depleted strength barely made any difference. He shook his head and continued to pull. Finn was finally back on the ice — safe, but in very critical condition. With lungs that strained to breathe, and body that writhed, non-responsive, as he laid there, stuck in place.

CHAPTER 8

Behind the Mask

I

"THIS IS ALL MY FAULT!" SHE SOBBED OVER FINN'S FROZEN NECK, staring into his weary gaze, fingers raking through his mane — now icicles trapping his burgundy hair. "What to do now!!" she cried, feeling her boy's shallow breathing against her ear — consumed by contriteness, as she should have never risked his life by trailing off into the unknown mountains.

The man walked over to them in stillness, and started loosening the cinch of the saddle, completely untacking him — irritated, as he did. Not able to grasp the lack of control of her emotions, he shook his head after glimpsing over at her pitiful self just sitting there, instead of using her naturally instilled survival sense.

"Please, sir…tell me he will make it…" she begged him for an answer she wanted to hear, with her bloodshot eyes staring at the man's covered face that seemed to have been frozen into place as well, for it didn't flinch. The man was quiet, as if in deep thought, until she was holding onto the fog that pierced through his wild rag, knowing he would soon mutter a word.

"Hm…" he shrugged faintly and she blinked.

"He is going to make it, right??" She gaped at him, insisting for that answer to not lose her last strand of sanity, and the man cut his eyes at her.

"Don't know." he finally answered in monotone, and turned around to pull a reddish elk hide off the back of his horse that was rolled up and tightly tied to the blemished brown saddle. He laid it over Finn and started rubbing his quivering body with it, all the while Charlotte watched her stallion protectively through squinting, suspicious eyes.

"Need to move him." the man spoke again, almost startling her as he did.

"M-Move him?"

"Hm." He nodded, avoiding her gaze.

Scanning the area around them, he spotted a patch of trees to give them some shelter from the horrendous snow. He knew a blizzard would be hitting sooner or later, as the brutal night approached, and the mountains only intensified it.

"Mount me horse." he said shortly, waiting patiently next to his steed. She blinked again, staring blankly at the steed that appeared all too familiar, and yet her memory was a smudge across the void in her head, frostbitten with no way to recover. "Yer deaf, lass?" he fussed, startling her again.

"I…I'm afraid I can't, sir." she said sheepishly, for she could barely move her hands, for she needed to warm up herself as soon as possible, for her whole body was benumbed, and the rush of adrenaline had waned, making her feel the effects of the freezing water — slowly descending her into hypothermia. Her blue hands were folded together, faintly rubbing against one another to warm up — he noticed.

"Hm." He bobbed his head, engrossed, and strode towards her, picking her up in his arms, and she hesitantly coiled her arms around his neck — not trusting his intentions, and yet not having another choice than to trust them.

"…and Finn?" she stammered, refusing to leave him back, as he lifted her over the saddle.

He was so strong; even after all the pulling and hassle, he didn't pause for a moment to catch his breath, yet his weathered skin across his forehead betrayed his age — or, the hardship that weathered him. He nodded in response, his coat drenching by her freezing wet clothes. He tied Finn's back legs with the rope, and looped it again around the saddle horn. "Roy, walk." he ordered, and he immediately strode steadily, dragging Finn behind him along the block of ice. They settled underneath a patch of pallid trees, cloaked in white dust, beneath a lattice of frost where stars slashed through them, and even they couldn't nurture her soul with a sense of companionship. The logs sparked, as he built a fire with staunch, calm hands — in complete muteness, with his gaze fixated on the logs before them.

II

IT WAS A LITTLE AFTER MIDNIGHT; THE MOON HUNG HIGH above the Mustang Valley, illuminating the trampled blooms of lavender, still faintly glowing in the dimming light. Will had successfully collected the gray mare, after hours of chasing her and luring her with carrots, as Charlotte showed him prior.

He returned to Longhorn Ranch, barely able to see the path before him, for the night seemed darker and gloomier than ever, or perhaps it was the reflection of his sensitive being, still rattled in the shock of a haunting adventure. He put up the horses in the stable and went to the guest house to check on Charlotte, as he thought surely she would have been home by now. However, glancing at the hitching post with a leaden chest, he noticed Finn was missing and his heart dropped to his very first pair of muddied boots.

"My lady?" He knocked on the door, twitching his mustache in fervid anticipation, as the critters of the night muffled his own hearing with their eerie lullaby — an owl's screeching, a raven's shrilling, a caterwaul of a bobcat lurking about. He swallowed dryly and turned his head around, piercing his gaze through the somber woods. The first trails of snow emerged from the mountains, and a dancing flake brushed against his fair cheek. "Charlotte?" he opened the door, tentatively.

Desolation.

III

THE FIRE EVOKED A FEELING IN CHARLOTTE'S HANDS AGAIN, yet she was still quivering, as collectively as she could, to not upset the man any further than she already feared she had. The wind was blowing wildly against them — competing with the swaying flames before them. They hissed at them, as if they too loathed them for having to keep them warm in the bone-chilling cold. The temperature dropped far below freezing, as the heavy whiteout swallowed the Lake of the Grizzlies.

She laid next to Finn, who was slowly regaining his vigor to everyone's surprise. His eyes appeared content, and he felt much warmer, however his energy was still drained and he refused to get up. She tucked his neck in the elk hide, like you'd tuck a baby with its blanket, and she prayed over him — prayed with every sinew of her being that he would make it. She wondered about the man, emerging through the fog like a ghost that she had conjured in desperate need. She had never witnessed someone in such harmonic cooperation with their horse, almost otherworldly, as if both of their minds merged with each other — into one. And although his quietness appeared menacing enough, she couldn't deny the fact that he rescued Finn and herself from the bear and the swallowing waters. She frowned in bewilderment, and rested her head against Finn's shoulder, waiting patiently for him to return.

The mysterious man came back after a suspicious while of being gone, and yet he didn't return empty handed, for a roll of bear hide was carried on his horse's back. Her eyes snapped back open, and after clearing her throat and straightening her back in defense, she glared at the man who was halted few feet before them. He untied the pelt, and tossed it before her feet. She gasped, and jolted at the abrupt notion.

"Is this…the bear?" she asked, aghast.

"Hm." He nodded.

"Oh…" she sighed, her eyes examining the bloody sinews of skin still attached underneath the fur. "What…what are we supposed to do with it?" she questioned him, troubled, for she felt shameful for the killed animal that was only protecting its territory after all.

"Yer clothes." he said, dryly.

"My…clothes?" she blinked.

"Off with 'em." he ordered, with a cold tone once again, and turned his wide back to her.

"Excuse me??" she exclaimed, surprised — the corpse's pelt repulsing her to the core, as a scent of virgin death engulfed her.

"Ye wanna freeze to death? If so, keep 'em on. If not, take 'em off." he fussed impatiently, his eyes piercing through suffocating fog that shielded him.

Finn snorted subtly at him, noticing his rude locution, and Charlotte caressed his muzzle to reassure him, and yet there was a knot in her stomach. Dithering, she slowly slipped out of her wet clothes, and wrapped the bear pelt around her bare shivering body, checking on the man every second to make sure he wasn't peeking. He wasn't. He was stiller than the writhing trees, as if cold could not penetrate his flesh.

"Thank you…sir, for saving my horse, and…myself of course…" she said, as she sat back down by the fire, feeling immediately warm and content from the bear's coat that now cocooned her up to her jaw.

The man turned around and started cleaning the hunting knife he used for the skinning, pulling his bandana down to light up a cigarette. Snatching one from the back of his ear, he held it in his mouth, and lit it up, covering with a large hand before it to shelter it from the wind. He pulled down on the tobacco stick, and continued scrubbing the blade with a cloth.

Charlotte watched him inhale and exhale the smoke; noticing his gaze never move away from the blade — hauntingly content and eerily calm once again, as if he didn't just kill a bear, fish out a giant stallion from a lake, and skin a massive animal. She was immensely confused at his everlasting silence, and the methodical behavior of his, and yet somehow she couldn't be bothered, for all that mattered was Finn's well being, and getting out of this frozen hellhole of danger.

Her thoughts wandered back to Will; missing his eloquent words and loving caresses. Wondering if he would even notice she was missing; if he would come looking for her here, if he was even able to do so, or if he even cared — for why would he, it was simply "her". She sighed heavily, and he cut his eyes at her with a raised brow, then bowed his head back down to the knife.

"Do you want to sit here by the fire to warm up?" she then offered him in kindness, tapping at the ground beside her with the palm of her hand, for it felt lonely and frightening in such isolated terrain, and wolves had started to howl in the very near distance, as if they could sense the bloodied pelt, or perhaps it was the fragrance of her fear they hungered after. "Sir?"

"No." he declined sternly, and she blinked once again in confusion. Her eyes squinted through her eyelids, trying to even make out a face, for all she could see was his shadow, since he'd never go near the fire's light.

"Okay…" she sighed, huffed and tore her gaze away with a frowned expression, drumming her fingers atop her leg nervously. "Well…do you have a name, sir?" She then persisted with her curiosity, somehow his silence urging her to speak more than usual.

"Don't we all?" he said snidely, putting his knife back in its case. A breath of smoke covered his face, as he got up to grab a bottle of whiskey, but before he was to fumble it out from his saddle bag laid out by the fire, she spoke again.

"I'm Charlotte…" she gave her hand for him to shake, the moment he neared to her — hoping to break whatever ice remained wedged between them.

He stared at her dainty hand, not knowing how to react, her fingers illuminated by the hissing flames, a lively red again. He reached out hesitantly, and shook it reluctantly — completely forgetting about the bottle. His grip was firm and rough, much different than Will's, and yet a familiar energy slithered through it, one she could suddenly recall. Then she noticed his black glove — the same one that the man who rescued her that night wore; with just one finger exposed.

"It's you!" she exclaimed before she even thought about it, and he looked at her startled, almost choking on his cigarette's smoke.

"I ain't." he scowled defensively, and strode swiftly back into the darkness.

"I can't believe you're rescuing me for the second time, sir! I…I truly owe you my life, and I just don't know how to ever repay you." she said relieved, in a sigh, and glanced at the fire, and back at Finn's restful face. Suddenly, a glimmer of hope gathered within her, knowing they would both escape this nightmare with his help and evident expertise.

"Sir, please do tell me your name, for I've been wondering since Marysville!" she said and he froze upon her words.

"I ain't who ye think, lass!" he shouted in response, and clenched his teeth, aggravated. Charlotte could not understand the secrecy nor the defensiveness that came from this man — after all, the only thing she did was thank him, yet it only fueled her stubbornness and curiosity.

"Why are you being like this to me?" she then fussed subtly, noticing him smoke faster in rage, as frosty waves of wind had picked up around them. "If you can't stand to even show me your darn face, or tell me your name — if you even have one, why do you bother rescuing me for the second time? Might as well let me drown in that iced w…"

"Just shut it, will ya??" he leered at her, and walked away in haste. Charlotte, baffled by the insulting command, oddly resembling all her mother's clients, she stood up hardheadedly, and walked after him with an angry frown scarred across her face and fingers cracking in fury. She grabbed his heavy shoulder and turned him towards her, with the smoke now lingering in the air between them — barely able to hear each other as the howling blizzard whirled around them. His brows snapped together, and his hero shaped nose crinkled in anger.

"Listen here big fella, you're not going to talk to me like this!" She pointed at his face with her newly warm, recovered finger. "I might be a worthless or useless little girl, that can't defend herself or escape a dang bear, but I don't deserve this type of treatment from anyone! Especially from someone that can't even have the decency to introduce himself!" she looked at him straight in his deep blue eyes, and suddenly they lit up by the cigarette's flame that freshly ignited by a breath he inhaled.

Then it dawned on her; in the cold, in the mist and in the darkness. Her eyes nailed to his well-defined jaw, lifting to his projected chin, his perfectly shaped thin lips, higher to that strong, haunting gaze of his — the face on the poster, the face in Boomtown, suddenly appearing before her eyes in sharp cut clarity. She gasped and slammed a hand across her mouth, taking a step back in shock, as he tossed the cigarette behind him, now advancing to her.

Stepping on the bear pelt, she lost her balance, and fell on the hard snow, now crawling backwards away from him in great haste — uncovering herself, as she did.

"Please...don't." she begged him as he was striding after her, with his stare not leaving her frightened eyes.

IV

MOUNTING HIS HORSE, WILL WAS HEADED TO ROCKVALE — the nearest and most well-financed town in Mustang Valley, right beside the ominous forestry of Kitunaha. This mountain town was void of saloons, gunsmith shops and fences of illegal trades; making it the safest place to visit, for lumberjacks, hunters, and gunslingers didn't reside here — instead it attracted settlers and wealthy visitors. Its mayor had been trying to convert it into a resort town, with great success, for it consists of a myriad of pretty log cabin style houses, with dome shaped and impressive timber arches that connected to one another. Its roads, clean and in the process to be brick-paved, with sturdy, quaint wooden bridges all merged to a landing overlooking an enormous water mill.

"What got ya rattled?" a deputy asked Will, noticing his obvious nervousness as he approached the jail's office — hands folded together, balling an anxious fist.

"I wish to speak to Sheriff Faust with utmost haste, sir; I'm here to file a report for a missing person." Will announced in earnest, as he slung his french imported leather satchel around himself.

"Alrighty. One moment, chap." he trod towards the back of the jail, with his gun-belt hanging loosely around his chap-covered bottom.

Sheriff Tanner Faust; a grumpy old man of few words — not so uncommon for sheriffs, as it appeared, for they loved nothing more than to nag about their occupation — yet enjoyed the occasional gossip they'd get out of it. He was almost sixty, and he looked it. His hair was surprisingly still a healthy brown with few strands of gray, short and tidied up with a lick of pomade, eyes droopy, cocooned by a veil of black circles all around them. There was a topaz tint to his face, albeit it didn't match with his fish-belly white hands. His muttonchops almost looped around his oval shaped jaw, and in contrast to his hair, they appeared carelessly disheveled. Neatly dressed to fit the town's fastidiousness, his boots came up to his knees and half of them had an old coat of mud glazing the surface.

"What can I do for ya, sir?" He strode towards Will, stroking his mutton chops as he did.

"Sheriff, I regret to inform you of a wonderful lady that went missing this evening. She was pursued by a grizzly in White Elk River, and was headed north last I saw her." he declared, hoping to convince him of the urgency, pointing with his hand over to the mountains.

"Grizzly? Chased by a darn grizzly? Ya ain't pullin' my leg are ya, son?" he rolled his eyes to him, and crossed his leg over the other in incredulity.

"No, Sheriff. I stand as witness, for I saw it with my very own eyes." His brows snapped together in worry. "I'm devastated to surmise, a horrendous tragedy must have occurred!" he insisted, now tugging on his neckerchief to take a breath, for somehow it felt like it choked him.

"Well, that's too bad; ya know, grizzlies ain't poodles — speakin' of which, have ya heard they sell some…poodles now down in Mon Louis? Folks been losin' their minds, tellin' ya…" his thoughts drifted off, his eyes stared up the sky with a lopsided pout.

"Sir, I am stricken with worry for my lady…" Will said, in a sigh.

"Oh, but of course! But them poodles, kind sir! Ever seen one??" The Sheriff locked eyes with him in earnest and Will stared blankly at him.

"May I *insist* that you now *desist* with the poodles and *assist* me in filing a report on my missing lady, Sheriff? I have an abundance of money; I will gladly pay myself for your deputies' time in looking for her. You don't have to worry about that." He pulled a check out of his satchel, already filled out and signed — knowing that's what it took for anyone to take him seriously; all he was to people was a walking check.

"Sure, dear boy, sure! What's your lady's name? Any specifics on her?" he questioned, fumbling out a notebook from his pants, and a pen to note things down — all the while side-eyeing the check within Will's fist, almost able to identify the numbers through the paper.

"Thank you, Sheriff." he sighed, feeling relieved. "Her name is Charlotte. She has long brown hair — she usually keeps it braided or completely loose; hazel eyes, fair skin, and a fit yet curvy physique." he said, as the sheriff was taking notes, bobbing his head absently as he did. "She also has a chestnut stallion, on whom she rode off." he described, then noticed the sheriff's abrupt pause in his writing.

"Charlotte, ya say?" he asked, engrossed, scratching his chin — tilting his head up to look at Will.

"Yes, sir…Charlotte." Will nodded, feeling the sudden silence suspicious. The sheriff walked away for a brief moment, returning with a poster clasped in his hand.

V

CHARLOTTE KEPT CRAWLING BACK TO A BUNDLE OF TREES as the man, now confirmed to be none other than the infamous Mac Kinnon, was approaching her steadily with an ominous leer that slashed through the ebony night. The blizzard had dimmed its wrath, as if to intensify his presence even more. He tucked his hand underneath his duster coat, and Charlotte's eyes flared in affright.

"No…please don't…" she begged him again, as she saw him pull his hand out torturously slow, as if he expected for her to confess. "I wasn't looking for you here, I swear!! The bear chased me up here!!" she avowed, petrified, for she recalled her hideous assignment — suspecting he was aware of it. "I…I have nothing to do with this…I…"

He slammed his rugged boot atop the bear pelt, heavy enough to thud against the snow, and carve a dent into it. Cutting her breath in her lungs, preventing her to move any further, silencing her trembling mouth, he threw a poster at her. Quivering, she glanced down at the paper, and back up at him. He didn't voice an order, and yet his menacing expression forced her to pick it up.

Charlotte gasped, aghast, as she picked up the paper; expecting it to be his — the one she carried all the way from Bisonhorn, thinking he might have found it in her coat when he rescued her from the O'Donnell drunkard, yet to her surprise, she saw her own face revealed on it instead.

"Welcome to me world…" He snorted sarcastically, and walked past her, tilting his stiffened jaw left and right — every crack, another slam in her stomach.

Shocked and horrified with the fact that she was wanted in three different states, she looked back at him, now just casually sipping on a bottle of whiskey by the fire, and her heart constricted. She glanced back at the poster, a blurred vision through her eyelids — the words were smudged, no longer able to be read clearly, as nothing made sense anymore. The ground shook beneath her feet. Spun. Felt hollow. So did she.

"I…I strangled a person??" stuttering, her mouth dropped to the ground with the accusations. "I'm wanted for…manslaughter?!" She stood up, dragging the bear hide behind her, absently pacing around, sinking deeper into the snow and yet she couldn't feel the cold trapping her feet — instead, she felt hot flashes within her chest. She gnashed down on her teeth and sat down by the fire in haunting silence, cupping her face with a hand — utterly lost for words.

She glanced over at him; he was looking back at her with the bottle resting on his lap, annoyingly content. "Why…how…do you have this??" She gaped at him with the question hanging from her lip, and in a sigh that followed, she noticed the night had calmed. She searched for his face, as if she couldn't grasp it was the same man she met in Boomtown. "Why did you save me, if you're this…merciless murderer?!" She bombarded him with every single thought that emerged within her rattled mind, "Why are they blaming me for what you did??"and "Have you been following me, or watching me, you…you psycho??" Her mouth, wide open — left speechless, frustrated, and in denial.

Mac cut his eyes at her as he gulped down the burning liquid, exhaling the burn in dark amusement.

"Answer me!!" she yelled, exploded, as she didn't care to upset him anymore, as she felt her questions being answered was more important than to fear this individual that could deftly silence her, ever so quickly with a slash of his blade, so that no questions needed to be answered. "Can you talk to me, please??" she persisted, and he kept on staring at her without batting a single eyelash.

Noticing his complete apathy, she wilted and burst into tears, hands pressed against her face, and legs pulled to her chest. "Lord, please help me. I beg you, Lord." she prayed in a sheer moment of vulnerability, longing to find the strength to continue to even breathe. A sudden snort of sarcasm hit her ears — a taunting, almost demeaning snort. She raised her head, lifting her sobbing gaze up to him. There was a subtle grin on his sharp lips, and her brows frowned in fury.

"What is so darn funny??" she leered and he side-eyed her briefly, then resumed back to his drink. "Hello?? 'Mr. Kinnon'??" she hissed mockingly, and another snort emerged.

"Hm." he smirked snidely

"What??"

"Ain't no Lord out there, princess." he finally said, and she froze upon his remark. Dark clouds circled above them, sailing all across the busted iced lake. A roll of distant thunder rumbled in the distance and a foreboding wind of frost brushed against their faces.

"What do you even know…" she snapped at him, tearing her gaze away from him in great irritation.

God had been the only one besides Finn she entrusted her troubled thoughts with, for her mother would never care to listen — never care to even try. He was the only that encouraged her to leave her hometown — with a single prayer, she was able to gather up her grit and do so.

"More than ye think…" he snapped back, his deep blue eyes following the clouds form above them; the horizon clearing for the distant thunderstorm to roll as nothing but faint snowflakes remained floating in the air.

"Perhaps you should try it, once…you know." she said, for she was stubborn enough to fuss back at him. "Maybe you wouldn't be here right now — hiding in these darn mountains, freezing to death in a freaking blizzard…" she grumbled, feeling the urge to slap him with the bottle he still sipped on, so irritatingly detached.

"Sure." he clenched his teeth, sending a menacing look over at her. "Let's see how the sky faerie saves ya; if ye get outta here alive, that is…"

"Oh, I will find a way to get out, I can assure you of that, mister…" She folded her arms in protest.

"Hm. Sure…" He bobbed his head with sarcasm.

Charlotte didn't have the strength to answer his sarcastic remarks anymore. She chose to remain in silence, stare at the flames as if they were a map of her route out of the secluded trap she found herself within.

"If ye do get out…them deputies gonna find ye, arrest ya for murder, lynch ya…an' laugh at ya as ye swing…" He shrugged caustically, cutting his eyes at her once more, briefly searching for her reaction.

She was quiet instead, feeling defeated. His words echoed in her head, morphing into visions before her eyes. *She swung with her head in the noose at the gallows of Marysville, and a myriad chattering faces clapped in triumph.*

Suddenly, she felt the scorching urge to end her life, for he was right — once captured, she would be hanged. Aside from that, she was stranded with a widely-known killer in the worst region possible; Finn wouldn't be able to make it out of there alive, and she certainly would freeze to death trying to do so, or be eaten alive by the wolves that kept on howling in the background for added drama.

Her gaze froze, benumbed with the realization — contemplating her options that weren't all that many. Dithering, she glanced at Finn, who was still resting, seeming awfully fatigued and fragile, and her heart sunk furthermore, adding to her decision. "Oh, Finn…forgive me." she said, and Mac's ear flinched her way. "I don't know what else to do. We are…stranded here, boy. We are…not well…" she said, her heart throbbed in woe, for Finn barely flinched an eyelash. "You're just going to die here, and…I don't have the heart nor bravery to end your suffering faster." she said and Mac frowned, bewildered with her monologue. "I'm so sorry, my sweet boy…but I know, you will simply…fall asleep…and somehow it will be more peaceful, in the end." she swallowed down a sob and coiled her arms around Finn's neck, kissing him softly on the cheek. "I love you, so much…thank you for everything you ever did for me…" she whispered in his ear, and tucked him in with the elk hide tightly, choking to do so.

Standing up, she grabbed the gun belt off the ground and pulled out her revolver. Mac's brow cocked at the notion, as she passed him in restrained silence. He watched her — paying full attention to every move she made, his sarcastic smirk slipped and set his lips on a straight line, now turned into deep suspicion. She walked away from the fire, trudging deep into the snow-cloaked woods with the gun's barrel bobbing against her leg.

Mac sighed in frustration, plopped the bottle into the ground, and strode right after her with an air of rage. He spotted the bear pelt wrapped Charlotte, as she was raising the gun up to her head, and ran up to her swiftly, grabbing her arm before she was even able to place a finger on the trigger.

"What ya think yer doin', woman?!" He scowled, and she turned her body harshly towards him, keeping an eye on the barrel as he did.

"What do you want from me??" She leered. "Do you think I will just hide here forever and ever until I turn sour, like you?? I will never be like…you!! I can't even hunt, or shoot a bear! My horse is dying — God apparently doesn't exist, so who the hell do you think will help me out of here? Myself? Ha!" She chuckled hysterically.

"Yer not thinkin' clearly now…" he growled, squeezing her wrist and locking stern eyes with her.

"I will be lynched IF I ever get out of here! You said it yourself, mister… mister murderer!" she hissed, trying to yank her arm away from him. "Leave me be!!" she yelled, feeling her wrist crack from his rough grip.

He kept her arm low, and kicked the gun out of her hand — firing a shot as it hit the ground beside them. "Listen to me, young lass." he tightened his grip, her eyes flared in shock, and her ears muffled by the sudden gunshot. "Ye need to learn to control yer self and yer goddamn emotions, or else that's gonna kill ya before I ever will!" he looked at her straight in the eyes, squeezing her hand even more.

"You're — hurting me!!" she yelled from the top of her lungs, pulled her arm back and raised her hand, slapping him across his face unapologetically. The echo of the clap was the only noise that was left around them, and Mac froze before her, stunned, for he never had a woman talk to him in this manner, let alone throw a stinging slap at him, after saving her life yet again — however this wasn't all that came out of her feisty mouth, to his surprise. "Oh and, to control my emotions! Ha! So I turn out like you?? Emotionless?! I'd rather shoot my brains out!" she growled, glaring at his scarlet flushed cheek with her fingers imprinted on it. She swallowed down, almost embarrassedly and tore her gaze away in shame, realizing how harsh her words sounded.

"Then feckin' blow them!" He grabbed the mucky gun and pressed it against her hand, cocking it for her, and sliding her finger in the trigger — his cigarette breath hitting her face as he did. Stinging her eyes. Smothering her senses. He spat on the ground and walked away, when he heard Charlotte burst into gut-wrenching tears. He halted — dithering. She whimpered. She cried. He rolled his eyes, and strode back towards her, as a breath of frustration escaped his chapped lips.

His hands balled a fist, not knowing how to comfort her. Not knowing why he even had to. There was an awkward, maddening circle of silence he stood within, trying to grasp her behavior — the sounds that her throat issued, only familiar to him from his begging victims. A shadow that reflected on the snow beside him, caught his attention. He glanced back at the fire, spotting her stallion slowly move. He looked back at her, and cleared his throat.

"Yer horse is…gettin' up." he said tersely, then studied Finn lifting his round hind in the air.

"He…is?" Charlotte asked in the most pitiful tone, glancing quickly over at Finn with her swollen, bloodshot eyes — as emotional as she was, she still couldn't suppress a smile.

Mac rolled his eyes again, and shook his head.

*What am I gonna do with her…*he thought to himself.

V I

"MAC, SON, DID YOU WATER THE CROPS ALREADY?" the farmer asked the young boy after walking through the door, back from his errands.

"Yes, sir." he answered, swiftly hiding the cigarette package underneath his shirt.

"Are you ready to read the word of God? To learn God's truth, and seek forgiveness for all your sins?" He looked at the boy with a cocked brow, examining him from head to toe, expecting him to sit down next to him.

"Yes, sir." he answered politely, knowing if he were to decline, he would get a hard beating again.

Mac sat down next to him, as instructed — as expected, as ordered every-day. Grabbing his bible book from the table, and clearing his throat from the sudden dryness that clogged it, he started reading the verses on the page, one after the other. Loud, slow, and clear — just like the farmer wished it.

"Well done, my boy." he said, his hands caressing along his neck, his fingers slithering down to his lower back. His throat, choking again.

V I I

"I REFUSE TO BELIEVE THIS, SHERIFF." WILL SAID as he folded the paper, and handed it back to him. "Miss Charlotte is not a murderer; she has clearly been with me all this time, and one could not hope for a more substantial alibi — she is most certainly not hiding anywhere up north…with Mac Kinnon, or otherwise." he defended her, while risking his reputation in doing so.

"Well, that's all well and dandy, but she been wanted for quite some time now, and I'm afraid the deputies down in Marysville ain't gonna give a rat's ass 'bout your lovey-dovey sob story, son; ya better tell 'em what they need to know in order to find her, and save your own arse." he raised his brows and turned his back towards him, not interested in hearing anything more.

"She is INNOCENT!!" He scowled, for the first time in his life raising his voice, and yet all he heard, was a sarcastic chuckle in response.

Will, disgusted by the sheriff's lack of empathy and cooperation to fight for justice — let alone seeing his personal bias, which truly repulsed him — decided to take matters into his own hands, and head down to Marysville to investigate the case. He had the money, the time, and the connections to help Charlotte if needed — but most of all, he had fallen. Fallen madly in love with her, and he was not ready to let go.

CHAPTER 9

Stranded Hope

I

MAC KINNON AND DESERTED CHARLOTTE MADE IT to the settlement of Hope during the night, just before the blizzard hit again. It was a strenuous journey, albeit not far from the lake, so Finn struggled to keep up the pace and carry her load. The thunder roared above them, slamming invisible spikes into the ground beside them as they rode. The cold took their breaths away, penetrating their lungs with a forceful fist to collapse them; and icy blast of wind froze their hands upon the reins, busting the skin along them.

In Hope they investigated all the buildings around, after stabling the horses in the still functional barn, tending to them with frozen limbs and benumbed legs. Thereupon, they settled in the only cabin that was still decently intact, with only a few loose boards clapping about on the timber walls.

Upon situating, Mac built a fire in the old bricked chimney in the middle of the cabin, and they sat around it in silence — warming up their fingers and toes before they would fall off, for the hoarfrost that enveloped them threatened as much. For the awkward night, they shared two spacious rooms with one bed each in it — which worked out perfectly for them, since they were strangers to begin with, and had constantly quarreled the entire ride towards Hope — or rather, she would fuss at him for ignoring her interrogative questions all along. There wasn't much to be said to each other, for Mac's silence betrayed as much, and Charlotte's stubbornness had succumbed to it.

Both dithering in mistrust and suspicion, they went to their rooms to rest up. Charlotte had dragged a whole cabinet before the door in attempt to block any possible amorous entrances during the night, and Mac, as he laid in the rickety bed, rolled his eyes and shook his head repeatedly at the creaking, and dragging sounds that she made while reorganizing the whole room for her safety — hurting herself in the process, as she would stump her toe on the corner of the bed and cuss at it right after. He snorted and crossed his arms behind his head, glaring at the fogged up window to his side, slowly drifting in thought.

All of Hope was snowed in. The paths leading up to it, unable to be crossed without a sturdy horse that knew how to navigate through such dangerous terrain. Mac was surprised how Charlotte was even able to ride through, all the way up to Lake of the Grizzlies. Albeit not willing to admit so, he was impressed, since even the deputies had failed to cross through successfully.

Finn was a stout stallion however, with a powerful hip and long smooth stride, as he had already observed — it was extraordinary for a horse that hasn't been exposed to such environmental conditions to be able to master them with such ease, and yet he did. He took care of his rider, it seemed like; he wasn't putting up a fight, but was trying to please so badly instead. Only a willing animal would leap over such a cliff, straight into an iced lagoon to escape a threat for his rider, he thought to himself — the window collecting snow flakes that slowly frosted their print atop it.

And she...she was unusual, he thought. Stubborn, certainly, slightly naïve and insecure, greatly annoying; and yet, there was a spark of bravery within her — ignited every time she tried to prove herself to him. Her worth, and her vigor. Her grit, and her sense. Albeit trying to shoot her own head off, she was able to push through situations after all. He noticed, Finn was at the very core of her try. And yet he wondered, *would she even fight for her own self, if she were to be smothered by utter loneliness?*

II

THE DOOR SNARLED OPEN, AND HE CUT HIS EYES AT IT from the main room. He spotted her hand trying to push the large chest of drawers aside, for somehow it had jammed beneath the pommel door knob, and evidently she had managed to lock herself securely inside the room.

"Darnit…" she fussed to herself mutely, and he suppressed a snide snort, turning his head away again, as she now tried to squeeze her way through the gap. She finally succeeded.

She cleared her throat and walked towards the main room, trying hard to stay composed and hide the embarrassment on her cheeks, meeting his shadowy being leaned against a desk, an arm crossed over him, a hand holding a metal cup, and his feet folded lazily at the ankles.

"Good morning…" she greeted him subtly, as he was sipping on the freshly brewed coffee, now looking out the half-broken window.

"Hm." He nodded, not moving his sight. She bobbed her head in awkwardness and fiddled with her braided hair, for that clump of hair appeared more talkative than him to her.

"Slept well?" she forced herself to ask, meanwhile wondering what was so interesting outside. He frowned and thought of her question. There was a moment of silence, and then he spoke.

"Sure." he buried his lips into the cup, stealing a swift glimpse of her, realizing he'd never seen her in bright daylight before. He tore his gaze away again.

"Aha…" she nodded, a defeated pout scarring her lips. His eyes darted back at her like a hawk.

"Yerself?" he forced to pose the question back after another long pause, for he noticed the disappointment in her gaze. There was loneliness within it.

She lit up.

"Kind of!" she exclaimed, and walked towards the coffee pot. "May I?" she asked him, and he cocked a brow.

"Hm." he said and she blinked, internally counting just how many words he really was able to speak out. She sighed heavily in thought, and poured herself some coffee in a dusty cup she'd swiftly blown out.

"Well…" she spoke again, and his brow rose now out of habit around her, for he wasn't used to being with any company, and the sound of her voice slashing his mundane silence, appeared eerie. "Not gonna lie, I had a more comfortable living arrangement two nights prior to all this mess…" She snorted, in a desperate attempt to lighten up the mood.

"Sorry it ain't perfect for ya." he snapped instantly, slamming the empty cup atop the counter. The coffee grounds bounced off the bottom of the metal, and appeared for a swift moment in the suffocating air, before they descended back downwards.

Charlotte, astounded by the abrupt reaction, quickly realized she wasn't able to joke around him at all, so instead of snapping back, she tried to keep the peace. She depended on him, and knew very well without him — she would not make it out of there alive, and somehow, during the quarreling journey towards the settlement, he agreed upon safely returning her if she quit the whimpering and the sobbing that drilled within his ears.

"Well…I was thinking…" she cleared her throat and he drew in a deep breath, in attempts to tamp down his anger. "To walk around a bit, and… check on the surroundings, I reckon. Perhaps I will find a hidden pathway, that isn't snowed in…" she said, drumming her fingers against the cup.

"Hidden pathway…" he snorted, and she bit her tongue. "Yer stranded, lass. Weather ain't good news for ye." he said and she peeked through the window.

"Well, I find the weather to be quite pleasant this fine morning, so…I'm not sure why you think otherwise." she said and he grunted heavily. "We can just, ride around, and…see if we can spot a road back south, or west… or whatever, and leave the mountains." she said hopefully, and he ground his teeth.

"Sure…and when the blizzard hits tonight, yer gonna curl into a ball and sob me a song again." he said snidely, and she blinked at him.

"But…how long will this blizzard situation continue for??" she gaped at him, not wishing to stay a minute longer by his side.

"Two weeks, I reckon…" he muttered beneath his breath, and her jaw dropped to the ground.

"Two…two weeks??? This cannot be!! I…I can't possibly stay here with…I mean, I can't!" she clasped her face in shock and he shrugged, detached and devoid of any emotion, other than the occasional annoyance she would evoke within him.

"Well, door's open for ye to leave." he said, and kicked at the door with a swift extension of his leg. The door slammed wide open with a chip of wood breaking off, and a gust of wind blew inside in an instant, slamming a billion snow specks atop her face. Mac's glare was nailed at her with a challenge, watching her shuffle towards the door with all her strength as the sudden violent wind kept pushing her back. Stretching her arm, she grappled the frame and reached for the door's handle, pulling it back shut.

"Are you crazy??" She turned to face him with a pant, her entire face and hair cloaked in whiteness.

He smirked in dark amusement.

She grabbed a chair and pulled it towards herself, plopping into it defeatedly. She rubbed her eyes and as she pried them back open, spotting the decayed map he had spread across the bookcase next to him. She stood up swiftly and walked towards it, halting beside him as her eyes studied the map. His brows snapped together, and his gaze nailed back on her, expecting to hear her speak again. Which, she did.

"So...what is the plan, then? For the next...days...weeks..." She bowed her head, squeezing her braid in a fist.

"The plan..." he grinned lopsidedly with her ignorant question, as apparently, she should be able to figure things out on her own, and apparently they should be able to find a clear path, polished and tidied up by the otherworldly mountain fairies of the Rockies.

Charlotte could barely stand his rude insinuations. She bit her lip again to prevent herself from fussing at him, but the urge was burning up inside her. It burned so badly, she could barely breathe.

"The plan is for ya to start learnin' how to shoot." he said unexpectedly, and she blinked, aghast. "Can't be riskin' me life 'round ye, when ya don't even know how to take care of yer damn gun." he grunted, and folded his arms, stretching his jaw towards the table.

Baffled, she turned around and glanced at her gun he had taken out of its holster, and taken apart into what seemed to be a million pieces — all that while she was still asleep, she furiously noted.

"What did you do to it??" she screeched and tugged on her braid, not knowing how to put it all back together.

"Cleaned it — for once, the mucky thing." he fussed. "Who the damn knows what kind of dirt it had collected all them damn years. That ain't how ya treat the only thing that'll damn save ye!" he froze upon her with a leer, yet pulled his eyes away immediately in sudden bewilderment, when he couldn't help noticing the beauty of her wake-up face.

"First of all, spare me with your damnations. And second of all, don't get me started on how YOU…" she pointed with her finger and poked his well-built chest that his vest so gently shaped, "treat your horse that saves you every single DAMN day — not giving him a single pat for carrying your murderous…ARSE." she made her point and crossed her arms, proud of her smooth comeback. She nodded, a satisfied smirk across her lips.

"Hm…" His lips twisted to the side, and her smirk only widened for she had silenced him, until he drew in another breath.

"Roy is glad to be alive still…" he said sardonically. "My mounts before him wasn't that lucky." he teased her, knowing this would get under her skin, pausing briefly as she stood before him, unintentionally forcing him to lock eyes again.

"You're so…argh! Pathetic!" she hissed and his brow cocked again. "I swear, it's like talking to a child in a man's body! A manchild!" she gasped and he frowned deeper in agitation. "How are you even able to do all the things you do and get away with it! How??" she wondered, subtly realizing the strange childlike innocence that he carried within him. She glanced away, and strode confidently to her gun — attempting to put it back together to make a point — to prove herself to him again.

He couldn't help but smirk with sarcasm, as he watched her try to figure out which piece went where — her fingers trying to grip at the oily parts, only for them to slip through them and fall off the table and into her lap.

"You just…oiled them too much…" she mumbled, flustered and embarrassed.

"Hm. Did I?"

"Obviously…" she picked up the fallen parts with trembling fingers, feeling his stare of judgment pierce through her back. "Haven't even had a proper coffee yet…" she nagged, displeased.

"When yer wanted, chased after, hunted, ya ain't got time for coffee."

"So why do you have time for it then?" she hissed, envious of his cup. Silencing him swiftly.

"Concentrate, lass." he ordered, his voice suddenly stern and cold.

"Concentrate, lass..." She wiggled her head, mocking him beneath her breath with her tongue sticking out as she rephrased his words.

He slammed his boot down as he unfolded his legs, startling her by the thudding noise, and walked up to her. Leaning with his chest over the table, he grabbed all the pieces with one swift large grip, and Charlotte glared at his vascular hand imprinted with old scars — with his veins popping out in every direction underneath his dried-up skin, almost able to feel his pulse thud through them. Her eyes traveled up his arm to find more scar tissue and all sorts of bumps that weren't the bumps her mother's clients carried. Bumps of sin to relieve the pain, whatever pain was strong enough to make them choose an outlet to destroy their life with. These bumps appeared different; deep wounds that were meant to heal, but were scraped open over and over again, almost in a torturous manner.

She couldn't help but compare them to Will's perfectly spotless hands, with the softest skin imaginable. She thought of Will often that night; *how things could have been if the grizzly didn't interfere. How she was so close to feel such tenderness — how strangely, unfamiliarly aroused she found herself, just thinking about his lips meeting hers. And now, she was stuck with this mountain man who could barely put two words together.*

Yet her pleasant thought was swiftly interrupted by Mac, the mountain man himself. "Here. That's how ye do it." he slid the gun across the table and placed it in front of her, side-eyeing her reaction with earnest suspense.

Charlotte didn't realize she had to pay any attention to it; she was lost in her own thoughts — thinking about Will's mustache tickling her nose, so she opted to act like she understood, to not offend him — if at all possible.

"Ah! Not so difficult, after all!" she grinned sheepishly, as his eyes caught her in the lie.

"No...It ain't." he straightened his back, huffed, and strode outside, slamming the door behind him.

I I I

Will was crossing the Sweetwater River, as a train was leaving the Smokey Hills Station — emerging on the old-fashioned, latticed metal bridge above him. His mare, although highly trained by professionals, was not used to the sudden noises or lurking, squeaking, screeching creatures that ran around outside the comfort of the stables; let alone the sudden loud blow of thick black smoke from such a massive engine that smudged the blue cleared sky.

Rachel was a dark bay thoroughbred with a little white star on her face, tall legs and two white stocks on the very back; she had the sweetest disposition and absolutely adored Will, for he was a gentle, albeit novice rider, and had a healthy supply of sugar cubes in his satchel.

However, her breed was prone to spook more than the stock-bred ranch horses cowboys typically used on their travels, and as she felt the vibrations from the train underneath her hooves, she raised her head, snorted, pawed, tapped on the ground, and finally bolted right through the bit across the river — with Will bouncing like a green bean atop her, hanging on for dear life as she sped up with every stride, leaping over rocks and bushes.

"Whoa!!! Whoa, Rachel!!" he ordered upon a loud yell, when he suddenly felt himself lift up from the unbroken-in saddle — feeling the breath flee his lungs as he flew over her arched neck, catapulting like a canon ball and descending rapidly into the hard ground.

Rachel hit her brakes the moment she felt him off her back, and turned to look back at him, wondering what the yelling was all about, for she had already forgotten the reason of her bolting. She softly neighed and nudged his face, nibbling at the raven hair that frizzed by the wind. He didn't seem unconscious, but the fall sure knocked the air out of him. Will walked away with nothing but a scratch on his cheek — his now dirt-speckled coat had a slight tear in it, and his back was covered in muddy soil — probably the filthiest he'd ever gotten in his life.

This was Rachel's first time out of the fancy barn and large enclosed paddocks she used to roam; yet being a well-bred thoroughbred, he figured she would be best suited for the long journey. Will didn't imagine this turn of events, the challenges he had already faced and surely would face further with his inexperienced horse, yet he was determined to reach Marysville and proceed with his journey.

I V

SHE SWIPED A FINGER ACROSS THE DUSTY OLD NIGHT-STAND, collecting the gray smudge on the tip of her finger. Somehow, this appeared more exciting than breathing his stillness and some odd type of arrogance within the cabin. After weeks of riding through the desert and lush meadows, being confined in the middle of nowhere felt maddening. It wasn't so much the boredom that came with it, but the uncertainty of her situation, let alone having to endure his shadowy aura, never knowing when it would morph into the murderous beast. Surprisingly, that hadn't occurred yet. He was dreadfully asphyxiating, awfully sarcastic, and yet he kept his distance from her. He never bothered her, he never talked to her, he never ordered for anything other than silence.

She sighed heavily, and absently looped her finger within a fine circular brass handle. She tugged on it, and the drawer pulled out. Her eyes flared, finding a leather-wrapped notebook within it. Curiously, she grabbed it and investigated it in great intrigue. It had two strings of leather coiled around it, and as she untwisted them, the notebook unfolded.

It was a journal. Evidently either forgotten, or tucked away to keep safe — and then forgotten. Someone had written within it, and there were draw-ings of horses, wildlife, trees, and lakes, all reflecting the environments of Rockies West. The drawings were beautiful, as if created by a talented hand. She dithered in politeness, wishing to read the written text, as if yearning for someone to speak to her more than a few caustic words, and yet she didn't wish to invade someone's privacy. Biting her lip in confliction, she tore her gaze away. Then her hazels darted back to the text. "Forgive me, stranger…I long for company…" she whispered, caressing the leather cover of the book.

December 12th 1896

And here, I find myself.

In the shallow void of no return. In the faint moment of life sparing me of the burden to see them again. Here I cower, and here I rot in woe, until my heart can mend again, if at all. There's pain within me…pain that morphs my thoughts into despicable visions. I detest this pain, I detest my imagination, for once it was so pure and blissful, for once I was…

Here, where I can smell the frostbite upon my fingertips, the coaled smell across my legs, so vividly alive still. Here, where I can see the leaves drown in pure whiteness, and the decaying of trees as they succumb to winter's harsh grip around them. I can oddly empathise to the notion…for I hardly recognize myself anymore.

I don't recognize myself anymore, for the mirror reflects another man. I am not me, not any longer. I shall be…me, no longer. Here, I will study the words imprinted on the pages, here, while I find the new me.

J.M.

Her heart sunk for the stranger's note, and guilt consumed her for reading such a personal piece of his heart. But before she could think too much of it, a violent thud of a fist slammed against her door.

"My God!!" she gasped, pressing the book against her chest in startle.

"What yer doin'…" Mac grunted before the door.

"I…I…what do you want??" she hissed, flustered to be interrupted so rudely. There was no answer back, as if he thought it over again. She blinked in silence. "Hello??" she called for him, and silence continued. "What is this man wanting again…" she growled under her breath, stood up, pushed the cabinet away from the door and opened it, only to meet his face inches away from hers. She gaped at him, aghast, paralyzed by his deep blue eyes, and pulled back swiftly. "What is it?" she cleared her throat, composing herself again.

He swallowed hard and glanced down at her hand, still gripping the book. "What's that?" he asked her curiously, and she blinked.

"Nothing..." she said, hiding it behind her back. "Nothing that concerns you..." she said sternly, lifting her jaw, locking daring eyes with him again.

"Hm." he tore his gaze away, in thought. "Sure."

"So? What is the reason of your...rude disturbance?" she asked him, standing tall and bravely before him. That brow cocked again with her attitude.

"Guns..." he said and her eyes shot left and right.

"Guns?"

"Hm."

"Can you be...perhaps more specific?" she asked, tapping her fingers against he frame of the door, noticing his dimples flinch in nervousness.

"Shoot...to shoot guns..." he said, awkwardly, and then frowned, agitated. "Ye gotta learn how to goddamn shoot, woman!" he leered and walked away, leaving her wordless with a knot in her chest. Somehow in all her confusion, he appeared more bewildered than herself, as if he didn't know how to speak to another human being.

V

"MY NAME IS WILLIAM GRIFFITHS, AND I'M APPALLED by the fundamental injustice within your legal system." Will confidently voiced, walking into the sheriff's office in Marysville. "This lady here is innocent! You should be ashamed for making up such rumors, and chasing down people who have nothing to do with crimes in this ill-managed muddy excuse of civilization you call a town!" he proceeded to say, then brushed off the last speck of dirt off his coat.

"Slow down, pretty boy..." the Sheriff muttered, striding to him. "This gal is wanted for manslaughter; she strangled an innocent man and tossed him into a pig stall to be eaten. Ya come here to defend this worthless whore? Wanna be eaten, too?" he stared him down, as if to appear more intimidating.

"You possess no proof of that; a myriad of factors must have been adduced to explain this situation, to neatly wrap the case up and off your docket — but I doubt you have any actual evidence. If I'm mistaken, please enlighten me?" Will said. He might not be comfortable shooting a gun or riding a horse, but he knew his way with impressive-sounding words to overpower any argument, or bewitch the minds of women with them, albeit he never much tried.

"Oh! We've got a city boy here, fellas! Where ya from, partner?" he mocked him, studying his tidily brushed black wavy hair. "For if I had to guess, I reckon you're from the planet of arse-licking elites! Haha!" he laughed and his deputies burst into laughter with him.

"So you are devolving into the ad hominem, instead of expounding any facts regarding your claims." he pressured him, verbally pushing him into a corner. The Sheriff twitched his mustache in irritation, and cocked his head.

"Listen here boy, things are simple. When ya lady gets captured, she be hanged together with her lover — a lover that ain't you, no matter how hard ya try for it to be." he stabbed him where he felt he was the weakest, as in his eyes no sane man would ever fight for a missing woman who was a stranger.

"Sir, upon this blatant expression of contempt towards a missing human being, please expect to receive a court summons. My legal team will gnaw through your petty career faster than any pack of wolves could ever hope to try. Suffice to say, this will *not* end pretty for you." he threatened, as he pulled a poster out of his satchel in great haste. "Upon my thorough investigation, I suspect that Charlotte might have been kidnapped by this degenerate...*Mac Kinnon!*" he growled, waving the paper before his eyes. "Instead of blaming the innocent, perhaps take a closer look into far more plausible possibilities that actually make sense." Will insisted, and the sheriff leaned closer to him, towering over him with a puffed out chest, intended to intimidate him — which surprisingly, it failed to do.

"Tell ya what, boy. If ya find her first, keep the gal. We ain't interested in her, but her partner, Mac Kinnon. However, if my men find her before ya, she'll be gone — in no time." he grinned wickedly, and marched away further back into his office where another sheriff was observing the whole ordeal.

"I'll find her. You can be certain of that." Will promised and mounted Rachel, pawing nervously at the muddy soil, appalled by the filth of the town.

CHAPTER 10

Warmth

I

"HOLD IT STEADY." HE PLOPPED THE RIFLE IN HER HANDS. "Cock it." he ordered firmly, and she rolled her eyes at him.

"I know how to do it…" she nagged as she slowly rotated and pulled on the bolt handle, only to jam the cartridge between the bolt and chamber.

"Hm." he cocked his head, shifting his weight on his leg, suppressing a sarcastic snort.

"This…you…you make me nervous, standing over here!" she fussed, and turned her back to him, trying to figure out the mess she created once again.

"Stop foolin' 'round, lass." He turned her around again, and grabbed the gun from her. He popped the cartridge out, as he reversed the bolt and tipped the gun swiftly before Charlotte could even blink — loading the round into the chamber manually with his thumb, and pushing the bolt forward in one smooth motion. Ready to fire. Charlotte stared in awe, as his methodical movements were flawless — realizing he must have done it a thousand times or more. *Which certainly he had, for he was rumored to have killed at least that many victims in his lifetime,* she thought to herself and crinkled her face in repulsion and great abhorrence.

Handing her the rifle again with an earnest expression imprinted on his face, the bright sun emerged from the gloomy clouds for a change, illuminating his dark blue eyes.

"Press the stock 'gainst yer shoulder. Lift and point the barrel to the bottles, focus through the front sight, an' keep the back sight centered around it." he instructed to her, as she was holding his heavy rifle, ready to shoot the dusty bottles he used as targets. Suddenly, the rude child within him disappeared; and the man she met in Marysville had returned. Solemn, calm, and calculated. "Pay attention. Breathe deeply in, let it out, an' pause yer breath while ya aim…then gently squeeze the trigger when yer sights are stable in yer eye." he stood behind her waiting for her to shoot, as she felt his hovering presence overlook every single breath she took incorrectly.

"So *now* you can talk suddenly, like a typical, ordinary adult of a human?" She poked her head around to face him with a bewildered frown and he twisted it around again with a firm push of a forefinger.

"Concentrate, lass." he said and she rolled her eyes, then fixated them through the sights.

Pow!

"Ugh!!" she fussed and her foot tapped against the ground.

"Again…" he ordered, and she shook her head in resistance.

"I ain't doing it, mister! Let me just die and rot here, okay? It'll do us both a favor…" she hissed, immediately giving up on herself as the shot carved a hole in the snow, although rather impressively deep.

She turned around, surrendering his rifle — briefly noticing his dark blond hair contrast against the slate gray sky in a way she never saw before.

"No. Ya need to learn this now. I didn't kill a whole damn bear for ye to waste me time now." he handed her the rifle back, suddenly beholding her green-tinted hazel eyes that would change shades of color every time the light would hit them — and somehow it hit them differently that morning, somehow hypnotizing him into a state of trance, as they stared right through him. "Concentrate!" he then fussed, pulling himself together from the sudden distraction. "Stop complaining. Straighten yer back, eyes on the sights!" he commanded strictly, as he pushed her back into position.

Lifting the rifle again, she fired.

POW!

The cartridge glided right above the bottles, brushing against a bristly tree. Her whole being clenched in disappointment.

"See?? I'm a lost cause." She huffed. "I'm not a hunter, or a gunslinger… or an outlaw-shootin'-thing like you! Gah!! Let's just…stop right here, before

I accidentally shoot anybody…as if there would be anybody out here to shoot…" She bowed her head, disappointed and frustrated with herself, and passed the rifle back to him again.

He clasped it tightly and glared at it, benumbed by her lack of inner vigor, as if someone had worked really hard on instilling a sense of insecurity within her. And somehow, it resonated with him for a split moment.

Mac strode towards her, and pressed his knuckles against her frosty chin — lifting her gaze up to his. "If ya don't believe in yer self, who else will?" he said hauntingly soft, his eyes unwittingly lowering down to her lips, for he hadn't seen a woman that up close since he was a young man visiting a working lady in a mucky town called Crowfoot — and even that wasn't engraved in his memory. This was different; being close to Charlotte felt different — intense; a feeling he could not control nor explain, yet always resulting back into rage.

"Pick up the damn rifle and feckin' concentrate now, will ya!" He lit up a cigarette to calm himself down, judging and studying every movement of hers.

Charlotte, as instructed, picked up the weapon and braced it against her shoulder. There was no way she could concentrate, feeling his pressure behind her. Let alone the menacing voice of his, drilling into her ears. His intense stare stabbing right through her. Daggers, slicing her.

Pow!

The bullet barely missed the bottle — again, piercing deep into the snow.

She sighed. "I can't do it. I'm sorry. I'm just wasting your time…" she said, raising her arms to hand him the rifle for the last time.

He grabbed her arm, and repositioned it.

"No. Ye *got* to keep tryin'." he insisted and adjusted himself, now standing behind her back; subtly pressing his chest against her, feeling her elegant shape touch his strong build. Even as curvy as she was, he was framing her body beautifully. He wrapped his arm around her shoulder, keeping the gun steady for her. All she could feel or hear was his hauntingly slow, warm breath brushing at the crease of her neck.

Raising her hair. Prickling her skin.

Sending a hot flush throughout her body.

"Breathe slowly, point to the bottle…" he whispered against her face, as if they had sneaked before their prey — not wanting to alert it. Her hands started to quiver, as did the barrel, albeit not due to the heavy metal, and the more she felt his body pressing against hers, the more she forgot there was even a rifle in her hands. He reached around her left side and placed his vascular hand oddly tenderly over hers, stabilizing the rifle.

"Always, pull the trigger on an empty lung…" he ordered within a sough — a soft voice trickling down her cheek, a feral breath now tickling the bareness of her neck, utterly paralyzing her. Feeling her chest begin to deflate, he stepped back for her to shoot.

POW!

The bottle exploded into a thousand shards of glass.

"Good…shot." he expressed his very first compliment to her yet Charlotte remained speechless, gaping at the shards, almost crystallized before her eyes.

She didn't even realize what had happened — she felt herself writhing from adrenaline, or rather some strange exaltation; she felt his raw breath against her face, against her now cold goose-bumped neck that somehow still remained. The sudden flicker of feelings utterly perplexed her, and as she turned around, she locked eyes with him tentatively.

"Thank you…" she said faintly, barely audible, as if her voice had evaporated in the sweet-scented air, as his cigarette was rapidly burning away to his lips and its smoke painted questions in the air between them.

Mac hushed; this time, he had a different kind of quietness to him. Ashes dropping atop his coat. Flying off. The wind was still. He was still.

His eyes were glued to hers; his feet felt frozen, unable to take a step.

"Uhm, here, your…rifle." She handed him the gun slowly, noticing his chest rise bigger the closer she strode to him.

"Sure…" He gazed out at the slivers remaining of the broken bottle.

II

"MAC, DID YOU FEED THE CHICKENS YET?" The farmer emerged next to the chicken coop — his shadow towering over it, knowing the young boy had stolen one of his hidden liquor bottles again.

Mac stood up, frightened, and hid the bottle behind his back with a quivering pout that betrayed his sin. "Yes, sir — doin' it now." He sucked in a stutter, grasping at his suspenders nervously.

"What you got there, son?" He limped towards him, with a salivating grin.

"Nothin', sir." He watched the obese man's grin get wider; his flabby flesh shaking with every step; his gold crucifix pendant swinging from his neck like the pendulum of a grandfather clock, relentlessly counting the moments before his punishment.

"Turn around for me, son, will ya?" His face, nearing Mac's.

His rotten breath, creating a cloud he could not escape from. Threatening. Two eyes of a black so rich, they were lifeless — the black of an ominous night. The black of his soul alone, reaching through Mac's chest to paint him with the same horrid dark liquid that swirled within his flabby mass.

The boy handed him the rum bottle reluctantly, as he did not have another choice. "I'm sorry, sir." he mumbled, as he watched the farmer's drool run down his mouth.

"Oh, Mac. Don't be *sorry* to me…be *sorry* to our Lord and Savior, for you have sinned. Again." he pouted snidely at the boy, with thick sets of brows that pulled together in an insincere frown.

"Lord, forgive me." the boy sighed with a sullen look, pretending he meant it, feeling the farmer's shadow now swallow him whole.

"Turn around, Mac, my son." He twisted his body, lowered the boy's suspenders, and undressed his trousers down to his knees.

III

"AAAAARGHHH!!! YE FECKIN' BASTARD!!!"

Charlotte awoke from Mac's horrifying screams, and rushed to his room as fast as she could push the cabinet aside, and adjust her vision through the dimly lit cabin. She found him in bed, drenched in sweat, locking his stiffened jaw tightly, his stained teeth clenched together and his fists wrestling in the chilled air. "Mister!! Wake up! Wake up!!" She grasped his shoulders, shaking him as fast and hard as she could.

"I'll feckin' kill ya!!!" he yelled in agony, chest and abdomen emerging through his soaking wet white shirt every time he'd arch his back.

"Mister!" she shook him. "MAC!!" she slapped him across his face and yelled. "Wake up!!"

"GAH!" He grappled her hand and pressed it against his chest, the moment he woke up by the sting of her hand. "Don't hurt me!!" he yelled — thinking he was still within a nightmare, an ongoing nightmare playing repeatedly in his mind for decades.

"It's okay! It's okay…" Her fingers brushed softly against his grip, quivering herself to be so close to him. "It's okay, Mac…it was just a nightmare. Nobody is going to hurt you."

She leaned over him in slight hesitation, and caressed his forehead with a free hand. She felt helpless to see this angry mountain man for the first time in such vulnerable distress. An expression of terror plastered on his face, and streaks of veins slashed through his forehead. He looked at her in equal shock, feeling his heartbeat burn up his throat, and his rapid pulse pounding through his veins, pumping him with a rush of adrenaline he couldn't control.

"I…I…" He exhaled heavily, bewildered, almost shy, for he wasn't used to waking up next to someone, yet she was here — holding his hand, as he held hers — not pulling away from his strenuous, sweaty grip. "I just…" he stared into her eyes, seeing the reflection of a murderer within them.

"Nevermind." he stuttered, tearing his gaze away, trying to catch his breath with a grimace full of woeful pain.

"Do you wish to talk about it?" she offered kindly, still subtly caressing his hand with her thumb.

"No!" he snapped, changing his tone again.

"Leave me." he said and pushed her hand away from him.

I V

WILL RODE THROUGH THE BURNT PINE HILL FOREST upon a steady trot, looking around himself at the lifeless birch trees and empty fields as he did. Rotten carcasses of animals were scattered around and greedy, ravenous vultures were working on the next victims as they finally succumbed to their injuries. He halted Rachel for a moment, as a deer with a burnt stomach limped across their path, dragging its intestines beside it as they tumbled out of a large gap; a pack of coyotes followed after it in sheer slyness, and yet they knew it wouldn't be too long now.

He thought of how Charlotte must have felt rushing through the menacing forest, trying to escape the wildfire with all the stubborn grit she possessed. That he was so infatuated with. He thought about how brave of a woman she was; braver than himself, braver than he ever was and ever would be.

He recalled the hideous way he missed shooting the grizzly down, realizing he could've prevented this whole mess — if he was just…*manlier,* instead of a cerebral bookworm of the Wild West that everybody mocked. Until they needed his expert advice on anything too complicated for their simpleminded brains to grasp, that is.

The road up north became more challenging; he could not find a path that was not snowed in, or cloaked with heavy rocks rushing down the moment he stepped over them, plunging off the lip of the cliff beneath them. Rachel had no experience with such terrain, and didn't have the best feet to begin with, only adding to the complexity of his problem.

He tried to ride up a rock wall, but kept on sliding down, dangerously fast and abrupt. He could not comprehend how Finn could have passed through such rugged terrain — while a bear was chasing after them, no less. Rachel pushed as hard as she could; sliding down with every try. Rocks smashing down behind them, spooking her as they rolled underneath her body.

Deciding it was not feasible, he turned to the other side of the glacial mountain. Dismounting in disappointment, he led his mare over a steep cliff that led to Rockies West — the very same cliff that the avalanche cleared, killing a dozen deputies. A dead end.

Will had to turn back again; he needed to set camp for the night, for the sun had started to set below the snow-capped mountains.

V

CHARLOTTE COULDN'T SHUT AN EYE THE NIGHT BEFORE. She listened to the wind rub its nails against the timber walls, glide them against them so the wood would rattle and creak to frighten her furthermore. Somehow she didn't place the cabinet before the door this time, in fear she needed to rush back to him again during another night terror. Somehow she felt a little safer in his company, or perhaps it was her compassionate side feeling sorry for him. She was utterly stunned seeing Mac struggle like this, as so far, she was convinced someone had sliced his heart open and yanked out every single emotion known to man.

His anguish reminded her of her own nightmares, growing up. How she would always wake up covered in a bed of musky sweat, fearing that one of her mother's filthy clients would be hovering over her, yet thankfully no-one ever did — they were too intoxicated or drugged to even walk after their sessions. *However, even being in hiding felt more peaceful than living with her own flesh and blood, and that had to count for something,* she thought to herself.

That night she wondered about Mac, and what his story could possibly tell, as all she knew so far was the apparent atrocities he had committed for decades. The curiosity tormented her, yet she knew she would never get an answer out of him — it shouldn't be important to her anyway, as they'd be leaving the mountain anytime soon; parting ways, never to be crossed again.

At dawn, she watched the ravens fly across Hope while she sipped on her coffee. They were picking on a rabbit's rotten carcass, taking turns, throwing their heads around as they pulled on the meat. Somehow the sight made her hungry herself, for she refused to eat Mac's elk meat he had buried within the snow, in fear he would try to poison her in some way or other. She feasted on the same canned beans instead, proven to be resilient to the iced cold water, for they sunk with Finn within it in the saddle bag.

She heard the wood floor crack as Mac was getting up from bed, strangely later than usual, as if last night had drained him. There was no door in that room to block her sight, and her sheer curiosity was guiding her eyes to him. She glanced cautiously at him taking off his sweaty shirt, and as he turned towards the light, her eyes flared, aghast, and her throat dropped to the pit of her stomach.

His wide, strong back appeared to be dented with deep scars — old burn marks mapped across it, or marks from a strong beating — permanently carved, for him to never forget. Forever to remember. She tore her gaze away, realizing it was the polite thing to do, yet her heart felt suddenly heavy.

After a while, Mac walked in the room with a relatively fresh button-up black shirt, with its collar loosened around his neck, and his shirtfront lazily secured. He poured himself some coffee, and looked at her briefly as the nutty scent traveled across the room.

She bowed her head, not knowing if he wished to speak this time, respecting it if that were the case. And yet, to her surprise, he spoke.

"So…" he huffed, as he leaned against the windowpane. Her gaze lifted up and nailed on him, and yet then, there was silence. Her mouth cracked open to ask, and yet she chose to give him more time instead. "Weather's better…" he finally said sheepishly, avoiding to look at her, as if he was still embarrassed for the vulnerability that slipped up from him. He then cleared his throat and spoke again. "So, I'm headed out to check on things…" he said, and her brows dropped into a frown.

"Check on things?"

"Hm."

"What things? The roads?" she asked, and he bit his lip.

"No. Deputies. They must be movin' up here." he said, and her face fell.

"What? How??"

"Anyway…I'll be back." he said, not wishing to elaborate, and walked out of the building.

Her fingers tensed up, and her hands balled into a fist. She looked around herself at the hollowness of the room and back outside the window, seeing him stride the opposite direction of the barn. Bewildered to see him walk instead of ride Roy to wherever he was headed to, she decided against her better judgement to rush after him.

"Mac! Wait!" she said, and he halted, aghast to hear herself speak out his name again. "Wait, please!" Her was voice now clearer as she neared him.

He turned around, and faced her with confusion.

"What?" he grunted.

"I…just wondered…why are you not riding Roy…wherever you're headed to?" she asked and he stared into her eyes, almost coldly again.

"Tracks, and uphill path." he said, and she bobbed her head.

"Oh…I see…" she said, and he turned away again. "Wait, Mac!" She clasped his shoulder ,and he yanked it away from her grip. "I'm sorry…I… can I…come with you?" She swallowed dryly, bewildered with her own self for even asking this. He glared at her, speechless.

"Come with me?" he repeated, and she shrugged shyly.

"I just…need to get out some. And weather is nice, finally…and…just wish to…get out some…for I haven't…for I'm…I'm going crazy, in there." she rambled, and he tore his gaze away.

"Hm. Bad business." he said sardonically, and she bit her tongue again.

"Please?"

"No."

"What? Why not??" She followed after him as he strode to a bundle of trees, chopping off two pine branches with his knife after he halted beneath them.

"'Cause, I said so." he said, bending them into a large shape to fit his boots.

"So? You can't forbid me to follow you…the land is big enough! Surely, you won't feel threatened by my presence." She cocked her hip with an attitude, and he continued to ignore her, coiling thick cordage around the branches for structural rigidity. "What is that you're doing, anyway??" she then asked, for curiosity got the best of her. He rolled his eyes, and huffed heavily.

"Do ye always talk so much?" he asked her in earnest, and she folded her arms before her chest.

"Actually…no. Not in the slightest! I never do…unless I talk to myself, or…my pony." She bit her lip, rehearsing her hideous answer that was every bit true.

"So, why do ye do now?" he asked her, as somehow he was intrigued to know. She stared at him blankly, for she had no answer to that.

"I…I am not sure…" she said, shying away.

"Hm." He retrieved himself back to his wood-crafting, lashing cordage across the branches to weave smaller pine leaves in between them.

"This…this looks just like snowshoes…" she said, watching him wrap them around his boots.

"Hm." he nodded.

"Well…I suppose I will have to make myself some shoes, then." she said, and he cut his eyes at her beneath a heavy frown. "If you could be so kind to wait on me for a few…minutes. It won't take long." she said and he blinked at her, baffled.

She leaped upwards and grappled a branch of pine, hanging from it in the pitiful attempts to break it, and yet it wouldn't break, no matter how much she tugged on it and twisted around herself. Mac rolled his eyes and shook his head, extending his arm and chopping it off with his knife, only for her to land abruptly on her bottom, sinking deep into the snow like an ice spike.

"Thanks…I guess…" she said and he snorted.

After a few minutes of struggling to connect the branches and tie them all together, she managed to create her own version of snow-shoes — which consisted of two half-bent branches that ended into a sharp point at the toe, barely able to fit her whole boot into one.

"See? They're perfect." she boasted, genuinely impressed with herself.

"Hm…yer gonna roll down the mountain with those." he said, and she cocked her head at him.

"How dare you? I think they look beautiful." she said, he shook his head.

Mac didn't have the patience nor the time to correct her design, and he knew she wouldn't let him attempt to do so anyway.

They started hiking up the hill. It was one of those rare perfect days in the mountains; as perfect as you could get them, in such a lethal environment. There was just enough clouds to lend them shade, and just enough sunshine to pierce through them, warming up their limbs and faces with a tranquil glow.

"It is, however, beautiful here…" she said, pausing to scan around herself. "The world just looks…different, dressed in white. Almost innocent and pure, and yet…it is nothing like that." she said, perhaps inappropriately for the company she had, and yet she didn't realize it at the time, and nor did he, for his gaze was nailed at her shoes with concern. "If it didn't have those deadly frozen lakes and temperatures, perhaps I would have myself a house built up here, not that I could ever afford one that is…nor be eligible to own one."

She chuckled with herself and took another step, only to stumble and have her legs spread widely apart, doing the splits. "Shit!" she fussed and he snorted, as she tried to pull herself back together. "This…this is not funny, Mister Mac…" she hissed and he shook his head with a smirk. "I was simply distracted…" she said, and took another step, only for one leg to slide back downwards, and as she tried to regain her balance, her legs scissored frantically not to fall down.

He didn't help her. He could have, but he chose against it. It was oddly a comical sight to witness, and for the first time this feeling of pure amusement registered within him. Somehow she made him feel this way, and he couldn't grasp what power she held to do so.

"Perhaps ye should wait here. Don't think yer shoes can carry ye further up." he said in earnest, and she frowned.

"Of course they can! Like I said, I was distracted…" she said, clearing her throat in shame. "I barely even sink! I don't even leave tracks behind, nor… leaves." she stammered, finding a trail of leaves after all.

"Hm." He cocked his brow.

"Just…let's continue, please." she said and trod now first, a few feet before him.

There was a nip in the air that slowly turned into a wintry squall the higher they trod up the mountain, a squall that now pushed everyone back. Charlotte leaned forward and slammed her snow-shoes harder against the snow, as Mac followed right behind her.

Completely ignoring the importance of not leaving any tracks behind, she chose to get on her fours and help pull herself up over the last lip of the mountain with her hands hooked into the soil before her. Mac made sure to go over her tracks with his snow-shoes, covering the evidence.

Arriving at the very top in strange success, she plopped herself on her back and inhaled a lungful of air. He looked at her, and shook his head again.

"Is this what you do every single day?" she panted, barely able to breathe.

"Sure…" he said, pulling out his binoculars and crouching at the edge of the cliff, now looking through.

She rolled around and crawled towards him, breaking a branch of her shoe as she did. "And?" she asked him, curiously, somehow excited to break the mundane routine of hiding in a cabin.

"Deputies appear elsewhere…there's a fire on the other side…so, they're here." he said and her heart skipped a beat.

"They're…here??" she gasped and he nodded, carelessly. "And now?? What do we do now??"

"We stay quiet." he said, cutting his eyes at her, and her breath halted in her lungs. "Then, we breathe." he said and she exhaled through her rosy nose.

Upon descending, the weather had started to change. Flurries of snow intensified, falling thick and rapid against their faces and yet the sun still glimmered proudly like a shield above them, preparing for its setting in a couple of hours.

"So…you always have to scan your surroundings, when you're out and about?" she asked him, her voice sincere and kind.

"Hm…" He nodded faintly, not wishing to discuss this.

"That must be tiring." she said, absently rushing down the mountain beside him, with her shoes slowly loosening around her boot. Yet her focus was on sparking some conversation for this man stirred her curiosity, and for whatever reason she couldn't grasp, she wished to learn more about his life-style now that he appeared kinder and slightly more talkative — by a relatively impressive two words more.

"Sure…"

"Mhm…" She sighed. As she took another step her shoe unwrapped from her boot, making her lose her balance, trip over herself in the least eloquent way, and start to descend rapidly towards a steep drop from the hill. Reacting upon instinct, he grabbed her from the shoulder and pulled her to him, only for her abrupt weight to slam against him, making them fall together — now tumbling down the hill like a pair of entangled tumbleweeds. He covered her head with his arms, pressed his forehead against hers, hooked his body into hers to shield her from any rocks as they rolled around. The downwards snowy trail appeared endless, and yet their bodies almost leaped along the blanket of snow, eventually landing with Mac's back against it, with her petrified being atop his, arms coiled around her and faces glued together. Both startled, more at the way their bodies were merged into one, they snapped their eyes open and glared at each other, wordlessly.

Every fiber of his being urged him to grapple her neck and yank her off of him, in this moment of vulnerability he was no longer used to find himself within. His whole body rattled on the edge of self-defense, for that was what his body had been trained to do; that was what his brain had been programmed to function like, and yet, somehow he couldn't move a limb, somehow he felt an odd, unfamiliar warmth radiate through his hollowed chest instead — and that frightened him.

She stared into his eyes, panting breaths merging into a mist of bewilderment. Her body ached from the fall, and it shivered to be laying atop his. Her hands were clasped on his chest, sucking out every breath he inhaled as discreetly as he could. Something felt coiled tight inside of her. She cleared her throat, and both tore their gazes away. "I'm…sorry." she said, barely audible, and climbed off of him in great haste.

VI

HE WAS GONE FOR A LONG WHILE. In the darkness and in the blizzard, evaporated like a ghost within the hazy veil of snow. He didn't say a lot after the abrupt, shameful fall, other than breaking her snow-shoes to feed the fire with, for he deemed them useless. She didn't say a lot, either.

There was embarrassment that lingered in the air of the cabin, a leaden silence that suffocated them more than before. The air had shifted differently this time, and Charlotte herself couldn't explain what it was. He let it be implied that he was headed back out again — this time with Roy, to check on the deputies, camped on the other side of the mountain. It was certainly also implied that she would be staying back in Hope.

She chose to nest before the fireplace, cocooned in a woolen blanket she found in one of those drawers; picking up the leather-bound notebook again for the sake of some company other than the crackling of fire and the bumping of timber wood against the shabby old cabin. A drawing of a woman was revealed upon flipping the page, and her eyes nailed with hers. "Wow…" she soughed to herself, for every detail was so lively captured, her face almost appeared real — trapped within a blank page. She searched the woman's face, as if expecting for her solemn eyes to blink back. Another note was below it.

December 20th 1896

*I've been practicing my speech, you would be delighted to know,
and I've been learning the arts of drawing, and painting…you.*

*For I still can envision your poreless face, and the youthful lines
of naïvety at the crease of your neck. For you were naïve, my
dear. You were naïve to abuse my love for you for the mere sin of
being different than you. For talking, different than you. For
dressing, different than you. For suffering, different than you…*

*But if there is one thing that this life of mine, of utter sorrowful
hardship, has taught me, is that I will never give up on hope.
My hope is for one day to find myself laying next to you, until
all our differences turn equal, until my shadow morphs into
flesh and bone, allowed to tower over you, allowed to be your
shield of protection, allowed to be the trigger you pull on him.*

J. M.

"Hm…" Her head cocked, and her lips curved into a pout of sadness. "I am sorry for your pain…stranger." she said, caressing the note with a forefinger. "But if you were to ask me…I would tell you to never settle for someone that doesn't accept you, just the way you are." She stared at the letters, and back to the drawing with a different pair of eyes. "And I feel like this woman most likely hurt your heart in ways you could never write down in such a journal…albeit, I don't really know how that feels like." She sighed and shut the book, wondering if that beautiful woman was deserving of such a man, one who appeared to be a loving gentleman with a most sensitive and loyal heart. She shrunk within the cloth, wondering about Will, and her own heart that hadn't much thought of him in the last couple of days. She cut her eyes at the room with no door and suddenly her heart constricted, startling her with the unfamiliar feeling. Then, in the midst of her panic, she heard a knock on the window. Her breath caught in her lungs, and swiftly she reached for the shotgun Mac had left her with — figuring it would be best for her to simply point and shoot with a barrel that didn't need much precision.

Clasping it in her hands, and forgetting to cock it, she trod towards the window, her bare toes sliding across the oaken floor in slyness. Her breath fogged before her face, and as she lifted the shotgun, she turned round the wall and aimed it at the window. Her eyes flared, and a sigh of relief escaped her as she spotted a raven nudging the glass with its beak.

"You silly bird…" She snorted. "I almost had a heart attack…" she said and the bird halted, turning its head to face her — perfectly still. She swallowed dryly and stared back at it, wondering what it even wished for. "Are you hungry?" she asked it, as if it could answer, and the bird cocked its head. "Well…I do have some oatcakes…I'm sure Finn wouldn't mind, if half of one went missing." She giggled, placing the shotgun down and fumbling in her saddle bag for the can of biscuits.

She grabbed a lantern, and trod outside carefully as to not to spook the bird. Her fist was crumbling up the oatcake in a myriad of sprinkles, and as she turned around the corner towards the window, the raven was still there as if waiting for its treat.

"You must truly be hungry…" she said, her lips quivered from the brutal cold and her lack of attire. The bird flew from the window and landed a few feet before her, hopping towards her, barely denting the snow. She tossed a few sprinkles to it, and it picked them up with its beak hungrily. Upon closer inspection, she noticed its upper beak was half-missing, and yet that didn't hinder it to scoop up and gorge down the cookie crumbles.

"What yer doin' here?" he asked, startling her so hard she dropped the lantern and broke it.

"Good Lord, Mac!" she hissed, and he folded his arms before his chest. "I was…feeding the poor bird you scared off!" she said, and he blinked.

"Feedin'…a bird."

"Yes! And the poor thing was injured, and…you scolded it away now…" she sighed heavily, and he shook his head.

"Ye know, if we was able to come here, then there's other folk 'round too." he said and she blinked, barely able to see him through the black veil that enveloped them.

"What's your point?"

"Where's yer shotgun…is me point." he said, and she huffed heavily and with complaint.

Settling before the fireplace again, he nursed on a bottle of whiskey and she unbraided her hair for the night in embarrassing silence. She couldn't grasp how he was able to sneak up to her without her noticing, and that alone was a scary enough thought to have. Then she thought of the stranger's note and the bird that appeared right after reading them, as if in a state of feverish hallucination — her eyelids felt leaden, and her heart, oddly content enough to let her guard down around him. It was the very first night to sit around the fireplace together, albeit in the usual silence. It felt peaceful.

"I've never had my heart…broken…like…*this*…" she said incoherently, her voice faint and feeble, the stranger's words flashing before her eyelids.

"Hm?"

He cut his eyes at her discreetly, noticing the absent movement of her fingers, tangling them within her lush brown hair as she slowly dozed off. The fire's light softly brushed against her face, illuminating even the faintest of freckles she carried on the bridge of her nose, and yet the flames contrasted his own face, creating streaks of shadows that slashed through his deep, intense glare. A wave of serenity wrapped around him the longer he studied her, and a tingling feeling slithered throughout him.

Her head was cocked and slowly her body leaned to the side, falling completely against the ground. She laid there, comfortably asleep, with her chest rising and her mouth cracked open, eyes locked from sheer exhaustion. An adorable snore escaped her as she drew in a heavy breath, and Mac bowed his head in thought.

Standing up from the ground after a lot of contemplation, he walked towards her and picked her up in his arms, carrying her back into her room. He laid her into the bed and placed the blanket over her. A last glance of her tranquil being was stolen by his eyes, for he knew the days of her company were numbered — and at that moment, a feeling was so keen it slashed him like a knife.

CHAPTER 11

Agreement

I

HE SET UP CAMP BEFORE TWO LARGE GRAY-SLATED BOULDERS with caps of snow atop them, shielding him from the penetrating cold that whipped against him the more the night roared its entrance. He lost hours of daylight wrestling with his brand new tent that he acquired from Marysville's general store, setting one up for the first time in his whole existence. Figuring he needed a few minutes to do so, for it shouldn't be all that complicated — he quickly regretted that decision, when he realized he needed to collect supple tree limbs to mount the canvas with, as well as craft spikes to drill it into the ground.

"I am certainly not equipped to be a man of wilderness endeavors." he sighed to himself, proceeding to make a fire a few feet before the tent, something at least he had some experience in doing.

Placing his imported Egyptian-cotton sleeping bag, filled with straw, upon the painted canvas ground cloth, he laid atop it and covered himself with a wool blanket, quivering to the very core by the harsh weather conditions he wasn't accustomed to.

"My lady...I am yet, by no means, discouraged by what trouble you have found yourself within — and therefore I shall hope this expression of effort to be an avowal of my fervent and honorable passion for you..." he said, sliding his thumb across the set of rings on his fingers.

11

"WAKE UP, LASS." HE BUMPED ON HER DOOR AND CHARLOTTE, used to his rude awakenings by now, squinted through her eyelids and slammed her hand on the night-stand beside her, pulling herself up by its sturdy support.

Grumpily, she stretched her arms back and felt the unpleasant tension release from her muscles. Shuffling herself into the common area with a head of bed hair and eyes still clamped together, she found him patching up a hole in his coat with his usual metal cup beside him.

"Good morning…" she said, somehow not as nervously as before.

"Hm." He nodded to her and put away his needle and leather thread, tucking it back into his satchel. He cleared his throat, and nailed his gaze at the window. "Deputies been campin' at Ewing Basin for over a week now, judging by the limited supplies I spotted at their campground." he said and she swallowed hard.

"Last night you found them?" she asked him, clasping a cup of coffee and sitting in a chair.

"Southwest of the lake where ya almost got yerself eaten." He took a sip of his coffee, after throwing the tease into his announcement. She let him have that small triumph. "What them eejits don't understand though, is this place is known for avalanches. Bad weather'll be comin' in soon, and surprise the feck out of 'em." he said, eyes analyzing the storm clouds on the far horizon. Charlotte bobbed her head, as if she was supposed to agree with that statement, suddenly emerging into the role of an outlaw herself.

"So…what do you suggest we do?" she then asked him with concern, as she had been trying hard to drown the thought of being wanted ever since she found out.

"We need to move." He cut his eyes at her, and she froze still. "We try to head east, in a few days." he said and walked towards the map, pulling out his knife and gently gliding the tip of it across a large secluded area. "We cross Black Wolf Lagoon." He showed her on the map, with his bruised fingernails clasping the wooden handle of the knife now guiding her gaze.

"I thought…I thought we can't leave, until two weeks from now…" she said, confused. "Because of the…blizzard?"

"Hm." he nodded, and she blinked. "We ride during the blizzard, so they won't be able to detect us." he said, decisively.

"But, the horses?" she gasped, for Finn hadn't recovered completely yet.

"Horses will be fine."

"But…"

"Roy's used to such weather, and yer Fox will just follow him. He already proved himself to everyone." he noted, as he slid the knife across the map further down.

"It's Finn." she corrected him, offended, watching him poke a cigarette between his lips.

"Fine." he gave her a sharp look, and lit it up. He pulled down on it and exhaled away from her. His eyes, nailing back to the map. "So from the Lagoon, we follow Sweetwater River, and go through Great Bend…"

"Great Bend??" she screeched, shocked to hear this location, pulling his gaze towards her with suspicion.

"Hm…towards Hot Springs." he grunted, seeing her eyes light up in an instant, and her cheeks crimson. "Why?" he asked, for her sudden silence engrossed him.

"Nothing…" she bowed her head, with a smile she couldn't suppress.

"Hm…" he frowned and lowered his hand with the knife, bowing his head as well.

"It's just…I have a friend there." She looked away briefly, as if he wasn't supposed to know — yet he knew.

"This Will lad, ye shouted for?" he clenched his jaw, for he'd been curious about it ever since.

"Yes…we…got separated from this…grizzly…when we were…well, we… and, well, that's where he lives." She stumbled over her words, not being able to hide her discomfort as she watched him put out the cigarette with his thumb.

"Hm." he went eerily quiet, as a gust of wind blew through the window.

"Can't be seen by no one, so ye can stay at Great Bend with the fine lad." he snapped abruptly and walked over to the chimney, tossing the cigarette inside and stretching his hands to the fire.

"I...I would, but I'm...apparently wanted now, as well?" she clarified, noticing his sarcastic tone yet again, wondering how to explain Will — how he would perceive it all.

"Not me burden to carry." he grunted, as he felt a knot swell up in his throat.

III

CHARLOTTE TROD THROUGH THE BARN WHERE ROY AND FINN were comfortably stabled and sheltered from the frost-land outside. She needed some fresh air to help clear her mind, for this sudden shift in her life overwhelmed her.

It was a beautiful barn; built to last for many years to come. The roof and walls were still intact, and miraculously there were no missing wood planks anywhere besides a few rotting boards. It was the perfect nook for keeping the horses warm and safe, and Finn certainly benefitted from the break against the horrendous weather. She was certain she had heard or seen a gang of chipmunks nesting in the barn's loft, and an owl hoot in the dark sapphire twilight of the evening.

She patted Roy on his hind to let him know she was passing him, just in case he would spook at the sudden movement behind him — for she didn't know him that well, yet she thought he was undeniably stunning.

"Hey, Finny boy!" She hugged his warm neck, which had started to grow a dark mahogany fuzzy winter coat — sliding her fingers through it, feeling the softness against her freezing palm. "Oh, sweetie...you already seem to be feeling so much better..." She sighed into him. "I know this is all new to you; it is for me too..." she said, laying her face against him. "But, at least...we're together in this...craziness..." She chuckled, and kissed his neck. "Remember that time we were talking about this man...? What a fool I was..." she snorted at the irony, for again, he had saved them both, in a strangely selfless way. He appeared a lot more selfless than what they made him out to be, and she struggled with this realization. Albeit an odd personality, there was something so innocent within him that would arise in rare moments, not a pure touch or word, but a gentle innocence within his wrath and silence. Her face fell as the map emerged before her eyes again, and a knot twisted her stomach, as if the new plot for their escape, benumbed her. "Crazy how things work out, huh…" she shut her eyes and buried her nose into his coat, taking in the best smell in the world to dissolve all her worries.

Roy nuzzled her back, envious of the attention Finn was getting, as he hadn't gotten any affection from Mac since many years ago — besides the occasional pat on the neck, that was more habit than devotion.

"Hey, handsome!" She giggled and petted his bald white face, staring at his bright blue eyes that portrayed an aged wisdom which Finn hadn't acquired yet. "You are one heck of a horse, Mr. Roy…" She hugged his muscular neck, and suddenly smelled *his* sweet, smoky scent imprinted on his coat. Pulling back, aghast, she drew in a breath — and dithering, faced him again. "Thank you for saving my Finn…" she whispered to him, and he let out a big yawn and licked his lips contentedly.

Finn snorted and pinned his ears, as he wasn't used to such competition, let alone that of a good-looking stallion. Charlotte glanced over at him, unable to restrain her laughter, as his annoyed and grumpy face stared right back at her. Finn turned his butt towards them, and snorted once more.

IV

"RACHEL, GIRL, I DO NOT KNOW WHERE WE ARE HEADED…" he petted her neck nervously as he was trying to find a decent road to take this early morning, as everything looked eerily the same dressed in white.

"I cannot believe I'm talking to a horse now, too." He realized he was mimicking Charlotte, feeling a sudden nostalgia reach through him. "Quite the majestic scenery; however, I see no way out of here either." He looked over the hill, wondering if he would ever find a way to the gloomy, dangerously lethal looking mountain. His throat felt tight.

Riding on a different path, upwards towards the mountain, a sudden snowfall bombarded them — snowflakes thicker than hail, harsher than stones, covering Will's dark coat and Rachel's hind; sticking to his well-groomed hair and her perfectly trimmed mane. He certainly wasn't dressed for inclement weather, nor prepared for such tough expedition — *what was I thinking*, he wondered as the cold shook his bones, aching within him.

A flock of ravens shot through a lattice of snowy branches, spooking Rachel just enough for her clopping hooves to trace a large circle and turn herself around. He pulled on the reins with his stomach up to his throat, and as she halted to his surprise in a more punctual manner than before — and suddenly from above the hill, he spotted an abandoned settlement. His eyes flared, swiftly clutching the reins in one hand and fumbling out his map with the other, he unfolded it over the cantle and compared the landscape.

Ewing Basin, it read. There was a campfire emerging from it. Black smoke, billowing up through the peaks around it. A glimpse of hope filled his heart. *It must be her…or the deputies,* he thought to himself, and swiftly his mind raced to figure out a plan.

V

THE FIERY GLOBE OF THE SUN SET LOW BEHIND THE SNOW-CAPPED MOUNTAINS; faintly reflecting its wrath across the glittering iced lake in front of Hope. The buildings within, now cloaked in crystallized hoarfrost, as if preparing for themselves for the ominous weather that was yet to hit them.

Charlotte stood outside, stretching out her arms liberally, taking in the fresh cold air — feeling the softest flakes of snow land against her face, chilling every inch of it. She wished to take in the last moments of her stay in Hope, even if that meant freezing from the cutting cold that tightly enwreathed her. Somehow she was used to it by now, as if her soul longed for the raw, cruel beauty of winter. Yearning to feel the wind wrap itself around her bare skin.

She would miss the sound of quivering shingles from the shattered roofs, and the creaking of timbered frames threatening to collapse atop her, but cowardly never did. She would miss the twisting of a keening wind between her and the covers, stirring her disheveled hair to the side of her head as thoughts of sorrow suddenly were able to vanish in its spell. She would miss the way the brutal cold would rise up her cheeks and nose, as if she had accidentally blushed shyly. She would miss the way her fingers would burn, oddly pleasurable before the slow-burning flames. And yet, that wasn't all that she would miss after all, but it was the closest feeling to it.

Mac observed her from the frosted window, as he kept to the shadows of his own lair. He was not able to take his eyes off of her anymore, no matter how hard he attempted to pull his focus away. It hurt to look, and it hurt not to. It confused him, and it utterly frustrated him. He dared to avow to himself, she was so beautiful to him, so enchanting — hauntingly gripping all his senses every time he stole a glimpse of her in sheer discreetness. The odd sensation of her womanly body pressed against his, lingered within him ever since — for it felt different than before. This time he was forced to breathe in her being, her company, her kind smile, her caustic snorts, and her menacing leer when she would get upset with him. Days passed, and yet they felt like seconds he desperately tried to cling on to. Any time spent in her absence felt like an eternity, and his sudden mind bursting into thoughts he never had before bewildered the entire character he had trained to be dull, and hollow. Chills made an icy trail down his spine as he tensed up, thinking of the way she looked at him when he got too close, and for he could read the eyes of a victim — her eyes were not amongst them. He couldn't read them.

He saw her stumble over herself once again, plopping into the snow and slamming a flustered fist beside herself. A lopsided smirk of amusement scarred his lips. She was certainly hardheaded, and yet naïvely forgiving. Frightened and insecure, and yet daring and feisty towards him. He loathed her rude comebacks when others writhed in agony upon the mere mention of his name, yet, perhaps that's what he valued about her too; she knew who he was, yet she still held his hand like no one ever did before.

The ebony cloak of night had now sailed over them, and the thought of leaving her behind at Great Bend strangely twisted something within him. Something so evil and rotten, an emotion so spoiled and tarnished; one deeper than the urge to pluck someone's eyeballs out or slit their throats. It was almost poisoning, as if a thorn was stabbed into the core of his heart, dripping indefinitely within it. *Will*, he thought to himself, clenched teeth and tight throat. *She apparently cared so much for him*, he thought. For her cheeks had crimsoned by the mention of his name, and her eyes lit up in the presence of his darkness.

He glanced over at his rope, feeling the sudden creeping urge to get his hands around his neck. Realizing the monster that lived within him. Not meant to be ever loved, or trusted.

V I

"THIS IS BORING…" A DEPUTY SIGHED, HANDING HIS BEER TO HIS PARTNER.

"Ya tellin' me. Been guardin' for some days now! Bout time ya came to help!" He lit up a cigarette with quivering hands, and lifted his leg onto the barrel before them.

"It ain't my fault. Dorman's quite obsessed with this Kinnon fella. There ain't no way we're findin' anythin' out here. This boy'll probably be swimmin' about some tropical island, all while we're out here freezin' our nads off!" he nagged, grabbing his beer back again.

"Yeah. Yer probably right. But, orders are orders." He huffed and puffed on the cigarette in deep thoughts.

"Gentlemen." Their conversation was interrupted by a sudden, confidently soft voice. The deputies lifted their guns slower than a snowflake would hit the ground, and pointed them at the man — none other than the elite and handsome William Griffiths. "No need for that, kind sirs. I am but a humble ambassador, here to visit your fine selves in peace on this lovely winter solstice." He raised his hands up and glimpsed swiftly at his surroundings, confirming that she hadn't been detained.

"What ya needin', boy? Name?" They kept guns pointed to his head, and the cigarettes bobbed in their mouths as they threatened him.

"Tom. Tom Williams." he said with confidence, glancing at their dispatch stars on their coats.

"What brings ya here, Tom?" the deputy asked, still uncertain of his intentions. Another deputy from the overlook tower lowered his rifle, for he noticed Will's expensive attire through the scope, thinking he must have been sent by a higher rank.

"It's my pleasure to inform that the esteemed Sheriff Faust sent me here, all the way from Rockvale. He intimated that you gentlemen might be in need of my assistance." he side-eyed the barrel from the other deputy, still pointed at his head.

"Help? Ya don't seem like much! How in tunk will the likes of ya help us?" They all burst into hysterical laughter, echoing across the Rockies West, dangerously loosening the snow atop the caps of the mountains.

"By the simple yet effective notion of pointing you lot of bally fools directly to Mac Kinnon's hideout." he raised his voice, silencing them swiftly by the mention of Mac's name.

Will had looked around the hills, and there was no way he would be able to cross through any of the paths, for they were each caked with a dozen of feet of snow. That meant, however, the deputies wouldn't be able to either. They were stuck in here — per orders, they couldn't leave. So it was the perfect opportunity to mislead them, or figure out a way to delay them.

Buying Charlotte some time, he wishfully thought.

VII

HE CLEANED HIS RIFLE AND REPLACED THE SPENT CARTRIDGES around his gun belt, then double-checked on his pair of Smith & Wesson Model 3 Schofield revolvers that he acquired from an infamous outlaw a decade ago during a shootout. Charlotte stormed through the cabin, seemingly refreshed from her embarrassing snow tumble and energized from nuzzling with Finn, who would always blow her worries away with a tender snort against her face. She had gathered up her grit to face Mac again, after his odd outburst that morning, not knowing what to expect.

"Hey…" she greeted him, as he was seated by the chimney with his faded black boots crossed at the ankles, tilting the Schofield revolver within his hand — watching the fire reflect on the shiny metal.

Yet, he didn't lift his gaze up to her — somehow, he couldn't.

"I just wanted to thank you again, before we part ways, for…" She looked at him flustered, for he completely ignored her once again, for he'd reverted to the form of a manchild; a rude mountain man, the quiet shadow of a murderer. "…for saving Finn, and myself…" She sighed, noticing his lips remain locked

— his eyes, fixated on the black gun that posed no threat to her anymore. "No one has ever done something like this…for me…" she mumbled under her breath. Silence. "And, I…appreciate you sticking to our agreement of…"

"Leavin'…" he said the word for her, and she tore her gaze away.

"I…" She bit her lip and stared at him, benumbed. His head, bowed, and eyes nailed to the barrel. She shook her head, and strode back outside.

He threw a sharp glance at her walking out — grunting a pent-up breath, balling a fist, for he felt his heart constrict within his ribcage.

She led Finn out of the barn by the reins, tossed the blanket over him, grabbed and threw the saddle right after. Pulling up the fender with the stirrup and resting it over the cantle, she clutched the girth and fastened it in a furious hurry — halting her fingers upon it when she noticed, for the first time, the intricately embossed letters *W.G.* — leaving her frozen in place.

Will had gifted her this saddle after she had lost her own. Her eyes stared at it, as her face fell in shame. She couldn't believe she had forgotten about this; she was never the kind to forget nor take things for granted, yet all this was making her numb; it was too much to handle, too much to figure out, too much to swallow down as if it was all but a suffocating lump in her throat; choking her, all the more she thought of it.

And *he,* he was too much…

Her eyes flooded; she couldn't take this awful silence anymore — she still didn't understand why she was suddenly wanted in three different states, and the unfairness utterly devastated her. She was disappointed that Will didn't even attempt to come find her after risking her life leading the bear away from him — as if she clearly was not all that important to him, not in reality amounting to all those colorful, pretty words that he painted her name with.

She couldn't accept why Mac was being so rude and hateful towards her for absolutely no reason, as if all these days they spent together in this torn-down cabin didn't mean anything to him in the end. *For whatever friendship they had built, or perhaps it was just her naïve imagination, for he was a wanted man, destined to kill his way through life, and such man was not to be befriended… nor trusted,* she thought to herself, trying to convince her heart. Then she grunted, and yanked down the fender with the stirrup. She was furious, she was confused; confused as to why she cared about this strange temperamental man who seemed to loathe and avoid her — who she should loathe in return, instead of longing for his company that felt eerily safe and at home. Why she felt sick to her stomach with the thought of staying back at Great Bend — of never seeing his chiseled, marred, yet unblemished face again; never smelling his sweet cigarette scented clothes and hair as he walked past her — never noticing his muted smirks whenever she did something stupid, never staring into those deep ocean blue eyes again, that always seemed to struggle to speak to her.

She hardly knew him, yet she craved to know more of him.

The air suddenly felt cold again.

A bile of nausea, reaching her throat.

She tethered Finn to the post and trod back to the building, finding him rinsing his face in a barrel of water — a few locks of hair dripping wet atop his muscular shoulders, as he turned his head to face her.

"My…my horse is ready to go." she stuttered as his piercing eyes locked hers, as she beheld every inch of his face, perhaps for the last time in tranquility. "Let me know when you are." she coldly spoke to him, and disappeared swiftly into her room.

CHAPTER 12

Just a Burden

I

THE NIGHTLY TERROR OF A BLIZZARD SLAMMED THE MOUNTAINS of Rockies West; the perfect opportunity Mac was waiting for to head east. The trees were howling and rustling, their echoes entangled with a howling wolf pack hunting elk in the night.

He knocked on the door before her room — impatiently stepping inside without her allowance as there was no time to waste, for he had calculated every mile they would be riding tonight.

"C'mon, we gotta get goin'. Blizzard hit." He squinted his eyes, trying to figure out what was taking her so long as the storm rattled the walls around them. Then he saw it, and curiosity grappled him.

"Okay." she hummed, unusually abrupt. She tucked the journal back into the drawer in the most tender way, after scribbling a few written notes within it that her heart urged her to express. She got up, finished braiding her hair, and passed by him, avoiding his eyes.

"Charlotte?" He paced after her with suspicion, for the very first time calling her by her name. She froze. Almost paralyzed beneath his voice, or rather the way her name sounded out of his mouth paralyzed her, for she had forgotten he actually knew it — let alone remembered it. She paused to look at him, suppressing any emotion as if she had forcefully made her decision. "This ride won't be easy; I'll need ya to be close to me, or else yer lost. One mistake, one false step, and yer either off a cliff or down a crevasse." He pointed down to his feet, before he fastened the wild rag around his neck to protect himself from the cold.

"Understood." She walked away, grabbed her coat, and left the shack.

They mounted their horses, the wind now vigorous and whipping, blowing their heavy coats over their horses' rumps. Finn pawed at the ground, raising his head in anxiousness for such a shifting gale reminded him of the accident, making him feel uneasy.

"Ready?" he questioned her, holding his leather hat down.

"No…Finn is…upset." She sighed heavily, tugging on the reins, pulling his head around to disengage his powerful hind.

"Yer got a good hold of him, lass. He'll be fine." he said, and her eyes cut at him with a frown, wondering if that was a rare compliment, and wondering what had changed for him to mutter one, and then wondering why it even mattered to her, for it shouldn't.

"Alright…" she mumbled and caressed Finn's neck, slowly settling down.

They started trotting away from Hope, as the dark fog rolled across their path. The snow felt mushy and slippery in certain places, and hard as a stone in others. Mac was leading the way, as if he knew exactly where to step, and she followed beside him as long as the path allowed.

"Can ye hear me well?" he shouted over at her, glancing down at Finn to ensure he was handling the weather calmly for her now.

"Yes." she grunted irritatedly, not taking her eyes off the path.

"I'll need to check ahead! Stay here!" he ordered and she bobbed her head, barely able to hear him.

Dismounting, he slowly moved across the sheet of snow, with the end of his rifle's stock probing the ground a couple of feet ahead of him, thrusting it within in a smooth motion. Charlotte observed him, squinting through the mist, choking in nervousness. The resistance lessened abruptly against his gun, and he halted swiftly. He bit his lip and looked back at Charlotte, shivering within her clothes, tensed.

With his hands coiling around his mouth, he shouted at her. "There's a hole! We'll take a sharp right up that hill! Keep yer horse close to the rock wall!" he warned and continued to step backwards, following his tracks, but as he stepped into the previous footprint, a cracking sound emerged — and before he could do anything, the earth itself split apart and sucked him inside.

"MAC!!!" she yelled from the top of her lungs, jerking the mountains around her with intensity. "Mac!!" Her fingers trembled, her legs went into shock. Dismounting swiftly, she followed his tracks as carefully as she could, and then his voice emerged like roll of thunder.

"DON'T!! STAY BACK, YE EEJIT LASS!" he scowled and she jerked away, startled.

"Are you alive??" she asked, nearing closer to the crevasse.

"No...me ghost's speakin' to ye..." he murmured as he was climbing himself out slowly and steadily, with the gun-stock pierced into the iced wall, and his boot heels hooking into any dents that he found along the way.

"Mac??" Her voice got stronger, and he leered at her to move away.

"Stay BACK, lass!! Don't feckin' come here! Just...take the right up the hill, and straight from there!!" he yelled and yet, in her typical stubbornness, she proceeded — now crouching and slowly moving towards the hole.

"I'm not leaving you!!" she shouted back, and he froze, harder than the ice he was glued upon. "I'm here...just...let me help you." she then said, a shadow of a face peeking down, and he frowned, aghast.

Her hands clasped his shoulders, and with all her strength she started tugging on him. He unhooked the rifle and pulled himself out of the hole, wrapping an arm around her and plopping her further up the path.

"I said to stay back!" he growled at her, panting from the rush of adrenaline — not so much from the entrapment in the crevasse, but the worry of her naïve, inexperienced self moving towards it.

"And I said...I'm not leaving you." she replied sternly, panting herself from the upwards spiral of anxiety that rattled her whole being. His face fell upon her words, as if she needed to repeat them a hundred times for him to believe them. "Oh, by the bye...I ain't no eejit." She snorted, and he cracked a smirk.

Mounting up again, they took a sharp right up the hill. The winds thickened, and the fog spread around them in a leaden veil, bound to smother any visibility.

He leaned over Roy's neck to help him get over the hill, and glimpsed immediately back at her. His heart thudded wildly, for no-one had ever cared about him enough to risk their own lives when they had the chance to escape from his miserable company.

Charlotte followed right behind him, yet Finn was exhaling heavily; he was not used to trotting in the snow — or rather, he was still recovering, however he tried his best to keep up with Roy's steady momentum and carry her weight over the hill as he did.

Now, they could barely see before them; everything was blacked out in darkness and a heavy veil of haze, for the snow blew relentlessly against their faces. Mac knew his way around these parts, but even he second-guessed himself under the conditions.

"Y'alright?" he questioned her again, Finn's huffing sounds hitting his ears. He cut his eyes behind himself, seeing Finn nervously pace all over the path and her hands quivering to control the reins.

"YES!" she shouted back, annoyed to be asked by someone she would split paths from after all. His brows snapped together by her sudden shift in tone, and then if that wasn't enough, she fussed again. "I'm darn great! This all is just wonderful!" she hissed, taking her pent-up frustration out on him.

"Watch yer mouth, woman." he warned her, and paused in his tracks. "Ya think I want ye here? Havin' to escort yer rookie arse all over the Rockies?? Yer just a burden!" he snapped, turning to face her for a fleeting moment, completely switching tone as well, as if it hurt the same within himself — then he kicked his horse to continue. Charlotte rehearsed his words in her head as she watched him almost disappear before her, and kicked Finn's sides to catch up with him swiftly. "We are passing east of Lake of the Grizzlies!" he shouted again, this time keeping his calm, considering the critical conditions. "Stay with me! There's ice close to the lake, underneath the snow!"

As wrathful as Mac was, he still made for a wonderful leader — giving clear instructions and taking care of his partner, always ensuring they were safe. Somehow, she felt admiration for that.

Charlotte rode and followed as instructed; she just wanted to get out of this treacherous area as soon as possible, as she had never encountered such terrifying chaos around her and witnessing the crevasse only heightened her terror. It was ominously dark and the earth shifted forebodingly underneath them, the frozen whirlwind slamming against their faces, forcing them to squint heavily during the entire ride.

The snowstorm froze their hands to the stiffened leather reins, and their bodies had been shivering ceaselessly for the last several hours. Frost had covered, almost bending, the horses' ears, and their faces were cloaked in snow. They weren't even close to the Black Wolf Lagoon, since Mac had taken them through unknown paths due to the wild conditions and the lack of light.

"Charlotte!" he shouted through the noise, as he spotted a dozen hoof prints on the ground before him.

"What?" she yelled back, covering her face with her coat to warm up her lips she could no longer feel — perhaps they had already frosted and fallen off.

"We ain't alone…" he muttered, as his incredulous eyes scanned around him — impossible to see through the darksome cloak of the ice storm.

"I can't hear you, Mac!!" she screamed at him nervously, feeling the blizzard's turbulence blasting within her ears.

There was a sudden silence coming from him as the murky wind muffled his voice indefinitely, and the whiteout made him vanish before her eyes. Finn suddenly crashed against Roy's hind, who had stopped in his tracks, making Charlotte brace herself against his neck.

"Mac?! What happened? Why are we stopping?" she yelled through the howling blizzard, yet no answer was received. She dismounted swiftly and led her stallion next to Roy, only to find Roy's rider missing. "MAC?!!!!" she screamed at the top of her lungs, feeling the world crumble beneath her feet.

I I

WILL HAD BRILLIANTLY ACQUIRED HIS OWN TENT within Ewing Basin; the deputies were kind enough to let him rest for some days there with the feeble promise that he would somehow lead them to Mac Kinnon. He was studying the map of Kitunaha; focusing on the region of Rockies West. There were three lakes in the area. *Possible fishing locations for survival,* he thought. Lake of the Grizzlies, being the closest to Hope's settlement.

He opened his tent and a squall of snow crashed against him, pushing him back down again. Standing back up with refreshed determination, he rushed outside and lifted his coat over his head until he reached a building where he could safely look outside without the snow blinding his eyes.

He examined the cliffs, the hills, and any possible pathways. He was convinced Charlotte would be staying in the abandoned settlement; just like she rested at his ranch before — she was smart enough to find shelter, however he couldn't grasp how she'd managed to get up there.

Mac Kinnon, though…he didn't give much thought about him; he didn't think he would be hiding here, knowing the deputies were after him. *Just another lowlife outlaw,* he thought, *moving from state to state so he never settles.* He was more worried about his lady being stranded with no way out, and so that was his primary focus.

"This goddamn bl-blizzard is never gonna give us a b-break!"

Will overheard a deputy complain upon a stutter, and covered his face with a green silk wild rag.

"All this, for the darn r-raaaat…" the deputy nagged.

"Sir, if I may…you don't seem to *really* accept the notion of Mac Kinnon residing here, do you?" Will started conversation, for he had noticed the deputy bumping into the barrels behind him, seemingly intoxicated.

"*Offff* course not! *Whoooo* would be *foooooolish* enough to s-stay here for *weeeeeks* with no damn supplies and such *lowwww* temperatures, nevermind this shitty weather every damn *ssssecond!*" he complained further, hobbling over to Will.

"Yes, sir. I find myself in complete and utter agreement with you; our beloved Sheriff Dorman most certainly is possessing of a rather wrathful temper and stubborn mind, is he not?" Will looked at the deputy, holding a bottle of whiskey as he walked funny through the whiteout.

"*Yeaaah!* He sure does; does not, doesn't he?" he bobbed his head repeatedly.

"I cannot help myself but to recognize, sir, that you've been working exceptionally hard in the line of the most arduous duty all these weeks. Why don't we all let our hair down, as it were; to have a little celebration of life, freezing as it might be at the moment — simply to reinvigorate ourselves, and clear our burdened minds a bit. This could be nothing but beneficial to our overall cause; for what are we if not in tip-top shape for the days ahead! Shall we?" He glanced at the boxes of liquor they had stacked up in the next building.

"But…what about them *o-orders?*" the deputy scratched his head, then gulped down another sip.

"Oh, for that much is simple! Blame it…on *me.*" Will winked at him.

"Fellas! Mister T-Tom here's kind 'nough to let us have some, some…some ENJOYMENT in this cocksuckin' blizzard tonight!" he wasn't able to finish his thought, so Will interfered.

"Gentlemen, why don't you rest for the night, as I will be happily guarding the camp? There's liquor for everyone!" he walked to the boxes and started handing bottle after bottle to a line of deputies, as the gust of wind rattled them within their grip.

Soon enough, they all started drinking, singing, brawling, dancing, and getting so drunk they couldn't witness Will mounting his horse and disappearing through the blizzard.

I I I

"MAC!!! WHERE DID YOU GO, DAMN IT??" CHARLOTTE SCREAMED, as she looked around Roy — checking the cinch of the saddle, as if that made any sense. She shoveled the snow with her hands underneath him, as if he was already buried deep into the ground. She trudged to the bundle of trees before them, looking through them and peeking over the cliff right after, her body utterly tensed.

He was gone — with no trace left behind, as if the man had turned into a ghost, turned into the blizzard itself. The realization grappled her senses like a helpless fish on a hook. She didn't care she was stranded, not this time. She cared about him having stepped into another crevasse, and yet around her there was only fresh fluffy snow, covering any evidence of such an occurrence.

Roy suddenly stomped his feet anxiously on the ground, and Finn pawed beside him. "Shh, shh…" She caressed his neck, trying to calm him down. "It's okay, Roy… where is your rider, sweet boy? What happened?" She held onto his reins and continued petting his muzzle, as she glanced around her in frantic panic — praying he would magically appear, praying he was safe and alive.

Drawing in a deep breath of courage, she turned her head back to the saddle. Her hands shook from the sudden rush of adrenaline as she examined it — noticing his rifle and rope were all there, still attached.

She stood there, aghast, as every possible scenario stormed within her mind. *There was no avalanche, for it would have killed us all, were there one. There was no crevasse, for it would have buried Roy with him. There was no gunshot that emerged, for deputies would have captured me as well…*she thought to herself, and took a step back.

"ARGH!!" she then yelled, in harrowing, agonizing pain, as she felt her foot suddenly stabbed deep inside. She glanced down tentatively, and lifted her leg — to find Mac's hunting knife pierced right through her. Immediately, a wave of lightheadedness washed over her as blood was now gushing through her boot. She grabbed Mac's saddle horn, desperately trying to keep her balance, yet her legs turned into utter nothingness underneath her. She grunted in pain, as it shot right through her with every move she made — feeling the blade dig deeper when she accidentally let her foot drop down.

The blizzard slammed her against the saddle, filling up her ears with fresh iced snow as her vision blurred and her hearing muffled, succumbing to her defeat. There was a sudden wing-beat of a bird echoing about, able to buffet through the fog and the roar of the blizzard. Her legs gave out, and she slowly started falling down — holding on to Mac's rifle, with her finger looped around the trigger. Pulling it, as she hit the ground.

I V

POW!! A SHARP SOUND AND ITS ECHO REVERBERATED through the mountains.

Will, startled, looked over at the hill where the gunshot had emerged with a vigorous, loud growl of black powder. *Charlotte.* He kicked Rachel and started loping towards the sound, hoping its echo would still remain in the distance long enough to orient to its direction.

An enormous, steep hill appeared before them — the hill that all the deputies couldn't cross over. The cliff felt like it stood at a perfect right angle to him, and Rachel was falling underneath her legs trying to cross over it.

Will wasn't an advanced rider, but he was intelligent enough to understand the geometry of rock formations and the manner in which horses moved along an incline plane. He subtly kicked Rachel and led her on the side of the rock wall, and she, loyal to his cues, positioned herself against it like a very expensive and well-bred mountain goat.

He kicked again, as he turned her head to the opposite direction —
urging her to climb with her front legs and push herself with her hind to the
second layer of the wall. He repeated this for what seemed an eternity, but
he himself could not believe his eyes when suddenly they found themselves
over the hill — staring in awe at a clear road ahead of them.

Dismounting swiftly with his legs shaking uncontrollably from the spark
of adrenaline, he led Rachel through the path. He had the map constantly
planted before his eyes — wiping it every second as the snow covered it all
over again. He squinted through the snowfall, steadily approaching the Lake
of the Grizzlies before them, and slowly walked through the featureless white
ground as the echo of the gunshot still lingered in his ears — following the
vestigial trace of sound through the whiteout.

CHAPTER 13

Life Debt

I

"WAKEY-WAKEY, MAC KINNON..." THE MAN TEASED HIM, with a breath of rotting fish that hit his nose.

Mac squinted through his eyelids, swiftly noticing that he was tied to a post before a frozen lagoon — Black Wolf Lagoon, in all its secluded glory. He snapped his eyes open and clenched his fists, finding the man swinging his knife slowly before his face as he waved his pale lumpy tongue at him.

Recognizing the mucky face immediately, he realized quickly what had happened, for only one gang could possibly be in hiding out here; the only ones sharp-witted enough to know the Rockies territory like the back of their hands, and have the proper mules to cross through them effortlessly.

Jose Chavez, notorious gang leader and regarded as one of the greatest gunslingers that ever lived. He was head of the Los Muertos gang and knew Mac very well, as they both crossed ways down at Great Desert Basin — making a deal for a Winchester 1887 lever-action shotgun in exchange for breaking out one of his compadres from the jail at Spanish Peaks.

Yet Jose had a mind of his own, and while he kept his word — there was no true moral compass or loyalty within him, traveling with a dozen men up the Rockies West mountains — expecting the arrival of Mac Kinnon, and anticipating the taste of his bounty's reward.

"Boythhh!! The gringo awoke from hith beauty thleep! Hahah." He laughed, and his decaying smelling saliva erupted from his toothless mouth. A large tent opened widely, and a brawny middle-aged Mexican man marched out, none other than the leader himself.

"Kinnon! My boy! My dear, old friend!" He trod through the blizzard and Mac remained silent, following the shadow sinking deeper and heavier into the snow before him. Jose kneeled down and pressed his thick, cold finger against Mac's jaw. "What did ya do again, ya wanted amigo?" He smirked at him, and his goatee widened across his face.

"Not much. Just killin' folk as I go." Mac smirked back at him, and his cigar-scented finger twisted his jaw.

"Aaaah…padre, padre my boy." He chuckled, and grabbed his neck tightly — locking his wildly-sick eyes with his. Mac extended his jaw and lifted his head up, searching for a lungful of air, yet still he remained calm. "Twenty-five thousand bucks is a lot of money, amigo…a *lot* of money." He bobbed his head, appearing deep in thought. "I know how to get it, too." He released his grip, letting his head drop back down abruptly.

"Sure." He smirked, and stared back into his eyes. "Can't blame ye." He leered, and glanced around him — hoping she wasn't here as well, yet not wishing to ask, in fear of revealing her existence.

"Oh, that I know amigo…that, I know. Ya see…I been waiting here aaall those weeks. And, ya lindo chico just walked into my arms…just like that. How could I resist, amigo? Such most valuable prize…and the best thing was, it was so very simple! Ha! You was distracted by the blizzard, wasn't ya, poor Kinnon?" He smiled, his own brand of breath smelling of salted offal and rum.

"Must be tough upon yer pride, all 'em years killin' folk, robbin', runnin' from the law…and ye still barely got two hundred on yer head." He snorted wryly, unclenching his stiffened jaw, and Jose's eyes darkened into a leer. "Although ye shoulda known better…folk don't care to see a man of yer kind swing — for a noose will be too big to fit 'round yer neck, judging by yer lack of size." He dropped his gaze down to his crotch tauntingly, and Jose slammed a fist against Mac's face.

"Watch your mouth, ya varmint…" Jose leered, and Mac spat blood to the side and locked eyes with him again.

"But me knife, I can already feel it fittin' perfectly in yer throat…I can already sense yer blood gushin' out of it…and feel yer helpless jitterin', as ye look me in the eye…" he said, eerily content, and Jose's balled fist unclenched.

Cowardly hesitant to hit him again, and cowardly petrified to keep eye contact.

"Keep an eye on our little friend! We ride at dawn to deliver the town a long awaited present!" He ordered, and strode back into his cozy tent.

Mac snorted and spat out blood again; suddenly shivering uncontrollably — more from wrath than cold, and yet his hands were stuck together and he knew he would die from hypothermia were he to fall asleep that night. He knew the moment they would attempt to move him from the tying post, he would have a chance to make his attack. His mind had been calculating his every movement for this opportunity, thinking the moment they would cut him loose, he would grab the knife from the man's hand, swiftly prop up, turn around and kill him, then rush to grab the shotgun that was stupidly planted twenty feet before him, and head behind the boulder sticking out from the snow like a shield. He nodded to himself in compliance, and drew in a deep breath as if to warm his insides.

He was covered in a white cloak from head to toe, for he could not wipe the snow off his face. He felt his nose and lips itch beneath it, slowly freezing until he couldn't feel them anymore. The blood pooled in his fingers felt like it was swelling, morphing into large clumps of stone hard mass, stretching the skin.

He thought hard about which mistake he made to get caught like this. It bothered him to no end that after all these years, he got captured by nothing but another outlaw, and yet he knew the blizzard wasn't his distraction.

His thoughts couldn't help but wander back to Charlotte; he thought about how she stretched her arms in the air, how she built her own snowshoes out of sheer stubbornness, how she was utterly quiet on their ride until she risked her life to rescue him, how he missed and longed for her voice to nag him again. How he "missed" something for the very first time in his life, unable to grasp how this sensation was able to smudge his thoughts, that were always so sharp clear.

He thought of how he failed to keep her safe.

How he failed *her.*

II

WILL HAD SUCCESSFULLY CROSSED THE RIVER CONNECTING to the Lake of the Grizzlies. He started galloping, as Rachel was obliged to do — for you could run thoroughbreds and they would never stop until you told them to, as she herself seemed to know.

Seeing an enormous shadow rush towards him over the hill, he swiftly raised his gun, worrying it was yet again another grizzly — not prepared to deal with it any more now than he was then, and let out a caterwaul of a warning. "Stay back!!" He pointed his gun to the mass and the sights shook before his eyes, yet the shadow kept on nearing closer. "I w-warn you!!" He sucked in a stutter and then his eyes flared, as the shadow turned into a shape. "Finn?!" The shape of a *fine specimen* he knew so well, now standing few feet before him.

He jumped off of Rachel, and stepped slowly up to him, clasping the reins in his aching grip from clenching it so hard — thankful and relieved to have found them.

"I never thought I'd be so happy to see you, young man!" He petted his neck, his fingers breaking icicles off his coat. Finn snorted anxiously, and threw his head in the air, pulling him back to the path he came from. "Charlotte?" he asked him, for he felt his urgency tug on him.

Striding next to him, Finn led him to another horse that was patiently standing still up the hill. Roy. "Whoa, it's alright, boy!" he said, and without another delay started frantically searching for Charlotte, meanwhile his fingers had turned purple and were feeling awfully benumbed — a feeling he could not relate with, for he had never the opportunity to.

Finn pawed at the ground in its own frantic way, uncovering Charlotte's body as much as he could with his hoof — carefully, as to not injure her any further.

"Lord have mercy!" His eyes widened in shock, his heart sunk in his gut, and the sight of her bluish face petrified him. He kneeled down before her and started pulling her out of the snow-covered ground.

She was still breathing, but unconscious and gruesomely frozen. He took his coat off and wrapped it around her body, rubbing her warm in the middle of the snowstorm. He prayed, and he rubbed, and he prayed. He blew hot air on her face, trying everything he could to warm her up while freezing worse himself.

"Please darling, wake up for me!" He choked as he held her now tightly in his tender embrace, squeezing her to radiate his heat to her.

"Will…?" She squinted her eyes open, recognizing his soft loving voice, yet her blurred vision betrayed her senses.

"I'm here, my lady. I'm here!" He kept on rubbing her, protecting her pale face from the wind with his the shield of his body.

"Help…" she whispered faintly, her eyes kept on drifting away.

"No, no, my love. I'm here. I will take care of you now!" he said, swallowing down dryly. "Is…is Hope where you've been staying, my lady?" he stuttered, suddenly feeling the weight on his shoulders he'd chosen to carry.

"Yes…but…" she mumbled faintly, and her eyes rolled to the back of her head.

He picked her up swiftly, and placed her atop of Finn — noticing the knife handle sticking out from her boot. "Oh no…" he gasped in horror, realizing things could actually get worse than he imagined. He mounted her horse right behind her and galloped back towards Hope, as fast as he could.

III

THEY ARRIVED AT THE SETTLEMENT AMONGST THE LOW CLOUDS, the blizzard, and the howling winds — after a strenuous, gut-wrenching ride across the hills and hidden paths, avoiding holes and cracks of crevasses, and frozen lakes that appeared eerie enough to hide mysterious denizens within their depth.

Will kept her face pressed against his neck, warming her still with his olive green shotgun coat wrapped around her body. He writhed relentlessly throughout the ride, yet he'd never felt more determined to carry on. The place was vacant of any life; he pulled Charlotte from the saddle, and carried her hastily to one of the beds inside.

"Will…" She kept on calling his name, reaching for his hands desperately, as the panic she felt intensified her fears — focusing in and out of hallucination. The room turned pitch-black and span around her.

"My love, it will be alright." He kissed her cold hands softly, worried if she would make it through the night as he grudgingly recalled witnessing such dimming eyes before. He scanned around the building, still clasping her stiff fingers in his grip. His brown doe eyes sought for what might be a medical cabinet, hanging somewhere, anywhere, yet then returned back to her swiftly, as she begged to feel him close.

"You…came…" she whispered with faint vigor, staring at his unusually disheveled face.

"Of course, Charlotte. How could I forget you, my beauty?" His frozen mustache stretched across as he smiled. "I will have to pull this knife out now, alright, my love?" His eyes glanced down to the dark walnut coffin handle, carved with a thousand perfectly symmetrical notches.

"Mac…" She sighed with an agonized voice, and twitched her injured leg.

"My lady?" He frowned, confused, meanwhile his hands quivered in fear to hurt her. Nearing the knife cautiously, while she grabbed the old sunken bed covers with her nails the moment she felt him touch the handle.

"It's Mac's…knife." Her lips writhed upon the words she tried to speak out, "He needs help!" She squeezed his hand in her fist. "Please…head northeast." she murmured, reminiscing Mac's directions, his guiding voice; *his* voice — before she lost consciousness again.

"Dearest…no!" He held her head up trying to wake her again, shaking her, panicked. "Stay with me, Charlotte! Stay with me, my love." He lifted her boot, and grabbed the knife firmly — pulling it out as carefully yet as fast as he could, freshly slicing the wound open again on the way as he did.

He took her boot off swiftly, while the blood was gushing out before him, all over his imported Italian woolen vest. He wrapped her foot with a cloth and tightened it with a piece of leather from the saddle, pulling on the leather string as hard as he could — his hands staining with blood for the very first time.

"It's done now, my lady. Stay with me please." He leaned over and kissed her on the forehead, and she opened her eyes subtly — sending him a shiver of relief.

"Will…please…help him." She sighed, clutching his anxious hand. "We have no time…left." She looked at him, as exhaustion took control over her.

"You mean Mac? Mac Kinnon?"

"Yes!" She gnashed down on her teeth, and he tore his gaze away, choking, rehearsing the sheriff's accusations in his head. "But darling, he is…"

"No, he ain't all that!" She fussed, suddenly finding the strength to defend him. "I will…explain to you later. Please! I owe him…my life." She squeezed his hand, and her eyes begged him to go find him.

He bobbed his head in compliance, covering her with a blanket. Making sure the leather was still tight around her foot, and that she was stable, before leaving the rattling cabin.

Mounting his horse outside, he headed northeast. He had tethered Roy to the cantle, thinking he might lead them to his rider, or at the very least, Mac could ride him back instead of holding on as a monkey behind him. He had no idea where to go, or what he would find. Still, the accusations from the sheriff, *and disturbing legend of the notorious Mac Kinnon,* lingered in his head.

CHAPTER 14

Courage

I

THE ROARING BLIZZARD HAD DIMMED ITS BLINDING WRATH, and the wind's rage slowly was lulled into tranquil waves of breeze, yet the bone-chilling cold still remained in the arctic air and his shadow was still nailed atop the frozen post. The crumbling snow fell from Mac's face each moment he jerked his head around, awakening himself every time his eyes would attempt to shut.

He glanced around the hideout to find Jose's men all sleeping in their enclosed tents — warm, and sheltered from the dreaded weather that coiled around him, burying him all the more deeply into its frosty embrace. He grunted, shifted, and twisted his tied-up wrists to see if he still felt his hands — miraculously, he did. Stretching his fingers out and flexing them to encourage blood to pump through them, he studied Jose's tent, recognizing his projected silhouette laying unbothered in bed, fast asleep — the lantern still glowing dimly within it. All he could think about was the gross shape of the massive shadow, approaching his bleak and windowless room as he hid beneath the covers; a pair of blue eyes peeking through the holed cloth.

"Mac, dear boy." The shadow now adopting trunks of legs, thudding all the more loudly in his head. *"Please explain to me, how these cigarettes appeared under your bed? What did we say about sinners like you?"* Adopting a scent, worse than a rotting corpse — spoiled, a soul oozing of malice. *"They deserve a beating, don't they, Mac?"*

He clenched his teeth together and started to pull his frozen hands frantically away from the post, yet was met with no success as the rope was brilliantly tied in methods of knots he'd need a knife to cut through and escape from.

The feeling of being confined evoked the buried terrors within him; he could feel his burn and lashing scars suddenly become alive across his back — burning freshly as the very first time, deep into his flesh; bruising it, scarring it, buffeting it, splitting it, bleeding it down to his bones. It was the mental torture rather than the physical that drove him insane, for a spark of the past still slithered within the crease of his being, carving at his heart with every passing day of his existence — forever engraved within his memory, like a curse branded in his mind.

Having to stand still and politely mute, sometimes tied up against the barn's sturdy timber post, as the farmer whipped him mercilessly with his leather belt or a special wood plank he kept next to his bed. Oftentimes he would light up a match — from the same matchbox Mac hid in his trousers, and let it glide against the open wounds of his bare back, cauterizing the ragged edges of the wounds so that they might never heal properly. A punishment…a lustful punishment, and yet these were but feeble pranks compared to what had yet to follow.

Mac smoldered with resentment, wrath only quickened his blood, a deep raw hatred thrummed through his veins as he recalled all these memories. His wrists began to bleed, as the rope rubbed against them unforgivingly the more he yanked his wrists away. *"Control yer emotions…"* he mumbled to himself, out of a strongly ingrained habit. *"Control…yer emotions…"* he repeated, his lips barely spliting apart from each other. *"Control…"* He writhed, fighting hard against the urge to doze off.

II

WILL RAISED HIS LANTERN BEFORE HIMSELF and halted at the crest of a hill after he had successfully crossed river after river, breaking through iced creeks and puddles, constantly riding up — constantly northeast. He didn't possess the mind of a mountain man, let alone the skills of an experienced horseman to weave through such terrain of utter bleak whiteness with invisible threats lurking beneath the ground; however, he was determined to tackle any challenge that would arise.

He was dismounting every so often, hunting for horse tracks on the way — inexperienced enough to not realize the blizzard would have covered them within seconds, or perhaps his otherwise sharp intellect had dulled by the rattling events. The full moon hung low between the giants of mountains, peeking through a faint cloud to make its glorious appearance as the gloomy night turned lively again.

Awooooooooooh!

Rachel's eyes dilated — halting swiftly in her tracks, looking around herself anxiously, snorting and stomping all four legs on the ground — spreading the snow around as she paced and adopting another couple of white stockings on her front legs as she did. All the while Roy kept still beside her, as if that threat was nothing compared to what he had lived through with Mac.

"Rachel! Easy! Easy, lady!!" He held the reins tighter as she circled around a thick layer of gnarly trees, bumping his head into frozen lattice of branches and tangling the rope from Roy tighter around the cantle, turning him into circles as well.

A threat in the air, she could sense in now sharp clarity, borne by the wind to reach her flared nostrils. She could sense the knotted coat of a predator — almost able to feel its hunger, rumbling within the sinews of its being, deep within flesh and bone. There was a sudden howl, low and long, carved out of starved lungs, resonating through branches and mountains, engulfed by a silver and titanium white cloak. A fragrance of a rotting breath, one betraying desperation; one caught in hunting for too long.

He lifted his gaze up to the amid ebony skies, the barbed crescent of a decaying moon hanging low into a dark glen, with charcoal clouds billowing around them.

There was a wolf that emerged behind them, hunched down with glowing eyes of menace, slowly sneaking towards them.

Hungry. Threatened. Protective.

"Back!! Back off!!" His hands trembled and his voice was scarred by fear, strengthening the animal's confidence all the more. He tried to reach for the rifle that seemed to be stuck in its stiffened holster, and lifting his gaze back up to the wolf, his breath cut in his lungs as it now advanced to them. "Back OFF!!" he yelled — his throat ached by the slashing cold, barely able to issue a sound threatening enough.

Rachel, against all her best efforts to remain loyal to her rider or as behave content as Roy, was unable to ignore the animal's looming pressure anymore. No matter how hard or how harshly the bit pulled against her lip, she ran right through it. Bolting, forcing Roy with her as she did.

Will held on to her, one hand clasping the reins, the other the cantle, as the wolf now sprinted after them in full speed and desperate vigor. The heavy clumps of snow plunged off the branches, landing right atop of them as the softest of rocks as they galloped hectically through them — scraping his legs against the coarse bark on the trunks as they did. The wolf was barely sinking in the snow; it was light as a feather, flying over rocks with its tall and slender build as it leaped over the ground, almost floating.

Yet a wolf without its pack is not a very brave one, and seeing the horses disappear in thin air, it let them go with a lonesome howl of defeat. Proceeding to gallop further away, Will noticed the previous noise of a growling breath and the sense of snarled teeth behind him had evaporated completely; so gathering up his grit, he glanced back, realizing the wolf had turned around. "Oh, th—thank g—goodness…" He exhaled a stuttering breath of instant relief, and unbeknownst to him, halted few feet before the Black Wolf Lagoon.

III

CHARLOTTE, FEELING THE WAVES OF BLACKNESS distort the room around her, lifted her head up and hesitantly dropped her gaze down at her foot — swiftly curling her lips in repulsion at the sight — feeling the light-headedness reach her once again. However the bleeding seemed to have stopped at last, and she eased herself back down, drawing in a breath of relief.

Thinking how she couldn't grasp the fact that Will not only came to find her, but even rescued her, through the most brutal blizzard she'd ever witnessed at that. The awful sense of guilt turned her stomach around, for she had assumed otherwise. She admittedly never expected this elite of a man — this poreless, unweathered, beautiful being of a man — would be brave or capable enough to do such a courageous thing. Much different than how he handled the grizzly incident, she admired.

She never realized she could actually be important enough to him, or to anyone, for that matter. Her mother didn't fail to remind her how any man would think she would be worth less than dirt, for she always thought so; and if she could, she'd trade her for dirt and be happy for the exchange. Somehow she suspected she had attempted to do as much.

As relieved as she felt about her worries and assumptions being disputed, her concern only grew the more she wondered about Mac's odd disappearance — trying hard to recall what he warned her about just seconds before. She simply couldn't imagine this man getting into a dangerous situation without being able to get out of it on his very own, but she couldn't risk waiting for that suspicion to be confirmed.

Tense from her inner deliberation, she glimpsed out at the fire-burning chimney, and somehow it didn't feel the same warmth about it. Somehow, something was missing to evoke its warmth again. She reminisced the sounds of him poking the fire around in the middle of the night, as he was inclined to stay awake — tending the deepest thoughts he held buried within him, guarding Hope, *guarding her,* she dared to imagine.

The image of his quiet self that night emerged before her eyes; his busy mind as he lounged on that squeaky three-legged chair, watching the flames grow and roar proudly as their burst of colors danced with each other inter-changeably. Sometimes he glanced over at her, seeing if she was sleeping, cocooned in that blanket he had given her. She knew he had carried her into bed that night, for she woke up still feeling his arms around her.

IV

"OH, BOY! OH…BOY." THE DEPUTY GRUNTED, holding his throbbing head with a hand as he was waking up from a long and heavy sleep. Upon cracking an eye open, and feeling his body oddly confined and restricted to any movement, he paused briefly. A moment of slow, spiraling panic brewing within his chest.

He then dropped his gaze downwards and yelled, aghast, when he realized he was covered in a leaden veil of snow up to his chest. Scanning swiftly around himself and noticing all his deputies buried by the blizzard as well, he started to frantically dig himself out, screaming and panting as he did.

After what seemed an eternity of claustrophobic mental torture he pulled himself up, swiftly climbing out of the hole. Standing up, listening to the wheezing of the winds and the eerie silence around the campground, he turned around sheepishly to find a few hands still holding on to their bottles through the snow — ominously frozen, ominously blue, ominously dead.

He rushed to them, hobbling with his feet benumbed and swollen inside his boots, aching with every step, barely able to even walk. He grabbed a shovel to dig them out, drilling through all the snow's different layers — fresh and soft on the surface, dense and strong the deeper he reached.

Once their faces emerged, pale, bluish and stiff, he shook them relentlessly to wake them up, but only a few did crack their mouths open to inhale a lungful of air. Sadly, most of his partners froze to death underneath the snow that night, for the liquor and the joy of extending those carefree moments of rest was stronger than their senses.

"This son of a bitch!!!" he yelled, and his echo shook the cliffs around them — awakening them again. "I knew not to trust this bastard!!!" he screamed, as he kept digging his lifeless partners out. "TOM!!! You traitor!!! Where are you!!!" He angrily searched for him inside the ruined buildings, when a sudden all too familiar *whomp* of noise froze him in his tracks. He turned his head towards the wild mountains above, and his vision was swiftly smudged by a thick wave of snow barreling down. An avalanche.

V

"RACHEL! LOOK!" HE POINTED AT THE SWIRLING CLOUD OF SMOKE on the horizon, exhilarated to find a sign of life out there; for so far he was certain the only sign of life, or rather sign of death, found in the Rockies would be himself buried somewhere beneath the snow. "Let's keep quiet, lady..." he whispered to her, tethering her up to a tree and leaving her with a pat on the neck and a calm, collected Roy to her side.

Slowly striding towards the iced lake, he noticed the lines of inhabited tents before it and his breath halted. He took out his fine binoculars — handcrafted and imported from Canada, promised to have the highest optical clarity available — and looked through their still foggy lenses.

"My Lord…" He sighed, as he counted a dozen men sleeping in their tents. He zoomed in further to find a man tied up to a post, with his head just barely sticking out of the tower of snow he was trapped within. "That must be him…" he mumbled to himself, and his legs started to quiver — not knowing who or what to fear more.

He took his rifle with him and slowly made his way to Mac in slyness, sneaking through the trees and through the knee-deep snow, always glancing over at the tents as he did. His feet moved as quiet as a hunter's, dragging his ostentatiously out-of-place coat behind him.

Dithering, he approached, and his arm reached for him. "S-sir?" He pulled in a stutter, as he touched Mac's shoulder from behind.

Mac, more than startled to hear a clear, soft-spoken voice bearing no accent, turned around to be met by a man's worried face, shaking from the cold — or rather his presence; yet he saw a sense of innocence imprinted in his gaze, as he searched through his brown doe eyes for a reason to trust him.

"Who are ye…" he asked him suspiciously, almost growled, squinting his eyes as his frozen eyelashes felt heavy over them.

"My name is Will, sir. William Griffiths." He proudly introduced himself, proceeding to shovel him out, trying to cut the rope off around his hands with his ornately engraved sterling silver pen knife.

Mac's eyes flared, so much so his eyelashes almost broke the ice off of them. Of course, he knew this name very well by now — *her* voice still repeated it in his head. "Charlotte?" he questioned straightforward — clenched teeth, tight jaw, feeling the rage slowly ignite within his chest.

"Yes, sir. She…sent me." he said hesitantly and cut through the rope, releasing his frozen grip after so many hours of restraint.

"Where is she…" he inquired, his sharp eyes cut at him with a threat.

"Sir, I promise to explain further on the road, but I can assure you she is safe." he muttered, equally suspicious of the obvious concern he tried hard to hide. "We need to get out of here, however. Please, let us go with utmost haste!" he whispered urgently, for he noticed the shadows of the men move.

"Not quite yet. Got some unfinished business to tend to." he noted as his blood flushed color back to his cheeks, now standing up swiftly and grabbing Will's rifle from his hands with his still-frozen grip.

"Sir! I must protest, as you will assuredly get us both killed in whatever endeavor you are set to pursue here! There's at least a dozen men of various stations here. We simply must leave. Revenge is but a fool's game in any regard, can you not understand?!" he urged him, and grabbed his rifle back daringly — still, his eyes staring at his, noticing the eerie darkness within them.

"I need to finish…this…business. Ya better not get in me way, lad…" He spat on the ground; a crystallized clump of blood, and went for the rifle again.

"No! Charlotte is injured! I must remain adamant that we return…NOW!" he insisted, this time with a stricter tone, as his lips trembled and his eyelids flickered nervously for he too knew the legends about him.

Mac gaped at him, aghast and in sheer bewilderment, for he was certain the men hadn't harmed Charlotte. They would have teased as much. His deep blue eyes overpowered his, trying desperately to find the answer in them, and yet all he saw was fear.

The men snuck carefully through the woods and mounted their horses, galloping swiftly away from Black Wolf Lagoon.

CHAPTER 15

The Stubborn Silence

I

"MY DEAR?" HE LEANED OVER HER FACE TO WAKE HER UP SOFTLY, fingers brushing against her cheek. Mac's glances pierced through the wall; his ears, muted shadows clasped against them, hands poking the fire once again in loneliness. Will had left the door open to her room, and Mac noticed she was cocooned in a blanket with her injured foot sticking out of the edge of the bed.

"Will!" she gasped upon prying her eyes open.

Her voice, clutching his heart.

"My lady…" He smiled to her, and yet her eyes avoided it.

"What, what happened to Mac? Did you find him? How is he? Is he alive? Please, tell me he is…" She propped herself up in frantic panic, and before Will could answer, she found Mac now standing in the back — hovering in the shadows.

They locked eyes, holding their breaths captive within their chests.

They stared, as their throats ached, struggling to swallow that unbearable knot that suddenly emerged — knowing they weren't alone in the room, knowing they couldn't come close, knowing they couldn't express their strange kind of relief in seeing each other again. A relief he'd never felt. A relief he didn't know how to even express, and yet there was this crumbling sensation within his rib-cage, feasting at his sole being.

Will noticed Charlotte's cheeks suddenly crimson unapologetically as she glanced past him, hooking her eyes to another man. He smiled awkwardly within a sigh of disappointment and tore his gaze away right after, not wishing to endure this all too familiar feeling.

"I...I'm alright, lass." Mac spoke, breaking the deafening silence with an oddly uncharacteristic stutter and a soft, almost defeated voice — somehow not knowing what his awestruck mouth muttered, somehow feeling her warmth reach through him the longer her hazels stared at him.

He cleared his throat and glanced at her wrapped up foot, and looked back at Will, who was patiently waiting for them to finish their exchange of gazes. Startled herself, she jerked her head away and clasped Will's shoulder. He lifted his gaze up to her, but his lips had sunken into a pout of an uncertain smile.

"Will, thank you so much...for everything..." She reached for his hand, realizing she hadn't thanked him yet and plastered a sincere smile on her face. "I can't believe everything you did for us already! You have so much to tell... us both." She looked back at Mac — his eyes staring right at her beneath two thick knitted brows.

"Don't mention it, my lady..." he sighed, cracking another smile of bravery, not wishing to appear broken-hearted, all the while his heart's shards collected in the pit of his stomach. "Shall we...perhaps cheers on a successful evening?" He offered in the midst of awkwardness, struggling to clear his mind and make sense of the exchange only a man and woman in love could have — refusing to believe the Sheriff's accusations were factual after all.

I I

1. *Haue mercie vpon mee, O God, according to thy louing kindnesse: according vnto the multitude of thy tender mercies blot out my transgressions.*
2. *Wash mee throughly from mine iniquitie, and clense me from my sinne.*
3. *For I acknowledge my transgressions: and my sinne is euer before mee.*
4. *Against thee, thee onely haue I sinned, and done this euill in thy sight: that thou mightest bee iustified when thou speakest, and be cleare when thou iudgest.*
5. *Behold, I was shapen in iniquitie: and in sinne did my mother conceiue me.*

Psalms 51:1-5
Old Testament of the Holy Bible
1611 King James Version

THE BOY, MOCKINGLY DRESSED IN A POTATO SACK far oversized for his starving body, stuttered the verse out loud as the farmer proudly exposed himself before the young boy's face.

"Mac, son, look at me." He lifted his jaw up with a fat thumb, and an overgrown nail that scraped against his skin. "You surely know this verse by now...repeat it for me, son, will ya?" The proverbial beast emerged through his mortal body, as he urged Mac to succumb to his mental torture.

The young boy, distraught by the reflection of the exposed flesh in his innocent eyes, started bursting into relentless tears — covering his face with the Bible.

"No, Mac, my sinning child."

He grabbed his hand, and...

III

"NOOO!!!!" MAC RAISED HIMSELF FROM THE BED, as his panicked heart almost leaped out of his chest — trying desperately to drill itself out of his body, as if it too drowned in repulsion and shame. He glanced around himself frantically, still sitting in bed, stiff and tensed, cloaked in a haunting cloth of perspire. He drew in a deep breath, grounding himself by fixating his mind upon the familiar wooden walls that rattled from the keening wind of dawn, by feeling his fingertips brush against the woolen blanket and swallowing down repeatedly to taste his own familiar being — anything other than the grossness still engraved in his memory.

He got up swiftly, tucking his shirt into his trousers with quivering hands and slipping into his weathered boots. As he walked out of the room he spotted Will; sleeping deep before the chimney, comfortably cocooned within a thick elk hide. He flung his coat around him and strode out of the shack, longing to feel the fresh, chilled air hit him against his face, for the crisp wind to carry away his heinous thoughts.

"Hey…"

He turned around, brows snapping together, stunned to see Charlotte right behind him.

"I'm sorry, I just…heard you." She exhaled, embarrassed to have followed after this stranger at the crack of dawn, and yet she couldn't ignore the pain in his screams.

"Hm…" He blinked, wordless. Benumbed.

"I just…wanted to make sure you're okay…" she said faintly as she shut the cabin's door behind her, taking a step towards him.

"Hm…" He bobbed his head, sighing with a brittle voice, then lit up a cigarette with the excuse to not face her.

"I didn't mean to…I mean… I'm…" she stammered shyly, nervously; somehow she could never find the right words under his intimidating presence, and yet somehow it appeared they barely needed any words. "I'm happy to see you…back here…" she huffed a pent-up breath, and frowned due to the sudden shooting pain in her extremity.

"How's...yer foot?" he asked courageously, as he spotted her lifting it off the ground.

"Foot?" Her head cocked in confusion, for the only pain she felt was the sudden realization of how attractively he puffed on that mucky cigarette, as he held it loosely between his thumb and forefinger.

"Yer sliced up foot, lass..." He snorted, and a gust of smoke escaped the crack of his mouth.

"Oh!" She blushed. "That foot! Right...it's, it's there, I mean, it's hurting, of course...making me a little more useless, I guess! Ha!" She chuckled awkwardly, stepping accidentally on her foot again, only to be reminded of the pain.

Mac couldn't help but smirk subtly at her endearing self, yet his nightmare still lurked within his mind, feeling his jaw ache from clenching it all night.

"Mac...?" she hummed gently, pulling his troubled eyes back to her. "Talk to me, if you want?" she hesitantly offered, somehow feeling as if he would open himself up to her.

He stared at her blankly. There was that stubborn silence again, dwelling between them. She bowed her head to not pressure him, and yet stood still before him like a rock of support, begging to be hooked with his confessions; begging to bear the pain, to lift up his burden.

He cleared his throat, dithering. "I just..." He exhaled heavily. "...sometimes, get these...dreams." he mumbled quietly, reluctantly, as if he still wasn't allowed or supposed to tell anyone.

Charlotte, amazed at his willingness to open up for the very first time, remained in entrusting silence as she quietly hobbled towards him.

"Yes..." she encouraged him, and paused before him, noticing his apparent discomfort hanging from his chapped lips.

"Dreams, that...still haunt me..." he paused briefly to catch another glance from her.

"I'm listening, Mac..." she reassured, glancing at his hand, begging to be held.

"He..."

"Yes?"

"Never mind." He shut down, as abrupt as gravity pulling down their weight. He had sworn himself his secret would be buried with him when the time comes, somewhere six feet deep beneath the rotten ground, for decaying soil was all the memory his corpse would deserve. "I guess, there's a reason why I'm the man that I am now…" he then added daringly, his eyes stealing a sharp glance from her, concerned if she would step away from him.

"Mac…if you allow me to say…" She bowed her head and drew in a deep breath, as his own shortened. "I…see a kind man, who was probably hurt by someone very much — so much, so that he let it shape him over time." she spoke softly to him, and daringly reached for his free hand.

Their fingers clutched together, palms pressed tightly against each other.

Mac stared down at her eyes…

They were honest and genuine; full of an empathy he'd never received ever before. It terrified him; something about it terrified him deeply.

The unknown…the undeserving.

"But the wonderful thing about shapes…they can shift again. Like the river's shape, when it reverses directions…" she said, glancing with him at the little creek flowing next to them, breaking the ice atop it — moving it to the side, for the next snow to come cover it. She turned her face back to him and lovingly smiled, as her fingertips brushed against his — feeling the hardened callouses on his skin, somehow so endearingly.

Mac's lips locked tightly — he couldn't harness the breath to push any words out, let alone his deep brutish voice to express them. His mind failed to operate or make any sense, as all he wondered was why this woman was still showing kindness and care after threatening her, calling her a burden, and avoiding her every time she tried to connect. Why did he long for her company, as if his life depended on it. Why was he feeling his heart dropping to the void of his stomach, just far enough only to ascend back to his throat again and choke him in the sweetest, most torturous way. Why could he not control this emotion. This tormenting emotion, paralyzing every fiber of his being just by her sheer presence.

His ears muffled, unable to hear the wintry squall blowing against them — rattling the barn doors beside them, as it did. He couldn't feel the freezing cold creeping up on him, benumbing his limbs and bare face, as he stood there motionless for it to consume him.

All he could notice was her sudden silence entangled within his. Her full attention, captured between their enigmatic eyes; her tender touch sending shivers — slithering through his skin. Her enchanting body that he protected with all his being, getting so close to his, with every breath he took.

Her flushed red lips, yearning to be met by his.

He leaned over her face, and his hands gently coiled around her neck — quivering, as to control his murderous grip. He felt her thudding pulse at the crease of her neck, hitting against his fingers. He could sense her nervousness, and smell the sudden sweat that broke beneath his palms.

They shut their eyes, and nearing so close a breath could be felt, he brushed his lips hesitantly against hers — caressing them softly with his cracked skin, feeling of her smooth fullness as a cold fresh gasp escaped her.

He pulled back, worried if he was forceful, and locked eyes with her. Both panting heavily, with a lopsided smile cracked on her lips, and yet her brows snapped together, frowning in an odd stubborn urge to feel him again. Worriedly, his gaze dropped back down to her lips, appearing just as beautiful as before, and before he could cower in shadow again, she grabbed his hair, pulled him towards her, and pressed her lips onto his — kissing him excitedly, lustfully, as if she'd been waiting for all eternity. They'd both been waiting... somehow unbeknownst to each other, or even to themselves.

As they bruised each other's lips, his chapped skin felt cold and sharp against hers, and yet somehow all the more she desired to kiss him, all the more she wished to breathe him in, hungering to taste him, as if starved. Fervently entwining their lips, pulling and sucking on each other, her hand reached inside his blood-stained duster coat, caressing all over his muscular chest that deflated by every stroke she gave. She could feel his breath hasten, and his muscles tense up beneath the palm of her hands. Mac couldn't handle this blood-curdling sensation; he hadn't felt a tender touch in so many years; a touch that wasn't paid. A touch that wasn't forced. He could feel himself throb as his heart beat faster, pumping his blood through his veins in such a pleasurable torment.

Then the voice of Will emerged within his head; and how kindly he spoke to her, how he rescued him from the gang, how he so desperately seemed to love and care for her...how he wasn't a sinner, but a blank page of innocence and of importance.

He started squeezing his hands around her neck tighter and firmer, hooking his fingers into her flesh, the more he thought of him, the more he thought he could never have her, the more he realized a man like him should never deserve a woman like her, for his shape had already shifted beyond change, and suddenly his nightmare flashed before his eyes again.

Charlotte, startled, pushed her hand firmly against his chest — letting go of his lips abruptly. She jerked her head away, and locked frightened eyes with him, begging for an explanation.

They stared, aghast, at each other.

An air of regret deepened between them.

The scent diluted from lustful tenderness to alerted defense.

"I…" He pulled back, leaving her swollen lips red and warm to contrast against the white snow that surrounded them, so much more pure than the lips that had engulfed her.

Confused, Charlotte felt of her neck.

Her pulse thudded differently now.

He hid his fists behind his back.

"I…I don't know why…" he said, stepping back, unclenching a fist and drying off his wet lips with a hand, now walking away in haunting silence.

"It's not your fault…" she muttered to herself. "I shouldn't have come… close to you…" she said, embarrassed, as she watched him disappear.

CHAPTER 16

Ghost in the Fog

I

"THEY WHAT?! IT CAN'T BE..." SHERIFF DORMAN SHOOK HIS HEAD speechlessly after the delivery of the devastating news by the only survivor. The avalanche had taken the life of all the remaining soldiers that had survived through the snowstorm, except for one.

"Sir...they all are gone." the deputy reassured him, lowering his head to pay respects to their loss.

"...and he's still...running free...he's still running FREE!!" He slammed his hand against the table, as rage hiked up his head through his elderly bones.

"Sir, we had an intruder." he said, and the Sheriff cut his eyes at him. "His name was Tom Williams; tall, black hair, well dressed. He said he was from Rockvale, and was ready to lead us to Mac Kinnon's hideout, he said, this poor bastard." he said, and the sheriff's eyes flinched in heightened rage. "Gave us official permission to drink, later that night..." he lowered his tone, embarrassed that he trusted him; feeling remorseful for his partners' deaths.

"Must've been the pretty city boy...musta been..." He glanced over at Charlotte's poster still hanging next to the cells, as he brushed through his cigar-stained mustache, untidily sprouted from his face in these days passed in misery and self-pity.

A throttling chuckle hit the deputy's ears; a wheezing noise. He cut his eyes to the left, spotting the prisoner cackling under his breath at the sheriff's obvious distress.

"Forget Mac Kinnon..." he whispered to the deputy. "We need the gal...

when we get the gal…the others will come, like a pig followin' to the slaughter…" He raised his pistol swiftly, and shot the prisoner dead through the bars. The deputy gaped at the shot man — a cracked smile had remained across his face. "He'd be hanged tomorrow, anyway…" Dorman muttered, as he span the pistol back into its holster.

I I

WILL MANAGED TO BREW FRESH COFFEE FOR EVERYONE — imported directly from France through his very close friend and associate down in Mon Louis, yet this time the layer of delicious clotted cream was missing atop his cup.

It was an unusually peaceful day outside; the snow was suddenly sun-drenched by the fiery globe of light that was shining after weeks of being in hiding and struggling to appear through the thick blanket of winter's gloom. Mountain wildlife, both small and large, was grazing through the snow — leaping over it and chasing each other playfully, for they equally enjoyed the positive change in weather for once.

It is a bright day to start fresh, he wishfully thought.

"Thank you, Will…" she hummed, as he handed her the cup of coffee. The blackness staring back at her, as if to portray her sin. She was wrapped by the silky soft elk hide that smelled of Will's expensive cologne — cuddled within it contentedly, yet her mind was buried deep in tormenting thoughts.

"How are you feeling this dayspring, my dear?" He caressed her cheek lovingly, and sat down beside her. She almost flinched away.

"I'm, I'm great…" she stuttered guiltily, her eyes drawn to the flames and crackling logs in the fireplace. "But how did you manage to get here, Will?" She made an effort to change the subject, worried he'd smell *his* lingering smoke on her breath.

"Oh, it was quite the grand adventure, I must admit! I'm rather surprised I made it in one piece, if I am being brutally honest with myself." He glanced back at her hazel eyes, noticing their usual spark had dimmed. "I, as you assuredly have noticed, am not so bold akin to the two of you — intrepid and venturesome daredevils!"

He chuckled innocently, feeling a stabbing gaze behind him. Seated by the windowpane, Mac was paying close attention to their words; quiet as usual, but calculating every move and breath Will took.

"You should be proud of yourself." she said kindly. "You truly were a hero last night." She smiled at him, secretly suffocating with guilt from what happened a few hours prior.

Mac bit his lip frustratedly; tearing his gaze away to compose himself. He was supposed to be the hero for her — *he was the hero all along before he showed up,* he naïvely thought — for the first time in his life feeling a sense of envy, realizing that was the thorn in his heart after all, poking him anew.

"Oh well, I could never leave you behind, no matter what misfortune that might entail for me. I was compelled to find you; I *needed* to know you were okay." His eyes sparkled as he looked at her, his hand daring to caress her leg. "Besides, that was indeed not exactly a small bear you had after you!" He chuckled again, bowing his head shamefully, and glancing down to his rings that glistened from the fire's light.

"Yeah…shot the damn beast before it got to her." Mac swiftly interrupted, when he saw Will's hand brush over her thigh. Then he wished he hadn't said a word, for this was unlike him, and yet the words spurted out of his mouth beyond his control.

"Thank you, sir. I sincerely appreciate everything you've done for her all those days." Will responded kindly, in a diplomatic manner as he always did.

Mac's tension dug right through her. The essence of his words, sucked in by the sinews of her being. He appeared enraged with her, and yet she didn't know why, for his hands were the ones choking her. She gave him a sharp leer — her eyes begging him to not start a fight, as she fiddled with her plaited hair nervously.

"So what's yer plan then, lad?" Mac crossed his boots — hitting the spurs against his pants. He raised his jaw and sipped on his coffee, his leather holsters screeching with every shift of his body as he stared him down.

Will, taken aback by the subtle interrogation from a legendary murderer, cleared his throat and adjusted his neckerchief as it felt suddenly too hot against his skin. "Well, it happens to be a charmingly beautiful day outside; it's not that cold — actually it is quite sunny, so I thought perhaps it would be an ideal opportunity to leave this gloomy place before those men come after us. How might either of you feel about that?" He glanced around, somehow expecting everyone to disagree with him.

"What 'bout them deputies, me lad…" Mac nailed his eyes on him. "Ye think they won't try travelin' through better weather, boy?" He snorted, his sharp eyes now peeking through the cup.

"The deputies…by all accounts must still be trying to sober up and gain their wits about them, for when I encountered their party I may have orchestrated a slight yet rather effective distraction…" he proudly noted, a confident smirk scarring his face.

"Hm." Mac glanced at Charlotte, who was still braiding her hair — avoiding everyone around her, and pretending she didn't exist in this conversation. "Guess the fine lad got it all figured out, Charlotte." Mac sucked in an irked breath, pulling her attention back to him. "We'll head east, follow the Sweetwater River, and then I leave ye two at Great Bend." he said, his voice so harsh it could cut through ice. "Yer lass already told me ya was livin' there." He looked at her again, swallowing down the sudden lump in his throat.

"That would be lovely!" Will exclaimed, and reached for her hand excitedly. "Do you think you will be able to ride, my lady?" he asked and her face fell, for suddenly she choked upon a thought.

She didn't wish to ride anywhere away from Hope.

Anywhere away from *him*. Anywhere without *him*.

"Yes…I'll be fine, Will." she finally said after a long pause, cutting her eyes back at Mac to capture his reaction. Yet she could not read him; his eyes seemed empty, and no matter what she could say to him, she would never be able to fill their void.

He lowered his leather hat over his eyes, and rested in the corner.

III

"DID THIS MAN EVER INFLICT PAIN UPON YOU, CHARLOTTE?" Will finally asked her privately as they had gone for a slow walk through the woods near Hope, with his arm wrapped around her, supporting her weight as she limped.

"No, I promise, Will." she swiftly answered — *too* swiftly. "He can be temperamental sometimes, or…most of the time, but he is not a danger to me…" She felt Mac's hands squeeze around her neck the moment she said that, and tore her gaze away in shame.

"Fair enough…" He nodded, watching the sun glitter upon the distant layers of snow. "When we have safely returned to the ranch, you will have to tell me everything." he said in earnest. "I feel as if I haven't gazed upon your fair countenance in forever and a day!" He turned around and wrapped her in his arms tightly, startling her bad conscience as he did.

He always had the kindest smile on his face; he was so peaceful to be around — he could make all her troubles disappear with his charismatic self, yet she always wondered if he ever had days where he too struggled, as he always seemed so unbothered and lighthearted. Then she realized, there was a sudden cruel power in the grip of her hand; in the corner of her mouth, on the tip of her tongue. A power to utterly destroy any lightheartedness this man possessed. Her heart sunk. It drowned in self-repulsion.

"I missed you too, Will." She gifted him a genuine smile, forced a try to reconnect, and forget about this man that shouldn't matter to her after all. "There were so many cold nights where my thoughts traveled to our picnic at White Elk River." She sighed in his arms, and the wave of guilt washed over her yet again.

"As did mine…" He tucked in a lock of hair behind her frosty ear. "We will simply have to repeat this blissful expedition, and hopefully…continue where we left it." He blushed adorably, like he usually did, braver than last she remembered.

She smirked tentatively, for she recalled whose lips she was kissing at dawn. She didn't have to remind herself. The sharp edges of his skin had scarred hers. A flame of anxiousness burned within her chest. She couldn't understand devilishness what got into her to let Mac, *out of all men,* kiss her; after years of waiting for the right one for her first kiss, and yet, it had never felt so right. As if their lips were created for each other, and each other alone. Locking together, in perfect harmony. *If Will only knew,* she thought, as she froze into place…*how could she slip like that from her senses…*

"But of course, we don't have to rush such matters…" he corrected, noticing her quietness, and then looked around searching for something to stare at in the wide-open land of ubiquitous snow scattered across it.

"No, Will, you're absolutely a delight to be around…" She avoided his eyes, knowing hers could speak the truth louder than the promising words she spouted. Words, forced to mean something. "I would love nothing more than to revisit this moment." She caressed his rosy cheek, praying this nauseating feeling would desert her once and for all.

IV

FINN NEIGHED THROUGH THE STABLE WINDOW from the moment he heard Charlotte approach. It was his feeding time, and he made sure everybody was aware of it with a kick on the wall and a steady pawing at the gate. A proud stallion should never skip a meal, let alone Finn, who tended to be a little on the heavy side.

Charlotte and Will entered the barn to feed and water the horses, after a long walk of conversation and sheltered secrets. All of the horses were lined up side by side in the stalls, continuing to paw at the doors and neigh in unison their sweet song of desperate hunger.

Yet the barn was already occupied by Mac's eerie shadow as he was brushing Roy; changing his water, cleaning his saddle pad, and stocking up the bags with supplies. The air now felt heavy around them; as if dark storm cloud hovered over his head — it rained within his mind, and it rumbled within his chest. There was tension, betrayed by Roy's uncomfortable body stance, having absorbed from Mac's well of confused emotions. There was a rapid pulse thudding at the crease of his neck; teeth were clenched in vexation when he noticed they had gone for a walk on their own while he slept.

"You know, my love…" Will slashed the silence with an awkward knife. "Finn was actually the true hero of the story." He beamed genuinely, stroking Finn's neck as he was eating his oats.

"He was?!" She side-eyed Finn like only a proud mother would, not surprised at all to hear this.

"Yes, yes indeed. He appeared as though he were an apparition, manifesting himself through the thick fog to alert me that you were in trouble. He must have caught my scent on the air, and recognized me." He fleetingly glided his thumb along her cheek, to remove a speck of dirt that she had collected after hugging Finn.

"I'm so proud of this pony; I told you he is something special, didn't I?" She hugged his warm, fuzzy neck again, peeking over his shoulder to steal a glimpse of Mac — who was saddling up his horse, pretending he wasn't observing them all this time. She tore her gaze away and bowed her head into Finn. Upon a sigh, she spoke again. "I also need to thank you for gifting me this wonderful saddle; I haven't forgotten about the gray mare and my promise to you, either…" she said, and Will responded with a tender smile. "How is she, by the way?"

"Well, I did manage to…collect the sassy lady that day." He raised his brow, as he reflected upon the countless carrots he lured her with. "It took some convincing at first, but we got her safely back to the ranch." He huffed, for even reliving the memory exhausted him. "However, I did instruct my stable manager to go ahead and…sell her at the auction, as I didn't know when to expect my return." he said sheepishly, feeling apprehensive about telling her the unpleasant news, knowing how much she cared about this mare.

"Oh…I'm sorry to hear that." She sighed in sudden wave of sadness, for somehow she had bonded with her just in those few hours of studying her soul through her eyes. "But, I understand. I didn't even know if I would survive that bear chase…" She shook her head, as her skin crawled by the thought — then her heart skipped a beat, and her eyes peeked over that shoulder again, meeting *his* for a brief moment. "Did I tell you already that Finn was stuck in the iced lake?" she interjected, and Will's eyes flared. "It was a wonder that I got out before I froze to death…if Mac hadn't come in time, we both would be gone." she said in earnest, as Mac was bridling his horse in silence.

"Goodness…I had no idea!" He faced her in utter shock — his gifted mind, still wondering how Mac was able to retrieve an entire horse from the water. "Thank God!" he exclaimed and bowed his head, still processing what sounded like a story from a novel. Then he raised his head back up and with a straight back, turned to face him. "Mr. Kinnon, sir, I owe you for saving my lady's life." he said, facing him as Mac leaned against the barn door. "If you ever change your mind about where you're heading, I have…invaluable connections, that might be of great help and interest to you." He offered kindly, feeling obligated to help him back. Charlotte lowered her gaze, knowing what was yet to come.

"Hm…" Mac smirked snidely. "Listen up, fine lad." He pulled himself off the door. "First off, ain't no such thing as God — where was the mighty eejit when her mount was struggling in the water, or when she was freezin' before a grizzly's eyes, ready to be torn into pieces for dinner." He leered as he strode towards him, while Charlotte was peeking sheepishly over Finn's saddle with a knot in her throat. "Second…ye don't owe me nothin'. I was just passin' by there, when I spotted the damn bear." He brushed off a snowflake from Will's coat, then pulled out a cigarette from behind his ear. "I didn't even notice 'yer lady', to tell ya the truth…" He lit it up, glancing over at Charlotte — her head hung as if coiled around a noose. "I just enjoy to shoot and kill, son, and that was a good opportunity to stain a bullet once more." He puffed on the cigarette, staring into his eyes. "Last, I need no damn connections — connections is why I'm where I am now — wanted, by more connections." He leered and walked back to Roy, fastening the cinch tighter on him, exhaling a thick smoke of irritation as he did.

Charlotte looked back at Will, who surprisingly was not fazed by Mac's ill-mannered attitude, as if he had dealt with such behavior before.

"Her name is Mrs. Marga Goodell; she oversees a moonshine operation under a successfully low profile. You see sir, she also was wanted for many years, until life gave her a second chance." he said and Mac snorted sardonically, yet Will continued. "She was tortured, by the most…" he paused, recalling Mac's wanted poster. "…she was burned by some men, as she was confined within a building…hoping she'd not survive, yet she did, and came back stronger than anyone I've ever known…and today, she bears the scars to tell the story." He sighed, and his gaze wandered off. "She's been recently managing her interests from an underground bunker around Rockies East, north of Holy Station. She can assist you, but you'd have to help her in return." Will, slightly annoyed, caressed Charlotte's arm and led his tacked-up horse out of the stables — leaving Charlotte and Mac behind.

By the mention of Holy station, something was triggered within him.

Something about this name, this word, received by a submissive mind that had been manipulated deftly in its most vulnerable state of development — bound to be entrapped by memories of noise, scent and taste.

Charlotte looked at him, almost petrified to find him standing so still, with eyes dilated and lips tightly taut across his face. His skin was goosed, and she could almost feel the heat it oozed through its pores. She searched for a flicker of an eyelash, but his gaze was frozen. Suddenly, as if shooting out from a state of numbness, he jerked Roy's reins — yanking the bit in his mouth, making him lift his head, aghast, at what he did wrong to deserve this. In turn, he yanked at the bridle again, making the horse back up faster.

"Stop! What are you doing to him??" Charlotte rushed to him, furiously taking the reins out of his hands, swiftly adjusting the bridle on Roy's head and turning to face him with a leer. "Why did you do this??" She insisted for an answer — one that had better be good enough to explain this abuse.

Mac stared back at her. It had felt like an eternity since he last saw her hazels in such close proximity. They pierced his skin, penetrated his blood, and almost poisoned his thoughts. His full gaze turned menacing.

"I need no connections, and no damn God." he growled. "And definitely need no helpin' from yer feckin' lover!" His face close to her, his cracked lips folded, his eyes haunting hers — choking her, to see his sudden mood swings for no apparent reason.

"Mac…"

He tore his gaze away and turned around swiftly, for being too close to her was triggering him as well. Feeling enthralled by her sole being, so much so, all his vexation prior vanished like magic. As if she held a candle of the purest light, to extinguish his darkness.

Charlotte, speechless and still upset, still caressing Roy's fuzzy white face, stared over at Mac — pouting, like a little child. She just couldn't understand him. She had met some odd behaved men in her lifetime, but *he*…Mac was something different altogether. So stubborn and set in his ways with everything he thought or did; so rough in his mannerisms and awfully rude with his speech, utterly devoid of any remorse within himself — and yet, the times he did let his shield down, he was a man you could entrust your very life to.

He was a man that did something to her heart.

V

"CAREFUL OF YER HORSES; IT'S STEEP." MAC WARNED THEM, as he had Roy on a loose rein. It wasn't his first time around this area; he knew exactly where to place his feet, and where not to.

Roy was an incredible steed; vigorous, proud and a picture of health and care. Mac first met him at the Holy Ranch's barn when he was just a little boy. He would make deliveries there for his adoptive farmer, and would ask for permission of Roy's owner to brush him. He didn't know much about Roy's background, only that he was a highly skilled horse — implied with eerie pride, to have been stolen from some "redskins" as they called them.

His adoptive farmer, however, was not enthralled or comfortable with the idea, for the concern sat on his chest that Mac would talk to the right person at the right time. It was a small country town, everybody knew everyone, and secrets were hardly kept. Nonetheless, with the mask of religion worn, he gained respect and power — and he could get away with anything.

There was one single gentleman, however, that had questioned the farmer's integrity and care regarding Mac — when he realized, time after time, how emaciated the young boy appeared. He never saw Mac again after that, and in turn, Mac never saw Roy until much later.

Roy was in his early twenties; he had started to slow down some, and Mac had to push him everywhere he went — he couldn't afford to lose a trusty mount like him; a horse that knew instinctively all the tricks and cues Mac needed him to know.

"Sir?" Will spoke, and Mac rolled his eyes.

"Hm."

"How is this area called, if I may inquire?" he asked curiously.

"Gah…" Mac grunted, his fingers drumming atop the cantle. "Black Wolf Lagoon." he finally said, in a sigh.

"Oh! Black Wolf Lagoon!" Will exclaimed. "Upon this realization, I understand why it seemed so awfully familiar! This is where the famous Saber Wolf hunter resided…now, what was his name…ah! James! James Godard! He passed away in eighteen forty-two. He was badly injured in one of his expeditions to find the beast, and died here in a horrifyingly slow death. Quite the awful ordeal, indeed!" He pointed at the cabin right above the frozen lake.

"Saber...Wolf?" Charlotte asked confused, as she'd never heard of such a creature before.

"Indeed, my lady...the Alaskan Saber Wolf, adduced to be the genetic product of Pleistocene Dire Wolves that survived in isolation. Not to be confused with the *Canis lepophagus*, which is the predecessor of today's grey wolves and even dogs, of course. The legends hold that a single Saber Wolf may be responsible killing dozens of people, just by biting their heads off — then expanding their territory over here, eradicating the remaining population in all of Rockies West!" he excitedly explained, his eyes sparkling in delight.

"How do you know all these things, Will?" she chuckled, stunned at his vast understanding of seemingly random history and knowledge.

"Oh...well, my lady. I've spent an overabundance of time consuming a great variety of books in my lifetime. It's a craft I strongly resonate with; reading and writing, that is — not Saber Wolf hunting, to be sure!"

He smiled at her, almost going off the path.

Will was the most entertaining, endearing, lighthearted gentleman imaginable. Always able to become distracted whenever he talked about a subject he cared about. His reflexes were feeble, albeit adorable, but he was smart as a whip to make up for his lack of practical skills and survival instinct. He could tell you virtually any modern history occurring long before he was born. He never complained, he loved to please people, and was a saint when it came to his patience — *he just didn't seem like he had a mean bone in his body,* Charlotte thought to herself, studying the blitheful smile across his face.

"Hobble yer goddamn lips! Or ain't ya not wantin' another bear comin' after ya, with all that noise ye makin' back there??" Mac agitatedly silenced them for he wasn't used to having company, let alone someone like Will, who couldn't keep his mouth shut longer than a minute.

"To say 'ain't we not' is not only linguistic tragedy that I fear to digress upon, but also a double negative; negating that we *do* wish for another bear, in which case you are absolutely correct that we *do not,* my good sir!" Will replied with the most innocent use of sarcasm, as he genuinely meant to be helpful.

They giggled in the background like teenagers getting into trouble, and

Mac rolled his eyes at them, leaping down to the main path.

Finn followed diligently right behind Roy, who was the lead horse of their group. Rachel right after them, slightly pinning her ears at Finn, not at all appreciating being left behind.

"This path leads to Great Bend, on the chance yer not familiar with it already." Mac took a dig at Will — since apparently, he knew everything.

"Lovely! I can't wait to be back home!" Will exclaimed, and Mac clicked his tongue in irritation. "You're welcome to stay too, Mr. Kinnon, if you need a place to rest for some days. It's very well secluded, and I'm sure you could benefit from the respite before continuing on into the wilderness." He looked over at him, expecting him to decline. Mac was quiet for a fleeting moment.

"Naaah…I really don't wish to bother ye two…after such a long time of being apart, and all." he grumbled snidely, as he made Roy leap over a fallen tree — noticing the bark was clawed out by some other bear.

Charlotte kept herself in muteness in the back, her lips sealed and her gaze lowered in shame and sadness. She inched forward, leaping over the log as well, with Will leaping right after her, shifting his weight in the saddle and re-adjusting himself for better balance. A gasp escaped him and it hit her ears, absently painting a smirk on her lips, for it was evident by now that he wasn't the most accomplished horseman after all.

She feared. She feared this would be the last time she would see him; her blue-eyed hero behind the black mask. She tried to block these thoughts, almost erase the memory of him, but it appeared even more difficult than galloping away from a charging grizzly. She looked over at Will, trying to feel what she felt before for him — but it just wasn't there, or perhaps it was, but a mightier shadow had swallowed it whole.

V I

"SIR, I HAVEN'T SEEN THIS LADY IN A LONG TIME. She just bought some jeans from here, and went on her way." the shop owner nervously confessed to the sheriff, as he was closing his shop for the evening.

"Did she stay at the hotel? Do ya know? Did she say anything about where she was headed?" Sheriff Dorman questioned him, groping a brand new cigar from the shop and pocketing it.

"Sir, yes, she was staying there for the night." He nodded politely, as he watched him steal two dollars from his savings. "No, sir, she never mentioned anything else." he then added, turning off the lanterns and shutting the door behind them. "But I would like to say, she was a very kind woman, sir. I highly doubt she had anything to do with the crime." He hesitantly defended, though he would bet all his savings on her innocence.

"Well, ya keep your doubts to yourself." He snorted. "See, that sneaky gal lied 'bout where she was goin' when I first met her down in Bisonhorn. Said she was headed to Birdsboro, to visit her family." he expressed, as he lowered his gaze to the muddy mess of a path before him — hearing Will's insults in his head. "Well, guess what, she AIN'T got no family! See, I went up to Birdsboro myself, and investigated the files with my fellow Sheriff Jordon — there AIN'T no Charlotte. So tell me, mister, would ya trust such a lying witch? No…ya wouldn't." He winked at him and strode over to the hotel, mud splashing against his boots, and the cigar bobbing along in his pocket.

VII

THEY PICKED UP THEIR PACE AS THE SKY TURNED TAR-BLACK ABOVE THEM; droplets of rain running down the brims of their hats, as others coursed down their necks, chilling their weary bodies and soaking their clothes. The clouds coughed out enormous gouts of water, flooding the river underneath the sharply shaped, almost evil-looking cliff they were slowly riding along.

An earthy smell rose from the slippery land, now being cleansed and washed from the heavy rainfall. Shredded pillows of clouds fought and raced against each other, forming an eerie light between them. Thunder, soon striking the trembling trees, rumbling across the midnight skies, slamming against the mushy wet ground; as if the sky raged and had a voice of its own.

The horses were squealing as the thunderstorm's wrath got closer, and raised its guttural voice ever louder, yet they loyally marched with their riders atop them towards Great Bend.

VIII

MAC HAD SAFELY LED THEM BACK TO WILL'S RANCH as the rain was pouring down, and the storm rattled every sinew of his body, yet that didn't faze him anymore. Instead, he felt numb within; empty like a hollowed vessel, and he himself couldn't grasp that hideous sensation for hollowness was all he knew.

Charlotte and Will stabled their horses in the barn, while Mac waited on them outside as the storm kept on clinging onto his clothes, winding itself around his limbs like a serpent's tail.

Will rushed outside with his coat pulled over his head, fancy riding boots clopping against the puddles of water. He halted before Mac and Roy, lifting his gaze up to him. "Thank you, sir, for guiding us through such a nasty storm!" he said, then offered his hand to thank him, yet Mac refused to shake it.

"Sure." Mac hummed shortly. "Ye better get inside the house, yer gonna catch a cold out here." he said with subtle sarcasm, pointing with his jaw towards the house door, as a pool of cruel cold water dripped off him.

"You're confident you don't wish to stay for the night, sir? There's more than enough room for everyone." Will insisted kindly, genuinely worried about Mac traveling in such weather. A streak of lightning slammed against the ground beside them, jerking Will off the ground in startled fright, as Mac sat still in the saddle with his eyes still nailed on him.

"Get on, boy." Mac pressured him, as if he was pressuring himself instead.

"Well…" Will sighed. "Thank you again, sir, and…it was a pleasure meeting your legend. Wishing you good and safe travels." he said, and Mac bobbed his head to him.

After one last glance of the barn, he turned around and kicked Roy into a trot, ready to leave the memory behind.

"My love?" He searched for her face, feeling fortuitous to share the night with her alone finally.

"Will…" She poked her head over Finn's rump, then slowly squeezed between it and the stable, squirming her way out of it. "Are you both okay?" she questioned him, wondering if Mac had decided to stay in light of the drastic weather change for the worse.

"Yes, we are." He cracked a smile on his lips. "I'll be making a warm fire inside, if you'd like to join me when you're ready." he offered excitedly, watching her water Finn.

"Oh…thank you. I'll be right there." she said, in thought, holding the question on her lips. "Did, did he stay?" she finally asked, upon turning her head to look at him, and yet he was already headed to the house — the whipping wind and icy, blasting rain muffling her voice.

"Dammit…" she fussed to herself, rushing to the barn's window and looking outside, spotting Mac trotting his way into the woods. Her face fell. Her legs felt chopped off into place. Her stomach dropped, and her body started to quiver.

Pulling back from the window, she squeezed her fists in exasperation and paced back and forth inside the barn, still with a limp, still heavily conflicted with her morals and her feelings. She halted her hideous moping and turned around to spot him again, now slowly turning into shadow, merging with the blackness of the somber woods.

"Mac!!! Wait! Please!" She stormed through the cracked barn doors, with a hand clasping her aching chest. Running frantically after him as much as she could, the relentless rain and unforgiving wind kept pushing her back. Her foot was getting stiff, and her wound painfully radiated throughout it, and yet she wouldn't stop. Her pace picked up all the more through the torment.

"Mac!!! Goddammit, Mac, please!" she yelled at him, and suddenly stumbled over herself, falling to the ground and into a puddle of mud. She stayed there, devastated, as the rain showered her woeful being, and the thunder rumbled above it, as if taunting her naïve behavior.

"*Ya need to learn to control yer emotions…*she had his words play out loud in her head — over and over again, as she was fighting back her tears, struggling to make sense of her own emotions — emotions she'd never felt in her life. Emotions that clasped her heart, and soaked it in a puddle of burning alcohol. She wilted in the mucky soil, few wisps of oxygen abandoning her aching throat as she sobbed in defeat.

"What yer doin' on the damn ground again, lass?" His boots planted before her lowered gaze, sinking in the same puddle she sat within. His voice emerging through the loud storm, suddenly muting any clasps of thunder around her.

Aghast, she lifted herself up swiftly, and launched to him, hugging him tightly without a word or second thought, without shame, without fear of feeling his hands choking her neck. She buried herself in his arms, with her muddy fingers squeezing his back as the rain came flushing down on them, soaking them even further. Their clothes stuck together, their cold bodies merged into one. She felt such relief, such warmth and serenity, even when all hell was breaking loose around them, even when he was Hell's greatest sinner.

"Please…please, stay." She sobbed in his shoulder, not letting go of him, forgetting there was someone waiting on her with a warm fire and stability.

"Charlotte…" He pushed her gently away from him — loathing to, as her embrace sheltered his soul for the very first time.

Forgetting who or what he was. Forgetting she barely knew.

"Mac…no…please." she begged and he swallowed hard, not knowing what these words even meant coming from her. "I…I don't want to see you leave…yet…" she dared to avow, and he stared at her, aghast. She lowered her gaze shyly, wondering if he understood, wondering if her words sounded so obvious. Embarrassment engulfed her, and yet she had nothing more to lose.

He cleared his throat and tore his gaze away. "Ye got a good lad there waiting on ya; don't be an eejit…ye don't know me, lass."

Lightning struck in the background, lighting his chiseled jawline, so sharp it cut through her soul. "Don't tell me that I don't know you…" she hissed, eyeing him with a threat.

"Ye don't…" he said again, feeling her choking neck within his hands, his victims' faces flashing before his eyelids, the innocent blood pumping his veins.

"Oh, alright…" She bobbed her head caustically. "So, you're just going to leave in this weather? When there is…a perfectly fine and spacious home for everyone, because I apparently don't know you, Mac Kinnon…"

"It ain't fair to the lad…he saved me life." he said in earnest, choking, and after freezing her gaze upon his, she bowed her head in shame.

She knew what he meant.

She knew he was right.

But her heart could not comprehend it.

"Be well." he said dryly, and turned away. She gasped and grappled him from the slick wet duster coat, pulling him back, for no other reason than to face him again, smell his tobacco scent, feel the mucky coat in her fingertips, be with him once more.

"Mac…" Her grip tightened, and eyes locked again with frowns shadowing over them.

"NO." he growled, leering at her, hoping she would leave. Hoping she would get scared. Hoping she would make it easier for them.

"You don't scare me…you will *never* scare me." she growled back, and his frown deepened.

"It's best for ya I keep goin', lass. Be well." He patted her shoulder and strode back towards his horse, leaving her standing with a knot in her chest; constricting the tighter his words, his actions, his absence twisted it.

"So that's goodbye, then?" She gulped, her eyes stung, her heart scorched. "Is it so easy for you? Just like that?? Didn't 'it' mean nothing to you?!?!" she yelled at him the more he ignored her. "You damn fool!!!" she screamed, as he now mounted his horse, kicking it into a lope.

She had no other words left. Her heart felt torn apart in a million sharp pieces. She couldn't breathe, she couldn't hold back her tears anymore, and she didn't care to either. She buried her face in her mucky hands and screamed in distress, writhing in sheer panic.

Mac could hear her; he could hear her pain in sharp clarity — it grabbed his heart and it slashed it like a knife was stuck within it. For the very first time, he felt completely unstable beneath his feet, unsure about any move he made — suddenly, his emotions could not be controlled, as he disappeared like a ghost in the fog.

CHAPTER 17

Kentucky Bourbon

I

THE FOGGED-UP WINDOWS WERE SHINING FAINTLY AT THE BREATH OF DAWN. Fire still murmuring a crackling sound in the barren room. Wood walls shifted as the humidity dropped, and the oaken floor creaked as he approached her.

"Good morning, Charlotte." Will briefly caressed her back, handing her a cup of hot coffee.

"Good morning…" she exhaustedly greeted him back. Her eyes droopy and weak, bloodshot scarlet from the endless tears she shed against her pillow.

"Bad night?" he asked her with an unusual, rushed tone in his voice, noticing her swollen eyes.

"What do you mean, Will?" She looked at him confused, clearly impatient to partake in any more guessing games.

"Nothing, dear. I just figured you had a bad night…I know this is not easy for you." He sipped on his coffee and glanced, engrossed, out the window — from where he could have easily seen them hugging fervently last night.

"What is not easy for me…?" she asked him suspiciously, wondering if he knew more than she thought he did.

Will was awfully quiet; he always had a carefully selected answer before someone had even finished their question, but this time, he was still. His lips sealed, not a smile escaping from underneath his freshly trimmed mustache. He flipped his pocket watch open — the same one hanging from his luxurious red vest back when they first met. He stared at the time in crippling silence, all the while Charlotte was feeling her throat cramp in a knot.

"Will?" she asked, selfishly worried she'd somehow lost him too.

"Would you like to join me for a ride? It's a beautiful morning — calm, after the storm last night…" He twitched his mustache, wetting his lips nervously. "It's just the two of us, and I would like to spend some…valuable time together, if you don't mind, of course." His eyes avoided her, turning red and watery — his dry throat swallowed down the dark caffeine abruptly, as it did nothing to dispel his feelings of dejection.

"I would love to, Will…" she sighed, her heart feeling a sudden relief; meanwhile, she loathed herself more than ever for the betrayal, for she noticed those brown doe eyes had turned raven black in sadness.

II

THE GROSSMAN FARM LAID DUE WEST OF HOLY RANCH. It was used for crop farming and hosted some cattle and chickens — not a big farm production though, compared to Holy Ranch. It was intended for personal consumption mostly, or for limited sales to the local town and family friends. The crops were the bread and butter for farmer Grossman, however, he oftentimes took in misbehaved children as extra working hands so they would be taught a strong work ethic, as well as resilience. As an avidly religious man, he would always spread the word of God and share it with them — forcefully, if needed.

"Boy, make sure the cows are fed and watered, ya hear? The chickens need moved to the chicken coop, and crops still need waterin'." he instructed, as he waved with his pipe around. "Do NOT leave any gates open again!" he ordered the young boy — who had just turned 8 years old that day.

"Yes, Mr. Grossman." he huffed politely, continuing on with his chores, pushing the pitch fork into a pile of moldy hay.

As the sun started to mellow over the fields of Freelands, the young boy strode through the crops with a bucket of water in his youthful hands, and foot by foot he'd slowly water them.

Suddenly he heard a quiet, held back cough in the back of the barn, right next to the stalls. The boy placed the bucket down to the moist ground slowly and crouched, hiding within the crops. He sneaked up to the barn and peeked through the warped boards of the stable, holding his breath in sheer curiosity.

"What ye lookin' at?!" Mac shut the hole with the palm of his hand, from where the boy was looking through.

"I'm, I'm sorry…I didn't know you was here." he excused himself, and went on swiftly to water the crops again.

"Wait!" he called him back hastily, letting out another strenuous cough. Mac was kept in isolation around the farm; he wasn't allowed to leave the property unless he had to make a delivery to Holy Ranch, where he would take the rare opportunity to visit with Roy. Meeting another boy close to his age was thrilling to him, as he felt so lonely with no one to socialize with; to shoot guns with, wrangle with, play-fight with — just the usual things young boys did growing up.

"Yes, sir?" the boy asked respectfully, as he could tell Mac was a little older than him from the deep breaking voice, and the height that towered over him.

"It's Mac. Didn't mean to scare ya back there!" he mumbled with a play-ful grin on his face, his full head of hair outlined by the sun setting through the cracks of the walls.

"Oh…not a problem, Mac!" The boy smiled back to him. "I just heard a coughin', and didn't know what that was! Mr. Grossman didn't mention you was livin' here." the boy rumbled, gaping at the cigarette Mac was holding.

"Yeah…" Mac smirked, and puffed on the tobacco stick. "The ol' man never cares to mention me. Not that I give a flyin' feck." He snorted. "What's yer name, lad?" he asked him excitedly while taking another puff, pretending to be older than he was.

"Mickey, my name's Mickey." The boy smirked widely in blithe spirit, as he too was quite the loner.

III

WILL AND CHARLOTTE TOOK A CLOSE MORNING RIDE THROUGH HOT SPRINGS, just east of Great Bend. The terrain was much rockier compared to the south-ern region, and the land mainly grew pale white birch trees.

"Did you know Charlotte, that in Celtic mythology, birch trees symbolize renewal and purification?" He pointed at the pale tree they were passing. "See, when the glaciers of the last ice age receded, these trees were the very first to colonize the rocky landscape. It's the tree of beginnings." He looked at her in hopes that she wasn't too exhausted, or rather too detached, to understand his romantic remark.

"That's interesting…they've always been my favorite types of trees." she muttered, completely disregarding his intention.

"Indeed…" His gaze dropped down at his saddle horn that had gained a few scratches from all the riding the past days; disappointed that he couldn't make her thoughts of Mac magically disappear. "Is your foot feeling any better?" he asked her, changing the subject.

"Well, it still hurts…" she shrugged.

"I am saddened to hear that…" he said with a pout and she bobbed her head in silence. He tore his gaze away from the woeful aura of her being, and fixated it at the small speck of his ranch in the distance. "Would you like to go back? We've been riding for the past hour; perhaps your foot needs to rest." he offered as he pulled the reins to change direction, already knowing her answer.

Taken aback by his abrupt reaction, she pulled her reins too and caught up with him. "Thank you for your consideration…I think that would be a good idea." she said, and he nodded in silence.

Everything felt so bewilderingly strange to her; she couldn't recognize her feelings towards Will anymore, for it felt like he had turned into a complete stranger; worse actually, an irrelevant stranger whose mere presence such as breathing was nagging her to the core. Thinking about the wanted man — that stubborn mountain man, without a break in her mind, she wondered where he lurked now, and if they'd ever cross paths again. And if by any rare chance they did, what would happen…what *could* even happen.

The more she noticed Will, and the more she was surrounded by his company — the more she felt the suffocating urge to run away, and the more she wondered, why she didn't run away last night. And yet, Will didn't do anything to deserve these malicious thoughts of hers, as he was a one-of-a-kind gentleman — intelligent, considerate, gentle, and very handsome, but he just…

Wasn't him.

She felt frustrated with herself. Repulsed to allow such emotions to arise. Furious that she couldn't just start desiring him again. *Perhaps she didn't try hard enough,* she thought, as she studied every inch of his face, while riding abreast back to his ranch.

IV

"THAT'S SOOOO COOL!!!" MICKEY EXCLAIMED, ASTONISHED, as Mac bragged about himself riding a wild stallion — which in reality was a bomb-proof ranch horse, Roy — and he'd only ever brushed him.

"Sure, it is!" He puffed out his chest proudly. "Do ye ride at all?" He noticed the spurs around his boots, that were only there to show off to the other boys in town.

"No…not really." he shrugged, and then his shoulders slumped. "But I wish I'd get a horse! It's my birthday today, you know, but here I am shoveling shit!" He scowled disappointed, since his family was the wealthy kind, never considering any of his wishes — they'd rather keep their money safe and take it with them to their graves.

"Hm…" Mac nodded in thought. "Here. I got somethin' for yer birthday, Mickey." Mac jumped off the hay bale and marched proudly with a swagger on his hip to a wooden box he had buried beneath a stack of black-tinted straw. He fumbled out a bottle of rum, and strode back to Mickey with a naughty smirk on his lip.

"Happy birthday, me lad!" He smiled lopsidedly. "Have a shot!" He handed him the bottle, daring him to not decline the gift. Mickey took a big sip and felt his lungs swell up with an unforgiving wave of the burning liquid; he coughed and burped simultaneously in front of Mac, making them both burst into laughter.

"I love this! That's some good…poison! Haha!" Mickey grinned, his eyes squinting to take the burn. "Maybe one day, I'll work at the saloon! There's no way I'll shovel shit all my life, or be a boring old lawyer like my pa either!" He chuckled with some reservedness, knowing he'd be disowned by his family were he to follow through with that plan.

"Ya know…ye can be anything ye want." He flicked his cigarette, throwing it down and slamming his boot atop it. "Don't let anyone make ya think otherwise, Mickey." he said in earnest, clutching Mickey's shoulder with a hand — being too wise for his young years.

"Thank you, Mac! You…you're my best friend now!" He hugged Mac abruptly; who looked around, embarrassed, making sure no one witnessed the tender moment — feeling an odd warmth within himself, that he had forgotten the sensation of.

V

"MIGHT I OFFER YOU REFRESHMENT, SUCH AS…A GLASS OF WHISKEY?" He took off his shotgun coat and hung it over the chair, pulling his cashmere sleeves up to his elbows. "I believe that's the only inebriant I possess, at the moment…" He added skeptically, as he searched in utter concentration through his cabinet with tightly sealed lips.

"Yes, that would be lovely, Will. Thank you…" She sat down on the oaken floor, before the fire that was still burning low, feeling her foot ache with every movement she made. "Argh…" she grunted faintly, yet reaching Will's ears.

"Your foot?" he asked shortly, as the blade nailed through it still reminded him of *him,* of *her,* and of *them;* embracing in the downpour of eerily depressing rain.

"Yes…" she huffed, glancing down at her bare foot, still wrapped in a cloth. "Perhaps the ride…strained it, somehow…" she explained further, as no reaction came out of him.

She turned her head towards him, for he was still being soundless, yet always soothing in the way he walked across the room. She couldn't help but notice his tall, lean body in steady calm motion pausing before a shelf, reaching for two glasses. His long raven hair now hugging slightly around his shoulders, shining like that of a young boy, she was unable to find a strand of gray within it. She watched him as he sniffed a bottle of whiskey in private concentration, almost touching his razor-sharp jawline covered in short stubble that he didn't have time to shave off yet.

He was such an attractive man, Charlotte thought, as she examined his vest that was so very well fitted around his small waist. His back was narrower than Mac's, but still was an enticing wall of lean muscle. His calm demeanor was so comforting to be around, and his distinguished charm was unlike anything she had ever come across. His smile was the flicker of light within a candle's flame; a flame you could swing your finger through and not get burned by its heat. For it was delicate in all its fierceness, and swayed beautifully in eternal contentment. Will was not a man to burn a heart, and somehow she worried she had already burned his.

She rested her head against the chair behind her in a sigh, and closed her eyes to let herself unleash for a fleeting moment. Will sat down beside her, caressing her cheek softly to get her attention. Startled, she found his hand offering a half-full glass of rich topaz liquid, swirling and splashing against the glass.

"This Kentucky Bourbon has been aged for twenty years…" He took a sip and licked his full lips, exhaling the subtle burn so attractively. "I must admit, it is my favorite choice of spirit…" He twisted the glass before the fire, watching the liquor turn translucent from the light. "It's strong…vintage… artistic…" He paused and lowered the glass on his lap. "…romantic…" He cut his eyes at her, freezing them as they pulled hers towards him. Charlotte, enchanted by his words, noticed his cheeks flush red the moment he unlocked his gaze again. "I promise, it is not kerosene…" He chuckled as he side-eyed her, looking worriedly to see if she had tried it yet. She took a big, burning sip and looked at him again with a brighter smile this time.

"I do hope you approve of it." he said, biting his lip in nervousness.

"It is delicious…" She winked absently, and his face froze.

"I'm delighted to hear that…" His cheeks crimsoned, and swiftly he tore his gaze away. "Charlotte…if I may…" He drew in a breath, and hers halted. "It has come to my attention, that you…you are a wanted woman now." he said and she choked on the liquid. "In three states, at that. Are you alright?" he asked, and she nodded upon another cough.

"Yes…that…that is true, I suppose." she said and looked at him, concerned.

"Hm…is it an accurate report that suggests…you murdered a man, down in Marysville? If it is not too rude of me to ask…"

He frowned, and faced her again.

"Will…no. I have never murdered a man before, and I never will." she said in stern honesty and he swallowed deeply, listening intently.

"Did…he…do so?" he asked finally, for that question had been tormenting him ever since he found out about them. She took another sheepish sip of her drink, one long enough to numb her lips, to burn and prickle them. She nodded, and his chest rose upon a heavy breath. "I am pleased to know that he was there at such a crucial time. I do not condone manslaughter, but in this case, I applaud him for it, for I would have done the same if you were in danger." he said and she smiled quizzically. "Charlotte, I deeply apologize for not succeeding to change his mind regarding his stay here." he said bluntly and she blinked, aghast. "It is no secret to me, that…you both have been acquainted in an ardent and sincere manner, nor do I wish to withhold such knowledge from your awareness — for that would insult your intelligence, and doing so would insult mine." he said, and the flames suddenly engulfed her whole being in a hellfire of shame. His honesty, thrusting daggers of admiration into her heart.

"Will…"

"I feel no hesitation in avowing, however, that I long to offer…a mutual warmth of affection, if not more…to you, my lady." He swallowed dryly and the words abandoned her. "And if I shall fail to do so, then I have not the smallest of hope for my character, for I shall deserve no attention from you." he said and she stared at him blankly, trying hard to even rephrase his words in her mind to even comprehend them. "I do not expect an answer, Charlotte. I simply felt it necessary to speak my feelings and thoughts, and I wish to be able to move forward in hopes of future happiness with the idea of you as my lady in them." He tore his gaze away, and buried his face into his cup as she sipped on hers sheepishly.

"Please allow me to simply say…I genuinely appreciate the way you're able to communicate your feelings to me, and I am…incredibly sorry if I have appeared distant…" she said, and he forced a smile to her.

"I beg you, my lady…do not apologize, for I am by no means discouraged."

He smiled wider, and her eyes held back the tears of guilt.

She took another sip, swallowing down the sob and shifted her weight on the floor, accidentally jerking her foot again. Her eyes squinted, and her whole face scrunched up from the pain that shot through her. His brows snapped together in worry.

"Is it dreadful?" he asked her and she faced him, perplexed.

"What is?"

"The whiskey…"

"No…no. Just my foot. I think I might have pulled a tendon, actually… or something like that, for it feels different than just the wound." she said, and he nodded.

"May I?" he then asked, reaching with his hands to her bare foot. She froze in embarrassment, for that would be quite an intimate gesture and yet she didn't wish to reject him again — not after burning his heart in the most demeaning way possible.

"Yes…sure…" she said shyly, lifting her foot to his grip. He clasped it tenderly with his hands, and she flinched, more from the cold touch of his hands than the pain.

"I apologize, my lady…" he said, now gently kneading her foot with his thumbs. She gasped, arching her back, and taking another burning sip from the whiskey as if somehow she required it. Suddenly the air she breathed became swelteringly hot, and sweat of nervousness ran down her sides. His fingers felt like steady ripples of water, strong enough to brush against her skin, but soft enough to not hurt it.

"Where…where did you learn how to do that, so…nicely." she soughed, lifting her head to face him.

"Hm." He chuckled shyly, cracking his mouth open, then released a hand, grabbed the glass and sipped whiskey instead, reconsidering. Somehow he didn't wish to answer this, as if she scraped a layer from his own secrecy. Yet she couldn't be alarmed by it, for suddenly she was noticing his wet lips and his slanted brown eyes, his sharp cheekbones, his divinely lean face that exaggerated every symmetrical detail on it, and suddenly she felt a tingly sensation slither through her. "Does it feel better?" he asked her and she cracked her mouth open, in turn sipping whiskey as she reconsidered her answer.

"Yes…thank you." she smiled, and retrieved her foot. "By the way, I… think this is the best whiskey I've ever had…" she sucked in a stuttering breath, trying to come up with things to say other than how *fucking* good her foot felt beneath his fingers, and how she could *see* him again through her blurred, fogged up vision. "…but I'm not surprised; you always choose the best stuff, it seems." She smiled, for the first time not thinking about Mac.

"Yes, I tend to, so it seems…" he hummed softly as he looked at her, making her cheeks crimson in an instant — a flaming scarlet flush. He leaned over and gently kissed her on the tender crease of her neck that was lit from the fire's light. "My apologies…I couldn't help myself, Charlotte…" His kiss leaving a sweet stickiness from the drink against her skin, his lips still lingering on her neck. "You look beautiful tonight; in fact, you always look beautiful…almost bewitching…certainly, bewitching." he soughed again with a soft subtle chuckle, tickling her skin, prickling it, erecting the fine hairs across it.

"Will…I'm sorry." Guilt pushed the gasping words out of her mouth unapologetically, and his lips pulled back from her neck.

Easing himself back into his seat, he glanced at the ground quietly, his hands resting loosely on his knees and she gaped at him within a panting lung. He had such a seductive, masculine, and intense aura about him tonight — much different than anything he portrayed before.

"You have nothing to be sorry about, my dear Charlotte. I am sorry; if I rushed things for you." He grabbed her hand to squeeze briefly. "You have known me a sufficient time to be a judge of my merits by now, dare I say… therefore, I hope you are consciously aware that I won't be holding you hostage under my being, and you are free to depart anytime…" He gulped down a big sip and looked up at the wooden ceiling, feeling it looked down back at him.

"Will…" She caressed his warm hand with her thumb. "I feel so honored to have met you…" she said, sipping on her glass hastily.

"What do you mean, my lady?" he asked, confused, not expecting such a compliment. "I'm not…anything that important…" he muttered, repeating his father's words subconsciously.

"Don't say such…" She frowned, and locked eyes with him. "You're one of the most interesting people I've ever met, I'm just…too ignorant to understand you, I suppose." She bit her lip in deep awkwardness, as she realized she wasn't anywhere near so educated as he was. "But, I would lie if I said you didn't arouse my curiosity." She smirked, proud of herself for coming up with such witty remarks — yet the whiskey helped make them flow.

Will chuckled as he lowered his gaze again, for her eyes were hauntingly captivating, too strong to be able to look at them for a long time. "You know Charlotte, I bear the wounds of many battles I've avoided in my life, yet you… you've fought every one of them, as far as I know, and that is quite admirable." he said with a wide smile, his dimples emerging through his stubble. "I suppose I must say, I'm quite honored to have met you, my…love." he said daringly, and she stared at him in raw silence.

"I…" Her lips froze, her brain struggling to understand what he meant. "What battles have you avoided?" she didn't hesitate to ask, as she noticed his smile slip beneath his pencil-mustache.

"I've…I've always wanted to be a writer." he said tentatively. "Yet, I fear I've wasted most of my years loathing my everyday occupation…" his mustache twitched nervously. "This might not seem like much, but it has crushed me, as the books I've written are all but spoiling in my dusty attic, instead of being published — somehow." he sighed. "Somehow, I let them go…"

"You've written books??" she interjected, propping herself up excitedly to learn more about him.

"Indeed…a long time ago." He looked into her hazel eyes, seeing them ignite in thrill. "However, this is minuscule compared to what you went through, and I can't even handle that." He chuckled with the irony.

"Promise me something, Will." she said, as an encouraging smile emerged on her lips.

"What's that, my lady?" His eyes trailed off down to her lips.

"Grab those books from the attic, and make it your life's purpose to make them known worldwide. If anyone should be recognized for such a gift, it is you, Will!" She caressed his hand and sat beside him again, feeling a sudden wave of disorientation. "For I will read them one day. That I swear." she nodded gravely.

Will, muted, rehearsed her statement in his head — conflicted and shocked by her sudden support. Charlotte gulped down another mouthful of bourbon, almost emptying her glass. She had started getting a little tipsy, and the timber walls appeared like dark waves closing in on her, so she rested her face against his shoulder and slammed her eyes shut in hopes for her senses to sharpen again. He smelled so fresh, and so…sweet to those deranged senses.

"Is this a cologne you're wearing?" She pried her eyes open and jerked her jaw towards him, grabbing his neck, and pulling it towards herself to bury her nose in it.

"It is…" His voice deepened, as a sudden shiver slithered down his spine. "Do…do you like it?" He sucked in a stutter, glancing down at her alluring bust that was always stretching her shirtfront, yet now it was nearing towards him — even a gentleman could not resist it.

"I love it…" she sighed heavily and started kissing his neck fervently, gently pulling on his skin with her teeth — grabbing and caressing his sharp jawline as she sucked on him. "So much…" she grunted, and he choked.

"Charlotte, perhaps we…" His neck arched back and his hands clung strongly on his knees — desperately trying to come up with all his intellectual words, yet they all failed him at that tense moment.

She lifted herself up swiftly, straddling him without a second thought, her legs wrapped around him and her arms coiling his neck. She looked at him with a promise, and he looked back at her with uncertainty. "Remember…" she said. "When you told me you hoped we would…continue where we left off?" She smirked, and he drew in a deep breath.

"Yes I do, my lady…I certainly do…" he said, as she breathed in his cologne again.

"What was on your mind right then…Will…" She gasped against his skin, as she glided her lips along his neck. His hands squeezed his kneecaps as he felt her. Her breath was hot. She was so hot…and he was melting beneath her lips.

"If I may avow to you…I surmised about those lovely lips of yours, that I longed to lovingly embrace." he said and she halted her mouth before his, breathing heavily her devouring desire into him.

"Oh, Will…" she sighed, and pressed her lips against his; kissing him long and deep, feeling the fullness of his lips entrap hers. She pulled back and rested her forehead against his and smirked in sheer bewilderment, for his lips felt different. "My apologies…" she whispered to him snidely, only to kiss him again — lustfully gluing to his mouth. Unclenching his hands from his knees, and succumbing to his weakened core, he wrapped his arms around her body, trailing them down slowly to her round buttocks above her cloth — feeling of their shape as gently as he could. She pulled away and continued to look at him lecherously, her fingers starting to unbutton his fine red vest.

"You cannot form any idea of my excitement at this moment, my lady…"

He sighed heavily. "But, I fear that…"

"I think…I can't resist you now, Will…" she whispered to him again, impatiently taking off his vest, unbuttoning his white cashmere shirt with hasty fingers.

Muffled, his eyes traveled down to her cleavage again, as it now revealed itself ever more before his face. "My love…" he grunted within a stutter. "I should…I should perhaps now make you aware, that you're exposing your… ineffable…bust, to my ardent gaze…" he said, and she halted with a tender frown of bewilderment. "Perhaps we shouldn't proceed…under your influence of spirited substance, my lady." he said in earnest, in this tormenting attempt to resist this temptation.

She paused in her own attempts to understand him in her all her fuzziness and blurred, now twisting vision, and noticed him ogling her, as she was opening his shirt's last button, exposing his lean, built body to her devouring eyes — a wave of cologne hitting her face again.

"You want to see them? Is *that* what you're saying…" she asked him shyly, while brushing her hands over them temptingly — imitating what her innocent eyes witnessed growing up, in great teasing movements, as if she had done it all her life.

"I…" she leaned over and started kissing him faster, and harder, searching for a feeling she had lost somewhere last night.

"Take them off for me…" she ordered him, guiding his hands on her pants, as the room span around her, as she felt for the very first time a bulge grow stiff and hard beneath her.

"Oh, Lord…" he gasped, pulled back and clasped her from the shoulders, locking stern eyes with her. "Charlotte, dare I say I would beg for relief from the tormenting stiffness that nearly bursts my virile member asunder, however, you shall give me leave tonight instead, and consider permitting me the honor to have that another time, for you are a very fine and desirable woman, and I am now advanced in life, and have bedded a few handsome women, but I

never saw a cleavage of that voluptuous form, and I am therefore convinced…
you must be just as desirable upon every other inch of your being, and if you
do grant me that cherished honor, you will find me worth knowing. It will be
a novelty exciting to us both, and upon that, I wish to…end this…wonderful
night, on a promise of equal wonder." he said, and her whole being gaped at
him, benumbed, unable to grasp a single word, and she didn't know if it was
the whiskey speaking in tongues or the elite creature reciting again.

Will, as much as he wanted to feel her so badly, felt it was morally wrong
to proceed — as he could tell she was intoxicated, and in fear of taking advantage of her without her sober and sharp consent, he pulled back. He lovingly
pushed her away from his chest and buttoned up his shirt again.

Charlotte, confused and disappointed, didn't understand why he would
reject her so abruptly — and yet she barely understood anything to begin
with. She slid off his lap and he helped her sit beside him, feeling dirty and
ashamed of herself, the bile of nausea slowly but surely creeping up on her.

"Do forgive me, Charlotte. I respect you so much; I do not wish to take
advantage of you in any way." He reached for her hand, and kissed it.

"I think I'm sleepy…" she said, lied, as a tear of embarrassment coursed
its way down her cheek.

"My lady…" He frowned, confused, noticing her sudden change of tone.

"Goodnight, Will." She stood up awkwardly, holding on to the chair and
his shoulder, and draggingly made her way back to her room.

Will remained on the floor with his shirt half undone, and his whiskey
spilled on the ground beside him. Part of him could not understand what
morphed her into this lascivious creature suddenly; was it revenge for Mac
leaving? Was it the alcohol affecting her judgment? *Or was it genuine attraction towards him,* he wondered, as he let the fire slowly die down.

CHAPTER 18

She is Dead

I

THE HERDER WAS COLLECTING HIS SHEEP JUST BEFORE MARYSVILLE; making sure they didn't wander off with his heeler right behind them, oftentimes jumping on their left and speeding to their right again, ensuring they're crammed in together on a straight line. There was a livestock auction happening in the town, and everyone was excitedly preparing for it.

Dozens of cattle that needed to be sold to other farmers; sheep that were ready to go to slaughter, and undoubtedly the finest horses cowboys could get their hands on. The bidding game was always a pleasure for the townsfolk as their life was quite a routine, and they loved the opportunity of possible drama that such an auction would bring between bidders. The cattle rattle had started; an enormous wave of bidders was standing in front of the auctioneer, ready to raise their hand if the price fit.

"One dollar bid, now two, now two, will you give me two?" The auctioneer hypnotized the bidders. Hands were raised, and the bidding price skyrocketed.

"Y'abletabid…twenty-five dollar bid now, y'abletabid thirty, bid thirty?"

He rhythmically repeated himself in a melodic manner.

"Going once, going twice, sold!"

The herd of sheep was first to successfully sell. Hogs were anxiously running around in the muddy pen by all the noise of the tow; cowboys already threatening duels as they were too poor to bid high enough to get anything.

"Forty-five dollar, bid it now, a fifty dollar, fifty?

Will you gimmie fifty, make it fifty.

Bidin' it on a fifty dollar, will you gimmie fifty?
Who'll bid a fifty dollar bid?
Fifty dollar! Bid it now, fifty-five, will you gimmie fifty-five?
To make it a fifty-five, to bid at fifty-five.
Sold that hog for a fifty dollar bill."

The farmer jumped up in joy, as he didn't expect his hog to sell for that much. He slashed the air with a triumphant fist and kicked his heels as he leaped lopsidedly. A horse for sale stormed into the corral pen, bucking and snorting frantically, charging towards the bidders that were standing outside; pinning its ears and striking at them, hooking its legs over the pens as it reared.

"One dollar bid, now two, now two, will ya give me two?"

The auctioneer looked around only for him to find the pale faces of the bidders; no hands were raised that time. The horse squealed, kicked its heels in the air, and snarled its teeth — reaching to grab the people around it.

"One dollar bid, now two, now two, will ya give me two?"

He repeated, considering if he should employ the chandelier bid now.

"Two!" A voice filled the unusual void in the town. A southern preacher, also a rancher down in Cottonmouth State, finally bid for the gray horse.

"Going once, going twice…gone!"

II

"FINN…" SHE SIGHED INTO HIM. "I made a fool out of myself last night…you'd be shocked to have seen me like this…so much, like…mother." She brushed along his well-built top line, which was still warm to the touch from laying down in the straw, flinching her shoulders and grimacing in repulsion the longer she revisited last night's memory. "I can't even look him in the eyes no more…how to?" She let her head drop onto him, as her mother's demeaning words hit her ears again.

> *"You'll end up just like me, Charlotte. Apple doesn't ever fall far*
> *from the tree. But perhaps this might save you one day; as you*
> *ain't good enough for anything else."*

Finn breathed out heavily, feeling her tension reach within him. "Men are only trouble, you know, sweetheart?" She shook her head, fixating her glare upon his shiny coat. She felt terrible realizing she hadn't paid much attention to Finn in the past weeks; how all this kept her away from him, and her mind was constantly preoccupied with her silly emotions or the hideous concept of *men*.

"Knock-knock?" Will said as he knocked on the barn door; her thoughts almost conjuring him.

"Oh, hey!" Charlotte, startled, invited him in. Quickly grabbing the brush again to act like she was busy, completely avoiding any eye contact as she did.

Will walked behind her, caressed her shoulders, and kissed her on the back of her head. "Good morning, my beautiful lady…somehow I had an inkling that I might find you here." He smiled kindly as he always did, and she sighed out heavily, feeling relieved. He felt gentle against her back, his voice soft and with no judgement, grazing lazily at the crease of her neck. He appeared oddly content, and not the least bit worried or repulsed with her.

Gathering up her grit, she turned around to face him. "Good morning, Will…" She sighed, with a tremble in her voice. "Listen, I…I am very sorry for what happened last night…" Her words stormed out of her mouth, like ants from a colony her guilt stirred up.

"I beg of you, do not…"

"No, Will, hear me out. Please." She threw the brush back into the bucket, ready to confess to him in hopes to save what little noble reputation she had left. "I am…I have never…I am just not like…"she stammered and gaped at him with crimsoned cheeks. The timbers of the barn creaked louder in her silence as the wind brushed against them, for she couldn't find the words to tell him she'd never slept with a man before — let alone have a relationship of any kind, and so last night's behavior was completely out of character for her. "I would never rush things, let alone…force you, and I'm…really sorry that I…" She quivered, and a loud voice suddenly horned in on her.

"William Griffiths!" The abrupt voice of a man, shouting as he was dismounting his horse outside Will's house, rattling every bone in her body.

"Down!" Will whispered to her, alerted, and they crouched swiftly to the ground. He strode quietly to peek slowly through the barn's window, only to see Sheriff Dorman knocking on the door right next to Rachel who was tied up at the hitching post. His brown doe eyes flared, calculating his options, and he glanced back at Charlotte with a pouted lip. "You need to leave, my lady."

"What??" She gaped at him, aghast.

"They will hang you, Charlotte! If they find you and arrest you! You need to leave!" he urged her, clasping her hand tenderly as tears formed in her eyes, never realizing she might find herself in such a position.

"Now." He sighed, heavily. "You…should climb out the window and go through the woods, and do not even contemplate turning back here! You *have* to persist in moving away! I will meet you to the east…shall we say, Birdsboro?" He thought of the furthest point she could be safe as he trembled, frightened, this time willing to face his battle.

"No…no, I can't. I told him I was headed there!" She looked over at the sheriff, who was looking through the glass windows of the building, wiping the fog away with his sleeve. She felt the time ticking from Will's pocket watch, yet this time it was snug within his vest.

"Mister Griffiths, I advise ya to open the goddamn door before ya don't have a door to open no more." He scowled, and peeked through the next windowpane. "My deputies will be arriving soon enough, and they wouldn't mind tearing the whole building down, with you in it!!" he yelled, still waiting for Will to appear.

"They will search the place once they arrive, Charlotte. You need to leave. NOW." His chest deflated nervously, his hands sweated and his panicked breath dried up his throat. "They will be suspicious of me." he said, and helped her climb out the window.

"What about Finn??!" Charlotte asked worriedly, as the idea alone of leaving Finn behind absolutely devastated her.

"I will sneak through the back door of the house, let him in, and you hurry to lead Finn out from the stable. Can you do that, my lady?" he asked her softly, his eyes screaming in fear at her.

"Will, will you be okay?" she asked him, squeezing his hand in case it was the last time she'd see him.

"Always, my love." He reached for her lips, and kissed her intensely goodbye. "Now, go…I will catch up with you. Let's meet…in Mon Louis — at the saloon's hotel. Tell them my name, and they will take care of you."

III

"SHERIFF DORMAN! HOW CAN I HELP YOU this fine morning, sir?" Will opened the door and a fist punched him right in his face, making his nose crack and bleed uncontrollably.

"Ya think ya can fool me, pretty boy??" The sheriff walked over him, pointing his gun at Will's face.

"I take it you haven't found Mac Kinnon yet, sir." Will responded wryly, pressing his aching nose with his fingers.

"Don't make me waste a bullet on ya, boy. Where is she…" he threatened him, as Will laid on the ground inhaling his own blood.

"She's dead." he said to him, feeling of his broken nose, a sensation he had never encountered before.

"Ha. How conveniently clever, aren't ya…and how do ya know she is?" He snorted derisively, cocking his revolver. The sound ringing in Will's ears, competing with his rampant beating of his heart.

"I found her…frozen to death." he said, spitting out some blood right after, his white pearly teeth now tinted of scarlet. "You're welcome to search my house if you don't believe me. Does this satisfy you now?" He locked eyes with him, as the barrel stared down at him. "I lost the woman I cared most about, and you're trespassing here violently because of some sick obsession over a wanted man I have nothing to do with!" He leered, his fine pencil-mustache almost as red as the sheriff's sleepless, bloodshot eyes.

"Oh, spare me with your poetry! My deputies will make sure they'll search every damn corner in your rotten place…" He shook the gun around as he threatened. "They will camp right at Great Bend, and will make sure ya don't have any…intruders, so ya can sleep well tonight." He winked at him snidely, pulling the gun away from Will's face, and started treading back to his horse. "Oh, and Mister Griffiths. Once we find your sorry arse guilty for the loss of our deputies up in Rockies West…you're gonna be hanged, my friend." He jammed his revolver back into his holster, and mounted his horse. "And everybody in town is going to be invited to watch the pretty-boy swing to his doom…"

Will, detached from any threats, watched the sheriff gallop away, then stood up swiftly and rushed to the barn. Finn was gone, and so was Charlotte.

IV

A SWARM OF ARMED MEN SPREAD AROUND GREAT BEND, blocking the path and questioning everyone who came through, particularly stage coaches that transported women passengers. A dozen deputies were searching Will's house — moving beds, opening wardrobes, and pilfering cabinets — anything they might find suspicious, anywhere possible Charlotte could be in hiding.

"Boss, we cannot find anything here." the deputy informed Dorman, after hours of rude investigation.

"It can't be! Look harder! The gal is here! If she wasn't, he wouldn't be here!!" he yelled at all his men, pointing to the house, ordering them to go search harder.

"Sir, we have searched every corner already…there is nothing we haven't moved or opened."

Will was clinging onto Rachel's reins outside. Holding his breath captive in his lungs, trying to remain as composed as he could under such pressure. His nose ached like it never had before, and it kept on reminding him of Dorman's immoral ways of dealing with his affairs — making him thankful that Charlotte got away in time, for had she been found, he was convinced Dorman would have treated her as a barbarian stuck out of time.

"Ya damn yokels! Can't do anything right here! Only drink and freeze to death by a damn blizzard! Costing me a fortune to replace every single bastard of you! Marshal Tilghman woulda hanged ya all!!" the sheriff shouted, as he now was stepping inside the house to take matters in his own hands.

He looked around, inspecting every speck of dust, every boot print on the ground, every strand of hair — that so far wasn't colored or long enough for a woman like her. After an hour of looking through he decided there was no evidence, *yet,* and proceeded to exit the building. Passing by the fireplace, his boot knocked over a glass that was hidden underneath the chair. He kneeled down to grab it and noticed another one right next to the chair, still filled with whiskey. His eyes widened in thrilled pleasure and glared back at the deputies, shivering in their boots.

"Arrest this man."

Deputies strode over to Will, who still appeared calm and confident, yet the way they marched towards him made his grip sweat around the reins, and they slipped as his content demeanor slipped with them. Without a word, they smacked a rifle against his head, making him drop to his knees. They tied him up as he was slowly becoming unconscious; the ground span around him, and daylight dimmed to jet blackness.

"Will, Will, Will…" The sheriff walked up to him, grabbed his hair, and lifted his head up to face him. "William Griffithssss, or do ya prefer…Tom Williams?" He cackled menacingly. "Too bad ya won't have the chance for another drinkie anytime soon, pretty boy."

A deputy knocked him out completely with his rifle, after the sheriff signaled with his gaze. A flock of ravens spooked Rachel, as they flew over them — disappearing within the bright sun rays of the sky, dimming them too.

CHAPTER 19

Boly

I

NAILS THAT SCRAPED THE BARK OFF A TREE; INGRAINED WITH DIRT, wooden splinters piercing through, deep underneath them. Struggling, frail hands tied together tight, stretched out stiff — cold; pale. Tips of extremities a shade of black; perished.

Crushed, resting head with a hawser around it; aghast face incised with tender strokes of a rusty blade. Blood now dripping harmoniously, after the flowing stream it gushed before. Body still, bruised and bare, hanging afloat.

II

"MICKEY!!!" FARMER GROSSMAN YELLED FROM THE TOP OF HIS LUNGS — a yell from the pit of his flabby throat, a voice so coarse and robust, almost inhuman as if rage had a voice of its own. Hunting for the young boy out in the fields, trampling down his crops with his boat-shaped boots, he kept on yelling.

"Sir! Yes, sir!" Mickey rushed to him, with a feeble trembling voice. Halting a few feet before him, close enough to be seen by him, far enough to be safe, feeling the farmer's heavy steps shake the earth underneath him as he halted as well.

"You left the infernal gate open!! All the cattle is gone!!! You worthless sinner!! C'mere!!!" He undid his belt and strode faster to the boy, as now the pebbles themselves bounced frightened atop the soil.

Mickey started running away from him through the tall blonde crops, but his leg got tangled up in them. He fell face-first to the ground; hitting his mouth violently against a rock. Blood suddenly pooled his mouth, and he burst into tears from the agonizing pain of biting his tongue, painting it red. The soil. Himself.

"Aw…ya poor thing." Farmer Grossman looked down on him, slobbering over the tortured expression the boy gave him. He grabbed his small body and twisted it, pulling down the boy's pants. He slapped his bare buttocks with his leather belt, beating them until they turned raw.

Mickey screamed, unable to remain brave, for how could an eight year old comprehend the concept of punishment that felt more like the endless torture of a slave. Distress colored his screams; there was a harrowing fear coiled around his stomach as he would look back at the monstrous, fleshy man and witness the sick satisfaction outlined on his face.

"Leave him, ye fat bastard!!!" Mac yelled as he jumped on his back, putting him in a swift headlock, squeezing as hard as he could with his innocent arms. "Run, Mickey!!!! RUN!!" he screamed at him tensely, still trying to suffocate the monster.

Mickey pulled up his pants and hesitantly started running as fast as he could, glancing back every so often as long as he could still spot Mac in the haze of the eerily still crops and the ocean of crows that stirred the clouds above them.

The farmer grabbed Mac's legs and pulled him around, slamming him to the ground and hitting him with a kick in his chest. He took his belt, grabbed him from the hair to pull him up again, and wrapped the belt around his neck.

"Ya trying this trick with me, son? Hm?? Is this respectful to your elders? Is this respectful to your…father?" He snorted tauntingly, and jerked on the belt. "Oh Mac, my dear child…you coulda been dead in them streets of Mon Louis…was I not who chose to adopt you…you was but a bag of bones, and I took care of you…showered ya, with abundant love…" He pouted ominously, and slammed a fist against Mac's face, mudding up his skin with fresh bright blood. "Let's see how *ya* like being choked now!" He slid the belt through the buckle tighter, and Mac swiftly struggled to breathe — turning purple with pressured veins popping all over his face and hands, until the hands stopped resisting. "Repent for your sins, son…" He shook his belt, disorienting Mac furthermore, tightening it all the way and yanking it towards him, rubbing his face against the rotten-scented crotch of his grimy pants.

"Repent for your SINS!!"

The last word that echoed in his head, before he succumbed to a state of trance, dozing off into a room of darkness with the belt still coiled around him, and yet that too was a more serene place to find himself in. The ravens kept croaking above him, almost a whimpering sound escaping their beaks. The crops embraced his young body, laying lifeless on the ground, sheltering it before the monster of a man threw it over his shoulders.

III

"HOLY RANCH, FINN!" A SIGH OF EXASPERATION HIT HIS FUZZY EARS, and they flinched by the air it stirred against them. After days of riding through Rockies East, going further south to reach Mon Louis, she spotted the infamous ranch — the nucleus of all surrounding towns for fresh produce. "Finally, a town to get supplies! I have one pitiful can of green beans left, and that's about it." she said, briefly reminding herself of her naïve decision to not have any of Mac's elk meat back in Hope. "I wish I could graze on grass like you, handsome…" She chuckled, and the thought of reaching safety gave her a vast sense of relief.

Finn grabbed a chunk of grass on his side, as the mention of it gave him a sudden appetite. Snorting in blitheful relief himself, they trotted towards Holy Ranch. As they advanced to it, she realized the town was certainly different around here. People would not greet, nor speak, nor make eye contact with her, but instead, look wary of her and rush to their homes. She spotted a stable boy in the distance, wrangling with a horse, or rather the horse wrangled him as it bolted, dragging him across a muddy pen. She chuckled for she could relate to that feeling, then hitched up Finn on a post in front of what seemed to be a deserted general store, and walked to it in hopes of finding some food.

Right before opening the door, she noticed a poster hanging next to it. Startled, she was met by her own face on it, side by side with Mac's. Her skin crawled, her face fell, her hair stood up all over her body, and her jaw slacked, dropped to her feet, as the shocking feeling she got when she saw Mac's face again, staring right back at her — evoked all drowned feelings within her.

That's why everyone here was walking away from me, she quickly realized, picking up her jaw off the ground. Not long after, a voice echoed all across.

"MCCOY!!! What in the world are ya doin' so long with the nag!!"

Rushing back to Finn and slipping her boot in the stirrup, hopping into the saddle and quivering in panic, they galloped as fast as they could away from the ranch before more people would recognize her. The reality started to kick in, sailing over her like a wave of woe; *she was a wanted woman in all of Hollenberg, and she couldn't stay here.* She had to move faster, push Finn to his limits, and reach Mon Louis as soon as possible in feeble hopes that she could start life anew.

"This is the life that Mac led, for decades…" she whispered to herself, stunned at how he still wasn't captured, for being wanted all over the nation was certainly a bigger challenge than three small states. "I cannot do this, sweet boy. I will never survive this long enough…" She sobbed, and her heart rattled in misery within her rib-cage. "…but I promise, I will make sure you do." She clutched his shoulder, fingertips pulling gently on his coat.

Her irrational thoughts brought her back to Will; concerned of his own well-being and safety, wondering if he would manage to meet her in time, before the deputies caught up with her. Her youthful hands shivered in fright as she glanced around herself, paranoid, scanning the shadows of the woods as they passed through.

CHAPTER 20

Fractured

I

BOP!! A HARD FIST PUNCHED WILL FOR THE HUNDREDTH TIME that bloodletting evening. A hundredth time, met with silence.

"Talk, ya filthy pretty bastard!"

He hit him repeatedly, throwing his head around left and right. Will's face, cloaked in blood, eyes swollen and badly bruised; his smooth skin, now scarred from the man's rough knuckles. A small piece of his lip, busted open, hanging loosely — burning every time his sweat would wash over it. He had never felt such pain in his entire life; for he never had to be under interrogation of any sort, let alone such demeaning torment.

"Boss, our pretty boy ain't talkin'." The deputy glanced back at the sheriff who was seated behind, watching the show of torture with eerie satisfaction.

"Use your goddamn knife, then." he ordered him, puffing contentedly on his cigar, with his piercing eyes hiding underneath his hat's brim. Will raised his head up and blearily saw the man pointing a knife at his neck, slightly pressing it against his throat.

"Speak, pretty boy...where is she..." he asked him with a leer, and Will coughed up a puddle of blood on his face unintentionally as he pressed the knife further against him.

BOP!! "You son of a bitch!!!" He yelled, hitting him with the pommel of the knife across his face, his dispatch star turning scarlet. "SPEAK!!!!"

Will, barely hanging on, drowning in his own blood, his lungs rummaging for a lungful of air, tried to pull in a breath so he could let a word out.

"She…is…dead…in the…mountains…" He shut his eyes, expecting to be punched again.

"Boss??" The deputy glanced back at the sheriff again, wondering how else he could torture him without knocking him unconscious, or rather knocking him to his death.

Sheriff Dorman yanked the cigar from his mouth, stood up swiftly, and marched to Will with lips aching from resentment. He groped for his neck, choking him in rage. "Listen now, ya son of a bitch! If ya don't speak soon enough, I'll put a mirror in front of ya, peel your damn eyelids open and cut your goddamn throat — and you're gonna witness every single damn thing!!" he threatened, and spat on his face.

Will did not react. He had no fight left within him; he was never the type to quarrel, and he could not comprehend this behavior. He was exhausted, defeated, and had accepted his maltreatment. The sheriff released his grip from around his neck, took his gun out, and slammed it on his head, denting a wound into it.

"SPEAK, YA SON OF A BITCH!!!!!" He slammed it again.

"SPEAK!!!" Again. "SPEAK!!!!!!" Again…"ARGH!!!!"

He would not stop slamming his revolver against his cracked skull, harder and harder every single time. Blood gushed out of it, painting Dorman's face with every hit, showering Will's as he continued to hit him. There were no brown doe eyes left, there were barely eyelids that were visible, now covered in thick scarlet liquid. A porcelain beauty of a face, now a canvas of dark madness.

"Boss…boss! His skull is opening!" The deputy clasped the sheriff's arm, and the sheriff halted with a disheveled hair hanging over his forehead and streaks of veins slithering through it.

Will collapsed in a sea of blood. His body seized.

I I

OZARK RIDGE IS A HEAVILY FORESTED TERRAIN just outside of Birdsboro, with a myriad of mountain hills, enormous waterfalls, and enchanting scenery. It is one of the most fairytale-like areas to travel through as the tall trees of oak guide a wanderer along their path; dimming the sunlight that pierces through by their dark, and deeply furrowed bark, oftentimes rumored to harbor an old and weathered human face when the moon hangs low enough to illuminate it.

However, Ozark's forestry is also known to be one of the most dangerous places to trudge through, as it is extremely isolated, and people always avoid passing through if possible, for too many have gone missing far too often around these parts.

Cougars and highly poisonous snakes are its notorious predators, as well as the Fiddler Brood who'll murder anyone that crosses their path. They're very territorial, and loathe any form of civilization — therefore living far away from it. Their sickly fascination is capturing travelers; particularly women, as they tend to be an easier target. They imprison them in their caves deep in the Ozark mountains, where they rape and torture them for days before eventually murdering them and dismembering their heads as trophies. Easily recognizable as they're "adorned" with limited amounts of ragged clothing, and their inbred deformities leave a haunting impression.

III

CHARLOTTE AND FINN WERE RIDING THROUGH OZARK RIDGE in the early morning. They had never witnessed such vibrantly green leaves on trees in the autumn, or such thick swaths of lush grass circling around them; nor ever drank from such crystal clear waters from all the streaming creeks and pure flowing rivers they crossed through. Birdsboro's forestry was certainly an enchanting sight to behold, almost bewitching the senses of man.

"Finally!" Charlotte exhaled a pent-up breath. "Such soft ground underneath us! No more rocks for us, Finn! Your feet will be able to enjoy this ride for once!" she said with excitement, leaning over his neck, locking it within the noose of her arms as he loyally marched forward on the path. They set up camp before the most majestic and craggy waterfall, gracefully showering onto the rocks before it, and tumbling its foam over a steep cliff — Cedar Falls, one of the most impetuous and full in the entire region.

"Alright, Finn…" She drew in a deep courageous breath in sharp concentration. "I have to do this now, or else I will starve to death…and if I do starve to death, then…you're gonna miss me! Hopefully…that is." She shrugged and Finn looked at her with little faith — snorting as if he was picking on her.

She prepared her gun, determined to try her luck with hunting — or at least whatever she thought preparation was, as she wiped the dust and dirt off the barrel with a cloth. Studying the herd of deer grazing across the deep pool of Cedar Falls, she slowly loaded a round into the chamber manually with her straining, shaking thumb, pushing the bolt forward just like Mac had shown her. She crouched and snuck towards them, stepping as lightly as she could, sheltered by the harsh sounds of the waterfall's torrent, covering the noises that would betray her footsteps.

Stand straight. Press stock against shoulder…eyes through the sights, she repeated Mac's words in her head; imagining him standing against her back again. She rested the foregrip against the split of a limb on a young sapling for stability, bracing the stock with her off hand. *Breathe in…*his whisper now stirring the loose strands of hair against her cheek, and a sudden shiver crawled down her spine — feeling his cold breath, so eerily real against her neck, now exhaling herself again.

POW!

The shot was fired.

The deer dropped dead fifty yards before her.

Charlotte, shocked, stood shivering from the rush of adrenaline as she had never killed an animal before and the deer certainly appeared lifeless. She could not grasp the haunting sight of death, of a last breath evaporating in the damp air around her; unable to convince her own self of her triumph. A tear escaped her eye, feeling she had proved *them* wrong; her mother, her mother's clients, and friends who all demeaned her since the day she could understand their words. Suddenly they too did not matter, for she made herself proud for the very first time in her life.

"This is for you, Mac…" she said, a nostalgic smile scarring her lips. It quickly slipped, when she realized how much she still missed him.

IV

"ONE DAY YOU WILL BE THE MOST INSPIRATIONAL WRITER that ever lived, my son. You are such a kind soul, don't you ever change. Don't let the world harden you." She hummed softly to him, caressing his long black hair, after she slowly read the boy's essay with a feeble voice.

"Mother…Father told me I would inherit his business one day, and I…I'm not so sure I want that." he stuttered worriedly to her, in a woeful sigh, folding the essay back into his coat's pocket.

"Don't you worry Will, my darling. This will just ensure you have a future; to not worry about surviving in these dark ages we live in. You are the most intelligent and loving young man, I've had such the honor to raise, and I'm so…so very proud to call you my son." she soughed gently, coughing heavily right after, laying still in her bed.

"Mother…" He glimpsed at her sunken eyes tentatively. "Are you…going to…Heaven?" he asked her, his young eyes shone in tears, his throat swollen into a bundle of emotions he could not process.

"Yes, son." she hummed, and caressed his soft, rosy cheek with a quivering forefinger. "A much more peaceful world than here…don't you worry about me…" She looked up the ceiling, with a hopeful smile on her face.

"How…how do you know?" he asked her, clinging onto her weakened hand, more bone than flesh.

"He calls for me, son. He tells me my ma and pa are there waiting for me; and I will do the same for you, when the time comes." Her head turned towards him, her gaunt face struggling for another smile. Her eyes suddenly shut and her brows snapped together, as if in concentration. "I see wide open lavender fields, guiding me through a dark forest beneath a starry sky; a crystal clear lagoon before me…promising peace, as the Lord's messengers — a beautiful flock of ravens, shelter my new home." She nodded, confused herself, and opened her eyes again to face him. "And I hear them…they croak almost a lullaby to me…and they tell me…they know of you, and that your heart is too pure for this world…" She swallowed hard and her throat started to ache, as if preparing for a breath in its finality. "But don't let yourself get discouraged…the cruel world needs your light, my sweet boy." She let her bluish lips taut into a smile of encouragement. "And you are beaming, of the purest form…"she said and he pressed her hand tightly against his cheek, sniffing against her jaundiced skin.

"Will we…meet again, right, Mother?" His tears started to flow and roll painfully down his face, as somehow her description was not the comforting Heaven everyone had preached about.

"Yes, my sweetheart…" she promised, squeezing his tiny hand in her grip with all the strength that was left within her fingertips.

"I love you…Will…my son…" The faintest voice, gently dimming like the candle beside her. Will leaned over to her and embraced her tightly; crying over her shoulder, as she took her last breath.

"I love you…"

V

"THE PATIENT HAS STRIATED FRACTURES ON HIS SKULL, multiple bruises, and as it seems, some internal bleeding and swelling of the brain; which resulted in his body seizing." the doctor declared. "He is fortunate to have survived this — you said he fell off his horse, sir?" he inquired of the sheriff with a cocked brow of suspicion, as he could tell the assertion was impossible.

"Yes, doctor. Indeed…" Dorman nodded sheepishly. "We found him down a mountain; probably tumbled over it, hitting rocks…multiple times, he did." he explained, covering his face with a mask of vague innocence.

"Aha…I see." His head bowed, conflicted. "He will need months of rest in order to recover. Not too sure if he will walk away from this without major consequences." he told him worriedly, wrapping Will's head with multiple layers of medical cloth, knowing better that he was most likely beaten to death.

"We will keep an eye on him, doctor." Dorman said in earnest. "Any possible amnesia risks?" he asked him, concerned they had lost their chance to get any further information out of him.

"Very possible to have post-traumatic amnesia, indeed. Fella is lucky to be alive, however." he said, casting a last glance at Will's miserable being, still laying asleep in bed. He sighed and shook his head. "Have a good day, sir! I'm afraid I have other patients waiting on me." he said and left the room, as if his suspicion had been just confirmed.

"For fuck's sake…" Dorman glanced over at the deputy, as they were both speechless from Will's diagnosis; he was their only chance to help trace Charlotte and Mac.

V I

"WE WILL NEED TO FOLLOW THE BUFFALO RIVER all the way down south, and cross it on our way southeast…then we will reach Mon Louis, and Will will meet us in a matter of days." Her fingers swiped excitedly across the map, her lips taut across her face in concentration, as she was rehearsing her plan to her trusted pony. Finn rolled on the ground, covering his glowing coat with tiny specks of torn-up grass. He was enjoying himself this quiet evening, and making sure Charlotte would brush him a little longer the day after. Fireflies surrounded them; lighting up the thick dark forest, tangling themselves in Finn's mane, and magically decorating Charlotte's plait. They almost glowed within their light. She laid on her back, right beside Finn, who had settled down to rest after his countless rolls. Taking in the peaceful moment of the eerie quietness of the hills, the distant growls of cougars echoing in the void, the smooth sounds of the misty falls lulling her to sleep; feeling serene watching the stars multiply the longer her eyes focused on them.

She was feeling a strange new confidence from her achievement — hunting down the deer successfully, and tasting the freshly cooked meat for the very first time, salivating over it as if she had never eaten in her life. *It would be hard to go back to eating beans after that,* she thought to herself, and smiled with sincere satisfaction. Her eyelids were heavy; exhausted from the strenuous ride, the suffocating thoughts and the benumbing worries within her. She rested her head against Finn's full belly, and covered her body with a warm blanket that Will had left in the barn. The sudden sound of leaves crunching and twigs breaking couldn't alert her, nor keep her awake — only the fireflies started vanishing within the gloomy darkness.

VII

"PRRRRHH!!" THE GRAY MARE SNORTED IN AGITATION. Squealing, she struck the pole with her front legs, chipping and splitting her hooves as she did. Pulling her head back to all sides, she tried desperately to escape the constant pressure she was feeling from the rope that was keeping her confined to the pole.

The rancher grinned in dark amusement, for he enjoyed witnessing the suffering of an animal, for to him, and as a preacher, animals bore no soul — they weren't created by the likeness or image of God; therefore, there was no sin in any form of ill-handling them, and he took pride in doing just that.

Fighting with every sinew of her being against the cruel restraint, the hard ground worked into powdery sand that disappeared against her soaking wet, sweaty body. She had a strong spirit; untamed, unbroken. A pride that not even a lion could surpass. She kept on fighting for hours, and days that followed — exhausting all her vigor and power, yet she wouldn't give up — not for a single drop of water, not for a single stalk of hay. The preacher watched her wrestling with the pole, day and night. Observing, he realized he had never seen such a strong-minded horse before, yet he was just as stubborn, if not dangerously more.

VIII

"YOU'VE DONE A BAAAAD THING, SON…" HE SNORTED, then cackled, then stood stern before him, noticing Mac slowly open his eyes. They flared.

"Wh…where am I???" He panicked upon feeling his hands tied up in chains against a brick wall, upon glancing around him only to spot a dark wall with an immense variety of corroded farm utensils, hung in an ironically tidy order. He was in the mucky cellar of the farmhouse, tied up, confined — captured in complete darkness. His hands jerked instinctually and his head turned to the side, searching for the feeble speck of light that came from the stairs leading up to the main floor.

"Mac, my son." He chuckled with amusement. "The question is…what did ya do...*to me?* Hm? My dear boy..." He looked at him with his malevolent eyes, a cocked brow of a challenge. Mac's breath cut in his lungs, and he abruptly pulled on the chains as hard as he could. His skin started to peel off and blood stained the metal, dripping on the floor.

"Sh, sh, shhh, Mac. No point in harming your lovely hands, my boy." He chuckled lecherously. "Remember, I still need ya to *work* for me, son." He winked, as slobber dripped from the corner of his mouth.

"What ye want from me??!! I did everything ye wanted or ever asked!! Please!! Let me gooo!" he cried, pressing himself against the wall, trying to escape the demonic silhouette before him.

"I want ya to learn to control your emotions..." He smiled at him, filling his chest up with a sick sense of pride to see him squirm. "But first, ya have to learn to control pain; learn how it feels to suffer through it..." He took a brief glimpse over at the utensils, and cut his eyes back at him. Another wink of a threat, another wink of a promise. He patted him on the head, slapped his sobbing cheek, and strode back up the stairs — locking the door behind him.

Darkness filled the hollow room, cold bricks making Mac's bare body shiver. Unable to lay down, unable to move his arms — only able to press his legs against his chest to shield himself from the cold, hoping to stay warm throughout the long night. There was a cloud of haze within his mind; confused and petrified, for that was a punishment he had not expected. For how could "man" rope the hands of another, let alone a child. How could "man" feed his desires, by torturing another. And how could "man" not feel remorse or guilt. How could "man" not feel...

He thought to himself.

Darkness filled him.

IX

WILL WAS RELEASED FROM THE DOCTOR'S OFFICE after a week of supervision; he was alert now and able to walk properly, yet he had a thudding headache that felt like a dozen bricks smashing his brain together at once. He was no longer under arrest, as the sheriff had no use for him any further; even if he knew he was the one that initiated the death of his deputies; he had no evidence to uphold his claims — he only offered them a celebration, after all. He could also no longer interrogate him, not under such a health condition. Having the doctor as a witness didn't help his case, either. Will was a wealthy man, and he had the connections needed to make the sheriff pay for what he did to him; besides, he threatened as much the day he first met him.

However, Will chose to go by the sheriff's before renting a hotel for the night; deeming it necessary to express his thoughts to him, as scared as he was, as devoid of strength and as traumatized as he felt — he had to ensure that he didn't have to worry about him anymore, so he could instead spend his energy on planning his journey to Mon Louis.

"Boss…the pretty boy's back…" a deputy quietly informed Dorman, who was examining the map closely.

"Sheriff Dorman, I won't be of disturbance for long." Will strode towards his office, squinting from the pain with every step. "I felt it important to thank you for taking me to the doctor, instead of letting me bleed out to death. Whether the catalyst was from the goodness of your heart, or…the worry of your mind, does not matter in the end." he said and Dorman blinked, flinching his mustache in irritation. "Deep down, you seem to have the best intentions in your heart for your fellow citizens. We may have our disagreements on the execution of intent, but I appreciate the humanity you chose to show towards me in the end." he said, and reached to shake his hand for the last time.

The sheriff, perplexed with his lack of rage and resentment, could not grasp how he could be so noble — completely disregarding all the needless suffering and abuse he had just gone through, suddenly making him feel less of a man, and somehow shame swallowed him whole. Yet there was still the bug of selfishness buzzing within his ear.

"Help me find Mac Kinnon, and I will make sure Charlotte will not be harmed." he made him a last, hopefully intriguing offer.

Will sighed heavily in exhaustion. "Sir, with all due respect, I give you my word — man to man, I do not know where Mac Kinnon resides. However, I truly need to rest tonight…" he said, briefly noticing the area where he was interrogated had been thoroughly cleaned out, as if that would erase the memory. "Thank you…again, for your compassion, Sheriff." Will bobbed his head to him, put his wide-brimmed black hat over his head, and walked away slowly — every stride, his head painfully erupted.

Will was not a fool to avoid seeking revenge against him; he was smart enough to know how to manipulate people's minds. He was a man ahead of his time — a man that was easily misunderstood among the simple people of the Old West, a man that was very similar to his father in intellectuality — although he loathed him deeply.

X

CHARLOTTE WOKE UP FROM THE RUSHED CHIRPS of a pair of bluebirds that flew right over her. Shooting their beautiful blue feathered tails from above her face, tickling her nose as they brushed against it. Cracking her eyes open in sheer contentment, her hand lazily reached beside herself to feel Finn's chest slowly rise, still asleep with his neck coiled around her; the grass was blowing and sweeping into his nostrils, as he snored right behind it.

"Sweet boy…" she soughed to him, caressing his short pasterns with tender fingers. She arched her back, and stretched her sore muscles along it, then stood up to look around herself, only to realize…her tent, rifle, and gun belt were all gone.

"Oh no…" she gasped and her eyes flared in high alert, aghast, for she expected to find the sparkling waters of the falls, winking back at her instead.

"FINN!! Wake up!!!"

She rushed to him, bridled him, and urged him to get up. Finn, startled, started lifting his body underneath him, balancing on his legs as fast as he could without falling atop her. She threw the saddle over him, grabbed the cinch, secured his breast collar, and…

"CLICK"

There was a sudden knot in her throat. A sudden pulse that thudded. A sudden vain that popped at the crease of her neck. A drop of sweat washing off the dirt on her face. She raised her hands, feeling a gun barrel poke the back of her head.

CHAPTER 21

Caged

I

*"Find him, hide him
Crush his bones to dust
Break him down to pieces
Leave his heart to rust
The secrets that he saw
Will never leave his trust"*

"WHAT DO YOU WANT FROM ME!!!" THE MAN SCREAMED and begged in great despair, as his shadow continued to chant silently with a deep, caustic voice; stroking his knife ever so gently, fingers gliding across the blade. Feeling all the worries of his life disappear in comparison, as his only focus was the next line to be delivered.

*"Me soul is filled with joy
When eyes are filled with fear
Come close and I will tell ye
Last words ye'll ever hear
Oh, oh"*

"Oh dear God, please!!!" he pleaded, now the shadow of a man advancing to him. "You…you, you're SICK!! NO!!" The man let out a caterwaul of despair, when the sharp knife was stabbed right between his startled eyes — twisting deep into his skull, as he still breathed a cry of anguish.

The bloody river splashed against the boats and the clouds raced above it, forming into distinct clusters, blocking any hints of moonlight that might light up a trace of villainy at the docks of Sailorman's Wharf.

Relief filled up his chest.

I I

"ITH YA LOOKING FOR THITH…?" Charlotte heard a hoarse voice behind her, realizing the man most likely had not a single tooth in his head.

"Please…I'm just passing through…I, I…I was already on my way out…" she pleaded upon a stutter, her voice shaking in agony.

"Oh, ya hear thith Jeremiah? The wath on her way out! Ahah-ahah. Ya heard thith??" the man mocked her together with his partner, still pointing the gun to her head.

"I have money! If you need that. And…a whole deer carcass, still fresh." She trembled, trying to find a way to convince them to let her go, yet somehow she feared they were there for *her*.

The man walked around her, and as he turned his head up, her face fell. Her eyes widened, freezing upon an unsettling expression. She was frightened, petrified to the core; she had never seen such a malformed face in her whole life — the wicked layers underneath it was intensifying the feeling of abhorrence all the more. As far as she was taught, such birth defects resulted from sin; not because of sins the parents had committed, but due to "sin" itself. Oftentimes she wondered, why does the almighty God allow malformations, let alone all the suffering her mother went through just to survive in the world she was born into. She could hardly look him in his face; a gruesome asymmetry covered in superficial burns and cuts. Her heart sunk for him in an odd compassionate way, and yet that feeling swiftly vanished with the following command.

"We wanth the pony…" He grinned as he looked over at Finn, who was nervously pacing back and forth, for his partner had now hobbled his feet.

"NO! You can't have him!" She leered menacingly.

"Hiiiihi. Ya hear that, Jeremiah?" The man snorted, cackling like a hyena.

"Take me instead." she then naïvely offered, trying not to raise her voice — trying to seem strong and confident. She wasn't. Deep inside, she felt the unbearable urge to curl up into a ball of misery and bawl her eyes out, pray that they would pity her and leave her be out of the goodness of their hearts.

And then she thought, *it likely too was malformed.*

"Why not both?" he said and they both burst into laughter, still the rifle pressed against her head by his partner.

Her teeth clenched, and her throat felt tight. She drew in a breath, and faced the man in earnest. "Because…because, I am expecting Mac Kinnon to come and pick me up anytime now." she hissed, in hopes they would fear the mention of him too. The mens' laughter suddenly paused, as they glanced at each other with great concern. Charlotte stared at them, feeling her heart bang hard against her chest and her fingernails almost fall off from squeezing them within her palms. "That's right…I am…his lady, and I know for a fact he will be very disappointed and upset if he notices me missing…" she added, as she saw them communicate with each other in their own language. Even Will's english made more sense. "Also…knowing Mac, he knows where to search around these parts, and he will not stop…until…he finds me." she emphasized, and crossed her arms before her chest.

There was a sinister moment of silence between them. Finally, the man walked up to her slowly with a snide grin on his face. "Princess, there is an itty-bitty, teensy-weensy little problem…" He smirked with pleasure at her apparent distress. "Mac Kinnon…does NOT care about NO one! Liar, liar, pants on FIRE!! Ahaha!"

The men grabbed Charlotte before she had a chance to escape, tying her legs and hands while she screamed for help with every breath she had within her lungs, yet her voice vanished in the loud stream of the waterfall behind them, and beneath a mucky cloth they stuffed into her mouth. Throwing her in the back of their wagon, Charlotte, still screaming her head off as a decaying scent of flesh engulfed her, looked around to find fresh guts and rotting human bones lying all around herself. A foreboding sight; one promising the nature of her own doom. "HLP!!!" she yelled again and again, yet her voice went muffled and unheard, deeper into the Ozark mountains.

III

WILL HAD ABANDONED THE TOWN OF MARYSVILLE, with the promise of seeing Charlotte in Mon Louis clutched tightly within his grip. He was crossing through Cottonmouth State now, making good time, even though his head was pounding with every single gait Rachel was in.

Mon Louis was located on the southeastern shore, and it would take him a couple days to reach. Cottonmouth State, despite being small in area, still had the biggest population. There was mostly farmland, plantations, and a small town called Amity. A swamp just south of it connected Amity to Mon Louis. Will was aware he had to ride through the swamps during the day, for the sun would light up every speck of suspicious darkness behind the thick willow trees and abundant brush surrounding them — many dangers lingered the moment the sun set, the moment eyes would get dull, and eyelids heavy. Dangers that weren't necessarily the alligators; kept well fed by the hogs, deer, and countless exotic birds that inhabited there.

Tormented by the humid southern climate, Will sweated underneath his luxurious woolen vest, and itch desperately beneath the medical cloth wrapped around his head. Flies would tear up sores on his flesh, as they hooked into his skin with countless bites, feasting on the blood and threatening to poison it. However this wasn't the only worry he had, for a sudden light-headedness would hit him recklessly, and a bile of nausea would shoot up his aching throat; his vision would blur, and limbs would sometimes turn benumbed. He had the map spread out across his saddle horn and Rachel's neck, ensuring he was not making a single mistake, for the fear of turning deranged after the assault lingered in the back of his head. Haunting him.

IV

THERE WAS A SMUDGED BLUR IN HIS VISION, shrinking steadily into darkness over a course of weeks. His skin dehydrated, his body feeble and deteriorating into a skeletal state of being. Weight fell off of him, and he had fallen himself. Sounds were but a buzzing in his head, sounds of eternal silence, or the clinking of chains that lulled him to sleep as he shifted them in loneliness. The walls around him, sucking the very essence of his weeping in the hollow gaps of its bricks, meant to entrap them to never let a memory decay. Fear was but a feeble veneer of emotion that had remained, a ghostly veil that swallowed him whole.

Mickey had gone to visit him, beneath the secure wing of his parents — he never told them anything about the abuse, but he stressed enough that he needed them with him there. Concern about Mac had plagued his soul, and after all, he knew he owed him. Farmer Grossman reassured them however, and everyone around town, that he had gone off for studies, pretending he was sentimental over it — missing his presence, as he thought of him as his own son. Boasting about the knowledge and skills he had acquired beneath his loving care.

Yet as his blue funk tangled with the night's cloak of darkness, he strode down to the cellar with a grin that promised another harrowing torment, a grin that only widened the moment he would choose the farm tool he would use on him that night. Now the grin slipped into a theatrical pout, untying one of his hands and flipping his body towards him, with his back bared to him. There was no sound to be issued from his throat, no scream that Mac's lungs could create, no plead for mercy that his heart desired to yell, for there would not be a point. Instead, he had decided the less he fought him, the faster he'd be done.

Clasping a small scythe with a rusty blade, he started brushing it all over his back — slobbering at the feeling of this torment, ogling the scars he carved in sheer lecherousness. Pressing it more harshly against his skin, it started peeling off, buffeting deeper lines of torture across the flesh, a map of diagonals, all now merging like bloody rivers and tributaries.

"Well done, son. You're learning to control the feeling of pain…for the devil wants ya to be afraid, Mac. He wants the fear to cripple ya, and when ya focus on fear, the devil is winning, son. Ya need to resist the devil, and he will flee from ya. Submit and resist. Submit to God. No more trying to control your life and make your own decisions, my dear son. He is Lord, and ya shall submit to his authority!" he yelled and dug the scythe deeper, gushing the blood out of his youthful being, exposing his fresh flesh to the filth covering the whole damp and dirty room. He knew the flies would soon come to feast on his wounds, and the rats that lurked within the brick walls threatened to rake their claws and teeth across him. He knew maggots would slither towards him, and yet perhaps shelter him from infection. There was no animal that intimidated him as much as the beast on two feet before him, for resentment only grew within him, and rage now morphed his soul.

There was a feeling of defeat in his heart; the feeling of a well of emotion slowly running dry. He suffered in utter, devastating silence — cursing God under his breath for allowing this to happen. A boy that once was witty, full of life, emotional, and empathetic…slowly turned into one of complete numbness and apathy.

V

THEY DRAGGED CHARLOTTE OUT OF THE WAGON AS SHE KEPT ON RESISTING, trying to kick them away from her, squirming, screaming, and writhing in protest. They laughed in response, grabbing her from the hair and twisting her face around to show her off proudly to the rest of the inbred family — tearing her clothes apart, tossing them into a pile of other victims' clothes, and shaming her bareness before their ogling eyes. Their eyes flared at the sight, and their teeth snarled, almost in great anticipation to feast on her flesh. Their hands jittered beside them, balling fists of self-restraint, for they knew the rules. They knew there needed to be a ritual first; a torment, a rape, and days of captivating her sole being by watching her starve.

Charlotte was dragged further into a dark cave, a lair of beasts, where human heads were impaled onto wooden spears, serving as ornaments, leading their way deeper into the cavern with a steady flame of torch that burned through their torn up mouths. Her screams turned into echoes of silence, for such an ominous sight she had never encountered, nor imagined to ever exist. She was tossed into and locked up excitedly within a cage that seemed part of a sheriff's old wagon, with blood-stained iron bars, and a floor filled with locks of old hair. Her breath caught in her lungs, and her face fell at the scent of death that surrounded her. A nightmare seemed like a fairy-tale compared to the Hell she was living in now, and the fear she felt utterly crippled her.

The Fiddler Brood celebrated around her; eating leftover human flesh, drinking mugs of a yellow liquid, tossing the bones towards her as if paying her for her revealing bareness They sang in their own language, in a high-pitched voice, almost demonic, so otherworldly it felt to be scratching at her ears. Drumming discarded bones against the cavern walls — they danced around the cage, hand in hand, leaping from their toes like the heaviest of swamp toads lunging from rock to rock, shaking the ground beneath them.

"Lord…you have abandoned me…" She cried silently, squeezing her hands together against her dispirited face, sheltering her eyes from their faces pressed against the iron — squeezing their slobbery lips and rotten tongues through it, letting out a bestial yelp that sliced right through her.

Hours went by, hours of celebratory screams and menacing glares. Hours of her body writhing in panic, and her hands clutching each other in mental support. There were prayers; so many prayers that spurted out of her mouth in sheer hopelessness, and yet there was no answer within the ironed walls she was confined. The gang had settled down for the night, huddled close to one another, snoring and coughing out substances as they choked in their sleep. Another disfigured man was watching her from the corner, set to guard the cage — as if Charlotte could ever escape from it. There was a glorious plan for the morning, a plan of raping and tormenting Charlotte before cutting her head off and piercing through it with a spear for good measure.

VI

THE MAN ROPED THE MARE'S LEG OUT FROM UNDERNEATH HER, making her hop on the rest with great difficulty. Starving her for way too long, in order for her to lose her tremendous strength, she still continued fighting against the rope, rearing and jumping towards the man with the hopes of pinning him down. The man dragged the rope beneath and around her belly, pressing it against his leg, gloves smoking from her pulling so hard — still resisting. With her leg now tied up to her stomach, he pulled ever harder behind her, and she slowly started falling down to submissiveness. The moment she hit the dusty ground, her head slammed against it, and a squeal of anguish escaped her.

She attempted to lift herself up again — this time, however, with no success. Her head crashed down, her knees fell beneath her, open and raw. The once-proud mare was now lying on the ground, on her side, breathing heavily from exhaustion and defeat; her eyes half shut, nostrils expanded, the spark within her, now a dimmed flame slowly extinguishing in her gaze. A skeleton of a body, a ghost more than horse. She had given up.

The rancher walked towards her, a grin of satisfaction scarring his face. His boots tossed sand over her, but there was no reaction from her side. He approached her. Kicking her chest, her coat flinched as if a fly brushed against it, but her eyes remained dull, empty. He sat atop her in a moment of triumphant silence. Determinedly, he had broken her spirit.

VII

WILL RENTED A HOTEL FOR THE NIGHT IN THE TOWN OF AMITY, successfully maneuvering his way through the swamps. He hitched up Rachel on a post outside, and went into the saloon to order a refreshment. His head ached, his body begged for rest, and his mind fogged up faster than the veil of mist that engulfed the meadows of Amity. "Gentleman, would you be so kind as to pour me a drink…for I've been riding all day under this heat and humidity; everything sticks on me, it feels like." He sighed, longing for the refreshment, as if water couldn't quench his thirst.

"Sure thing, partner! Where ya headed?" the bartender asked him, picking out a dusty glass from underneath the counter, checking to see if it was clean. He spat on it, and swiftly swiped it with a cloth.

"Mon…Marysville, sir." Will said, thinking it would be wise to not give away any information.

"Oh, not very far now then! Comin' from?" he asked as he lifted a bottle in the air, catching it facing down, and poured the drink into the glass.

"Birdsboro, sir." Will muttered, and grabbed the glass from him, not looking forward to a long conversation.

"Ah! That's quite a way, then! Ya here to stay for the night? We have a free room, and we also offer *deluxe* baths with uhm…some extra helpin' hands, if ya know what I mean." He chuckled upon a dedicated wink in his direction, clearly already intoxicated himself — which Will despised, generally.

"I'll respectfully decline, sir. I only require a regular bath, and a room for the night. I'll head out at dawn…" He politely turned down the offer, and gulped down his drink, satisfying his built-up thirst only to dehydrate his blood furthermore.

"Aaaah, must be a very important lady then! Alrighty, sir! We'll get ya situated!" He clapped his hands in blithe, and ordered his server to prepare the room.

"Yes…that, she is." he mumbled, staring at the whiskey — recalling that night they drank together; envisioning her face in front of his, feeling the softness of her lips brushing his own, admiring the shape of her body against his hands — a shiver went down his spine, as he readjusted his thoughts.

He hiked up the spiral stairs slowly and steadily, the boards creaking beneath his boots, and he briefly wondered when would anyone replace them, knowing in Amity it was cheaper to patch up cracks with more rotten wood, than afford a renovation. Supporting his head with a hand, as it was still bothering him madly, thudding with every step he took; a line of working ladies was hovering over the stairway and noticed Will coming upstairs, on his way to his room that was already prepared for him — *southern hospitality was unlike any other,* he always thought.

"Janet! Janet! Look at that huuuuunk!" the lady whispered to her coworker with utmost urgency, lusting over Will's long hair and tall, leanly built body, draped in an attire that screamed of proper wealth.

"Oh my, oh my! We don't ever get any good lookin' boys like *this* one 'round here!" she whispered back, waving her folding fan faster in front of her chest that was almost popping out of her corset with every breath she took.

"Ladies…excuse me." Will said as he passed them on the stairs, leaving his fresh cologne lingering in the air behind him. They inhaled it, as if it was their last breath of air on Earth.

"Hey sugar…are ya here for some fuuuun?" Janet asked seductively, as she now followed after him with her friend.

"Oh no, no, madam. I'm just…headed to bed." Will blushed and started to pace faster towards his door, that all of a sudden seemed a mile away.

"Well duuuh honey, we didn't think anywhere eeelse."

They both giggled, now hanging from his shoulders.

Will sweated shyly, his discomfort growing all the more as he felt their fingers rake over his arms; he wasn't about this way of living, for he felt he wouldn't be a man of honor — a man he would be proud of. His heart sunk for such women, as this was a demeaning way to earn some money in order to survive, yet he recognized not everyone was dealt such a fair hand in life as himself. "Here, ladies…" he said in earnest, halting swiftly beside them. "Twenty dollars to each of you. I'd be honored to recommend a phenomenal book of literature for you; one I believe you would be thrilled to own and take great pleasure in reading. However, I truly need to rest, as I have a special lady waiting for me." He respectfully handed them the money and rushed inside his room, locking the door behind him, feeling his heart drumming wildly within his rib-cage now easing in relief.

"Well, Janet! Whatcha think 'bout that, girl?" she asked her friend as she was left speechless, and quite annoyed he had turned them down.

"Well, Pattie! I think it's such a shame! Guess we gonna need to start on some readin'!" They chuckled together like hyenas, as they waved their fans before their faces, waiting for the next victim to fall into their booby trap.

Will stripped off his clothes and soaked his exhausted body in the warm bath; the dirt on his long arms completely melting away, and the swampy sweat on his hairy chest stained the water a muddy tint. He stretched his arms behind his head, and laid there until the water turned cold. He felt the scent of the sheriff, the doctor, and the working ladies completely evaporate, and thereupon, felt a wave of relief finally escape his chest.

He stepped out of the tub and started to dry his body off in repetitive motions, absently looking at himself in the mirror across. There was darkness surrounding him, and few lit up candles that guided his eyes around. The mirror reflected in his gaze, and somehow he felt the urge to stare right through it. A candle blew off, jerking his head to that direction. Suddenly he felt a sharp pain in his head that shot right through him, and a violent energy slithered through his veins. His blood pumped rapidly, and it pulsated at the fresh lavender-soaped crease of his neck. Yet, somehow he couldn't lift his arms to it, and upon glaring down at them, he realized they had balled a fist, his fingers rolled into his palms involuntarily, and his limbs now started to twitch.

Not long after, he collapsed to the ground as his legs gave out with no warning, and his whole body convulsed together uncontrollably. Clenching his teeth, he bit through his lips, and his eyes rolled back into his skull.

He seized, his head banging on the ground repeatedly.

VIII

CHARLOTTE FELT HIS HIDEOUS GLARE GLUED UPON HER, and after hours of refusing to face him, she side-eyed the guard, who now squinted with his swollen red eyelids. The torches inside the deep, twisting cave, highlighting every shadow his deformities would naturally create on his face and exposed, flabby upper body. In his grip, a machete, tightly clutched. He'd pet it all over with a forefinger, merged together with another, raking his overgrown fingernails all across the blade, taking a deep whiff of the blood that was imprinted upon it — as the memory of the murder excited him all the more.

Charlotte noticed him ogling her bareness, as if she were a piece of meat; which in the end, she was, beneath the layer of clothes and grimace of emotions. There was flesh and bones, veins and blood rushing through it. Perhaps a soul of unknown purity, for it appeared to tarnish the longer she was trod on this earth. Cutting her eyes at him again, she reflected upon how her mother's clients would ogle her in the same lascivious way, wishing they'd have a chance at her youthful form, yet somehow her mother did not let them, as if somehow she cared deep down within her own layer of meat.

She felt the sense of repulsion reach up her throat, a bile of nausea, and as the guard grinned wider in lust, she desperately tried to hide everything she could, crossing her arms and limbs. Yet, suddenly, she perceived her only chance to get out of there. She gathered up some grit, and after convincing herself to loosen up every fiber in her being, and fight against her instinct to shrink within the cage instead, she uncovered her body and pressed herself against the cage. Her eyes locked with the guard's, pulling his attention swiftly towards her with a slow shift of her legs in front, and a seductive flex of her right thigh to him. The man immediately stood up, startled, not expecting her to provoke him in this way, and pointed his machete with slight uncertainty to her.

"Aw…you don't like what you're seeing?" she managed to ask, forcing a tender voice to him. "I thought you were staring at these before?" She subtly brushed her leg against the cell.

"Me-me-me??" he stuttered with every breath; suddenly his evil demeanor turning into curious innocence.

"Yes, you big boy, you…" She lured him to her as a mermaid would lure sailors, ready to drown them deep into the dark ocean. The guard was still speechless, yet his excitement was quite apparent — it didn't take long for him to be hypnotized by Charlotte's bare breasts, or the way she talked — the way she moved for him, meanwhile her soul tarnished a little more.

The Fiddlers were sleeping with each other — all inbreeding together, over many generations — the lack of diversity in their genetics limiting intelligence, comprehension, and the ability to see through such simple mind games.

"Too bad I cannot be closer to you…" She pouted, disappointed. "…and this mean…mean cage, that separates us." She cocked her head, staring at him as composed as she could, yet deep within herself, she was frightened for she didn't know how to escape the cave filled with so many of him and his kind.

The man took a careful glimpse around himself with his protruding eyeballs, noticing the others still sleeping deeply. Dithering for a brief moment, he strode towards Charlotte and unlocked the cage.

Charlotte, baffled to have achieved as much, showed him the rope around her legs and hands — acting still disappointed, yet her whole being shivered in fright. The man was now inches away from her, and the scent of rotting teeth, layers of fecal matter along his body, and years of perspire turned into a thick dark crust across his skin hit her like a brick wall.

"Wh-what about these, handsome?" She sucked in a stutter. "I can't please you wearing these, can I?" She forced the words out of her mouth, the thought of it repulsed her.

The man blinked, and excited to feel wanted for once by someone that wasn't his own kind, cut through the ropes without a second thought. He grabbed her roughly from the arm, unintentionally — as he did not know how to control his emotions, or rather, he didn't learn properly how to treat a human being that was quite different from him, pulled her towards his own nook of the cave — a boulder, offering a place to be seated, one with strands of thinly sliced meat across. His eyes glowed big as he twisted Charlotte around, and jerked her on top of him; her naked body now touching his, now both covered in the murderous blood and evil stains of human debris.

Feeling the urge to vomit all over his face, Charlotte thought of her mother who always forced herself to sleep with filthy clients she never cared for. She thought of her, for the first time, as someone to idolize, someone to gift her the vigor to pull through her task.

She grabbed the man's malformed face and kissed him on his lips, feeling his cleft palate splitting wider against her mouth, and his enormous sharp teeth chasing after her tongue. The man whimpered strangely, like a dog who got a bone as a treat after being starved for too long. Yelping, for he felt such innocent gleefulness he couldn't express it, almost falling for this stranger that he wasn't permitted to be ever romantically involved with, yet the sudden thought crossed his mind as she kissed him, a sudden revelation of a thought; *what if they weren't all that different after all, what if they should seek out tenderness from townsfolk that rode through their forest, instead of trapping them in the hopes of killing them all off?*

Charlotte pried her eyes open, and cut them at the machete he had forgotten next to them, calculating her moves smartly, all the while swallowing down the vomit that kept on surfacing, suppressing a gag every-time his tongue touched hers. As she was kissing him, she tried to reach for the weapon, but he stopped her by flipping her completely over and onto the ground under him.

Shocked, jerking her head back to see him already preparing to penetrate her, panic set in. He took out his flaming red and abnormally swollen genitalia, with large lumps hanging from his sheath and a fountain of green discharge gushing out of it, pumping it excitedly before her. There was no gag in the world she could suppress now, as she felt her insides twist into a knot. Stretching her body, extending her arm, she reached for the machete, and before he had a chance to make a sound, she swung it towards his head with the most vigorous force.

His throat sliced open, a deluge of blood exploded on her.

The large man, eyes full of horror, fell on top of her as his whole body shuddered and convulsed to its death. She pushed out a gush of vomit as quietly as she could, clogging her throat with it, trying to keep quiet to not wake anyone else up — disregarding that she had just murdered a man for the very first time.

Unable to process what had just happened, still feeling the slime coating her lips, and the scent of his being now imprinted on hers, she grabbed the machete with her, and made her way slowly through the cavern. Fiddlers were scattered everywhere; some covered with pelts, or stolen clothes from travelers, and others lying completely naked and exposed. She spotted her clothes upon a pile and sighed within herself, for that would a task too risky. She snuck carefully by a dozen of them, holding her breath and praying they couldn't hear her thumping heartbeat before she reached the opening of the cave.

She spotted Finn tethered next to some other horses. Her heart exploded with relief for she did not expect to ever see him again, fearing he would have been skinned alive. Approaching the exit in slyness, she halted, as another guard was making the rounds right in front of her. Rushing back into cover behind a boulder, she observed him. She did not think she could try the same trick of seductiveness with him, and she certainly didn't wish to repeat it. This guard appeared much smarter than the other; much meaner too, judging by the way he held his body, or the confident way he guarded the cave. Shoulders and back straight as an arrow, chest puffed out like a rearing bear, and arms inflated beside him like two rocks ready to smash anything that came in his way. She could attempt to sneak past him, or kill him — either would be a risk.

CHAPTER 22

The Orchid

I

"WHAT WE DO ON A SMALL SCALE, is what the government does on a large one." he said, following the lady of the night. "Killin' ain't just a poor man's sport."

"I saw you, sir, killing that innocent man, you did!! And I will ensure you get caught!!" she yelled to him, pacing faster away through the alleyways.

"Oh no…ye didn't, and no, he wasn't — ain't nobody all that innocent…" he grunted, grabbing her hand and silencing her with a swift move of his blade across her neck.

Her dying body wilted and writhed in his embrace; slowly fading, as he patiently watched the lantern right above them — counting the flashes of light, feeling her pulse weaken by the second. His gaze locked hers. His hand covered over her eyes, swiping the lids of judgement shut.

II

UPON THE FLASHING OF AN ORANGE DAWN, Will had reached the last part of swamps he had to cross through. He barely slept the night before — not so much due to the actual event, but having to digest the fact that he now had to deal with a sudden and quite major health issue that there was apparently no cure for. Disturbing thoughts lingered in his head, detesting the way this uncontrolled illness made him feel and appear — both helpless and weak. A fragile being, living in a moment's time of constant uncertainty. He was embarrassed to meet Charlotte with such a frailty as she already admired Mac's vigor and independence so much more than his own; and now he had to compete while enduring this.

Slashing his thoughts away with a gentle shake of his head, he paused in his tracks, then noticed a beautiful orchid clamped on a tree, impressive enough for him to dismount his horse and take a closer look at it. It had large white spread-out petals, and rewarded the sweetest scent.

Orchids "steal, lie, cheat"
And look impudently good while doing so

He recalled a quote he memorized from one of his books, regarding all rare species of plants. "Rachel, see that?" He pointed with a forefinger. "This is an extremely rare find indeed! See, orchids trick their pollinators into pollinating them, and stick the pollinarium onto the animal without offering them any nectar, unlike most flowering plants." he told her with a gentle smile on his face, besotted by its beauty and fragrance. He stepped on the tree trunk to reach it. He plucked it and placed it carefully in one of the saddlebags, stealing a last glimpse of it. "I think Charlotte is going to love it." He smiled and mounted his horse, proceeding to ride through the damp, musky swamp.

III

CHARLOTTE, HIDING BEHIND AN INK-BLACK ROCK perfectly blocking her whole body from the light of the torches, her eyes followed the bold steps of the guard with her mind racing to come up with a lifesaving idea. She couldn't just sneak past him, because she needed to get Finn out of there as well; and Finn being the vocal stallion he is, would certainly "help" to escalate the situation.

*Charlotte, you have to concentrate now…you have to keep your calm, and you have to…figure a way out of this damned cave. For if you don't, you're gonna turn into a torch…with your head sticking atop it…and worst of all, Finn… Finn is going to suffer…*she said to herself, pepping herself up. *Oh, my Lord… what do I do now?* Her teeth clenched in distress as anxiousness now spiraled through her. The guard's steps thudding all the more louder within her head. *I need to…I need to get his attention…somehow without killing myself in the process, that would certainly be nice…* she continued, and looked around for a distraction.

She glanced down at the rocky ground and grabbed a large, roughly pitted stone, waiting for the perfect moment to throw it out and down into the forest before the guard who marched steadily back and forth, his heavy feet dragging on the ground — pausing to look suspiciously in every direction, and continue on with his trudging right after.

Charlotte gulped down a knot, and with a trembling hand of reluctance, she threw the stone as hard and as far as she could, hitting the lip of a hill, and tumbling downwards right after. The guard immediately noticed and lifted his gun, striding slowly towards the noise. Without a second longer to spare she pulled her legs beneath her, rushed out of the cave, and went to unhitch Finn; who neighed immediately the moment he saw her.

The guard glanced swiftly back at the horses and spotted the naked figure standing there, staring terrified, right back at him. He sprinted. He sprinted in the strides of a giant she had never encountered. Sprinting right towards her — every loud echo of his steps would radiate across the cave, and benumbed, she stood there with Finn's rope in her grip. He fired a shot in the air to warn the others, and that was enough warning for Charlotte to mount Finn in haste, making him pick up a full blown gallop, leaving the guard behind in a wave of dust. He started shooting at them, barely missing as Charlotte weaved and maneuvered through the barrage of bullets. Suddenly she heard a herd of horses galloping right behind her, their hooves in unison rattling the tree trunks around her. She spared a glance behind herself, only to find the entire Fiddler Brood in hot pursuit — with their guns pointing right at Finn.

"Oh my god!!" she gasped in horror, the shadows of them enlarging against the trees as they neared them. "Finn! Run!! We need to go through the woods!!" She swiftly yanked the reins and turned his head to the side; taking a dangerous leap over a steep hill towards the magical forest of the Ozarks.

With Finn's sure-footedness and Charlotte's sturdy balance, they rode together like dancing partners, weaving through the trees with such ease, merging into one united shadow — leaving the Fiddlers miles behind them.

However, Charlotte would not stop riding away, further and further, and as the somber woods sucked them deeper inside, a white raven shot right before them — slashing through the foggy air with its pallid feathered wings. Her head jerked its direction for she had never encountered such a rare being, and as it did, her eyes spotted what appeared to be a ramshackle cottage tucked in within a lattice of brush and trees. She halted tentatively, as if a voice urged her to go take shelter, and yet she couldn't trust it, she couldn't trust these woods anymore. She was determined to reach Mon Louis overnight, for she would no longer stay in this dreary, iniquitous place.

She didn't know exactly how to enter such a civilized town buck naked, but at this moment, she didn't really care to figure it out either. Unable to grasp how she was able to escape that cave of hell on her very own, or to have sliced the throat of a fellow man, as different as he may have been, she briefly thought of the kind owner of the general store in Marysville.

If he only knew who is probably wearing my Levi's jeans right now...

I V

A CHARCOAL CLOUD ENGULFED THE LIGHTS OF MODERNITY. Smog polluted the air, as the factories continued producing it to the open sky. A usual landmark for Mon Louis, as well as the overall industrial noise welcoming all sorts of travelers to the city. Thieves, traders, sailors, workers, and beggars all bundled up in this fancy metropolis. The business sector was booming — which is where Will handled most of his dealings; most of the industry magnates knew of him, and respected him, thinking very highly of his vast knowledge in all matters. He was also known for selling some truly exquisite horses at the auctions, a far cry from the sale yards of other towns. It always felt like home for him; the paved streets intensifying the clopping of the hoofbeats, and hanging lights on the towering buildings decorating the dark streets at night. It created a very romantic atmosphere — as long as you remained in the more affluent areas.

Will excitedly arrived at Mon Louis in the early evening, cutting his trip in half. He had successfully crossed through the remaining swampy terrain without any ambushes from wandering raiders or "others". He glanced at the bright lights fastened around the trees, and an overwhelming joy rushed through him. Even though he felt the exhaustion from the journey, he couldn't wait to wrap Charlotte in his arms, and show her every corner of his most beloved city. He made his way to the barber first as he felt his mustache had gotten a tad too long, and right after, to the tailor to change into fresh clothes.

"Mr. Griffiths!! Mr. Griffiths, my dear friend! Where have you been all these months!" The tailor, overjoyed to see him again, rushed to welcome him through the door.

"I've been on quite a journey, my friend. How's the shop doing? Business still going strong?" Will questioned, as he looked through the fine selection of vests he had hanging behind the counter.

"Fantastic, thank goodness! Mon Louis just installed a network of tram lines! Bet you've never seen such before!" he said with a beaming smile.

"Terrific; I will have to visit that." He nodded to him.

"Yes! Indeed you have! Our dear mayor sure has put some effort into making this town a better place for everyone!"

"Hm..." Will bobbed his head again, this time in silence as if he knew more than he wished to say. The tailor leaned close to him and held a hand to the side of his mouth. "There's been rumors, Mr. Griffiths..." he soughed and Will cut his eyes at him.

"Rumors...how *unusual* for Mon Louis..." he said, snidely.

"Indeed...that the mayor...has some...uhm..." He coughed, and cleared his throat. "Romantic...affiliations, with our Sheriff Tom..." He wheezed and Will looked at him with a cocked brow of irony; as if the tailor wasn't himself romantically affiliated with a person of his same sex.

"Sheriff Tom is an exceptional gentleman. He has managed to influence a great deal of good in this town." he said, not wishing to get involved, and the tailor shrugged his shoulders.

"That he has...what...what's wrong with your head??" he then asked him, as Will lifted his hat for a moment.

"Oh...I had a bad fall...from a horse." He cleared his throat, placing the hat back on his head in embarrassment.

"Oh, my heavens..."

"But I'm in a bit of a hurry, my friend…" he said and the tailor nodded.

"Well! What may I help you with today?" the tailor then asked, noticing Will's gaze darting back to the vests.

"I'm looking for a new vest…perhaps a new dress-shirt, and I suppose we should complete the ensemble with some pants while we're at it." He chuckled excitedly, thinking of Charlotte without a break in between.

"I've got exactly what you're looking for!" he said and handed him a black cashmere shirt, a gray ash vest, and a pair of black town pants to try out in the changing room. After a while, Will walked outside, and the tailor's eyes flared, hands clasped together and pressed against his cheeks in awe. "Grandiose!!"

"Thank you, Pierre. You're very kind." Will hummed, as he admired himself as well in the squeaky clean mirror.

V

CHARLOTTE RODE AND RODE WITH NO INTERRUPTION, all the way along the Buffalo River, between gigantic forest-cloaked cliffs that towered over her. She had managed to grab a fallen tree limb that still had all its leaves intact, making a perfect temporary cover for her bare body — it must have been the silliest thing she had ever done, but nothing mattered more to her than being free, and far away from the horrors of the Fiddlers' cave. They had reached the northern side of the perimeters of Mon Louis, spotting the massive blanket of fog over the city. Her brows snapped together in the mediocre excitement.

"Wow. So that's all that it's about? Interesting." she muttered to Finn, disappointed as she watched the evening clouds collide against the leaden smog, swiftly merging into one massive veil of blackness.

She lingered there, in the shadows of the willow trees, trying to figure out a way to make it to the hotel. *Without being seen, without being arrested for indecent exposure, without being followed by any more perverted minds, and certainly not by any inbred creatures,* she chuckled in dark amusement at the thought. For dark humor was all that was left within her, or perhaps the relief of seeing civilization fueled her heart again with hope. She dismounted Finn and covered her most sensitive areas the best she could with a branch full of leaves — slowly moving towards the town, hiding herself behind Finn's shoulder as she did. In slyness, she would choose to position herself next to buildings or slip down streets where there were no townsfolk — which was nigh impossible in this busy, over-populated town.

"Now that I think about it, a quick decapitation of my head would have been less embarrassing." she said in a sigh, as she noticed how many people were standing on every single corner.

Thankfully the sun had already set, gifting her some more privacy, but interestingly the actual citizens seemed too busy to notice what was happening around them, which she found great relief in. She didn't even know where the hotel was, nor where to go — all the streets seemed of the same confusing labyrinth to her; loud, busy, and bright — with far too many unfamiliar smells and sounds. It felt like she had stepped in a completely different planet, for the roads were perfectly paved in brick, the familiar mud puddles were nowhere to be found, and everything glimmered and sparkled around her.

She had found herself in the wealthiest neighborhood of Mon Louis.

CHAPTER 23

Forever and Always

I

"GOOD EVENING, ANTOINE!" WILL GREETED THE SALOON OWNER with a big smile on his face, thrilled to see him again after so long.

"Will! What brings you here, my friend!" he asked him enthusiastically, ready to take care of his wishes. "How long has it been?! You look well!!" he said, glancing over his freshly hemmed attire.

"Thank you, my friend. It has been a little while…" he said, biting his lip.

"I know you've had some uhm…problems, last I heard from you! Have they been cleared?" He winked at him and Will stared at him, blankly.

"That detail remains to be seen…hopefully sooner, rather than later." He sighed, and Antoine nodded with a frown of concern.

"Well, I know it has been a most…unfortunate time for you." he said, and Will swallowed dryly.

"Well, I hope you might be able to inform me if a very special lady has arrived as of yet? She should have let you know that I'll be meeting her here." he spoke confidently, changing the woeful subject, letting his excitement rise again and feeling his heart beat faster from the great anticipation.

"A lady? Hmmm…" Antoine lowered his gaze, trying to recall. "No, Will, I hate to disappoint you my friend, but your lady must have not arrived yet." he said, resting over the bar counter with crossed hands and entangled fingers.

"It…it can't be." He gaped at him, aghast. "She should have been here days ago. Are you…are you of absolute certainty?" Will's heart sunk to his stomach, fearing the worst.

"Yes, sir. But you're welcome to get a room, and wait for her here?" he offered, as his brow raised in confusion. "We also have a deal on our prime rib tonight!" he added, trying to cheer him up.

"I…I think I will have a whiskey instead, if you don't mind." He sat down on the stool in front of him, slamming a hand against his face, trying hard to understand what could have possibly gone wrong.

I I

"THIS MUST BE THE MOST EMBARRASSING SITUATION I've ever found myself in!" she fussed to herself under her breath. "Ugh! Finn! There's people every-where!! This won't work!" she whispered intensely to him, as if waiting on him to introduce a better plan. "What to do??"

DING-DING-DING-DING!!!

A blinding light froze their senses; an otherworldly sound ringing in their ears. Finn jerked his head up high, terrified, and Charlotte glanced swiftly behind her to witness a metal machine barreling right at them.

"Goodness!! What in the world is that!" She gasped, still blinded by it, her eyes meeting the driver's in mutual shock, as the light penetrated easily through the leaves that covered her. She pushed Finn's shoulder out of the way, so the strange-looking machine and the benumbed man driving it could pass through. They rushed into a dark alleyway — Finn's round hind barely fitting through it, as the paved ground led them to a small private garden belonging to one of Mon Louis's many lavish mansions.

"Wow! Would you look at all this…how do you even call…*all*…this!" Charlotte's eyes lit up as she studied the enormous aristocratic balconies of the ionic pillared mansion, the perfectly trimmed trees guarding the sumptuous gardens, and the glamorous stairway leading up to each floor of the build-ing. Finn snorted, disinterested, and started nibbling on a neatly polished tree. He wasn't that impressed with it, either.

"No! No, Finn! Don't!" she whispered harshly, and picked up his rein. However, then she noticed a line stretched from the side of the nibbled tree to another — the line had clothes on it, all spread out to dry. She bit her lip, and a grin widened on her face. "You...you are such a brilliant pony!" She squeezed Finn's soft muzzle in her hands with great excitement and he blinked tightly at her in bewilderment, thinking she surely owed him a bucket of fresh carrots by now. She picked out a set of clothing — a long cream cashmere shirt, with some loose cream bloomers, and put them on hastily. "Not particularly my style, but it'll do for now. At least we won't get arrested — well, unless they find out we stole their clothing." She giggled, as Finn continued munching on the trees.

III

"MR. GRIFFITHS?" THE BARTENDER SHOOK WILL'S SHOULDER in an effort to wake him up as he laid on the counter, head planted atop it and hand still clasping the glass, raking it with his rings as his fingers twitched.

"Cha—Charlotte?" Will squinted at the light above him as the blurred figure slowly sharpened, revealing his old friend. "Oh...My apologies. I must have...it's been a long day." He let out a pent-up yawn, disappointed to not see her there instead of the balding man who woke him up.

"Will, please get a room. I will notify you as soon as I hear from her. You don't look so well." he said and took him by the arm, leading him upstairs.

"Thank you Antoine, my friend. I didn't mean to be an embarrassment in front of your clients." Will said, patting his shoulder. "You know I've stopped drinking like that, a long time ago, ever since..." He folded his lips in awkward silence. "...well, the exhaustion just got the best of me." he apologized to him instead, ready to shut the door to his room.

"Don't even worry, my friend. You deserve some rest. Was a pleasure seeing you again!" Antoine nodded, and returned downstairs to take care of some patrons that were making quite a racket around the poker table.

Will took off his brand new vest and stared at it for a moment; he started to wonder if Charlotte was in trouble, or if she had chosen a different path after all — one Will would not be able to follow. He glanced at the cigar they had placed on the bed as a welcome gift. Over the years they had learned his favorite whiskey brand and particular choice in cigars, even though he rarely smoked and he rarely drank in solitude. He smiled within his sadness, and lit up the cigar. He walked out onto the balcony, and looked out at the view of his cherished city. Lights were competing with the hidden stars behind the fog; he stared at them as if he were searching for answers, dazzled by the almost foreboding sight.

He sighed deeply and dropped his gaze down at the road, letting his arms hang absently over the rail. There was a gasping sound of horror that hit his ears, with another one following right after. He jerked his head to that direction and after tracing circles around himself, looked back down to the road, only to see a very familiar chestnut pony. He squinted hard till his head started to thump again from the strain, yet then he noticed an oddly adorned woman walking right beside it — townsfolk changing their route, staring in repulsion, or otherwise ogling her attire— gasping as they did. "…Charlotte?" he whispered to himself, almost letting the cigar slip through his lips.

IV

THE PIANIST PAUSED HIS PLAYING AS CHARLOTTE TROD INTO THE SALOON, devoid of any emotion, other than exhaustion and relief — making a record time from Birdsboro to Mon Louis, and yet she couldn't tell that to anyone, nor did she care much to celebrate her triumph. Everyone, even if already intoxicated, stared at her strangely. Charlotte tried to ignore the unwanted attention, rushing her way as elegantly as possible to the bartender, for how much worse could it get — she smelled like horny inbred Fiddler, had blood smeared across her body beneath aristocratic clothes that were awfully transparent, and most certainly her hair had random leaves stuck within it in the best case. She cleared her throat, halting a few feet away from the bartender.

"Uhm…sir, excuse me…" she called him over to her, this time she had practiced her words the whole way to the saloon.

"Oh! Madam! Your…" he stuttered as he glanced over her revealing outfit, pulling his gaze swiftly away again out of respect.

"Yes. Yes, I'm aware, and I don't have much time to explain about that." She waved her pointy finger around. "I'm here to rent a room, sir. Uhm…I'm expecting a kind gentleman…William Griffiths, to meet me the upcoming…"

"Will!!! It's YOU!!" he interrupted her, making a happy dance around himself of celebration as Charlotte blinked at him in bewilderment. "Of course!!! Of course, madam!"

"Shhh! Sir…please, not so loud." She took a hurried look around, noticing everyone staring and whispering to each other, with a few ladies scowling and frowning — their focus locked instead on their men, for peeking.

"Charlotte!" Will's voice suddenly broke the awkwardness in the place, reaching her ears with the softest gale of wind. Charlotte turned her head to face him striding down the stairs, startled, as she spotted his medical cloth coiled around his head, but also quite amazed by how handsome and sharp he looked in his complete black outfit that contrasted with his fair skin. There was no doubt that Will was blessed with genes from the elite pool, for his face was carved in perfection; uniquely designed where flaws could not take hold.

"Will…" She smiled widely, ready to leap into his arms in such relief to feel safe again.

"Goodness, Charlotte. What, what are you wearing, my lady?" he asked her, stunned, as the clothes she stole were actually rather expensive lingerie that only an aristocrat could afford.

"Oh trust me, it's not my first choice of clothes, but it was the only choice I had!" She snorted sarcastically. "However, perhaps we could discuss this somewhere else…somewhere more private…Will?" She nervously urged, as everyone continued to stare and tried to observe their conversation, eavesdropping with flared ears and awkwardly leaned bodies.

"Certainly! Of course, my lady. Thank you, Antoine!" he said with a big smile; suddenly all his groundless thoughts disappeared, gently placing his hand on her waist and helping her walk up the stairs.

V

HE HOPPED INTO A SMALL WOODEN BOAT, and pushed it with the chipped-off paddle away from the cold, stony shore. Slowly paddling down the Ouachita River, the thunderstorm struck through Mon Louis's cloud of smoke, lighting the way for him. Rain harshly washed off the boat's mossy surface, revealing its lively shine again. Powerfully, the thunder hit the shoreline along the river; spreading its fury over the water. The rhythmic ripples of water banged brutally against the boat's hull as he rowed gently further into his own eclipse against the light of the storm.

VI

"I...I AM IN SHOCK." SHE SHOOK HER HEAD, GAPING AT HIM, aghast, squeezing the soaking wet hair from her first ever luxurious bath that he insisted upon ordering for her. "I don't quite know what to say. Surely there must be a way to punish them?!" Charlotte asked him furiously after he avowed to her what happened to his head; meanwhile, the storm regularly lit up the entire room through its windows, as if it too was enraged.

"Yes...there is." He planted an anticipated kiss on her forehead and her face melted, cheeks crimsoned, for she had forgotten how his full, tender lips felt. "I plan on visiting my friend here who is a very knowledgeable doctor; studied in France, actually! Phenomenal man..." He looked away, convincing himself of the potential success. "He at the very least can help me build a foundation for my case, and I will take it from there eventually. A remarkably brilliant lawyer resides down in Marysville, out of all places, ironically..." he hummed softly, and glanced at her endearingly worried face.

"I just feel so horrible that you had to go through such evil torment...all because of me." She caressed his head softly, making sure her touch was as gentle as it could be.

He held her hand. Kissed it lovingly.

"I would give my life for you, Charlotte — if that act but meant you could live forever freely." His thumb fiddled with his rings subconsciously, as he meant every word he said. Charlotte melted once again with his captivating words, and the winsome smiles he would lend her.

"Will...you cannot imagine how thankful and relieved I feel to be by your side tonight. Promise me, we will never lose each other again?" She held his hands in hers, locking eyes with him in earnest.

"I promise you, my love. As long as you'll let me, I'll be by your side, forever and always." He leaned over to her, and brushed his lips tentatively against hers, until she confidently locked hers onto his.

"I missed this…" she paused to note, brushing her finger across his lips.

"I missed you, my lovely. All of you…" He wrapped his arms around her waist, and pulled her towards him. "If I may…say so…do so…"

He blushed, and she smirked.

"You may…Will…" she soughed softly, and he found his aching pain suddenly benumbed by her loving voice. They kissed passionately for as long as the thunder roared that night, eventually falling asleep in each other's arms.

CHAPTER 24

Death Rattle

I

THE TEMPERATURE LOWERED IN THE ALREADY ICE-COLD CELLAR. Harsh weather was rolling in, blowing the crops in every arbitrary direction. The cattle had taken shelter, packed in like a can of sardines underneath an empty shack, fallen limbs slamming aggressively against its roof. Croaking ravens sailed across the green glen and meadows, merging into a solid mass of darkness before the menacing clouds.

A silver key unlocked the chains of his hands; making his arms drop abruptly beside him. His haggard face sunken and dull; leaning over his frail shoulder. "You have repented, son." he said softly. Clothes hit the boy as he tossed them over to him; now walking away — gifting him privacy he never had before. "The crops have been dying under my care…somehow they prefer your tender touch — and who can blame them, for I do as well." He snorted and Mac stared blankly at the brick wall before him. "There has been a wave of birds slaughtering them, and I've been slaughtering them in return with my rifle." He chuckled, and turned his head to face him. "Yet, they keep coming back…as if they're waiting for your return. Have you been feeding them, Mac?" He grinned snidely, and yet Mac's eyes were dull, for he couldn't even recall. "Do get dressed, boy…it is such a shame to witness your demise. I had expected more from a youthful body of yours. But, you are forgiven…"

Mac thought long and hard how to find the strength to dress himself; just the clothes alone felt too heavy on top of his defeated body. His hands quivered in attempts to clasp the cloth, bony fingers shook as they unfolded the white shirt.

"Ya see, Mac, God forgives us all in a way." Farmer Grossman said, moping around. "We just have to suffer for our sins first — to prove to him we are willing to make changes; to repent, and give ourselves to the Lord." he said, halting in his tracks, staring at the dark wall of the cellar, patiently waiting for him to get dressed.

Mac managed to put the shirt over his head, and pull it with his hands over his emaciated body. He shrunk within it, letting the fabric swallow him whole. He didn't feel a sudden rush of relief to be freed after months of torture. He didn't feel a sudden sensation of warmth engulfing his body. There was still cruel coldness around him; within him. There was still a lifeless entity moving his eyes, his limbs and body. The heart had been rotten, the soul, tarnished.

"He died for our sins, son. Let us not let him have died in vain by sinning again." He continued preaching, glancing over at the farm implements that were now stained with the boy's blood. Rusted too.

Mac pulled up his pants slowly; they fit loosely around his now scrawny legs. He went on to tighten the belt that was still attached, yet he paused, sternly. He looked, and stared — examined that thick piece of leather; his cadaverous blue eyes suddenly turned intensely vibrant. He stared at it, as all his senses came back to him at once.

"I am proud of ya, son. I didn't expect ya to survive to tell ya the truth. Not for so long, that is. Indeed ya have the devil's force within ya, but God is almighty…" A tear ran down his face, feeling overwhelmed with emotion.

Mac took the belt off his pants, and tried to balance his weight in order to get up without snapping any bones in the process. He waddled towards him; his lack of mass rendering him utterly silent, bare feet gliding in lithe muteness, slowly sneaking right behind him as he proceeded to preach.

II

"YA GOD DARN ANIMAL!!!" HE YELLED, running after the mare, hitting her body with the end of the lasso — punishing her for defending herself; for listening to her instinct that screamed loud and clear, *this man was not to be trusted.*

"Wasn't even worth the two bucks I wasted on ya! Darn Griffiths! Here me was thinkin' ya was worth somethin'." He kept on roping her neck, legs, and body as she ran around him in the corral. The horse, terrified, would lope as fast as it could, until the man pulled on the rope flexing her neck towards him. "LOOK AT ME!!!" He rushed towards the mare, the rope kept tight in his grip, with the mare holding still as this somehow was easier than resisting to the pressure — at least that's what she understood from being tied up for so many days. The man launched energetically towards her face, and the mare pinned her ears, biting a chunk off his straw cowboy hat with the last grit within her. "YA SOULLESS SLUT!!!" He now yanked and jerked on the rope, punching the mare's face, chasing after her as she backed up fast to get away from the constant pressure, from the harrowing pain that drilled right through her skin. He kept on hitting her soft gray muzzle, banging across the bridge of her flea-bitten nose, until it swelled up twice in size and blood gushed out of her nostrils. He took his fist and punched against her belly — forcing her to yield away from him, "respectfully".

"Ya ain't even worth a bullet." he yelled and loosened the rope around her neck, letting her go. The mare shook anxiously; her lips quivered, chin locked tight in panic. She couldn't comprehend why his aggression and violence was endless; as this was not a natural behavior amongst her own kind.

III

"I'LL MAKE SURE THESE DEGENERATES PAY FOR THIS...IMPURE EVIL!" Will huffed furiously, as Charlotte explained in turn what happened in that odious cave, somehow benumbed by the experience, as if the joy of rescuing her own self was bigger than the trauma.

"Will, how? You don't understand, they are not...like us, these...people. They don't even speak our language." she said, shaking her head, remembering. "Besides, do you really think anyone will defend a wanted person — let alone a woman?" She sighed in annoyance, reminding herself of that fact.

"We will remedy this too, my dear. Please, do not worry." he said, stealing a kiss from her luscious lips.

"Will?" she asked him, with a question reflecting within her bright hazels.

"My love?" He stole another kiss; somehow it was even harder to resist her.

"Will you…protect me, next time?" she asked hesitantly, as the thought of being alone again terrified her.

"Always, Charlotte. I will always protect you, my beauty. That I swear to you." he promised as his brown doe eyes locked hers solemnly, now a tint of raven-black, shadowed by his own medical cloth.

"I've…sent out a letter already, regarding your 'wanted situation' to a close acquaintance of mine. I believe I have mentioned her to you…and…well, to Mac Kinnon also." he muttered, hesitating to bring up his name again.

Charlotte felt a sudden wave of discomfort rush through her the moment he voiced it. An instant memory of their kiss giving her immediate goose-bumps, prickling the skin all across her limbs and body.

"Uhm…Mrs. Marga?" She quickly composed herself, clearing her throat and shifting her weight in the bed.

"Yes…she has a spare room in her moonshine shack, however, I would hate for you to stay there; it would be temporary, until I figure things out with my lawyer. As far as the sheriff knows, you were incapacitated…frozen, to death…" He brushed his mustache with his finger uncomfortably, not knowing how she would react to that.

"Frozen? Well…that's different, I suppose." She chuckled awkwardly. "But, if I stay there…what about you? What about…us?" she asked, bewildered.

"I am afraid I cannot answer this for you right now…I have some…dealings, in Bisonhorn, coming up — so the timing would be perfect for you to stay there for some weeks until things calm down, or you can stay here in Mon Louis if you prefer?" He swallowed guiltily, dreading to have this conversation.

"*Weeks?* What dealings in Bisonhorn? Can they not wait? I mean…we just now got together, finally, again. When are you supposed to head that way? So this sheriff doesn't hunt you any more? I just want to stay with *you*, Will." She bombarded him with questions, confused and disappointed by how everything changed again, especially after his heartwarming promises not even a minute before

"My love, calm down." He caressed her leg, as it quivered nervously. "Unfortunately no, they cannot wait as I've already…ignored it, for a while. I have to leave in a couple of days, so let us focus on us, and our time together this beautiful city." he said sheepishly, as he gripped her hand lovingly.

"Couple of days…last night you promised me we won't lose each other again…some minutes ago you promised you'll always protect me, and now? Now I have to see you go, again, so soon." She shook her head, tearing her gaze away, heart racing again. His head bowed in shame. "I'm afraid, Will. I'm afraid to be out on my own again. I just don't know where to go anymore — I haven't had a single break in months, it seems." She took her hand away from him, and a pout scarred her lips.

"My beloved Charlotte, I completely understand your frustration…but my promise still holds true and strong. Just please let me take care of some things that need taking care of…urgently. You stay here in Mon Louis; this is the safest place to lay low for now. If Mrs. Marga responds in a timely manner, and you are willing to live with her — I will come, or send a stage coach to escort you to her. I promise, *nothing* will ever happen to you again. You have my word." He looked out the window, his eyes turning a soft brown again.

"So…what are we gonna do before you leave? I need to make sure Finn is settled well at the new stables, before we go anywhere…" She sniffed, clearly on the edge of bursting into tears.

He wrapped his arm around her, and leaned close to her face.

"My love, it would be my honor to introduce you to my tailor friend and have you fitted in something very special to wear…for there is a ballroom dance, at the mayor's party." he said and her eyes flared, petrified. "I have been invited for some months now; as serendipity would have it, only now do I have the perfect partner to escort. Upon your acceptance, of course…"

I V

HE LOOPED THE BELT AROUND HIS NECK AND PULLED TIGHT, with all the strength he had collected in the last few minutes, gaping at him with a calculated eye. Farmer Grossman tried to grab him from his body, but Mac knew better than to change his strategy this time. He needed to be swift, choking him as fast as he could, no gap between leather and skin, no room to inhale another breath. He pulled tighter.

"D…dev…devil's child!!" he yelled, struggling, as his Adam's apple pierced through with the leather belt's force in a saw-like motion. His knees collapsed, sending him down to the ground, but Mac kept on pulling tighter.

"I never…was…yer child." he growled, a voice of sudden maturity, a voice of bravery yet devoid of any emotion. He pulled harder and the belt dug deeper into his neck. The body constricted against him, violently slamming to the ground beneath him. There was a sound of a wheeze, unlike the keening wind that brushed against his youthful face, unlike the muted laughter that was shared between he and Mickey in the sacred barn, unlike the train wheels that halted at the Holy Station, unlike the whimper of his own breath after every beating, raping the last wisps of air out of him. His hands filled up with blood; for the very first time, blood that was not his own. His eyes, widely awoken and alert, stared at the drips running down his arms. He felt the last warm breath of death reach his face; he heard it leave the farmer's mouth, like it was the most enchanting music ever to reach his ears. *The death rattle.*

He never realized how much he longed to hear this agonizing pain; followed by the peacefulness of death caused by his very own hands. A feeling of pure ecstasy rushed through his body, as the man's weight got heavier and limp. He let his head drop to the ground, like the heavy stones he threw out of the crop fields. He stared with an eerie pleasure at his work, carefully inspecting the deep ravine created within in his obese neck.

His brain's chemicals danced differently that night — they waltzed unbalanced through its structures as the endorphins exploded like fireworks; flaming up and burning down any emotional system — burying it down to the very bottom of his brain; laying it there to rest, until the waltzer would eventually die down himself.

V

"THIS IS FABULOUS!! BELLE! BELLE!!" Tailor Pierre admired Charlotte's bell-shaped red dress; still measuring how the gored skirt fit around her smaller waist. "You have an exceptional…aaah *physique,* ah?" he said with a thick

French accent, conspicuously winking over at Will right after — who was stunned by Charlotte's extraordinary beauty, yet blushing again for staring speechless at her low-cut neckline that was struggling to cover her large bust.

"Thank you, sir…you're too kind…" Charlotte said shyly with a scarlet face, and bowing her head, she cut her eyes at Will to capture his expression. He was beaming in awe, and yet somehow she couldn't see it, as if her mother's demeaning manipulation made her always believe otherwise about herself.

"Certainly, madame!!" Pierre said, and clapped his hands in excitement, then left to grab a pair of velvet gloves to go with the outfit. Will took the opportunity, sneaked behind Charlotte, and grabbed her from her waist.

"You look irresistible, my lady." he whispered softly, caressing her on the neck, his hands traveling down to the swell of her hips, daring as ever.

Charlotte, startled, blushed from the sudden compliment she was not used to receiving; caressed his brave hands, letting her fingers fiddle with the silver rings he always wore. "Do you…do you really think so?" she asked him, still her head bowed in shyness.

"I am certain of it, my lady…" he whispered.

It was so different for her to be treated in this way; to have someone buy her the most expensive, fancy clothes man has ever made. Designers whose names she couldn't even pronounce; garments she couldn't understand how to put together. Just in Bisonhorn, she was admiring the dresses women wore, mocking her own self for never being able to wear anything close to a beautiful flowing gown other than a potato sack. She only had a single pair of jeans back in Nephilim Cove, and two shirts. Yet now she was here with Will, preparing herself for a ballroom dance — draped in the most elegant red dress, seeing for the first time her own body squeezed within a corset, accentuating the most alluring womanly shape she didn't even know she possessed. She had been blind to it, and suddenly, she wasn't. *Perhaps it was all God's plan,* she wondered and smiled big, turning around to steal a kiss from his lips before Pierre would return — shocking him pleasantly, for it was against any public etiquette — and yet Charlotte couldn't have known, nor could she have cared, for Nephilim Cove *had* no etiquette.

"These! These here will be peeeeerfect!" Pierre slipped the glove over her hand, making sure it fit appropriately.

"May I?" Will interrupted Pierre.

"But of course, monsieur!" he said, happily handing him the other glove.

Charlotte looked away, embarrassed, feeling the butterflies in her stomach fly all over within her, as Will caressed her hand deftly, slipping the glove softly past her dainty wrist. "Fits…like a glove." They both giggled playfully at his silly yet witty remark, and locked glimmering eyes.

CHAPTER 25

The Waltz

I

EVENING SIGNALED THE LANTERNS TO BE LIT IN ALL OF MON LOUIS. Boats were lit up, embellishing the dark river as they scattered all across it. There was an invigorating cool air beneath a granite sky, serene enough to not threaten another storm, and yet a layer of fog billowed around the ships — sheltering any shadows that approached it.

He paddled towards the famously luxuriant Caddo River Boat, which was still anchored at the shoreline by the marina ramps. He threw his lasso over a pillar on the boat, and slowly pulled himself up to the main deck. All the guards were still stationed on the bow of the ship; disarming everyone who entered for the evening ride, and yet the whole boat was steadily filling up with the elite of society. Lauded officers of the army, the occasional foreign diplomat, and even a member or two of the monarchy. He sneaked through and rushed up the stairs to the boiler deck; opening every door to find the room where the valuable ruby was locked away in, still lingering himself in disbelief.

The fence in Mon Louis was known to receive private information through the higher ranks of society, perpetually in petty competition with one another, then send out outlaws to steal from the rich; then upon returning their valuable finds, he would reward them with guns, ammo, and rare explosives. A necessity for any outlaw that was trying to survive, as a piece of paper was not of any use in trade and therefore not of any interest. All this illegal opportunity was known and shared between the outlaws, thieves, and gunslingers in Sailorman's Wharf. There was no sheriff to look over the town;

there existed only chaos and shenanigans. Not everyone had the skills to go out on a mission like this; as the risk was too high to get captured — so most outlaws preferred to kill common travelers that rode through, or steal from them instead. But most outlaws, were not *him*.

I I

"WILL!" CHARLOTTE GASPED. "I AM SO NERVOUS!!" she said anxiously, squeezing his arm tighter. She had never gone to such a public gathering, let alone one that the mayor had organized himself. She had never worn such luxurious clothing, and certainly never acquired knowledge of how to dance the waltz.

"You are absolutely without reason to be nervous, my dear. You look absolutely ravishing, and I cannot wait to show you off…" He winked at her, as they walked towards the mayor's mansion that looked suspiciously empty — wishing to plant a crooked kiss on her cheek, but "etiquette" was to be obeyed. "Hm…hold on a moment here, Charlotte."

He strode to the guard, worriedly. "Sir, excuse me for bothering you this fine evening. I have an invitation to the ballroom dance at the mayor's…"

"It ain't happening here, mister. You gotta go to the Caddo River Boat. You still have time, but I recommend you hurry." the guard interrupted Will since he already knew what he was going to ask, as so many had the same question before him. He was bored and agitated to the core to have to inform every single one of them of the very same thing — so agitated, he failed to recognize the infamous elite standing before him.

Charlotte and Will hired a stagecoach that happened to pass by, and they rushed to the boat ramps of Mon Louis in unbeatable time. "Will…I…I have never been on a boat…" she huffed nervously as she stared at the enormous, intimidating ship before her, almost hyperventilating, watching the ripples of water splash against the ramp.

"You haven't? Oh, it is lovely! Just don't look down as you walk across, as you might become dizzy from the waters below." He caressed her shoulder to reassure her, walking towards the ramp to enter the ship.

"Invitation for William Griffiths, and I have special company with me."

Will pointed his hand to the guards, as he handed them the letter.

The guards looked at Charlotte with a cocked brow, measuring her from head to toe. Her breath was halted in her lungs, trying to compose herself before the eyes of the law. Her bust barely moved, and yet the corset made it quite a challenge to not gasp for a lungful of air through its constricting force. "Welcome, Mr. Griffiths." the guard finally said, nodded sheepishly, and stepped aside for them to board.

III

"BOSS, WE RECEIVED AN EXPRESS LETTER from Sheriff Jordon up in Birdsboro!" the deputy said as he stormed into the office, informing Sheriff Dorman who was oiling the cylinder of his revolver.

"Get on with it…" he ordered impatiently, eyeing the piece of paper from the corner of his eye.

> *Sheriff Dorman,*
>
> *I need to inform you of a suspicious criminal activity down in that shit hole, Sailorman's Wharf. A sailor was found strangled to death and hanged by a tree, with strange knife carvings across his face and body. Then there's a negro who was found drowned with a large knife wound on his face, right underneath the boat he lived in. His eyes had been carved out. Plus, a working gal was found decapitated in the alleyways of Sailorman's Wharf. Not much more was done to her.*
>
> *We suspect it's the man we're all after, Mac Kinnon, but could very well be the Fiddler Brood — however, they ain't so smart to leave no trace behind. No fingerprints were found.*
>
> *Sheriff Jordon*

"Ha…well, would'ya look at that." He snorted with dark amusement, placing down the oily cloth beside him. "Sailorman's Wharf…all the way to Sailorman's Wharf, our little boy." He put his gun down, yanked his legs off the table and marched to the deputy, patting him on his shoulder — ecstatic to hear a word from a fellow sheriff that tacitly expressed more brains than the whole bunch of deputies combined.

"Ya see? We need no 'Pretty Boy Will' — little Kinnon's doin' for us, all on his own!" He chuckled, satisfied, and poked a rancid, cheap cigar in his mouth to celebrate the good news.

"Boss…do you want us to…"

"Ya know what to do! Get the horses ready! This time, trust NO stranger! Ya hear!?!" he shouted at him, and the deputy nodded in earnest.

I V

IN SLYNESS, HE CRACKED A HEAVY WOODEN DOOR to a large office that seemed to match the description they gave him back in Sailorman's Wharf, or at least it appeared expensive enough to fit the image. Ensuring no guards were lurking around, he slowly entered the office with his knife gripped tightly in hand, black wild rag covering his face. His hands started feeling of the walls; pulling out books from bookcases, expertly trying to place a hidden safe. He glanced every once in a while out of the window, watching the guards slowly remove the ramp. Not long after, the boat started moving away from the shoreline, sailing further away by the minute, and the lights of Mon Louis started to dim. Guards were trooping through the main deck, on their way to protect the mayor as he would hold his welcome speech. The ballroom dance would be starting any moment, so the guests could enjoy the rest of the evening around the numerous poker tables and multiple bar counters to quench the thirst.

V

THE HIGH CEILINGS TOWERED OVER HER. She stood there, aghast, breathing in the sumptuous air that every important entity around seemed to stir. The ship's ceiling was resting upon pillars, upon pillars, connecting to an internal, open-air balcony, where spiralled staircases of glimmering gold led upwards to. The oaken wood floors, shining as if they had been mopped down to the very fibers of the wood; she was terrified to scratch them with her heels, and barely dared to take another step atop them.

"What do you think thus far, my lady?" Will leaned in to her with the question and she swallowed hard, drawing in a breath to find the words to answer.

"It's…quite incredible." she stammered, still dazzled by the gold and shine.

"Well, it is exceptional indeed." He sighed, glancing around him. "However, do not feel discouraged by certain people, and their lack of manners…" he said in earnest, and she cut her eyes at him in bewilderment.

"What do you mean, Will?"

"They will be curious about you, my lady…they hunt for new faces to gossip about…and intimidate." he said, and she blinked.

"Intimidate?" She snorted. "They have no idea who they will try this on…" She rolled her eyes, and he smiled at her.

"Certainly." he said, yet deep down his stomach ached with the thought, as he spotted faces already cocking a manicured eyebrow of judgement.

"Why would they do so, anyway?" she then asked, in sheer curiosity.

"For no reason, other than having the need to know everyone and everything about everyone…it satiates their pitiful craving in a way, dare I say." he said and she rolled her eyes again, then she noticed a bundle of decorated officers staring right at her. She tore her gaze away swiftly and gulped down a knot, somehow concerned if they recognized her.

His fingers coiled around her arm in an attempt to get her attention, and yet her eyes remained nailed on a wicked painting that hung between two candelabra. "This must be Marshal Bill Wheels…from Texas." he said, squinting through the loud crowd of chattering mouths and insincere faces. "He is not a man of strong character…not genuine, that is." He shook his head, observing the way he waved his hands around energetically, betraying that he must be boasting about himself once again. His brown eyes scanned around the faces of the officers. "I don't think I detect the infamous Marshal Tilghman, this time…that's a shame." he said to her, and yet she was too occupied with her own thoughts of concern to hear him, as if the ominous painting was siphoning the last ounces of purity out of her soul. "I never managed the opportunity to engage him at previous events, at least for long enough to entertain a conversion…then again, he is not a man of proper morals I wish to associate myself with…" he said absently.

Charlotte shook her head, as if pulled back from a state of trance, and faced him, realizing she had not heard a single word of his. Then he went on to ramble further, as if he knew the deepest insights into everyone around him.

"Right next to the marshal, our dear Sheriff Tom…I believe I see Agent Mills glued to him as per usual, and a whole army of Pinkertons in the very back…" He nodded to himself, and she swallowed hard for all the law was not the most comforting company she longed for in a boat with no means of escape — other than the ocean, to drown within.

"Perhaps we should move away? You know…" She cleared her throat, and he nodded.

"Of course, my lady." he said, and led her with her arm in the noose of his, when a voice halted him in his tracks.

"Mr. Griffiths!" A voice very familiar, erecting the hair on the back of his neck. Charlotte turned her head to her left, spotting a relatively short man. As he approached in great haste, she locked eyes with him, a pair of narrow-set eyes of a dark brown color, swiftly observing the odd, perfectly-trimmed brows over them right after. "What a pleasure to see you here! Glad you made it in time!" the mayor greeted Will with a big smile on his face — one no-one ever knew if it was genuine, if he meant a word he said, but he always tried hard to appear as if he did.

"Thank you, Mr. Lemaire! The pleasure is all mine!" He shook his hand, rubbing against the diamond rings on his fingers. "May it be my pleasure to introduce you to Miss Charlotte — my beautiful lady." He stepped to the side to reveal her, who was cowardly hiding behind him.

"Ah! Wonderful, indeed! A pleasure to meet you, madame." His roman nose flinched with judgement, as he grabbed Charlotte's hand to kiss upon a bow. "Are you new here in Mon Louis, madame?" he asked her, and Charlotte swiftly looked back at Will.

"Sir, if you might allow me to elucidate. I have the honor of showing her around your beautiful town for some time, but we most likely won't be staying for long." Will interjected, and Charlotte nodded in silence.

"Oh my, how fabulous! How does she like it?" he asked, and Charlotte suppressed a snort, for she loathed Mon Louis's modernity, and yet she grinned politely in response.

"I am certain she is just as infatuated with it, as I am, sir…" Will said and Charlotte nodded with slightly sarcastic cocked brows.

"Terrific…" He grinned insincerely. "Well, I would love nothing more than to converse with you further, but…as you know, it is time for a demonstration." He winked at Will, and Charlotte frowned with suspicion. "Mr. Griffiths, would you do us a favor and demonstrate the waltz for all of us?" he asked of him loudly, so all the guests could hear — a wonderful tactic to ensure declination is not an option.

"It's an honor to do so every year, so it would be my pleasure again, sir." he said, as he walked to the round open space the guests made for him, circling all around in great anticipation.

Charlotte glanced around herself to see the gentlemen all dressed formally in black tailcoats, white shirts, and proper vests — pulling it all together with a classic bow tie. The ladies had a little more variety; low-waisted gowns, off the shoulder with small sleeves — some white, some dark; skirts were universally full and bell-shaped with lots of petticoats, all lavishly decorated with flounces, ribbons, and lace. She definitely felt out of place, as even though she longed for such beautifully elegant dresses, she didn't feel like herself within them — however, she was happy to be with Will on her very first formal occasion.

"Ladies and gentlemen! It is my privilege that I may introduce to you…the smoothest, most elegant dance known to man; one that only uses…four steps. It has a distinctive three-quarters timing, boasting a gracefully flowing style."

Charlotte stared at Will, stunned to see such flow in his speech — such attractiveness that radiated from him, making her blush as if she was holding that speech before dozens of the elite herself.

"Indeed, it is the very first 'closed' dance, in which people moved 'arm in arm', hand to the back — slightly down, to the waist…" He moved his hands accordingly, as he glimpsed around the crowd whose attention was captured by him. "…though it was *not* socially accepted." He paused briefly to create a suspenseful aura in the soundless room. "It is here tonight, if you are lucky enough to find the perfect partner to dance…the legendary 'waltz' with…" He glanced over at Charlotte after he ended his speech, and strode towards her with his eyes locked on hers, possessing a powerful confidence that captivated her the smoother he walked. All guests' heads jerked in his direction, eyes darting at his hand, that gently reached out before the woman in a red dress.

"Would you be mine, Miss Charlotte?" he said loudly, as he held his hand out for her. All the guests now surrounded them, anticipating Charlotte's answer — and she couldn't recognize if Will's question was more pressing, or the hundreds of protruding eyeballs almost kissing her from all directions.

Charlotte looked at Will nervously; her hands started to shake.

"Will…I can't…" she whispered as quietly as she could, desperate not to make a fool of herself or to embarrass him.

"I would love nothing more than if you would grant me this dance tonight, no matter how it goes." he whispered back to her, still holding his hand out.

The ladies, almost falling over from stretching their necks so far towards them, trying to find out what all this whispering was about. They all adored Will's mannerism; he was well known and desired by the many aristocratic women in Mon Louis, but he was not easily willing to commit to someone. They didn't pose a chance, for that matter — so they were quite envious of Charlotte being his partner that evening. A face, a name, whom nobody knew.

Charlotte placed her trembling hand on his, still feeling his cold rings underneath it. He smiled, and she forced a shy smile back to him. Leading her smoothly to the middle of the room; he placed his hand around her back, and stretched his other out, holding hers. She placed her hand behind his shoulder, still shaking, glancing around to notice everyone watching — expecting to either to witness something outstanding, or the catastrophe of the century.

"Look at me, my love." He lifted her gaze to him with his tender voice. "Imagine it's only us." he whispered to her softly, the dimples of encouragement emerging on his face again.

"This is so difficult, Will...*everyone* is staring." She sighed, her eyes glancing over at the pianist who was getting ready, stretching his fingers — the cracking of them hitting her ears, as all the little sounds intensified around her.

"Follow my lead...don't look down." he said and before she could draw a breath, he started swaying with her within a circle; choppily she moved with him, struggling to understand where to place her feet, almost stepping atop him after a couple or more circles, and yet he kept encouraging her with a smile in his eyes, and soon enough his smooth movement swiftly guided her legs, her hips and her whole being, now flowing across the room in complete harmony, moving their shoulders gently while lengthening each step.

Forth. *Left foot.* Sideways. *Right foot.*

The people around them smiled involuntarily, as even they couldn't resist admiring how much they complimented each other. Charlotte couldn't help but giggle when she noticed Will blushing once again, trying to remain serious in front of his important audience. Will took her hand and twirled her back into his arms, falling back into step; letting his lead control her movements.

Charlotte's hazels glistened as she smiled in his eyes, feeling her nervousness dissolve like ice in sweltering water — as did the staring people around her. A deep brown lock had escaped from her hair — simply styled, drawn up into a knot on the back of her head, decorated with a velvet black ribbon.

He spun her around once more, feeling her dress brush against his legs, his tingly fingers holding on to hers as she returned back to him. "Thank you, my lady." he hummed, and kissed her hand lovingly.

A loud round of applause followed, from all around them.

CHAPTER 26

The Pocket Watch

I

THERE WAS NO SAFE IN THIS ROOM, AND MOST LIKELY, there was no precious ruby in that Caddo River Boat either. Frustrated at himself for trusting the rumor that was spread throughout Sailorman's Wharf — out of desperation, for he was in urgent need of new ammunition — he tried to figure out a way out to the main deck without being spotted by the myriad of guards that lurked around.

Said guards had started to get into their usual positions, scattering across the different levels of the boat. He heard sudden steps approach the arched oaken door, as one of them was ready to stride right into the office. He noticed the knob twist, and swiftly hid behind the door. His dry lips folded tightly, breath held within his lungs, no sound escaping him. As the guard entered with his brows raised in suspicion to find the door unlocked, he immediately grappled him and pressed his gun against his head.

"Say one word…and yer dead…" he growled against his ear, and the guard raised his hands before him.

"P-please…I'm just…a hired man." he stuttered.

"Sure…" His brows pulled together, as though considering. "What's yer name, lad…" he then asked, kicking the door shut behind them.

"R-Rudolph…" He gulped down a knot, clenched eyes shut, the barrel denting his head from the pressure.

"Rudolph…how's yer day, so far…" he asked, cocking his head to observe the taut lips on his face, painted with terror.

"I…I…I think decent, sir…I mean, decent until now!" he said, quivering.

"Hm…bad business…" His shoulders shrugged with sarcasm and the barrel shrugged with them. "Well, I'll tell ye what, Rudolph…me day ain't that decent so far…" he said, his face set and grim, and the guard forced his eyes open, dithering to turn around to face him. "But I hope…yer gonna make me trouble worthwhile." he said. "Where's the goddamn ruby, Rudolph…" he growled and shook him by his uniform.

"R-ruby??"

"One more time ye repeat me word, and yer dead, boy…" he said and the guard wailed.

"Please, sir! There is no ruby that I know of!!" he cried. "For I would tell ya!! I don't give two beans 'bout the mayor and his wealth!!"

"Where's the safe, me lad…" he growled again, cocking the gun.

"I…I don't know! I don't think there's a safe in here!! For he had been robbed not too long ago, and therefore d-decided to not keep any of his belongings on the boat!" he stammered in a cutting despair.

"Hm…this answer don't satisfy me, boy…"

"I…I have a watch!! I have a watch to give you!! But please…let me go…" he begged, patting a hand on his chest, feeling the watch beneath his cloth.

"Rudolph…it may just be yer lucky day…" he said, twisting him around with a force, facing him.

The guard's eyes flared, aghast.

"My…heavens…" He gasped, and a smirk painted on the gunman's face.

"The watch…Rudolph…" His eyes set in a leer and the guard nodded, swiftly fumbling out a golden pocket watch.

"Hm…not bad." he said, flipping the watch open and shut, the guard's eyes flinching by the sound. "But I do have another request…Rudolph." he said, and the guard choked in fear. "Ye see…I can't trust ya…"

"No…no, I…I won't say a word!! I swear it to you!!"

"Swearin' ain't good enough. Not in me book…"

"Please!!"

"Hm…" His brows cinched and his head cocked, studying the tremble on his lips. "Nah…not today, lad…" he said, and knocked him out effortlessly with a forceful bang on his head, dragging him behind the desk, sparing his life for the trade he offered.

Escaping the office, he slunk down the stairs slowly, trying to blend in with the shadows of the boat. Another guard was walking straight towards the stairway, so he rushed back upstairs into another room, finding himself in a hallway that led to the ballroom. His fingers fiddled with his knife, calculating his next move.

He spotted a crowd of people walking in at the end of the hallway, as he also heard the door slightly crack behind him. He examined the area he was trapped inside, but noticed another door to his right where he vanished within.

I I

"BRAVO!! BRAVO!!" THE MAYOR CLAPPED FERVENTLY as he walked towards Will and Charlotte. "Terrific job as always, Mr. Griffiths! Ladies and gentlemen, you may now begin…to dance!" he ordered and the pianist resumed hitting the keys again, and the dance room flooded with the army of aristocrats starting to waltz. "Mr. Griffiths, I have a business proposition for you, if you have a moment to discuss it over in my office." the mayor said in earnest, fixating his glasses over his dull brown eyes, setting his gaze atop Will and Charlotte.

"I understand, sir." Will bowed his head, knowing this was an opportunity that could help fund some of his future projects and yet he had no inclination to be involved with the mayor more than needed. His head turned to face her with the words hanging from his lips. "My dear, I will need to discuss something with the mayor for some minutes. Perhaps you can look around the main deck while I'm gone. It has some remarkable art pieces hanging on the walls." he offered her, ready to follow after the mayor.

"Sure…" she mumbled curiously, wondering what the mayor could want from Will. She didn't trust his sneaky smile, nor the way his tiny brown eyes wandered all over him, as if he was ogling Will's body lecherously the whole evening. In fact, she didn't get a warm and fuzzy feeling from any of those "higher-up" people, for even the flourishing dresses of vivid colors couldn't warm up their souls.

She walked around. Her eyes set at the painting that drew her attention prior, luring her in with an invisible yoke. Dithering, for somehow a shadow stood right beside it, yet it slowly morphed into her own as she approached. Eyes squinting closer, she studied the painting; it was unlike anything she had ever seen before, and certainly not fitting to the others around her. It was ominously dark, gloomy, and yet deftly created with the most nurturing hand. Every detail upon it was as if carved from reality, and plastered atop a canvas. It was the back of a woman of a strong hourglass shape, draped in a dark cloak that reached her bare ankles, flexed as she stood on her toes with gracefully crossed legs. There was a trail of a scarlet tint that coursed down her ankles, bright and ominous, betraying it climbed down her legs. There was no face to be seen, but a flock of raven feathers descending atop her before a glowing silver moon, bathing her with light. Her skin stood erect; it held for a while.

"So, Miss Charlotte, I presume?" a French accent startled her from behind, a shrill voice that cut through the painting.

Charlotte turned her head around swiftly, to see a lady's face covered in white powder and dressed in an oversized fluffy white dress that looked like it had swallowed her whole. She blinked in awkwardness.

"My name is Victoria!" She winked proudly, shaking her shoulders as her back straightened. "Quite a strange piece of art, don't you think?" she giggled and Charlotte blinked again, for she felt it was the most beautiful painting she had ever witnessed, and yet something told her not to admit as much.

"I suppose…" she said, clearing her throat, her voice low and suspicious.

"I simply cannot fathom what artist could possess so dark a soul to even consider such an idea for a painting! Although, I do have my suspicions…" She rolled her eyes, and Charlotte bowed her head, somehow feeling compassionate towards the man. "My Heavens! I'm surprised to see the macabre showcased on the Caddo River Boat!" She snorted, almost fumed at the fact.

"Right…" Charlotte said, swiftly disinterested.

"Anyhow!" She chuckled, again in a shrill voice, flinching Charlotte's eyes. "My dear?" Her eyes set back on Charlotte.

"Yes…" she answered sharply, not trusting her mischievous gaze.

"Brilliant dancing there, my child!" she complimented her, yet her tone of voice betrayed her genuine intent.

"Thank you, ma'am…" she said politely, wishing Will was back already.

"Where are you from? You look…well…so out of place, here." she giggled, her fan waving before her powdered face.

"Thank you…I suppose…" she smirked snidely. "You're correct, I ain't from here…I come from Nephilim Cove." she muttered proudly, not afraid to scare her off, hoping it actually would.

"Oh…that explains your…well…the lack of…never mind…" She smiled widely, as if she didn't mean to insult her. "So, you and Will are married, yes?" she added, reaching for information.

"Uhm…no." Her eyebrows snapped together, baffled. "We are just… together…ma'am." she said, already annoyed at the lady's audacity to press for details such private matters.

"Oh! What a pity! But, I understand…Will has a hard time committing again, after his *scandalous* divorce that is actually rumored to not be final yet." She shook her head in disbelief — as though she didn't plan already to interfere with Charlotte's feelings and senses, for they appeared far too happy of a couple to be left alone.

"Divorce…? Why scandalous? Not over yet?"

A knot emerge in her throat, choking her.

"Oh well, it is not really my place of course…I thought surely you must already *know* that he had a wife. Pardon me." she said with a high-pitched pompous voice that annoyed Charlotte even further, watching her prance and giggle away from her, merging with the rest of the powdered faces in the room.

Charlotte, speechless, didn't really know how to react to this news about Will's second — *or first?* — life in secrecy, and a wave of emotions blazed so strongly within her it burned every inch of her skin. Her sense urged her to find Will and bombard him with questions, and yet her heart simply wished the dance floor would swallow her whole.

"Mr. Griffiths is such a fine young man. Lucky you!" another lady whispered to Charlotte, as she passed by her, hand briefly clasping her shoulder with a white laced glove.

"Are you and Mr. Griffiths together?"

"Are you and Mr. Griffiths married yet?"

"Are you promised to Mr. Griffiths??"

"What about Elizabeth?"

Powdery faces interrogated Charlotte like a machine gun, only the bullets were gasps of powder, stained with scarlet lipstick. The ladies swarmed her, faces swallowing her whole being. She stood there, benumbed. Stood there, grasping desperately for air and for answers.

The bile of nausea shot up her throat, face becoming blanched. Blood darted downwards, feeling light-headed and claustrophobic. The powder blinding her view, the wide bright smiles stinging her gaze. Crowded around by women who once seemed so elegant to her, they now felt like witches adorned in white cloaks to mask their evil.

"Excuse…excuse me, for a moment." Stammering, she squeezed through them, inhaling a lungful of air, tripping over her long dress, tearing it up to her knee. Leaving the ballroom, holding back her tears; she couldn't believe what she heard back there about Will and his scandalous divorce, and some kind of lady owning the most elegant name that sounded something like …*Elizabeth, certainly that was it* — after finally starting to fall for him, and forgetting about Mac; somehow forcing herself to forget.

III

"I'M CONDUCTING A RE-ELECTION CAMPAIGN." HE SAID, slumped back and bowed jaw, pouring himself and Will a glass of bourbon. "I don't want to ask for it to be fundraised…" he said, twisting around, handing him the drink. "You know, in a way, this shows both weakness and greed." he snorted, implying he was not the greedy type at all.

Will waited patiently for his turn to speak, standing there before the fireplace, and took a sip — yet still, fiery glimpses of Charlotte and her dress as she spun around him flooded his mind.

"You're very liked here, Mr. Griffiths." he said, stealing a bewildered glance of Will's obvious dent in his head, visible upon closer inspection. "Everyone speaks highly of you. Everyone knows you more than they actually know me. Ha!" He cackled, and yet it was factual enough to not be too amusing to him. He bit his lip, tapping his fingers against the glass, his eyes resting atop Will's chest, as if intrigued to see through the cloth. "I can only wish to have such fame as yours." He bobbed his head, thinking. "Your father did an excellent job in raising you, Mr. Griffiths…"

Will's thoughts turned into a line of images of his father, deeply assailing him. Images of him being often intoxicated, angrily tearing apart every essay or small novel he ever dared to write as a young boy. He thought of the countless days he never was home, and he pictured his sick mother taking care of him; supporting every ambition he had to become a writer. His father didn't raise him, but he certainly instilled an insecurity within him to never follow after his dreams. He succeeded, well after his death.

"Thank you, sir." Will said coldly, sliding his lip through his teeth.

"You're certainly a wealthy man at such a young age, but I can ensure you stay that way." he said, his eyes cut at him.

"I don't quite understand yet, sir." His mustache twitched in confusion.

"Fund my campaign, and I will make you my assistant. Once I retire, you will take my place as mayor." he offered, chugging down the last drop of his drink, expecting him to jump onto this once in a lifetime chance, and yet Will stood sternly before him, eyes dull.

"Sir, I truly appreciate the extraordinary offer, but…I'm afraid the horse industry is keeping my hands tied for now." he respectfully declined, knowing very well he would loathe himself as a mayor, let alone being the assistant to a corrupt one, knowing he already had more money that he knew what to do with, knowing somehow he abhorred that too.

"Fair enough. Just know the offer is still here, were you to change your mind." he shook his hand, clutching it for a moment too long, and handed him a cigar.

Upon escaping the voracious mayor's lair of insincere opportunities, he strode along the blessedly dim hallway, for the shadows it held within it somehow eased the thudding migraine that emerged. Turning around the corner, he crushed into a lady of dirty blonde hair, dressed in a red gown as well.

"My apologies, my lady." He bowed his head in impeccable grace, and she turned to face him.

"Oh, my! If it isn't Mr. Griffiths himself!" She gasped, and then her mouth settled on a wide smile.

"Forgive me, for I do not wish to be rude, but…"

"Jane." she said, handing him her hand to kiss. He clasped it and pressed it against his lips.

"Jane Tilghman…I should have known as much." he said kindly.

She huffed. "Indeed! I haven't attended a ball for some time…well, ever since my…dearest ex-husband attended it with me, many moons ago!" She snorted, and Will swallowed shyly. "Thankfully, he isn't attending this year, serendipitously so…for I'm sure I would have detected him." she said and Will kept on bobbing his head. "But! What do you know! Perhaps he is hiding in some of those closets, doing unspeakable things with anything willing enough, maybe even a sensual-looking mop. He so tends to do, nowadays… apparently." She rolled her eyes, trying to quell her rage.

"I understand, Mrs. Tilghman." He nodded, somehow still holding onto her hand. She retrieved it and chuckled with crimsoned cheeks. "Well, I fear that I have a special lady waiting on me…so I should make myself scarce." He smiled lopsidedly, subtly besotted by her enchanting beauty, knowing the marshal would never settle for anything less than that — yet also knowing the rumors he never appreciated it once he had it.

I V

HE CRACKED THE DOOR SLIGHTLY OPEN TO TAKE A GLIMPSE at the golden hallway. The light of the candles filling up his blue eyes as he watched guards march up and down, couples blabbering loudly as they walked past him. Hiding inside a tight utility room with no way out. Most likely, he would have to wait until the ship returned to shore, and the guards stopped trooping around, in order for him to escape. Wearing a thin black long-sleeve shirt and ragged, worn down black pants — he would stand out in a second, were he to sneak through the crowd.

He sniffed the dust of the room inside his lungs, and scrubbed the pocket watch against his pants, setting the gold finish ablaze. He flipped it open, watched the time pass, listened to the slight, unpredictable irregularities in the ticking and rested his head against the wall.

His eyes, distant. In thought.

V

WILL RETURNED TO THE BALLROOM, EXPECTING TO FIND CHARLOTTE admiring the wall of art, yet Charlotte was nowhere to be found. He searched through the white and black blanket of guests, passing all the uninteresting, same-old faces, as his worry grew that something must have happened to her again.

Charlotte rushed through the hallway and exited to the open deck, gasping for a hint of fresh air, for her lungs had collapsed and her breath had vanished somewhere within them. She yanked the knot from her hair, and released her brown waves — falling over her shoulders, covering her back. She burst into tears, feeling an unbearable pressure crushing down upon her chest. The wind blew harshly against her face, tangling her hair, lifting up her dress to the knees as waves slammed loudly against the ship. Covering the sound of her weeping.

"What a fool I am…" she cried, glanced down at her dress, thinking back to them dancing intensely, carelessly; recalling Will's promise to her, to always be by her side — *"forever and ever."*

"Sir, have you seen my lady?" Will frantically questioned guest after guest, breaking out into a sweat of nervousness — messing up his perfect coiffure of long black hair.

"No, Mr. Griffiths." The answer was repeated again and again, only building up his concern.

She sucked in a deep breath, wiped the tears away with her sleeve, and cleared her throat. Determined, she entered back into the long hallway, remaining calm and unbothered, for she wouldn't give the pleasure to those powdered witches to see her in such distress.

VI

THE CLOCK KEPT ON TICKING, AND HE KEPT HIS EYE GLUED to the gap of the door — watching everyone pass every other second, mentally noting the faces and the number of guests. Walking in the hallway, she halted the moment she heard a faint noise. *Tick-tock-tick-tock.* Frozen in her tracks, feeling the ticking buzzing in her ears — immediately she scanned around herself, terrified, for she suddenly felt a strange presence watching her; eyes that felt like nails on her, nails that felt like soft feathers brushing against her — yet both eerie enough to prickle the skin.

A single deep blue eye stared at Charlotte from the dark, turning her slowly back towards him. His watch kept on ticking, his heart now beating faster. She slowly neared the cracked open door, her quivering hand reaching out to open it further. He leaned back, still studying every move she made; holding his breath, and yet a wisp escaped him when the familiar face bared in his gaze. His throat, dry. Hands, soaking wet. His body froze into place the more she approached timidly. Slowly, his sharp hooded eyes emerged, dark in the shadows, revealing to her upon a foggy view; the same intense eyes that locked onto hers from behind the strangled man. The same black cloth, covering nose and lips — yet she knew how they looked behind it, how they felt against hers. She could feel the ticking of the clock pulsate within her; the closer she got, the stronger it did.

"…Mac?" she whispered to herself in doubt — doubt that grew into hope.

Hope that had died, long ago.

He stood still, feeling the strongest urge to pull her inside the room with him — just for a moment; just for a split second to feel her warm, inviting aura fill up the coldness within him — his darkness, that only she could light.

"Charlotte!! Charlotte!!" Will startled her as he ran up to her, wrapping her into his arms without any thought of decent etiquette. "I was so worried about you!! Thought something happened again…" he said, his body trembling in fright. Benumbed, frozen into place, she blinked over his shoulder, then pulled back to face him.

"Will…I just…needed some fresh air…" she spoke shortly, stealing fleeting glances back at the door.

"Everything alright, my dear? Your eyes seem…"

"Yes, I'm okay!" she hissed, the powdered face flashing before her eyes, the sound of the elegant name still ringing in her ears. *"Elizabeth".*

"We can walk around, then…and I can show you some art?" he worriedly offered, feeling a strange distance from her.

"*INTRUDER!!!*" a guard screamed upstairs, after finding the tossed body in the office, still unconscious, squeezed beneath the desk like a sardine within a tin can. Charlotte immediately glanced back at the door, hunting for those deep ocean blues again, more concerned for his safety than her own, and yet darkness prevailed through the gap.

"*MAKE HASTE! EVERYONE GO DOWN TO THE MAIN FLOOR! DOWN TO THE BALLROOM!!*" the guards ordered, pushing the guests towards the floor; cocked rifles, ready to defend.

"Charlotte, let's go!" Will grabbed her hand and rushed with her to the ballroom, as she kept on glancing back — hoping to see him escape to safety — hoping to confirm what she felt, was indeed there.

VII

CHAOS RULED IN THE BOAT; A CATERWAUL OF TERROR stripping the golden finish off the rails, ladies hiding in the arms of their partners as they desperately pressured the guards for further information, running to the mayor demanding an immediate solution.

"Mr. Lemaire, what happened?" Will questioned the mayor, rushing to him for answers as well.

"A body…was found…" he whispered, as to not upset any more his guests. Looking up to the balcony; making sure no one was pointing a gun at him, plotting his assassination.

"A body? Who could be the intruder? Why here…" he asked himself, more than the mayor, as his curiosity spiked. Charlotte jerked her head away from them, not wishing to give away who she immediately thought of, as if it were possible for them to read her mind.

"Don't worry Mr. Griffiths, we will be berthing soon…let's just stay here as the guards make the rounds." he said in an effort to quell his panic, for there was an offer still lingering in the air between them.

Will led Charlotte to the side, to have some privacy. Taking out the cigar the mayor handed him before, he hoped to get some instant relief, for the unknown intruder wasn't all that was tormenting his being.

"My dear…I can sense something is troubling you…" he said, placing the cigar in the corner of his mouth. Hanging loosely from his lips. His worries, too. Eyes now setting on her, in earnest.

"I just…don't really like these folks here…don't mean to offend you, as they seem to be…your kind." she said snidely, wondering if that *Elizabeth* was their kind too, for she certainly sounded the part.

"My kind? Hm." He grinned, lighting up the cigar. "They're not my kind…it's strictly business. If you think I have any friends here, you're greatly mistaken, my dear." he said in unusual defense, confused with her sudden change of attitude.

"Oh well, they sure seem to know a lot about you, though — for them not being your friends and all." She stared wildly about, unable to hold her tongue any longer, feeling her chest crush again, realizing they were quarreling for the very first time. She shrunk in shame.

"What are you implying, Charlotte, my love?" His eyes fell upon her, stunned. Knowing very well how gossip traveled with fervor between the aristocrats, his suspicion grew.

"Nothing, Will. I guess I'm just saying, these people aren't very genuine, or honest. They all just seem…the same." She sighed, thinking of all the elite clients her mother had sleeping with her, while their wives stayed up waiting on their return late at night. She loathed them, and yet even the mucky Los Muertos weren't any better. Perhaps it was just a man's habit, after all — to stray like an emotionless entity, bound to break ones heart.

Her heart felt broken, or bent. She couldn't tell. It still beat.

"In fact, I agree with you…" he said, trailing off as he puffed on his cigar, acting distant himself.

VIII

The Caddo River Boat returned to the shoreline of Mon Louis much earlier than planned that evening. The town was asleep, with the exception of the occasional beggar counting their earned coins from that day on the side of the streets, only to be stolen by a gang of children that tended to lurk around through the town's gloomy alleyways on the west side of it.

"Will." She tugged on his coat. "I think I left my glove outside, I will be right back…" she mumbled to him, her glove hidden within her other hand.

"But…the intruder, Charlotte…" Will gaped at her, aghast, as a glove certainly wasn't worth risking her life for.

"I'll be right back! It's just around that corner there…" she grunted, still not being able to look him in the eyes, for his words appeared as a big lie, drenched in white powder.

"Let me come with you, then." he insisted, grabbing her hand softly.

"Leave me!" she fussed abruptly yet unwillingly, for her heart couldn't muffle the pain any further. "Please…" She tore her gaze away and he stepped back, nodding.

A desperate urge to go by that cracked door again flooded her with coldness; she didn't care to consider Will's feelings at the time, for hers were deeply hurt already. She imagined all the secrets he must have kept from her; a current or previous wife, a whole life he had certainly built with her, a possible divorce, realizing that she herself was a secret to him, to her, to *Elizabeth.*

She longed to stay away from him that night.

She yearned to forget.

She neared the door. It was already shut.

She waited impatiently, trying to hear the ticking noise; but there was disappointing silence. She coughed softly, in case someone would recognize her and open the door again, but there came no movement from inside.

She reached for the knob, terrified to find someone other than who she thought it was; wondering if it was all in her imagination, if she was starting to go delirious — *certainly, after inhaling so much powder,* she thought to herself.

She squinted in fear, standing still before the wooden door. Snarling it open, a rush of anxiety spiraled through her. Inside, there was nothing…nothing but a golden pocket watch, carefully laid on top of a black piece of cloth.

Her heart stopped; she could barely breathe. Lungs collapsed.

This was where the ticking noise came from that she heard before, yet this time, the watch was shut closed — it was dead quiet. She picked it up with a shaking hand, and held it tight, clutched against her chest. Her hand reached to grab the piece of cloth that was folded underneath it, clasping it and pulling it closer, the cloth unfolded in the air — revealing itself as a black wild rag. Stunned; mist shone in her eyes, fingers trembled as they felt of the cloth ever so gently — recognizing exactly who it belonged to.

Smoky tobacco scent.

Rough texture.

Faded color.

All the same.

It was *his*.

CHAPTER 27

Promised

I

SHE STARED IN THE MIRROR AS SHE BRUSHED her long ginger hair, eyes distant and glazed. She pierced the heirloom pin through her bun, curling and affixing the remaining hair that peeked out around her face. She walked out from the ranch house, breathing in the view before her as the sun rose and glistened through the trees, bathing the freckles on her cheeks, drenching vibrant color into her pallid skin.

She fumbled out her diary from her gown's pocket, flipped it open, pulled out the pen, and wrote a couple lines. Clasping a teacup in her elegant hand, she took a walk around the ranch, visiting with the horses in the stable. She sipped the tea as she watched them eat their oats in contentment; their satisfied munching sounds calming her soul, an absent smile scarred her face. She glanced at the stall next to them, still empty; the brush in the bucket, still untouched for far too long. Her smile slipped.

Empty, and untouched. So was she.

II

"IT WAS QUITE THE ADVENTURE YESTERDAY, WASN'T IT, DEAR..." He rolled over to her side and whispered to her ear, caressing her shoulder lovingly, knowing she had been awake for a while.

"Yes...indeed, it was." she muttered, her eyes absently staring at the closet, almost piercing through the wood, almost able to see her secret gift from *him* — not particularly caring about it either that morning, as the words of the powdered witches tormented her mind.

Spinning it around; waltzing with it.

"This is our final day together here, I would really love to spend it however you desire. Perhaps, waltzing wasn't the best idea…" He chuckled awkwardly, hoping to break the sudden ice that had formed between them. She rolled towards him, looking him straight in his big, brown doe eyes that flared upon her challenging gaze. "My lady, I suspect you must have a question for me…" he said jokingly, and yet he genuinely feared as much.

"What will you do in Bisonhorn, Will?" she asked him directly, unable to talk about any other subject that seemed so miniscule in comparison.

Will blinked at her. Tearing his gaze away, his hand still caressing her shoulder. "I…I have some important business to tend to, my love. I've been putting it off for some time…" He pulled in a guilty stutter, and cut his eyes at her again, aghast, as someone must have warned her.

"I see." There was sarcasm painted on her smirk. Displeased with his sheepish, cryptic answer, she poked him further. "New oil business? Horse business? Waltz business? What is it?" she persisted.

"None of that, dear. I have a…friend, who I need to see." he said sheepishly, for he could hide things well, however, his ability to lie was the same as his talents for shooting at a bear — pitiful.

"A friend…what *kind* of friend?" she asked, feeling the awkward knot form again in her throat, and her chest slowly tighten.

Her airways, blocked. Smothered.

"Charlotte, don't tell me you are worried now, silly?"

"What to worry about? I can trust you…right?" she asked him, not breaking eye contact.

Will delayed his answer; he sighed uncomfortably, staring into her beautiful eyes that had started to water. Tears that burned, tears that stung. He caressed her cheek, and leaned over to kiss her lips. She pulled back, still expecting an answer from him.

"Will, I can trust you…right?" She choked, suddenly reminiscing all the wonderful moments they had shared. Realizing how close she had let him in;

how she had started to fall for him, and she didn't even know it until she felt her heart break into a million pieces the night before, or perhaps it was but a harrowing forewarning of how a broken heart could feel.

"You have my word, Charlotte." He grabbed her face, pressed his lips against hers and kissed her fervently, his heart stinging with guilt as he did. Burning. Sinning, furthermore.

He pulled back and clasped her hands. "Please, give me time to deal with some matters…once and for all." he said, squeezing her hands in his fist, clutching them against his chest.

Charlotte stared at him beneath cinched brows, trying desperately to read between the lines. *Perhaps he meant to finalize the divorce*, she thought wishfully, eyes studying the way his dimples twitched in an unusual manner. She felt his heartbeat pick up pace, pulsating rapidly against the palm of her hand — almost able to hear the keening sound it made; his breathing raced, eyes flickered, fist squeezed her hand, twisting it as his body suddenly spasmed uncontrollably.

"Will!! Will! What's going on!?!?" she yelled, struggling to unlock her hand from his fist, feeling her fingers slowly crush within it; he squeezed harder. "Please, talk to me!!"

He broke into a sweat, spilling an endless blood-specked froth of saliva, screaming as someone trying to escape from their own body, eyes flared widely and mouth constricting, slamming shut, teeth gnashing down on it. Managing to untangle herself from his grip, she rushed down to the saloon owner to seek help. She leaped down the stairs, holding on to the rail, bumping into working ladies, and accidentally kicking the stool where the pianist sat — making him miss his notes.

"Please! I need somebody!! I need a doctor!!" she cried to him, her hands shaking in panic.

"Madam, what happened?!" Antoine asked, shocked to see her so rattled.

"Will!! He needs a doctor!! Or a priest!! I don't know!! Help him, please!!" she yelled, recalling a few verses she had learned in the Bible.

14. *And when they were come to the multitude,*
    there came to him a man, kneeling to him,
    and saying,

15. *Lord, have mercy on my son: for he is*
    epileptic, and suffereth grievously: for oft-
    times he falleth into the fire, and oft-times
    into the water.

16. *And I brought him to thy disciples, and*
    they could not cure him.

17. *And Jesus answered and said, O faithless*
    and perverse generation, how long shall I
    be with you? how long shall I bear with
    you? bring him hither to me.

18. *And Jesus rebuked him; and the devil went*
    out from him: and the boy was cured from
    that hour.

Matthew 17:14-18
New Testament of the Holy Bible
1881 English Revised Version

Rushing back upstairs to the room, she found Will lying in bed in frightening silence, as if the whole world froze around him, unable to differentiate whether it was an illusion of her own, or a sickening prank of his. She approached him timidly, to notice his eyes pried wide open. Her heart sunk, thinking he had died — that a demon had taken him, or worse, that a demon was still here, inside him, morphing into his charismatic being.

"Will...?" she mumbled, her voice trembled in fright.

"It's all right, now, my dear..." he said, voice weaker than ever. "Forgive me...for scaring you..." He sighed with all his strength. She stood, dithering of what to do, examining every inch of him.

Gathering up her courage, she climbed up on the bed beside him, making sure that it was indeed Will speaking. "What...happened?" she asked him, not able to hold back her emotions seeing the pure exhaustion on his face.

His mouth, bleeding like an eerie calm river. His tongue adopting a few more scars. "Remember…my…head…injury?" His head bowed, his arm wiping the bloody foam from his mouth. "Well, that's…just the result…of it." He huffed, exhausted, ashamed, repulsed with his own self. "The…doctor said…my body…seizes from it." he spoke with delays in between — something that he never did before. He seemed so very frail now, his speech so awfully slurred, and her heart shrunk with every word he spurted.

"So, you're not…possessed?" she whispered, petrified.

"No, my love." He forced out a chuckle with her innocent ignorance. "Science…has come a long way…I don't know…how to explain it yet, but… my friend I was telling you about…I'm sure, he will." He grunted subtly, trying so hard to come up with the studies he had read, yet his brain was not cooperating. There was a pulp of information within it, trapped and obscured beneath a layer of haze.

"Ah!" she exclaimed. "The doctor! Yes! He will be here soon!" she said excitedly, hoping to resolve this issue with a one-time injection cure. "And… and then you will be fine, Will." She smiled at him, and leaned in to kiss his forehead — all of a sudden, *Elizabeth* wasn't so important anymore.

"You…you went to notify…the doctor?" he asked, aghast.

"Yes. Well, I told Antoine to get him as soon as possible, so we can take care of you properly." she said, and he clasped her hand abruptly.

"Charlotte…you…would be a fabulous wife…to someone, one day." he said in earnest, eyes sternly locking hers.

She blinked with a knot in her throat, for that was such a far-fetched conception for her. He smiled at her within her silence — wishing he could call her his tonight, tomorrow, and for the rest of eternity. She forced a smile back, reminding herself he was already married, *or was he divorced?* She wondered, suddenly worrying if she had caused his seizure with the pressure she put on him earlier.

"Will…thank you." she said politely, not wishing to upset him any further.

She felt a huge responsibility weigh on her shoulders; it was because of *her* that he was badly injured, because of *her* that he kept quiet towards the deputies; tormented until he seized almost to his death. And now he sat here, stiff and depleted from any energy, devoid of any emotion other than a wave of woe and sorrow, staring back at her with a gentle smile, as if she had never been the culprit of his demise. She wished, so badly, to had been captured instead, to be able to rid him of any pain he suffered.

III

"SHERIFF JORDON! PLEASURE TO MEET YOU, SIR." He shook his hand, and walked abreast into the sheriff's office of Birdsboro.

"Sheriff Dorman received my letter, I assume." He sighed heavily, plopping himself into a creaking chair. "How many of ya boys did he send?" he asked, cutting his eyes at a dozen deputies waiting outside his jail.

"Plenty, sir. We have been ordered to search the towns of Sailorman's Wharf, Birdsboro, and all the surrounding woods, sir." the deputy explained in detail, noticing Sheriff Jordon's judgmental frown.

"I see. Smart. Smart thinking." He cackled, and the deputy joined him sheepishly, not knowing if it was genuine or sarcastic. He turned stern. "Ya know what ya dealing with, right?" He locked eyes with him solemnly. There was no sound of laughter this time.

"Mac Kinnon, sir?" the deputy, confused, asked to confirm.

"Devil himself, son." He bobbed his head, his leg crossed over another at the knee, wiggling in irritation. "Are ya a smart bunch? Don't know how he's still runnin' free out there all them years." He wondered, his face scrunching up as he observed some of the deputies goofing around with each other.

"Yes, sir. We are well-equipped and have a solid strategy, sir." he answered confidently, meanwhile a deputy got bucked off his mount for poking his fingers into its ears.

"Yeah…" Sheriff Jordon huffed heavily, realizing they were all but a lost case. "Well, best of luck to ya. If ya need anythin' ya know where to find me." he muttered, ready to take care of his own outlaw dealings.

"…Sir? How dangerous is the man, really?" the deputy, who was a new hired hand of Dorman's, inquired with slight concern. Sheriff Jordon glanced down with a bowed head, bursting into snide laughter with his stained, chipped-off teeth rattling within his mouth.

"Son, Kinnon has murdered men stronger and smarter than the bunch of ya combined. He has murdered women, young men, elderly folks — all in cold blood. He could be in this office right now, without us ever noticin'. He would kill us both with one swift bullet, and even God couldn't explain ya how. He is a master of his craft, and like I said — the Devil himself." he said, flipping his pocket watch open and shut again repeatedly, eyes hooked on his. "He murdered an innocent preacher once, down west of Holy Ranch, hid his body down in the cellar — all that as a young lil' boy. He was found decapitated, with his mouth cut wide open to fit an entire Holy Bible into it, and a cross carved with a knife across his face…" He bobbed his head, lip sucked in beneath a row of teeth. "Do ya realize, now, what ya dealin' with?" He chuckled, resting his legs on top of his desk.

"Yes ssssir, Sh-Sheriff Jordon!" He sucked in a terrifying stutter, for Sheriff Dorman never deemed it necessary to share such information.

"This…*evil,* requires a specialized bounty hunter, not a dozen foolish deputies as cannon fodder." He snorted, shaking his head with Dorman's pitiful crew. "Ya can't outsmart him." He shrugged. "Wastin' your time, wastin' mine…no offense." He winked. The deputy nodded in cowardly compliance.

IV

"THAT'S A HELL OF A THING, MR. GRIFFITHS." the doctor said, shaking his head after explaining to Will what seizures technically are, and how science was still trying to figure out all the many ways the body or mind can trigger them.

"Yes. I figured, my friend." His shoulders slumped, and his head lowered. "There is no cure, correct?" Will asked, still hopeful, swallowing down all the bad news so far.

"No, Mr. Griffiths. Not as of yet. I'm sorry." He patted his shoulder, devastated to see his friend suffer like this, for he was the last person that deserved it.

"Thank you…I had hoped there would be something…Mon Louis is more advanced than Marysville, let's just say." He chuckled, yet his sadness shone in his eyes.

"Mr. Griffiths, do you happen to have any…delusions, or amnesia?" the doctor questioned him, as he'd received such claims from previous victims who suffered from head trauma far less severe than Will's.

"Oh no, sir. Thank Goodness, that part of me is intact." He chuckled again, pleased to not be as damaged as the doctor thought he might be.

"Good…however if anything changes, please do come by and see me, Mr. Griffiths." He pleaded in earnest, for Will meant a great deal to him ever since he was a little boy.

Charlotte rushed inside the room when she saw the doctor leave, anticipating to find a fully renewed Will. *Cured. Healed. Exorcised, by the power of modern medicine. Whatever.* "And? Did he give you an injection? What did he say? You will be okay? Right, Will?" She flooded him with a dozen questions.

"Sit by me, my lady." he spoke calmly to her, reaching for her hands. Charlotte sat down by his side, still carrying a hopeful smile on her face — *doctors were supposed to heal someone up,* so she thought — even though she had never been to one, as it was too expensive to ever afford. Or rather, she wasn't worth the expense. Or, because the only doctor she had around in Nephilim Cove was a rusty old gunslinger — making a living by identifying "miasms" behind disease, and selling spoiled water labeled as homeopathic remedies to combat them.

"I will be okay. I promise." He kissed her on the cheek, holding back his drowned emotions. "Sometimes, I might have these…episodes, but rest assured, I will be okay." he explained, disappointed. Shying away from her gaze, as shame for his weakened condition was suddenly overpowering him.

"Does…does it hurt you, Will?" she asked curiously, fingers grazing softly across his tender hand.

"At first, but not really after that. I kind of…travel into a darker place for some time, and come back again." he said, with a crack in his dry voice.

"I'm so sorry, Will…" She choked. "Oh, how I wish I would have been captured instead…How I wish I could take this punishment away from you! I'm so sorry, Will." she cried to him, loathing herself for causing him such irreversible damage.

"No, don't even think like that." He lifted her jaw with a forefinger and wiped her tears with his thumb. "It was my choice to protect you, Charlotte. My choice to fall for you, and do such silly 'brave' things I've never done before in my entire life!" He laughed to cheer her up, realizing how much he grew as a person, as a man, since meeting her.

"To…fall for me?" She blinked, blushed, not expecting to hear these words, not ever having heard them to begin with.

"Isn't it apparent so far?" He smiled, sat up, and wrapped his arms around her, letting out a big sigh. "I will miss you so much, my lady…That journey is awfully dreadful to me…" he said, clutching her tight against his chest.

"I will miss you too, Will. I just wish you could stay…" she sobbed faintly into him, burying her nose in his scent again. That woodsy, pungent scent of his cologne, still able to drill within her.

"Look at me, my love…" He cupped her face, lifting her gaze to his again. "I give you my word, no matter how long it takes, I will come back for you. With the breath of dawn or the gloomy whisper of dusk, I promise, I'll be there. Even if I must go through the wildest blizzard again, I'll be there." He chuckled with his silly remark, since Mon Louis would never have a blizzard like Hope. "You know what I mean…I suppose…" he mumbled, embarrassed to be out of character, realizing he didn't deliver his point very smoothly.

V

THE STREET GUITARIST STRUMMED HIS WEARY OLD STRINGS, played his five usual chords, not missing a note. The sun set low in Mon Louis, bathing the mansions in a golden light. A beggar opened his bottle of rum excitedly, enjoying the atmospheric music not four feet away from him, singing along — at the very least, clapping to the rhythm with a hand raising the bottle and the other banging against his pot for good measure.

Well-dressed couples trod along the paved streets, arm in arm, headed to the lavishly elegant theatre which was lit up with lights in an exceptionally inviting manner. The police, guarding every corner of the streets, some making the rounds with steady marching strides. Mon Louis was known for having the best law enforcement in the state; not many dared to cause any trouble. The officers were endless, and all were equipped with modern, fast-shooting pistols compared to the standard revolvers typical of deputies in other areas.

Everything was moving and growing faster in this city; however, the class divide between wealth and poverty was starkly evident. Neither Aristocrats or the rich ever visited the darker sections of Mon Louis, where criminal activity was habitual. Far and away from the fancy saloon Will and Charlotte stayed in, there was a shabby, smelly bar squeezed between the fence and another run-down building. Its interior was decorated with erotic photographs, empty whiskey bottles, old worn-down boots, collectible guns, and all sorts of animal hides — albeit barely visible through the dense air, filled with a blinding fog of tobacco smoke. The floor was gritty from all the filth the cowboys dragged in with their boots over the years, and sticky from the drinks they spilled and never washed off. Yet, it was the only true saloon breathing life into the city, when the northeastern side of Mon Louis dimmed its burning candle at night.

V I

"Did you notice any suspicious activity in the last week? Any…strange man, looking like this, lurking around?" the deputy asked a one-eyed gunslinger that was looking at Mac's wanted poster.

"Nah. He is too pretty to be hangin' 'round here." He fixed his black eye patch, exhaling the smoke from his cigarette into the deputy's face.

"Sir, there were three innocent people murdered here; we need any information we can get to protect other potential victims." The deputy persisted, coughing from the smoke that drilled through his nostrils.

"Protect? Us? HA! We ain't need no protection, child. We're all doomed sooner or later, anyway." He chuckled, noticing the perfectly clean-shaven face of the young man, hair kept short and neat beneath his hat.

"I understand, sir, but…we are going to need to make some investigations in those…buildings." he stammered, glancing about, swiftly wishing he wouldn't have to. "Ya ain't gonna find Mac Kinnon here, chum. If ya did, ya would already be seconds from death, partner." He winked at him snidely, and limped away, bronze spurs jingling with every step.

VII

"YOU HAVE EVERYTHING? GUNS ARE LOADED? Spare clothes for cold weather?" Charlotte paced within the barn, going through her list of things to ensure Will had a safe journey, sticking a few carrots in his saddle bag as she did.

"Dear…" He smiled in a sigh, poking his head over Rachel's back to face her. "Please. I will be alright; I've done this journey so many times — I know it like the back of my hand." He teased her worry lovingly, winked at her, and ducked to tighten the cinch on Rachel.

"And…you will write me when you arrive, right?" she asked him, feeling her heart drop when she watched him lead Rachel out of the fancy stables of Mon Louis.

"I promise you; I will write you the most beautiful letter you have ever received." he pledged as he held her hands, squeezing to let her know he meant it.

"Will…please don't forget me…there, in Bisonhorn…" she cried to him, imagining of the worst — thinking of that foreign name again.

"How could I ever; I couldn't, even if I tried." He leaned in close and kissed her cheek, lingering against it to imprint the soft texture in his memory.

"Please…kiss me." she whispered.

With a swift scan around the barn, he laid his soft mouth on hers, kissing her lips long and deep. She pressed herself against him, raked her hand slowly through his perfectly curled long hair, feeling the way his smooth skin contrasted against his sharp cheekbones. He smelled fresh, earthy — almost like the clearest creeks that flowed wildly up in the mountains.

"Ch…Charlotte?" he mumbled between the kissing, yet she wouldn't let loose. She pulled him closer to her, taking him all in as much as she could, before he had to go. "My love." He smirked, pulling himself back. "I will come back, I swear." he said, looking around himself, making sure nobody witnessed them.

"Fine…" She pouted playfully, cocking her head with a complaint.

"I will write you…my lady…" He promised, and mounted his horse. "However, give me leave to make one request of you, which is, that you will take care of yourself, for the sake of one whose happiness is centered upon you alone…" he said, and she smiled with a knot in her throat, watching him trot away from her — glancing back every so often to blow a kiss her way.

He disappeared around the corner. A corner that seemed a lot more hollow than the rest around it, as if all its brick's color had suddenly drained, replaced by a veil of shadowy blackness. She felt the emptiness consume her again. A different kind of emptiness, this time — for she couldn't compare this to the way she felt when Mac left her back in a puddle of mud, beneath a storm shower, with not a single promise on his lips for he didn't even kiss her.

Both goodbyes were completely different for her. The men alone were different for her. Even the way their kiss grasped her heart was so divergent from each other. She couldn't quite understand it herself; something torment- ing her ever since Hope. His kiss, almost choking her, sucking the soul out of her as if he depended on it, and yet deep down, she knew she would will- ingly give it up for him, for somehow it felt she depended on his entire being in turn. And Will's…Will's was the tourniquet around her wounded soul. A fine layer of cloth covering it softly with the most tender fabric ever created, and yet, it was feeble enough to blow away.

One was a cold-blooded murderer that pretended to care about her, or rather took pride in rescuing helpless women in all his heroic ways, then disappearing like a phantom into thin air; and the other — a one-of-a-kind gentleman that any woman would give anything for, yet, carrying a deep secret within him. A secret she chose not to talk about. A secret that wouldn't allow her to give her whole self to him. Now both were gone, and all that didn't really matter.

It was only her, and Finn.

However, memories still dared to linger.

CHAPTER 28

Autumn Leaves

I

"The iron clad hoofs of my horse spurn the sand.
The wide spreading desert is peaceful and grand;
My good lance at rest, at my side hangs my brand.
My brave Arab comrades come at my command.
For a son of the desert am I."

YOU COULD HEAR THE PIANIST FROM AROUND THE BLOCK, singing as loud as he could, completely out of tune or rhythm with the music he played.

"None so dauntless and free on land or on sea,
For a son of the desert am I.
None so dauntless and free on land or on sea,
For a son of the desert am I."

Now the whole room of drunkards cheered with their drinks in the air, swaying as they sang along, which explained the sticky floor of the saloon.

It was Friday night; the west side of Mon Louis was either asleep, enjoying themselves with a content walk in the gardens, or attending a watch party at the theatre. The northeastern side was lurking around the alleyways, trading drugs, spirits, and other valuables.

In a way, both sides were lively.

Some more than others.

II

"WELL, IT SURE IS NOT AS LONELY WHEN I'M WITH YOU, FINN." She gave him a soft pat between his ears, as they trotted in the early morning down to the local butcher of Mon Louis.

Will, after firmly insisting upon it, had left her with a handsome stack of money to last her in relative luxury for a whole month or more; which she fought hard to decline, and yet he worried about her — not wishing to risk her getting herself into trouble just to find some food to eat. Again. He had already prepaid Finn's stay at the stable, to Charlotte's surprise, plus her own stay at the fancy saloon. *For a wealthy man, he certainly was not the greedy, selfish kind,* Charlotte thought to herself, dismounting a few feet before the butcher.

"I would like some of the dehydrated venison, please." she said, feeling a strange confidence to actually be able to afford it, yet she wouldn't even think about touching the finer cuts of meat. Having so much money in her possession rather petrified her by its exotic nature alone.

"Only the finest meats for you, lady! Highly recommend some elk cuts we have, straight from Ozark Ridge!" he offered, grabbed and wiggled the meat before her flaring eyes.

"…No, no, thank you. You're very kind, though!" She forced a smile, immediately thinking of the Fiddler Brood, the hacked-up neck, and all the other meaty parts she tried hard to forget about. Just the mention of that area repulsed her. She almost gagged, and the butcher cocked a brow at her.

They trotted further around the neighborhood, exploring the city Will loved so much, in some sort of way to honor his sudden absence. She couldn't contemplate his obsession with it, she could never feel any comfort here; everything was too polished in a way, too perfect, too…superficial — or perhaps, she just thought of those nasty "witches" once again that left a bitter taste in her mouth.

The hairdresser was right around the corner, she noticed, then dithering, glanced down at her brittle brown plait — fiddling with the ends that stuck out like barbed wire. She never put much effort into her looks; just a quick brushing and a fresh braid, and she was ready to go on about her mundane day; for what else did she need to prepare herself for? Other than cleaning the mess of her mother's clients, or riding through the desert with her trusty steed. Besides, prettying herself up would only attract the wrong attention, she always thought. She never could afford it anyway even if she wanted to, and if she could, she would rather buy a new saddle pad to spoil her pony.

"Oh well Finn, if he don't like me like that, he can just stay in Bisonhorn… with his *friend.*" she said to Finn, flustered, who snorted in response, feeling her exasperation clasp his heart. It ate her up to the core that she didn't make an effort to express her feelings to him, or even to at least ask for an explanation, for now she was left with nothing but a vague promise — uncertain if she was ever going to see him again.

"Miss Charlotte!" A very familiar, shrill voice emerged from the side, slashing her thoughts like nails dragged across glass. Charlotte twisted her body around herself, confused as she couldn't see anyone. "Down here, my child!" The voice now rang within her ears in closer proximity.

Charlotte glanced down to spot the same powdered face she'd tried hard to not think about anymore, and alarmed, hair stood erect all over her startled being. "Oh…" she exclaimed, brow cocked, a subtle nod when words failed her. "Hello, Mrs…" she muttered, trying to recall her name, as she dismounted Finn at a rather slow pace.

"Mrs. Victoria, my child!" she proudly reminded her, folding her arms before her chest, somehow offended.

"Of course…my apologies, Mrs. Victoria…" She smirked, setting her eyes on her. "I ain't good with remembering names." She snorted snidely, knowing *damn* well she could never forget Elizabeth's.

"Oh, that's alright, sweetheart." She giggled, that shrill voice only adopting an even higher pitch, so that Finn's ears jerked away from it. "So, where's your fine gentleman, Mr. Griffiths? Is he around?" she asked suspiciously, unapologetically frowning in repulsion with Charlotte's riding clothes.

"No. He had some business in Bisonhorn to tend to…" she repeated Will's words to her, for she had no input of her own.

"Ah, he's probably checking on his ranch, the horses and…*oh, well.*" Another snide giggle escaped her, the knife twisted in Charlotte's stomach.

"Yes. That's what I thought too, Mrs…Victoria." she said, raised jaw and confident stance, attempting to appear unfazed by the psychological assault. However, the shock of him having another ranch there benumbed her legs.

"You know, my child, you're *very* young still." She sighed, slipping off her white-colored kid leather gloves. "Mr. Griffiths…he…he has a complicated life; perhaps a little more complicated than you'd prefer. Now, things are still fresh and exciting for you two, but *believe* me, he has a lot on his plate. And…in fear of offending your character, dearest, I have to declare that… Mr. Griffiths could not be associated with someone…of *your* kind for long, before…eventually succumbing to the dreaded realization that…you are ruining his reputation and undermining his charming character." she warned her, putting on a caring face, painted with a scarlet pout, lips exaggeratedly pressed together — a nauseating sight alone, without the malevolent words.

Charlotte blinked with odd amusement, for this was the slimiest attempt she had ever heard from someone to insult her. She was utterly impressed, and yet couldn't help but feel the ridiculousness challenging her patience. "You know…" She cocked her hip, bowed her head, and nodded to herself as though in sudden sharp concentration. "Mrs. Victoria, I have quite the complicated life myself — perhaps more complicated than you could ever imagine." She cut her eyes at her, shadowed by her tattered hat. "To tell you the truth though, 'dearest', Will is quite attracted to that aspect of my char-acter — the adventurous…filthy clothed, utterly disgusting woman that I am. I'd go as far enough to say that he is infatuated by it, for at least, honesty prevails in such a mucky character — instead of the same old, same old elite bullcrap he has to deal with every single day that is caked with white powder to hide a lying, obnoxious face, for I'm certain…you are aware, 'dearest', a vague veneer of pretentiousness, slowly fades as well in time, and all that is left then, is but an empty vessel with no character at all." She smiled snidely to her, flattering her eyelashes. "Now if you would excuse me, I have some things to take care of, so I'm ready when Will returns." She bowed her head to her, turned, and as she was ready to mount Finn the shrill voice spoke again.

"Meet me at the 'Bucket of Blood' saloon on the northern side of Mon Louis!" Victoria said in great haste. "I will tell you everything you need to know about Mr. Griffiths. I'll be there, just before midnight." she said, leav-ing Charlotte speechless with one foot in the stirrup, and the other still on the ground. Suddenly the whole paved street shook underneath her; heart submerged low into the ground, mind raced wildly to imagine what she could possibly tell her. Curiosity spiked.

III

"MAKING GOOD TIME, RACHEL! SO GLAD TO BE OUT of those filthy swamps; always has been my least favorite part of the journey." Will sighed as he rode through Hollenberg, admiring the sunset that showered the rocky hills.

Glancing over at the town of Marysville, he wondered if he should ride around it instead. *Surely, there would be Sheriff Dorman waiting on that one unlucky traveler to interrogate regarding his obsession with Kinnon,* he thought to himself. *I wonder what he's up to these days, anyway?* His thoughts trailed off to Mac, and the intruder at the Caddo River Boat. *Surely not…there's just too many fugitives running around, it couldn't have been him…* he assured himself, not wishing to believe he could possibly be anywhere near Charlotte.

He rode through a thin patch of forest leading to the Sweetwater River. Set his camp for the night in a secluded spot; strapped his tent together, and secured it to the soft ground. He made a fire and cooked his evening meal over it impatiently, exhausted and starved from the long journey. His eyes set at the distant haze of Caledonia Territory, and his heart sunk within a pit of resentment.

IV

THE DEPUTIES WENT ON TO INVESTIGATE THE ALLEYWAYS and run-down buildings of Sailorman's Wharf, having the residents evacuate their homes for a whole day as the law plowed through them, under the order and supervision of Sheriff Tom. There was no trace of Mac Kinnon, as per usual, and the outlaws and sailors residing there would not give them any clues or necessary information. They knew very well of Mac, more or less; they admired his unmatched surviving skills — and being able to make anyone that came across his path so effortlessly disappear.

Sailorman's Wharf was a brotherhood of wanted men — yet the bounty on their heads was not worth the trouble to chase after them. They were poor thieves, drunkard murderers, but murdering their deprived uncle or wife didn't really interest the law that much. Aside from thieves, there were mostly sailors, and yet they too were involved in illegal trades of rum and cocaine.

However, Mac had lived amongst them since he was still a young boy. After escaping the farm, he stole Roy from the stables and galloped his way north. When he reached Sailorman's Wharf he crashed from exhaustion, falling off his horse in the middle of the road. A sailor ran up and carried him to his boat, providing him with some water and bread — slowly nourishing him back to health over the course of many months. He grew up amongst sinners — yet Mac felt they were more honest than all the preachers and "godly" people he had to be around before, for they never flogged him, they never dared to touch him. He was taught how to fish off the docks of Sailorman's Wharf instead; how to tie all the strongest nautical knots, how to steal from the rich to trade his finds at the fence for ammo supplies.

He was like a son to the community; who slowly grew into a man everyone respected, and oftentimes feared, for stealing was not his limitation. For his morality knew no boundaries. For the scars across his back, albeit healed within the bleeding cracks, and the torn flesh that sprouted anew again, still burned in his memory, still reflected on the mirror as he studied them at night, loathing himself, reliving the harrowing torture, igniting an unbearable urge to unleash the beast that grew within him; a beast that the farmer nurtured all along, a beast that kept him company when the echoes of a keening wind cowered in the shadows. He stared with menacing eyes in the glass, searching for a soul within him, but darkness was the sole reflection that prevailed, for a tarnished soul was never able to unsully, and the more the beast grew, the more it tarnished in return.

V

SHE BLEW OUT THE CANDLE AS THE STARS SHINED BRIGHTLY above the land, glimmering upon the swath of grass in the early dark hoarfrost of fall. Watching the wind blow the umber leaves off the trees, descending in waltzing motion, burying deep into shadows.

"When the autumn leaves begin to fall, you'll find me here...you have my word."

His soft voice engraved within her head, colliding with the echo of her own guilt; her pallid thumb rolled the emerald ring around her finger, eyes nervously glaring out the polished window, still waiting — still hoping. She fluffed up her laced, goose-down feather pillow and rested her head upon it; her long ginger curls embracing every corner of opulence, her being sinking within. She placed her lithe hand on her chest, breathed in deeply; somehow sensing his presence getting closer.

His leather-bound book laid beside her; his cologne still infused within the pages — for the endless sleepless nights he spent writing it, he vanished within his words of comfort, within the purest of company he could ever have.

VI

FIREFLIES SURROUNDED THE DEPUTIES AS THEY CREPT through the woods of Ozark Ridge. The air felt thin, the wind was still, and the frogs were croaking atop the larger rocks in the river. Trees held their shadows as they sneaked past them, only to be ripped away from their bark the deeper into the forest they strode. Guns raised and pointed, stepping steadily over branch after branch, moving limbs aside with their barrels still aimed as they advanced closer to the hidden campsite.

"John!" one whispered to the other, crouching in sync. "Stay close, I think we got him...look at the shadow in the tent!" he said, pointing with the barrel.

"Remember, don't be hasty! We don't want to screw this up again." he warned him, his frightened eyes scanning around him, only finding shadows from bark to bark. "I told ya what Sheriff Jordon said 'bout the scum…he could be anywhere…"

"Don't be so gullible! He is in the darn tent!" he fussed, pointing the barrel again. They marched quietly, closer and closer, until they reached the front of the closed tent. Glancing at each other, dithering, nodding, quivering in doubt, they raised their guns up proudly, thinking they had almost captured the legend — almost tasting the honor and glory they'd receive for doing so.

"Me lads…" A playful voice suddenly revealed itself behind them, freezing the deputies, the breath, the air, the wind, the life around. The deputies glanced at each other, alarmed, aghast, carefully turning their heads back to be faced with a silver shine.

Two blades kissed their flesh, one each drilled right into the middle of their faces — capturing their expression of terror, eyes crossing, setting on the knives. "…God bless yer sorry souls…" he added sardonically, yanking the knives from of their faces. He shoved them inside the tent and threw a burning log on top of them. He watched.

CHAPTER 29

Levi Krog

I

"JUST WHOOOOO DOES SHE THINK SHE IS, THIS…this pompous old crone!" Charlotte scowled, flustered, as she was scrubbing Finn with a bristle brush, ready to saddle him up for the night's unusual outing in a vast, busy city. Jittering in anxiousness, the more she thought of it.

Finn was munching on his oats, unbothered by Charlotte's sudden foul language, for he was simply gleeful to receive such deluxe care in this barn; with new bedding every single day, fresh clean water, and an unlimited supply of high-quality hay that ensured his belly would never hunger — not that he ever had such an issue before, however the strenuous journey through the desert must have left him with a worry, for at one point he had to share her horrible canned green beans with her.

"Oh goodness, Finn!" She gasped, and Finn cut his eye at her. "That cinch is getting *tight* on you!" She giggled, realizing he had put on some weight from his luxuriously lethargic stay here in the stables. Finn snorted, offended, and tilted his head towards the cinch as if he was checking to see if it were true.

"Alright, handsome. Time to go to the 'Bucket of Blood' saloon." She mocked Victoria, imitating her high-pitched voice, wiggling her head in the air, flourishing her mockery with an exaggerated eye roll.

They walked along the street, trotted a little towards the northern side of the city, and slowed down once the scenery changed rapidly, as if a gloomy cloud suddenly swallowed the whole town, chewed it up and spat it out into scattered pieces of filth. The buildings no longer reminisced mansions; all the gardens' fruitfulness of manicured bushes and trees, now but deserted back-yards, sometimes fencing in small groups of hogs and goats. Chickens were flapping their wings around the streets, helplessly trying to lift their plucked out hinds in the air. Spooking Finn every so often, who was not able to take his flared eyes off of terrifying creatures. Beggars were reaching out with their empty hats to Charlotte, as she evaded them.

Why...would she send me up here... she suspiciously asked herself, as this area seemed more similar to Nephilim Cove than Mon Louis, and all she could think about was the man in Marysville. Or any man she saw, who could morph into his rotten corpse and tackle her to the ground again. Her skin stood erect, looking frantically in the dark alleyways. She picked up their pace.

The saloon revealed itself in all its vile glory, welcoming them with a thick cloud of smoke before it. Dithering to dismount, she eventually hopped off and tethered Finn on the very first post, making sure she could always keep an eye on him or mount him in case she needed to leave swiftly. Scanning around herself for a fleeting moment, she spotted a man across the street, leaned against a tall shadowy wall with what appeared to be a notebook in his hand. Cloaked in darkness, yet calm and contented, scribbling away. She cleared her throat, shook her head, and convinced herself that she was safe; *not every man was a Fiddler or an O'Donnell,* although everyone around her seemed to blend into this kind of threatening aura.

Gathering her senses, she opened the saloon door, and her breath cut in her lungs, asphyxiating. Shocked, baffled, witnessing such a dirty interior as she strode in and glanced around herself carefully — suddenly, even the bar in Nephilim Cove gave a more warm and inviting feeling.

Burly men were wrestling in the very back tables; arms hard as rocks, covered with thick patches of manly, sweaty hair, as their musky smell wafted away from their skin, hitting her nose from across the room. The poker table was laid out with a full detail of worn-down cards, so much that you could barely recognize any numbers on them, and yet that didn't stop any gambling.

"Ma'am, women aren't allowed here." The bartender startled Charlotte, as he spoke strictly to her, stern eyes hooking hers.

"Excuse me, sir?" She blinked at him. "I literally have an invitation from an elite woman that should have been here...or will be here any minute, at least." she defended herself, her suspicion growing.

"Elite woman? *Here?* HA!" He burst into laughter, slamming a bottle atop the counter, and her brows snapped together in shame and irritation. "Gah. Who the hell cares. Want a drink, lady?" he murmured, thinking money is money after all — no matter where it came from.

"Yes…I could use a drink." She sighed, again glancing around herself, eyeing Finn through the fogged up window. "Whiskey, please." she ordered timidly, wiping down the bar stool with her sleeve in order to sit somehow comfortably atop the stickiness.

Charlotte looked around herself, examining the erotic photographs hanging all over the walls, which seemingly examined her shyness in return as though in bewilderment. Her eyes became wide in embarrassment to be surrounded in such a heavily "male-influenced" environment for she avoided such back in home, as much as she could during her rare times of solidarity. Everything stank like armpit sweat, the cheapest tobacco brand you could ever get, and intoxicated vomit; she gagged a bit from the fumes, and chugged down her whiskey.

She couldn't grasp why Victoria had invited her; *perhaps she couldn't or didn't wish to be seen with her by other aristocrats,* she thought wishfully. She sipped on her second drink, attentively poured by the bartender again, letting herself relax for a brief moment. She was anxiously waiting to hear more about Will's secret; and wondering how this lady knew more than she should, knowing Will was pretty private, and yet Will had more to lose with Charlotte than her; mind raced, a deep exhale merging with the smog around her.

Glancing at the broken pocket watch that hung as decoration from the shelf, she absently watched the time pass. At this point she didn't expect her to appear as it was already after midnight, so she gulped down the last sip, clenched her teeth in frustration, and stood up to leave. Turning around, she crushed against a wall of muscle.

"What makes a pretty young thing like *you* come to these parts?"

A stinking, rotting breath of alcohol and tobacco alarmed Charlotte, immediately reminding herself of the monster in Marysville. "Leave me alone, sir. I warn you." she leered angrily, instantly suspecting his intentions.

"You…warn me?" His brows cinched and his jaw slacked, mouth cracked open. "Ahaha!! With what?" He burst into mocking laughter, cornering her between the bar counter and himself. Her throat tightened and her chest heaved. "Ladies first…" he said with a sickly grin, stepping a foot back, but as she attempted to slide past him, he slammed his hands on the counter, dropping her back into her chair. His hands now hooked on the bar, with Charlotte trapped in between them.

"I said, leave me alone!" she yelled, but the men around her did not seem to pay much attention. They were rather entertained by the game the burly man played with her, witnessing a helpless woman be teased by him. As if a cat would step on a mouse's tail, release it for a brief moment, and hook its nails atop it again as it attempted to flee its menace.

"Oh…poor thing…how *awful* of me…" He pouted and lifted his hand off the counter. She stared at the freeing gap beside them, calculating the speed in which she should use to escape. She launched to the empty void, only for him to plop his hand back atop it. The men now screeched in sheer enjoyment and the man smirked, darkly amused by both her torment and the crowd.

"Either you move away, or…or…"

"Or…else?" He leaned in closer to her face, feeling Charlotte's body quiver in fear, sensing her pulse outlined in the crease of her neck.

FTTT!

She spat on his face, freezing all the gazes around her. Now the man stood embarrassed before her, clutching a fist, the slippery drop of threat coursing down his cheek.

"She got ya good there, Bobby!" They laughed, almost falling off their chairs and slamming their hands atop the tables, wheezing hysterically.

The man, aggravated, wiped the spit off his face and before she could escape, he slapped her across the face; an enormous hand, feeling like a brick smashed her against the wall. Her head twisted to the side, jerked benumbed in whiplash. Eyes forcing open to compose herself, cutting back at him.

"Bobby, let's calm down now, will ya." the bartender interfered, feeling for her as the situation escalated and it wasn't just a teasing prank anymore.

Charlotte stood strong, looking straight into his eyes. She would not run away this time, and she would not cry either. She had enough of people taking advantage of her innocence and weakness, and she wouldn't mind hacking a head off again if she could. However, there was no machete this time to hack one with. There was only her, and her writhing shadow, slinking away.

"I...won't say it again. Leave. Me. Be..." she growled, and the man spat to the side.

"I think...you went with it too far, woman, for me to let ya go..." he leered, and raising his hand again — a swift blade slashed through his malice.

TAK!

Bobby and Charlotte, both startled, looked to their side to notice a Bowie knife stuck deep in the bar top between Bobby's fingers.

"You heard the lady...leave her be." A deep, raspy voice warned. Bobby recognized the man in an instant, and annoyed, backed off slowly; taking his eyes off of her, bowing his head and slipping past him with a grunt of defeat.

"Th-thank you, sir." she stammered, barely audible, still trembling from the rush of adrenaline that paralyzed her into place, into that sticky seat that had now adopted her sweat of panic as well.

"Are you all right?" he asked her, collecting his knife back again, flipping it and shoving it into its sheath around his belt in sharp finesse.

"Yes..." She bobbed her head in absence, trying to ignore what could have happened if they weren't interrupted; if she hadn't been rescued. Again. "I'm just a fool, is all." She sighed, embarrassed, realizing she fell into a trap, eyes gazing dully, hooked on Bobby as he settled around a table of poker, proceeding right along with his evening as though he hadn't just hit a woman.

"Aren't we all, though?" He smiled at her, ordering her another drink to help her calm down. The wave of his hand, the tap of his finger atop the counter, catching the corner of her eye.

"Oh, please sir, I don't need another drink. I just came here to meet someone, and well, that someone never came, so..." she talked in circles, not making any sense.

"Who would stand *you* up?" He snorted, baffled. "It's their loss, then, and definitely they're the fools for not meeting up with such a...brave woman." He shrugged, chugging down a drink, exhaling heavily as she rehearsed his remark in her head, in denial.

"No, nothing like that." She rolled her eyes, stinging with the reminder of Will's absence, his ranch, his mysterious *Elizabeth*.

"Well, if not that, I at least bet that slap left quite a pain behind, and nothing better than to drown it with some good ol' medicine." He threw her a discreet compliment, sliding her drink across the counter.

"It really don't matter anymore, to be honest." she said and clasped the glass in odd habit, took a sip, scrunched her face as it burned all down her throat. Her cheek still scarlet like the robes the ladies in the photographs wore, or rather, let slip teasingly off from them.

"Be careful around these parts, especially at night. It's no place for women like you." he warned her, his eyes glancing over her body as it was leaning against the counter — her back arched, legs crossed, and head cocked to the side in sheer defeat.

"Like me?" She frowned swiftly, pulling herself out of a state of trance. "What do you mean by that? And thank you, but I can take care of myself." she nagged, offended, and turned her head to face the stranger for the first time.

"Oh, you can?" They locked eyes, and he smirked teasingly, reminding her of Bobby's disturbance. She blinked, almost bewildered at the sight, for even though he sounded the way he looked, she didn't expect anyone around here to look the way he sounded.

"You would be surprised." she managed to say. "Besides, you don't look like you're from here, either." She glanced at his dark leather coat, rugged pants, and leather vest. There was no way anyone around here could afford this, and she highly doubted the French tailor would carry it either. He didn't look like an aristocrat, didn't speak like one either, *and he certainly didn't behave like Will did*, she thought.

"I am not. That's correct." He winked with an air of confidence, blowing every air of hers away; whatever crippling air that still floated around herself. "I grew up in Petit Jean — Red Giants area, if you've ever heard of it." His eyes set on her sharp hazels, ordering another drink for them. Charlotte thought of her mother that she found dismembered in Red Giants, and coughed from gulping the burning spirit too fast.

"Yes…I've heard of it. Close to Bisonhorn…" She snorted with the irony.

"Ah, ya. Good ol' Bisonhorn. Not much there for me really; it's like a smaller version of Mon Louis. Too many perfect people…" He bobbed his head, leaned over the counter, his back stretched widely as he did. "We

Norwegians prefer simplicity." he noted, then cheered his drink to hers. Her glass almost slipped through her sweaty grip; somehow her slammed cheek wasn't the only benumbed thing on her body.

"Norwegian? Impressive. And what brings you here, then?" she asked, certainly feeling a little tipsy by now.

"Well, my parents immigrated from Norway. I was born here, but the roots run deep in my blood." he said, gulping down another drink like it was water, cutting his eyes at her as she kept an absent smirk on her lips. "I was assigned a mission, that's why I'm here. What brings you here?" he returned the question, for he had noticed her different manner of movement and speech compared to anyone else he'd encountered.

"Must be an important mission…to be so secretive." she teased him, burying her face into the slippery glass, lifting it up only for the vacant liquid to hit her with stinging fumes. He snorted and ordered her another drink. Taking another sip from the refill, she huffed a sweltering breath and turned to face him. "Well, I'm just waiting on…" she stopped herself briefly, not knowing what Will really was to her after all; not knowing how to even describe him. "On someone to return." she whispered insecurely and he leaned in close to hear, then pulled back and nodded with a cocked brow, amused.

"Ah, interesting. Must be an important someone…to be so secretive." he teased her back, cracking a smile on her face.

Since she possessed a speck of sense to know not to drink any further than she already had, as the light-headedness assailed her, and the room spun around her, the erotic ladies slipped back into their robes, and the clock had multiplied by now, as well as the bartender, she stopped him before he ordered any more drinks for her. "Oh, boy…" She cackled, then worriedly froze, for she didn't expect it to happen that fast, for she thought she'd never repeat this mistake again, and yet here she was, drinking together with a stranger, surrounded by possible Fiddlers and O'Donnells.

"What's wrong?" He cocked his head, studying her grimace of shock.

"What time is it, stranger?" she asked him, staring at him with the question, then searched for a single clock that didn't sway before her, realizing time had passed swiftly within a blink of an eye.

"Most likely time for you to go home, or get a room…" He chuckled, as he noticed her wobbly legs.

"Very funny…I have no idea how to ride like this." She glared at the window, now a smudge of glass with a chestnut silhouette through it. "Finn will think I'm crazy…" she mumbled, holding herself up on the counter.

"Finn?" he asked, still with a smirk on his face.

"My horse." She pointed to him as he was nibbling on the reins with his playful lips, knowing very well he wasn't allowed to do so, yet boredom got the best of him.

"Let me take you home." he said, and her eyes flared, cutting sharply at him beneath snapped brows. "I promise, no funny business." He swore to her, holding out his hand for her to hold onto. She stared at it, calculating her options.

"Ahem…sure…why not." she timidly agreed, hoping she wouldn't get herself into trouble again.

I I

"HE AIN'T NO GHOST, WHAT A LOAD OF BULLCRAP. He is just a dumb bastard, who clearly wasn't fucked enough. Ahaha." The deputy mocked Mac to his partners, as they rested around a camp fire in the woods, tossing sticks into the crackling fire, bumping the logs with the toe of their boot.

"Dorman sure would give him a try, as he still seems hung up on him after all them years!" another added his remark.

"Oh just wait till he hears we couldn't find his little boy again, he will damn us all!" another deputy chimed in, snorting along the way.

"Ya really still think Kinnon is a danger? Where the hell is he?? He is NOWHERE! We are the fools to chase after him all this time!" he said, as he cleaned his harmonica. "Booooooo! I'm Mac Kinnon, the ghost of Ozark Ridge! Nobody can find me! Wooooo!! I'll cut your throats open!" They poked fun at him, drinking a little too much again.

Their taunting laughter echoed through the forest, disregarding anything Sheriff Jordon warned them about. They cheered their bottles into the air, as some started playing the harmonica, dancing around the fire, with the noise of the party carrying all the way to the deeper woods of Birdsboro.

A swift arrow slashed through the celebratory smoke, landing in the fire before them, silencing them instantly. They stood up slowly; felt the air stir, wide smiles sinking deep into their cheeks, bottles slipping through grips and a gale of ominous wind playing through their harmonicas.

They neared the fire with caution, looked deep into it, noticing a burnt head pierced by the arrow roasting further in the flames. The sickening scent of human flesh slowly took over their campsite, infesting the pores of their skin with a layer of repulsion, making them gag, choke, quiver in fright; their chests swelled with instant regret, for they knew, they felt *him*. Dithering, hands clasping their guns on their hip, they looked closer to inspect the head, eyes flared upon the sight of a stick of dynamite wedged into the eye socket, already ignited by the fire.

Without a second left on the fuse, a loud explosion catapulted the dozen deputies in every direction, dismembering limbs and killing most instantly. A burst of caterwauling voices now erupted in the woods for a fleeting moment, and yet one prevailed; one screeching survivor, crawling away with his one arm still attached, gripping on the ground, pulling himself up, bit by bit, until he felt a knife drill into his back.

"ARGH!!" he yelled in agonizing pain, the blade slicing through the spinal cord between his vertebrae. A shadow leaning up close, a breath brushing against his head.

"Have ye been…*fucked enough?*" he asked snidely, and flicked cigarette ash over his wound.

"Pppp…pleassee…" he stuttered, a fountain of blood spurting out from his mouth. "Shhhow sssssooome mememerrcy…" Writhing, he slowly felt himself get cold.

"Mercy…hm…" he soughed, and walked away into the darkness, letting the paralyzed deputy bleed to his fate.

III

"I LIKE YOUR HORSE…" SHE SAID TIPSILY, HICCUPING ABOUT, still tasting her drink in her mouth.

"Thank you! He is one of many I have; he just can handle the humidity better than the rest." he said, and petted his horse's buckskin-colored neck.

"So, you choose your horses based on your…secret assignments?" she teased him again as she tried to collect her loose reins, stubbornly slipping through her grip every time her fingers clutched them.

"Haha. You're smart as a whip!" he said and she snorted, for she didn't think so. "Yes indeed…" he cut his eyes at her, resting his gaze at the intriguing swell of her hips. "And 'Finn' is your 'one horse do-it-all'?" He frowned with concern for she barely held on, trying to balance herself on the saddle as she did.

"Yup." She nodded with a lopsided smirk. "Just like a man should be. I think…" She wondered, counting Will and Mac on her five, ten…twelve fingers.

"You think?" He chuckled, enjoying her unreservedness, then went silent. Eyes setting on her again. "You have a lucky one?" he curiously asked her, then worriedly noticed her foot leave the stirrup.

"Oh, I don't know about lucky…" She laughed hysterically, almost falling off of Finn.

"Whoa!" he halted. "Alright, I think you might need to ride with me. Still a ways to go." he said as he dismounted his horse, and strode towards her. She frowned and stared at him, a blurred shadow approaching her. He stopped Finn, clutched the reins, and tapped her thigh. "Off, lady." He snorted and she clicked her tongue in annoyance.

"I'm really…really fine." she muttered, then dismounted in a wobbly, ineloquent manner. *This would make Victoria's face fall to the paved road,* she thought, she chuckled, and he suppressed a remark. Boot slipped through the final stirrup, and she fell into his arms; plopping like a rock, the weight of her body clutching against his chest, testing the resistance. It held — he held her, strong and tight.

"You have some strong…strong arms, like…" she halted, suddenly feeling Mac's sturdy arms of support around her. Her smile slipped, and her eyes glazed, set dull and grim.

"And you've drunk a little too much! Thought you were a tough cowgirl, madam!" He poked fun at her, carrying her to his horse.

"Oh I'm just…I'm just a wanted 'cowgirl'." she confessed, not realizing the risk she took.

"Wanted? You don't say…for what?" he asked earnestly, lifting her up on his horse, tethering Finn's reins to the cantle, and mounting right behind her. "Get!" he ordered Finn, and he quietly followed beside them.

"Oh. Long story. Veeeery long story. Apparently!" She pointed heavenwards with her forefinger, clutching her eyes shut as if to recall every detail. "…I strangled a man! Down in Marysville! The mudtoe! I mean, the mudtown!" she said, tripping over her words, confessing even more, as she leaned her body on his, feeling the cold leather vest against her white linen shirt.

"Oh, that doesn't sound too good cowgirl…you do such things too?" He poked his head around her shoulder, eyeing her briefly with the question. "Maybe Bobby back there should've been worried, after all." he noted teasingly, while perfectly recalling the posters he passed in Marysville with a woman's face on them — one able to catch any man's attention.

"Yuuup! That's what I told you, mister!" Her finger waved in the air. "Although I never did strangle the son of a gun!" she leered, frustrated at the unfairness, the emotions sweltering her insides all over again; her chest swelled, and her lips pouted in fury.

"Who did, then?" he carefully inquired, and she blinked tightly.

She went quiet; suddenly it dawned on her what nonsense she was blabbering, and chose to remain in deafening silence. She wasn't about to snitch on Mac, no matter how annoyed and disappointed she was at him for leaving.

"Miss?" He tilted his head to look at her again, and startled, she locked eyes with him.

"You…you have beautiful green eyes, sir." she said, half-way genuine, half-way hoping to change the subject, as she gazed into his eyes. "Somehow I couldn't see them back…back there, as if they were missing." She snorted, recalling the blinding fog that swirled around them.

"Haha. You're quite the mess, girl." He shook his head, and yet a smirk remained plastered on his face. "But tell me, really, who strangled that son of a gun?" he persisted subtly.

"I did…that's what the posters say, don't they?" she said, annoyed, then randomly looked back, making sure Finn was still following behind, then getting dizzy again, nauseous, repulsed with herself, all together.

"Okay, don't bite…so you're staying at the saloon on the eastern side, correct? For if so, it's right 'round the corner." he said, hands clasping her waist to turn his horse without her losing her balance.

"Yes…that's…that's the lonesome nook of mine." She sighed heavily, wondering if Will had ridden past Hollenberg already.

"Well, we're here." he said, halting the horse.

"Thank you! For…bringing me here!" she muttered, and rushed to mount off on her own out of habit.

"W-wait! You will kick me in the head!" He chuckled as he stopped her boot inches away from his chin, deftly stealing a quick glance at her raised-up butt right before him.

"Oh. Right…sorry. Go ahead." She giggled light-headedly, clasping the mane from the horse. He dismounted, sliding off the rump of his steed, then grabbed her from her waist, and pulled her down towards him.

"Here you go, miss!" He smiled in her eyes, somehow really enjoying her company all this time.

"Thank you, cowboy!" She winked at him, then frowned bewildered with the fact that she did, and awkwardly turned away from him, grappled for Finn's reins, and strode away all independently. Not many steps after, she fell to the ground, planting atop it. Her finger lifted again up to the sky, and a sigh escaped her. "Well, darn it." She snorted, defeated, staring at the hitching posts right before her.

"Let me carry you inside, and hopefully we won't terrify too many of the elite." He chuckled and picked her up with one try, tripping over the hitching post as well. He grunted, as the post hit right at his knee. "You're a mess, girl…" he said through clenched teeth, unable to let go of her.

"Hey…" Her finger skyrocketed again before his face, and his eyes set on it, glaring past it, lowering to her lips that subtly split apart to talk. "I told you…I can take care of myself…on my own, that is…" she said and they burst into laughter, as though they had been long-time friends.

He opened the fancy double-wooden doors of the saloon and strode right in, pulling all the blanched faces towards them as Charlotte's head pressed against his shoulder, eyes peeked at everyone around her, senses spinning.

"There's too many pianists in here! Something ain't right!" she whispered to him suspiciously, wrapping her arms around his muscular neck, burning breath coiling his own senses.

"Don't worry, cowgirl. I got your back!" He played along, seeing only one pianist staring strangely at them. He nodded to him, assuring him they were okay.

"Miss Charlotte! Is everything alright?" Antoine rushed to them, asking her with concern, at the same time studying the stranger dressed in black — looking like anything *but* William Griffiths.

"Just grandiose!" She buried her face in his chest, and giggled embarrassedly with her own answer, hoping Antoine wouldn't be too offended, yet impressed with herself for even remembering such a word.

"She just had a little bit too much to drink; I'm just taking her up her room, sir, and will leave her to it." he reassured him, and walked up the stairs with her. Antoine stood there, glaring, jaw hitting the ground.

"Alright, 'Charlotte', we have arrived!" He put her down, back on her feet, and shook her hand; his grip was firm, warm. "Was a pleasure to be your guard tonight!" He chuckled once again, her hazel eyes glimmered beneath the lantern on the wall.

"How do you…know my name?" She cocked a brow, bewildered, in sudden defensiveness.

"Oh, the bartender mentioned it." He shrugged, calm and collected.

"Ah…right…" She bobbed her head, and went about to twist the knob of the door, relieved to find it unlocked, shocked to have left it that way.

"Well…seems like you're safe now." he said, pulling her back to him with his voice, as if she'd suddenly forgotten he was there, present, inhaling the same intoxication she exhaled. She looked at him, brows drawing together, eyeing him from head to toe with suspicion. He snorted, cracking a wide smile.

"Is it that bad?" He smirked, and she swallowed hard.

"You are a very…a very…" She squinted, trying to think of the right word.

"A very?" He grinned, amused, waiting to hear a drunken bit of nonsense.

"You laugh a lot, mister. I like that. I needed that tonight. Thank you." she mumbled, a smile on her face, blowing back the lock of hair that persisted in blocking half of her vision.

"Life is too short to always be serious." he said, tucking the loose strands of hair behind her ear. She bowed her head shyly, blushing. "I'm thankful for every minute I'm alive. You have a good night, Charlotte." He shook her hand again, yet it felt final this time.

"But! But what's your name?" she asked urgently, delaying his departure.

"Levi." He winked at her, and left the room.

CHAPTER 30

Yours Devotedly

I

"THESE COCKSUCKING, GOOD FOR NOTHIN', goddamned yokels!!" Sheriff Dorman slammed his hand on the table after re-reading the unpleasant news from Sheriff Jordon's telegram. The walls shook around him from the impact.

"What are we doing now, boss?" the deputy hopelessly asked him, staring at Dorman's flustered being as he exhaled deeply, brushing his hair back with his hand, composing himself.

"Jordon…" He drew in a deep breath, teeth gritting against each other. "Apparently, has hired a bounty hunter, knowing our deputies would fail us once again, as he so politely pointed out here…" He waved the paper in the air, annoyed by the fact. "Problem is, if goddamn Kinnon gets captured by this…'bounty hunter'…we can *forget* about any recognition or fame. Might as well retire in this godforsaken town!" He exhaled again; more disappointed, more exhausted than ever before. The few streaks of blackness along his hair had turned a dirty gray, and the few patches of tight skin that remained had morphed into wrinkled flesh.

He could not swallow the fact that he had lost so many deputies to a single man's game, unable to afford losing any more. There was a foreboding feeling that lingered in the stirred air, one betraying he had lost a battle he fought hard for. Over many decades, seeking revenge for the gruesome murder of his brother — farmer Grossman.

II

"WE ARE ALMOST HOME, RACHEL…" WILL SIGHED ANXIOUSLY as he saw his ranch from a distance; still standing there, just like he left it. Only not as proud anymore. His fingers sweated from untenable worry and tension, cold and yet hot to the touch, sliding against the leather of the reins as he held on to them tightly. Too tight; squeezing a balled fist around them, almost able to smell the ignited fumes, the charcoal ash left behind, the hay that kept burning low in an intense smolder long after. Almost able to hear the screams, the anguish and the harrow; deaf to his benumbed ears. Rage spoke louder.

He didn't know how to look her in her beautiful deep green eyes, after everything that happened between him and Charlotte, and yet her eyes had avoided his as well. His heart was torn in half, as the reality hit him more harshly the closer he got to her. He watched the leaves from the trees slowly fall beside him, and he knew he had at least kept his word to her. Yet the man of honor he always strived to be, had disappeared a very long time ago.

III

CHARLOTTE WOKE UP WITH AN UNBEARABLE HEADACHE; thumping with every move she made. Grunting, she forced her eyes open with a hand clasping her forehead. "So, *that's* what it feels like…" she cried, pressing her fingers into her temples, wishing she didn't drink so much the night before. The light shined too bright through the tall windows of the room, squeezing through the gap of the heavy red curtains, illuminating the flourishes atop them as it did.

Her eyes lit up as she looked around herself, making sure she was where she was supposed to be — alone, as she was supposed to be. "Levi…" She smiled, reminiscing last night's silliness; the uplifting personality and the fun they had together — even if intoxicated. "What a silly, fun man…" She chuckled on her own, blushing for no apparent reason known to her.

She stood up slowly and painfully, her face grimaced in repulsion, realizing the need of a desperate shower judging by the fumes that escaped her clothes. "Ugh…Charlotte…you stink…" She snorted, for she smelled worse than a pig stall, and while she was no powder-smelling flower like Victoria, she always made an effort to take care of her basic hygiene.

Adjusting her blurred vision, she noticed a yellowish flower on top of the little night-stand beside the bed. Underneath it, a handwritten letter with the most beautiful calligraphic handwriting she'd ever seen. Her breath held deep in her lungs, her chest rose with anticipation. She gently picked up the flower and took in the smell of its petals; so beautifully honey-sweet and fresh. She grabbed the letter carefully, as to not damage its corners, and let her eyes glide across it. Her cheeks crimsoned upon his name.

My beloved Charlotte,

This marks the very first letter I have ever written for you… rest assured, many more are bound to follow. It is with pain I write to you however, in fear of underestimating the clarity in putting into words how heavy my heart feels — crushed; for having to leave you behind.

I am off, and yet not altogether, for I hand over my heart in your gentle keeping. You need not place a guard over it, however, for it is as impossible that it should stray away, as for a single starved bee to deny a the nectar of a blossom. In fear of employing mockery, I wish to declare I am that bee, and dare I say, I starve for your nectar. I feel confident your knowledge of my character will lead you to understand the sentiment behind that statement.

My mind still travels back to our first picnic in White Elk River — right before the bear interrupted us, of course. The evening that followed weeks after; our first kiss — the most sensual moment that ever possessed me. I remain honored to have felt the softness of your lips — the warmth of your godly body against mine.

You gave me a small taste of who you are, and ever since, I've been longing to explore you more. Not only in a passionate way; but I'm dying to know who this beautiful woman is, behind the hard shell. Believe me, dearest, this is no puerile fancy, but the matured result of a warmly cherished admiration regarding your many charms of person and mind.

My dear Charlotte, I will cherish our first dance for all eternity, hoping that it should never be our last. Wait for me, please, as I shall return back to your loving arms upon the very first opportunity I have. For this sheet of paper, though I hope I have successfully enveloped it with enough loving words of affection, could never tell you truly how I long and yearn to see you again with every fiber of my being.

I'm aware your heart is worried, yet my heart belongs to yours, and forever it shall.

Yours devotedly,
Will

Charlotte's jaw dropped to the floor, to the void, to whatever her feet touched for at that very moment, there was no floor, nor feet; she floated. She didn't sit, she didn't stand, only gentle pools of tears stood in her hazels. She wilted; turned into mush. There was a smile on her lips, a rich curve of disbelief, and yet awe. She had never imagined anyone would ever write something so meaningful — something so perfectly expressive, just for her; *her,* a whore's daughter, created to be equal with the cheapest of dirt. Born to be belittled, broken down, never to be showered with the most tender words known to man, let alone to have any man even write a letter to her; it felt otherworldly, felt odd, non-deserving. She stared at the words, begging for them to make more sense, begging for confirmation they were indeed meant to describe her.

She hugged the letter tightly against her chest, tears coursed down her face, heart bursting from joy; chest welled up with emotions she herself could not imprint on paper, yet contentedly now feeling better about Will, and stronger about *them*. She needed to trust him, and not listen to envious Victoria, who already had set her up for failure last night. Deciding to not worry about rumors, and simply wait patiently on her romantic prince, she tucked the letter safely into the drawer.

I V

HE FILLED UP HIS LEATHER POUCHES WITH A MIXTURE of gravel and sand, making sure they were equal in weight and size. Measuring his vascular arm, he cut off the cord to match its length. He tied up the pouches to three strings of sturdy cord — all bound together, in the end becoming a powerful bola weapon. He counted his bullets and pushed them into the loops of his gun belt, one by one. He loaded his custom-made revolvers, and slid them into the holsters of his belt. Three separate lassos were already tied onto the saddle, with a bolt action rifle secured in the front, and a double-barrel shotgun hidden underneath the saddle's fender. He lit up a cigarette, doused the match with his thumb, and drew in a puff — fogging the intense stare of his eyes, cutting at the folder.

V

WITH THE FIRST BREATH OF DAWN, WILL ARRIVED west of Bisonhorn as the sun slowly flooded the sky with streaks of colors. Nearing his ranch at a timid pace, he cast a glance over the well-cared horses grazing in the paddock; knowing she had to have already been awake to let them out of the stables. His stomach twisted; it had been a while. He nervously glanced around the land, to see if he'd spot her sipping on her luke-warm tea by the campfire, or feeding the chickens by the brand-new chicken coop, or sweeping the front deck of the house; yet she was nowhere to be seen. Swallowing down any remaining cowardliness, he neared the house slowly, not able to delay his purpose any longer. Not able to pretend she never existed. That they never existed.

He hitched up Rachel to the all too familiar post, took the saddle off, placed it on the rail. Briefly wondering if she could hear all the noise he made, or tried not to make. He took his wide-brimmed hat off, clutched against chest, ready to greet her politely like the gentleman he was — or used to be. He stood; before the heavy oaken door, riding boots a lot muddier and scratched up than when he left. He stood there like a different man, one portrayed in his novels. A survivor of immense abuse, a horseman of the Rockies West, a lover with a throbbing heart, and yet, she would never know.

Inhaling deeply; a courageous breath, he pulled down on the handle.

VI

"FINEST FISH HERE, LADIES AND GENTLEMEN! Fresh fish! Finest fish! Sturgeons, muskies, trout! We got it all! Come get it first, ladies and gentlemen!" the fisherman yelled proudly, luring in the townsfolk of Mon Louis on a beautiful chilly morning; a strong fragrance of briny water, grass and fresh cut leaf steamed out of his collection of fish, so fresh they almost jittered still. A sturdy bay draft horse was pulling his large wagon, filled with countless fresh catches from the day. They were on their way to the fresh market that took place every weekend at the docks of the town's eastern side.

The fisherman kept on yelling out loud, and townsfolk poked their heads out of their apartment windows. "Fresh fish, everyone!! Caught by the finest of sailors!!" He cackled excitedly, glancing back at the sailor who was flipping the fish around in the baskets, noticing his dog sniffing at the fish heads, licking its lips in great intrigue. "Mr. Lee! Get your darn dog outta them fish!!" he then yelled with flared eyes, and the sailor snorted, pulled the dog away, and kissed it on the fishy snout.

Charlotte was already in the stables, brushing Finn's pampered self. She stared in awe out from the barn window as she watched the enormous draft steed prance by. "Wow! He is massive, Finn!" she exclaimed to him, flipping the saddle over his chestnut fuzzy coat, tightening the cinch right after.

Her curiosity only spiked to visit the fresh market; see the variety of fish he so very well advertised, smell the ripe fruit from the local farmers, as well as the newly harvested vegetables. She was in such a pleasant mood after reading Will's heartfelt letter; finally feeling a hint of contentment staying in this town; an inkling of the warmth she craved to feel since Hope.

After the soothing bath that she finally could afford to take; a first in her life to experience such luxury, she further spoiled herself by wearing her nicest white crop top and brown riding pants, an attire Victoria's stable lady would wear, *if there was a stable lady that is,* she snorted with the thought. She unbraided her hair, it fell loosely in lush waves over her shoulders. The many shades of brown highlighting her thick curls at the ends, the admirable length of it gently touching her lower back. She was ready.

VII

HE LAID AWAKE IN HIS HAMMOCK, HUNG AND TIED between two tall pine trees south of Ozark Ridge; one leg swaying outside of it in sharp concentration, smoke slithering out his mouth. Debating whether he should rob the weakling of a gunsmith in Mon Louis, for he had only one bullet left in the chamber, and a spare bullet hidden on his belt. He decided he couldn't do much with his knife, in case an army of deputies were to find him — which would only be a matter of time now, considering all the close calls and traces of evidence they were leaving lazily behind them.

Swinging off the hammock, he climbed down the tree, almost glided against the bark, and mounted his horse with a swift leap atop the saddle. He snatched the rugged leather hat off his cantle, fastened it atop his head, flicked the brim, and covered his eyes with its shadow from the blinding early rays of sun. He followed the Buffalo River, hiding himself between sun-baked boulders; it was always a risk to travel during the day, but evidently the deputies caught up with him, so he had to move faster and smarter regardless.

A couple of black bears, harmless to people if left unbothered, were feasting on the carcass of a deer right before him. He paused for a moment to study them; somehow inclined to do so, taking in nature's cruel beauty — the desperate need to kill in order to survive. Then he reflected upon the grizzly bear's unreasonable chase after Charlotte; what seemed to her like an eternal torture; and wondered if animals did feel resentment towards others they didn't even know, wondering if he wasn't all that odd after all for revenging those who never harmed him; they were all equal beasts perhaps, some more estranged from instinct than others.

Her cries slashed through his thoughts with an echo, still remaining engraved within his memory; sobbing in sheer devastation over Finn's critical condition, wilting and writhing into a ball of defeat. Unable to grasp how she could have such empathy towards an animal in struggle; *wasn't this part of nature's cold way?* Didn't they all have to struggle — and who is there to care; *who was there to care in that hollow cellar…* yet, deep down there was bravery and kindheartedness that he admired in her; risking her life for a horse with all her heart and soul — and then he wondered why he risked his own life to save him for her, why he ever risked his life to save her.

He thought of *her*. He still did.

VIII

"FINEST FISH HERE, MA'AM! BUY ONE, GET ONE FREE!" the fisherman attempted to entice Charlotte, as she studied all the different types of fish.

"Thank you, sir! I'm just here to visit the market." she politely declined the offer; somehow she didn't know what to do with a slimy piece of scales with tail still attached.

"Finest fish ma'am, finest fish!" he emphasized, wiggling the fish in front of her face, making her feel guilty for declining as she looked into the glassy eyes of the fish. "No? Maybe…salmon would be better, ahh?" He winked and grabbed a freshly cut fillet, now it wiggled before her mug as well. "All the way from Mayhaw, madam!" His brows flickered at her, and a snort emerged from the back.

She poked her head around the flabby pink fillet with gray scales that shined brighter than her future, spotting a sailor gutting a whole bucket of fish, in swift finessed movements; her eyes set on his inked arm as he jerked it back and forth with a blade, back turned towards her, and yet his voice radiated across. "Let the lady be, Oscar. She doesn't want your fish…" He chuckled caustically with the most melodic voice for a sailor she could imagine.

The fisherman huffed, grunted in disappointment. "Ya don't want no fish, ma'am?" His brow cocked at Charlotte and she blinked tightly, shaking her head in politeness.

"No, sir...I appreciate you, however..." she said, and the fisherman rolled his eyes and plopped the fish back into the counter; a stray scale catapulted and her eyes followed with it as it descended atop a young boy's disheveled head of hair. Contemplating if she should make him aware of the fishy dandruff, his mother made the decision for her, as she wiped it off his hair with a swift brush of a forefinger.

"Alex, we cannot afford this fish at the moment sweetie..." she said, and the boy pouted.

"But the fisherman said it is...the best...and fresh...and all..." His pout sunk further, curving down to his tiny boots.

"Yes...but so are the beans and potatoes over yonder." She sighed and Charlotte cleared her throat without even thinking.

"Excuse me, ma'am?" She approached the mother, already jittering from shyness and embarrassment.

"Yes, ma'am?" The mother looked at her, perplexed, hand clasping the boy's shoulder, clutching him against her protectively.

"I...I uhm...please forgive me, but..." she stammered, somehow forgetting how to even speak to a creature of her own kind. The mother continued to blink at her. "I would truly love to buy you some fish, for you and your son." she said, swallowing hard. The mother's jaw dropped and the boy's eyes flared, staring at Charlotte as if to imprint the kindness of her face forever in his memory. "It is...truly a beautiful fresh catch, and...since I cannot cook to save my life, I am certain that you will be able to do more with it than I ever could. Please..." She nodded to her in earnest, handing her a five dollar bill.

The mother's eyes dropped atop it, as if she had never encountered such generosity before. She clasped it timidly and burst into tears.

"May God bless you..." she whispered aghast, and the boy leaped up from joy.

She moved towards the vegetables, with a chest swelled up of blithe and contentment; she couldn't ignore the boy's sunken cheeks and the mother's disappointment in her face, and even though it wasn't money of her own, she knew Will would have done the same. To continue her charitable cause, she asked to buy a handful of vividly bright orange carrots.

"These will be for you, Finn, my pretty pony!" she whispered to him, thrilled to spoil him even more. Finn's eyes dilated with excitement; the earthy flavor of the carrots tingling his nostrils, his tongue, almost able to taste their sweetness. He reached with an arched neck over them, snarled teeth, mouth wide open, and couldn't help but snatch some carrots from the table — the ones that she didn't even pay for.

"No no no! Finn!" she yelled at him, clasping the reins tight to try to reach his fluttering, slobbery, smacking lips. She grabbed the leafy green stems still sticking out from his mouth, and pulled on them hard in hopes for him to let the carrots slip through. Finn pulled back instinctively and bit off the carrots instead, resulting in Charlotte falling over a table behind her, filled with an army of angry-looking potatoes.

"Nooooo!! Not my potatooooooes!!" a German farmer shouted, devastated seeing them plunge off the bench, tumbling down and rolling in every direction possible — looking equally angry as them.

"I'm, I'm so very sorry, sir!" Charlotte stuttered, embarrassed, not believing her unlucky start of the day.

"The potatoooooes!!" he yelled again, face-smacking himself, clasping his head in disbelief. Trying to reach for the last potatoes that were rolling off, he leaned over — and with the force of his belly, he flipped the whole table upside down. *Oh my God...* Charlotte's breath sunk in the pit of her stomach.

"Sir, I will collect them! One by one! I promise! I will collect everything!" She hyperventilated, kneeling down to pick them up immediately, shocked at what had just happened, all the while the farmer nailed a stink-eye on her. Grabbing potato after potato, a vascular hand reached in front of hers, clutching a potato as well. Halting, she looked up to see a familiar smirk on a quite handsome face.

"Are you getting yourself into trouble again, girl?" He chuckled, studying her eyes in the bright daylight.

"Of course...I have to keep you entertained, as it seems!" She snorted snidely, and placed the potato in an empty bucket.

"Let me help you. It's quite the battalion of potatoes you've released here!" He couldn't help himself but to chortle with her awkward situation.

"You don't have to do that, Levi. It's my mess." she said as she grabbed another one behind Finn's hooves, thankful and surprised that Finn didn't spook at it.

"I don't have to…but I want to." he smiled at her, and picked up a dozen potatoes, carrying them to her bucket.

"Well, you must like potatoes then." She teased him, grateful for his help — yet somehow guilty to be talking to a stranger some days after Will left, mere hours after reading his heartfelt letter.

"I do, in fact." He bobbed his head. "Do you fancy dinner tonight?" he asked her without hesitation. Boldly.

"Pardon me?" she gaped at him, dropping a potato back to the ground.

"Careful there. Haha." He picked up the fallen potato, tossing it into the bucket. "I said, would you like me to take you out for dinner tonight?" He clarified and she blinked, speechless.

"But…I…I am…" she stammered, unable to find the words to politely tell him she had a partner in her life. It was such a sudden, random question that she certainly did not expect to receive — certainly not over a bunch of stray potatoes, anyway.

"You don't have to if you don't want. I will be dining at the saloon anyway, so thought I might give it a shot." he said subtly, as he filled up the bucket of potatoes.

"As friends, right?" she asked, making sure he understood the boundaries, reassuring herself that she wasn't being naïve and gullible again.

"As what else? Strangers?" He smirked, swiftly noticing her bust weighing down against her shirt as she was bending over.

"Erm-erm! The po-ta-toes!" the German farmer interrupted them with a flustering leer, one hand folded against his chest, and the other held out, expecting them to hand him the bucket.

They giggled together and returned him the potatoes.

"Meet you there at seven." He winked at her, abruptly disappearing in the crowd that was still shopping around in the market. She stood there, benumbed, and yet somehow her cheeks were crimsoned.

CHAPTER 31

Someone Special

I

"ELIZABETH...?" WILL WHISPERED COWARDLY, one foot stepping into the ranch house, the other forced to follow right after. It echoed across, bouncing off the thick timber walls, the domed ceiling, and the spider-webbed glass; appearing vacant, almost woeful, and yet, her flowered perfume still floated like a ghost. Staring blankly at his homestead, a red slick robe hanging off the wall like a feeble sign of life; he wished it had been deserted.

Footprints now merged his echo, and his gaze turned towards them. She emerged like a deity, gowned in the purest of white; walking out of their bedroom, with muffled tears running down her face. Locking eyes in mutual disbelief, for she had begun to think he would never return, and he had begun to wish he didn't.

"Elizabeth..." he hummed softly, now standing a few feet before her.

"William...you came." She walked closer to him tentatively, as to take a better look at him — fearing he had changed over all these months of being gone, fearing she had forgotten him, or adopted a different face in her memory — one of malice, one of resentment.

"I always keep my word, dear." he muttered, feeling the urge to step back the closer she got to him.

"May I...may I hold you?" she asked, barely audibly with a reluctance in her trembling voice, as somehow she noticed his brown eyes flare and glaze in uncertainty.

Kindly nodding to her, he took another step and embraced her; arms coiled around his waist, fingers nailed his back, eyes burst into tears — she held him, and he held her back. He sighed deeply, for he felt her pain dig through him, he felt her chest rise and deflate rapidly the harder she sobbed into him, and all he could think about was how estranged they had become, how an embrace didn't feel like home, but a torture chamber instead; with the only escape left alone back in Mon Louis.

"It's been so long, William…" she cried, squeezing him tighter; suffocating him, choking him to the core. He patted her back, reminding her they'd been holding each other too long already and his head turned away, for he did not allow for his heart to be probed by her again.

"I apologize…" She sniffed, and pulled herself away.

They walked together to the living room. Will took off his coat, and hung it on the wall. Drawing in a deep breath, he turned to face her. She sat silently on the delicate brocaded couch, not wishing to make a wrong move or say a wrong word; somehow she owed him that respect.

"How have you been, dearest?" he asked her, putting a disingenuous smile on his face.

"Oh…it's been, you know — the same." She shrugged, lifting her right dainty shoulder; holding the gown by a fine thread of lace. "The horses have maintained excellent condition, and — the chickens, have been steadily producing eggs…Mr. and Mrs. Miller have been kind enough to visit me, and check on things…" she stuttered anxiously, her fingers fiddling with her cloth.

"I'm glad to hear that, Elizabeth. I've been worrying a great deal about you." he expressed genuinely, still avoiding her emerald eyes, feeling their gaze hooked upon him, weakening him as though a spell was cast to do so.

"Thank you…my love." Her lips trembled, throat felt tight. "I feel relieved to have you here…it's been…lonely, William." She sighed, staring at his dull expression, almost able to count the nights they spent apart within his eyes.

Will dropped his gaze to the floor, bowing his head in shame as Charlotte's face flashed before him; he knew he had to tell her one of these days, as a respectful courtesy towards all the promised years spent together.

"And, your business? How did it go? Did you sell that feisty mare?" she forced conversation, for things went eerily quiet. He was quiet; more than ever.

"Yes, I did." He nodded and cut his eyes at her, as if to realize he was really in her presence. "I can't recall how much she sold for at the moment." he said, tearing his gaze away, knowing very well he was stuck in the mountains looking for Charlotte when she sold.

"Oh, good…" She exhaled deeply, feet wiggled nervously.

"I think I need to rest some…if you don't mind, Elizabeth. It's been a long journey." he said in earnest, not giving her a chance to declare otherwise, for he strode now towards the room, caressing her shoulder as he walked past her.

She felt his woe wrap around her neck, choking her. A shadow of a man's grip bruising her tender pallid flesh; stabbing her heart with his bare hands, for his language was clear; he didn't long for her company, he wasn't here to heal them back to what once was — for she shall never be forgiven, for she choked him first.

I I

I expect you to find further information, as soon as possible. Our time is running out. Dorman's men were all murdered within a single night — now you know with what kind of monster we are dealing with.

This won't be your usual bounty hunt; be alert at all times; it's only a matter of time until he will chase you down and try to strangle you as well. Last murder was in Birdsboro, Ozark Ridge; go from there.

You know the protocol.

Sheriff Jordon

HE FOLDED THE LETTER AND TUCKED IT IN A SMALL CLOSET, beneath a heavy layer of clothes. He slipped into his black cotton shirt, draping all muscle with a cloth of darkness, buttoning it up to his neck; he pulled his black leather suspenders over his torso, and adjusted them evenly, snapping them against his chest. "I'm going to get you, mister…" he soughed, leering eyes staring into the mirror, an expression almost shattering the glass. "…but first, I have a lady to take care of." He smirked, and sprayed the cologne around him; a sharp herbaceous fragrance engulfed him, filling up the air with a wishful craving.

III

STUDYING HERSELF IN THE MIRROR, she tucked her black blouse into her long, velvety laced skirt that she bought from the tailor that afternoon; not exclusively for this particular occasion, however, she wanted to look at least presentable in front of all the elite that were dining downstairs — aside from not being able to wear her fish-scaled riding clothes, or the smoke engraved ones from the saloon that night. She briefly glanced at Will's letter, still laying there, unfolded; for the sole endearing purpose of admiring it throughout the day. She stared at it, feeling as though it judged her. "He's just a friend, Will…" she explained, as if he was able to hear through the paper and ink.

She threaded her hands through her hair, collected it all up in a knot, let a loose lock fall beside her face; and yet her whole head of hair appeared disheveled, still with wet strands from the bath prior, blending awfully with the wiry dried up frizzy hair. She clearly didn't know how to style it properly and tidy to the extent of "Mrs. Victoria", she mocked her out loud, lip curled up in repulsion and brow raised, and yet again, it was just a dinner, a friendly dinner at that, and it shouldn't matter if her hair stunk or glistered. Her eyes cut at the letter again.

Striding down the stairs timidly, she felt a pang of sudden guilt rattle her chest, as she peeked over the rail — spotting that tall, brawny, strange man "Levi" punctually standing there, leaning on the bar counter, already sipping on a drink. Her heart throbbed a little, pulsed a little, ached a little, skipped a tiny beat, and even she couldn't comprehend why. Maybe it was that wall of muscle glaring back at her; muscles she had never encountered before; maybe it was sheer intimidation, *certainly not admiring him,* she convinced herself; planted beside the rail, foolishly benumbed. She tore her gaze away from his sharply v-shaped back, with suspenders wedged between those "intimidating" protruding muscles of his shoulders, and proceeded to walk further down the stairs.

"Hey!" she greeted him in almost an insecure whisper, tapping his shoulder, as she did, then leaned on the bar beside him, her arm almost slipping off; it felt stiff, somehow. She felt stiff, awkward, guilty.

"Well, hello again, miss!" He turned around, met her gaze with a greeting, gave a friendly handshake, smothering her entire dainty hand.

She swallowed hard, his green eyes popped against his black shirtfront, and it wasn't the only thing that popped. Somehow she had failed to notice the firm wide chest with the dark cloth taut across it, somehow unable to notice through the army of potatoes that morning, and the night before she was too drunk and wasted anyway. Her mind rambled, and thankfully he spoke again to slash through her inexperienced lecherous thoughts.

"I needed a drink first, to calm the nerves — hope you don't mind!" he said, gulping the last bit down.

"Why are *you* nervous?" She raised her brow in confusion, expecting her to be the only nervous one.

"How not to be?" He snorted, his eyes falling atop her unapologetically. "Look at you!" He winked at her, stood up, and led her to an already reserved table, as his confidence pushed everyone aside.

"Well...thank you." She blinked, eyes struggling not to ogle that back, bewildered with herself, for any man had a back, and she had seen many "men" with a "back", just not...this one; she glared, her lip parting off the other — besotted. "You're too kind." She cleared her throat, and sat down on the side opposite to him, still baffled by the random compliment.

The server came to take their orders; flipped his busy notebook out of his pocket, pressed his pen against the page, ready to write everything down.

"Sir, I'm thinking of having some...potatoes for dinner. Just plain potatoes." he said in sheer earnestness and Charlotte's face fell; then he leaned over the table and locked eyes with her, freezing her into place. "What you say? I know *you* like potatoes..." He chuckled, not able to keep a straight face, noticing her cheeks flash scarlet in an instant.

"Are you starting again?" she nagged playfully, unapologetically ordering the prime rib, suppressing her laughter.

335

IV

"YOU'VE SLEPT FOR QUITE A WHILE…are you alright?" Elizabeth questioned Will as she was seated beside him in bed, waiting for him to wake up, her hand clasping his leg.

"Goodness!" he exclaimed, startled. "Yes…I, I'm feeling better. Would you like to meet me outside?" he said, subtly ordered, not wishing to be so close to her, feeling as though his privacy had been invaded.

"Of course, my love." Her head bowed, then her gaze lifted back to face him. "Around the campfire? Like the old times?" A smile scarred her lips, hand now caressing his leg lovingly.

"Campfire? Is it that late already?" He sat up, rubbed his sleepy eyes, forced them back open only to briefly take in her aura; still enchanting, still engulfed by a ginger veil of beauty.

"I'll be outside, making the fire." she hummed softly, letting her hand slide off his leg temptingly, as she knew it would get his attention like it always did. Will stared at her as she walked out of the bedroom in slow, seductive movements, in case he would notice — which he did. Her ginger curls bounced on her back, hips wiggled with every gentle stride. Turning around the corner, she halted at the door frame, her head turned to face him once more; her eyes in heavy shadow and yet she let her gaze trail off all over him… all down on him, as though she longed more than just his company.

He tore his gaze away, swallowing down a sudden lump. It was still his wife, and he was still married, and there still was something deep within him, feasting at his heart.

As the sun sunk behind the forestry of Kitunaha, he met her at the campfire outside their home. She was seated before a burning pile of logs, holding his favorite bottle of whiskey and two glasses with a beautiful crystal decanter that brilliantly reflected prisms of the fire's light — both in the style of the classic bulbous snifter, intended to enhance the bouquet of the whiskey inside. And yet, beneath all that sparkle, it was still only the same glass, bound to shatter. As did they.

As much as Elizabeth wished for the fancy life of an aristocrat which she now led, Will, on the other hand, loathed it — as with fame and wealth, came consequences regular people never had to worry about — as simple as never knowing who was a friend, and who a fiend. Oftentimes he wondered if Elizabeth married him for that same corrupted reason, and later on learned to love him — or did she? *Did she ever love him...*

"Here, to celebrate your return!" she exclaimed ecstatically, knowing he enjoyed a good whiskey.

"Dear, you're aware I do not wish to drink around this place anymore." He pushed the glass away, apprehensive for any long-drowned emotions to arise, yet still felt frivolous in doing so.

"Just tonight. For us. Just one glass, William." She poured him a drink, and pressed the glass against his hand.

His mustache twitched in thought; he had sworn to never drink on that property again, as if the ominous aura to his right challenged him to do otherwise. As though he could feel his presence still lurking behind the brush, the windows, the building. His eyes cut at it; it looked still the same, grimy and smoke-stained, only this time it held shadows of memories. He accepted the drink, and took a sip to swallow them down, and her voice slashed through the cloud of past again.

"Sit by me, please." she begged him, crossed her legs elegantly before his eyes, pulling his gaze into her.

The fire was burning wildly before them; warming up their boots and expressionless faces. The owls hooted loudly, hidden in thick branches of trees around them. Corvids seated atop the shingled roof, taking in their movements closely, as the shining of their rings enticed their thieving hunger. The horses' grazing hit their ears softly — rhythmically munching on the grass, plucking it from the ground, breaking it into a million pieces — and repeating that process for as long as the night allowed. Coyotes howled a caterwaul from a distance, celebrating their kill as they pranced around it energetically, expressing their joy in unison.

Will sighed, he missed all those sounds around him; he loved his ranch and enjoyed the quiet countryside they chose to build a life within. It felt like home again, and in this feeble moment of serenity, she felt like home too, he cowardly thought. He stole a glance of her, still nursing on her first glass of whiskey uncomfortably — for she rarely drank. Her finger still carrying his ring faithfully; the necklace he gifted her, hanging around her dainty neck.

She looked back at him, smiled, and caressed his dour face.

"You…you still wear it." He cleared his throat, eyes setting on the ring.

"How could I not…" she said, stretching her elegant hand out before the fire, the flames shone through her palm, and the diamond on the ring sparkled with the reflections of all the many colors it possessed. "You are my husband, William…my beloved husband." she said in earnest, and turned to face him. There were tears standing in his doe eyes, throat choking tighter the more he rehearsed her words. "And I am your wife…and I long to be your wife, until the ground buries me whole…" she said, and he stared at her again, tormented.

"You are to understand, Elizabeth, that I came here with the determined resolution of…"

"Yes…I understand it, but…I think we ought to give ourselves some time, before proceeding into such…irreversible…"

"I will not be dissuaded from it, dearest…" he interjected in turn, and her head bowed in defeat.

The wind brushed against them; it was numbingly quiet, maddening. Her brows snapped together, and determined, she turned to face him again, clasping his leg with a firm grip.

"I missed you so much, William…" she whispered with heart, meaning every word of it. "I feel grieved and anxious at your unusual neglect…" She sighed, darting her eyes on his lips. Her chest rose, a leaden breath escaped her cracked open mouth.

"I have never been selfish or unmanly to wish to deprive any lady on whom I had so firmly fixed my affections upon…Elizabeth, but my peace of mind and serenity would be lost forever, had I not left…" he said sternly, eyes lowering to her mouth in turn.

"I wish it were in my power to clothe the feelings I held for you during your absence, William!" she cried, squeezing his leg. "The entirety of my hopes of happiness are centered upon you, William…and I may truly add that without you no place can be a home to me, and this place, suddenly feels like home again, and therefore, I implore you to consult your own heart, for you have known me a sufficient time to be a judge of my character, and what happened…did not merit me any compliments, that I am fully aware of, and I do not expect to hear any, however, I beg of you to understand, that I have no inclination to share my affections with half a dozen others, for nothing less than a whole heart will satisfy me, and I beg of you to reconsider…for hearts should not be exchanged in the dark." She leaned closer to his lips, her hand now cupping his jaw. "You had and still have my entire and undivided affection, and I looked forward to your return with the most pleasurable emotions…don't…let it die. Don't let *us* die…"

He couldn't let a word out. His voice suddenly was lost somewhere deep inside him, muffled deep inside the memories they had created and shared over the past years, deep inside the timber walls; built upon a structure of lust and love, once so pure and strong, almost unbreakable. But it bent, and it broke beyond repair, and yet a fine thread was still holding them together.

She breathed him in, gasping before his mouth, craving him, weighing his soul. Her elite beauty, unmatched, so elegantly torturous, drawn by an artist that wished to imprint the epitome of beauty atop his canvas. She fleetingly brushed her scarlet lips against his, luring them unto hers. A frown of conflict wrinkled his brows, and dithering for a fleeting moment, he pulled back; leaving her breath to dance between them in the chilled air.

Her eyes pried open, they flooded. She drowned within them.

"I fear I can't…Elizabeth…" He yanked his face away, tears coursing down his cheeks, recalling the way she broke her promise to him; in the back of the barn — in the middle of the night — right before he set it ablaze.

V

HE RODE THROUGH THE FOG-CLOAKED SWAMPS, slashing through them like a shadow on a midnight steed — stepping over massive snapping turtles that moved in slyness through the damp layer of simmering smog, maneuvering through alligators that growled at his horse as it passed them — throwing a kick at their faces if they ever got too close. Reaching Mon Louis, the town's sudden light illuminated the shape of his shadow, as if suddenly formed by blood, sinews and bones; shaping a man of muscle and fearless pulse.

Leaping off his horse, he tethered it underneath a tree, hidden expertly in between tall bushes. Crouched, he slowly snuck through the darkest alleyways the city could offer, infested with rabid rats that ran through his feet as he carefully stepped over them; they squeaked and nibbled on his boots, as he skidded to a halt. Face masked, eyes merging with the darkness, he watched them; guards marching across the street, the sheriff sneaking away from his office, scanning around himself frantically as though he dealt with his own worry to be seen.

They moved around the corner, and he shot through another domed hole of rat filth, leaped atop the brick wall, and rebounded from it to the other within the narrow alleyway, fastening a grip on a shaky stairway ten feet above ground, barely attached to the desolated building. Pulling himself up, he climbed it, and paused when he reached its crooked roof.

Now he ran, leaping from roof to roof, surpassing all the guards underneath him who were marching absently around the streets. Spotting the closed gunsmith shop with the lit-up sign lettering above it, he halted again at the lip of the building's edge. Calculating his following moves as his ocean blues studied the people as they passed. He lit up a cigarette in contentment; still he had plenty of those — and waited for the streets to darken and desert.

Resting his head against the smokestack, he glanced at the horizon, taking in all the sparkling night lights of the town; somehow it made him feel peaceful in his ordinary loneliness; a sense of rare serenity clutching his heart — and yet even that sentiment couldn't last longer than a fleeting moment, slipping off the arteries of his being, for he realized he would never be a part of it; only from afar, only as long as he hid in darkness.

VI

THEY LAUGHED ENDLESSLY AS THEY ENJOYED THEIR DINNER TOGETHER, all the while the aristocrats gaped at them in utter disgust and contempt for disturbing their peaceful, quiet evening; menacing eyes meant to sting, and yet they provoked further more laughter.

"Levi…they're looking over at us again…" she said in embarrassment, and yet she couldn't suppress the urge to laugh, for somehow she hadn't dissolved into such laughter ever since she left her hometown.

"Well…let them look at us…" He shrugged with the widest smirk on his lips, enforcing one upon hers as well.

"We really can't be laughing like this here…they need to enjoy their dinner too." she leaned over the table as she whispered, side-eyeing the crowd.

"So? It isn't our fault they're so dry and dull, is it now?" he whispered back, still grinning from ear to ear.

"I mean…if you put it that way…but, I do think it's getting a little late for me…" she said, drumming her fingers on the table, not wishing to admit how much she enjoyed his company —so freeing, raw and honest. "I still need to check on Finn!" She gasped, eyes flared in shock for she forgot. "Oh my goodness…he will be livid!" she said and he snorted.

"Never feed a horse at the same time of the day…it's alright if he waits a bit longer, teaches him patience and manners." he said in earnest and she blinked, appalled, and yet deep down she knew he was right. "Besides, he won't starve for…let's say, an hour longer?" He winked at her and a knot sat in her throat.

"Well…" She cleared her throat and he cocked his head, staring into her eyes with all his being. "Finn isn't just a horse to me…but…anyway, I need to go, Levi…" she said, stood up in great haste, bumped her hip into the table as she did, grunted and tripped on her way to the door, as he followed after her, suppressing a chortle.

"Charlotte…" he said, and she skidded to a halt before the door, turning around to face him, briefly setting her eyes on that powerful chest that towered now over her.

"Y-yes?"

"May I be your guard again?" he asked and her eyes widened. "I'm headed that way anyway." he added; standing before her, hiding most of the saloon with his large frame.

"Uhm…sure. Why not?" she agreed sheepishly, not really having time to think about it, or rather the confidence to decline it.

Antoine stood behind the counter, eyes glued upon the windowpane, arms folded and ears sliding against glass; watching Charlotte and Levi head out together; although nothing alarming was said between them during dinner, he had his guard up — suspicious of the way they sometimes glanced at each other. Being a loyal friend of Will for many years, he was protective of him — and he didn't wish him to go through any betrayal again.

They walked down the street quietly, striding side by side. A smile cracked on their lips, and yet both mouths were sealed in sudden shyness. Her fingers fiddled nervously with her new skirt's burgundy ribbons, tangling them up, accidentally cutting her blood supply with them as she did.

"You're fun." He broke the silence, finger poking her in the back teasingly.

Charlotte, startled, yanked her hand from the tangled mess, almost pulling the whole ribbon out with it, then looked at him with a playful nag, suppressing a screech of harrow as her finger throbbed the blood back into it.

"Don't cut your eyes at me, girl…" he nagged back, and stepped before her, his tall frame towering over her again, and yet this time it felt a lot more personal, forced and yet inviting, exciting and yet terrifying — she couldn't tell, she couldn't understand the sudden flush of lustful feelings, for what she felt for Will was nothing like it, and what she felt for Mac…appeared a lot deeper, and what she felt for Levi was a fiery spark of a fleeting moment, ignited by his laughter, and the cheerful way he made her feel.

She froze in place — his cologne circled around her, suffocating her sweetly. She felt his eyes crawl all over her, and her breathing grew leaden. "We…we should be close to the stables by now, I think…" she stuttered nervously, not able to think straight, not able to pull her gaze away, for he was torturously handsome.

"We're right here, Charlotte." he whispered with a smirk, as they had indeed paused right before the stables.

"Oh…" She chuckled awkwardly, feeling like a fool. "Well…great…I… I think that Finn is probably waiting, and…" She swallowed hard, almost sweated beneath the fluffy layer of skirt, for heat rose between her legs, unbearable heat; they almost quivered. "Levi…thank you for the delicious dinner." She managed to say, to her surprise without a stutter. "I had a wonderful time again! And…and you're fun too…" she said, standing close to him, getting lost in his bright green eyes.

"My pleasure, cowgirl." He leaned closer to her face, as if he were ready to feel the luscious lips he'd been staring at for the whole evening, so boldly unbothered by the etiquette of the elite, or any etiquette for that matter. "But I have to say...I can get a lot more fun." he whispered and her skin stood erect, her mouth gasped for a lungful of sense to drill into her mind, for she had never encountered anything so enticingly confident before, completely wiping what little confidence she possessed.

"I...I need to let you know of something, Levi." she said swiftly, as she felt a familiar tension between them that she didn't want to accept.

"What's that?" he asked her with a whisper, leaning closer — taking in her scent, breathing against her neck, choking her with his shadow that washed over her face. She plopped a hand on his hard chest, feeling the buttons of his shirt poke her underneath her palm.

"I have...someone special in my life...I don't wish to hurt him." she confessed to him, tilting her head away from his face. He lingered there for a moment, speechless, nodded, and pulled back.

"I understand, Charlotte..." he said, plastering an insincere smile, taking a step back respectfully, looking over at the stables to compose himself.

"Thank you..." She swallowed dryly, barely finding a voice to speak. "And I'm sorry...I hope we can still remain friends..." she said with a knot in her chest, for she genuinely enjoyed his refreshingly different company; swelling her lungs with laughter with every silly joke, lifting her spirits up when she would spiral into the void of loneliness and woe.

"'Course! I didn't mean anything more than that." He breathed in the lie awkwardly, fearing he had rushed things, wondering about her experience after all, for she dressed and looked the part.

"Oh!" she exclaimed, nodded, snorted, and nodded once more. "Good then. Perhaps, I misunderstood." She slid the toe of her boot across the pavement. "I think Finn is calling me for more of those carrots..." She giggled, after she heard Finn neigh in the background, grateful that he did this time.

"Don't starve that pony! He waited long enough unnecessarily!" He chuckled and yet it sounded bitter. "Have a good night, miss." He flicked his hat to her, and rushed to leave the area, slightly embarrassed. "Oh I...I almost forgot!" He turned back to say, not wanting to leave things awkward between them. "If you ever feel bored with all the dull and perfect people around here, you're welcome to come meet me at my camp base, just outside of Mon Louis."

he said and she blinked at him, ready to take a mental note of the directions. "There's a good stew with *plenty* of potatoes, cooking every morning." He winked, chuckling again.

"That sounds wonderful! Thank you! I will!" she answered excitedly, feeling she didn't lose this friendship after all.

Grateful and relieved to have instilled some healthy boundaries between them, she couldn't help but wonder why was she so close to betraying Will again; why was she allured by Levi's very being, as if Will wasn't enough for her, as if he hadn't captured her whole heart in every fiber. For a lover wasn't meant to be like that; he was meant to be devoted to one partner, blind to all the rest, and yet she wasn't blind to Levi's humongous structure, enchanting green eyes, and confident aura. Then she wondered if Will was blind to Elizabeth, and her heart sunk with worry again. Why was she capable of turning into the woman that stranger wrote about on that journal back in Hope, and why did she feel utterly and solely devoted to a man that had abandoned her in the cloud and the rain.

CHAPTER 32

Cost of Mercy

I

HE JUMPED ATOP THE GUNSMITH'S SLIPPERY ROOF, sliding down skillfully to a square balcony sticking out from the second floor of the building. Leveraging the window open with his knife, he slipped right in through the gunsmith's upper floor. He rushed down the stairs, not expecting anyone to still be here, yet he remained alert and cautious. Grabbing several boxes of ammunition, as much as his satchel would hold, examining the scopes behind the counter as his had long been damaged, and eyeing the sticks of dynamite atop the shelf, he halted, froze still, as a sudden sound hit his ears. Stairs creaked and squeaked from heavy footsteps, nearing closer and closer. He counted them with every breath he held in, and realized it was more than a single pair. Searching for a dark corner immediately, he hid in the shadows of the shop — waiting with his freshly sharpened knife ready between his fingers — his free hand held steady over his cocked gun. A couple of thieves had spotted the broken-in window, and rushed inside the building to steal whatever valuables they could find to sell.

"Ya sure nobody ain't here?" one thief asked the other, speaking loudly as if there was no question they were alone.

"Do ya see anyone — no, don't ya? So let's hurry now, ya milksop." he scowled agitatedly, holding out a lantern, lighting up his path. All five toes stuck out from his torn boot, and two on the other that was busted. He wore a slouched brown hat, with the top caved in. The other thief had a few less toes sticking out, but still bore the same attire of poverty and struggle.

His eyes followed their silhouettes on the wall as they neared the shelves; studying them, breath held within to not make a sound. He knew he could take them down if he wanted to, but he felt an odd sensation, reminiscent of pity — after all, they all were there for the same reason; to steal for survival.

He watched them carefully, as he waited for them to leave.

"Look at thaaat! That's gonna get me some fiiiine money, right there!" he exclaimed excitedly as he picked up a Parker side-by-side shotgun.

"What ya mean it's gonna get *you* some money?? We split everything evenly! Fair and square!" the other thief argued, and pulled on the shotgun.

"But I saw the window! It was my idea to go in here!" he pulled the loaded Parker back towards him, his fingers absently gliding down to the trigger.

"I don't think so, brother! Deal is a deal!" he pulled the shotgun back to him, barrel now pointing to his face.

He watched them quarrel, noticing the lantern wiggling back and forth. His face furrowed, for he feared this wouldn't end well were they to continue, and yet they stubbornly did.

"Give it back, Johnny!" he yelled at him.

"No, ya give it back!" he yelled back.

POW!!

The thief pulled stronger on the gun, resulting in his fingers pulling on the trigger itself as hard as they could — blasting off the head of his brother, exploding like a melon, painting the walls a blood-curdling red. He dropped the gun, aghast, as he realized he had just murdered him — his own flesh and blood, over a simple weapon, now planted on the ground, as his face was spread across the wall in every direction he could look.

Their lantern, thrown in the air — the burning oil, spilled all over them. There was darkness, then it sparked as the flame caught fuel in the open air. Light, heat, then he felt, then his heart sunk; his eyes dropped down as heat started to feast on his flesh, crawl slowly and torturously hot along his limbs — a burst of flames, burning the dead body of his brother, and he was now engulfed by fire himself, screaming in agonizing pain, smothered by the most crippling slow death a sinner could hope to receive.

He rushed to unlock the door, but there were no hands he could feel, no fingers he could use, all burnt to the bone. He stood there, legs in flames, smoking and digging deeper through layers of flesh. His face was falling, hanging lopsidedly from tendons still attached to the bones of his skull. He stood there, only able to feel his skin melt off his flesh; his eyelids liquefy into nothing — his eyes soon blinded, plunging from their sockets. His whole face now dissolved; and his excruciatingly painful voice was the last thing left of him.

A sudden bullet put an end to his misery — that one bullet saved in the chamber. The whole neighborhood had heard the horrifying screams of the man along with two gunshots and ran to break into the door, slamming planks of wood against the glass, others calling out for the law.

Rushing up the stairs as the fire was now chasing after him, burning everything in its way with its ferocious force, he found the large window before him was jammed. He took his rifle and hit it against the old, heavy glass — breaking it into large, sharp pieces; one piece from the top landing like a guillotine on his arm, piercing right through it. He groaned, aggravated, and squeezed himself through the broken window as the remaining shards scraped his duster coat like giant stalactites ready to drop on him.

Sprinting as fast as he could along the rooftops, passing balcony after balcony; he held his arm tight, yet blood gushed out of him like a fountain, filling the gaps between the shingles with red liquid. He spotted an empty building right across the edge of the roof, glancing behind himself to make sure he wasn't being followed, picked up his pace, and jumped inside it, landing on his feet. He slammed himself against the wall, slowly easing downwards it, now laying on the ground, hand still clasping his arm. Relieved to be safe for a moment, he glimpsed down to his wound only to witness himself losing far too much blood by the second.

II

SHE CLASPED THE POCKET WATCH WITHIN HER HAND, brushing around its rounded corners ever so softly with her finger. She gently flipped it open, listened in odd contentment at the ticking sound it made — reminiscing the way it steadily ticked in *his* hands. She realized he had left it there for her, and yet she wondered why he would…

She wondered about him…often.

She thought of him, often.

Yet she always forced herself to drown his memory, deep within her feeble hopes of starting a life together with Will. For perhaps that was all she needed after all; a man to forget the other. Her mother never appeared to have any strong bonds with any man, nor any issues to forget them — certainly not, if they failed to pay her enough. So, she thought she simply needed more time with Will, and Mac's presence in her mind would naturally vanish.

Being around Levi was selfishly helpful as well; for she needed the comfort of having a friend here that wasn't covered in smothering powder, and was actually genuine and not in the least way judgemental towards her. She never had such a friend, *besides Finn;* her face furrowed sadly, thinking. She cared about him, albeit she barely knew him; not in a romantic sense, however, for if he had decided to never see her again, sadness would not linger for long.

There would be no nail in her heart that suddenly would puncture through it in the way it did when Mac left her — as much, she could differentiate by now. Love, if that was what she had felt, was nothing like she imagined all those years. It hurt. It punctured. The nail rusted within her with his name engraved upon it.

Levi was dangerously attractive; she couldn't deny that she studied his tall, muscular build that night, his adorable slender nose, or his dimples that intensified every time he laughed — and he did that a lot. She couldn't help but stare into his soulful green eyes every time he spoke to her — forgetting her own words, utterly hypnotized by them. She felt an innocent curiosity to seek what laid beneath his cloth, as innocent as someone could call that line of thinking. Somehow Will had never ignited that curiosity, and Mac; he never appeared to care all that much — *for he almost choked her instead,* she thought, and rolled her eyes. "Oh, Mac…" She sighed to herself, allowing herself a brief flash of his memory.

But besides all her odd curiosity feeding into her vast inexperience and stirred up lustful emotions she didn't know how to handle, Levi was just that — a friend to her. A friend she desperately needed in this town. Picking up a mighty pen of her own in all her determination, she couldn't wait to write Will about him, the ridiculous incident with the potatoes and the farmer, how Victoria set her up in that bloody bar — *or should she even give her the recognition she didn't deserve?* So she thought to herself, taking out a piece of paper to write a couple lines.

It was exciting for her; she had never written a letter before — and certainly not towards a lover. She was aware her writing skills, let alone the hideous appeal of her handwriting, could never compare to Will's, however she eased her worries into the belief it might make him happy for her to at least try. Plopping in bed, chest and stomach pressed down upon the covers, with a book before her hazels — buried beneath the loudly empty paper, she wiggled her bare feet in the air, pen kept in her mouth, thinking hard of how to even start.

Dear Will…

The ink dropped.

III

"GOOD MORNING, DEAR." WILL GREETED ELIZABETH, who was reading the morning's newspaper on the porch, back straightly pressed against the chair, head slightly inclined, legs kept together.

"Good morning, William." she hummed, focused, as she flicked through the pages.

"I brought you some coffee…" he said sheepishly, handing her a cup, noticing a frown emerge on her face.

"William…" Her head cocked harshly towards him. "You very well know I don't drink coffee…or have you forgotten?" she asked him with subtle sarcasm, confused.

Will, shocked with that fact, retrieved his hand and the simmering cup, realizing he had mistaken her habits. "No…no, I haven't." He cleared his throat, tearing his gaze away. "Tea, correct?"

"Yes…I've already had, though. Thank you." she muttered skeptically, feeling him tense up with guilt.

"So…is there anything worthy of my attention? Not much happening in Bisonhorn, so I don't know why they keep on writing the papers…" he complained, awfully missing the busy life in Mon Louis.

"Well, not in Bisonhorn thank heavens. The…gentleman of a marshal down in Cougar's Tooth apparently captured few of the Los Muertos degenerates…it says he lost his eye for it." Her face scrunched up in repulsion and Will blinked at her with a cocked brow.

"Marshal Tilghman is not to be confused with a *gentleman,* my dear…" he said, as if her admiration stung a bit.

Elizabeth cut an eye at him. "How dare you to insult the only marshal around, that has ridden the West of so much corruption…"

"My intention is not to insult his character as a marshal, my dear Elizabeth, however, I was simply very much displeased with the rumors of his own personal shenanigans…" he said sternly and she swallowed down a knot.

"Rumors…can be an envious man's wicked imagination…" she defended.

"Certainly, until said 'envious man' turns reveals itself to be in the shape of his very own wife…previous wife, as I stand corrected…" he said, and she looked at him, bewildered.

"Are you speaking of Mrs. Jane Tilghman right now?"

"Certainly…"

"And just where and when would you have found her to converse with her, especially regarding such a personal matter, William?" Her brow cinched, and his lips folded in return.

"The ballroom…at the Caddo River Boat." he finally said, averting his eyes back to his cup.

"Oh…you attended?"

"I was invited…"

"In my absence…" she said, and then there was silence.

"Do proceed…" He sighed and she set her eyes back on the gazette, as he leaned against the rail, sipping on the cup, drowning his secrecy in the brown liquid.

"Perhaps this would please your ears more, for there was a building that burnt down…in Mon Louis." Her eyes flared, as she read aloud the town.

"What?" The cup slipped a bit through his fingers; he clasped it just in time not to hit the ground. "What do you mean? Which building? How?" he pressured, instantly worried about Charlotte.

"The gunsmith shop." she read. "They say, they found two bodies...shot and burned to death."

"You mean to imply, an actual *murder?* A very gruesome one, at that..." Mac flashed before his eyelids, now he paced on the porch; with every anxious step, Elizabeth's heartbeat thudded along with it.

"Are you alright, William?" she voiced her concern, noticing his face in distress; fallen, distorted, taut across pallid skin.

"Read more!" he fussed, and she stared at him, aghast. "Please..." he corrected, anxious for further information.

DUE TO THIS MACABRE NATURE OF THIS MURDER, WE ARE SUSPECTING WANTED MAN MAC KINNON. CITIZENS OF MON LOUIS: BE ALERT, AND DON'T LEAVE THE HOUSE AFTER DARK UNTIL WE'VE SEARCHED EVERY SINGLE BUILDING. THE POLICE DEPARTMENT IS EXAMINING THE MATTER, AND HAVE APPOINTED THE DETECTIVE AGENCY FOR FURTHER INVESTIGATION.

She read the last paragraph to him, folding the gazette in relief to hear they're taking matters into their own hands; eyes darting back at Will. His face was blanched; the soft pallid color of his skin had drained into nothingness. Putting down his cup, he sat on a chair, fingers scratching his face, pulling on his chin nervously.

"William? What is wrong?" she asked him, realizing there was something more than just empathetic concern regarding the lost building and lost lives.

"I will need to write a letter..." he muttered faintly, barely a sound to issue, his gaze trailing off.

"To whom?" she asked, for his eyes glazed with worry, dozing off into a void of ominous thoughts.

"I cannot declare to you, at this moment and time..." he said shortly.

"What is going on, William?!" She raised her voice, disapproving of his sudden secrecy.

"I cannot explain this to you now, Charlotte!"

There was a moment of silent astonishment in the air between them, perhaps a wave of shame, merging with a scent of guilt, twirling around them with a gale of nails, hooked into each other's necks. Buffeting their breaths. Will's eyes were set upon hers, as hers gaped into his. The air deepened the longer silence prevailed, and throats tightened in a smog of resentment.

"I…understand." she said, throwing him a dejected look, breaking the quietness. "I suppose I need to let the horses out…" she added, squeezed her grip, turned her back to him, now gazed over at the barn, unable to even see one through the fog in her brain, the mist in her eyes.

His lips folded in distress; his whole being shook and shattered within. Raising a hand, balling a fist, he slammed the wooden post next to him to release the rage that surged through him — something quite unusual of him to do. The guilt had consumed every sinew of his being; he loathed to hurt Elizabeth in this way, and he loathed to imagine that Charlotte might hurt him too. He loathed to think of Mac being anywhere close to her, now knowing he was in Mon Louis. His hand ached; the soft pine dented. Eyes once gentle and kind, now adopting a deep, dark leer; he was envious for he remembered the way Charlotte held Mac that night; tight arms wrapped around his waist, shamelessly breaking any barrier of etiquette, let alone respect and honor between them.

He had sworn to his proud self to never let another woman betray him the way Elizabeth did; yet here he stood, numbed, with rage emanating from his pores, bending like a feeble branch, bound to be cracked by a woman's tender heel.

CHAPTER 33

The Others

I

IT WAS A WINDY MORNING DOWN IN MON LOUIS; cloudy, gloomy, with a chilled breath of upcoming winter. The streets and balconies were decorated with a row of glimmering lights, and the air felt festive enough to plant a smile on the grimmest of faces.

"Whoa, boy! Whoa there!" She held the reins tight, collecting this massive chestnut stallion beneath her thighs, as softly and yet as sternly as she could. He snorted in response and lifted his head up high, flicking his ears in all directions, eyes focused anywhere but straight ahead, ears deaf to her cues. With a flamboyant attitude, he pranced proudly — showing off to the riding mares that passed by them — who were clearly distracted by him, some even tilting their hinds towards him, squealing a lullaby of lust.

"Oh my goodness, Finn…seriously?" She rolled her eyes, apologizing to the riders right after. "Is that what it is all about? You're…horny?" she whispered, then chortled, and he nickered and neighed, feeling the wind pick up his mane and blow against his face, flooding up his nostrils with all the exotic smells swirling around him.

"You're feeling good, aren't you, sweetheart?" She smiled, giving him a loving pat on his hind. "But you better remind yourself…mares cannot give you fresh carrots, so you better not dump me now…" She snorted, and they trotted beneath the line of flickering lights, eavesdropping upon a group of townsfolk — appearing elite enough; they were fussing before an art gallery.

"*It is every way horrible! A disgrace to society!*" "*Who would even surmise they have the right to paint such…atrocity! What is he even trying to represent, aside from a filthy…character, one no real lady should possess!" "It is of such terror! I find the brushwork…baffling to portray such…macabre detail! I cannot find words to express…certainly not in mixed company."* They continued to fuss, and Charlotte, unable to perceive the art hidden by their feathery hats and fluffy bustles, proceeded to ride around the city.

An army of law suddenly emerged before her gaze, blocking her path, surrounding townsfolk, and examining building after building. "Oh no…I hope they're not after us, Finn…" she soughed; what a strange feeling or thought to even have.

"Ma'am?" A policeman's voice startled Charlotte; hands jolting the reins.

"…Sir?" she hesitantly asked, eyes sweeping around herself to find a quick way out if needed, then glanced down upon him; it wasn't a deputy, it was the actual sheriff of Mon Louis, judging by the sparkling starry badge on his coat. "Sheriff…" she corrected, choking furthermore.

"Any suspicious activity you noticed last night? There was a…horrific homicide in the gunsmith shop, and we need any information we can get." he explained, briefly glancing at Finn's muscular jaw, veins popped across it as steam escaped from his nostrils.

"Oh goodness…no, no Sheriff…" She swallowed hard. "I was in my rented room, all night at the saloon." she explained, relieved to know he wasn't about to capture her, yet her guard was still up.

"Alright, ma'am." He nodded to her, scribbling a few words on a notebook. "We advise everyone to stay home after the sun sets. There's potentially a very dangerous man in the city, but we are working on his capture." he promised, doffing his hat and bowing his head to her.

Halting her train of thought, as if a scenario flashed before her, she wondered if Mac was the potential murderer, and if so, she found herself oddly, genuinely hoping he could escape into safety once again. Her concern about him had never faded; sometimes she prayed for him to find his undisturbed rest in the shadows, albeit knowing he would loathe her for it. She could no longer judge or hate him for his atrocious acts; for he revealed a hidden side of his to her that she could never forget, one that contradicted with all the rumors enveloping his name. One that merged her heart to his.

II

"HEARD THE NEWS YET, LEVI?" ASKED AN ELDERLY BALD-HEADED MAN, dressed in a light brown duster coat.

"Sure did…" Levi muttered, concentrated, brewing some herbs together over the campfire.

"Do we need to pitch the camp?" He cocked a wiry brow to him. "You just say the word! In a couple days, we'll be back down in Mon Louis." he said, absently pulling on his rowdy grey beard as though in deep thought.

"He won't be staying down there long, JB…question is, will he be coming back here, or going further south…" he wondered, pouring the herb potion into a small bottle, sealing it tight.

"Mon Louis is a biiiig place, son…he could be hidin' anywhere!" He sighed, and sat back down, pressing a mucky harmonica against his lips, blowing the first couple notes; almost choking by the dust he inhaled. "Darnit!" He coughed and Levi cut his eyes at him with a chortle. "Can't trust any hole nowadays!" he said and they burst into laughter. "Ya know…back in the army…"

"JB…" He chuckled. "I do really appreciate you, my friend, but…I need to get going." he said and JB shrugged and blew into the harmonica some more — a cough hitting Levi's ears again, as he walked away.

Striding into his tent, he fumbled for the map, unfolded it and spread it across a table, studying it in sharp concentration. He wasn't all too familiar with the area here; however, you could blindfold him in the woods of Red Giants and Hollenberg and he would still find his way out effortlessly. As a little boy, his father wrapped a cloth around his eyes and dropped him off on the other side of the forest. Having to prove to him and the rest of the kin that he was capable of returning home, it was not a surprise to anyone that he did.

Levi grew up to be an adventurous soul; loving to be challenged in life, craving that feeling of satisfaction whenever an issue was solved by his own judgement and actions. His father taught him how to remain calm and collected in all uncomfortable situations; how to think for himself, and how to be a protector with the right morals and priorities in life. They had formed an unbreakable bond, for he meant everything to Levi — his most cherished role model; admired and respected.

One night upon a wolf's keening howl, when the woods of Red Giants had silenced, and the trees had bent and formed unusual spines upon their bark, he was found murdered — hanged by the neck within the cabin. Levi; a young man at the time, cut the rope around his father's neck, releasing his heavy body from the noose of death's arms. He gave him his word upon his burial, that he would chase down every single man who was even harboring a thought about committing such acts of barbarity. Becoming the most sought-after of all bounty hunters years later; there hadn't been a single wanted man that he was assigned that he couldn't capture or kill. His record was flawless... and in his mind, Mac Kinnon was next.

I I I

"ARGH..." HE GROANED QUIETLY, pulling the broken shards of glass out of his arm. The wound burned; felt tingly and irritatingly numb. The more he moved his arm, the sharper the pain slashed through him, and the more blood gushed out of it as the wound tore wider.

The deep cut stretched a hand's length across his forelimb with dark blood pooling underneath, covering himself with it. Soaked. The iron smell evoked memories he tried hard to ignore, for he now hung by a thin thread of self-composure, fighting more against the harrowing past that assailed him than the injury itself, and yet the scent was different; it didn't stink of malice and abuse. Albeit not fazed by the excruciating pain, he naturally started going into shock; the blood drenched the life out of him, flooding the ground he sat within; a dark cesspit of never-ending demise.

Pulling out the last fragment of the glass, carefully as to not break it off, he pressed with his fist against the wound — yet his fist was not large enough to cover the wide cut. Weakening, the room darkened around him, held in shadows of his mind, spinning, fogging up his vision. Pressing as hard as he could, he tried to wrap his bandana urgently around his arm — squeezing it tightly. His eyes hunted for his satchel, dropped few feet away, knowing his sewing supplies were within. Albeit a man devoid of any emotions, the veritable name of legend, nature's cruelty still prevailed. His eyes glazed over; set, out the broken window — faintly watching the clock slowly tick on the spire of Mon Louis's dark cathedral.

I V

"FINN!" SHE GASPED AS HE SKIDDED TO A HALT, lifting his head up high, alert, focused on some tall bushes that must have looked especially terrifying to him. He kept his nose pointed towards them as Charlotte kicked him to proceed in moving forward, yet he refused to take a step further; he stood there like a frozen statue of masculinity, and...excess padding around the belly.

"What's gotten into you, boy?" She dismounted, knowing this was no fight she could win against her proud stallion, and caressed his worried face.

Finn kept on staring at the bushes, and let out a loud neigh. Charlotte looked towards that direction, but couldn't spot anything. Mounting up again, Finn bolted before she even had a chance to grab the reins.

"Finn!! Wh-wh-what...are you do-doing?! Whoa!!! WHOA!!" she screamed from the top of her lungs, galloping unwillingly towards the bushes with every will and power he possessed. She attempted, struggled, quivered in panic to collect the split reins, yet they were flowing loosely beside them like wings of his own, only enforcing the face-whipping speed. Holding on to the cantle for dear life, Finn stopped right before the bushes, almost catapulting her into them. A wisp of air escaped her lungs, as she sat still in the saddle, panting with frizzy locks of hair sticking out of her braid. He nickered softly, as though in self-admiration.

"What in the world was in your oats this morning??" She dismounted again to compose herself, legs shaking from the unusual behavior, briefly wondering if her breeches were still dry. Finn stretched his neck through the bushes; a wave of an anxious nicker rattled his whole being.

"Alright, alright, let's check what monster hides behind those teeeeerrify-ing plants!" She rolled her eyes, moved the branches apart to examine what could possibly hide behind it — stretched her hand through them, fumbled between fall-colored lattice of leaves, when she suddenly felt something cold and fuzzy. Startled, she jolted and jerked her hand away, and yet Finn kept on nickering ever so softly. Trusting that his senses were not misleading her, she stuck two hands through the brush again. Her eyes flared as she pulled the branches apart and spotted a black horse hitched up, covered in sweat, with a deep hole excavated in the ground before him from relentless pawing.

"Roy…" She gasped, her throat tightened, her jaw dropped, and her legs slashed at the knees. She could not believe her eyes to see Mac's horse here, alone, hitched up, in Mon Louis, and in unusual distress.

"Easy, boy…it's okay! Easy…" Tears shone in her eyes, a stab in the stomach twisting every emotion her heart could spurt out. Trying to calm him down, she realized Mac must be in trouble, for he would never leave his horse unattended, in bright daylight, in a city at that. "Finn…good job, once again." She hugged him tightly, and tethered him next to Roy to keep him company. Thinking back on the Sheriff's warning, she knew the gunsmith was right around the corner of the street, and rushed to it. "He *must* have been the one…" she muttered.

Arriving, she noticed the shop was closed for further investigation. All the dark red walls, now a tint of ashy-black. Looking around, she spotted a dark alleyway, and dithering, she approached it, squeezing through it, between the gunsmith and a half-ruined building, narrowing into her, smothering her with a veil of blackness the deeper she crawled, threatening to collapse. She felt she almost did…

She noticed a ladder leading up to the roof, one high enough to tighten her chest with a knot of nervousness. Scanning around to see if anyone was watching her, she gathered up her bravery, climbed up; writhing, pausing every so often to grasp for a lungful of air, for the ladder shook with her, rattled with every step she took. Drawing in a deep breath, gnashed teeth and tightened being, she pulled her trembling body up and over the roof, instantly noticing dried-up blood drops across it, staining the weathered shingles. "Oh no…" She sighed, breath cutting in her lungs, cautiously following the bloody trail as the sun started to sink behind her.

V

HIS EYES REFLECTED IN THE MIRROR, STRAIGHT RAZOR pressed against skin, slowly trailing down, shaving off the stubble that had sprouted in the absence of care. The candle beside him lit the side of his face, a warm, supple orange hue; he rinsed cream from the blade and placed it back against his skin.

Will's body had seized a few hours prior, right at the moment he was brushing Rachel after their self-reflective ride; suddenly dropping beside her on the ground, spasming in darkness, in a void, until he awoke — ashamed to notice his bladder had released in the meantime. Accustomed to the sudden episodes by now, for they had sadly multiplied in frequency, he had learned to deal with them; adopt them as a part of his self — self-consciously embracing the fragility that now portrayed him. Shaving the last bit of stubble from his cheek, he suddenly heard a voice emerge right behind him — a brash, vitriolic manner of voice.

"Charlotte is with me, Will…"

He turned around swiftly, his shiny wet razor held out, ready to threaten the intruder. Water dripped down the blade and a shadow shrunk within it — yet, no one was there; not a man of mass, not a man of visibility, only the dark empty void filling up the timber-framed room before him. Shaking, he frantically checked the walls and corners with flared brown eyes — again, to find nothing. His heart raced, grew leaden, grew fast; drummed faster, then faster; the familiar voice felt too real — too raw, to just have vanished into thin air.

"I'm still here, Will. I'm always here…"

The sarcasm hitting his ears again — behind him, closer — coming through the mirror still lit by the flame. Eyes now set upon it, he strode carefully towards it — slowly, a thump in his chest, another, almost constricting the muscle within it. A drop of sweat fell from his forehead, hitting the sink; somehow it echoed across, bounced off the walls and intensified; it clinked, it rang within him. He hesitantly leaned close to the mirror, staring at it in denial — its glass slowly fogging up by his deep breath, another snide whisper.

"Closer, Will…"

He neared the mirror, as though hypnotized; hand quivering, holding the blade, now the shadow spreading across it, larger. Squinting through his eyelids, almost touching the glass with his freshly shaven face, he forced his eyes tighter to recognize the sudden shape that formed within it. His face furrowed, heart sunk to his stomach when his own reflection started to peel off; as if skin was paper thin, gray, flakes of ash, lifting up before him, merging into another man's face, one still cruelly engraved within his memory. Slit eyes of a serpent, shaping into deep holes of blackness and void, until the candle's flame sparked beside him and eyes turned a deep blue.

"Kill him, William."

Another voice slowly emerged, shrill and yet low, sitting with a vile pressure atop his chest, suffocating him.

"ARGH!!!"

Screaming, he hit the mirror with a fist, again and again, slamming the knife into it, until the face disappeared into the sharp, fallen shards of glass.

"William!?!?" Elizabeth rushed into the room, only to find him hunched over the broken mirror — hyperventilating, trembling from the rush of adrenaline, razor still gripped tightly within his bloodied knuckles, and yet now glimmering brightly. He turned around quickly to face her; eyes flared aghast, barely of a brown tint — staring right back at her.

"My love…?" she whispered, taking a trembling step back.

CHAPTER 34

The Devil Himself

I

HE ALWAYS CARRIED HIS REVOLVER OUT as he rode through the town of Sailorman's Wharf, knowing gunslingers and thieves were waiting for the perfect opportunity to ambush travelers — yet they knew better than to try this with him.

He glared at the outcasts with great disgust; constantly reminding him of the ones that murdered his father, albeit he never saw them, nor found them, for there was no trace left behind. He never felt an ounce of pity for them, their misery never clasped his heart, for in his mind, they *chose* this way of disruptive living and he strongly believed in everyone being capable of becoming the best they can — despite the cards they'd been dealt. He passed them, their menacing glares, and pitiful leers; there was no gaze he wished to exchange with them, appalled enough already to breathe in the same air.

His guns bounced with every stride his horse took, lassoes slapped against the hard brown leather saddle; he retrieved his gun and galloped his steed as fast as it could, with subtle spurs against its skin reminding it to not take a break. It was already pitch black outside — the sky, moonless; hiding behind thick grey clouds that formed. A sudden lashing rain poured on them, fell in torrents, beating them down — creating mud puddles along the path, trapping the horse's feet for a brief moment before releasing them again to the rocky ground.

I I

"OH, DEAR GOD…" SHE FEARFULLY SIGHED, calculating the distance to the next roof. "You can do this, Charlotte…you might be inexperienced, but…you're agile. You have to be. In fact, you have no excuse to *not be,* at your age…" she said to herself, then took a giant leap to reach the adjacent slippery roof, barely making it over in one piece. Falling to her knees, she rolled around it, clasping at the shingles with tooth and nail. "I'm…I'm alive…" She gasped, stuttered, lifted herself up, picking up her jittering body, securing it atop two limbs she barely felt.

Looking ahead, she noticed an open window and as though her survival instinct had suddenly awoken, she was almost certain that he was hiding in there. The trail of blood had vanished — washed away by the harsh rain right before her. She couldn't detect any other evidence, besides the last drop of blood she witnessed dripping down the lip of the roof. Stepping closer, calculating again her movement, considering her agility in self-doubt, she realized she would have to sling herself into the window, for there was no balcony attached to it — promising a sharp fall right below. The rain suddenly sat atop her chest, and controlling her breathing was suddenly a necessity.

Slowly letting her legs hang from the roof, with her body following right after, she clung onto it; hands slipping from the wet roof, clothes soaked, only sticking uncomfortably to her body, only weighing her even more. "Dear God, I ask for your guidance and strength…" she prayed, forced her eyes open, and slung herself successfully into the window, landing on her feet, right before a familiar man's shadow — freezing before a gun's snarled teeth.

Charlotte, stood there, aghast, seeing *him* after all this time, after fighting so hard to extinguish his memory in her mind. There she stood, petrified more with her own emotions that swelled her chest than the barrel's threat.

"Mac…please." she issued a sound, yet his senses and cognition were beyond any form of comprehension — all he knew was that he was hunted, being found was inevitable, and the gun was ready for his last defense.

CLICK

"No!!!" she screamed, frightened and panicked, ears feeling muffled; an echo of silence thudded within her. He'd pulled the trigger, forgetting he had shot the last remaining bullet to relieve the thief swallowed by the flames. There was a grunt that escaped him, and a clop of metal slamming the ground.

Charlotte, quivering, squinted through her eyelids, feeling of herself; still whole and standing. Forcing her eyes open in a state of shock, she set them upon him; the gun had dropped to his side, and Mac's eyes were slowly shutting. "No no no!!" she yelled as she rushed, petrified, to him; kneeling before him, cupping his sweaty face harshly, trying desperately to shake him awake. "Mac!" She shook him. "I need you with me now. I'm here to help you, I…" she paused, noticing his injured arm; bandana, clothes, floor, all soaked in blood. "Oh no…oh, dear God…" She choked, examining his benumbed arm, untying the wet cloth, squinting through the heavy veil of darkness or the shadows that engulfed them.

Crying, she was left speechless, seeing the deep and wide cut across his arm; blood flushing out, showering her own. She pressed swiftly with her hands against it as hard as she could — all the while making sure he wouldn't lose consciousness more than he already had, as well as trying to stay strong and unfazed by the terrifying sight. She felt his pulse pounding wildly, yet feebly, his heart desperately trying to make up for the long-lost blood volume.

"Stay awake now, okay? You have to stay awake!" she ordered him, sobbing in fear; shaking whole from adrenaline. This wasn't how she imagined meeting him again, certainly never wished to see him so vulnerable. Suddenly she prayed for the cranky mountain man, the dreadful manchild to emerge, but his sarcastic grimace had drained from his face.

"Mac, I beg of you!! Look at me…look at me, darnit…" she fussed, shaking him harder. "Look at me goddammit!!" she growled deeply, and his face suddenly flinched in response.

His eyes slowly pried open; realizing whose voice was pestering him, whose being was crouched before him. Locking eyes, again, in the dark, in the threat, in the odd serenity that emanated from her, he felt a sudden strength within him — a will to desperately prove to her that he was the usual strong and independent man she always knew; a will to protect her, despite all his vulnerability. "How…did ye…" he spoke; deep, yet weakened voice.

"Yes!" She gasped. "That's right! Talk to me, Mac. T-talk to me!" she said, holding on to him. "Finn found Roy, and then, then…then I tracked your blood across the rooftops…and…talk to me!!" she encouraged him upon an anxious stutter, grabbing her cloth between her teeth, tearing her sleeve apart, and wrapping it around his wound.

"Leave, lass…" he grunted, stealing a glimpse of her horrified face, still as beautiful as ever. "Better like that…than hanged." he growled, fighting the urge to go into a deadly shock.

"NO." she exclaimed firmly, struggling to think how to help him next.

"Yes…"

"Stop, Mac!! Stop being so darn stubborn…"

"Hm." He huffed and Charlotte, jittering in panic, scanned around herself.

"I need to get this cut closed somehow. I need to call a doctor, but how to leave you here…" she cried to him, finding herself with a great dilemma she had never encountered before.

"No!" he growled, straightening his back in annoyance, only for shoulders to slump back down. "They…they will…" His eyes clutched, his head tilted to his shoulder.

"Mac! Talk to me! Please, talk to me!" She shook him awake again, trying to remain composed, as she waited for his blood to finally clot. His eyes forced back open, locking hers again, moonlit through the window. "Good…now you stay with me, you hear?" she fussed, brows snapping together as though upset with his unintentional disobedience.

"Hm." He smirked caustically, and his mouth cracked open. "Where, where's…the fine lad?" he curiously asked, remembering the way their bodies entwined on that Caddo River Boat, as if that was the most important issue he was dealing with. Charlotte blinked, then tore her gaze away.

"He…he…he is not here, right now." she stuttered, feeling a sense of guilt once again consume her.

"Hm."

"But I'm here, and we will get through this together. I just need to find something to stitch this up with!" she anxiously said, scanning around the empty building.

"Me satchel…" he muttered, jerking his jaw to its direction, pulling her eyes with it as well.

"Okay! Okay! Got it." She drew in a rapid breath, and he kept staring at her in faint denial. "You stay calm, and keep your hand pressed on it, alright? Can you do this for me, Mac?" She grabbed his other hand gently, placed it on the cloth, and stood up to clasp the satchel.

She looked through it; hands sorting through ammo boxes, dehydrated meats, when suddenly her fingers got poked by a sharp hook needle used for stitching leather — right beside it, a suture thread wrapped in a buckskin hide, unfortunately not sterile enough for a wound.

Charlotte sighed, disappointed, not wishing to cause an infection on his arm, yet she had no other choice. "Alright…" She turned around and walked to him. "I found something…well, you probably know already, since it came from your satchel…" She rambled in awkwardness, almost shyness. "Let me see the wound again." she said, kneeling back down before him, swallowing hard to be so close to him again. "Because…it should…it should have clotted by now." She sucked in a stutter, unwrapping the cloth.

Mac kept quiet; watching every move of hers as much as he could. He felt her warmth radiate again within him, making his unbearable loneliness fade away in the only way she could. It felt strange to see someone take care of him for the very first time — unusual, unimaginable, almost like he didn't deserve it.

"Yes!" she exclaimed, startling him. "We did it, Mac! The bleeding has stopped!" she yelled excitedly, and cupped his jaw in gleefulness. He flinched, jerked by the sudden intimate touch, and she swiftly retrieved her hands, lowering her gaze in shame.

"Hm…" He hummed, attempting to make a sound as though to pull her hands back on his face, as though begging to feel such tenderness again.

"Okay…I will start now with the needle, and the…thread…" she said and as she approached his arm, he tensed, and a growl escaped through clenched teeth. She halted, and her head came up to look at him with a question. He breathed heavily; it wasn't the needle, nor was it her, it was the threatening act of it. "Please…let me…" she said, as if she understood. His face furrowed, her hand reach out daringly, softly brushed against his shoulder. They slumped, wilted beneath her touch. He nodded, and she smiled in his eyes.

"This might hurt, however, so take a deep breath for me…" she said kindly, slowly piercing the threaded needle through his thick skin and flesh, cutting her eyes back at him every so often to capture his reaction.

"Ye ain't…gonna hurt me." he mumbled, finally easing himself to her care. Trusting in her.

Pulling the needle all the way through, while tightening the thread each time, Mac stared at her focused face, a troubled frown wrinkling it. Utterly freezing his gaze upon her pure beauty, the dark strands of hair swinging down past her cheekbones, resting subtly beside her elegant nose — his breath got tight in his throat. Infatuated with her; every time he studied any complex expression she made, his heart burst with an immense emotion he'd never felt in his life. She made his heart beat again, not for the sole purpose to keep him alive, but rather a much deeper one than that.

"Just a few more pokes, and you will be fine, Mac." She looked up to comfort him, finding him staring right back at her. She blushed; crimsoned cheeks the color of the blood that stained the thread. Mac never had to say much to her; his eyes spoke for him instead.

Deep. Blue. Soulful.

His intense gaze always sucked out all the words and thoughts from her mind, she thought to herself and shook her head with a smirk. His brow cocked, noticing that too. Her hands still trembled; she had never sewed something before, let alone a human arm — yet she did it, and Mac was still alive. She briefly hoped her mother could see her from above, realizing she was so much more than what she implied her to be, then she realized, she was probably staring up from below her.

"I think…we are all set!" she proudly announced. Sighing in relief to have it over with, she tucked the needle and thread back into the satchel and faced him cautiously.

Mac glanced at his stitched-up arm, quite impressed by her suturing skills in the middle of the night with no light source around, his cocked brow that persisted told as much. "Good…job…" he hummed with a frail voice, the sound of the gloomy deluge outside overpowering it.

"Thank you…" She smiled, bowing her head again, forgetting what she was about to do next. "Oh! Here, eat this jerky — I think it will help you." she said. "You lost a lot of blood, and I don't know how you made it, to be frank." she said, and poked the meat in his mouth, accidentally sliding her fingers in there too. They both went quiet, for the slightest inappropriate touch created such an intense tension between them. Looking at his face as he was still chewing on the stringy meat, she noticed his dark blond hair had gotten longer; it was busy, messy, yet perfectly suiting his striking face with some straight locks of hair falling over the side of it, framing his masculine jaw. She couldn't take her eyes off of him — he couldn't stop staring at her, either. There it was; the feeling of the nail twisting within her heart, and yet somehow it didn't hurt this time, somehow she begged for it to stay there.

"I...we..." She bit her lip, trying to rephrase. "So, we meet again..."

She chuckled awkwardly, lowered her gaze, embarrassed.

"Hm." he smirked lopsidedly, and kept chewing on the meat.

"You've...you've changed..." She smiled, not realizing how much more handsome this man could get, and yet this was never the core of her attraction to him; for it wasn't just attraction.

"So have ya..." he grumbled, recalling her in that fancy dress, surrounded by elites; surrounded by Will.

She went quiet. Her smile slipped and her eyes glanced away.

"I...I will try to get some medicine tomorrow, as soon as they open in the morning..." she said, swallowing down a lump.

"I won't be here, lass." he said sternly. "If ye found me, they will too."

"But...you can't just leave like that! You need medicine, Mac!" she fussed, concerned she would lose him again to his stubbornness.

"I can. Ya know I can." he insisted, during an attempt to get up.

"No! Please." She clasped his shoulders, pulling him back down. "You need to rest now! You will kill yourself out there in the storm!" she fussed, and a sudden voice slashed through hers.

"You heard the lady." A voice, as robust as a clap of thunder, emerged behind them, in the darkness, in the storm, covered by the sound of his heavy footsteps.

Charlotte turned back to spot the silhouette of a tall man, backlit by the faint visage of a moon, as Mac reached for his knife, and pulled Charlotte towards him — protecting her with his freshly sewn arm coiled around her.

"Lady, move aside, please. This man is a worthless piece of shit, and it's about damn time he be brought to justice." the man said firmly, gun pointed at Mac's head, slowly yet confidently walking over to them. The closer he approached, the more the shadow morphed into the shape of flesh and bone.

Her eyes flared, aghast.

"Levi?" She gasped.

III

"William…I beg of you, put the knife away, my love." she said, as calmly as she could, feet kept pulling her away from him as he followed her steadily, in sheer bewilderment — eyes dwelling someplace else, in shock.

"Where, where did he go??!" he yelled at her, his hands tensing beside him.

"Who, sweetheart? There is no one around here." she said, baffled, noticing the glass shards on the ground.

Will glanced behind him, to his side, everywhere he could lay his eyes upon; his ears almost tearing apart from his skull, as though to hear more clearly. There was no voice, only a buzzing sound around him. He exhaled heavily, dropped the knife on the floor; it hit and it slid right to her feet, her own reflection smudged atop the blade. He moaned within a gasp of desperation, releasing his state of panic as he kneeled down to the floor, bursting into gut-wrenching tears, hands jittering atop his face.

Elizabeth stared at him, stunned, for she had never seen him so bewildered, for his mind could never be one to bend or derange, for it would insult his brilliancy. But, ever since he returned, he didn't appear like the same man she married. She went to him and hugged him tightly; he sobbed on her shoulders, shivered against her chest.

"I don't understand, Elizabeth! I *saw* him, I *heard* him…" he cried to her; cocooned in her arms.

"Saw who…William?" she asked, lovingly caressing his smooth face, contented to finally find herself so close to him, breathing in his sorrow, feeling his flesh beneath his cloth.

"The Devil himself." he whispered earnestly, peeking back at the broken mirror, in dark resentment.

IV

THE SLASHING RAIN DRUMMED WILDLY ON THE RATTLING ROOF; chilling the air around them. It splattered ferociously against the open window, washing off the dusty floor beneath it. Droplets of rain leaked through the gapped wooden ceiling, manifesting in a pattern right beside them. The earthy smell lingered in the dark room, and the freshness of the wind gushing through the gaps heightened their senses. The cathedral's clock clanged loudly across the city of Mon Louis, as midnight struck unforgivingly.

V

"CHARLOTTE??" HE GASPED IN RESPONSE, equally as surprised. "What…what are you doing here, and with *this* son of a bitch?" He frowned, confused, appalled by the turn of events.

Mac remained still, facing the gun that still pointed at him. He was curious enough to listen to their conversation; curious enough to find out who this obviously attractive and strong man was to her — one certainly not of his kind, yet not of Will's either.

"It's…it's complicated, Levi." She swallowed down a stutter. "Please lower the gun…there's no need for that." She begged softly, lowering Mac's arm that covered her.

Levi gaped at her concerned face, and resumed focus back to Mac's challenging stare; baffled at her words, baffled to find her in the arms of a murderer, baffled to even stand now before such a legend. He felt his eyes crawling all over him, felt his core weaken a little.

"Charlotte…he is…you know who he is, right? You *must* know!" He warned her, conflicted, still directing the gun to him.

"I do, Levi…" She huffed. "But he is not a bad man. He is, he is…misunderstood." she mumbled, and Mac cut his eyes at her, baffled himself to hear these words come out of her mouth.

"Misunderstood??" Levi snorted snidely. "He…is a *killer!* He has murdered innocent folk in every state, Charlotte! He will murder you too, when he feels like it!" He raised his tone, agitated with her defensive position towards him.

"No, I won't." Mac growled, finding the strength to get up and walk towards the gun, with Charlotte jumping up swiftly to clasp his shirt.

"Mac, please. Don't. Let me handle this, please!" She pulled on it, yet his chest now pressed against the barrel.

He stared at Levi, and Levi stared at him — intensely challenging each other, like two stallions measuring their opponent before a fight.

"You don't want me pulling that trigger, son." Levi threatened, cocking the gun.

"Nothin's stoppin' ye, or is there?" Mac argued back, scarring a sarcastic smirk on his lips.

"Your head is worth more alive than dead, or else I'd have pulled it a long time ago. Doesn't matter to me if you rot in here, son, but folk…they wanna see you swing." He leered, spitting his chewing tobacco to the side.

"Hobble yer lip, ye filthy excuse of a deputy or whatever yer supposed to be…" Mac snorted, feeling the light-headedness come and go in waves. "For ye make me blush, embarrassed, with yer threats."

"I can keep your face blushed by blasting your goddamn head, and make my apologies to the government for doing so, later…" He growled and Charlotte grunted in loud frustration.

"ALRIGHT! Enough with this nonsense now! Can we just handle things in a…in a civilized manner?? Levi! Please! Mac!" She shouted, scolded them, feeling a flicker of immense irritation.

"Put the knife down, boy." He ordered Mac, knowing he was quick with his blades; quicker than a simple man with a gun.

"Mac…please. Do it for me, if you care at all." The words spurted out of her mouth without thinking, then swiftly tore her gaze away from him and faced Levi. "You won't shoot him, right?" she asked him, feeling swallowed by his giant being, somehow intimidated by it; worried that a beast within him would unleash at any time.

"What do you expect me to do, Charlotte? Let him free, so he goes on another killing spree to satisfy his sick and twisted mind?" He leered, brows snapped together in disappointment. "And is he *really* that special someone you were talking about??" The bitter question hung from his lips for too long, annoyed by the fact she would choose Mac — a degenerate, a cold-blooded killer — over someone like him.

Mac's eyes cut at her to capture her guilty expression, yet never leaving sight of Levi's face.

"Levi, please." She left the question hanging, unanswered, and deflated her chest upon a leaden breath. "Lower the gun. He is badly injured, and needs a safe place to rest. Please." she pleaded, suddenly remembering Levi's secluded campground.

"Oh, that son of a bitch isn't nowhere safe." He snorted, not giving up his catch so easily. "They're *all* lookin' for you, partner — in every single state."

Clenched teeth, he poked the barrel harshly against him.

"They've been lookin' for me for years. Nothin' new to me, lad. But if ya miss me soon enough, I'll come find ye…don't ye worry 'bout that." Mac growled, feeling the urge to slice his throat open, already able to see the thudding pulse at the crease of his neck.

"Levi, let me remind you that I'm also wanted!" Charlotte interjected, flustered. "Why don't you shoot me, then? What is the difference? Why didn't you arrest me at the bar?" she said; Levi's face fell and Mac's brow cocked heavenwards.

"Charlotte, that is different." He rolled his eyes, side-eyed her, taken aback for a moment. "Besides, you didn't kill the man, or did you now?" he returned the question.

"You will never know." She shrugged, defeatedly. "You will also never know what Mac had to deal with, in order to kill someone. Because…because let me tell you, he never…touched me, and he could have, for he had plenty of days and opportunities to do so!" She hissed with heart, and they both gaped at her, speechless. "Levi…please." she persisted, and his brows sunk deeper.

"What exactly do you want me to do, Charlotte?" He exhaled roughly, playing her words over in his head.

"I…I know this is going to sound like the worst idea possible, and I'm… utterly ashamed to even suggest it, but…you mentioned a campground to me? Why don't we move things over there, and just try to get along until he heals up, and then forget about everything?" she awkwardly asked him, knowing very well how terribly dumb this sounded, and yet she didn't know of another place he could hide until he heals, definitely not in Mon Louis with all the police and detective department hunting after him like a prized item; a legendary animal to slaughter, and hang on their wall as a trophy.

"What???" They both turned to look at her in shock, and she blinked at them, then her finger pointed at Mac.

"Mac, you cannot travel on your own, not like that. I won't let you!" Finger swayed left. "Levi, please! You know I would never ask this of you if it weren't important, if his life wasn't in danger! He cannot go to a doctor, and, and… infection will kill him!" she said and he tore his gaze away, as Mac stared at her; his leer, softened. "But if you can't, I understand as well, for I don't wish to take advantage of you, or for you to feel like I do…I just…I guess I just don't know what the hell to do…and…" Her head bowed, gaze nailing the pulled up oaken boards of the floor, able to smell the mold beneath them. "I guess I could ride him someplace else." she said sternly and they both blinked, baffled.

"Charlotte…" Levi sighed, festering with enviousness and irritation.

"I'm sorry, Levi…I just thought the campground to be the best solution, and I would have gladly paid you for the stay, as well as all the trouble." she said, meaning every word of it and Levi stared at her, aghast.

"I'd never ask you to pay me anything…" he said softer. "I invited you, Charlotte, but I did not invite this scum…" he leered, looked sharply back at him and her heart jerked in worry.

"B-Besides…" she stuttered nervously. "I really wanted to try that potato stew…" she tittered awkwardly, hoping to remind him of the good time they had on their last visit, hoping to avert his eyes back to her, and yet Mac's gaze now hardened in the foggy vision, in the scent of blood and sweat, in the sudden spike of weakness — nailing upon her; like a hawk studying her every move, as she suddenly walked towards Levi.

Levi's gaze lowered to Charlotte; standing there before him, hand stretching, clasping him, caressing the arm that held the gun, gently lowering it little by little. He followed her eyes, the lips that neared closer to him with every step she took.

"Please…cowboy." She tilted his wide-brimmed hat up, so she could look him in the eyes; her honeyed voice softening every frown on his face.

"Fine…" He exhaled heavily. "I'll do it, for you only. But after he's healed up, the chase is on; fair and square." He menaced as he lowered the gun. "Don't want to fight an injured man, anyway." He added proudly, and yet Mac was too puzzled by Charlotte's slick behavior to notice the remark, for this was unlike the flowered being she always portrayed herself to be, or perhaps he was wrong after all; perhaps there was another side of her she had kept hidden — a darker story, untold, swept beneath the rugs to mold into past.

"Thank you so much, Levi…" She planted a genuine kiss on his cheek, grateful for the favor, for she knew the risk he agreed to take and the shame she felt, crippled her.

Mac's teeth gnashed in frustration, lip curled in repulsion, hands gripping a fist tightly, wishing he had been shot instead of having to endure this sight; somehow more irritating than the elite's hand rubbing against her thigh; somehow, something quickened his blood.

"You are my *friend,* Charlotte. But he ain't, and he won't ever be." he said firmly, patting her shoulder, while subtly letting her know he saw through her tempting behavior, reminding of her own boundaries she set between them.

CHAPTER 35

To be a Gentleman

I

THE RAIN HAD SUCCUMBED TO THE OPEN STARRY SKY; wind turned a fresh breeze that gently picked the leaves off the ground. Small dusty sandstorms built up before them, circled in the open space, as they sat around the fire.

"Well, the wind certainly picked up tonight!" Elizabeth muttered to Will as he seemed to be distracted; lost within deep thought, tormented, confused with his own self.

"Yes. It certainly did, indeed…" he shortly answered.

Her fingers were entwined in her plait, nervously unbraiding it and braiding it back again, eyes piercing through a faint curtain of ginger strands, side-eyeing him. "William…do you wish to declare something of great importance to you…perhaps to me, as well?" she asked him solemnly, hoping for an honest response.

Will sighed, and glanced over at the barn; the replaced timber wood almost glimmered, as if the stars nested in the sinews of its body. Drawing in a deep breath, he stood up, and her heart skipped a beat. "Perhaps it is time for a drink, Elizabeth." he declared, and went to grab a bottle of their favorite whiskey — imported straight from Kentucky.

She sat in silence, feet tapping against ground, stirring the sand with nervousness, wondering what he might confess to her, yet the name he spurted out still clinked in her head, and yet again, there was still a candle burning with hope within her. Upon a leaden sigh, she glimpsed over at the chickens peacefully sleeping in their coop; all in a line, cuddled up with puffy feathers keeping each other warm, sheltering themselves from hungry coyote snouts that would occasionally poke through the gaps of the coop. Her eyes swayed towards the barn; still the tiny speck of shadow lingered in the loft; still there it was, seated, claws hooked on the lip of the window — the stubborn raven, still there, eyeing her back, making its appearance every single night since Will's departure from the ranch.

The snarling of a door hit her ears, and as she turned, she spotted Will, striding out of the house with a bottle and two glasses — an oddly familiar sight to her, one her heart had longed to see. Her beloved husband, his confident stance and attractive aura he always radiated. She stared at him as he advanced to her; heart swelled with pride. Admiring him.

He filled up their glasses and cheered together, oddly like they used to do to celebrate an expensive sale or successful investment, yet there was no wide smile scarring his face this time. This time he sat down, planting himself in the chair as though prepared to depart again; he faced her, eyes of concern.

"Elizabeth…" he said, voice low, coarse like barbed wire. "Remember that time…when you broke our promise?" he asked straightforward, took a sip of whiskey, and lifted his head to face her.

"Yes…" She sighed, voice dry, tangled up in wire. "William…but I'm trying to forget…" she added, gaze dropping to her feet as though remorseful.

"I need…" he swallowed deeply, cleared his throat, took another sip, wetting it for the words to come. "I need to avow to you, my dear." he said, heart fell heavy like a rock; shattered somewhere in a foreboding vision. There was a knot formed deep within her throat, choking her, as if she could see the vision herself.

"Elizabeth, you are aware by now that I despise false delicacy, and therefore shall not pretend that I have been blind to the state of your feelings since the mention of the lady's name. Albeit, I should have treated them with the degree of coldness which you say I have shown ever since…the fire." He swallowed hard, eyes briefly darting at the barn. "I am not accustomed to speaking plainly, and know little of such, so therefore, do not think the worse of me for opening my heart to you abruptly, for I do not wish to hurt you, and yet I fear I will no matter the niceties of etiquette…" he said, cutting his eyes at her flushed cheeks, as though she wore the tightest corset, tightening furthermore, as if slender fingers were tangled within the velvet cords, tugging on them with every breath she took. "Despite everything, my dear, you are a good, kind-hearted woman, and you do not deserve to feel this pain, and I for one have always regarded the pleasure of calling you my wife as the greatest that earth could afford. However…" he rambled, not knowing how to start.

"William…please, get on." she said shortly, for his pretty words didn't mean a thing to her right then.

"There is another woman, Elizabeth." Mouth sealed cowardly to catch her reaction. There was none. As if her sculpted face had suddenly turned to stone. "I met…another woman…"

She folded her lips, stomach twisted — a suffocating knot, clogging her. She couldn't stand to look at him any longer; the lips that confessed such woe, eyes that dared to lock hers. She jerked her head away. Stared at the fire. Dreading to hear his next words.

"It was not…my intention."

"William!" she hissed, interjecting. "I will tell you first hand — it's *always* your intent." she said, poured more whiskey in her glass, chugged it down.

"Elizabeth…I won't disagree nor argue with that statement; however, she appeared suddenly within our ranch up at Great Bend, and…"

"She did what? And how, William? Who is this lady you're referring to? Charlotte? Is that the name? An elite of Mon Louis?" She bombarded him — tears stood tall in her eyes, only ones to not cower in her presence.

"Charlotte, her name indeed." He sighed, feeling a weight leave his chest. "It's just too complicated to even start to put into words, dear. I so wish I could, but…there's too much that happened, in such a short period of time." he said, hands slashing through the chilled air nervously.

"So much that happened? *What happened*, William?" she asked, sobbing a river of tears, sobbing her whole soul out, pain she never knew existed; pouring more, drinking more, drowning the bitter taste of betrayal.

"Easy with the whiskey, please, Elizabeth."

"Get on, William!" she insisted, eyes flaming red, words slurring, a jitter on her flushed face, gaze glazing dull and grim. Tears.

"We shared a kiss…that led to more fervent kisses, however…there was nothing more, and that I swear to you with heart." he confessed, frustrated.

"Nothing more…as a kiss means *nothing* to you, William…" she wiped her tears, trying to remain strong and eloquent, as Will always knew her to be, but somehow she was faltering, dropping into a drunken cesspit of misery.

"No, I did not say that, Elizabeth. I hate to admit, and I hate to be the cause of your suffering any further, but…I…the truth is…the favorable emotions I received the moment I laid my gaze upon her, have gradually deepened, as my intimacy with…her, matured, and it would be false modesty in me now to disclaim a feeling of the sincerest and most affectionate regard for her in pitiful attempt to shelter your heart after you've shattered mine, therefore, I'm afraid that it is love — pure, devoted love — and I wish to proceed with the process of the divorce."

The words escaped his mouth voluntarily; a relief he longed to feel ever since he met Charlotte, ever since their lips locked that night, and yet somehow, as he stared at his wife's furrowed face, shadowed lines he had never noticed before, a well of regretful emotions flooded him.

Elizabeth gaped at the gloomy horizon; feeling hollow inside — the small flame of hope she had left for them, put out completely. Doused.

Evaporated, like it never existed.

He tore his gaze away, in thought, emptying the whiskey into his glass.

"So, *that* is why you returned. For the papers…for the…divorce." There was apathy in her voice, a heart suddenly turned cold.

"Yes…Elizabeth. And, I wanted to ensure you were alright…" he added, dithering, making sure he remained the gentleman she always knew.

"Well, you sure did a…*fabulous* job, William…how could I possibly ever be any better?" She snorted snidely, then stood up to leave, slamming her glass to the ground. Shattering. A large piece landing before him; his face reflected upon it, in shadow.

He chugged down the last burning drop of his drink, briefly wondering if Charlotte was even waiting on him; if breaking Elizabeth's heart was even worth all the fight and harrow. Dropping his head, he stared into the feeble reflection. His eyes appeared dark, almost black like the sweltering logs within the circle of glowing stones, yet there was no warmth around him, and he now rarely felt any within. He barely recognized himself anymore; there was no face of familiarity, only skin and hair.

I I

THEY MOUNTED THEIR HORSES IN THE STORM and the downpour of rain —
patiently waiting next to each other, still hidden in the brush and trees, only
soaked in the deluge. Mac gave a quick, tentative pat to Finn's neck before
anyone could notice, for he knew without him, he would have most likely
died in the mucky dark room — never seeing her again, never being stitched
by her quivering fingers, nor feeling her warmth against his skin. Finn's eyes
locked with his for a freezing moment, as though to portray gratitude as well.

"Good ol' Roy..." He patted him in turn; mounting wobbly and weak —
as climbing down the buildings exhausted him even further, trying to keep up
with Levi to not seem frail, all the while keeping an eye on Charlotte; mostly
crawling across the shingled roofs, petrified of the heights.

"The camp is just outside of Mon Louis...pitched in the swamps. We
will ride through the crop fields north of the city, as every corner is guarded
here." Levi instructed, feeling like a fool himself for protecting a murderer;
something that went completely against his deeply set beliefs.

Charlotte, seated in saddle, muffled by her own thoughts and concerns,
gazed out before her in a state of benumbed trance . Thinking of Will, feeling
torn to leave the saloon he's been paying for without even a word of explanation to his old friend, Antoine; feeling guilty as though she betrayed him yet
again, *but what was she to do? Leave Mac to his irreversible fate?*

She glimpsed over at him, arm clutched to his chest. A squint of exhaustion to his eyes. Broad shoulders unusually slumped; hunched over the saddle
horn, trying to keep his balance without falling off. She sighed, heart tearing
between them. Again.

They galloped through the crops, the fields and the swath of grass of a fall's
meadow, in the night's darkness, covered by its thick ebony veil. Passing farmers, sleeping in their huts and barns, dreading to continue their work when
sun would rise to burn their necks again, tinting them a cancerous red; they
plowed through their fields in slyness. Finn, awfully agitated by a fat water
moccasin passing briskly before his mighty hooves, stomped and snorted a
couple times, then continued to follow the more seasoned horses ahead of him.

Gnarled cypress trees welcomed them with ghostly Spanish moss hanging from their branches, like slender fingers reaching out to touch a mortal's head just to feel the living hair. Rotting vegetation embracing their thick black trunks, sinking all the more into the scummy waters. Smoke of fire billowed up through the thick, stagnant air and the dark, leaden silence that eerily persisted through the trees, creeped up in hollowness within them.

III

Sheriff Dorman,

Mr. Levi Krog is on his way to Mon Louis, to investigate the criminal scene at the gunsmith shop. I've given him all the necessary details of what was found — he is a smart son of a gun, and this won't be a challenge for him to find any possible trace that was left behind. Sheriff Tom down in Mon Louis gave me word last night, that he and his police department have been working together with Agent Roger Mills, and Mr. Dickinson of the Pinkerton Agency, and they have identified the bullet. Matching it with Mac Kinnon's revolver; the very same Schofield. No telling why this degenerate keeps on using the very same gun that is already in our files. Anyhow, the other bullet was matched to a Parker side-by-side shotgun from the store — the gun was not fired by the degenerate, based on the fingerprints instead corresponding to the victim. I expect to know something in the upcoming days. If Mr. Krog doesn't find Mac Kinnon, I will be very surprised. Like I said, he is the best there is at his craft. That being said, the case will move forward to the marshal up in Cougar's Tooth, said Sheriff Tom, if Mr. Krog fails us.

We'll find him, Owen. I guarantee it.
Sheriff Jordon

SHERIFF DORMAN FOLDED THE LETTER, scrunched it up within a fist; it crinkled between his fingers and jaundiced nails subtly poked through it. Exhaling a breath of frustration, he refused to believe the highest trained police department in the entire country could not find a single man. *How could a bounty hunter manage to track him down, if they failed to do so…*he wondered, hand squeezing the letter tighter.

He didn't have much faith in Levi; he feared Mac would forever escape right under their noses, and nobody would ever notice, for he had done so for decades. His thoughts trailed off back to Will and Charlotte, simmering with rage the more their faces flashed before his eyelids; anger coiling in his stomach, flaring his irritation, for the pair's story appeared all too suspicious.

I V

"LEVI! LEVI, MY BOY!" AN ENTHUSIASTIC VOICE ECHOED across the whole campground; taking form into a pear-shaped man with a steady limp on the left side, hobbling their way. Halting, slamming his round boots into the muddy soil, when Mac's shadow took presence in his sight; face blanched.

Loyally lifting his gun, he pointed it at him.

"It's alright, JB. He is with me…" Levi grumbled, dismounting, cutting his eyes at JB's grimace of confusion and quivering frightened limbs.

"Levi?" He shuffled towards him, as though in discreet slyness. "What in the world? Is this…is this…" he whispered, again in attempts to be discreet, only to blow loudly in Levi's ear instead.

"Don't even ask me to explain; I don't even know…" Levi muttered, embarrassed, pulling him aside to speak more privately.

"Levi, this ain't M-a-c-K-i-n-n-o-n now, is it?" JB spelled out loudly in sheer disbelief, casting glimpses at the legend himself. Levi rolled his eyes at his evident admiration that overpowered any fear he should have instead.

"'Course he is…" he grunted, tethering the horse to a post. "But I'm keeping an eye on him; won't be sleeping tonight." He assured him, yanking a shotgun out of a holster, planting it next to a chair.

"And the lady…?" JB whispered to him again, flickering his eyebrows, a sneaky smile scarring his plump lips as he glanced over Charlotte.

"Uhm…that's uhm…Charlotte. That…*friend.*" he said swiftly, as they neared behind them.

"Ohhhh Lordy!! She *is* a busty one, indeed!" He cackled loudly, and Levi leered at him.

"JB!" He growled, slamming a hand over his slobbery mouth. JB shrugged, all the while his eyeballs protruded all the more as Charlotte neared them with Mac beside her.

"This is JB Chott…my loyal friend, of many years…and best camp guard dog you could find!" He joked, and JB burst into laughter.

"Oh, Levi boy!" he wheezed, then looked over at them. "He ain't wrong, ya know? I might have a limp or two, but boy can I blast some intruders outta here!" He winked at them and Charlotte smiled with his oddly endearing self, as Mac stared at him, unimpressed, somehow already pre-annoyed. "I oughta be a marshal — 'Marshal Chott', that would suit me, aaah?" He flickered his brows at them and Levi drew in a deep breath of patience, tapping him on his back. "Alright, alright! You can just call me 'JB'!" he said, hands lifted before him upon a shrug. "Welcome to my swwwwamp ass laaaair! HaHA!" He turned around swiftly, hobbling towards a campfire with a large cast iron pot hanging from a sturdy branch. "We've got some fresh stew, been brewin' three days, if anyone's still hungry! Let me tell ya, I'm always hungry for a fine stew, and this son of a gun is the best out there!!" he rambled, and Charlotte suppressed a giggle, and yet her flushed cheeks betrayed her amusement.

"Thank you so much, kind sir!" she said, shaking his hand for a proper greeting. "My name is Charlotte, and I've heard so many good things about your stew!" She smiled kindly at him, and JB's cheeks crimsoned by her alluring presence, shaking her hand rapidly.

"Oh Lordy, I've heard lots of…huge things about, uhm…your uhm…" he stuttered, eyes scanning all over her, fixating on the shirtfront that stretched taut across her chest; a stern cough slashing through his awkwardness as Levi approached nervously.

"I told JB about…your great talent in getting into trouble." he interjected, Mac's eyes nailing on him with suspicion. Charlotte snorted and JB bobbed his head, giggling in sneakiness.

"I see…well, I hope you will not judge me badly for it, for I can be useful, and I would love to help you out around here, in return for our temporary stay." she said, pointing over at Mac.

JB's eyes followed the trail of her finger, only to jolt, aghast by Mac's sly shadow merging with hers. "Oh, Lordy!!!" He cackled anxiously. "You're a sneaky one, ain't ya?" he said, and Mac blinked at him, grim. JB stared at him, his smile slipping into a pout of awe, jaw slacking and eyes protruding in shadow, witnessing the ghost of a man everyone spoke of in haunting stories around the campfire, standing now in his very own campground. "Well! You… you certainly don't need to work 'round here, ma'am! This is JB's territory, and I have my routine. HaHA!" He winked at her and Charlotte sighed heavily. "Let's eat some stew, ahhh?? We don't want it to spoil! Well…I don't much care if it does, for the extra flavor is otherworldly, I tell ya! But Levi here, he has a sensitive tummy! Always had since he was little." He cackled and Charlotte no longer could suppress her giggle, as Levi rolled his eyes in embarrassment. Serving them bowls of alligator and potato stew, they dug in swiftly, scarfing it down like a starved pack of wolves.

"This is absolutely delicious, Mr. Chott…" Charlotte said and JB dropped the spoon into his bowl, splattering the oily stew all over his gray wiry beard.

"Ah-ah-ah! Call me JB, madam!" he said, Charlotte nodded with a smile.

Levi looked over at her, holding back a tender smile — not wanting to seem relaxed about the situation, and yet her kindness radiated across, besotting him furthermore.

"Oh! Well, it's honest work, I'll tell ya! Only the finest gator meat 'round here! And…some stolen potatoes from the fields, but, oh well! Oh, well!" He tittered as he limped towards the pot of stew, still simmering over wildly burning logs — serving everyone a bowl full again. Seated around the fire, keeping the relentless mosquitos away from them as they gobbled down the stew, JB's eyes flared in pride, and his chest swelled with joy to be able to feed a hungry mouth.

"Y'all a hungry bunch, aren't ya!" JB muttered with a wide grin on his face — excited to see they enjoyed his terrible cooking. "You see…Levi here has been helpin' me out with supplies; he hunts down anythin' I tell him to — gators, cougars, bears, ya name it! But this stew — this stew right here — I shot this darn gator in the head, prayin' it wouldn't chase after me! The big bastard growled as the bullet planted into his skull! Ha!" He slapped his thigh upon a chuckle, and took in a large breath to proceed.

"But tell ya what, sure can't run that fast no more, not with this crooked son of a gun!" he wiggled his knee cap back and forth, smacking it with a hand to locate back into place, making Charlotte's eyes bug out in repulsion, feeling faint all over again.

"You did good, JB. Stew is exactly what we all needed, I think…" Levi said, then glanced over at Mac, silently eating in a corner, his wounded arm barely able to lift the spoon.

"Well, Levi my boy…you're an excellent hunter — don't matter if ya take down animals, or killers." He laughed on his own, then noticed, to his surprise, everyone was quiet around him. "Should *not* have said that…sssshould *not* have said that." he mumbled to himself, and continued poking the fire awkwardly.

"So Charlotte, you can sleep in my tent tonight." Levi began to say. "I have my bedroll out here…I assume you have one yourself?" he asked Mac sharply, without even mentioning his name, faintly cutting an eye at him.

"Sure." he confirmed shortly, throwing the empty bowl in a barrel of water.

"Thank you, Levi, and JB." Charlotte stood up, throwing her bowl into the barrel as well, giving it a good scrub right after. "It's been a long night for everyone…a strange night." she said, biting her lip in deep thought. "Thank you, for letting us rest here." She glanced over at Levi, worried she had broken his trust, and betrayed their friendship. He nodded to her coldly.

"You go ahead and rest, sweetheart!" JB smiled at her, feeling thrilled to have a woman at the camp — *one of such a pretty caliber at that,* he thought to himself, suppressing an innocent giggle of infatuation.

Charlotte strode inside the tent and shut it behind her, relieved to be finally safe with no dead body to grieve over, yet puzzled and benumbed by tonight's events, so much so, her brain was unable to form a thought; a quiet sense of relief prevailed.

Levi's eyes tracked Mac, struggling with his own tent he was setting up underneath a tree. He studied his calculated movements — so brilliantly adjusted, since he couldn't use his injured arm freely. *No wonder he hadn't been caught in so long; his instant ability to adapt in any situation was simply impeccable,* he thought, fuming.

Mac glimpsed back at Levi, through the lattice of a willow's branch, meeting the emerald eyes that pierced through him — holding the impressively customized shotgun beside his chair. For the first time, however, he was able to let himself unwind in the wilderness; knowing that nobody would come after him here. He didn't trust Levi, yet his intentions were already known and clear, and this made a strange difference to him.

CHAPTER 36

Old Love

I

WILL GULPED DOWN HIS CUP OF COFFEE, inhaling the grounds in all his haste, then mounted Rachel, and anxiously left the ranch upon a gallop. Riding through the endless fields of tall yellow grass, curved soil slowly flattening the more he approached the town. Pronghorns grazed within a glen, hunted by silent rifles that spread the grass apart with their barrels; packs of coyotes wrestled with their pups within a crevasse of tall black boulders, shooting out from the fields, herds of wild mustangs galloped away as he trotted through, separating them into countless pairs. Passing by a familiar oak tree, once symbolized tender memories he thought he'd never try to bury, he swiftly glanced away from it as to not be reminded. He finally reached the town of Bisonhorn with great anticipation; hitched up Rachel before the post office, and made haste into it.

"Mr. Griffiths!" the postman exclaimed in awe. "What a pleasure to see you again, sir! How d'you do?" he asked, scarring an inviting smile.

"I'm doing well, sir. I wish to check on my mail; if there's anything…I've received, in the last days…" he inquired, worriedly, fingers drumming against his woolen pants.

"Just one moment, mister." the postman hummed politely, now sorting through a stack of mail sitting on top of his dusty counter.

Will counted the seconds that turned into minutes; glared at his pocket watch, wondering why it took so long.

"They're looking at you, William. They're talking about you. They know what

you did." A sudden, low voice startled him, jerking his head back up, slamming the watch shut. He glanced back at the elderly man sitting patiently on the bench, waiting for his stagecoach to arrive.

"He knows, William. He will let everyone know…"

Will stared back at him; face furrowed in bewilderment, brows snapped together as the voice kept on pressuring, persisting, drilling deeper into his senses. He walked towards the frail man, and halted before him with a cocked head to the side, uncertain.

"Sir…what…what do you know?" Will asked him quietly, noticing his frailty, the quivering shoulders, involuntary bobbing head, glassy eyes that squinted up to him.

"Excuse me, mister?" the man asked, confused, a faint fragile voice.

"You were staring at me. What do you know??" Will persisted, coldly, quivering himself, as anger poured through him. The old man gaped at him, frightened, seeing his black pupils dilate in rage.

"Mr. Griffiths! Mr. Griffiths!" the postman called him repeatedly, for he seemed to not have heard him before. Will, as though snapping back into a state of consciousness, turned to look at him, noticing a letter being waved in the air.

II

CHARLOTTE AWOKE TO THE SOUNDS OF SLURPING MUD, frogs croaking, and flies buzzing around her head. Sitting up, she stretched her arms and twisted her back in all directions, feeling the pleasurable pull of sore muscles and cracks along the spine. She glanced around herself, it was a spacious tent, almost the size of a room — it *was* a room, Levi's, and he lived in this movable homestead since he was a very young man. There were ropes hanging about, a plethora of shirts that lulled her to sleep with the cologne imprinted upon them, coats, boots, guns planted all over, bolas tangled around wood, which Charlotte could not imagine what purpose they even served, *other than reminiscing Finn's jiggling jewels;* she snorted with the thought, then yawned and proceeded to walk out of the tent.

Peeking through, the first thing that appeared to her gaze was JB, moon-ing her gloriously as he bent down to pick up more firewood, and startled by the curly, hairy, tangled mess of a sight, she tore her gaze away, suppressing a screech. Her eyes nailed upon Levi, seated atop a log around the fire, and after daring to scan around for Mac, she failed to find him; panic, setting in.

She rushed frantically to Levi, who was sharpening his knife steadily, leg cocked and resting atop a chair. "Levi! Where…where is he?" she asked him with hair half braided, feet sinking slowly into the mud.

Levi looked at her, rolled his eyes, pointed his knife towards a tethered Finn, who was surprisingly being brushed by Mac. Her face fell, jaw dropped to the ground to see him caring for her horse, unable to comprehend what urged him to do so, in the middle of his sickness at that, however her panic was quelled, relieved to know he was around, standing on two feet, as though he wasn't on the literal bleeding edge of death last night.

"Oh…okay." She bobbed her head in absence, still staring at him in awe.

"Have a coffee, madam!!!" JB emerged behind her, startling her to the core — the suppressed screech now leaping from her lips. "Oh, Lordy! She's got some lungs on her! HaHA!" He cackled, and Charlotte swallowed hard.

"I apologize…I didn't know you was here…" she said shyly and Levi smirked, amused.

"Oh sweetheart, it's hard to miss me! HaHA! All this paddin' is meant to be seen and admired! Yes ma'aaaam…mhmmm." He cackled and handed her a cup of coffee. "Watch out for them grounds! For they'll come the same way out, as the way they went in!" He winked at her and she blinked, trying hard to understand this man's personality, for half of the things he muttered could be taken as jokes, and yet he appeared utterly earnest.

"Thank you, JB…thankfully, I'm quite used to…such coffee, where I come from." she said, bartender Nusbaum appearing once again in her mind. She sat down beside Levi and set her eyes on his knife, then the thrilled voice spoke again.

"So, dear lady! Miss Charlotte! Where *are* ya from?" JB asked her, sitting down next to her, and Charlotte almost choked on the coffee. Levi was silently fiddling with his knife, pretending he was still busy with it, yet curi-ously awaited to hear her answer, for he didn't quite know Charlotte either.

"I grew up around…Nephilim Cove." Her head bowed, ashamed, knowing exactly the bad reputation this place had — filled up with criminals and working ladies of every kind.

"Oh! Wonderful!" He clapped his hands together into a firm grip. "You've got family there?" he asked curiously, and another knot choked her.

"I…no." she said shortly. "My mother is deceased…" she said, and JB bobbed his head with pressed lips in sharp concentration.

"Oh! Well…who needs family after all! Ah?" He cackled.

Levi rolled his eyes.

"Right…"

"Besides! Nephilim Cove…eh…fittin' with ehm, your partner, ah?" he said, in a pitiful attempt to make her feel better, but only managed to make matters worse. Levi threw a warning look at him, almost slicing his thumb with the blade. "Should *not* have said that…" he mumbled again, burying his mouth within his beard — sealing it, to not say anything more.

"It's alright." She chuckled. "Mac…is not my partner. He is…just an important friend to me, I suppose…" she spoke faintly, as if she didn't want to believe it herself.

Levi frowned in confusion; *perhaps Mac wasn't the special one she had talked about.* His fingers drummed against the blade, wondering.

"Oh, my bad! Well, I've got to keep the fire goin'." he said, hands clutching his knees as though prepared to make an important speech. "Levi, I need some more meat for the coming days — we have more mouths to feed now… you knooooow…" He winked at him repeatedly, failing to remain discreet.

"'Course." He nodded, watched him hobble away, then looked over at Charlotte, still sipping on her coffee.

"Levi…" She drew in a deep breath and faced him, locking earnest eyes. "I hope you're not upset with me…" she said, voicing the concern that had been tormenting her all night.

"I am not…" he said, in a sigh, eyes squinting in confliction. "You're a good woman, with a kind heart. I guess, I just don't understand how…" He stopped himself, not wishing to dwell on it further, as if somehow it bothered him deeply in ways that shouldn't.

"It's complicated…I don't quite understand it myself…" she said, and he bobbed his head.

"So…Nephilim Cove…"

"Mhm…"

"That's not too far away from where I grew up." he said, and she forced a smile, side-eyeing Mac who was now walking in their direction. Her breath sunk within her chest; words hanging from her lips, and yet her tongue appeared tangled up.

"Hey!" she managed to say, and his blues nailed sharply upon her.

Mac bowed his head, nodded, lit up a cigarette and passed by them. She swallowed hard, in shame, and averted her eyes back to her hands, fingers entwined in bewilderment.

"Not the talkative type, ah?" Levi teased her.

"No…he ain't."

I I I

WILL, SEATED BENEATH A LUSH WING OF AN OAK TREE planted at his ranch a long time ago, held the letter in a tight grip; hands shaking and mind dithering to unwrap it. Gathering up an ounce of bravery, after staring at it as long as it took a gale of wind to blow off a leaf from the branches, he opened the letter from Charlotte, not knowing what she could possibly confess since Mac was definitely in Mon Louis.

Dear Will,

Please forgive me beforehand, as I will never be able to write so eloquently like you do, but rest assured, this is my best try.

Will chuckled; already wishing she could be here, wrapped tightly in his arms.

This room sure feels empty without your presence, and so do I. I will never understand why you had to leave so early, but I trust you enough to patiently wait for your return.

I'm longing to hear your soft voice in my ear, and feel your fresh breath against my skin, for somehow I miss that kind affection of yours, dearly.

Thank you for everything you did, and sacrificed for me, as I do not believe I deserve it. You have opened my eyes and proved to me that good people still exist — and you, Will, you are one of the best. I miss you, handsome, if it wasn't clear enough already.

Yours,
Charlotte

Almost able to hear her voice, feel her breath stir his hair beside his face, Will re-read the letter a dozen times; worshiping her handwriting, as it was the closest piece of her he had.

And yet, there was a knot in his stomach; an uncertainty.

What he once felt for Elizabeth had sunk deep within an hollow abyss, left there to tarnish every emotion that he still held for her — *and he did,* he did love her still, as a husband loves a wife of many years spent together. However his heart didn't flourish with joy any more, as it did in Charlotte's presence; for it ached, it rotted the longer he inhaled Elizabeth's fragrance of bitterness, and yet, memories still lingered in a feeble veneer of happiness.

Elizabeth was different from Charlotte, and yet not so different from him. Charlotte on the other hand was quite different from him; and he couldn't help but wonder if he deserved her, if a life devoted to him would ensure her happiness. She was an adventurous soul, young, with her whole life ahead of her, and he was…faltering.

He walked back to the house, a long walk of calculation, a content walk of reminiscing, comparing, and forgiving. A walk of responsibility, maturity, and honesty. He opened the door, and a stack of papers eyed him back. Approaching, his eyes set upon them, trailing all over them to find her elaborately intricate signature at the very bottom. She had already signed the divorce papers, and his heart suddenly sunk. "Elizabeth?!" he shouted.

A voice of distress and regret, echoing through all the rooms.

CHAPTER 37

True Berserker

I

"WE'RE GOING HUNTING." HE SAID, HANDING HIM A RIFLE. "Could use some help carrying more than one carcass. You eat for nothing here, anyway."

"Wasn't me choice to be here, remember that." Mac said, standing up to follow after him.

"Didn't know you were taking orders from a lady." he fussed back, as he led his horse around the hitching post.

"Didn't know ya did either." Mac silenced him. Even a blind dog could notice Levi had a soft spot for Charlotte, and Mac was certainly aware of it, yet he couldn't understand how Charlotte felt towards Levi, let alone him, and yet somehow it didn't matter; *it shouldn't...*

Riding away from the camp, into the dense swampy trees, they vanished behind a solid curtain of moss, leaving back a backlit row of silhouetted trees.

"Where are they headed to, sir??" Charlotte, aghast at the sight, asked JB swiftly, as he was scraping a deer hide. JB poked his head around the stand, and squinted through the haze.

"Who?" he asked her, perplexed, and she blinked.

"Levi...and Mac..." she said. His eyes flared, lit up like a Christmas tree.

"Oooooh!! But of couuuurse!" He cackled, and wiped his bloody hand against his shirtfront. "Huntin' it seems like." he said, looking back at the missing rifle in Levi's tent. "Levi always hunts with that particular rifle, and... it is gone, ain't it?" He winked at her and her face fell down to the fleshy piles of deer remains.

"Together?" She gasped, losing her balance. "Hunting…together?" Petrified, she repeated herself, for not too many hours ago they tried to murder each other.

"Yup! They make quite a pair, these two! HaHA." He joked; meanwhile, Charlotte was worried to the core if they'd come back in one piece. "They'll be fine, miss." He patted her on the shoulder, staining her white blouse scarlet, imprinting the scent of a rotten deer. "Levi never gets out of control; surprisingly for his young years. I could argue with a dull knife all day, and here he is, huntin' with a…" He stopped himself, as he saw Charlotte side-eyeing him with a raised brow. "I did *not* say that!" His finger lifted heavenwards, proud of his accomplishment.

Charlotte chuckled; JB was quite a character. He never thought before he spoke, and when he did speak, he spoke a lot. Yet he always made everyone either burst into tears of laughter, or feel awkwardly uncomfortable. There was never an in-between.

"Are you related to Levi?" she asked, cocking her head, staring into his eyes to find a resemblance; there was none. "For you two laugh all the time!"

"Oh no…Lordy, no…" He tittered. "I mean, it's a shame he couldn't inherit my good looks, but…I think he's doin' fine for himself!" he said, and Charlotte snorted. "I…I adopted Levi, in a way."He shrugged his rounded shoulders, hairy and wiry just like his beard, baring through the denim overalls he wore every-time he skinned a deer. "Well, his daddy was murdered when he was still a young boy — he found him hanged by the neck in their cabin…but perhaps I shouldn't have said that." He bit his lip, snarling his teeth in confliction. "Oh, Lordy…forgive me, Charlotte." he mumbled, realizing it wasn't his place to say.

"I'm sorry…" She sighed, feeling embarrassed for him. "Please, do not worry, I'll pretend I never heard that." She ensured him, noticing his sudden discomfort, his smile slipping within his gray beard.

"Thank you." He huffed an offal scented breath. "Sometimes, words just plop right out of my mouth! Hehe." He giggled, then sat down to play his harmonica, which guaranteed to keep him quiet.

II

"ELIZABETH!!" HE YELLED A LITTLE LOUDER, then from the top of his lungs, now searching frantically through the whole house, cellar, attic; she was nowhere to be seen. Running to the barn, dithering to enter it as if a flash of memories threatened to assail him, he jerked the oaken doors wide open, and found the horses all still locked up in the stables, all but one — hers. The proud white Arabian mare they bought together, at the auction in Mon Louis.

A knife dug into him, twisting, scraping every sinew of his being, realizing she was completely gone, for the very first time ever — his wife left the ranch, and him behind — voluntarily, without a word; without a warning. Gone. His legs failed him, his core weakened; he plopped down, sat on a square hay bale, suffocating in genuine concern, devastated to feel such emotional confusion, as if it confirmed everything that long walk revealed to him.

"Oh, Elizabeth…" Tears broke out, they flooded him. "Oh, my dearest…" He reeled into a sob, crying in utter loneliness, feeling his heart convulse, tear, shatter, and crumble into hollowness. Suddenly feeling the pain she nurtured all along, planted in this soil as though to keep her company, suddenly realizing how wrong it was of him to abandon her like a selfish coward.

A croaking voice hit his ears, followed by another one right after. Forcing his eyes open, he glanced up ahead at the timber frames of the barn's ceiling. Light shone through them in hazy rays, blinding, dazzling him; in the middle, a shadow, stood small and proud. It croaked again.

III

"KNOW HOW TO HUNT FOR BOAR?" LEVI ASKED HIM, spotting a herd of them grazing in the distance, pulling out his rifle and slinging it around his shoulder.

"Sure." Mac said shortly, taking out his own rifle in all its gloomy glory; weathered, scratched, adorned with a broken scope.

"We can either run up to them and shoot from the horse, or sneak towards them on foot. Your call." he offered, looking through his scope.

"Depends how good of a shooter y'are." he teased him, throwing him a sharp glance.

"Don't worry 'bout that. You'll figure that one out, soon enough." he threatened, and Mac couldn't help but smirk, amused. "So, do you want to fool around or hunt?" He grunted, as anything Mac said or did agitated him to the very core.

Mac bowed his head, and Levi stared at his caustic smirk, holding on to his silence as if it too was too loud. His eyes nailed across, his ankle tilted, his boot pressed, rolled a spur against Roy's belly, sending him into a full gallop, shooting off together like a bullet into the damp air; throwing muddy chunks of ground on Levi's face in response.

Levi wiped his face, gnashed down on his teeth, gripped reins firmly, and followed right after. The ground shook, mud splashed against willow bark, a symphony of hoof clops merging into a clap of thunder, as both riders plowed through in a morbid dance of foreboding fate.

Mac clasped the reins in one hand and carried the rifle with the other, feeling the stitches stretch taut across his flesh. He extended his hand over Roy's neck, encouraging him to go faster, moving his body with his rhythm, feeling every stride underneath him, seat glued to saddle, legs steadily pressed against it with firm control.

"Stay on their right!" Mac shouted from the other side, nearing the herd.

Levi kicked the horse's side and loped around to their right, taken aback by Mac's sudden orders. The boars squealed in fright, tumbling over each other as they rushed to escape, leaping into brush, squeezing through gaps of fallen trees, bolting ahead.

Mac rose in the stirrups, raised his rifle with his healthy left arm and looked through the sights, calculating the lead of his aim with the bolting animal before him. Levi, loping on the other side, stared in denial.

POW!

He shot the boar down; dropping it dead on the spot, leaping over it to continue on as it inhaled its last breath. Levi, benumbed by awe, realized Mac wasn't just skilled with blades; he was able to shoot a heavy rifle with one non-dominant arm, while riding a horse at full speed, and not miss with a single shot on a wildly running target.

"What yer waitin' for?" Mac pressed him, staying on the left side of the herd, pushing them towards Levi, all the while studying his maneuvers, judging them, capturing them in his memory, in case it would ever be needed.

POW!

Another one dropped instantly, and Levi turned his horse's head to a full stop and Mac skidded Roy to a halt, sliding sideways across a cesspit of mud. There they stood still, with two boars plopped on each side, with green eyes locking blues, facing each other.

"Alright…" Levi tore his gaze away, spat some mud out to the side, and faced the animal. "Let's drag them back to camp." he said, and Mac threw the lasso around the boar's feet, pulling it along.

I V

SHE TROTTED THROUGH RED GIANTS; nervous hands clinging onto reins as tightly as they could, quivering in a seat not ridden in years. Sun sunk behind her, vanishing beneath the ominous layer of red tinted trees, fog thickened, sounds emanated from the depths of the woods. Owls screeched as they flew over, descending on deserted buildings buried deep in the somber forest, blending with the early hoarfrost of the year cloaking the trees. Shadows held upon red bark, almost appeared to be crawling from branch to branch, racing with her, guiding her along the lonely path. A wolf's steady howl alerting her, pushing her away from its starving lair — its sound, lonely and upset — as though to reflect her feelings.

V

"GOOD HUNTIN', BOYS!" JB COMPLIMENTED THEM, over and over again, as he inspected the large boars in great delight, licking his lips, salivating over the flabby mass, already able to taste the rich stew he would make out of them.

"Yeah…bet we are stocked up now, don't you think?" Levi said, relieved to have it over with. He placed the gun down and wiped the mucky sweat off his forehead, peeking through his fingers to spot Charlotte approaching in curious haste; a statuesque figure silhouetted by the hazy light of the sun.

"Of course! I will get right to it!" JB happily pranced to them, pulled out his skinning knife, then slammed it dramatically into the animal's flesh.

"Good job, you two…" Charlotte noted, a wide smile of relief plastered on her face.

"Thanks…" Levi flinched a smile back to her. "Have you been enjoying the silence? Or has JB been keeping you busy?" He chuckled, hands gripping his sweaty shirt of mud and swamp debris, pulling it over his stomach, over his chest, his head, over him; completely disregarding there was a woman at the campground now.

Charlotte's eyes froze upon him; as he stood there, fronting her. A sudden trail of chills crawled down her spine. She stared, involuntarily, yet she stared for she had never seen a man's muscular body, certainly not in such close proximity, certainly not drenched in a steaming layer of sweat. For her body suddenly tingled, rattled, flushed with heat. There were tight, bulging abs, a rippled stomach, lines vertical and horizontal everywhere she looked, dents of shadows, contrasting against his fair nordic skin, padded pecs, a chest embosomed with thick, coarse, dark curls, dripping from hot perspire — slowly, torturously slow, trailing a line of hair along his abdomen, down to his pants, down to his…

"Charlotte?" his voice, a dim echo within her, swiftly slashing through her wildest of thoughts.

"I…" She pulled her gaze back up to him, unable to drain the scarlet color of her cheeks, only to be met by his emerald eyes, staring deep into hers.

Mac strode up right behind them, arm held against his chest; it felt painfully sharp from the exertion, and yet that pain subsided when he noticed Levi's athletic physique and much bigger frame than his own — towering right over Charlotte's awestruck eyes.

"Oh…uhm, yes…I've been enjoying the…silence." She sucked in an awkward stutter, trying to compose herself before his bareness.

"Silence? Haha. Hard to imagine that, girl…" He snorted, and grabbed another shirt — his abs flexed as he twisted his body to reach it, and she tensed in return; biting her lip, ogling like a fool, wishing he'd stay a little longer bare before her virgin eyes.

"No…it was…he didn't disturb me…" she muttered, tearing her gaze away, trying to compose herself as he pulled the fresh shirt over his head, tucking it into his pants that had a large natural bulge to them, one more detail she didn't fail to notice.

"Good." Levi smirked, amused, for she was greatly distracted.

"Excuse me for a moment, Levi." She forced her eyes, limbs, and being away from him, shaking her head with her naïve self to slip like that. She strode to Mac's tent; nervously fiddling with her hair, for she hadn't really talked to him since she stitched him up, and she feared he was distant due to that, or perhaps it was the awkward sight of her admiring Levi's body as if it was a Greek statue, locked up in some kind of museum overseas.

"Mac?" she called him and lingered in silence. "Can I come in?"

Mac, startled, went quiet — thinking about them being together in such a tight space. His blood pumped faster, pulse thudded hard. "Sure." he said uncertainly, scooting closer to the side.

Charlotte, dithering, drew in a breath of courage and crawled into the tent, as Levi watched her from a distance, puffing out in annoyance, leaving the sight to unsaddle his horse, brush it, feed it, water it, anything to keep his mind in a state of sanity.

Mac laid there on his back, head resting on one arm, keeping his eyes to himself in sheer reservedness. Charlotte squirmed in and sat beside him — instantly feeling the tension between them.

"Hey…" she greeted him, a soft low voice, a shy smile on her lips, eyes hunting his, searching his face.

"Hm." He hummed, avoiding her eyes.

She chuckled at the awkwardness, and he couldn't help but crack a faint smile on his lips. Feelings flooded them, as if they had never been apart. They drowned within them, enveloped in silence, and yet they were built upon silence, deafening, suffocating, smothering silence.

The sun set behind the campground, reflecting on the swampy green rippled waters. JB scurried about to light up the lanterns, hanging around Levi's tent, igniting torches he had pierced into the mud…

A fresh fire ignited.

VI

TEETH CLENCHING VIOLENTLY; HE DROPPED DOWN to the wooden ground, helpless, frail, alone. Back arched indefensibly, limbs retracted towards his body — twisting like rusty wire; bending, bending…bending all the more, hands folding tightly into fists. His whole being convulsed — head shook rabidly, slamming against the table's legs repeatedly — blacking out into a dark, hollow hole; lost to void…

Tongue, trapped between teeth, crushed vigorously with every spasm; bloody foam gushing out, wetting his torn-up lips. Squinting through the dark haze of confusion, paralyzed, breath imprisoned within his lungs, he saw him; in shadow, yet in flesh and bone, approaching.

A hand, fumbling out something of a finger's size.

A feather brushed against him; scraping his pallid skin, ever so gently, as if the softest of blades kissed his cheek.

Blood dripped.

VII

"WHAT'YA THINKIN' BOUT, LEVI, MY BOY?" JB ASKED HIM with concern, for he noticed his unusual quietude; his smile, buried beneath a grimace of woe and agitation.

"Not much." he said, oddly abrupt, then poked the burning wood with the black tip of his boot.

"Any trouble back there?" he asked, hinting at their hunt as discreetly as he could, pointing his protruding eyeballs dramatically towards Mac's tent, almost popping them out as he strained to do so.

"No…" he said, cutting his eyes at the tent. "It was strangely alright…"

"Oh! Wonderful! Oh Lordy, we might just make a huntin' pair out of ya two! HaHA!" He cackled, saying it far louder than needed.

"JB…please…don't test my patience…" he growled, then sighed in sorrow. JB blinked blankly at him, realizing there was something else bothering him.

"Charlotte?" JB then asked, betting anything that this was his torment.

Levi exhaled deeply. He didn't need to say anything further — JB was already convinced about it, for he knew him well, and his awful luck regarding women and relationships.

"Ah. Women. Beautiful tender creatures, yet never worth the trouble." JB said, sat beside him, tapping his shoulder a couple times. "Ya know...my dear Margaret was worth it though, but I was a fool to not see it. Lost her to a better man than I; and at that point, it was too late..." he sighed, crinkled his lip to the side, and half-shrugged in silence.

Levi looked at him, smiled gently, and wrapped his arm around his soft shoulder. "JB, you're a good man — you might have some quirks...or a lot of them, but without you, I'd have been lost." he said with heart, meaning every word he spoke.

JB lifted his gaze up to him, two heads above him, and held back a tear. "You always was like a son to me, Levi." He sniffed. "Your father would be proud to see you now. Everything you have become, in such a short amount of time...a true Berserker!" He clutched a fist and thumped it against Levi's chest.

Levi swallowed hard, tears misted over his greens. "You moved me, old man!" He thumped a fist back on JB's chest, almost pushing him off his seat, and they burst into laughter, now pushing each other around playfully, almost falling off the log together.

CHAPTER 38

Swamp Ghosts

I

"I JUST WANTED TO CHECK ON YOUR ARM, BUT…we can do this another time, if you want to rest now." Charlotte said softly, noticing the exhaustion on his sunburned face.

"Hm…" he smirked snidely, and she cocked a brow.

"What is so funny about what I said?" she asked and he cut his eyes at her.

He stretched his throbbing arm out to her and continued to smirk lopsidedly. "Here." he said to her, waiting to capture her shocked expression.

Charlotte leaned closer, clasped his arm, and pulled it towards her eyes.

"Oh my…" She gasped, horrified. "Mac!" Her eyes nailed him. "It's getting infected, Mac! It's…it's freaking infected!!" She sighed, disappointed, glancing back to it and back to his face.

"Bad business…" He shrugged, carelessly, like he didn't already know.

"'Bad business'? Mac! You silly fool!" She hissed and he cocked a brow. "You shouldn't have gone hunting! You should have rested, and kept it out of this swampy…swamp! You…you really are a stubborn, stubborn man, Mac Kinnon!" she fussed at him, annoyed, and he snorted in response. Her eyes flared, aghast, freezing upon his grin. "What in the world is so funny? Do you realize you can die?? Or do you have a death wish? Is that part of your… legend??" She continued to fuss, twisting his arm to inspect the red swelling around the sutures; fingers gently pressed into his skin, feeling it more precisely. "You will need medicine…" she said, contemplating how to get it without him having to be examined by a doctor.

403

"Imagine that." He snorted and her eyes cut at him again. "After all them damn years, I die from a glass shard, and a bad sewing job from a…"

He stopped himself, as they accidentally locked eyes.

"From a *what?*" she asked him agitatedly.

Mac was quiet, tearing his gaze away from her.

"What were you about to call me, Mac?" she asked with a leer, expecting to hear the dirtiest insult imaginable. "And besides, I saved your butt back there, and I haven't even received a single remark of gratitude." She hissed and his brow cocked back again, resuming back to the same habit in Hope.

"Hm…"

"Really? Is that the best remark you can give me?" She snorted, and shook her head.

"Thanks…" he managed to say, somehow that word felt foreign.

"You're welcome…" she said, eyeing him in deep thought. "What were you about to call me, Mac…" she then persisted and he rolled his eyes, shutting back down, avoiding to answer. "Don't look away! Tell me…it can't be worse than an 'eejit'." she said, and he snorted, then went quiet again. "Mac??" She jerked on his arm and he faced her sternly. She held his eyes, forbidding him to turn away.

"From a fine lass." he said, muffled, shying away again.

She stared at him, speechless, voiceless, pulse echoing between them. This must have been the only time she heard him say a kind word to her, even if discreetly, and somehow she begged to hear it play in her head over and over again, for it sounded so utterly perfect coming from his mouth, his cryptic nous that he carried, and heart that was coiled by stones. Her cheeks crimsoned; fingers slipped off his arm, for she couldn't feel them.

"Never mind…" he added, for there was no response, nor did he expect one. "I'm aware of the infection, I'll take care of it. Not me first one, nor me last one." he said, sat up, leaning forward to grab a cigarette, and she snapped out of her tranced state of mind.

"Well…thank you, for not insulting me after all." she said shyly, still hearing his compliment in her head, still internally bursting with happiness, smiling, heart fluttering and blood quickening through her.

"I'd never." he murmured, poking the cigarette in his mouth. She blinked at him for a brief moment; finally grasping the odds of finding each other again, now seated together within a tent, contentedly, trusting, not afraid of harming each other anymore — rather not afraid of him harming her, that is.

Her smile slipped as she studied his dull grimace, devoid of any emotion, cold and bleak. "I'll let you to it, then…" She sighed, feeling as though she disturbed him, for she couldn't get more than a word out of him, remembering he was the one that left her after all.

His head perked up swiftly, feeling her body scoot away from him, ready to crawl outside. "Where's the fine lad gone to, anyway?" he then asked, pulling her back to her seat, not wishing her to leave, dreading to feel her absence, loathing the awkward being he was within, unable to form a sentence that wasn't menacing. Charlotte, halting herself, gazed back at him.

"He is…he is home. In Bisonhorn." she said, wondering what that meant to him. What that meant to her.

"Hm…Bisonhorn, huh? Business?" he asked curiously, puffing out a cloud of smoke, *somehow so attractively,* she thought.

"I guess…" She nodded, bowed her head, shrugged, avoided him, knowing very well he was possibly visiting a wife. A wife with the name, *Elizabeth.*

"Hm…" He bit his lip, something within him nearly consumed him. It crawled and it slithered, coiling him to choke. "So, he'll be back? Or, ye'll go there, and…" He paused again.

"I…don't know…" she said and he blinked.

"Ye don't know…" His throat felt tight, drying the longer she didn't speak.

"I just don't know, Mac…for I'm…confused." She paused briefly, head turning to lock eyes with him once more. "I feel like…I feel torn, torn in so many directions — all the time." she said, swallowing hard, feeling brave, yet a coward dressed in disguise. "Once everything is peaceful, and normal, and the next moment, then…" Her eyes set on him, his blues drilling through hers, clasping her heart, squeezing it, twisting it like never before — feeling the sudden wave of immense happiness and sorrow all together, slither through her, bounding higher, almost too much to bear. There was no emotion stronger than what she felt being next to him; no godly shaped body, no tender words could compare. Her heart wilted in his presence, and all he had to do was to be there. He was torment, in flesh and bone.

"…then you suddenly appear out of nowhere." she dared to say, not understanding what she felt anymore. "And I…get confused…" She choked.

He stared at her in silence, flicking the cigarette butt beside him in sheer absent thought; denial. "Didn't realize I was part of yer confusion…" he muttered, looked at her intensely, pulled down on his cigarette, stared.

"You…you've always been, Mac. In a strange kind of way…" she said, whispered, barely audible, as she studied the way he loosely confined the cigarette between his lips — feeling dangerously envious of it.

"Hm." He nodded, surprised, skeptical.

"And I…" She halted, quivered in nervousness; his breath cut in his lungs, feeling the sudden rise of her chest compete with his. Her eyes fell upon his mouth as he clasped the cigarette, pulling it out, resting between his fingers. "Mac, I…" she stammered, blocking any thought, barely able to breathe, for his eyes suddenly dropped down to her lips, as though to read her stutter, yet he yearned to feel their softness once more instead; the sweet release of his rage, the creeping sin wash away for a fleeting moment, as long as eyes could clutch shut, as long as lips could entwine, as long as she could breathe light into him.

Charlotte, unable to voice her thoughts, leaned in to him and his eyes flared; alive, raw, stabbing hers, until they shadowed by her face. Her mouth neared his, lingering before it to breathe him in, just for a moment, stealing the scent of his lips. His chest inflated, hands balled a fist, squeezing the tension back into his own flesh. He felt her; felt her pulse, her heat, her leaden breath, sighing heavily before him. She leaned closer, smiled, shy, and pressed her lips against his cheek, kissing him tenderly, timidly, long enough to imprint her lips on him; for him to remember for the rest of the night.

"Please take care of yourself…" she whispered against his ear, and his eyes rolled back into his skull, chest deflating, tension flushing through him. "Good-night, Mac…" she said gently, pulling back to face him once more, yet there was no expression on his face; keen, emotionless, even a rock would scar a grimace of corrosion by a tender brush of rain. She stared with a leaden chest, wishing for him to translate this mystery that covered his eyes. Smile slipping in disappointment and embarrassment, she tore her gaze away and crawled cowardly out the tent.

Mac felt of his cheek, trembling fingers clutching the skin; still warm, rugged scars almost healed by her touch, still the soft veil of her lips covering it. His fingers traced circles around it — forever capturing the memory of her tenderness.

Levi's eyes had followed the shadows of their faces, lit by the lantern, as he oiled his rifle around the campfire, betraying the sense of privacy they thought they had within the tent. Teeth clenched.

II

A SLOW BURNING FIRE, BILLOWING FROM THE DEPTHS of the somber woods, invited her warmly through the dominant redwood trees; like an eerie speck of petiteness she stood against them. There was no blackness staining the wall of her memories, for she knew the path well, and yet there was a haze that encircled her, pushing her away.

Quivering, she fought against it, kicking her horse to push through the sudden gush of wind. Her eyes scanned around, pierced through the heavy, foreboding cloak of mist, only for her clouded illusion to paint faces in the walls of her head; faces atop the bark, shifting, evaporating upon a flutter of an eyelash. She loped away, slashing through the smog, unleashing her imagination, abandoning it at the end of the path.

Dismounting in haste, she hitched her white Arabian to a post, and went on to knock on the door of a wooden cabin, secluded ever deeper into the forest of Red Giants. Heart aching, standing before it; memories tangling her misery furthermore.

An elderly man opened the door, shotgun in his hand, and lantern in the other, only to face her frightened self. His eyes flared, swiftly lowering the gun. "Come…come in, Mrs. Griffiths! Come in!" he said, pulling her in with his kind invitation, stunned. Hobbling inside the cabin, he led her to the fireplace, for she appeared to be shivering from the sudden drop of temperature outside and he was rather certain she was.

"Thank you, Mr. Miller." she said, a voice trembling in woe. "I apologize for imposing a disturbance so late; I just…have nowhere to go, anymore." she cried to him, feeling her heartache intensify upon nailing her gaze on the photograph, still hanging on the wall, still the same haunting, still the same she resented.

"Mr. Griffiths?" he asked her, concerned, throwing a blanket around her trembling body, rubbing her shoulders warm.

"William…he…he's…I left him!" she screeched, turned, and sobbed into the elderly man's arms. The man's jaw dropped, face furrowed in sadness; her heartbeat slammed against his frail chest, and the walls turned into them.

The lantern extinguished.

III

"HOW'S HIS ARM?" LEVI ASKED CHARLOTTE, as she was walking towards the campfire, suspiciously saddened, eyes dwelling in thought.

"It's not good…getting infected, and he is too stubborn to do anything 'bout it!" she said, flustered. "He needs rest…for he is exhausted Levi, and… perhaps today — the hunt I mean, it pushed him too much…" she stammered and he cocked a brow.

"I see." He nodded, twitching his lips from side to side in irritation. "Doesn't he need medicine?" he asked, wondering how long he would have to endure him at his camp, how long he would need to be sheltered from any of his bullets.

"Yes. I'm afraid so. I might need to go back to Mon Louis, and speak with the doctor." she huffed, exhausted to the core, or rather weighed down by the disappointment. "Will…uhm…he is a friend of someone I know, so perhaps I will get it without him having to examine Mac." she stuttered, and tore her gaze away in shame.

Will, she thought. *Oh, darnit…oh Will, what the hell am I doing to your heart…to us…yet again?* Her gaze glazed, stared blankly at the flames, chest breathing heavily in further guilt and confusion.

"Aha." He nodded, engraving the foreign name swiftly into his mind. "You know, Charlotte, I won't stand to have him here longer than a few days." he said sternly, pulling on his suspender that was pinching his shirt uncomfortably; the snapping sound reeling her attention back to him.

"I know, Levi. I am so thankful for your help thus far; I just pray things go well for everyone…" She sighed worriedly, not knowing where Mac would end up next. "And I simply wish for everyone to get along…if at all possible." She rolled her eyes and he stood there, staring.

"I guess I haven't really told you, but…tonight might be as good a time as any…" he said, and she blinked at him, benumbed.

"What haven't you told me…"

He drew in a deep breath, and faced her in earnest. "Remember that assignment I was telling you about?" he asked, bit into the whiskey cork, pulled it out.

"…Yes?"

"Well, Mac Kinnon *is* my assignment." He chuckled, then took a gulp out of the bottle. Her face fell, and eyes blinked, wordless.

"What do you mean…your assignment?" she asked, not able to interpret the joke this time.

"I've been hired to capture Mac Kinnon, for quite some time now." he said bluntly, staring at her, bold.

Charlotte stared back at him, and yet words failed her. Her mind traced circles within her head, calculating, flashing all the past days before her eyelids; *him randomly finding them in that building,* suddenly it made sense, for he either must have stalked her or followed the same blood trail she did, which was quite impossible since the rain had washed it off.

"Is this…is this why you took me out for dinner?" She swallowed hard, chest tight and heavy.

"What? No! No, Charlotte." he said, brows snapped together, whiskey swishing frantically within the bottle as he jerked a hand.

"Of course it is! Why else? You *knew* that I knew him!" She leered, clutching a fist, buzzing with anger.

"No. I did not! How do you come up with that now?" he leered back, aghast at the accusation, all the while JB was sneaking behind a barrel, trying to hear the argument, almost bumping into the glass vessels he tended to collect with the intentions of using them, yet never did, and so they just piled up collecting dust.

"How?" She snorted snidely. "What are the odds we meet at that bar, that this witch sent me to??" Brow and hip cocked, she stared at him menacingly.

"Witch? What witch? What are you talking about, Charlotte?"

"This witch, Victoria! Is she paying you?? And also sending you to the farmer's market? All that…for Mac?" She hissed, her breath stinging his face.

"I think…I think you're making things up now, lady. Please calm down. I know no Victoria! And no, it was definitely not about him, all this, you silly goose!" He fussed, flustered, then gulped down some more whiskey.

JB's crooked knee trembled from kneeling down for too long; it gave out on him, planting his butt to the ground, causing an explosion of a sound behind the barrel of cover. Levi and Charlotte, startled, looked behind them only to find JB covered in mud, with an awkward smile across his face and a shrug to his shoulders. Charlotte glanced back at Levi, staring with sweeping disappointment.

"I need…I need to ride." she said, and hastened to Finn.

"Wait a moment!" He rushed to her, plopping the bottle into the ground. "We can't just leave things like that, Charlotte." he said, his voice coarse and anxious — reaching to grab her hand.

She yanked her hand away from his, and started to saddle up Finn.

"Where, where are you going now in the middle of the night?? Do you realize what lurks out there?" He warned her, grabbing the reins away from her.

"Yes! I'm aware! But even an inbred human-eating malformed thing sounds better than being around a *traitor!*" she scowled, fighting back the tears, trembling whole as the betrayal sat on her chest, weighing her further down into a muddy pit.

"I'm not a traitor, Charlotte." he said, stunned, not knowing how else to prove his innocence to her.

"Get!" She kicked Finn's sides, and loped onto a path through the swamps, shooting through a gate of willow trees.

"Damnit!" He yelled agitatedly, hand raking through his dark hair, kicking the mud on the ground, glancing back at her riding off into the heavy sheets of fog drifting around the swamp.

IV

"Oh, beat the drum slowly and play the fife lowly,
And play the dead march as you carry me along;
Take me to the green valley, there lay the sod o'er me,
For I'm a young cowboy and I know I've done wrong."

WILL SANG, SEATED, DEVASTATED, ON THE FLOOR in his bedroom; uncorking every dusty old bottle he could find to drown his thoughts with. Waking up in a haze, he laid there until no light was emanated from the world outside. For suddenly it too shone too bright, too blitheful, and darkness was the company he yearned for, he was left with. There, he laid, bottle in hand, eyes nailed upon him. The once intelligent, success-driven man, now had lost the plot. A weakling; an ill individual, solely controlled by his very own brain and body.

The voices, they still lingered — somewhere in the hollowness, in the dent of his head that had remained. He heard them, still, tormenting him, day and night — never knowing which was reality, and which a living nightmare he could not escape from. His head buzzed; it rang and it rattled.

Staring across the bookshelves, he realized there was no ink dark enough to smudge a page with his emotions, and yet he wondered if he should smear a paper with what little was left of him; with what little sensible explanation there was, stick it within the pages of his most treasured book, bound to be found, to be understood. Elizabeth was gone; leaving him behind with a house built upon shadows and delusions — a house once warm by her female touch and presence; now begging to be torn down, for the bitter coldness that remained, crept around his heart.

V

"THAT'S...THAT'S VERY UNLIKE MR. GRIFFITHS, though, Miss Elizabeth." Mr. Miller said, utterly baffled to hear about Will's mistress.

"I just never thought he would do such a *sinful* thing to me…" she cried, forgetting to mention how she sinned, and yet he knew too — everyone knew.

"Well…it is a horrible thing, indeed…" He bowed his head, still unable to believe Will would ever betray someone. "Perhaps, this explains then, why he left you for so many months on your own, miss. I know you never could understand why. You must be feeling devastated, Miss Elizabeth…" He sighed, concerned about her delicate feelings, hand clutching her shoulder for support, delicate too.

"Indeed, Mr. Miller." she said without a sense of regret; completely wishing Will would rot in Hell for loving another woman. Her eyes cut at the photograph again, the sharp cheekbones, the full husky beard enveloping them, the flannel shirt — still able to smell his woodsy fragrance.

"Try to rest tonight, miss. My wife is going to take care of you in the morning, while I'm at work." he said and she looked at him.

"Mrs. Miller…how has she been?" she asked and he drew in a deep breath.

"She is…she hasn't been doing very well, these last weeks." He choked, cleared his throat, and faced her again. "A horrendous, stubborn cough that just won't go away…and doctors, well…you know how expensive they are nowadays! Let alone in Bisonhorn." he said, limped towards the guest room, inviting her in.

"I'm so terribly sorry to hear that, Mr. Miller…" she said, staring at the guest bed, the clumsy, desolated room, a knot in her throat. "I promise I will not be a bother for too long; I will make my accommodation at a hotel room tomorrow afternoon." she said, tentatively sitting down on the bed.

"Oh, Elizabeth; you ain't no bother to us. Stay as long as you wish. You've been through a lot." He smiled in her emerald eyes and she stared at him with the question on her lips.

"How…how is your son, Mr. Miller?" she asked and Mr. Miller bowed his head, as though briefly considering his answer.

"He…he is doin' alright. Haven't seen him in some years, to be honest… ever since…you know." He shrugged with an awkward smile, swallowing down a lump.

"I apologize…" she said and he bobbed his head.

"Last he wrote us, said he would move to Mayhaw…even further away from us, I reckon." He chuckled bitterly, coughed within his frail lungs.

"Mayhaw…" She bobbed her head absently, stunned.

"Mhm. Said he needed to see the mountains, the ocean…the sailors, for some kind of inspiration, I reckon…" He sucked in his lower lip, tears stood in his eyes.

"It sounds as if he has…left the nest, to explore wider horizons." she said, oddly impressed, and he tittered gently.

"That he has, miss. He…has rather made some changes that I ain't so sure I understand the reasoning behind." he said dryly, glancing around the room.

"Changes, Mr. Miller?" She gaped at him in curiousness.

"Yes, miss…he is just…he don't sound like himself, let's just say. He appears rather shut down, and…as though he lives in his own little world of creation! Hm…" He chuckled, hands shivering beside him. "But he's done well for himself, I hear…dealing with a few conflicts and contradictions here and there in his line of occupation, but he is quite successful…he is certainly not a lumberjack anymore!" He laughed and she flinched a nostalgic smile.

"I am too happy in knowing how well he has done for himself, for I had worried about him…from time to time." she said, tearing her gaze away from him, and Mr. Miller nodded in silence.

"He was…very fond of you, Miss Elizabeth, if you allow me to say so." he said and she stared at the flimsy covers.

"He was a very generous and helpful man." she said shortly. "If you could excuse me, I would like to rest for the night." she said and Mr. Miller jumped up swiftly, as per command.

"Of course, miss. Have a wonderful night." he said, then shut the door behind him.

Her eyes cast a glance at the fogged-up window; the moon shone brightly over the dark silhouette of sharp treetops; seeming like pitchforks ready to pierce through it. She had never strayed away from the ranch since the marriage; it felt oddly revolutionary for an elite like her — and somehow oddly satisfying to cause havoc to Will — she knew she did, for Will was not a man of strong resilience.

VI

"IF HE THINKS FOR A SECOND THAT I'M STUPID ENOUGH to believe he cared 'bout our 'friendship', and didn't use me instead for his stupid 'assignment', he is in for a real treat!" she fussed, mocked him, still heated by their argument, venting to Finn the whole way through the foggy swamps.

"Gah! He is just so…so…pathetic! Why would he play with my feelings like that?!" she hissed. "Why would he, Finn?? Why would anybody play with anyone's feelings…I don't understand…" She sighed, briefly wondering if she played with Will's, and yet she rather tried to figure out her own feelings.

Her mind switched back to those poor potatoes they collected together; or the jokes they made a little too loud around the saloon during dinner, or the way he always smiled and laughed unapologetically, filling up her soul with so much life and energy she had lost back in Marysville. Her teeth clenched with the memory, rage surged through her.

Finn twisted his ears back and forth repeatedly; trying to pay attention to everything she rambled about — even though he couldn't understand a single word, he could feel her heart rhythm change as her mood swung all over the place. Realizing she was clearly upset, he refrained — as much as he could, that is — from spooking at random things, to not upset her any further. Yet, he picked up a scent of something unfamiliar; there twirling through vine and moss, something menacing, ominous, that posed an enormous threat to them. He paused in his tracks, between brush and willow fingers, reaching like a spider web across the path; front feet stomped, urging them to turn around.

"Could you just not, Finn?" She sighed, growled with a lack of patience, unable to accept his temper tantrums right now. Yet Finn stomped further, nickered with a forewarning, torn between obeying his rider and listening to his instinct. "Quit!" she fussed, collecting his head and kicking him to move forward. He did, striding reluctantly deeper into the eerie dark path.

Yet a sinister whistle alerted Charlotte, pushing Finn over his threshold. Eyes flared in fear, side-eyeing the dark surroundings. She scanned around herself frantically; Finn moved in a circle, stomping tensely, yet all there was, an ebony veil of fog, swallowing the ghostly vines, dripping down the trees.

A whistle emerged again behind them; this time, a little closer.

"L…let's turn around, perhaps…" she stuttered, finally realizing she should start listening to her stallion more often, for he always had a good reason when he'd act up.

VREW-VREW

A whistling hit her again, intensified through the thick bushes right beside Finn…and her. Charlotte grabbed her gun, pulled it out of her flimsy holster, cocked it, ready to shoot.

VREW-VREW-VREW

The whistling sound multiplied when she turned Finn around; it repeated, it rang in her ears, now circled around them — getting closer, still hidden behind the humid haze. Her breath hastened, heart thudded, whole being drenched in perspire; she could barely find the courage to cue Finn to run back, as though frozen into place by a spell.

A man, covered in bloody streaks all over his bare body, jumped out of the bush, hand holding a machete — ready to slice Finn's face open. Charlotte screamed in terror, her trembling finger pulling the trigger without being prepared to do so.

BANG!!

Her gunshot echoed all through the swamp, barely reaching Levi's campground, muffled by the thick willow bark, the dense waters, the suffocating air around her. She shot the man in his shoulder, and before she knew it, another one jumped out right behind her, followed by a few more.

"Run, Finn!!!" she yelled from the top of her lungs, urging him to go.

Finn bolted, trampled over the man — knocking him into the scum-filled waters behind, leaped over a bush, feet slashing through the mud and water. He bolted on his way back to the campground, as the strange men slinked swiftly behind the bushes and trees.

She rode as fast as she could, slicing the fog as she passed through it, barely leaving any hoofprints behind, for they almost floated. The camp's fire reached its reassuring hand out to her, and her eyes clung onto it for dear life. She never dared to look back, for the image of the wicked man assailed her, making her whole body tremble fearfully, freezing in panic.

"Levi!" she yelled at him from a distance, spotting his recognizable silhouette just outside of the camp, sitting on a log in silence, waiting all this time for her return. Levi stood up, alarmed by the distressed voice, and rushed to meet her. Dismounting swiftly from a huffing Finn, she sprinted to him, plopping into his arms, hooking her nails into him, hugging him tight — writhing all over.

"What…what happened?" he asked her, baffled, holding her firm, feeling her heartbeat race within her rib-cage, denting a hole in his chest as it slammed against it.

"I…I shot a…thing; a man…or something like that!! I don't know!!" she stuttered, bursting into tears, crying against his chest.

"Hey, it's alright now." He caressed her, fingers softly spreading across her back. "Calm down. You're safe now. I'm here." he said and she bobbed her head, quivering. "Where is the man now, Charlotte?" he asked her suspiciously, preparing to defend the campground.

"I don't know! I never looked back! I just rode away from them!" she cried, squeezing his shirt within slippery fists.

"Men? Was it outlaws? Drunks? Deputies? I need to know, Charlotte." he said, persisting, squinting with scanning eyes through the fog around them.

"No! It was none of that!" She gasped, grasping for air. "They had…bl… BLOOD!! Blood all over them, and they were naked!!" she yelled at him in panic, face burying back into his warm chest.

"*Swamp Ghosts…*" he mumbled, clenching teeth.

"What ghosts??"

"Don't worry, they won't be coming here…" he said, caressing her head, fingers tangling within her dark waves.

"How do you know, Levi? What are these things?" she asked with a quivering breath, face tilting up at him, tears standing in her eyes, and yet she felt oddly serene to be cocooned in his strong arms, feeling his body, heavy upon hers. He smiled gently in her eyes, and wiped her tears with a thumb, freezing for a fleeting moment in her gaze.

"Well…" he soughed calmly. "You're lucky to be alive, as they're pretty slick with their ambushes." he said, gently sliding a finger across her cheek, tucking in a lock of hair behind her ear. "It appears, however, you're pretty slick with *escaping* ambushes…" He tittered, her lips flinched a faint smile.

His hand slid back on her waist, holding her tight. She let him, somehow craving to feel close. "They are…a group of Vodou killers; rumored to have immigrated all the way from Crowfoot." he said, his eyes coloring the rage he felt upon the thought. "However…I'm not sure if Vodou is all they practice."

"I have…never heard of this…" she said, embarrassedly; he nodded.

"Growing up in Red Giants…I've seen a lot of witchery." he said in earnest and her brows pulled together in bewilderment. "Murders…with no traces left behind. Rumored to be Shamans, shifting shapes…shadows…but I find they're nothing more than cowards." he said, and she gulped down a knot.

"This…scares me. I don't wish to believe in any of this, Levi…" she said, burying her head back into his chest, thinking absently of his words. "I don't believe in witchery…nor any malediction."

"I'm sorry…but I need you to understand, witchery or not, there are lunatics out there, lurking in these swamps as you found out…and at night, no one should be riding through." he said, sighed, biting his lip, squeezing her tight. "I should have never let you go…I just, I was frustrated…" he said, and she pulled back to face him.

"It's not your fault, Levi…I was pretty frustrated myself." she said, in a sigh. "I just can't believe you would use our friendship like this." Her head turned away, hands retrieved, slowly letting go of him.

"Charlotte…I never ever used our friendship! I would never do such a thing. I swear to everything I hold dear, I did not know you two were…" He paused briefly, chest rising. "…together."

Charlotte sensed his discomfort; almost able to hear the pain in his voice, and yet she still wondered about his intentions.

"Then…why all this? Why did you appear magically at the bar to help me? Why the dinner, and the invitation to come see you here? Then you all of a sudden find us, in one of the hundreds of buildings in Mon Louis? I just don't understand how, Levi. Make it make sense to me…why?" she asked, her face furrowed in confusion, arms folded and eyes staring right into his.

Levi was quiet; he didn't know how else to explain the situation and his clear intentions to her. He stared back at her, fingers slid through his messy brown hair with frustration — for he recognized the oddly serendipitous manner of the incidents.

"Levi, please. Tell me why." She persisted, a pout scarring her lips.

He stepped forward, towered over, and she looked with confusion.

Hunting for her face, as the fog grew thicker between them — challenging them to see each other clearly, he grabbed her from the jaw — sharp and slippery against his hands, planting his lips on hers intensely, forcefully, without hesitation — pressing so hard, he could feel her pulse vibrate from them. He kissed her quivering lips, bruising them lustfully, thumb caressing her cheek — shaking himself, from the pressure he now felt within him; the dreadful fear of rejection. His mouth — warm and soft, gliding on hers; wetting her lips, feeling their teeth subtly meet, as they breathed in each other — tasting the feeling neither of them could ever explain.

He kissed fervently, and she kissed him back, tensed.

"Explanation will do for another time." he whispered, as his inflamed lips unhooked from hers, locking his green eyes on her hazels that tortured him for far too long — studying her uncertain, guilty, yet pleasured expression.

CHAPTER 39

Deranged

I

HE TIED HER HEAD TO THE SADDLE HORN, forcing it to the side as hard as it would go; there was no release from the relentless pressure, yet she was too weak to care — too run down to notice. He whipped her hind, forcing her to move forward, yet she could only twist in circles, like a senile old man, lost in the middle of nowhere, sinking into a quicksand of his mind.

Determined to make her *"broke as you could get 'em"* — both in mind, and in soul. Her legs quivered in attempt to keep her balance, knowing if she didn't, she would get bludgeoned across the face with anything the rancher could find. "Atta girl!" A prideful smile scarred his lips, witnessing the horse break further and further by his barbaric actions.

II

THE EARLY SUN FLICKERED ACROSS THE GROUND PLAYFULLY; flaring against particles in the air, shining through the window pane. His eyelids fluttered from the irritating brightness; squinting, he checked the time on his pocket watch still hanging from his vest. He held his head steadily, feeling the whole room spin around him; making him retch by the intolerable motion.

Tumbling over to the wall to support himself, he walked little by little to reach the door. Stepping outside, he grasped for a lungful of air, drawing in the deepest of breaths, lungs filling up with the scent of plants hunkering down for the winter; the musky-sweet smell of broken-down leaves gathered up into piles.

Yet, there was not a single hint of cedarwood scent — burning slowly as she sat down before it with her cup of warm tea, every morning before dawn. There was not a sound of a loving greeting, that he was accustomed to hearing from the other side of the land. Nor a welcoming wave, inviting him to sit beside her — with his coffee already brewing fresh and blazing hot for the morning.

Croaking crows, the only sound he could detect; flying over him, black feathers elegantly stretched out — matching with his raven-black hair. He studied them as they flew deeper into Red Giants before him and a phrase from a book emerged in his memory. It was believed that ravens were birds of death, and uncleanliness; *a symbol of diabolical evil,* he recalled, and glanced at the barn. The stubborn raven was no longer seated at the edge of the loft.

"You must follow them, William…"

The now familiar voice urged him to go.

"Death is coming upon them."

Tone was ominous, odious, and caustic.

"LEAVE ME ALONE!!!" Will screamed from the very top of his lungs, fingernails hooked into the sides of his head, forcing the voice to get out of him. "GOD!!! HELP ME, LORD!!!" He begged desperately, looking up at the dull sky, eyes burning by the sweltering rays that pierced through a gray-slate cloud — longing for relief, remorse, redemption.

Countless red cardinals flew, startled, from hoarfrost branches they were resting on, coloring the pale cloudy sky with their vibrant feathers. Dancing with the rhythm of the wind, blowing them in all directions; they circled in pairs to form their peaceful group once again and adjust their momentum. They, too, followed the raven's trail into the redwood forest before him, chirping excitedly as they did.

Will looked, stunned, at them — wondering if it was a sign from God, wondering if Elizabeth had run off into the woods after all. He burst into tears, chest retracted, hyperventilating from his distress and misery, clinging onto a feeble thread of hope, shortening the longer he lingered at the ranch.

In the shadows, in the voices, in the pit of woe.

III

SHE STARED AT THE COTTON CEILING. EYES PRIED WIDE OPEN. Mind racing, as she replayed the incident. Charlotte couldn't shut her eyes that night, for she was more shocked with Levi's impulsive kiss than she was with the Swamp Ghosts almost hacking her up. She laid there, in her own air of buffeting silence, wondering if she slowly turned into an odd version of her mother, *or maybe she always was, and didn't know it?*

Yet, she never asked to be involved with all these men who came pouring down on her like rain — nor did she ask for Levi to kiss her, even though she undoubtedly chose to kiss him back.

"Oh, Will…what a mess…" she mumbled, feeling like the dirtiest woman on earth — one he certainly did not deserve. "How will you ever forgive me…how will I ever be bold and rude enough to ask for such forgiveness…I shouldn't be here…and I shouldn't have rescued him, and I shouldn't have k…"

"Miss Charlotte?" JB called her, startling her to the core again. His voice, suspiciously coarse and worrisome, trying hard to cover it with a kind smile, as he stood before her shut tent, waiting.

"Y…yes sir?" she answered swiftly, rushing to button up her shirt over her silky white corset, the only undergarment she owned.

"Ehm, your partner, ehm, he, well, he is…the fella ain't doin' so well, miss!" JB strained a stutter, not knowing how to deliver the news; face flushed red from the struggle.

"You mean Mac??" She gasped, crawled out from the tent, the other boot still in her hand.

"Yes. That one." JB said, not feeling yet comfortable to voice the legend's name out loud.

"What's wrong with him??" Charlotte rushed to Mac's tent, not giving JB the opportunity to answer as he hobbled after her in great curiosity.

"Mac?" she called calmly, slithering into his tent.

Mac was cloaked in sweat; a horrifying ill smell escaping from his trembling body. His eyes cut at her, a guilty smirk on his face, knowing she had warned him about the infection on his arm.

4 2 1

"Mac, let me look at your arm." she ordered, grabbed it authoritatively, then noticed the infection had gotten far worse — yellow pus oozing out of the flesh, incredibly swollen, red, feasting at his skin. She felt of his head — it was blazing hot to the touch. In that fever, he shivered relentlessly; battling it all throughout the night.

"JB!" she called him frantically, and Mac kept his gaze upon her. A vein popped on her forehead, panicked.

"Yes ma'am!" He hopped up, startling her, for she didn't expect him to be all this time immediately behind her.

"Bring me a wet cloth and a bucket of water, please." She commanded kindly, one hand feeling of Mac's wet clothes. "And as many blankets or hides you can get me!" she added and JB shot off like a bullet — one crookedly leaving the chamber. Turning back to Mac, she lifted his head up and encouraged him to lift his upper body as well to take his shirt off.

"Hm." he grunted, tugging on his shirt.

"Mac? Please…let me just…"

"I…I'm alright!" he growled, barely able to speak.

"Your clothes are soaked! You need to take them off, Mac!" She fussed, grabbing the cloth again. "JB is bringing blankets, and some water to rinse the sweat off first." she said, hand attempting to pull his dripping shirt up, yet he wouldn't let her.

"I'm alright!" he growled louder, snarling his teeth at her like a wolf. She stared at him, aghast, yet her brows snapped together in determination.

"Mac…I won't say it again…not so kindly, at least." she said, pulling on it; he resisted, grabbed her hand harshly and yanked it away from him. He leered and she leered back, snarling her own teeth back to him. "You're gonna take this shirt off now, and I don't want to hear otherwise, you…you stubborn fool!" she fussed, and pulled his shirt up and over his face — yet her eyes widened in horrifying shock to witness a myriad of deep burn marks and ragged scars all over him, all across his muscular chest and abdomen, just like on his back.

A muffled gasp escaped her; and yet it hit his ears. Noticing the sudden terror in her eyes, his heart shrunk within him. Huffing agitatedly, he folded his arms together — hiding everything he could discreetly with the swell of his arms. She tore her gaze away, and so did he.

"Mac…" She reached for his hand, he jerked away. "I'm sorry…I didn't know…" she said, worried to have upset him. He cut his eyes at her, they stared at each other with mutual concern — *concern that he repulsed her; concern she made him distrust her again.*

JB delivered the bucket of water and rushed back to grab the blankets, hopping along on one leg to speed up. Charlotte averted her eyes to the bucket, dunked the cloth into the water, and placed it over his burning forehead.

"I…I will leave this with you, and you can…wash yourself if you choose to do so, which…would be good for you to do." she said softly and yet stern, and he swallowed in shame; easing himself back to the ground, grunting in great relief, feeling the coolness of the water drip all over him.

She tore her gaze away to not cause him any further discomfort, and yet her eyes stole a discreet glimpse of his flog marks again. As though someone wished to overlap his ripped abdomen with lines, carved by a menacing hand. Her heart constricted. There was a story dented in his flesh, still imprisoning his entire being in mind. A feral animal trapped within a vessel of scarred beauty; he was.

She swallowed down a sob, turned away, crawled out of the tent, when JB arrived with all the fur blankets, plopping them before her very eyes. "Thank you, sir. I have to head out to Mon Louis, and try to get some medicine for him, if you could…hand them to him. I will be back as soon as possible." she said, glancing back at Mac, still quivering uncontrollably.

"Oh! Well! Levi, actually…is takin' care of that!" JB informed her enthusiastically, placing the blankets next to Mac; his eyes freezing upon his scars, unable to pull them away from them. His face blanched, and it fell, and it flushed with sadness.

"He…is?" She gasped, surprised, reeling JB back outside.

"Indeed, miss! Now — haha, I don't know what he might replace the medicine with, but oh well!" He snorted, and Charlotte blinked at him, disturbed, hoping he was joking again; as this would be a perfect opportunity to kill Mac effortlessly and without suspicion. "Ah…guess I should not have said that…" he said, scratching his bearded chin awkwardly, loosening a piece of bread stuck within it.

"…JB???"

"I'm just kiddin'!" He wheezed, slapping his thigh for added sound. "He should be back anytime now, he's been gone for a good while already." he reassured her, and limped back to the fire he was preparing to start cooking a stew with.

I V

"MRS. MILLER, GOOD MORNING!" ELIZABETH SAID TO HER as she walked into the main room of the cabin; a cramped ramshackle of a room, yet cozily personal, decorated with frames of family photographs, a few pelts and proud elk mounts, all hunted within the deep woods of Red Giants.

"Mrs. Griffiths! Good morning, ma'am! How very…" She let out a cater-waul of a violent cough and Elizabeth's brows snapped together in repulsion. "How very good to see you again, ma'am…" she said, smiling in her cold eyes.

"Delighted to see you too, Mrs. Miller…" she muttered, avoiding to come close to her. "I heard you're dealing with a nasty cold?" she said, eyes scanning all around her, for once able to see the cabin in better light.

"Oh…" She chuckled bitterly. "Yes. It is a nasty cold, indeed, Mrs. Griffiths. But…our family has certainly been through a lot worse." she said and Elizabeth flinched a vague smile, for nothing was worse than her own situation; losing her husband to a woman named *Charlotte*.

"Yes…so I've heard." she said, disinterested. "Mrs. Miller, I'm afraid I may need my coat to be washed, as there is an unsightly speck of dirt on it from last night's riding." she then said, since Mrs. Miller was often taking care of her laundry back at the ranch.

"Of course, Missus." she agreed instantly, grabbed the heavy coat from her, and walked slowly — awfully fatigued from her chronic illness, to the barrel of water she used to wash their clothes in.

"You understand, I'm sure; I *cannot* be seen like that in Bisonhorn." she added, as she brushed her ginger curls repeatedly, glaring at her torn up slippers and the bluish veins that protruded through her frail skin.

"Of course, Mrs. Elizabeth." she said, and coughed heavily; a few droplets of bright red blood landing on her coat.

V

LEVI MANAGED TO RETRIEVE SOME MEDICINE SUCCESSFULLY from the doctor; he had a good reputation in every state, as everyone knew of his meaningful career — weeding out the murderers from every town, so asking for such a favor was not uncalled for. Trotting away from Mon Louis, he came across Sheriff Jordon on his path, and swiftly hid his face with the brim of his hat.

"Mr. Krog!" he called after him, and Levi bit his lip in guilt.

"Sheriff!" he greeted him, pretending to be surprised to see him here.

"How're things goin', son?" he asked him curiously, parking his large grey thoroughbred horse next to his.

"Busy, as always." he hummed calmly, brushed his full beard, itching from the unbearable humidity trapped within it.

"Any hints yet?" he inquired straightforward, avoiding pointless small talk.

"Working on it." he said, swallowing nervously.

"Wonderful!" He smiled, bobbed his head to him. "Sheriff Dorman will be pleased to know this. Keep your eyes peeled. He is a dangerous man." he warned him, kicked his horse, making his way into town.

Levi waited on him to completely vanish in the distance, for the last thing he needed was for the sheriff, who laid all his trust upon him, to follow him up to the camp and witness Mac being doctored up by *Levi, the Bounty Hunter* — instead of laying on the ground with his hands tied, ready for an overnight delivery to Birdsboro.

"What a goddamn mess." Levi sighed to himself, glancing down at the bottle of medicine, thinking back on the kiss last night; Charlotte's lips; the way his heart beat like never before as he tasted them, the way his whole being fluttered upon holding her in his arms.

She kissed him back, he thought, he smiled.

He hoped.

VI

MOUNTING RACHEL HASTILY, WILL RUSHED TO FOLLOW the faint croaks of the ravens still echoing in the forest. He couldn't believe this absurdity, yet he already felt he was going mad and had nothing further to lose. A bug had drilled within his mind; a poisonous thorn stinging his thoughts repeatedly.

Charlotte, he was convinced, had been deflowered by the arms, lips, and heart of Mac, someplace in Mon Louis…perhaps the very same room he paid for her stay.

The voices told him everything; therefore it must be true.

How else would they know?

> *"He is taking such good care of the mistress…she loves his barbaric ways; the way he strangles innocent souls — the way he fucks her, in the bed you seized beside her, like you could never do — for she admires how strong of a man he is, William. She is telling him you're weak, William; your body depleted, your mind delusional. Deranged. And they laugh at that fact, as you cry in a corner of your room. You lost her, William…"*

They kept on buffeting his serenity with verbal assault, every time he tried to think of her, or reread her letter he had torn apart. Dithering to deny the words anymore, he had to let go of her concept, still secretly bewitched by it.

Elizabeth, however; he was determined to find her, drop down on one knee and ask for forgiveness, beg to revert back to the life they once had built, before the flames of the barn, and the sin within it, burned it to ash. Even though he adored Charlotte with every fiber of his being, still beholding her in high regard, he could not forgive her betrayal, and the words she said behind his back — the mockery she and Mac made out of him and his condition, who they were to blame for. He cried in loneliness, he sobbed in pain, he yelled in an outburst of emotions; he laughed upon a nervous breakdown.

He laughed, because they thought *they* wouldn't tell him.

He laughed, because they thought he wouldn't find out.

He laughed, because they thought he would go crazy without her.

He laughed, as he trotted deeper into Red Giants.

Guided by the voices; encouraging him.

Leading the way to his beloved. *Elizabeth.*

VII

SHE SAT BESIDE HIM, WET CLOTH HELD ON HIS HEAD — falling asleep every other minute, since she had stayed awake the night before. She watched him squirm and shiver, for the fever spiked higher, and her heart throbbed within the chamber of her ribs, worrying to the core for him. Studying the woeful expression on his face, she realized he too was just a person beneath the blood-stained layer of sin that clothed him; with feelings just like her or anybody else — no matter his past, he too felt pain, albeit different than the rest. Perhaps unable to show it, speak about it, or even consciously feel it. Sometimes she forgot of that fact, as everybody feared him. Everybody longed to see him swing; the monster, *the devil's son,* as they called him. Sometimes she forgot, for he hid his emotions so very well, as if there never were any…at least, she wished to assume he had any to hide.

"Charlotte? Charlotte?" Levi repeated a dozen times, for he received no answer from her.

"Oh!" She gasped, forcing her eyes open. "Yes! Levi? Come in." She cracked the tent open, dunked the cloth in the water to freshly wet it again.

"Here. Give him that. That should do it." He handed her the bottle, peeking through the tent to see Mac lying there asleep.

"What is that, Levi?" she questioned him, making sure JB was kidding.

"Willow bark." He sighed, cocked his head, and faced her with a cinched brow. "Don't worry. I want him back on his feet more than you do." He teased her, winked with a smirk.

"Levi!" She hissed within a whisper, glancing over at Mac, still resting, not able to pay any attention to them. She leaned over him, uncorked the bottle, clutched the back of his head and raised it up. "Mac…drink this for me." she soughed softly and he squinted through his eyelids, cracking an absent smile to find her face before his. After administrating the medicine, she walked out the tent together with Levi; slowly, and awkwardly — in uncomfortable silence.

"Thank you, Levi…" she said, clearing her dry throat. "For getting the medicine. I would have done it, if I had known earlier." She sighed, his hands accidentally brushed against hers as they walked abreast, close.

"Don't mention it. Like I said, I don't do it for him." he said earnestly, cutting his eyes at her to capture her reaction.

"I know…" she said, bowed her head in confliction. "I actually also need to leave, back to Mon Louis in a few days. I just want to make sure he is… healthy again." she mumbled, secretly dreading to leave him, not knowing if she would be so lucky to ever find him again — albeit, also knowing she shouldn't anyway.

"Oh." He nodded absently. "You are?" he asked, confused, pausing, sitting down on the log before the fire, facing her.

"Yes…" A heavy breath escaped her. "You see…I'm…I'm awaiting some-one fairly soon, and I want to make sure he doesn't return to find an empty room." She tittered awkwardly, trying to lighten up the heavy mood — all of a sudden wondering when Will would arrive, and realizing she hadn't even worried about that since she left the town.

"Right. The special someone." He grinned back, and averted his eyes back to the logs.

"Right…" she said, nodding.

"Feel free to go anytime, Charlotte…I will take care of him. I promise I won't do anything you wouldn't agree with. Yet." he said, realizing he was already rejected. Again.

"I will definitely keep this in mind, Levi…thank you." she said, fiddling with her sleeves nervously, thinking about that sudden kiss they exchanged, contemplating to address it, choosing to bury it beneath a rug with other sudden kisses left untold.

"Levi!! Levi!!" JB waddled as fast as he could through the tables, hopping clumsily over logs that were spread around the campground. Levi stood up swiftly, turning around to face the unusual sight of his jog.

"Relax, old man! What's going on?" he asked suspiciously, for he rarely found JB so flustered.

"They...the..." He gasped dramatically, arched back, chest inflated, mouth split wide open, inhaling an army of flies within his lungs. "Gotta catch my breath, Levi boy!!" He wheezed, from running like a madman across the swampy ground that sunk with his weakened legs at every step.

"Calm down, JB! Take your time." he said calmly, as he looked around to spot any intruders.

"The deputies!!" he then yelled. "They found me, plucking some herbs from the ground just north of the camp!! Some oregano that never grows here!! I thought it would make for a perfect stew, but it wasn't enough, so I walked a little further, and found some more! But then the gators was eyein' me from the damn waters, and ya know I cannot run with this goddamn knee, so I thought to shoot the sons of bitches, which then alerted the goddamn bastards, and ya know that gun ain't no quiet piece of weaponry, which reminds me I really need to find a suppressor for it — ya figure the fence in Mon Louis carries something like that?" JB asked him, lower lip hanging down, upper curled and raised up, as though posing an important question, then he took in another deep breath to refill his lungs after talking so much.

"JB! Where are the deputies?? What happened with the deputies?!" Levi fussed, reminding him nervously.

"Oh!!! Oh, right!! The deputies!! Oh! Well! They stopped me! They, they asked if I had seen the man — ya *know* which man!" He exaggeratedly pointed with his bulging eyes over to Mac's tent.

"JB! I know! Tell me what they said!"

"They said they was lookin' for him! And are investigating every building around, campgrounds included!!" He wheezed again, let out a big sigh, as all this effort exhausted him to the core.

"Shit!" Levi looked at Charlotte, who had turned pale from fear.

"And now? What do we do now, Levi?" she asked him, petrified, expecting to hear a clever solution immediately, for she had none.

"We don't have time to pack the camp. We gotta move him, somehow." he said, thinking hard of a solution.

"And go where? Please, don't tell me deeper into the swamps..." She begged him, as just the thought of the Swamp Ghosts terrified her, and the sun had started to set again, and darkness would soon envelop the whole area, blinding them from any threat.

"No. We need to leave the state…" he said, then thought of a secluded cabin up north that he used as a hiding spot when he was tracking down outlaws. "Pack him up — somehow. I will get the horses ready." he instructed her and rushed to them. "JB! You pack the camp tomorrow; meet us at the hideout cabin in Rockies East!"

Charlotte trembled from the upwards spiral of adrenaline; she wasn't planning on leaving anywhere but back to Mon Louis, yet now she would be going even further away; somewhere she didn't even know. However, being also a wanted individual, *she could never trust that the law was hunting only after Mac,* she thought to herself, somehow excusing her decision to go with him again.

CHAPTER 40

Stay

I

THE LANTERN SHINED BRIGHTLY IN FRONT OF HIS FACE, illuminating the eerie stillness of his gaze; eyes that darkened by the hour. A face, furrowing, wrinkling in absent rage, not felt within his heart. They took dangerous shortcuts, straying far away from the safe path, and yet Will's hands weren't steering the head of the horse. The mossy hills, slumped soil, and fallen trees made for an unappealing atmosphere, while posing a threat to any horse's legs that would try to cross through. The bark of the trees shifted once again as they passed them; creaking and bending, as though ears sprouted within the black gaps, listening to his thoughts, listening to the heart knocking like a fist at a door, with no face to greet it back.

Will would always calculate ground formations, or any of nature's obstacles, to ensure the safety of his mount — just like he did up in Rockies West, yet the voices in his head commanded him to go ahead and move forward; to kick, spur, kick, spur, for Elizabeth was in great danger, and he didn't have much time left. So, he did. He kicked Rachel to go into a lope, slapping the split reins against her withers, but she refused for she couldn't feel confident enough to trust him; he who would never expect her to rush through such challenging terrain, he who was not acting like the rider she always knew.

"Spur the horse…harder." they ordered him, and he dug his spurs deep into Rachel's sensitive flank, making her bolt from the pain and sudden surprise, leaping over the mossy log, galloping downwards a sinking steep hill, squeezing through a bundle of trees, bucking him off of her, as the spur

had completely penetrated through her flesh. He fell off of her; landing on the mossy ground, slamming his head against a rock; knocking him unconscious. His guns, still attached on Rachel's saddle — she kept on galloping away, disappearing into the somber forest, as he laid there, unresponsive, with the blood-stained spur still spinning with the keening wind.

I I

"HOW'S HE HOLDING UP?" LEVI ASKED curiously, crossing through Ozark Ridge.

"He is…" She paused, hand feeling off his forehead. "Goodness, who are we kidding. He is burning…he is terrible! I've never seen him like this! So… so unresponsive, and…" She choked, cried to him, holding Mac tightly before her, struggling to see where she was going over his large frame.

"Well, get used to it!" He teased her in bad taste, as he started to cross a little river.

"Please, Levi, this isn't funny anymore." she hissed, crossing right after him, trying to balance Mac's large self on the saddle that was awkwardly too tight for both of them.

"Lighten up, cowgirl!" He snorted. "He'll be just fine. Didn't realize how much you cared for him anyway." he said bitterly, hopping over a rotten tree crossing the path.

"Wouldn't you care if someone rescued you so many times? I'd be dead without him…" she said, whispered to herself, reminiscing all the times he was there for her. Strangling the man that almost raped her, killing the grizzly that was inches away from slamming her into her death, rescuing Finn from drowning in the frozen lake — *how was she to forget?* Her heart crumbled like a feeble stone, arms squeezing him tight, as though for him to sense her gratitude once more. Levi remained silent; he didn't think this man was capable of having the slightest hint of empathy, or any feelings for that matter, besides the thrill of killing.

"I just don't think you really know what this man has done with his blood-stained hands, you're so eagerly protecting, or worshiping…" he grumbled, his tone stern and stone cold, thinking about all the victims that were found hanging by methods only Mac could invent; dismembered and decapitated in the most inhumane ways, burned or drowned alive so they could still hear themselves suffer. "You'd be shocked to find out…" he added, squeezed through a tight gap between trees.

"Not much shocks me, anymore…" she said after a particularly long moment of silence, clutching Mac's being protectively. "I've had my fair share of evil I had to deal with…and he is *nothing* like that." she mumbled, suddenly feeling the Fiddler's slobbery mouth pressing against hers again — his filthy, slimy body behind hers; a repulsive sensation and horrifying image she could never forget. She swore to herself to never ride through the Ozarks again, or Birdsboro for the matter, yet life did not care about her plans, nor feelings. *God didn't seem to care either, no matter how hard she prayed for his guidance,* she thought to herself. Bitter.

Levi nodded, disappointed with her stubbornness, and chose to remain quiet for the rest of the trip. He couldn't argue with Charlotte any further, as she was clearly not the kind to be persuaded.

I I I

Sheriff Jordon,

I'm headed to Bisonhorn to visit with a man that was last seen on the Caddo River Boat, by one of my retired deputies who served as a guard for the mayor of Mon Louis. He claimed he was together with a woman that could be the one we've been looking for — possibly, thinking she might lead us to Mac Kinnon, if captured and interrogated well. I got word that he returned alone to his ranch down in Caledonia Territory, as apparently, he is a married man. The fool…The man is a horrific liar, and I'm convinced he and the woman know all about Kinnon's atrocious plans — or else, why would he lie about her being dead? He is fond of the lady, so he'll speak if he knows we got her.

Forward this information to your bounty man; he needs to be aware, as she must reside in Mon Louis. I include a wanted poster of hers, so he knows exactly who to look out for. Lastly, his name is William Griffiths; a wealthy son of a bitch who thinks he's above the law. He will learn differently.

Sheriff Dorman

JORDON REREAD THE LETTER, AS HE COULDN'T BELIEVE that the well-respected William Griffiths, known and adored by the vast majority of people, was possibly covering for Mac Kinnon — protecting him and his crimes, all this time. He felt it was urgent enough to go find Levi at his campsite; not wishing to waste time writing a letter in light of this new information.

I V

THE MUSKY GROUND SHOOK GENTLY UNDERNEATH his resting body. Pebbles bounced up and rolled closer to his face, slightly tickling his nose. The deep red tree trunks trembled around him, as the footprints approached closer, stepping heavily and confidently into the mushy soil. A subtle noise of a groan woke Will up softly, now trying to adjust his vision in the dark, feeling the dent in his skull ache mercilessly.

He heard a sudden huff of complaint and looked around, startled to find a gigantic grizzly sniffing the surroundings. Sealing his lips as though to not scream from the depths of his core, he crawled hastily underneath a fallen log, and watched the bear carefully, now nearing the fallen lantern on the ground — miraculously still lit. Holding his breath, he felt his pulse shoot up in his throat; praying the bear could not feel it too.

The grizzly snorted and growled, as the uninviting smell of man agitated its senses. Danger is all it could get a whiff of, and yet a scent of fear intensified the closer he swiped its nose at the soil where Will was laying moments prior. Snarling his teeth, large yellow canines protruding from its mouth. Upon dropping its gaze back to the scent, he launched at it with its enormous furry paws and impressive muzzle, digging swiftly into the dirt with large ebony claws.

Will swallowed fearfully as he tried to contemplate in a state of trance and panic, where he was, and why he was in the middle of Red Giants, without his horse of all things, nor a gun around his hip, with yet another grizzly hunting him down. Laying as still as he could, not flinching a muscle, not breathing in any air, he gaped at the bear's chilled breath, lighting up in the darkness by the glow of the lantern's flame as it sniffed all over it. It reared its enormous body with its thick coat blowing in the wind; standing like a statue, sniffing intimidatingly, hunting for Will's scent. The sudden concept of loneliness clung onto his bones, clinking in the stillness like a wind-chime in his woeful heart.

V

"I CAN NO LONGER, LEVI...I HAVEN'T SLEPT ALL NIGHT...I'M FADING." SHE complained, as her head was crashing repeatedly onto Mac's back; falling asleep every minute.

"We gotta push, cowgirl. Ring Lagoon is just up ahead, just past those hills." he reassured, pointing with his lantern in the distance.

"What is this place..." she mumbled faintly, struggling to keep eyes open.

"It's an isolated lagoon, with a hidden path leading to it. Once, a notorious hunter built a cabin there; rumors say he had divorced and left civilization to live out his life in nature — away from women, and trouble..." he rolled his eyes, thinking back on the kiss embarrassedly, and the rejection that came right after it. "Anyhow, he lived a good life, until an angry bear took him." He chuckled, as their horses built up their speed to trot over the hill.

"Well, sounds quite ideal..." She smirked snidely, thinking about Will's divorce and the whole messy situation she was in. "Sometimes, I too want to just disappear..." she added, still struggling to stay awake.

"That would make for a lonely world." he said, seeing the cabin from a distance. "We're close, Charlotte. How's he holding up?" he asked, relieved to have arrived, as he was quite exhausted himself.

"He seems less warm…but still trembling a great deal." She sighed, feeling of his head again

"Well…luckily there's a whole lagoon we can dump him in, you know, to cool off…" He snorted and she rolled her eyes, too exhausted to respond.

Rushing down the rocky path, Finn's feet struggled to step on the giant stones. He would slip and snort, and huff and go off the path, somehow unusual for him to do so.

"Easy, Finn. We're almost there, sweetie." she encouraged him, as he hopped, agitated from the pain he felt underneath his hooves.

"Not that sure-footed, is he?" Levi teased her with a chuckle.

"Sure he is!" She perked up swiftly. "You should've seen him up in the snowy mountains! He was phenomenal!" she defended him, instantly thinking in sharp clarity again.

"Haha. Easy there, girl. Just teasing." he smiled, for he secretly loved to see her get annoyed by his taunting remarks.

V I

"GOOD EVENING, SIR!" SHERIFF JORDON APPROACHED JB, who was packing up the camp wagon hastily.

"Oh!" he screeched, startled, swinging around a wooden spatula as if for self-defense. "Howdy do, sheriff!" he then said, surprised to find him there, retrieving the spatula as Jordon stared at it with a cocked brow of disapproval.

"Can't complain…I'm here to speak with Levi, yet — it seems you are packin' up?" he inquired suspiciously.

"Oh! Lordy…oh, Lordy…" He tittered nervously. "Well, kinda. Perhaps." he stuttered, knowing he wasn't the best person to lie, then resumed to packing the wagon in sheer cowardliness.

"How come, mister? Where you headed to?" He persisted; looking around the campground for anything odd.

"Ehm…just, a little over there. Them gators are just gettin' too close, if ya know what I mean." he pointed now with a deer leg that he was packing up in the supply wagon.

"So, where's Levi at? I need to speak with him urgently." he said, tired of talking to what he considered Levi's clown.

"Levi?" He blinked at him and Jordon nodded stern. "He…he…he is, well, it's…personal." he shrugged, then folded his arms together, defending Levi's absence.

"Personal…" Jordon's brow raised to him, striding slowly towards him.

"The gal!" he squeaked. "He has a gal…he is takin' out for dinner." he said, curling his yellow-nailed toes inside his musky boots nervously.

"What…*gal*…mister." Jordon neared closer to his face, towering over him, intimidating him — clearly noticing the lie scarring his plump flushed face.

"Ch…a busty one!!" he exclaimed, as he didn't know what else to say, and that was his first impression of Charlotte anyway, figuring a fellow man would understand as much.

"I see…a man of great taste he is, ah? Ha ha." Jordon laughed snidely, and soon enough JB followed in after him.

"Ha ha! Indeed, dear sheriff! Indeed!" he agreed, then sipped on a bottle of whiskey, relieved to have survived the interrogation. "Too bad her partner is a blood-thirsty killer, however! My boy Levi would've been perfect for her!" He sighed with the realization, still chuckling with his hand on his belly, the other waved around — spilling the bottle.

"He is…a what?" Jordon cocked his head, in great surprise and confusion. JB blinked. Brows flickered unintentionally, lips quivered and eyes protruded ever more.

"…should not have said that. Should absolutely, most definitely, *not* have said that…" JB murmured faintly to himself, backing away slowly, until Jordon took out his pistol, and pointed it to him.

"You're comin' with me, ol' man." he threatened, anger burning a hole within him, realizing his lauded bounty hunter was not the loyal and trustworthy hired gun he thought he was.

VII

THE ALMIGHTY GRIZZLY CAUGHT THE WIND with its nose and followed it off into the forest; leaving Will behind, still petrified, frozen underneath the log. Gathering up his grit, he crawled out from his hiding spot and grabbed the lantern, rushing in the opposite direction of the bear. And yet he was utterly lost in the woods, for he never had explored Red Giants before, despite living right next to it.

A sharp pain hit him from the back of his head, rattling his whole body in harrow. Groaning in agony, he felt of the area, his fingers soaking with blood. "Darn it." he fussed, as he felt at the gash the rock left behind, wondering what other ill-effects it would gift him, suspecting now everything was a prank of his own imagination, unsure of who orchestrated it. A waltz through a feeble maze, yet this time he danced alone.

He walked further into the woods, with no particular direction; slowly lighting up his way — desperately hoping for a road to magically emerge in the distance. Shivering cold scraping his bones, violently through the silky long sleeve shirt he wore, for he was totally unprepared for the frigid night. His breath lingered in the air as he tried to quell his panic; it blended with the foreboding mist around him, a company of muted colors, faded scent, and yet he found himself lonely again. Even the voices had subsided; abandoning him, as though he was not even worth being tormented any longer.

VIII

DISMOUNTING AT A CRYSTAL CLEAR LAGOON, illuminated by the hanging moon above them, Levi hitched up his horse before the deserted rustic cabin. He grabbed Roy that he was ponying along the way, and tethered him next to his steed. Stepping back, he discreetly studied the black stallion, noticing the thick boning on his legs, and the powerful hip he was blessed with — *Mac sure knew how to choose his horses too*, he thought to himself enviously.

Charlotte followed right after, and Levi rushed to her, holding on to Mac while she dismounted. Pulling him down, they carried him into the chilled cabin, maneuvering through the darkness, around the chairs and table, bumping into them as Levi led them to a room.

"I'll start a fire real quick. I always kept firewood in the chimney here for my next return — luckily, I see no one has been here since." he muttered, as he glanced over at the pile of wood still stacked up in the corner, then proceeded towards the room.

They laid Mac onto the bed, and Charlotte hurried to light up the candles in the house with a match Levi gave her, as Levi worked on the fire, tossing logs inside the chimney, blowing a small spark that ignited.

"Mac?" She kneeled before him by the bed, his eyes struggled to pry open.

"Hm…" He breathed heavily, eyes clutched shut again.

"We are safe now." she said, swallowing hard and his brows snapped, not understanding why they even left. Her hand brushed across his forehead, and he flinched beneath her touch. "You don't feel so warm anymore, either…" she said, relieved, subtly caressing him.

"Stay." he soughed, grabbed her hand firmly.

"W…what did you say?" she asked him, in great disbelief, in sheer denial, yet his fingers coiled around her arm, not letting go.

"Stay…" he mumbled, shutting his eyes again — falling asleep in an instant.

Charlotte stared at him, stunned, feeling his fingers slowly pull her hand down upon his chest, softly unwrap from around her. Blushing, she bowed her head, subtly raking her fingers against him as she retracted them to retrieve her hand. She glanced back at Levi who was starting the fire — conflicted, doubting her own ears for she couldn't grasp his words.

Levi glanced back at her; his eyes as sharp as ever, noticing her hand resting on top of Mac's chest. She tore her gaze away, stood up swiftly, and left the room. Approaching, she sat beside Levi to warm up by the fire; hands reaching out to it, rubbing against each other before the inviting flames.

"Thank you…again. For everything you're doing." she said in earnest, tilting her head to face him, yet his eyes were nailed into the burning logs. "I know it's not your place, and you'd rather just…" she paused, not wanting to remind him.

"Let's not repeat ourselves; let's get some rest instead." he said shortly, stood up from the chair, exhaling deeply, feeling his whole being clench again. "Good-night, miss." he added politely, and left the room.

Charlotte accepted his wish and stared back at the roaring fire, yet her mind suddenly felt restless, and her legs jittered in anticipation, for Mac's words still rang in her ears, pulling on her heart strings in utter bewilderment.

Unable to stay still, and yet emotionally and physically drained, feeling as though ready to collapse, she went back inside to check on him; still restlessly trembling, clutching the blanket with his fists as the sweat started to drip off him.

Dithering, she took off her boots, which now felt like a part of her feet after hours of endless riding, then glanced down at her mucky pants in shame. She set her eyes back to his writhing self, and hesitantly climbed up on the squeaky bed beside him, pulling the heavy blanket over them — guiltily feeling the carefreeness overwhelm her. Scooting close, body touching his, feeling him, breathing him in.

She had never been so intensely close to him; at least not in this tender way, certainly not after him asking her to stay. *How could she even refuse; she burned for this moment.*

Every sharp detail of his face was highlighted by the candle's light, and for the first time she was able to admire him in all his rawness, up close. Every subtle scar hidden behind his blond stubble, wrinkles that had started to crease the corners of his eyes, now bared to her gaze. Blushing, she thought how much she longed to glide her fingers all across his face, trap them within the dents of his cheekbones, the subtle split of his cleft chin, the dark gap between his lips. She longed to explore him in the purest way, as though he were a weathered map, only visible to those capable of reading it. *Oh how she loved his rugged face,* she thought to herself, getting lost in it.

Gliding her eyes downwards his neck, they set on his open shirtfront, a line of a flogged wound exposed to her, and she knew this only led to a maze of further lines — deeper, darker, rougher, all across his chest and abdomen; how only someone receiving weeks or months of relentless torture could adopt such deep injuries — yet, oddly, she adored every inch of him without judgement, with not a trace of repulsion.

For besides the wounds, there was a pattern of darker blond hair hand-somely spread across his square-built chest, curled, scattered around the scars, there were protruding lines across his ripped abdomen, so wide and thick, betraying a vigorous core. His back, a wall of muscle in itself, and although she never had the chance to glance for long, his body was hauntingly striking, yet that was not the reason why she couldn't forget him.

For he did something to her. Something no-one ever had been able to do. Something a chiseled body would never be adequate enough to replace the emotion he evoked within her.

Staring at him, a besotted smile captured her face, wondering if he had ever laid with a woman before, and if so…how many did he lay with, and did he ever feel what she was feeling towards him right now, in this bed, next to him, beside him, close to him…with him.

Her eyes slowly and finally started to shut, feeling a serene relief take over her — demolishing every ounce of anxiety she had felt prior. Scooting the furthest she could, she cuddled up to him, feeling the warmth of his body escape through his clothes; both mucky from the travel, yet she couldn't be bothered to care. She had never felt her heart feel so content while laying next to someone; not even the night she spent laying next to Will.

She tentatively, wrapped her arm around his chest, holding him tight next to her, feeling the beat of his heart gently brush against her palm. Daringly, she buried her face into his neck, and suddenly felt like the happiest woman alive.

Her heart, still scarlet, throbbed.

CHAPTER 41

Confession

I

HE WALKED, AND WALKED, AND WALKED…until feet benumbed, froze and stiffened, for the bitter cold permeated through his boots. Clinging onto branch after branch, pulling himself further up the steep hill of moss, he halted. A voice flushed in the air around him, sending shivers down his spine.

"William…son, how have you become?"

Petrified, quivering into place, he turned around himself, lighting up the way with his lantern, yet there was no-one to be found, no face imprinted upon bark, no cloak swaying with the wind, no limbs scraping the soil.

"Fa…father?" Will asked, horrified to hear his intoxicated voice again.

"You've failed me; my whole reputation is ruined…over LUST!" the voice scowled, a shrill screech echoed, needles beneath Will's skin.

"I…I did my best, sir." Will stuttered, lips trembled in fear, lips of a little boy — heart raced as though his father returned home again after midnight, empty bottle in hand, gun threatening to shoot, yells, screams, violence, mother dropping to her knees, begging, offering to be assaulted instead.

"You'll never become someone. Only a weak man of silly words, written in secret, cowardly protected underneath your mother's wing." it said snidely, reminding Will of all the times he expressed his imagination upon empty pages, as his mother watched out the window — guarding, ensuring he had not returned yet; frail hand caressing his shoulder, instilling bravery within him.

Tears stood in frightened eyes, reliving these dreadful emotions he fought so hard to bury within the pages he never published; books that piled up, collecting dust — all decaying in his ranch's attic, left there to rot, all but one.

"You've failed me, son." the demeaning voice growled, wind shifted, shirt felt suddenly taut across his chest.

"NO!" he yelled, clasping the shirt, shaking it frantically. "YOU'VE FAILED ME!! YOU FAILED US ALL!!" His screams filled up the void in the forest — shifting the wind, rattling the fibers of the soil, scratching the deafening silence; he screamed. "YOU KILLED HER!!! YOU KILLED HER SPIRIT, BODY AND SOUL!" He screamed gutturally; menacingly, with all his soul and being — screams carved out of the purest of hearts. "I LOATHE YOU, FATHER!!! I LOATHE YOU!!!"

A caterwaul of words; words he had never dared to express, all those years, kept away, locked deep within himself. Words that turned into silence, crippling him, crippling his mother, noosing her into her death. For once, feeling powerful to erase that blood-curdling voice with words he dared to unravel — etching over his father's voice he loathed so deeply. Yet, he sobbed in agonizing despair, finding himself back there again, in the mansion, in the lavishly painted walls, shades of red and emerald, in the floral patterned wallpapers, in the clutter of wealth fighting for space to breathe.

As young William, he now crumbled, feeling the excruciating pain tear his heart apart. The voice that shuddered him; the voice that forced him awake at night, hearing it assault his fading mother; the voice that built a coward, cocooned by a layer of reservedness, the voice that blamed, degraded him, for the simple sin of loving art. The horrifying voice that could never be forsaken within his mind, yet always there to remind him of its existence, slowly lurking in his nous, slowly emerging from the empty pages like vines shooting out from the ground; he slashed through them, drowned them with the heavy ink of his pen he held so steadily.

I I

"SO, MR. CHOTT!" SHERIFF JORDON HUFFED, pulling out his chair in front of JB, seated behind a cell in Birdsboro, and plopped right into it; eyes locking his. "They'll take the cloth off your mouth, and you will cooperate with me now, alright?" he said, gesticulating with his head to the deputies to untie the cloth that Jordon placed halfway through the journey, for he couldn't handle JB's constant rambling — regarding his job as a young boy in the circus, or the bad food recipes he almost poisoned people with, or how Margaret left him for a younger man, or how his knee got injured, as well as the daily struggles he had with hemorrhoids that only worsened with the colder weather.

"So, Mr. Chott, now that we are situated…"

"Are we?" JB asked in earnest, and Jordon cinched a brow.

"Are we not…Mr. Chott?" He sighed, on the edge of losing his patience.

"Well…I could imagine it to be more welcoming inside here! Ya know… perhaps a pillow, on that rough chair! Remember what I told ya, 'bout them hemorrhoids…"

"Well, Mr. Chott…it ain't really *meant* to be welcoming here, so perhaps ya imagined wrong." He grunted. "Now, tell me where Levi Krog was headed to before you packed up camp." he asked him, stern tone, cocked brow, and JB blinked, fluttering his eyelashes in nervousness.

"Sheriff, I already told ya! He is out for dinner with the gal." JB said, side-eyeing the deputies around him, eyes bulging out, round cheeks flushing red.

"Hm…" Jordon bobbed his head, smirking. "But why don't I believe you, Mr. Chott?" he asked snidely, staring into his soul.

"I, I don't know why, sir! Perhaps you…you have trust issues?" JB said solemnly, scarring a saddened pout on his face.

"Haha…you're funny. Is that where Mr. Krog gets it from? Or from his father? God forgive him." He teased him, lighting up a cigar. Rage flushed through JB, for he didn't tolerate anyone mocking Levi, hands clutched a fist within the shackles and eyes squinted in menace.

"Listen, ya filthy rrrat! Ain't nobody's fault your soul stinks, and ya can't get yourself a busty gal like my boy!" He leered, throwing the only witty remark he could come up with.

"Oh don't worry 'bout that, sir. I've got plenty 'round here, and let the Lord decide 'bout my soul, alright?" he boasted, slightly agitated as though JB hit a nerve. "Where…is Levi Krog?" Persisting, he neared JB's face, mustache almost touching his wiry beard.

"I-don't-know!" JB exclaimed, flustered, squaring his eyeballs at him.

"Alright…Alright…" He sighed, easing himself back into the chair. "Let's try another way…what's the gal's name?" he questioned him, recalling Dorman's letter.

"Gal?"

"Mr. Krog's…gal…" he said, clenching teeth, finger squeezing the temple of his head.

"Aaaah! But of course!!" He snorted. "Oh, Lordy! Ch…Samantha!" JB stammered, correcting himself instantly, yet his lip started trembling again.

"Samantha…alright. Let's pretend it's that." He grinned lopsidedly. "And she's seeing Mac Kinnon, correct?" he asked, jaw raised, eyes nailing him, tasting the confession on his tongue.

"Correct, sir!" He bobbed his head in earnest, then halted. "I mean, correct, if it *wasn't* Samantha! Hehe…for the gal *you're* thinkin' 'bout, could possibly be seducing the men before Kinnon skins them, as far as I'm concerned!" he said, gnashing his teeth, sweating all over.

"This must be the easiest, yet most frustrating, interrogation I've ever lived through…" Jordon laughed as he pulled on his brows, shaking his head, wheezing.

"Wonderful!" JB exclaimed. "Can y'all let me go now? For I feel a sudden urge to crap my pants, and it ain't gonna be pretty here!" he warned, as his tummy suddenly rumbled.

"We ain't done, old man…" His chest launched back forward, face inches away from his. "So, when was the last time you saw the gal?" he asked, then detected a sudden foul smell coming from the cell before him.

"Ah, gee…" He huffed, exhausted. "Yesterday!" he said, toes curling within his boots, face flushing a scarlet warning. "Sir, I really really need to ssshit!" he whispered to him, embarrassed, in strong urge.

"I can tell…" Jordon covered his nose, waving a hand before his face. "But we ain't done, I'm afraid…so yesterday she left with Levi Krog?"

"Yes!! Like I already said!! For dinner!" he shouted fervently. "And lemme tell ya! It wasn't my dinner, for sure! These beans ain't kiddin'!" JB yelled, toes now wiggling, trying desperately to not release his bowel.

"So, they rushed through the night…Ozark, or Cottonmouth State?" he persisted, not planning to let go of him now that they were progressing.

"Sir! I need to SHIT! I will crap all over the place, if ya don't let me out pretty soon!!!" JB urged him, stood up, hopped on his leg.

"Ozark or Cottonmouth State, Mr. Chott?" he insisted.

"For God's sake! Don't ya have a heart?!" He strained. "I pray to God ya never come across such beans! Or, perhaps it was the rotten deer carcass? Well, I didn't want it to go to waste, and the kids wouldn't have eaten it anyway since they left — perhaps the fellas, but definitely not Charlotte. I mean, Susan!" JB paused his ramble, realizing what he had just unwillingly confessed again.

Sheriff Jordon smirked with dark amusement, for he didn't have much to do other than let the fool speak on his own. "How very interesting, Mr. Chott." he hummed, ordering the deputies to continue the interrogation with more forceful measures.

JB's eyes set at the knifes the deputies pulled out; an evil smile cracked across their faces; wickedly anticipating to cut his confession out of his throat. "Oh...*shit.*" he whispered loudly, and the poorly digested stew escaped through his pants, unintentionally and forcefully.

III

SHERIFF DORMAN KNOCKED ON THE STURDY WOODEN RANCH DOOR, sickeningly expecting Will to jump out in great surprise. Envisioning the wicked methods he would use to interrogate him, hit him until his last breath, confession or not, dump him into the secluded depths of Red Giants, bury him deep into the mossy soil for no-one to ever uncover his bruised body.

He waited for a solid minute, then was greeted with his eerie absence. Striding around the property in attempts to find him anywhere else, he spotted the barn empty, and the land deserted, yet a faint nicker behind some bushes hit his ears, and carefully he walked to it. Will's horse, Rachel, standing there, petrified, quivering in shock; a wide cut across her chest; bloody flesh exposed, skin hanging down, a sturdy piece of branch piercing through her gut, intestines coiled around it.

"Dear Lord..." Dorman sighed, as he approached her calmly. She stomped, snorted, raised her head, panicking by the slightest movement and yet his eyes were nailed at the saddlebags. Swiftly passing by Will's guns still attached to the saddle, and a canister with fresh water hanging loosely around the saddle horn, he gripped the saddlebags, searched frantically through them, fumbling out an unopened letter signed *Antoine Van Alstine*, owner of the Windmill Saloon in Mon Louis.

IV

EYELIDS FLINCHED, JAW JERKED, MOUTH FELT DRY, and when moved, he felt a resistance, yet the lulling sound of water splashing harmonically against the lagoon's rocks eased him back in serenity. His fever was reduced, and his arm was not throbbing anymore. Lazily prying his eyes open, he glanced down to it, then suddenly saw Charlotte's arm around him instead. Tightly coiled.

Startled, he jerked his head to the side, finding her lying next to him. Asleep. Huddled close. Head resting upon his shoulder. Touching him. Warming him. His breath cut in his lungs, freezing himself still as though to not awake her, as though to not scare her, as though to not risk hurting her. He laid there, benumbed, lost for words, petrified of the sudden flush of emotions, twisting his stomach, yanking his heart down to it, a nerve racking feeling, for he never had such closeness with someone that he didn't try to strangle, drown, murder, and he certainly didn't expect to find her there.

He stared at the ceiling, dark timber wood staring back down at him. He laid there, passing the time, holding his breath until his throat got tight. His eyes cut cowardly at her, and daringly, he tilted his face towards her as though her beauty reeled him in, with the softest of force.

Gaping at her, his breath slowly released, a soft humming wind escaping through the gap of his lips, tickling her skin, and yet his prickled instead. He swallowed hard, studying the peaceful face resting next to his; the pale skin contrasting with his dirty black shirt, somehow not shadowing it with filth. His eyes trailed down to the faint veneer of freckles painted across her cheeks; specks of sweltering sun engraved within her pores, betraying long rides beneath the summer skies.

Fingers quivered, longing to feel of their softness, for he had never before;

yet his sinful hand was too rough. Scarred. Stained, with the innocent blood of too many. He feared to scar them, just by the force of his menacing fingertips; for he'd loathe himself to ever do so.

He noticed an endearing birthmark on her chin; one that not even her mother knew existed; it was faint, it scarred an endearing smile on his face. His eyes cut at her generous lips, scarlet, sharp, curved, sensually outlined in perfect symmetry; instantly reminiscing the way they felt against his; sensitive, fervent, soft, trembling and yet hungering to lock for eternity, taking his breath the deeper she kissed him.

His heart raced faster upon the memory. Fluttering. Thudding. Rattling within the chamber of his ribs. Unable to be tamed. His eyes dared to drop lower, down to her rising chest, faintly baring to him through the corset she wore underneath the low-cut cotton shirt. She breathed in, out…it expanded, deflated. The swell of her breasts, fair, round and full, shadowing a tight gap between them. He pulled his gaze away, not wishing to be *that* man, not wishing to stare at her as though she was a piece of meat, for she was so much more than flesh to drill his blade within; she was a bloom of a winter's honeysuckle, bound to be guarded by his thorns.

A murmur escaped her lips, her sharp brows drew together, and his eyes flared, jerking them away swiftly, nailing them back to the ceiling, shutting them, clutching them tight, not knowing how to handle himself as she started to wake up. Charlotte grunted, wiggled against him, stretched her arms that slammed against his face, then arched her back — almost falling off the bed as she bumped into him.

"Whoops!" She gasped, startled, glancing back at him, still pretending to be asleep. Staring, aghast, as if she had forgotten, as though she fell asleep upon a wish, her cheeks crimsoned. It was real, very real…scraping her heart raw with joy. Tearing her gaze away, bowing her head in deep thought, she suppressed a gleeful titter, hardly able to contain the happiness that surged through her. Swallowing down her shyness, she leaned back into him, hand gently clasping his forehead; it was cool.

She cracked a smile of triumph and relief and hugged him excitedly, feeling his heartbeat slam against her body. "You're going to be okay…you stubborn mountain man…" she whispered against his ear, and his heart convulsed by the warmth of her voice. Pulling back, she lingered before his face, as though in thought. Her hand slid daringly down to his jaw, cupping it tenderly. "You're going to be just fine…Mac…" she said, soughed his name, and leaned into him, brushing a deep kiss against his forehead.

Mac snapped his eyes open the moment he felt her move out of the room, gripped his chest firmly as though feeling on the edge of collapsing. His heart, ready to tear through him — a light-headed, blood-pumping sensation he had never experienced. All those years he thought he couldn't feel a single emotion, not even a thrill to kill, nor satisfaction or pleasure when he slept with a woman. Benumbed and hollow, he was, developing into the murderer he is now; yet when around Charlotte, he couldn't stop…*feeling.*

V

"Good morning, Levi." Charlotte greeted him upon a jolly prance; he was still resting on the ground before the fireplace, burly arm over his face, shadowing his eyes from the piercing dawn.

"Mhm." he mumbled, half awake.

Charlotte glared out the window, stunned by the immense beauty of the lagoon before her. The clear turquoise waters reflecting the early morning sun beating upon them, and the isolated island standing tall, like a rock right in the middle of the pool.

She felt of the crusty skin on her arms; dried up dirt from the messy riding last night, and realized she hadn't bathed since Mon Louis. She glimpsed back at Levi with a cocked brow of confliction; he snored contentedly, and knew Mac was still sleeping as well. A cheeky smile scarred her face, and she rushed out the door, undressed hastily, throwing her mucky clothes in a pile between two gigantic rocks.

Her toes wiggled excitedly, feeling the temperature of the water — slightly cold, chilling, yet awfully refreshing after inhaling the humid south for so long. She dipped her foot in, concentric ripples spreading away from her, an instant satisfaction crawled up her limb, evoking the memory of all the times she swam carelessly in the Sweetwater River growing up, staying in the water for hours at a time. There was a strange serenity it provided her, clearing her mind from all the bundled up thoughts she carried within herself.

She hiked up a boulder and without hesitation leaped inside the water, head first; waves slammed against the slippery rocks — catapulting like a shot of bullets upon the cabin's windows.

Levi, startled, woke up from the sudden sound, grabbing his revolver instinctively. Ironically, Mac had done the same; hopping up from the bed, sneaking with his back against the wall towards Levi.

"Trouble?" he asked Levi, who jolted again to see him up, awake, evidently feeling a lot better.

"Don't know. Heard a loud noise." he said, cutting his eyes at him bitterly, knowing exactly where she had slept last night. "Where's Charlotte?" he then asked, getting up himself.

"Thought she was in here." Mac answered, bewildered.

"No, haven't seen her…" he said, yawned.

Another wave of water splashed against the window, startling them both, lifting their guns towards it. They advanced to the window, in slyness, breaths held in, Mac's gun pointing at the door and Levi's at the casement. Nearing it, heads tilting, eyes peeking through the glass, both spotted Charlotte instead. Stripped naked, carefree — swimming in the lagoon, wiggling her legs in the air, diving back underwater, re-surfacing, flinging her wavy hair behind, with arched back, bust baring to the world — for a fleeting second, one second too short for eyes to truly capture anything.

"Oh." Levi's eyes flared in shock.

"Hm." Mac followed.

The men instantly turned their heads away from the seductive, all too alluring view, and stared at the ground awkwardly.

"Well…" Levi cleared his throat, drumming fingers against goosed arm. "At least, we know now, right? We know she isn't…in danger." he said, snorted, turned stern, wishing he could peek some more.

"Hm…" Mac nodded, pulled a cigarette out of his pocket.

"Mind to share one?" Levi asked, longing for a distraction.

Mac cut his eyes at him. "Sure." he said, cocking a brow, handing him one, side-eyeing out the window for a brief sheepish second.

BANG! Another splash of water slammed the windowpane; another leap she took off the boulder.

"She's…sure having fun out there, ah?" Levi chuckled, lit up the cigarette, feeling the urge to look even stronger now, for his imagination turned wild, torturing him to the core.

"Seems like it." Mac said, confused as to why he was suddenly smoking together with this bounty hunter hunting after his head.

"Yeah…"

"Hm…"

"You know, somebody needs to poke that fire, ah?" Levi said, cutting his eyes at him.

"Hm. Sure looks like it's dyin' out." Mac said, cutting his eyes back at him. They stood there awkwardly, guarding their spots at the window, puffing on their tobacco sticks.

"Don't you need to take your medicine, boy?" Levi asked him pretentiously.

"Nah. The lass usually gives it to me, me medicine…" He teased him.

"Oh. Right…" He snorted bitterly. "So, you guys are…?" he asked, and Mac paused for a long moment, not wishing to admit they weren't.

"Not sure." he said dryly.

"Ah. But you fancy her?" he asked, chest flushing with heat.

"Sure seems ye fancy her, me lad." He threw the assumption back to him, exhaling a cloud of smoke before him.

Levi swallowed awkwardly for he didn't realize it was that obvious, and yet his pride, bent and broken by her rejection, wouldn't let him admit to it. "We're just friends, partner. No need to worry." He winked at him caustically. "Besides, I know she's expecting someone back in Mon Louis." he added, twisting the knife on him.

"Hm."

"Name wasn't ever mentioned, however…" Levi added, continuing to stir Mac's curiosity.

"It's the fine lad." Mac said, cutting his eyes at him. "Will…the lad's name. Good lad…wealthy son of a gun." He snorted, then turned bitter upon a sigh of disappointment, figuring they must have gotten closer in Mon Louis, figuring she should choose that stability over the uncertainty he cocooned her with, meanwhile Levi bobbed his head, realizing it confirmed the same name Charlotte had mentioned.

"So, how's that fever?" Levi then asked, not wishing to hear about her mysterious lover, as there was no hope for him anyway.

"Don't ya worry. Ye'll chase after me soon enough." He smirked, unbothered by his threat.

"Deal is a deal, son." Levi shrugged.

"How ye imagine it…" Mac snorted snidely. "Yer gonna point a gun at me, on me way out?" he said and Levi clicked his tongue in irritation.

"Don't know about you, Kinnon, but I'm fighting like a man. Not a pussy."

"Don't underestimate the fight of a cat…might just claw yer eyes out." He winked at him and pulled down on his cigarette.

"I don't underestimate you…but I fear you underestimate me." he said and Mac bobbed his head, amused.

"Haven't spent much thought on ye, me lad. Sorry to disappoint."

"You'd better start…" he said, and the door snarled open, widely, as Charlotte stormed in with a sigh of contentment. Turning around upon shutting the door, she faced them, startled to find them standing together, so quietly by the window.

"Oh!" She choked, surprised. "You…you're all awake, I see." she stuttered nervously, not expecting to find them both right in front of the window she just got dressed outside of.

"Well…yeah. We just woke up, right?" Levi glanced at Mac.

"Hm…" he nodded shortly, as always.

"Okay…" She strode inside slowly. "It's good to see you feeling better, Mac…" she said, instantly blushing and he bowed his head, nailing his eyes anywhere but upon her wet hair, dripping across the taut white shirt.

"Sure…" Mac said dryly, puffing on the last bit of cigarette that remained.

Levi clenched his teeth, tearing his gaze away from the asphyxiating sight.

"Is JB coming anytime soon?" she then asked Levi, thinking it was strange that he hadn't arrived yet.

"He should have been here…" He sighed. "I might need to check on him; he usually is never late…" he said, and looked out the window; peaks of white fluffy clouds shadowing his greens.

"What about the deputies…" she asked as she squeezed some water out of her wet hair, twisting it around, releasing it, letting it plop over her shoulder.

"They aren't gonna capture me, cowgirl."

He chuckled.

"I am not the wanted one…" he said, looking over at Mac teasingly.

"Yer the government's loyal puppy dog…" Mac teased him back sternly.

"Okay! Enough, you two!" Charlotte interjected once again, now habitually doing so. "Levi, I'm worried about JB, perhaps you should head out before it gets too dark." she said, and he nodded in compliance. "Mac, we're going fishing!"

"You are?"

"We are?"

Both men uttered simultaneously, stunned, blinking blankly at her.

"Yes…" she said, flushing scarlet again. "If you feel like it of course, with… your fever, and…arm." she said, a knot clogging her throat. "I'm not the best with fishing, nor hunting, so…I might need your help." she said, briefly glancing back at the countless times she tried to catch a fish, yet only catching a branch instead, or seaweed monsters as Finn would view them. She looked at him, and he looked back at her. Tense.

"Sure." he said, shortly again and she tore her gaze away, suppressing a gleeful smile and rosy cheeks.

Levi bit his lip; loathing that he had to leave them alone, especially anywhere near the water, after what they both witnessed. "Darn you, JB…" he grumbled to himself, mounting his buckskin horse, loping away beneath the beating sun.

V I

Dear Mr. Griffiths,

I hope this letter finds you well, with your business booming over in Bisonhorn. I do not wish to disturb you with this news, but I felt obligated to let you know about your lady, Miss Charlotte.

There has been a man visiting her at the saloon, even having dinner with her, not too long ago. I did not witness anything of a romantic nature, besides some worrying looks here and there, but she completely disappeared after that. All her clothes were left behind as well, which is unusual for a woman.

I am worried that perhaps she ran away, or was kidnapped by him, Mr. Griffiths. I hope this letter won't worry you, and perhaps it's nothing but a big misunderstanding.

The entire town of Mon Louis is missing you, and we cannot wait to have you return soon.

Best regards,
Antoine Van Alstine

SHERIFF DORMAN FOLDED THE LETTER, grinning in dark amusement; *this must have been the most convincing proof he'd held in his hands thus far,* he thought, and tucked it into his warm coat. "Frozen to death...ha!" He snorted, mounted his horse, leaving a faintly nickering Rachel behind. Bleeding out further, in the bushes, drop by drop. Fading.

VII

"C'MON PARTNER, TELL US WHERE THEY'RE AT." the deputies repeated themselves, after the hundredth time of JB remaining quiet.

SLAP!

They smacked him across his elderly face, bare fists, rough knuckles across them. JB, already bruised all over, thought it wiser to not say a word than to start rambling again.

"Come on, old man!!" Sheriff Jordon encouraged him in the background, fiddling with a pen between two fingers. Yet JB remained stubbornly silent; feeling devastatingly guilty for not being able to cover for Levi.

455

"Cut him, will ya? He don't need all that fat, anyway!" Jordon ordered them; a chuckle of pleasure escaping from his paper-thin lipped mouth. They took out a knife, wiped it across JB's belly, pressed it menacingly with a leer.

"Slice the damn son of a bitch open!" he yelled at them.

"No!! Please!!" JB begged them, quivering whole, losing the strength to remain brave. Jordon waved his hand up suddenly, slashing through the sweaty air, signaling them to halt.

"Yes…Mr. Chott? Is there anythin' ya remembered?" Jordon walked towards him, a satisfying smirk on his face, grabbing the knife from the deputy, flinging it in the air.

"I beg you, sir. You have to understand!" he stammered, glaring at the blade's reflection of his very own sorrowful self. "Levi, he is like my son!" he exclaimed, reeling into an uncontrollable sob.

"And Mr. Krog was hired to do a JOB!!" he yelled at him, hitting him brutally across the face.

"Sir! Please! It's not his fault! He, he, he is in love, goddammit!" JB spurted out a confession. "He don't know what he's doin', he don't think right. And when he don't think right…he…he don't know what he's doin'!" he said, and Jordon cocked a brow.

"Oh, haven't we all been, once upon a time? Come ooooon, Mr. Chott… time's a tickin'!" He pressed him, raising a hand, threatening another hit.

"If…if I tell you, ya swear to God you won't hurt Levi?" he stammered, staring at him with a miserable pout.

"Depends on what ya tell me, old man…" he said, without a commitment.

"Please, forgive me…" he cried to himself in guilt, thinking of Charlotte, thinking even of Mac. "Ozark Ridge, sir…" He sighed in suffocating shame. "But that's all I know…"

"Better." He smirked with satisfaction. "Take care of him…"

"Wh-what?? But, I told you!!" JB yelled as the deputies carried him to the back cell. "You ain't any better than him, ya filthy bastard!!" His weary voice faded into the background, amongst the iron and darkness.

VIII

"MRS. MILLER...THERE'S STILL A SPOT ON THE COAT!" Elizabeth yelled at her, agitated, for she was moments away from leaving the cabin, and felt she had spent enough time sleeping in such a ramshackle living arrangement.

The elderly woman limped towards her to see which spot she missed when she washed her coat. Coughing with every step, she approached her. Legs quivering, getting weaker by the day. So was she.

"This here! What is this! Why is it red!" she asked her, clearly upset, slender finger pointing at the red spot.

"Perhaps I coughed accidentally on it, Mrs. Griffiths." she admitted guiltily.

"Coughed?? You mean to tell me...that *this* is BLOOD??"

She gasped, horrified.

"My apologies, Mrs...my eyes are not the best anymore, and..."

"Oh well, don't demean my intelligence with your petty excuses. You know what you need to do, for I cannot be seen like *this* out in civilization!" She threw the heavy coat on her, leaving the house to get some fresh air. "Such coarse barbarians...nincompoops...just like *he* was...filthy, disgusting, poor peasants." she fussed to herself, striding down a secluded path, turning into a ginger speck, contrasting to the lush green moss that spread across the soil.

Mrs. Miller adjusted her glasses and waddled towards the barrel again; dropping the coat inside it, hands sinking into the water, fingers clutching it tight. Her eyes set on a frame before her. A young boy holding an axe, clutching the hand of hers with the other. A smile on his face. Happy, within the clumsy shirt, the busted boots, in the muck and the poverty. Her gaze trailed off to the next one; now a decade older. A bearded man, arm wrapped around his father's shoulders, adorned in flannel shirt, torn-up jeans and work boots up his knees, a heavy wood log carried over his back, yet still the same smile.

"What did you do to my boy...you witch..." she cried and drowned the coat deeper into the barrel, rubbing it furiously until her breath got tight in her throat. Suddenly she stopped, as a wave of a relentless cough assaulted her, collapsing her lungs together. She laid down, arching her back, hitting against her chest with a frail fist, hoping to find the strength to get up again.

IX

"HELP!!! SOMEONE!!! PLEASE!!!" WILL CRIED OUT LOUD, looking for any sign of civilization in the deep forest of Red Giants, utterly lost, tracing circles around himself, bewildered within nature's maze. Pulling his exhausted self up over the same looking hills, grasping at thick branches of the redwood trees, some snapping, some holding his weight. "HELP!!!" he yelled from the top of his lungs, until his soft voice turned to raspy nothingness; lost, as well.

The whispering forest broke him down; passing trees over and over again, deranging him furthermore with faces that weren't there, yet he swore they stared back at him. He did not want to stay another night here, for he most likely would not survive the dropping temperatures again — if he survived his own mind's games first, that was.

Suddenly he noticed gray smoke up ahead; swirling through the backlit leaves of trees. A faint silhouette of what appeared to be a woman, dressed in a thick cream cloak and bearing long blonde hair, facing him up ahead. Jaw dropping and hands clutching a fist of victory, he started to run towards her, leaping over logs, trampling down herbs, and stumbling over himself, unable to find a voice to scream anymore, yet now a line of timber framed rustic buildings appeared before him. *Finally*, he thought, he cried. Hiking up the last hill of spongy moss, "Petit Jean" a sign read to him, and he collapsed beside it, before the red clayed road; collapsing out of relief and exhaustion.

A couple of men became alerted when they saw him drop, and rushed to him with axes resting upon their shoulders. "Who are you." one asked him with a strong accent, stern, cold, towering over him; a massive silhouette, backlit by the sun, pointing the axe at him.

"Please, kind sirs, help me. Please. I'm…I'm lost…" he pleaded, fading, eyes rolling into the back of his skull; now seizing before them, body releasing all the tension it carried the past hours in sorrowful torment.

CHAPTER 42

How to Feel

I

MAC AND CHARLOTTE STRODE DOWN THE PATH TO THE LAGOON, together with a couple fishing poles they found in the cabin — oddly reminiscent of their time in Hope, shooting guns together, or rather forcing her to shoot one. They stood atop an enormous black slate boulder, and threw their lines into the crystal clear waters, using dehydrated meat as bait, for there wasn't a better option and Charlotte was proud of herself to suggest it.

"Thank you for…agreeing to fish, with me." she said, and he cut his eyes at her. "I hope you're not feeling too sick…" she said, side-eyeing him from the corner of her sharp eyes.

"Hm." He nodded quietly and her lips folded.

"I…I felt of your head this morning, and…" She halted, blushed. He remained still, yet his blood suddenly quickened. "And you didn't feel as warm…" she said and he cleared his throat.

"Hm…" he hummed, and she tore her gaze away, bowed head, and drew her brows together in confusion.

He cast the line again.

"Do you know how to fish?" she asked him, noticing how smoothly he threw it, longing to invite conversation, in this rare occasion of being alone, after so long, after not quarreling anymore, after sleeping beside one another.

"Hm." He smirked.

"Is that a yes?" She chuckled.

"Sure…" he said. "I do know how to fish." he said, wetting his dry lips, concentrating on the line.

"Well, I don't…and you'll find that out soon enough." She snorted, trying to lighten him up a bit, by somehow mocking her own self.

"Figured it must be as good as yer huntin'." He crinkled his lip with a tight smile.

"Why, thank you!" She rolled her eyes and gave him a playful stink eye. His smirk jerked again. "You'd be happy to know, I actually shot a deer." she said and he cocked a brow.

"Hm…"

"Indeed…and it dropped dead. Immediately." she boasted, jaw and nose touching the sky, eyes searching for his reaction.

"Sure…" He teased sarcastically.

"You don't believe me, Mr. Kinnon?" She gasped, and he sighed heavily.

"Hard to imagine…ye barely ate any of me elk meat. Why would ye want to kill somethin' ye wouldn't eat…" he said in earnest, and she let out an ironic chuckle.

"Well, that was because I thought you would poison me…" she said and he turned to face her, both brows snapped together, aghast.

"What?" She shrugged, flicking the line as she did.

"Poison ye…"

"Of course." She cocked her head, and he cocked his.

"Yer wild, lass…" He snorted.

"I'm wild? I thought I was an useless eejit…" She chuckled.

"Yer imagination's wild…" he said, suppressing a snort.

"Oh, so you wouldn't poison me with elk meat?" She cinched a brow at him, a playful smirk scarring her generous lips and he stared at her for a fleeting moment, taking in all her attitude, feeling his heart skip a beat.

"Hm…no." he said in earnest, averting his eyes back to the fishing line.

"I suppose I should have eaten it, after all…those canned beans do get tiring after a while." she said and he cut his eyes at her.

"Ye was afraid of me…" he said. "Perhaps not such an eejit, not to eat me meat…" he said. "Me elk meat…" He shook his head, flustered.

She looked at him innocently, not understanding why he grunted, then briefly recalled the heavy cabinet she dragged before the door every night; still a toe felt broken ever since then, after slamming her foot against it.

"Perhaps I had just misunderstood you." she said, and he locked eyes with her. "For I feel like…we're past that point now. For I feel like…I can trust you, and hopefully, you can trust me too…" she said daringly and his chest rose, the pole almost slipping through his grip.

"Hm." he hummed and tore his gaze away swiftly, clearing his throat. "Where…ye shot the deer." he asked, changing the subject swiftly.

"In the…shoulder? Isn't that what you told me?"

"No, lass…which location ye found the deer…" he asked, and she blushed in shame.

"Oh, in Ozark Ridge…" she said. "It was the most delicious meal I ever had…believe it or not." She smiled, yet her smile slipped. "And yet…I didn't get to enjoy the rest of it, since…" She paused herself, a trail of chills crawled all over her.

"Since what?" he asked curiously, noticing her beautiful smile vanish abruptly.

"Well…I…some inbred folks…ambushed me, and…"

"The Fiddlers?" he asked her solemnly, worried about what they did to her, eyes cutting back at her in response.

"Is that what you call them?" She frowned, repulsed.

"Hm…"

"Anyway…" She sighed. "Yes, they captured me, and…let's just say…" She paused, not knowing how to tell him the way she escaped, for it shamed her just to think about it. "…you'd be happy to know that I killed a man, for the very first time in my life…" She huffed, feeling nauseous at the thought of the man's sliced neck, spurting blood all over her.

"Why would I be happy to know that? I wish ye didn't have to…" he grumbled, bothered by the fact.

"Well, I mean, don't you…*enjoy* killing?" she tentatively asked him, stealing a swift glimpse from his chiseled face that seemed hauntingly distraught.

"Is that what they say?" he asked her, casting the line again, further away.

"Kind of…" She shrugged, casting the line again as well, which wasn't really necessary.

"Hm." He went quiet for a moment, and the clouds formed above them, counting the minutes he lingered in silence. "And ye believe them?" he asked her earnestly, curious to hear her thoughts, yet dreading to hear them.

"No…" Her head bowed. "I don't know…you tell me?"

"Does me answer matter at all?" He snorted snidely, knowing she would never believe him.

"It matters to me, for I want to…get to know you…Mac…" she hummed softly, as her line flickered.

"Yer line." he mumbled, agitated.

"My what?" she asked perplexed, eyes still nailed at him, searching for an answer.

"Yer line, woman! There's a fish bitin'." he fussed, grunted, rolled his eyes.

"Oh!" She gasped, aghast, for it didn't feel like a seaweed monster this time. "And, what do I do now?!" She trembled anxiously, pulled on the pole, and started to reel in the line.

"Steady. If the fish pulls, hold on, but stop reelin'." he instructed, watching her carefully.

"So don't fight the fish. Got it." she repeated nervously, reeling the line in even faster.

"Steady, lass! Don't want the line to break!"

SNAP!

"Damnit!" Mac grunted, flustered, watching the snapped line sway in the air before them.

"I'm…I'm sorry." She bit her lip, embarrassed.

"It's fine." He sighed, feeling a sudden wobbliness from the fever.

"Mac?" She looked at him.

He looked back at her. Stared at her.

She stared at him.

Eyes locked, tensely.

"Please, tell me. Do you like to…kill folk?" she asked him the dreaded question again, as somehow she needed to know, as though it would make a difference, as if murder could be excused depending on the motivation.

"No." he said firmly, then fumbled out a cigarette.

"Then…why do you?" She sighed, putting the fishing pole down.

"…'Cause I have to." he grunted, dropped his fishing pole to the side, sat on the rock, lit up the cigarette with a swift movement.

"…Why?" She sat beside him. "Aren't they…innocent?"

"No." he growled through clenched teeth, looked at her stern, then bowed his head as though in deep thought. "Don't know…" He sighed heavily. "In me book, we're all sinners. Some more than others." he said, wiping the sweat from his forehead as the fever started to spike. She blinked at him, not knowing if that was the answer she was hoping for, realizing he didn't know himself how innocent or evil his victims really were.

"Do you have family, Mac?" she inquired curiously, wanting to find more about him, feeling rushed — as though he would shut down again, at any given moment.

"Thought we was fishin'." he grumbled, avoiding the question.

"I was raised in Nephilim Cove." she began to say. "My mother was a working gal, and my father…well, some man from Bisonhorn who disappeared once he found out I existed, at least that's what ma always said, along with a few more lines…" She snorted bitterly, yet hoped he would feel comfortable to share his story too, if she shared hers first.

Mac looked at her with his full attention, devoted, for he'd never led any conversation with anyone before, not since his younger years around Mickey and the few sailors that could barely make him speak.

"I was never allowed to meet any friends; and the ones that I did meet… well, they…they ended up mocking me for my ma's occupation, and my ugly self of course." She sighed heavily, as she recalled those dreaded memories and his brows snapped together, realizing how she viewed herself, realizing her past was also not the kindest; suddenly feeling as though she too had struggled like him, in a way.

"Then, my ma's clients were…drunks, and drug addicts, not the best men a young girl should be raised around. Thankfully, I was never harmed…even though she threatened she would let them 'have a piece of me'…if I didn't behave, which I always did…" She choked, and shook her head. "I never would want children, but if I ever were to have, I would never be able to treat them the way my ma treated me…" she said and he stared at her, nodding in thought. "Anyhow, my ma ended up a drunkard herself in the end, abusing all sorts of drugs, therefore, her fate was…foreseeable, of course. I…I found her body, dismembered, tossed away like…like it was trash." She glanced at him, knowing he did the same to others. "I will never forget that sight…" she said and he bowed his head. Charlotte's words affected Mac deeply; although he didn't feel an ounce of regret or remorse of his own atrocities, he felt for her.

"Bad business." he said, shortly.

"Yup…bad business, indeed…" She snorted absently, shrugged. "So then I ran off, because the drunks around Nephilim Cove knew where to find me. My bartender friend helped me sneak away, and…I ran off, for weeks rode with sweet Finn across the desert, surviving on canned beans!" She chuckled and yet his face was stern. "I have no idea how the Los Muertos didn't get a whiff of me…"

"Hm." He smirked. "They had their eyes on me…" he said, and she cocked a surprised brow.

"Well, then you rescued me once more." she said and he blinked, bowing his head again.

"So I headed further west, crossed through Cougar's Tooth, got interrogated by…whoever that marshal was called again."

"Tilghman…" he said, and she nodded.

"Yup…That's the one!"

"Hm."

"I heard he is quite intimidating, so naturally I was glad I survived my stay in his town. Barely saw him, actually." She snorted, he bobbed his head. "Then…I arrived at Boomtown, and…I found you." She recalled, blushing at the memory.

Mac was quiet.

Her words clogged his throat with a knot; he recalled the embarrassing way he was thrown out the window, drunk himself, and the way he fussed at her — yet never forgetting how beautiful she looked. "Yeah…sorry 'bout that." he apologized for the first time, avoiding to face her.

"Don't be sorry, you silly man." She chuckled. "Although you spooked my pony, and I still am upset at you over that." she said teasingly and he snorted.

"Yer pony almost trampled me…" he said, cutting his eyes at her.

"Well…aren't you glad I didn't let him?" She winked at him, and his eyes dropped to her lips. She blushed and he tore his gaze away, huffing. "Mac?"

"Hm…"

"I will forever be thankful that we crossed paths, no matter how…" she hummed in earnest, and he swallowed deeply.

"I…hm…" He paused himself, not knowing how to express his emotions, hands clutching a fist, flustered, for it was as though he had forgotten how to speak, for it was as if he didn't know how.

He didn't know how.

"Tell me about you, Mac. Please." she begged.

Her hand, gracefully placed on his knee.

II

LEVI GALLOPED THROUGH THE FORESTRY OF OZARK RIDGE, scanning through the only trails a wagon could cross, yet there was not a single sign of a destroyed, ambushed wagon, and no sign of a stranded JB. Reaching the gloomy swamps in good time, he spotted the campground, deserted, half collected, and his worry only grew, realizing he could have been indeed ambushed.

Dismounting in haste, he strode through the campsite, realizing something horrible must have happened to JB, for he was nowhere to be found. "Shit." He grunted, finding his rugged brown hat plopped on the muddy ground, half covered with mud. Kneeling down, he placed a hand upon footprints beside it, of a very familiar boot; long, narrow, with a pointy toe.

"This isn't good…" he mumbled, eyes following the tracks that turned into horse's hoof prints, leading east towards the town of Birdsboro. Whistling for his horse, it came running to him; mounted, then followed after the tracks with his gun held out as the sun started to set behind him.

III

"HE IS WAKING UP!" THE MEN SAID TO EACH OTHER IN SYNC when they saw Will's eyes pry open, lying in a guest bed. "Who are you?" they asked him immediately, still the same cold, stern voices, only multiplied.

"My…my name is Will, William Griffiths." he stuttered as he was adjusting all his senses, looking around to find himself in a cozy cabin. "Thank you, sirs, for saving me…" he sighed, devoid of any strength and spirit.

"Where are you from…" a tall, blond-haired man asked him, stepping inside the room, every stride rattling the heavy timber frame of the building.

"Bisonhorn, sir." Will said, raising himself up to face him respectfully. "I…I got lost here, my horse…I don't know where it went. All my guns, too, gone. I'm just so…lost." he repeated himself, confused as to how he ended up in Red Giants.

"You hungry?" they asked him, as they were preparing some assorted meats on the fire, flipping them around upon a cast iron skillet. The scent of burning muscle suddenly appealed to him, for his stomach had been cramping the whole night prior; starving, hungering, as though he hadn't eaten for ages.

"Yes, sirs. Very much so." Will answered, unusually short.

"Red Giants is no place to get lost in, mister." the burly man said. "Feasters everywhere, waiting for easy targets like you." he said, politely degrading him.

"Feasters?" he asked in shock.

"Bunch of cultist criminals; they torture people, skin them alive, burn them, cut off their limbs, eat them, and it goes on." the man said to him, as he looked at Will's expensive clothes.

"Goodness…I have not the smallest chance out there…" he said, and the man snorted.

"No, you don't." he agreed, and Will blinked.

"Do they ever give you any trouble here, sirs?" he asked them worriedly.

"No. They know better than to mess with us." he boasted, then adjusted his bear pelt around his shoulders.

"Where are you from, sir? I detect a different accent — if you don't mind my asking, sir." Will inquired, for he always was interested in history and other parts of the world, and he had already noticed these men had limbs stronger than oak, their height seemingly taller than a pine.

"Norway." he said proudly. "We all share the Nordic blood here. We are a small community, that tries to stick together in this evil world." he said. "My name is Jari Enberg, and these two are my guards, Sven and Viggo."

"Delightful to meet you all, kind sirs." he said, and they nodded to him on their way out of the building. "You have certainly an impressive line of history, more so than all Americans combined." he said and the man bobbed his head.

"That we do…"

Will looked around the cabin, his awestruck gaze reflecting upon the blades of a dozen axes, all hung on the wall. His eyes studied frame after frame of photographs, falling upon a picture of an adolescent boy, standing beside a fallen grizzly with a rifle over his young shoulders.

"That's Levi Krog…" the brawny man said to him, observing every eyelash that fluttered around his brown doe eyes. "Grew up here, with us. A boy with a heart of gold." He nodded, mist glazed over his eyes. "He is a well-respected bounty hunter now, across every state. Making us all proud." he bragged, stood up, took down the photograph, and handed it to Will.

I V

"…GREW UP IN THE STREETS OF MON LOUIS, after me parents was murdered. Originally we lived in the woods of Birdsboro…Ozark Ridge." he said, drumming his fingers nervously against his leg. "Started tradin' rum for money to buy food, as a wee lad, along with some other scums like me. Sometimes drugs, although I did never care to touch 'em…" He paused, heart felt oddly leaden — swiftly glancing over at her, to see if she was still listening. She was. Devoted.

"It's okay…" she encouraged him, a gentle smile painting her lips. Her hand, grazing sheepishly along his leg.

"Some damn nuns collected me, and a bunch of other boys. Sold us at an auction. Ended up west of…Holy Ranch, as a…rancher's hand." he said, gnashing down on his teeth.

"I'm listening, Mac." She daringly rested her head on his shoulder, somehow she felt he needed that comfort, for his tension slithered through her, sucking it all in within her being.

Mac looked at her through the corner of his eye, he didn't flinch this time by her touch, as though last night, holding her for what appeared too short of a time, healed that defensive reflex towards her — as though he had started to trust her himself.

"What happened next?" she asked, hand caressing tenderly.

"Hm…" His jaw clenched, tight; a host of paralyzing memories assailed him, lucid and visceral to the bone. "The goddamn…farmer…he…" He paused, flashbacks crippling him, bending, breaking him. Charlotte felt his being quiver, rage surging through, eyes distant, yet traveling in some other dimension; it was dark, grim, a maze of blackness with no escape.

She looked at him with worry, clutched his hand tight, pulling him back out of that hollow void. "Mac, I will not force you…" she said tenderly. "I will never force you to tell me anything or do anything." she said, hand squeezing his tighter. "I understand it can be…difficult, or…painful to look back."

"I don't, feel, pain." he growled sternly, twisting his hand away from her grip; a pout scarring his face, a sharp curve of wrath.

"I understand…" she soughed, concerned to see him so flustered; snapped within seconds. "Mac, I admire you for that." she said, trying to lift his spirits.

"Hm."

"I feel too much." She snorted caustically and his eyes set on her, a troubled frown wrinkled his sharp brow. "I can't control my emotions like you've told me so many times to do…or like you do." She shrugged and he blinked. "Whether it's worry, sadness, pain…*love*…as of…recent, I think…" She paused for a moment, instantly thinking of him, wondering if this was what love felt like. Mac swallowed nervously, noticing her cheeks, crimsoned.

"How?" he asked her daringly, yet timidly.

"How what?" she asked him back, not understanding his question.

"How is it like…to feel?" He shied away, lowered head and frowned.

"Oh…" She blinked, baffled. "Well…to feel worry for example, is… uhm…" She paused and looked over at Finn, grazing in the lush fields next to the cabin in sheer contentment, far away from any seaweed monsters.

"…is like a kick in your stomach when you worry about life, or how to take care of your precious pony; how to survive in this cruel world that keeps on challenging you…"

"It's like your insides twist in a knot, making you nauseous, and ill — similar to the way you must have felt with the fever. You panic! You start to tremble like a lunatic, and start thinking and acting irrationally; fearing your whole world and being will collapse and crumble to the ground; your feet sinking deeper into it, eventually swallowing you up whole." she said, and he stared at her in bewilderment, for these were not feelings he could relate to.

"Then…when you're sad, it's like someone reaches within you; grabs your heart with the roughest hands possible — squeezes it, until it's torn in half. It's a different kind of pain than just the physical; it's debilitating, numbing your whole mind and common sense; it just makes you want to scream as loud as your lungs can manage, and seek for an answer, yet that answer never comes. You just lay there in sadness; alone, feeling…empty?" she asked herself, wondering if she described it well enough, then looked back at him, still the same confused frown plastered on his face. "Does this…make sense?"

"Hm…" It didn't.

"Good…Now you know why I'm such an unstable mess most of the time…" She snorted, then frowned with her own self. He didn't laugh, for the one question still lingered in his head, and she didn't describe it.

"And…the other?" he asked, with a knot in his throat.

"Other?"

"L…lo…"

"Love…?" she said and he stared at her, chest heaved vainly, fighting for breath, unable to grasp what was happening to him just by the mention of this word, just by seeing her lips speak it. "Well, to be honest…I have to think about that myself." She chuckled, blushed, looked at him again as though to catch a swift glimpse of him for inspiration.

"Hm…why?" he asked her, curiously.

"Because…it's something I haven't really felt either…besides my love for Finn." she said and he tore his gaze away. "My ma never loved me, and perhaps I loved her out of necessity or politeness, however…this is not the type of love I'm uncertain of." she said, fingers pulling into her fist; nervously.

"Hm…uncertain?" He gulped down a knot, wondering.

"Well…love is confusing; blinding…and recently I have found out, it can be quite painful — torturous." she said and his breath cut in his lungs, yearning to hear more. "I actually never realized how much it can make your heart…tear, a bit." She shrugged awkwardly, and cut her eyes at him. "Yet, it is one of the most powerful and beautiful feelings someone can be lucky enough to ever experience…" she said, stealing a glimpse of him again, this time deeper, sharper. Her eyes hung upon him, unable to unhook.

"And ye did?" he then asked, locking eyes with her, hanging himself upon her lips.

"I…think so…" she said, breathed harder, unconsciously nearing him an inch, as though a magnet pulled her towards him; a rusty, corroded magnet, yet stronger than any other.

"How…does it feel like?" He leaned over to her with genuine curiosity, expecting to find darkness in her eyes, and yet they were dazzling with a gleaming light, uncertain of where it came from.

"Mac…" She sighed, soughed his name and his eyes clutched for a fleeting moment. "It…makes your heart race wildly…as you stare at the one you love." She blushed, staring into him, unable to tear her gaze away this time. "Everything around you freezes in time…only chaos exists within your chest, as love tears down your defenses, leaving you vulnerable for someone to so easily destroy you…and yet somehow, you hand them the permission to do so, for being destroyed by them, hurts less than to find yourself with someone you don't love." she said and tears shone in her eyes, his pupils flared, and she neared him closer.

"Love is when every inch of your body tingles the closer you are to someone; anticipating a word of affection, a tender touch…any touch, an awkward brush against one's sleeve, one's hand…" She paused, as his stare was once again too intense to handle.

"It feels like you're losing yourself…or, finding who you really are." She paused again. Suddenly, she felt overwhelmed, suddenly there was no patience within her left, her heart throbbed, pumped. "Have you ever felt like this, Mac?" she asked him emotionally, feeling the urgent need to know his feelings, yearning to finally confess to him.

Mac's eyes flared. Everything muffled around him, everything but the constant clop of his heart, pulsating in his head. He pulled his gaze away; sighed, struggling to answer.

CHAPTER 43

Cowardice

I

LEVI REACHED THE TOWN OF BIRDSBORO, in the evening sky that glowed with the city lights of Mon Louis far away. The roaring freight trains passed him by, ready to deliver supplies to the town; oily waters painting a colorful river flowing next to his path, a rainbow of colors, smudged and yet oddly enchanting.

The miners coughed as they drank a sip of water, hoping it might clear their coal-filled lungs. Levi cast a swift glance at them; it was a terrifying sight to behold, men, children with ash-cloaked faces, in a line to climb down a ladder, dropping meters deep into the cold, black depths of earth, into the uncertain death that was promised to them; and even more terrifying was to know a friend of his own struggled day and night just to be able to feed his family. He was grateful to hunt after outlaws instead, for somehow the mines appeared to kill one faster.

"Sheriff Jordon!" he called for him, storming into the building.

Two deputies raised up their guns, pointing them to him, already expecting his entrance. "Stay right where you are, partner." they ordered him, yet Levi was not fazed by their threat.

"I don't have time for this, boys. Where's Jordon?" he persisted, marched towards them, pushing them back with the shield of his muscular chest.

"STAY RIGHT THERE!" They cocked their guns firmly, and it registered to him. *Something had happened.*

"Why, what for?" he asked, sternly. Hand slowly lowering to his hip.

"…what for?" A smug chuckle emerged from the lower floor. "Your man spoke, Mr. Krog." Jordon informed him as he walked up the stairs, amused by his arrival.

"Don't know what you're talking about, Jordon." He leered. "Where is JB?!" he asked him angrily, fearing they had interrogated him in a torturous way, knowing they had no remorse whether it was an elderly man, or a young woman.

"Oh, he's here. Old man's here." He walked up to him as he spoke. "Just needed to get some…more information out of the old clown, regarding where you're hidin' our good ol' boy…Kinnon!" His revolver filled hand lifted rapidly, ready to slam Levi's head with it.

Levi grabbed his arm instantly, punched him in the face, dropping him unconscious to the ground. The deputies stared, aghast, and before they started to even think about shooting him, Levi had already pulled out his dual revolvers, pointing at them both.

"Don't want nobody to die here, but I'll be damned if I won't shoot you both down if you don't bring me to him." He threatened, eyes looking back and forth between them.

"And why do you think we'll do as you say, milksop?" the deputy asked him snidely, as though he behold any power to intimidate the wall of muscle.

BANG

His bullet shot the man right through his head; killing him instantly.

"You really want to play this game with me, son?" He threatened the other man, as he now pointed both revolvers to him. "Or shall we just play nice?" he added; an enticing offer he could not afford to decline. The deputy quivered, nodded, moved with his hands held up, right towards JB's cell, behind a heavily locked door. "That's better…" Levi told him, towering over him as he unlocked the door.

"Levi!!!" JB called ecstatically the moment his eyes set upon him.

Levi's eyes flared, shocked to see his camp companion bruised all over his face, with sharp cut wounds through his delicate elder skin. "You did this to him??" He grabbed the deputy by his neck, pressing his gun against his head.

"N-n…no!!" he stuttered, writhed beneath his grip, eyes clutching in fear.

"Get lost…" he ordered him, tossed him to the ground, not wanting anyone else to die today.

"I'm sorry, JB!! I should've never left you back there alone…" he growled to himself, furious to have not protected him.

"Ah! Don't worry 'bout a thing, my boy!" He chuckled, as Levi untied his hands. "I'm…I'm sorry for rambling to the men. I…I told them, Levi…I was weak." he confessed, ashamed, tilting his head to the ground.

"No, you aren't." He sighed, realizing his reputation was now bound to be ruined. "Let's get out of here. Fast." he urged, and helped him walk faster; JB's arms coiled around his neck, supporting his weight, almost floating in the air as Levi picked up the pace, stepping over Jordon's knocked-out face. "What's this smell, anyway?" he questioned, confused, unable to ignore the rotting scent that hit him with every stride.

"Oh well, that's quite a…a long story, one for the road!" JB chuckled, then sniffed the air to ensure it was indeed himself.

II

"I SEE…" HE HUMMED. "THE BOY CERTAINLY MUST HAVE HAD a dangerous passion for adventure! I know I surely wouldn't enjoy chasing after…degenerates." Will noted, thinking back on having to endure Mac's awful temperament in Hope — not understanding how Charlotte could handle it more than a second, let alone fall for it as it appeared she did.

"Not sure about that. Boy rather had a passion for revenge." Jari said sternly, staring at the photograph Will held. "In his mind, there's only good, and evil, but nothing between the two." he added, recalling Levi's words before he left.

"Well, at least he is doing something good for humanity, I guess; the world needs more of that." Will nodded, handing him the photograph back.

"He sure does. We're all missing him around here…he grew up way too fast. Had to." he muttered, as he handed him a plate of grilled meat.

"Thank you, sir…" Will nodded and yet Jari's mind dwelled someplace in the past, someplace darker, someplace with questions unanswered, someplace where riddles sprout from the ground, turn into vines, strangling the sense.

"He is a good man. A true Berserker at heart. One of the few I've met in my life." He thumped a fist against his burly chest and Will's eyes blinked with every thud. "He doesn't care about fame, reputation, or materialistic things... that clearly don't shape a person's soul." He glanced over at Will's expensive pocket watch, which could possibly pay for everything he owned. "He looks for peace, in a world that is starving for war." he said in earnest, fiddling with his braided beard in deep thought.

"I'm afraid peace...is not a concept easily understood, for it appears each man has a different perception of what 'peace' should be..." he said, and wiped his mouth with a cloth, and Jari stared at him with a cocked wiry golden brow. "Mr. Enberg, I'm...needing someone to take me back to Bisonhorn. Is it possible to hire any of your men?"

"We Norwegians don't ask to be paid, to help someone out." he answered solemnly. "All we ask for is clear intentions; and to not fuck with us." He gave him a sharp, threatening gaze, for he wouldn't blindly trust any money-thirsty elite. "And...sure, we will." he drawled upon a heavy sigh. "I will alert the Twin Wolves." he said in earnest and Will blinked blankly, watched him leave the building. The door slammed shut, rattling every bone in his body. He cleared his throat and waited patiently, wiping his greasy hands clean with the cloth.

The door snarled open, yet this time it creaked quietly, politely, gently. Will, somehow taking note of that, remained seated, eyes nailed on his empty plate. A hand suddenly brushed against his shoulder, fingers soft as feather; a matching voice followed right after.

"Traveler..."

A voice so dreamy, silky, it was hypnotizing. His head turned around to face the voice's host, his gaze dazzled by her gleaming fair skin, the mossy green eyes piercing him with intent.

"My...lady..." he soughed, as though in a state of trance.

"William..." she said, sat beside him, hands clutching his.

Will, benumbed, stared at the blonde woman, a canvas of youth and angelic aura, feeling her fingers entwine with his. "Do...do I know you, miss?" he asked, perplexed, and she cracked a gentle smile.

"No...but I do know you, weary traveler." she said contentedly and his brows drew together. "Do not stride back into these woods, William..." she said and his heart constricted. "Here, you shall rest your mind...sleep the journey from your eyes, until the sun beams higher, brighter than the shadows the bark breeds..." she said, and his hair stood erect. "For the shadows you turn loose...bring back your tears and woe..."

"I...I'm afraid I do not understand, miss..." he said, somehow intimidated by her, wondering if it was once again an illusion of his mind; yet for once an enchanting, kind presence.

"Your illness has started a long time ago, traveler...and I sense that you are tired, depleted, far beyond your travels..." she said, caressing a thumb across his hand, feeling his prickled skin, nails against hers. "But you shall not feel this way, William, for you have so much vigor within you, for your heart is as pure as the clearest creek...you shall not listen, to *them*..." she soughed softly, and his eyes flared in horror.

"You...you can hear them...too?" he asked her, baffled, looking around him, tapping his boots against the ground to ensure he was alive, seated where he was before, conscious.

"They are dimming your light...Darkening the candle to your pathway. But you shall not let them..." She leaned into him, pressed her mouth against his ear, feeling his breath release from his chest. "You shall lift the candle, and fight the darkness that has crept up within you...it's crawling to your core; I can feel it...I've been feeling it." she whispered and pulled back to face him. "Among the edges of a stream, behind corners of descending snow, between sharp winds, I've heard them too..." She then stood up, released her grip and bowed her head, striding softly back outside of the building.

He stared at the door, heart racing, chest oddly feeling lighter, vision in sharper clarity. *Who was she...*he asked himself, quivering in strange serenity. But before he could form another thought, Jari trod back inside.

"Viggo and Sven are preparing the wagon for you." he declared coldly, and Will bowed his head in graceful gratitude, then a knock rattled the heavy oaken door behind them.

"Come in!" Jari shouted swiftly, as if he were expecting someone.

"Sir, I'm here to pick up my wife's medicine." the elderly man said to him with a frail voice.

"You must be the kind man living up ahead?" he questioned, and Will turned to face him, for the voice sounded eerily familiar. "Hope this will help your wife's cough some." He handed him a vessel with homemade medicine within; an ancient mixture of many different healing herbs.

"Mr. Miller?" Will interrupted them, aghast.

"Mr. Griffiths!" Mr. Miller gasped, stunned himself.

III

"NO." HE SAID SHORTLY. TONE COLD, VOICE COARSE. His cigarette ash flicked before them, blackening the air they shared, suffocating her every breath. "I don't feel nothin'." He pulled on the stick, inhaled his lie, exhaled it, tossed it deep into the lagoon, shadowed by the drowning sun. It drowned, too. He drowned. Cowering within the rippled waters, for somehow that sentiment was more familiar.

Charlotte stared at him, wordless, limbs benumbed, heart drowning with him; not expecting to be that wrong about him — about *them,* the man she laid beside that morning, all night prior, hand clasping his chest, heartbeats merging in the purest of serenity. Staring at him, replaying their kiss in her mind, distinctly remembering how he intensely kissed her back, how she could feel every fiber of his being pulsate in the same rush of adrenaline that fed her excitement; how his eyes had brightened, livelier again every time gazes were exchanged — from being dead and hollow for so long before. A blood-curdling, nerve racking shock to hear him mutter those words, as if all this time she was "nothin'" to him. *But perhaps that's all she ever was indeed,* she thought, as she watched him smoke without flinching, without a single damn blink, a single bat of an eyelash that could betray a lie.

"I see." she said, slightly grunted, fighting back the tears, gazing away from the most beautiful blues she'd ever locked eyes with, realizing she'd never look into them the same way as before.

Mac sat in silence; staring at the waters, reflecting the vacancy across his face, aggravating himself with it as well. *Feelings,* he thought, unable to grasp how to express such a concept. He didn't understand them to begin with — it was the oddest sensation for him to be completely void, eerily cold and hollow inside, then suddenly upon meeting the most stubborn, infuriating woman, to feel so much, as if someone flipped a switch within his heart; it utterly bewildered him, for he was not supposed to feel. Ever. For that rule was deeply engraved within him.

"I think I…will have a ride with Finn." she whispered, barely audible, as though her voice had lost all vigor, as though the dry sobs she swallowed smothered her, a tight barbed wire coiling her throat, lynching her. "It's been long since we ventured off somewhere; just the two of us." She nodded to herself, pulled in a breath with a quivering chest, and stood up.

"Sure." he answered shortly, unknowingly upsetting her even further, as he stomped the cigarette with his boot and grabbed the pole again. Charlotte hopped onto her stallion's bare back and wandered off away from the cabin, letting her pent-up tears flow freely, bursting into a well of emotions. Teeth clenched in frustration, Mac felt the usual loneliness consume him. He threw the line back into the turquoise waters, watched it sink, ripple them apart, as his thoughts wandered back to her.

"Finn…you're the only one that matters to me, you know?" Her tears distorted her vision, barely missing the beautiful flock of bluebirds that shot before them in the dusk. "Perhaps I shouldn't have gone looking after him… perhaps I should have just stayed in the saloon, waiting on the man that actually cares about me!" she fussed, realizing she had forgotten entirely about Will. "Oh dear God, Will…" she sobbed even stronger, disgusted with her selfishness, disgusted with her lack of emotional control. "I completely abandoned Will…" she cried, gut twisted within her. "…he must be thinking the worst, or…or worrying to death about me! Perhaps he didn't even receive my stupid letter…" She gasped, and then went silent for a long moment.

"Why is this man coming into my life, every time my heart tries to settle?!!" she growled, yelled, then fumed, huffed hot air through her mouth, and adjusted Finn's lock of mane that was tangled in the leather reins with quivering fingers. "Why is God sending this man to me, Finn?" she asked, glimpsed up at the cloudy sky above her, slowly getting darker as the shining stars gently emerged through it. "Why…does he not feel the same…why does he not see how I burn for him? Why do I expect him to feel something for me…he is not…obligated to do so…" She choked, and broke apart. "That kiss was a mistake…perhaps we both were simply curious…nothing more." She nodded to herself, and proceeded along the narrow path.

Suddenly, multiple horse hooves clapped hard against the rocky trail, vastly multiplying the closer they got. "Whoa, Finn…" she whispered, and hid rapidly behind some birch trees, looking out to see who was passing in this secluded path. A dozen deputies were racing down towards the cabin, with their rifles held to the side, and lanterns dangerously attached to their horses.

"Oh no…it can't be." Her breath cut in her lungs, swiftly thinking of Levi's absence and JB's mysterious disappearance. "He didn't set us up…did he?" Her face furrowed in disappointment, eyes leered. "This can't be true!" she growled, and started riding in slyness back towards the lagoon, spotting Mac down at the waters — still fishing. "Damn it!!" She jumped off Finn, and swiftly started hiking down on foot so they couldn't hear her.

CHAPTER 44

Pierced

I

"WHAT DID YOU TELL THEM, JB?" LEVI ASKED HIM, as they were galloping through the Ozarks.

"I…well, they was about to cut my nuts off!! I had to say somethin'!!" he defended himself, holding on tightly to the cantle of the saddle, belly pressed against Levi's back, making him sit over the horn for both didn't fit in the seat.

"JB, it's alright, just tell me!" Levi pressured him again, arm kept before his face to protect himself from all the sudden branches that tended to whip against him.

"Told 'em 'bout the cabin!!" JB screeched, eyes bulging like a swampy bullfrog's as he did. "I'm so sorry, Levi!!" He sobbed guiltily, bouncing on the seat with every stride of the horse, holding on for dear life.

"Damnit…" Levi grunted, blood quickened in concern. *Charlotte…*

"We gotta hurry, hold on tight!" Kicking his horse harder, JB now bounced like a leaping frog after it swam in a pool of whiskey. His short, stubby feet wiggled in the air beside the horse, bumping against its flanks unforgivingly — Levi realized that night, he had a saint of a mount.

"What you say 'bout dropping me off at Ravenheart Pond?" he offered, somehow sense blessed him, for he was afraid to cause any further trouble. "And we meet back there…"

"…and Kinnon?" Levi worriedly asked him, not wanting a murderer around any of his people.

"He'll be fine, Levi. He could've already strangled me — I mean, not

479

everyone can deal with my…ramblings." He chuckled, realizing perhaps he indeed tended to talk too much; too much for his own good.

I I

"WHAT ARE YOU DOING HERE, SIR?" MR. MILLER QUESTIONED WILL, bewildered to see him so dirty, disheveled, untidy for the very first time, as though he was pommeled, tossed into a muddy pig pen.

"I fear I was lost in the woods…somehow." he said, eyes glazed in thought.

"What a terrible ordeal! I'm sorry for your struggle, Mr. Griffiths…" Mr. Miller said, briefly wondering if he had tried to follow after Elizabeth.

"Well…I was fortunate enough to have come across this…welcoming place." he said. "However, I overheard that Mrs. Miller is unwell?" Will inquired, concerned, for he always thought she was the sweetest old lady.

"Yes indeed, sir. She's been having a dreadfully stubborn cough that just won't go away, and…the doctor down in Bisonhorn doesn't have the slightest clue." he said, clearly upset by the fact.

"Mr. Miller, Bisonhorn is not blessed with a doctor of vast knowledge; however, if I may, I shall recommend my friend down in Mon Louis…" he offered kindly and Mr. Miller sighed heavily.

"Mr. Griffiths, thank you, sir, but we ain't got the money to travel that far; and definitely not to see a doctor." he confessed, eyes pooling with tears — concerned to the core for his wife's fate after sixty strong, unbreakable years.

"Mr. Miller, in fear to employ discomfort, please do allow me to help you." Will flipped out his checkbook, fumbled a pen from his coat, and scribbled an extremely generous number upon it. The Norwegian man stared, stunned by the sight of it, certainly enough to pay for the entire settlement Petit Jean.

He signed it off, flipped it around and handed it to him.

"Sir, I could never accept this!" Mr. Griffiths gasped, aghast. "I could never in my lifetime pay this back to you, Mr. Griffiths!" he argued, hands shaking from the generosity.

"I insist, Mr. Miller. You don't owe me anything; you took care of my wife, Elizabeth for me while I…while I was gone." Will stuttered awkwardly, suddenly reminding himself why he got lost in Red Giants. "I don't need the money anymore...please, accept it, for I insist upon it." he said sternly, tucking the check within Mr. Miller's coat.

"Mrs. Elizabeth...she..." Mr. Miller drew in a guilty breath, on the edge of confessing, for he noticed the hopeless gaze dim within his dull brown eyes. Will glanced back at him, surprised, waiting with suspense for him to finish his sentence. "God, forgive me..." he mumbled to himself, covered his face with his hands. "She is staying with us, sir. She...she came to us, all distraught and frightened. She cried you was seeing someone else." he avowed as the man behind them listened carefully as well, and Will stared at him, aghast.

"I need to talk to her, Mr. Miller...I...I've made a terrible mistake, I'm afraid, but...I'm here, suffering for it." he said, clenching his jaw. "I need to speak with her, please, Mr. Miller." He begged him, stood up swiftly; ready to follow him home, ready to win Elizabeth back, ready to confess, explain everything, ready to leave Charlotte in a void of the past. Ready to force himself to love his wife again.

"I ain't sure if it's a good idea, sir." he said, feeling protective of the privacy she asked for. Insisted for. Demanded.

"I have to, Mr. Miller. Please." Will insisted, grabbing his hand pleadingly.

III

CHARLOTTE'S FEET FLEW OVER THE LOGS BEFORE HER; leaping, hiking down, sprinting frantically, she ran faster than she knew her legs were capable of. Heart bolted with her, shivering all over from the upwards spiral of adrenaline, setting into the unbearable feeling of panic. A vine trapped her boot on the rocky ground, pulled her down to it, slamming her hands against rock and hardness; bones sunk into the soil, twisting her wrists against the stones. A groan of harrowing pain escaped her, yet she got up swiftly and proceeded to run even faster towards the cabin.

The deputies had arrived; sneaking around the timber building, cocking their guns — pistols, shotguns, rifles, all ready to capture Mac — certain this time they'd find him here. Charlotte had no weapon around her hip, yet she carried a small pocket knife within her boot, mostly used for cleaning Finn's hooves, picking out pebbles that would trap within them.

She spotted the men peeking through the windows, waiting before the door, anticipating; suspense radiating through the ruthless chill of the air around them — ready to blast the place down. Unable to find Mac anywhere outside anymore, she leaped over broken logs and rough hills; letting the stones roll freely underneath her as she climbed, grabbing what sturdy vines and branches she could, pulling herself further up and faster to him.

Signaling to each other silently, they counted with their fingers, before kicking the door open and shooting endlessly — blasting the place into thousands of wooden splinters. An echo of bullets, crashing against the bookshelves, drilling through the timber walls, windows exploding from the impact, the laughter of deputies all around Ring Lagoon reaching her ears.

"NOOOO!!!!!!" Charlotte screamed, devastated, arriving at the cabin one minute too late. "You MURDERERS!!!!!" she yelled at them, bursting into gut-wrenching, heart-twisting, mind-sickening tears she'd never cried before. "You goddamn SWINES!!!"

The deputies paused, turned, finding her with her small pocket knife held out defensively, quivering, yet this time not out of fear. There was menace in her eyes. They looked at each other and burst into laughter, mocked her innocent ignorance. They signaled to each other, and Charlotte stared at them with a leer, not backing down as they approached her steadily, while the rest entered the cabin to search for Mac's corpse.

"Would'ya look at what the cat dragged in…"

IV

"MRS. ELIZABETH…" MR. MILLER SAID, dreading to betray her trust. "I…I have someone with me, who requested to speak with you." he said to her, entering his cabin.

"And who exactly might that be?" she asked suspiciously, inspecting her coat once again, waiting for it to dry, realizing she would have to endure another night in their ruddy surroundings.

Mr. Miller cracked the door open, and Will strode right inside, wide-brimmed hat against his chest; remorseful eyes locking hers.

"William!" She gasped, aghast to see him here, in this cabin, in this pit of forbidden memories.

"My darling…" he hummed softly, and walked closer to her.

"What are you doing here?" she hissed, folding her slender arms before her chest.

"Let us sit down…for I have come here with the determined resolution to give you the explanation that you deserve." he spoke softly, tender, yet there was pain and hesitation in his voice.

"I don't wish to speak with you." she fussed sternly, tearing her eyes away from him.

"Well, I will leave you two to it." Mr. Miller politely interrupted, and exited the cabin upon a weary limp.

"And how do you dare to appear to me, in such…attire! So…filthy." Her face furrowed, scrunched up with an air of arrogance, as it often tended to do.

"My apologies, my lady…" He swallowed dryly, drowning in embarrassment. "I've been…I've been sick, Elizabeth. I think…I'm losing my mind, perhaps…" he confessed insecurely, recalling the doctor's warnings he chose to deny for they insulted his intelligence.

"What do you wish to imply??" she asked annoyed, carelessly, as though the whole world revolved only around her.

"It's too complicated to explain…my lady." He sighed, twitching his mustache, like he always did when nervousness smothered every sense of his.

"That's what you always say! It's too complicated to explain about your mistress, too!" She growled, leered, sending him a look of utter abhorrence.

"I'm here, standing before you, to sincerely apologize to you, my dear. For everything…for the horrible ways I made you feel since my return. My stubbornness and selfishness; living in a dream that killed ours. I'm sincerely sorry, Elizabeth…please, forgive me." he pleaded, reached for her dainty hand, clasped it with the sole tenderness only his fingers possessed.

Elizabeth looked at him with eerie pleasure, with eyes that judged him; eyes, blind to anyone's feelings but her own. His desperate depletion reflected within them, her hand pressed against his lips. He kissed it, tenderly. Yet when he looked up to face her cold green eyes, nothingness coiled his heart — the same nothingness that guided him when he left her.

V

MAC HAD HEARD THE ARMY OF HORSES AND RIDERS approach before, and rushed swiftly into the cabin to pick up his guns, hiding them behind the boulder they were fishing from, diving into the now ice-cold water of the lagoon, holding in a deep breath — counting the freezing seconds. Hearing Charlotte's ear-shattering caterwaul, vibrating the icy waters around him, he realized she had returned, now surrounded by deputies.

"What'ya gonna do with that, lady?" A deputy approached her, pistol pointed at her. Charlotte, still sobbing, unable to quell the panic, raised her knife higher, hand trembling agitatedly as a sudden urge to take revenge slithered through her veins.

"You're gonna rot in Hell, for what you did!" she yelled at him, lips shaking from the sudden drop in temperature; panic intensifying, paralyzing her legs, internal turmoil carving her whole heart out, breaking each rib of her rib-cage one by one, and yet she stood there. Knife, against a dozen guns.

"Hell is for sinners like your buddy, Kinnon…" He snorted, and strode closer to her. "…and damned whores, like yourself." He winked with a smirk, eyes ogling her body lecherously. "What do ya think? Should we see what Kinnon's been devouring all this time, as we poor bastards been lookin' for this son of a bitch?!" He joked, and the deputies burst into laughter.

"Don't even think about coming near me, you sick bastard!!" She waved her knife around, aiming at his face, teeth snarling.

"Oh, are ya gonna pinch me with it?" He pouted with a cocked head, snidely. "I might *like* it." He grinned, and yet a voice slashed through his joke.

"Boys! There ain't no damn corpse in here!!" The deputy yelled, rushing out after examining the entire shot-down cabin, panting in worry.

"Shit!!" he growled, eyes slamming back upon her. "Where is the damn son of a bitch, you goddamn whore?!!" The deputy launched to her, grabbed her hand firmly that was still gripping the knife, gun pressed against her head.

An instant relief flushed through her, yet she knew this would most likely be the end of her own life, the pull of a trigger just moments away, unable to shield herself from evil, bound to receive the consequences of her bravery, *or rather naïvety,* she briefly thought. A stone of worry sat atop her chest; she could either let it smother her, or push against it. She chose the latter. She jerked, yanked herself in every direction, wrestled with his hand, trying to dig the knife into him, while the man pressed the gun against her head harshly.

"You piece of worthless shit, ya're gonna tell us where he is at!! Ya hear?!" the deputy slapped her face with his elbow, still pressing the barrel on her temple. Charlotte spat at his round, disgusting face, snarling her teeth at him, hand trembling, knife swaying back and forth, still eyes aiming at the crease of his neck.

"You'd have to kill me first!" she growled, posing a challenge she could never win. The deputy smacked her across the face again, though now with cold metal; suddenly her legs weakened, vision blurred — dropping soon after to the ground from the forceful impact. A kick in the stomach followed right after, and the rest of the men circled around them, letting out a peal of immoral laughter, as she curled up in a ball, arms embracing herself, dwelling in fear and pain.

"I won't say it one more time…either ya speak woman, or ya're gonna meet your savior tonight!" he threatened her, looked up swiftly at the others, as though waiting for their laughter of approval.

"If I'm going…" she mumbled under her breath, wheezing from the harrowing pain. "…then so are you." she growled, stood up, and leaped on him with all her swiftness and strength, slamming the knife into his chest repeatedly. He dropped his gun in surprise, yelled, groaned, as she punctured him everywhere she could. Chest, lungs, throat — making blood gush out of tiny little holes.

The deputies rushed to grab her off of him, when a loud explosion startled them all, catapulting some of them in the air, slamming them against the trees, gruesomely dismembered. Jerking their heads at the direction of the cabin, blown up in flames by dynamite, they raised their guns towards it. Charlotte took the opportunity and let the moaning man go, but as she rushed to escape, yet another deputy tackled her to the ground. She screamed in frustration, kicked him, tried to slice his face up, yet he was too strong, pinning her down effortlessly until a bullet hit him in the head — making him drop dead atop of her.

Charlotte, benumbed, in a state of utter shock, breathless, glanced behind herself to find Mac walking out of the dark waters. A sturdy silhouette, back-lit by a decaying full moon. Long, wet hair touching his muscular shoulders, clothes soaked, dripping icy water with every step he took. Hand holding a revolver, still losing smoke from the barrel of his last shot.

"Mac!!!" she cried, screamed, warning him with the coarseness of her voice of the rest of the deputies, pointing their guns towards him. He kept on walking, calm and steady, shooting one deputy after another before they even had the chance to raise their guns towards him — he had already reloaded as they struggled to adjust their aim. Other thunderous shots were heard behind them, taking two more men down.

Mac and Charlotte turned back, stunned to find Levi flinging his bolas at the armed men; hurling them off his horse as it loped around them in an impressive maneuver — making them drop to the hard, rocky ground with legs tied up in an instant, unable to get up.

"RUN!!" he yelled at them, reloaded the cartridges in his rifle, standing steadily on the stirrups as his horse kept a lope underneath him. He aimed at their heads, forming clouds of blood in the air as he shot them off.

Mac rushed to Charlotte, who was shocked and frozen into place with the knife still glued to her grip, staining it scarlet. She had never been involved in a gunfight before — and this was utter chaos; this was war. There was no grand oasis in this vastness of gloom. Picking her shivering body up in his arms, sutures burst from his skin with the sudden strain; a harsh slicing sensation against flesh, a mouth of a wound, screeching in harrow, spurting out blood.

She buried her crying face in his chest, praying for all of them to come out of this alive; panicking for she couldn't control her fear, and the rush of adrenaline had worn off, subsided; ears rang from the loud gunshots going off near her, and wrists started to ache. "Let's leave, please!!" She begged him, pulled on his wet shirtfront frantically, unable to breathe, on the edge of losing control of her senses.

"Soon." he spoke calmly, without a hint of nervousness, or concern, as though they took a midnight walk in the lushest park of Mon Louis. He hid her behind a boulder, handing her his heavy shotgun. "Point, and pull." he instructed, then peeked over the rock to check on Levi.

"But, where you going!!" She trembled, petrified by the thought of being left alone in the midst of death, in the midst of a bloodbath.

"He can't do it on his own." he said, watching Levi now hide behind a thick tree, four last deputies gunning him down; shooting the bark off it in the process.

"Please!!!"

"It ain't his place to keep 'em off of us…they're after me." he said.

She choked. "Mac…Mac!! I don't want to lose you again!!" she yelled, still gripping tightly at his shirt. Mac froze, eyes set upon her worried face, streaks of blood muddying it from the deputy's hit, his anger rose even stronger.

"Ye ain't goin' to, me lass." he reassured her, reloaded his gun once more, ready to leave their cover.

Charlotte peeked over the rock as she saw him run towards the scene; shaking all over, she held the gun in her small hands, paranoid of every slight shadow that tree branches formed on the ground, crawling towards her, as though to merge with hers. "Mac! More are coming!!!" she screamed at him, spotting another dozen galloping down the hill.

Mac jammed his revolver within his trousers, slung his rifle from around his shoulder. Cocked it. Aimed at them, taking down one by one before they even reached the burning cabin. Slinging his rifle back, he pulled out his revolver. "On yer left!" he yelled at Levi, hip-shooting the deputy before him, clearing his path to him.

Levi aimed with his rifle, looked through his scope, shooting the men off their horses in the distance. Aim was shaky, shots too quick, as the pressure to perform was high, making him miss a few as he rushed. "Kinnon! We gotta go! There's too many!" he yelled back at him, as he scanned the area around them.

"That ain't fun!" He smirked, striding, taking his knife out, flipping it in the air, eyes nailing *him*. Kneeling down, he grabbed the man's hair, pulled back, and pressed his head against his, scenting him, still breathing, still hearing, still watching, still faintly existing — bleeding out, from Charlotte's multitude of punctures.

"Have bad news for ya, me lad…" he said, and he trembled, wheezed, choking in his own blood. "There ain't no savior." he whispered to him, sliced his throat wide open, then stuck the knife through the middle of his skull, cracking it, pulling it out again.

Levi rushed to him, freezing upon the macabre sight. Mac stood up, flipped the knife back into its case around his belt, and rushed with him away, taking cover behind two rocks, as Levi whistled hurriedly for his horse. "We can't do it, Kinnon! We need to leave now!" he urged him to listen, as he tried to catch his breath.

"Where to?" He smirked snidely, knowing no single state was safe for him, nor Charlotte. He took out a cigarette, ready to light it up.

"You aren't seriously gonna smoke now, are you??" Levi glanced at him, stunned and annoyed at his dangerous lack of urgency.

Mac looked back at him, cocked a brow of confusion, not understanding why he could barely breathe; expecting a bounty hunter to be calmer around such occasions — almost enjoying to have found such a weakness in him.

"Whatever!" Levi grunted. "There's an isolated ranch just west from here! JB is waiting on us there with some of my relatives — my cousin's family." he informed, as a bullet scraped against the rock right above their heads.

Charlotte spotted Finn in the distance, a silhouetted speck, still waiting loyally for her return. She whistled for him, yet he was too far to hear her, too terrified himself from all the unfamiliar noise. She crawled slowly away from the safety of the rock and wandered off into the jet-black darkness, heavy shotgun still in her hand — dragging beside her. *There was no way she would leave her stallion behind,* she thought.

"You can't be hidin' for long, Mac Kinnon! Your time has come! There's too many of us; surrender!" Sheriff Jordon ordered him upon his arrival, dismounting his thoroughbred, revolver pulled out, cocked.

Mac snorted tauntingly, for he had heard this line before. He exhaled a patient cloud of smoke, listening to the cocking sound of the deputies' guns.

"How do we leave now that they're here?" Levi asked him, agitated. "What's the plan??" he persisted, as he looked over at Mac, noticing his eyes freeze in eerie silence, calculating all the different barbarous methods he might use to murder Jordon, ticking him off the list of sheriffs murdered. "Kinnon!

We need to leave!" he urged again, as his horse appeared beside them.

"Ye go. I'll hold 'em back." he said in earnest. "The lass is behind the…" He paused, realizing she had disappeared. "Gaaah!! Dammit, woman!" he growled, agitated, frantically looking over the rock to spot her as the rounds kept on firing.

V I

"SO? YOU'RE NOT PLANNING TO FOLLOW THROUGH with the divorce, William?" she inquired coldly, expecting him to beg for her return even further, for suddenly she loved the attention and abrupt shift of events in her favor.

"No…no, I am not, my dear." he whispered, uncertain if he really meant it. "I…am not." He nodded to himself, glancing around the cabin as though to find a meaning in his words.

"But what about the betrayal?"

"Hm?" He jerked his head around, faced her. "Excuse me, Elizabeth?" he asked, staring into her eyes, searching for the answer.

"What, William?" she looked at him, ginger brows raised in confusion.

"The…the betrayal?" he repeated, biting his lip nervously, somehow glancing around himself again, as though a force hooked a claw on the back of his head, jerking him towards a wall; a wall holding a shadow; it now reached the ceiling, taking the form of a man. It vanished upon a blink, turned into a frame. "Who are you…" he soughed, nearing the wall.

"William?? Are you talking crazy again??" She leered, flustered, watching him approach the frame, hand reaching out. Her breath cut in her lungs.

"I am the dust, the maggots, and the soil…"

"What…" He cocked his head, tilting it, eyes squinting, struggling to see the photograph beneath the glass.

"William, look around…"

He twisted around himself, only able to lock eyes with Elizabeth again.

"She betrayed you again, William."

"With…who?" he asked and she blinked, frightened, taking a step back.

"The face of your nightmares…the face beneath the layer of your skin, drowned

in tears, buried beneath unspoken words."

"James…" he whispered eerily.

"Pardon me?" She gasped faintly, heart raced within her by the mention of his name.

"You went off, with James…" he repeated, slowly getting agitated, pupils dilating black.

"I did not! I've been here, all this time!" she defended herself, suddenly not amused by his attention.

"But *they* know…*they* knew you were here. Why would *they* lie?" Will cried, realizing the ravens led them to her, just like the voices instructed. Walking closer to her; the wooden planks of the floor creaked underneath his custom-made boots, imported all the way from Nova Scotia.

"William! Who is…they??" she whispered in sheer bewilderment, frightened, grabbing the knife from the counter behind her, studying his expression, slowly turn into something unholy — something unrecognizable.

VII

LEVI SHOT AT THE MEN AS THEY FIRED BACK AT HIM, swiftly peeking from the sides of the trees — hiding in shadow. A smoky trail of their fired cartridges betrayed their location in the vast darkness that engulfed the whole area.

Mac, without much further thought, swiftly pulled a slim, sharp knife out of his rugged leather boot, threw it forcefully over the rock, landing precisely with the blade embedded deeply into Jordon's scrawny neck.

Jordon gripped his throat in great surprise, hands were instantly cloaked by the streaming gore from his sliced jugular vein. "You…you…" He gargled, choked on his own scarlet liquid, kneeled down before them. Eyes of horror, bulged out in shock, body losing its balance, mind devoid of any fight — dropping like a sack of rocks to the ground.

The deputies, stunned, glanced at him; watching him succumb to nothingness — lifeless within seconds, so unexpectedly. Mac sprinted away from cover, arm extending towards them he shot at them, moving smoothly from rock to rock, shielding his whole body as bullets chased after him. Levi took the opportunity, mounted his horse and rode in the opposite direction, trying to locate Charlotte, dodging bullets as he dived to the side of his steed.

"Be a man, and face us! You coward!" they shouted at Mac, losing track.

"I ain't the one comin' with a whole damn army against one; yer callin' *me* a coward, ye eejits?" he scowled, shot at them some more, swiftly glanced around himself.

"You're a wanted man, Kinnon! You deserve the consequences of your monstrosities!" they yelled, then fired back, still cowering behind the trees.

"No one decides what I deserve but meself, me lads!" he shouted, looked around again in hopes of spotting Charlotte anywhere possible in the woods.

"The Lord has the last word, boy! Ya better get ready for it!" They snuck ever closer, now hiding in a different cluster of trees.

Levi couldn't find a single trace from Charlotte; not a single footprint painted in the soil, not a strand of hair trapped in branches; he couldn't spot Finn's large hoofprints either. Nervously raking his fingers through his beard, he thought intensely of ways she could have escaped, yet the possibility of someone capturing her greatly concerned him. Squinting through the veil of fog that cocooned them, he spotted Roy, standing in the middle of the woods, a black shadow camouflaging with the dark, waiting patiently for his rider.

"Mac!!! GO!!" Charlotte's quivering voice suddenly emerged from within the gloomy, brittle woods, prickling Mac's skin in relief. His eyes hunted anxiously for her through the dark; soon noticing the shine of his shotgun's barrel pointed at the two deputies before her. "LEAVE!!!" she screamed urgently, as both deputies raised their hands slowly, knowing the shotgun shells would blow a memorable hole in their backs instantly.

"Charlotte…don't do nothin' stupid, lass." he demanded calmly, seeing more deputies come riding down the hill in the distance behind her.

"Dro…DROP Y-YOUR GUNS!" she commanded them, a cold flow slithering down her spine, finger trembling upon the trigger, shotgun shaking back and forth. There was horror, fear, in her voice.

The men obeyed as ordered, watching Mac walk up to them, his weapon pointed at their heads. Before anyone made a sound, he shot one of them dead; Charlotte tore her gaze away, as the man plopped before her, bleeding out from a hole between his eyes.

"Wh…why did you do that? He was…he was surrendering, wasn't he?" she asked him, stammering.

"No man alive surrenders willingly…" he said calmly, pressing his barrel against the second deputy's head. "…no man." The trigger, pulled victoriously. Blood exploded in a fine mist from his skull, painting Charlotte's cheeks bright red. She froze in place, ears ringing again, staring horrified back at Mac.

"C'mere!" he urged hastily. "Got yer horse?" he asked her, seeing the new army of deputies dismounting by the cabin, swinging their rifles over their shoulders, eager to hunt them down.

"He…he…yes. F-Finn!!" Frozen in overwhelming panic, she called after him, alerting the deputies at the same time. The men started shooting their way, swarming the lagoon like an army of ants, as Finn galloped to them. "M-Mac…they're…they're coming…so…so m-many!!!" she grappled his arm, squeezed it tight.

"Calm down, lass. Yer horse is comin'. We mount, we ride off." he said sternly, grabbing Finn's reins to halt him. He stood there, beside her; snorting and stomping every time they shot towards them.

"Whoa…shhh…" Mac soughed to him, and Finn lowered his head. "Can ye ride okay?" he asked, noticing her quivering legs, not able to move off the cold ground.

"I…I don't know." Tears stood in her eyes, lips unable to mutter a single thought; writhing uncontrollably, she attempted to jump on his bare back, yet slid back off. Mac hopped over him, pulled Charlotte up before him, shielding her with his arms from any bullet that could land on her torso.

Clutching her tight against his chest, they galloped off, rushing through a variety of pine and birch trees, steering between them, scraping Finn's legs against gigantic rocks, trampling down thorn bushes before them; they rode away in the dim glow of the moon.

VIII

"I AM UNCERTAIN..." HE MUTTERED, JERKING HIS HEAD LEFT AND RIGHT.

"Of what, darling?" Elizabeth asked him, capturing the bewilderment upon his face.

"I know I've been alone...I know...but...someone has been watching..." he said, cutting his eyes at her, crying.

"William, please let us just...go back home, and...forget about everything!"

"You shall not...ask her..."

"Ask what?" he whispered to himself.

"William??"

"How did she enjoy sleeping in his bed...the one they fucked in..."

Will's breath cut in his lungs. He stared at her; a menacing leer, a pout of devastation, taut across his face.

"You...slept here...in his bed." he said and she blinked at him, blankly.

"William...where else should I have...slept? Look around you, darling!"

She quivered, and his eyes flooded.

"They fucked in the same bed...William...remind her."

"No!" he growled. "NO!"

"No what???"

"I don't want to hear you!! I don't want to ask my wife that!!!" He yelled from the top of his lungs, and she gripped the knife tighter.

"Hear who, William?? Ask me what??" she cried, praying for an escape, yet the door was past him, down at the dark glen of the cabin.

"I hear voices, Elizabeth!!! But no-one's talking!!!" he said and her eyes flared, aghast. "I can hear its breathing!! Its coldness against my skin!! Elizabeth, help me!!!" he sobbed in despair, screaming in agony, and yet she shook her head.

"William...I, I fear that I can't..." she whispered, sobbed, clenched her whole being.

"Did she love him, William..."

"No...she didn't..."

"Did she love him...dare to ask...you COWARD. DARE!"

"I am NOT a coward!!"

493

"ASK HER!"

"William, please!! Stop!!! You're scaring me, please!! I beg you!"

"Did you...LOVE HIM???" he yelled, and her heart halted. "Did you, Elizabeth?? Did you love him?!!" he cried, dropping to his knees. "Did you... love him...darling?"

"No...no, William. I never, ever loved him...I always loved you." she said in earnest, and he looked up at her with the last glimmer of innocence in his eyes. Then they clutched. Shut. Pulse echoed, thudding at the crease of his neck. Tears cloaked his gaunt cheeks. Darkness. A sweet scent brushed against him.

Eyes forced open. Glancing at hunting arrows, mounted on the wall — the arrowheads, razor-sharp, meant to penetrate through a bear's thick skin.

He stood up. Approached them.

Her eyes dilated, knife clasped firmly not to slip through her sweaty hands.

"William...no. Please, darling." Elizabeth stuttered in panic, as he pulled a single arrow off the wall with a steady grip. A wicked smirk, scarring his lips. "Mr. Miller!!!" Elizabeth screamed in despair, yet nobody could hear her, as the elderly couple had left them to their own.

"Elizabeth...why?" Will questioned her slowly with a raspy voice, as though it wasn't his own.

"I didn't love James, William! Nor was he here! I swear!!!" she shouted. "Have you lost your mind?! You just spoke to Mr. Miller!"

James is here, William. He is here...hiding in this very cabin. She betrayed you, once again. She is a woman full of sin and deceit..." the voices continued tormenting his mind, pushing him further towards her.

"Where is he!?!?" he yelled at her, walked closer to her — now, his confident chest almost touching hers.

"He's not here, William!! I swear, darling! Please! P...please!" she stuttered fearfully, eyes down at the arrow's point before her.

Will looked in confusion — his expression that of a senile man; lost in his own mind, with no control of his own thoughts or actions. He smirked at her maliciously, yet a sincere tear rolled down his face.

He knew he would. He didn't know why.

"Look closer, William...James is right here."

Will squinted before himself, staring with uncertainty into Elizabeth's green eyes that slowly turned raven black.

Her elegant thin face, now square and robust.

Her tiny shoulders, now those of a large man.

"Do it."

Will's hands shook in anguish. Eyes cried, yet heart felt no emotion.

He raised the arrow, and dug it swiftly into her heart. Pulled it out. Pierced it back. Again, and again.

His once expressive, soft doe eyes — full of joy, tenderness, and kindness — now a hollow black, eerily cold. The voices roared demonically with laughter in his head, and yet there was a silent weeping that echoed in the background, uncertain if it was his own, somewhere deep in his subconsciousness.

He dug the arrow ever deeper, finally not being able to pull it back out anymore. Stuck. A sharp pain suddenly awakened him, as he felt the searing warmth radiating from a knife that was drilled through his own body.

CHAPTER 45

Bloodletting

I

"ATTENTION, BISONHORN CITIZENS!" SHERIFF DORMAN SHOUTED across the town, standing atop a hill before the old town's cathedral. "Ladies and gentlemen, most of ya probably know all too well of this 'righteous' man, up on the hill...a Mr. William Griffiths!" he grumbled and the town folks stared at him, confused as to what could have happened to their beloved friend and caring neighbor, Will. "Well, he ain't there no more! He is guilty of deceit; dishonesty towards the law! He is a lying, cheatin' snake in the grass!" he scolded, and the people goggled at one another with great surprise. Will was never one to be dishonest, he was rather a helpful, generous young elite; a law-abiding citizen, who helped people in need with his immeasurable funds. An ethical business man who kept his dealings clean and fair. However, this very same kindness was taken advantage of, and friends quickly turned into greedy hands.

"And he is in hidin'! So! If anyone has any information, or knows this man's whereabouts, we request ya to come forward! There will be severe consequences to anyone who'll cover for this man! And be sure, we *will* find out if ya do!" he threatened, snatched his hat off the saddle horn, and put it on. "Justice...justice, will be served! No matter if ya're a filthy degenerate hidden behind generational wealth, or the more obvious breed of poor ungodly scum."

He protested further, then strode back to his office, glimpsing at Mac's wanted poster still hanging there — collecting dust on the board for so many years. "We never forget..." He leered, walking with a vast determination and confidence inside the door, ready to take matters into his own hands again.

II

THE MILKY WAY GALAXY SHINED DRAMATICALLY behind the sharply carved mountains of Rockies East; formed by billions of bright stars — each one born within the clouds of dust; the same fundamental elements scattered throughout most galaxies — flashing and flickering like so many beams of hope for the lost souls of the world, looking up at them for guidance.

Charlotte stared out at the twinkling and dazzling explosion of the night sky, so vibrant with details only revealed by their remote path through the wilderness; feeling Mac's arms still shielding her — even if they had already escaped the army of deputies. She felt his body shiver from the cold, yet he would not make a complaint. She glanced down at his arm; sutures sticking out like untuned guitar strings. Her heart sunk with worry again, finding herself unable to rest or celebrate their escape, knowing his arm would get infected again, and fever would feast at him whole.

The haunting exhaustion hovered over her; still trying to grasp everything that happened just a few hours before. She wondered how God put her in such a situation; what she did to deserve to be a wanted woman, for no reason — to be constantly hiding from the law and society, afraid to visit her favorite towns just to have a simple walk around the block. Finally, she wondered, *how in the world did she end up in the arms of a murderer, and why did they feel the safest yet.* She looked at his blood-stained hands gripping the reins softly; riding Finn as he would his own horse — hands gentle, loose rein, with the utmost care, and respect — not out of sympathy, rather for insisting upon himself to be perfectly skilled with anything he did, knowing his life depended on it. Finn moved freely, balanced underneath them — content with Mac's gentle cues.

"Mac…where are we going?" Charlotte sighed from enervation, cuddling up to his chest unapologetically.

"Ain't sure." he hummed contentedly, feeling her warm body against his, sending shivers down his legs — benumbing feet and sense. "There's a ranch or somethin' where the lad offered us to stay…" he mumbled, blowing her hair out of his face so he could see better.

"Lad? What lad?" she asked him, a little confused, collecting her hair.

"The bounty hunter…" he grumbled, agitated.

"…Levi?" she asked, somehow too exhausted for anything to register.

"Sure." he grunted, then spotted smoke billowing from the horizon, leading to a fire from what appeared to be a two-story house at Ravenheart Pond.

"Did he…did he get out of there alive?" she asked, and he sighed heavily.

"Hm." He nodded, bumping subtly into her head and she released a pent-up breath of relief for she had been too afraid to ask. "How's yer head…" he then asked and she brushed a finger against it.

"It hurts…" She snorted absently. "I've never had a gun hit against it; perhaps I will be less of an eejit now…" She smirked, feeling a heavier breath escape from him, as though he suppressed a chuckle.

"Hm. Perhaps." he said, casting a lopsided smirk.

She smiled gently, and rested her head against his chest.

"Mac?"

"Hm?"

"Thank you…again." she said.

He swallowed hard, recalling the agony in her voice that rattled every bone in his body. His arm pressed tighter against her.

I I I

WILL GURGLED, GROANED, AGHAST AS HE GLANCED DOWN at his shoulder, noticing a knife handle sticking out of it. He grabbed it tentatively, pulled it out swiftly, vision blurred and legs turned shaky, numb. Stumbling over himself, he balanced his body against the wall, gasping for a lungful of air, for his lungs felt collapsed. His hand slid against a frame, and eyes set upon it, then reality dawned on him; he was in a cabin, a now familiar cabin. There was a slippery sensation atop his skin; a scent reminiscent of iron; fingers rubbed against each other, fresh slimy blood tingled on his fingertips.

He glanced before him, and an overwhelming urge to regurgitate sent a shiver down his spine; he lost his balance again, upon recognizing his beloved wife, Elizabeth — lifeless on the ground, with an arrow pierced right through her chest. Stepping backwards, he tumbled over his feet in utter shock, gripping at everything he could find to support himself — trying not to pass out from the harsh realization that hit him like jumping into icy water.

"No…it, it can't be…I did not do that, Lord. Surely, I didn't." he mumbled to himself, taking a cowardly glimpse at her again. Heart raced rapidly, as if it were to yank itself out of his tightly contracted throat.

"Eli…Elizabeth?" he whispered, praying for an answer to come out of her cold, blue lips.

He stared. In silence. In uncertainty.

He regained the courage to go closer to her, in slyness he neared her, kneeling down before her snow-white face — her freckles, disappeared in the vast paleness. Her eyes, still sparkling in fear and agony, looking right back at him — expression one of shock and confusion; one that would haunt him for the rest of eternity.

His eyes pooled with tears, crying over her, gently tucking a still vibrant ginger curl behind her ear, escaped from her bun as she wrestled him frantically in hopes to survive. He cried, for he never expected to ever harm a man; let alone murder his helpless wife. He cried, holding her limp hand in his, stained with her own blood. It coiled, slithered and traipsed around his fingers, tucking slow truths within his pores.

I V

"AH!! WONDERFUL! WELCOME, WELCOME!" JB GUFFAWED when he finally spotted the exhausted figures of Charlotte and Mac arrive at the ranch.

"JB!" She waved at him, barely with any energy. "Thank you so much for having us here…" she said, in a leaden sigh, eyes starting to shut, ready to fall asleep atop Finn's neck.

"But of course!" He smiled widely, then the smile slipped. "Well, actually it ain't my place, but Levi's cousin!" He rubbed his neck, observing them halt right beside a shack. "They're right inside, waiting to meet y'all!" He chuckled excitedly — also somewhat guiltily, as they didn't know he snitched on them, and that he was to blame for anything that could have happened. "Oh! And the legend himself!" He cheered as Mac was dismounting Finn, giving JB a stern look of disapproval, as if he knew. "Well...maybe not." He shrugged, rather frightened by his sharp gaze. "Where's Levi at?" he then asked, not spotting another horse anywhere near them.

"Ain't here yet." Mac stated abruptly, tethering Finn to a post.

"He's alright, though, right?"

"Bet he is." Mac huffed, for he didn't really care to put much thought into it.

"I mean, he found ya right?"

"Hm."

"Before any deputies, right?"

Mac snorted snidely, leaving him with the question on his lips.

"JB..." Charlotte approached him. "The deputies found us first...but everything is alright now...at least, for now." she said, swallowing down the cruel realization.

"I...I am so very sorry, Miss Charlotte..."

"Don't be. It is not your fault in any way..." She smiled into his eyes and he flickered his eyelashes nervously. "And as far as Levi...Mac told me he saw him leave...so, don't worry, JB. I expect him to be here any minute." she said, and JB sighed heavily.

"Well...let's go inside, shall we? There's a fresh stew brewing!" he said, lifting his own spirits up. "And don't worry! Not the kind I had the, uhm... natural explosions from." He cackled, reminiscing. "Good Lord! That was quite a relief, after all! Let me tell ya! I ain't never cookin' with a rotten deer leg no more! Even Jordon couldn't handle those fumes! I'm surprised they didn't knock the poor bastard out!" he rambled, as he led them to the house.

"Jordon?" Mac asked him suspiciously.

JB halted into place, blinking tightly in guilt. "...should *not* have said that..." he muttered beneath his breath, embarrassed, not knowing how to explain to them everything that happened and was said.

"What yer talkin' 'bout, ol' man?" he snarled, forcing his strong build between him and the door.

"I...I can explain!" he squeaked, jolted beneath Mac's being. "It was, well, it's all over now! So, it don't really matter, right?" JB stuttered, glanced at

Charlotte, who was shocked to see Mac switch like this, even after everything they just went through, to have the vigor within him to threaten another man.

"It matters to me…" he growled, drilling his blues into his eyes. "It matters, to all of us! Do ye realize we was about dead back there?!" he scowled, frustrated, brushing his hand over his knife.

"Mac, please! Stop!" Charlotte fussed, and yet his eyes sucked in JB's trembling reflection, not willing to let go.

"Well…I was almost dead myself, let me tell ya!" He raised a finger, heavenwards. "Actually, worse!" he explained, thinking of the threats they made regarding his private parts.

"Let JB go, Kinnon." Levi's raspy voice emerged behind them, as he trudged confidently towards them.

"Levi!!" Charlotte gasped, delighted to see him alive.

"Ma'am." he greeted her with a wink, flicking his hat politely, yet eyes cut at Mac.

"Your ol' man spoke." Mac growled, walking furiously towards Levi.

"So? You think he had a choice?"

Menacing eyes locked in shadow.

"Just didn't realize he would put the lass in danger." he said, glancing swiftly over at Charlotte.

"No no, Mr. Kinnon! This ain't true! Miss Charlotte, please forgive me." JB interrupted, frustrated by the accusations.

"Mac, please stop!" she fussed again, advancing to them. "He didn't have a choice!" she said and JB bobbed his head in compliance, sobbing as he did. "JB, don't worry; I understand and I'm sorry for what you went through because of us." She sighed, eyes shutting from weariness. "Can we just…rest… please." she soughed and Mac looked at her, conflicted.

"You better be thankful you'll be able to sleep somewhere safe tonight, boy." Levi grumbled as he hitched up his horse, untying Roy from the saddle horn as well. "'Cause as far as I know, there ain't no state you're not wanted in." he said sternly, snatched his hat off to wipe the dried up sweat from his brow, and faced him again. "So, my family is waiting for you I'm sure, let's not disappoint them." he added, and stretched his back that was awfully stiff from the long ride.

The ranch door snarled open with a slow creak. A beautiful woman with straight black hair, deep brown eyes, cloaked in an olive blouse, black skirt, moccasin shoes, appeared from within, holding a little boy in her arms who gaped in awe at them all.

V

HE PICKED UP HER DEAD BODY; IT WEIGHED twice as heavy as he remembered when he lifted her up at their wedding, right after they lovingly kissed to tie their vows for eternity.

> *"In faith, in honesty, and in love, I take you, Elizabeth, to be my*
> *wedded wife, to share with you God's plan for our lives together*
> *united in Christ. And with God's help, to strengthen and guide*
> *me, I will be a strong spiritual leader for us in our life, for better*
> *or for worse, in sickness and in health, in joys and in sorrows,*
> *until death do us part."*

His tears cleansed two paths from the blood staining his gaunt face; reliving the moment they first met under that immense oak tree outside of Bisonhorn. She was reading a book as she laid there, elegantly on a blanket, stirring his curiosity, for it was unique to see a woman of elite society such as herself wander off on her own. He approached her tentatively, and kindly introduced himself — asking if she were lost, offering his help to return her safely home. They both giggled innocently, instantly felt a connection between themselves as they sat down together discussing the book she held in her gentle hands.

She was the only one who had ever read all the books he wrote; the only one who believed in him, besides his mother. She encouraged him to write, yet he always had to prioritize his father's business which depressed him in a way. *They wouldn't be able to afford all the things they had otherwise,* he always thought. In the end she was the one, the only one, who supported him; who got to know him, all his quirks over the years — from the slightest twitch of his mustache when he got worried, to the sneaky gleeful smirks he gave when he hid a nice surprise away from her. The handwritten notes he so lovingly placed on his side of the bed when he had to leave early for work, excited for her to wake up and read them.

Yet, he knew her, too…

The way she would always brush her hair steadily, starting from her left side, as she checked herself in the mirror — making sure everything was perfect and symmetrical. The way she put her make-up on, patiently and so quietly, longing to always look impressive for him. The way she brewed his coffee at the fire as she sipped on her tea, waiting for him to wake up with no disturbance on days he could rest. The way she sang around the campfire every evening, as he drank his glass of whiskey, admiring her soft voice. The way he could sense her heart break, every time he left — how her lips trembled sadly, eyes, scarlet from the endless wailing she did the night before. *He knew her all too well*, he thought, noticing his ring still loyally attached around her finger.

V I

"THIS IS AMARA, AND HER SON JONATHAN." LEVI PROUDLY introduced them to Charlotte, as if it was a significant step into their *friendly* relationship. "She's my cousin, and has lived here for some time; quite an independent woman, she doesn't need my help too often I should say." He winked at Amara and Amara snorted snidely. "Amara, this is Charlotte, a good friend of mine, and… and…" He paused, somehow not wishing to mutter Mac's name, knowing he was a wanted man, risking his family's life by bringing him here — let alone how it annoyed him to the core, since it seemed Charlotte loved to pronounce it as often as she could.

"Mac Kinnon, correct?" She smiled gently, her monolid brown eyes locking his. Mac looked at her, surprised, not expecting to hear his name in a pleasant tone from a stranger who apparently already knew of him.

"JB must have informed you, then." Levi hummed, glanced over at JB, who was stirring the stew excitedly, dressed in fresh clothing — a extremely puffy Norwegian sweater, hand-sewn by Amara.

"He did." She rolled her eyes. "He said you was quite a legend, however. It's nice to have you here!" Amara greeted him, grabbed his cold, rough-feeling hand to shake without warning.

Mac stared at her, not able to make a sound. This kind of treatment was unusual to him; nobody ever invited him into a warm house — for he always had to sneak inside one, and usually, kill the homeowner while he was at it.

"Ah, he did?" Levi teased him. "He can shoot, I give him that." He snorted, then strode into the house, ready to get a bowl full of stew.

"And I've heard a lot about you, Charlotte!" She slipped her arm around her shoulder, guiding her to the cozy fire in the house, unusually friendly; *nothing like the powdered faces back in Mon Louis*, she thought, heart throbbed in warmth.

"Well, it's so wonderful and kind of you to let us stay with you and your family." she said, smiling in exhaustion. "I promise it won't be for long, and we won't cause any trouble." she said, and sat down before the fire, instantly feeling her limbs swelter, comfortably melt.

"Oh dear, I have a young boy; believe me, I know trouble!" She chuckled, then looked for Jonathan, who was still quietly staring at Mac outside. Her brows snapped together in bewilderment. "Won't you come in, sir?" she asked Mac, who was awkwardly looking back at the boy, not daring to stride through the house, as though there was a barrier within his mind.

"Sure." He swallowed hard, walked around Jonathan, who was blocking the entrance with his small frame, tumbling over his feet as the light-headedness hit him again.

"Mac?" Charlotte pulled his gaze to her. "Everything alright?" she asked him, concerned, noticing his unwell expression.

"Sure…" he muttered, yet he knew that feeling all too well — his fever had returned, spiking again as the rush of adrenaline had succumbed to prevailing sickness.

"I know your sutures will need some fixing…" she stated, as Amara was handing them bowls of stew.

"Sutures?" she asked, as though her motherly instinct kicked in the very moment she heard that. She was a practiced nurse down in Bisonhorn, after all, before she moved across the country.

"Yes, he had a pretty bad injury…"

"Nah! It's fine!" Mac interjected with a grunt, hiding his arm behind his back — not wishing to be the subject of discussion.

"Don't be so stubborn, Mac!" Charlotte fussed. "Like I was saying, he has a pretty big and deep cut in his arm, I tried to stitch it together, but…well, it didn't last that long." She sighed as she glanced over at Amara, whose eyes were studying Mac — who was pouting, already annoyed.

"Let me see, mister." Amara reached for his hidden arm.

"Nah…" he nagged.

"Please, sir…I'm certain a legendary gunslinger such as yourself can't be all that shy." she said, and Levi snorted his stew out of his nose. Mac huffed, and agitatedly bared his arm to her, exposing his torn-open cut, oozing pus again from the ragged opening of the wound.

"Dear Lord!" She gasped and Charlotte's heart skipped a beat, Levi's brow cocked and JB's feet wiggled, besotted by the stew's taste. "We need to debride this and stitch it back up — right now!" Amara ran swiftly to her bedroom, to grab her utensils. Mac looked at Charlotte in pure disapproval, curling his lip to the side, clearly agitated.

"Don't cut your eyes at me! Stop being so stubborn." Charlotte argued, then took a spoonful of stew, making Mac pout further in his usual silence.

Amara rushed back to him, reaching to feel for his forehead, yet Mac flinched, jerked away. "Please, sir…" she said and he glanced at Charlotte, oddly longing to find reassurance. She nodded to him with a gentle smile, and he turned back to her, clenching jaw, as she felt of his swelteringly hot forehead. "Dear Lord, you're burning, mister…" She wiped the sweat off his face with a wet cloth, as he side-eyed her worried expression.

"Charlotte, would you please pass me the tourniquet?" Amara ordered her swiftly, and Charlotte's eyes searched for the word she didn't even know.

"The…the what?" she embarrassedly asked her.

"The leather tourniquet…" her voice hurried, pointed to the well-used strap with her sharp jaw. "Here! Give me your arm." Amara ordered Mac, and he continued to clench his jaw, balling a fist, fighting with his own self not to defend himself from her touch. She wrapped and tightened the tourniquet around the swell of his bicep, and grabbed a scalpel.

"What is that for…?" Charlotte asked worriedly.

"Removing excess blood…for his infection." she muttered sternly, as she precisely finessed the scalpel against his vein.

Despite the memories that arose to assail him, the relentless pain, and the horrifying view — Mac managed to remain calm, stealing a swift glimpse from Charlotte, who had covered her eyes — feeling light-headed from the sounds of his thick blood gushing out.

"Charlotte, the scissors and forceps." she ordered again, as Mac stared ominously at his blood flowing down like a river. Amara expertly trimmed back the already necrotic tissue, allowing a clear wound bed to form. "Keep on breathing for me, mister. You're doing great." she encouraged him, and he cracked a cryptic smirk on his face — *if she only knew*, he thought.

"Iodine, the dark liquid in the corner." she asked as Charlotte was already preparing for the next step. "This will keep the infection from returning; soak the needle and thread in the solution while I prepare the wound."

Levi watched them closely from the wobbly table he was seated at beside JB, completely ignoring JB's rambling — yet it didn't bother him, as he was pretty good at talking to himself. He stared at Amara being so close to Mac, chewing restlessly at the tobacco in the side of his mouth.

"Take a deep breath now, we are almost done…" She smiled at him, pushed the needle through his flesh carefully to not hurt him. Mac did as instructed, while his eyes noticed the boy staring at him again, holding a little otter pelt against his tiny chest. "He is infatuated with you." Amara giggled, as she looked back down at her machine-like stitchwork already bringing the freshly trimmed walls of his cut neatly together.

"Hm?" Mac hummed, confused.

"Jonathan." she whispered softly. "My boy…he never stares at strangers for so long; he must really like you." She smiled, enjoying the moment as she maintained focus on her work.

"Did I hurt you?" she worriedly asked, as she felt his hand flinch.

"No. Yer fine." he grunted, locking eyes, both forgetting the needle within his skin for a fleeting moment.

Charlotte couldn't help but listen to their conversation; feeling a sudden knot form in her throat when she saw how close they both were, pausing to look at each other — she had never seen another woman in such close proximity to Mac, and oddly, it worried her. She shook her head to clear her irrational thoughts, reminding herself she was kind to work so hard in healing his wound, let alone allowing them to stay here, and besides, Mac had already rejected her.

VII

WILL CARRIED ELIZABETH THROUGH THE THICK WOODS, following a little stream of water along the path. Forcing his legs over the same mossy hills he traced circles around himself, pulling them over logs, hiking up, hiking down. Bewildered. Panicked and frightened, for he knew the Millers would soon return, only to find a bloody mess in their cabin, he kept on pushing beyond his capabilities, beyond the strength of a mortal man such as himself. His legs benumbed, they wilted like a weak branch, bending, giving up on him little by little, for the dead weight felt heavier by the minute, her body stiffened in the cruel cold air.

The sunrise shone in his eyes in the hazy distance; a faint reflection on clear turquoise waters, flickering at him through the dark lattice of branch. A river smoothly flowed north through the endless wooded landscape of Red Giants, reaching the deserted lake of Flat Bow; ears followed the echo of pebbles tossing about with the force of stream, and eyes nailed to the sun. The dense forest surrounded a derelict shack, fronting him through a dark glen of woods, luring him in with a line, bound to coil around a secret. Eyes set upon it, he rushed to it, mind wilting in shame with the thoughts it allowed.

"Ah, my beloved Elizabeth…what are we doing, darling?" he wailed nervously, expecting still to hear her gentle voice. He placed her softly on the grassy ground before the still water, hand gripping the arrow tightly. Pulling it out of her chest, he broke off the shaft, now stuck inside her chest indefinitely — to always remind him of his act of savagery. "My darling…"

He sobbed uncontrollably, caressing the cheek of her cold face with trembling fingers. "Please forgive me…they…they misled me. They…made me, my love…" he stuttered, failing to speak the words he so eagerly tried to yank out of his chest — words that buffeted his heart; words that would prove his atrocity — words that made him owe an explanation to her.

He kissed her on her lips; deep and long, the first time for them to never kiss him back. Tears dropped on her dry eyelids, gently dripping down her cheeks, slowly tinting blue. Arms clutching her back, he pulled her up one last time, for her to hopefully feel his warm embrace; squeezing her tight, as her limp neck dropped her head back loosely — catching it with his shaking hand, burying it within his shoulder.

"You have my heart, Elizabeth, forever and always…my heart will belong to you." he cried, breathing her in, merging his body with hers, feeling her rib-cage against his, yet only one heart thudded in the chambers of their ribs. He laid her slowly into the water, pushed her body deeper into the lake — vanishing, after stealing one last glimpse forever to remember, forever to haunt him.

CHAPTER 46

Temptation

I

POKE-POKE! MAC TWITCHED HIS NOSE from an irritating sensation he felt while still deeply asleep in the guest room.

POKE-POKE!

Squinting through his eyelids, he saw a silhouette hovering before him, steadily poking his hero-shaped nose. He swiftly grabbed for his knife, pulled it out before him, awakening with instant alertness, finding the boy staring at him with big flared eyes, glancing at the gleaming blade. Mac, stunned, snapped his brows in confusion, trying to adjust his eyes in the bright sunlight.

"Wooow! That's a big knife!" The boy gasped, then tittered with immense happiness to finally inspect one of Mac's legendary weapons.

"Feck…" Mac exhaled a deep breath of relief and annoyance, sliding the knife back into its scabbard.

"Feck?" Jonathan mumbled with a pout, disappointed to not fiddle with the knife. Mac cut his eyes at him, figuring he probably shouldn't learn that word, figuring he didn't care if he did.

"What does this mean?" he asked him and Mac blinked.

"Gah…" Hand slammed against his face, scrunching it up in annoyance.

"I will ask mommy…" He shrugged and Mac's eyes rolled.

"No. Don't." he said, conflicted.

"Why not?" His eyes got big, now in great intrigue.

"'Cause."

"Is it a secret? Like…*a gunslinger's secret?*" he whispered intensely, and Mac set his eyes on him through his fingers.

"Sure…" he said and the boy chuckled, slamming a tiny hand atop his mouth as to not be heard.

"Feck!" the boy repeated and Mac's face furrowed, briefly contemplating where he found himself again; almost feeling as though he was baby-sitting a child.

"Gah…" he grumbled with the thought.

"You are a gunslinger, sir? Right? You are??" he then asked with immense pressure. Mac tilted his head to face him in utter earnestness.

"No." he said. "I'm a child eater." he said and Jonathan's eyes flared, aghast.

"Wooooow!" He gasped, unbothered. "Mister, I am not a child! So, we will be fine." he said in earnest, smiling into his eyes, and Mac blinked.

"Hm."

"What's your name?" the boy asked him excitedly, beaming to finally be talking to him.

"Nahhh…" he grunted, not willing to have any conversation with anyone, then he side-eyed him — eyes that glimmered in blithe. "…Mac."

"I'm Jonathan! I'm only six, nearly nine!" he smiled at him widely, glancing down at his guns hiding in the holsters.

"But you must be older! *Very* old!" he said.

"Sure." he murmured, pulled his arm over his head, laid back down again — ready to rest some more.

"And you stink, mister!" He chuckled.

"It's the children's fumes leavin' me body…" he said, and Jonathan laughed hysterically.

"You talk funny, mister." he said, noticing the Irish accent.

"Better we don't talk at all, then…" he offered and Jonathan pouted, then stood there, glanced around him, as ideas raced in his mind.

"This is Olaf!" He abruptly pressed his otter pelt to Mac's chest, expecting him to receive his gift.

"Hm." Mac frowned, snapped his eye open, startled by the sudden fur laying atop him. He clasped it, held it before his face, inspecting it.

"This…*was*…Olaf." Mac mumbled, cutting his eyes at him.

"It's yours now!" The boy smiled widely, his heart jolting with happiness, unable to contain himself. He clutched the pelt and wiggled it before him.

"I…uhm…sure." He grabbed the pelt from his tiny little hands and stared at the wall behind him, avoiding any eye contact, as if his innocence could judge him.

"Jonathan! Jonathan!" Amara called for him, rushing up the stairs. "What did I tell you?!" She stormed through the wide open door, after following the little trail of bread crumbs leading to Mac's room. "I'm so sorry, sir. He… he is a pretty respectful child, in general." she apologized, giving Jonathan a warning look only a mother could give.

"Hm. It's fine." he said, just now noticing her face's sharp features in the brighter morning light, realizing he hadn't seen or spoken in a civil manner to another woman since meeting Charlotte.

"Feck, mommy! Feck!" Jonathan giggled and Amara's eyes flared, as Mac's mouth crinkled to the side.

"Jonathan! Hush!" she fussed and he pouted. "Don't say this word here, you hear me??"

"But…it's a gunslinger's secret, mommy…and I know it now!" he said, and her eyes cut at Mac. He cocked a brow.

"I see…well, you aren't no gunslinger, so you better stop saying this word." she hissed and his pout deepened.

"But what if I want to become one? Like Uncle Levi!"

"Uncle Levi is…well…anyway! Enough now. JB is waiting on you at the breakfast table — no eating away from the table, Jonny!" she asserted, pushing him gently outside the room. "Whew! These kids!" She exhaled, stressed, and Mac blinked in silence.

"Oh! Olaf!" She gasped, as she saw the otter pelt in Mac's lap.

"Hm? Oh. Yeah. Wee lad gave it to me…" he said, handing it back to her.

"Oh…that's interesting." she said, clasping it. "He must reaaally like you, then." Her gaze turned dull, as though sorrow consumed it. "His…his daddy gave this to him for his birthday; sadly, we lost him too soon." she said, eyes wandering off silently.

"Hm. Bad business." He coughed awkwardly, speaking out the only words he knew were appropriate to use.

"It happens…a lot happens, when you raise a boy around Red Giants…"

she said, handing him the pelt back. "We should've left this criminal-infested place a long time ago." she muttered, then halted. "I mean…*bad* criminals."

"Hm." He snorted. "Ain't no such thing as good criminals. Not gonna lie to ye, woman; I ain't the good kind." he said caustically and yet in earnest, not wanting to pretend innocence.

"Well, I believe children can recognize the good in people before we do. We are too influenced by the cruel world around us, too worn down, and so tired we can barely notice the good or the evil anymore. I choose to trust my son's intuition, and I believe you have a lot of good to offer." She smiled softly to him, noticing his deep blue eyes, illuminated by the piercing rays of sun emanating from the window.

"Hm." He nodded in silence, squeezing the pelt.

"Did the fever settle? Hopefully, the treatment will take care of it…" she inquired, yearning to feel of his forehead.

"Sure."

"Good…there's fresh breakfast on the table, if you want to come and join us. We would be glad to have your company."

II

"GOOD LORD! WHAT HAPPENED IN HERE?! DARLING!!" Mr. Miller shouted for his wife to enter the cabin, inspecting the blood-stained walls and wooden boards of the floor. Thin strands of ginger hair scattered around the ground, Elizabeth's coat still present, yet this time soaked in a pool of blood.

"My goodness! Mrs. Elizabeth?!" Mrs. Miller yelled with her frail voice, letting out a raspy cough, followed by another, and another. She spat out droplets of blood, covering her mouth in shame.

"Sit down, my love. You need to rest." Mr. Miller guided her to a chair in another room, not wishing for her to witness this gory mess any longer.

Searching through all the rooms, expecting to find a dead body somewhere hidden, scrunched up between cabinets, hanged, or wickedly exposed, he found nothing. Everything was untouched, tidy and clean, just like they left it. He instantly thought of Will, convinced something terrible must have happened between them. Blaming himself for letting him close to Elizabeth; for believing all the honeyed words he always knew how to use in manipulating those around him, at least that's what his son always said.

"Darling, I'm heading to Bisonhorn for the sheriff's office! Lock the doors, and keep the shotgun by your side. You'll be okay, and I'll be right back." he ordered her, wrapped his coat around himself, and rushed out to his horse.

III

Sheriff Dorman,

The Sheriff's Department of Birdsboro regrets to inform you of the murder of Sheriff Jordon in a skirmish at Ring Lagoon, on November 4th, 1899 at roughly two o'clock in the morning.

He was killed by Mac Kinnon; his death confirmed by the deputies who buried him. The degenerate was seen with bounty hunter Levi Krog, and a woman — we suspect she was Charlotte.

They sadly escaped, suspected to be headed due west of Rockies East. We are sending our deputies, and working closely with both the police department of Mon Louis and the Pinkerton Agency.

Sheriff Tom has indicated he will send a letter to Marshal Tilghman, but noted too, that the marshal will not wish to cooperate with any law department on this matter.

We ask of you to alert the departments of Marysville and Bisonhorn. They need to troop the states closely, as they could be anywhere by now.

Chief Deputy John

DORMAN SAT IN HAUNTING SILENCE, STARING at the choppy handwriting, almost piercing his teeth through his lips from biting too hard.

He suddenly jumped out of the chair, tossed the paper across the office, slammed his fist against the wall, making the cells rattle beside it, startling the prisoners who were anxiously waiting to be hanged any day — soon, to end their misery and boredom.

He loosened his tie to breathe better, panicking, wilting beneath a pressure, beneath a thudding pulse rushing his blood. Cursing Mac Kinnon for yet again being able to escape an army of men, and a much more experienced sheriff than himself; murdering him in cold blood. "Son of a bitch!!! Devil's son!!!" he yelled and threw the books off his desk, kicked the chair down before him, pulled on his hair and yelled some more.

"Sh…Sheriff Dorman?" Mr. Miller knocked on the door politely, shocked to hear the sheriff in such distress.

I V

"WHAT ARE YOU THINKING, AMARA? RECKON HE WILL cause any trouble around here?" Levi whispered to her, as Mac stepped outside the house.

"No." She smiled. "He seems a kind soul. Hurt, but kind. The boy really is bonding with him." she muttered to him as she glanced over at Jonathan, quietly munching on some bread and cheese contentedly, repeating the secret forbidden word in his mind with sheer amusement.

"Keep the boy away from him. He is not to be trusted." he warned her, side-eyeing Charlotte, who was listening to JB's long-winded speech regarding the cure he invented for infected toenails, all while she was attempting to enjoy a slice of cheese.

"I'm not worried about him, Levi. The boy needs a father figure." She sighed hopefully.

"Wh-what is that supposed to mean, now?" His eyes bulged out in shock.

"No! Not what you're thinking, of course…" She huffed. "But at least grant him that; last night all he talked about was this man, and how brave he seemed to be — it really helped him fall asleep — you know how he still has those nightmares…" she mumbled, slicing the block butter with a dull knife.

"Yeah, brave enough to murder innocent folk!" he growled, frustrated with her blindness. "Remember Amara, he isn't that much different than the Feasters…" he reminded her, for her husband was found murdered in Petit Jean, and yet there was no trace to confirm it was actually them. Amara shook her head, pouted, and tore her gaze away.

"That's…quite interesting, JB!" Charlotte said, acting impressed to know his secret remedy for toe fungus.

"You bet it is! Oh! I need to tell ya 'bout that time I fought in the army! Lordy, oh Lordy! I had the meanest, biggest ingrown toenail ya ever laid eyes on! That son of a gun hurt like the dickens! I could not get it to stop, no matter how hard I slammed it, or twisted the rotten bastard!" he said, and Charlotte suppressed a gag.

"JB…I apologize, but I think…I have to check on Finn." she said. "He was kinda stiff last night, when we returned…" She stood up, not able to stand the repulsion any longer, nor smell the aroma of the cheese either.

"Oh. Okay. Well…I'll tell ya later then!" He cackled. "Remind me! It's a good one!" he said, then sighed, disappointed, as nobody ever seemed to want to listen to the end of his stories.

"Miss, thank you so much for the lovely breakfast. It was delicious." Charlotte greeted Amara, hand gracefully clutching her chest as she did, then walked towards the door before JB would reel her back into his rambling.

"She is a beauty, isn't she Levi?" Amara asked, catching his attention instantly.

"Oh…" He cleared his throat. "Well, I guess." he mumbled, trying to seem disinterested, side-eyeing Charlotte's statuesque body before she strode out.

"Oh come on, Levi! You can't hide things from me. I'm a mother; I can read you boys immediately." She chuckled, as she elbowed him teasingly.

"Sure, she is! But nothing more." he answered earnestly, bowed his head, and swirled his coffee in the cup in thought.

"I can talk to her if you want…" Another elbow in his rib. "I'm sure she would appreciate to speak to another woman for once, after being stuck with you smelly lot!" She snorted, and he did too.

"Haha. Noooo, Amara. She is…promised, or somethin' like that." he said, nervously wetting his lips.

"To who? Mac?" she curiously asked him.

"Agh, not really. I mean, hell, I don't know! This woman confuses me too much. Why are you asking?" He cut his eyes at her, noticing her sneaky smile.

"Nothing…I just thought you would make a wonderful pair." She grinned and shoved the last bite of bread in her mouth.

"Well, you're the only one who thinks so. I gave up on that a long time ago." He stated, standing up to check on what they were doing outside, briefly patting Jonathan's round head as he walked past him.

V

"OH, FINN!" SHE GASPED, HORRIFIED. "What happened to you, sweet boy?" she asked, concerned, palpating his hoof that was incredibly sore to the touch. Finn snorted, agitated, not appreciating the feeling of her hand pressing against his sole, pulling his hoof away repeatedly, not letting Charlotte examine it. Mac watched from a distance, brushing Roy along his jet-black topline, thinking she was a wonderful horsewoman, and yet way too soft when it came to schooling Finn.

"Abscess?" Levi came behind her, startling her with his sudden question.

"I'm worried so." she grunted, trying to keep him balanced, hoof shoved between her thighs. Finn would hold it just enough for her to get a good grip of it, then rear upon a bunny hop and toss her away from him.

"May I?" he asked politely, knowing he was not allowed to touch her pony without her permission.

"You know?" she asked him suspiciously, cinched brow and cocked hip, and he snorted.

"I own five horses, been riding since I learned how to walk, worked at ranches all my teenage years — I'm pretty sure I may have an idea, cowgirl." He teased her with a wink, towering over her again.

"Gah." She huffed, patting Finn's hind.

"I'm sorry, it's just…everything." she said, a breath of frustration escaping her. "I guess I'm just tense from all that happened yesterday." she explained, and moved over for him to pick up Finn's leg.

"Of course, I understand. I'm quite rattled myself." he mumbled, grabbed Finn's leg, pinched his chestnut, picked it up. Finn snorted in protest, and reared again. Levi repeated it, jamming his hoof between his legs, cupping it, poking around with his finger, while Finn continued to snort in disagreement.

"Yup. Seems to be an abscess. Got to cut it open — let it drain, put some remedy on it, and let it heal. No healthy feet, no horse." he confirmed, placed the leg back down, then faced Charlotte, who seemed quite flustered this morning.

"Great…" She sighed shortly, took out her pocket knife, and handed it to him, noticing her wrists were rather swollen and sore.

As Levi was slicing up the abscess on Finn's sole, or rather attempting to do so, as he fought against him, her eyes drifted off to what appeared to be Amara, walking slowly towards Mac, holding Jonathan beside her. Her heart halted; it didn't thud irrationally yet, but it halted.

"Damnit!" Levi fussed, frustrated as the abscess exploded all over him with tarry black liquid. Charlotte glanced back at him, and couldn't help but burst into laughter.

"Haha!" She cackled. "That looks good on you, Levi!" She teased, noticing his frown.

"Ha-ha!" He mocked, tapping the knife against his palm. "You find this funny, ah?" He walked towards her with a big handful of the gross liquid, then smeared it on her arm.

"Ew!" She screeched. "Levi! How dare you!" She leered at him, then halted, and they both released a loud laughter.

"What did you say?" He cocked his head in earnest. "You want more of it?" He chased her around Finn with a big grin on his face, while Charlotte hid behind her steed, poking her head over its back to locate Levi — then running around again, screaming playfully when he got too close — forgetting, for a fleeting moment, all the heavy burdens she carried.

V I

"EXCUSE ME, SIR." DORMAN STARED AT HIM, BLANK. "There was…we received some devastating news regarding a colleague." he said, clearing his throat, composing himself again, brushing his hair back on his flustered head.

"Sheriff, I didn't mean to disturb, but…I need to report a missing person." Mr. Miller muttered tentatively, fiddling with his round fingers nervously.

"Get on with it." Dorman said, took out his notebook, ready to write down his complaints, only for them to be shoved inside a drawer, buried underneath a pile with further complaints.

"M…M…Mrs. Elizabeth Griffiths…she…"

Dorman froze, looked up, startled to hear that name, suddenly gifting him his full attention.

"She was in the middle of a divorce, and she ran away from her ranch just west of here, sir." he said sheepishly. "She, she came to us to stay for a few nights…up in Red Giants — and, now she's completely gone." he informed him, a worried expression furrowing his face.

"Anything suspicious she might have said or done prior to that?" Dorman asked, as he brushed his mustache with a trembling forefinger.

"No sir, just…her husband, William Griffiths." he exhaled a deep breath of guilt. Dorman stared with suspense, one brow raised in immense curiosity, one boot clapping against the floor impatiently.

"He…he asked to see her, sir. He said he needed to talk to her urgently… so, I didn't think much of it, and brought him to my cabin." He began, thinking how to continue. "…I don't know what happened after that, as I still had some errands in town. I returned and found the place flooded with blood, that I suspect, came from dear Elizabeth." He sighed, devastated.

"Very well." Dorman bobbed his head, wordless. "Thank you, mister. My deputies and I will head to Red Giants and investigate the scene; surely we will find some traces we can track through the forest." Dorman promised, beginning to pace the room as he lit up a new cigar that had been sitting for too long on his desk. "Surely this time, we'll find Mr. Griffiths." He puffed on it, in deep thought.

Suddenly a throaty and gurgling croak amplified around the sheriff's building, wind slammed against the windows repeatedly, rattling the glass. Mr. Miller and Sheriff Dorman walked hastily out the door to witness a dozen flocks of ravens all flying nervously above them, picking frantically on the ground before them, croaking loudly, echoing in the streets of Bisonhorn — a few, staring eerily at Dorman.

VII

"WE HOPE WE DON'T DISTURB YOU, SIR…" Amara approached him. "The boy really wanted to see your horse." she said, petting Roy's enormous hind.

"Hm." Mac cut his eyes at them. "Sure." he said shortly, and went on about his business — saddling up his mount with his worn down leather saddle.

"Mommy, mommy, can I ride it?!" Jonathan asked excitedly, holding on to Roy's hind leg.

"No, sweetheart. You can't." she said, pulling him away from the kicking zone. "One day you will have your own horse to ride, but right now you're still a small child." she said, and Jonathan pouted.

"I'm not a child, mommy! If I was, Mac would have eaten me!" he said and Amara blinked bleakly at him, as Mac cinched his saddle.

"What?" she asked him and Jonathan huffed.

"Moooommy…he is a child eater!" He said, appalled that she didn't know.

Amara snorted, and glanced over at Mac whose expression was unexpectedly cold, hauntingly neutral.

"I apologize for…my son's imagination." she said, and he cocked a brow.

"Hm." He nodded, figuring it was best not to get into it.

"You're not leaving yet, are you?" she then asked, concerned, noticing his sutures holding up well on his vascular arm.

"No." he said dryly, fastening the breast collar to his saddle.

"Goin' huntin'." he added.

"Hunting? With your arm like this? And the fever…" She gasped, horrified, and yet impressed by his resilience.

"Ain't got no fever no more." he said, shoving the rifle into its holster.

"Can't stay here doin' nothin' in return."

"Well…that's very kind of you…"

"Kindness has nothin' to do with it…" he said sternly and she blinked.

"However, I don't wish for you to feel like you have to provide for everyone right after surgery…" She chuckled and he swung the reins over Roy's head.

"Mr. Kinnon…" She clasped his shoulder and he halted, nailing a leer upon her hand. "May I join you?" she offered with an excited smile on her face.

"No." he grunted in annoyance, twisting his shoulder away.

"Why not? You don't think I can hunt?" She snorted snidely, folding her arms before her chest. "How do you think I've been surviving all them years out here? The boy can't hunt for himself, if *that's* what you're thinking." She hissed, offended, cutting a sharp glance at him.

"Listen woman, I…" he paused himself, as he caught a glance of Jonathan, pouting, upset to hear his mother emotional. "Gah…" He jerked his head away for a brief moment, lips folded agitated. "Sure."

Amara jumped up with excitement, thrilled to get a short break from her little boy, intrigued to be hunting with a legend. "I will be right back!" she said, clasping the boy's shoulders.

"Jonathan, let's go to JB; he has some amaaazing stories to tell you!" She grinned from ear to ear, and Mac cinched a brow in confusion.

"Nooo, mommy! I don't want!" Jonathan cried, now holding on to Mac's leg, making him flinch in great discomfort.

"Oh, yes you do!" She smiled earnestly, unhooked her son off of his leg and dragged him gently to the house.

VIII

THEY CHASED AROUND, WITH FINN STANDING in the middle, slightly irritated and envious of Charlotte's sole attention dedicated to the abscess slicing man. "Okay, okay! I give up! I can't breathe!" Levi chuckled, resting against Finn's hind, feeling his tightened abs ache from the laughter. "You're a swift one!" he said, and she snorted.

"Well, serves you right! Now you know not to chase after me like a fool…"

She cackled and he shook his head, somehow in earnests.

"You got that right, cowgirl…" he said and she bowed her head, dropping her gaze on her mucky clothes.

"Now I need a bath! Look at this mess!" she complained, yet still amused by their antics, for she had never laughed so hard in her life, nor ever played around with someone. Somehow she missed that feeling, for her inner child had been buried deep within her way too soon.

"You and me both!" he said, then blushed, realizing how awkward this could have sounded — although he didn't mind the thought of it — didn't mind at all. His eyes cut at her, resting at the swell of her hips, the fine curve climbing up her waist, climbing up to her…

Finn snorted and shifted his hind to his other side, making Levi lose his balance and trip over his leg. Charlotte rushed to grab him, clutching her hands on his arm, yet his heavy weight strained her wrists even more.

"Ouch!" she groaned, yet still held his arms firmly.

"You okay?" he asked her, noticing her face furrow with pain.

"Yes…just…I think I strained my wrists somehow, last night." she sighed, and glanced down at her hands.

"Let me take a look."

"You're no doctor, Levi." She teased, feeling too shy to show her hands.

"Well, that's mean…" He winked at her and she bowed her head, blushing. "I might be no doctor, but I *am* the closest thing to a doctor you can get right now." He joked, teasing her back.

"You're an annoying man, Mr. Levi!" she nagged playfully, and placed her petite hands in his. He clasped them tenderly.

"I get that a lot." He smirked, and went on to inspect her wrists. "There's definitely some swelling on those wrists, judging by how small your hands are." he said, cutting his greens to her and a chill crawled down her back.

"Right…*doctor.*" she said, somehow frozen into his gaze. He pulled his eyes away, averting them back to her hand.

"Did you fall on them?" he asked, and she nodded.

"Yes…"

"How did you fall? How did you land on them, I mean…"

"Just flat on my palms…"

"Mhm…"

"Ouch ouch ouch!" she yelled as he was twisting her hands in all directions.

"Sorry." He paused, lifted his gaze up to her, drawing in a breath. "Good news is, I don't think you broke anything." he said, and she blinked, anticipating what could be worse than that. "Bad news is, it looks damn painful, and don't know of what we can do about it really, except bandaging it with a cloth." He proudly reported to her, and she snorted snidely, as he went to grab a cotton bandage.

"Ah…lovely. That much, I figured already." She teased, watching his tank of a back march to his saddlebag.

"Yes, but my service isn't done yet, miss." he said, returning with a round box and a cloth in his grip. "You're very impatient."

"Of course, doctor…I apologize for my impatience. Please do proceed, with your expert care." she said, and he smirked, suddenly wishing they could pretend a little longer.

"This is a balm of herbal medicine…I've used it for swelling and strains more times than I can count. It works wonders." he said, tilting the box for her to peek at the balm.

"Wow…It smells wonderful." she said, taking a whiff of it.

"You made that?"

"No…Not this one. This is special…only for special occasions." he said, smiled into her eyes. Blushed. "I get it from a friend up in Red Giants…she is a phenomenal young woman, wise beyond her years." he said and she nodded, intrigued.

He applied the silky balm all around her wrists and hands, and gently rubbed it in. She halted, breath inhaled deeply, undeniably feeling an inappropriate tingle rush through her. Carefully now rolling the cloth around her wrists repeatedly, in a way it would hold them steady and safe, Charlotte stared at his manly fingers fiddle with the fabric, so gently yet so strong at the same time, carrying rings she had never seen before; dark with cryptic letters between beveled edges.

Levi locked eyes with her, noticing her sudden silence, noticing her gaze studying his rings. He blushed, heart beat faster. "What is on your mind, cowgirl…" he asked, his voice low and deep, pulling her gaze back up to him swiftly. She cleared her throat and issued a noise, a word.

"Rings…" she said. "I mean, I was…"

"My rings? What do you think about them?" he asked, still wrapping her wrists.

"Well…they look intriguing, to say the least." she said, scarring a lopsided smirk on his lips. "But, I don't really understand the meaning behind them, I guess."

"They're runes." he said. "Elder Futhark Runes…"

Her eyes flared in awe. "Runes…"

"Mhm. Remember, I'm Norse after all. Ignore the brown dirty hair…" He snorted and she smiled absently.

"So…what does it mean? This writing, or runes?" she asked, embarrassed by her ignorance.

"The word 'rune' means both letter and secret. Runes allow one to access, use, and change the world shaping forces they symbolize." he said and she blinked, aghast.

"Wow…sounds…important." she said, unable to think of a better word.

"It is, for runes do not reveal themselves to any but those who prove themselves worthy of such fearsome insights and abilities." he said and she frowned, perplexed.

"And what happens when they do reveal themselves?" she asked sheepishly.

"Well…in Norse lore, it is said that runes revealed themselves to the god, Odin, after his sacrifice to find their meaning. A part of him died, but another fertilized…then he learned chants that allowed him to heal emotional and bodily wounds, to bind his enemies, to free himself from constraints, to expose and banish practitioners of malevolent magic, to protect his friends in battle, to wake the dead, to win and keep a lover…" he said and she swallowed hard.

"Hm…" She nodded, speechless.

"Don't worry…they have not revealed themselves to me yet…perhaps I need to sacrifice myself first, however." He snorted and she flinched a smile.

"Well…thank you for explaining all this to me. Didn't realize my doctor carried such secrets around his fingers." she said and he chuckled.

"You're…you're ready to go, cowgirl with swollen wrists." he said, still feeling the softness of her hand through the cloth.

"Wonderful…how much do I owe you for the service, Dr. Levi?" She tittered sarcastically, pulling her hands back, thankful.

"Fancy a walk tonight in the forest?" He couldn't help himself but ask her out one last time, feeling as though they had rekindled what was lost.

Charlotte felt a weight sit on her shoulders; trampling her down with guilt. Mac's rejection the other day flashed before her, stomach twisted. Will and their relationship floated somewhere in the uncertain, the unknown, not imagining when they would ever meet again, nor if she would be able to check her mail, *for he surely would have written something back by now*, she thought absently. *Unless he was sleeping next to his beloved wife, "Elizabeth".*

"I'm sorry…" he muttered beneath his breath.

"I…let me think on it, Levi." she said cowardly, hoping to not upset him, and his eyes flared in hope.

"Take…take your time. I'll be out chopping some firewood."

CHAPTER 47

The Cougar

I

"SO, JONATHAN! YOUR MA WENT HUNTIN' with the legend Kinnon, is that right?" JB asked him, still shocked to hear about this.

"Yes. And they wouldn't take me with them! I know how to hunt, JB!" He climbed down the chair hastily, hurried to his bedroom, bare feet clapping against the wooden boards — bringing back proudly a flimsy bow made of wooden sticks tied together, and tiny sharpened branches to use as arrows.

"Look, JB!" He pressed his bow to his chest, which was feeling cozy and fluffy from the sweater.

"Oh, yes. Very nice, dear boy! Did uncle Levi show you how to do this?" he inquired sweetly, pretending to be impressed.

"No! Daddy did." he said excitedly, staring intently at the bow with an innocent gaze.

"He was a good hunter, wasn't he, Jonny?" JB muttered, as his eyes misted.

"Yes!" he exclaimed, mouth cracked wide open to speak further. "He said once he tried to take down a giiiiiaaaant bear, but it was too strong, and big!" he boasted, clearly able to talk about his father again without tearing up.

"Oh, Lordy! Let me tell you about that time in Red Giants! Oh Lordy, oh Lordy, Jonny boy!" He wheezed with excitement. "See, I'm quite a fast son of a…a good hunter, myself!" JB bragged, preparing to exaggerate a story.

"A son of a hunter?" the boy questioned him in confusion.

"Aaaaah…no. That's not what I meant, but anyway! Like I was saying, there was this enormous bison! Bigger than this house!" He stretched his arms widely as to measure its size. "Ran right towards me and my dear Margaret, so I formed a tight fist and punched him right in its angry face!"

"Wow! Feck!" he said and JB blinked at him, all the while Jonathan appeared to have naturally understood the correct usage of the word. "And what happened next, JB?!" Jonathan's crystal blue eyes got real big, enjoying the story to the fullest, and JB poked a finger in his ear, scratched it, twisted it real good, thinking he had misheard. Jonathan bounced up and down, anticipating to hear the rest of the story.

"Then! Then my boy, we had a good ol' bison stew! HaHA!" JB chuckled, as he couldn't figure out how to end his made-up story to make any sense and Jonathan pouted, thinking there was more to it.

"Feeeck…" he said upon a sigh and JB's eyes bulged further out. Now he rubbed them instead, as if that would clear his hearing. "Mac is a good hunter, right JB?" the boy asked him, imagining all the monsters Mac could take down with a swift hit.

"Well, he sure is good with luring in a cougar right now!" JB winked at him as he giggled, tittered, wheezed, then he paused and looked at him. "Eh… perhaps, I shouldn't have said that…" he said, as he saw the boy stare with great confusion.

I I

DISMOUNTING AT A DARK DITCH, MAC PULLED OUT HIS RIFLE and glanced over at Amara who grabbed a bow instead. He cocked a brow, somehow intrigued by it, and went on to study the trail of deer scat and prints. They sneaked quietly through the trees; spotting the herd of deer grazing under bright sun rays. Mac raised his gun, ready to aim at the neck of a magnificent buck, when Amara grabbed the barrel and lowered it to the ground. He looked at her, confused and slightly agitated, since he would have already shot it dead if she didn't interfere.

"Shh…" She winked at him, raised her bow with a relaxed grip, and placed the arrow gently on it with her fingers entwined behind its feathers. She drew the string slowly, hypnotizing Mac with her steady, confident movements;

the string now touching her long slender nose, subtly caressing the corner of her thin widowed lips.

He stared at her, benumbed, for he had never seen a woman so confident around a weapon; especially one that required such finesse. He stared, finally realizing she had already pierced the arrow flawlessly through the buck's heart.

"Impressed?" She winked at him again, noticing his surprised expression.

"Hm." He nodded gravely.

"But, you're gonna do all the dirty work!" She tittered, then froze for a moment, noticing his chiseled jaw filled with short blond stubble, sweat dripping from his sharp cheeks and stern forehead. Her hair stood erect, skin prickled, somehow she didn't know why.

He was intense. Cold, feral, yet so intriguing.

They made their way to the deer, glancing over the clean wound as the rest of the herd leaped over bushes, yearning for their safety. Her eyes set on his sharp v-shaped back as it widened every time he leaned down to the deer; she stared at the way he grabbed onto the buck's antlers, making veins pop across his robust arms, and she couldn't help but admire the way his muscles swelled and striated against the strain, the more and more he pulled.

"You're very strong, almost like us Norwegians!" She chuckled, throwing him a sudden compliment, as he threw the buck over his horse, detached from her presence. "Even with an injured arm…" she said.

Mac looked at her with a frown, and adjusted his leather hat on his head that got shifted by the buck's legs brushing against it. She stared back at him, realizing she had crossed a line.

"Thank you for letting me join the hunt!" she added, filling in the void of his awkward silence.

"Ye did most of it." he said, mounting his horse.

"And you didn't expect that, did you?" She sneered in confidence, mounting hers as well.

"No." He pulled out a cigarette, pushed it between his teeth. "Not really." he added, lit it up, looked back at the road to her homestead.

"Well, we should be getting on…don't want anyone to start worrying about us." she said, realizing he was not an easy man to talk to, somehow bewildered by it.

III

"WHAT DO YOU MEAN, SHE WENT HUNTING WITH HIM??" Levi questioned JB angrily, balling a fist beside him.

"I tried to tell her not to…but, but she insisted! Ya know how women are, Levi!" JB defended himself as he held Jonathan, asleep on his lap after bombarding him with countless variations of "feck", racing around the table, screeching in joy as he did.

"If she don't return, JB. You'll be in trouble." he warned him, imagining the boy growing up without his mother, knowing this would be the last straw for him, for Amara was all he had and Jonathan was all Amara had.

"What's going on?" Charlotte asked them, concerned, as she walked into their yelling.

"Guess what's going on…" Levi grunted, paced back and forth, flustered.

"What?" she asked, eyes following Levi across the room, realizing Mac and Amara were nowhere to be seen.

"Goddamn Kinnon is out on a hunt with my cousin!" He fumed, fearing he killed her and left her in a ditch, escaping with what little money she had saved up.

"What?" She gasped. Jaw dropped to the ground. "What do you mean? Out on a hunt? You mean, hunting? Them two? Them…together?" She sat down, shock washed over her, for just the idea alone of them being together made her heart cramp agonizingly.

"How did this even happen??" Levi asked JB again, who was inspecting a mole on the boy's arm. "JB!" he finally yelled, after waiting a few seconds that felt like hours.

"Oh!" he squeaked, startled. "Yes. Uhm, well, she just rushed in here and told me to take care of the boy; she was goin' huntin' with Mac. Then I stayed right where I am now, and told Jonny some stories! Have I ever told you 'bout that time I almost got trampled by a bison?" He wondered, looking up the ceiling as to remind himself how it went.

"JB!" Levi leaned over the table, fist pressed against it. "Where did they head to?" he asked upon a leer, expecting an immediate answer from him.

"Oh! Ahhh...north, perhaps?" JB shrugged, not having the smallest clue where they had gone to hunt, yet he didn't want to worry Levi any further.

"How long ago?!" he grunted, slid his fingers through his disheveled hair.

"Hello, everybody!" Amara's excited voice emerged behind them, silencing everyone instantly. Levi and Charlotte looked at her swiftly in utter surprise, and before anyone could greet her back, Levi marched to her with a leer.

"Where were you, Amara?" Levi questioned her, already knowing the answer.

"We was hunting...with Mac. Got a really nice buck!" she said, and Charlotte's heart sunk, for they never hunted together; *she was too useless to do so*, she thought to herself bitterly.

"Oh! Thought it was a cougar." JB giggled inappropriately in the back, while everyone ignored him.

"You was hunting...just like that, alone, with a murderer! Have you lost your mind, Amara?!!" Levi yelled at her, frustrated and concerned.

"Levi, I think I can take care of myself just fine. Besides, he is quite...the gentleman, in a strange kind of way." she defended him, and Charlotte's eyes flared, trying to understand what she meant by that, giving her thoughts the permission they needed to turn irrational.

"You have a *boy*, Amara! You can't be risking your life like this! You want him orphaned?!" he grunted with a passion, thinking how it was for him to grow up without a father.

"How dare you, Levi! Of course not! Can a woman not have fun anymore?" she yelled back, went to pick up sleeping Jonathan in her arms, and walked to her bedroom.

Amara's words rang in Charlotte's head repeatedly; creating untenable images of them; Amara cuddling up to him upon the lushest grass while waiting on a deer to appear, head pressed against his chest, arms coiling his waist; Mac talking intimately to her as he'd never talked before, words of endearment, perhaps even learning a few Norwegian ones; holding her arm to walk with her like the gentleman he never was. Kissing passionately, after a victorious hunt...*or worse.* Her stomach twisted in unbearable, nauseating pain and her eyes trembled to not release a single tear.

Levi took the initiative and rushed out of the house, door slamming shut as he did. Charlotte glanced over at JB, and not a second later, they both worriedly rushed to the windows to peek, one upon a limp, the other upon a long stride, both climbing up the bench. He approached Mac as he was cutting the last meat off the deer, placing it into buckets Amara gave him outside.

"Good hunt?" Levi asked him earnestly, walking confidently towards him.

"Sure." he said suspiciously, then lifted his head to face him.

"Good, good..." Levi paused for a moment, trying to remain calm.

"What are they sayin'?" JB asked Charlotte, and Charlotte looked at him perplexed, for neither of them could hear behind the glass.

"So, why exactly did you need my cousin with you? Can't hunt alone, no more?" he asked him, hands quivering in rage, feeling the urge to brawl him, stomp him to the ground, skin him like the carcass.

"Not me doin', lad." he said, standing up, tossing the bony carcass to the side. Completely unfazed by Levi's aggressive stance.

"Must be somethin' 'bout the deer..." JB muttered, and yet Charlotte's heart raced, reading Levi's body language. "Perhaps he thinks it was a dik-dik!" He cackled.

"Explain yourself!" Levi pushed Mac's chest, but Mac grabbed him swiftly from the neck.

"Don't try me, lad." Eyes speared through his. "Haven't strangled someone in too long, don't test me urges." Mac threatened, lightly squeezing around his neck.

"Oh Lordy!! Most definitely, it *musta* been a dik-dik!!" JB squeaked, as Charlotte slid off the bench and rushed to the door.

Levi swung his fist towards Mac's face, yet he ducked instantly, avoiding the hit with uncanny reflexes. "Maybe you should try to keep your goddamn urges to yourself, you sick bastard! You've risked all of our lives already! Look at this mess!!" he yelled at him. "If you come too close to Amara, I swear it to you! You will not get out of here alive!" Levi warned him, still with Mac's hand around his neck.

"Mac!! Stop it!!" Charlotte jumped between them, arms extended, hands gripping their chests. "Just stop it, already!!" She leered to him, agitated herself at this childish behavior.

Mac released his hand surprisingly and willingly fast, leaving a trail of deer blood around his neck. Levi tried to compose himself, feeling the urge to murder him right here and then — as Mac washed his hands in a bucket, drying them against his pants, like nothing ever happened.

"Yer buck's ready." He smirked snidely. "Amara killed it with her bow." He teased Levi, unknowingly upsetting Charlotte even further.

"Yes. I've taught her well." Levi mocked him back.

Mac ignored him with a sarcastic grin, picking up the buckets full of fresh meat to carry inside the house.

JB tripped over himself when he saw Mac approaching the door, accidentally pulling down the curtains as he held on to them for dear life, trying to find his balance again. "Oh!" he screeched, gasped, startled. "Hi!" JB waved at Mac with a big awkward smile, when the curtains landed over his head. Mac shook his head in disbelief, and proceeded to walk into the kitchen to soak the meat in salted water to pull the blood out.

IV

"THIS AIN'T LOOKIN' GOOD, SHERIFF!" a deputy informed Dorman as he pulled a ginger lock of hair off the ground, stuck inside the dried-up blood. Kneeling down before the bloody crime scene, Dorman inspected the hair with his glove-dressed hands.

"Must've been a redhead; Irish woman?" Dorman asked Mr. Miller who was seated behind.

"Y-y-yes sir! Born into a wealthy family. Aristocratic, yet different from the rest." he informed him honestly.

"I see." He looked around the ground, noticing faint footprints within the blood trails, leading out the door.

"He sure don't have Kinnon's brains." he muttered, seeing as he didn't bother to cover any of his traces. "Alright, boys. Let's mount up." he said, groaning as he lifted himself up from the ground, stretching his weary knees to do so. "Tim, light the lanterns for us." he ordered his deputy, looking closely around to find any other hint.

"And ya've known him long?" Dorman asked Mr. Miller, cocking a brow as he spotted Elizabeth's blood-soaked coat.

"Yes, sir. For many years now. He was…always a good man, and good neighbor to us. Never caused any trouble. Always donated his funds to good causes, or to the poor. This is all very surprising to us." He sighed disappointedly, lighting up the candles since evening approached.

"He was going through a divorce, ya said?"

"Yes, sir. Mrs. Elizabeth mentioned he was seeing another woman." He sat down again, as the interrogation wasn't over yet.

"That much we are aware of…" he mumbled, dryly.

"His father was a great man. Successful, honest; you'd think he would raise him the same. Just can't wrap my head around all this." he rambled, as his eyes studied Dorman's every move nervously — as if he was hiding anything himself.

Dorman remained quiet; he wondered for a brief moment if Mac was here with Will, and this was all his doing. He didn't care about Elizabeth, or this old man's rambling about Will. He didn't really care about Will either — all he wanted was to put the puzzle pieces together, and find his way to his brother's murderer.

"And Mrs. Elizabeth…she always was such a fine lady. Polite as can be, except when she requested something from my wife — she was…pretty particular about things." He shook his head, bowed it. "But my son, James, always…had the best things to say about her. The best things…" He choked nostalgically, glancing at his framed photograph. "Sadly, Mr. Griffiths never got to meet him, as he moved up in Mayhaw not too long ago. Perhaps he would've put some sense into him; not to go lookin' for another wife." He shrugged, then noticed Dorman looking at his son's photograph hanging over the chimney.

"Alright, Mr. Miller. I need to get goin'. My men are waiting for me outside." he said, shook his hand. "Thank ya for all your information. We will be sure to find the man, and serve him his justice." he said, and Mr. Miller nodded in nervousness. "Ya have a good evening, sir." Dorman tilted his large brimmed hat to him, and left the cabin hastily.

V

Charlotte laid in bed, dejected; trying to process everything she just heard. She had never felt this kind of irrational wrath within her; feasting at every fiber of her being, crawling beneath her skin, scraping against it, making her clench her teeth every time she heard that name of hers in the same sentence as his. Muscles tightened, hands formed a fist, every time she thought about them being close to each other. Her temperature rose, her chest constricted, barely able to breathe.

She hadn't even talked to Amara, and definitely didn't have much time alone with Mac, ever since they came here. She wondered if she was exaggerating, yet — as a woman, she detected the familiar way she looked at him; the unforgiving way her eyes glimmered with the slightest move he made. The way she so anticipated the luring of any word she could coax out of his mouth, for his deep, rich voice made up for the lack of words he spoke.

However, you couldn't read him; the map would fold shut, no matter how hard you tried to notice the tiniest wrinkle formed by a genuine smirk, or the slightest red tint to his cheek when his blood flushed from shyness. There was nothing coming from him — nothing you could detect. He was always so expressionless, cold, grim. The only time he spoke a little more than a few words is when he was threatening someone, especially Levi; somehow Will didn't bother him as much. Her mind trailed off back to their fishing day; how he tried to open up to her, "speak" to her for the very first time.

She missed it. She missed him; his voice, his cigarette breath touching hers as they neared close, his gentleness when his guard dared to let itself down; she was so close to gaining his trust, *and now this "Amara" was ruining everything*, she thought, clenched her teeth again, loathing herself for even detesting her — the idea of them, *them together,* for it wasn't fair. Amara was beautiful, generous, intelligent, independent, and she…she was nothing like that, and a gunslinger like Mac deserved better.

"Darn it…" She choked, rehearsing her own thoughts, shutting eyes, daring to look back once more, back at the lagoon, back at him. Mac was clear with his feelings, or rather his lack of, and she, she had Will, somewhere in Bisonhorn, in the woods of Caledonia Territory.

The door knocked. The walls rattled, dust evaporated from them.

Charlotte jumped up, startled as she glanced at the door, composing herself swiftly. "Come in." she said with a coarse dry voice, barely able to issue a sound.

"Hello, Charlotte!" Amara stepped in, a big smile across her face, dimming hers — her whole soul's light that clung onto her sinews by a thin thread of hope that remained. Eyes flared in shock.

V I

"WANT A BOWL OF STEW, MR. KINNON?" JB ASKED HIM KINDLY, as he heard Mac's stomach rumble from the other corner of the room.

"…Sure." he said.

Levi stood up from the table, rushed outside, lighting up a much-needed cigarette after the previous argument. His blood boiled, loathing the thought of sitting beside him — still furious with Amara's immaturity and selfishness.

JB handed Mac a bowl of stew and sat down before him; unable to restrain his curiosity, he just stared at every gulp he took, noticing the tiny scars hidden behind his stubble.

Mac lifted his gaze, nailing him, cocking a brow of annoyance.

"Oh!" He gasped. "I didn't mean to…I…how's the stew?!" JB chuckled awkwardly, fingers fiddled nervously with the table.

"Warm." he muttered coldly.

"It better be! That fire was sure tough to start! Back in the army, I was the one responsible for it, and let me tell ya, starting one in a storm is a whooooole different story than poking firewood in the chimney!" he said in attempts to ignite conversation, yet it felt like talking to a stone-cold wall. Mac continued eating his stew in an irritated manner, avoiding any eye contact, grinding the spoon harshly across his teeth.

"So what's your story, mister?" JB asked, smothered by one minute too long being forced into silence. "I tend to ramble a lot I know, I know…so I'll let ya do the talkin' now, how 'bout that?" He giggled again, leaning back in hopes to hear him talk.

"I ain't got nothin' to say to ye, ol' man." Mac said sternly, as he inhaled his soup.

"Well, I've heard otherwise. Apparently you're quite the legend, ah?" He winked at him excitedly, encouraging him to speak.

"Legend? For what?" He snorted eerily, crossed his arms together, cocked his head to the side — looking straight into JB with a single blue eye that was lit up by the candle beside them.

"Oh…well. You know…for the…*activities* you do…" JB stuttered, toes curling up anxiously.

"Ye mean killin' folk? Strangling them to their death? Chokin' them unconscious? Then enjoyin' the sound of their last breath, as I slice their throats open?" Mac looked at him intimidatingly, without a single bat of an eyelash. JB's eyes dilated in shock; legs felt restless all of a sudden, and a strong urge to leave the table flushed through him.

"Well…there's surely worse out there, right?" He gulped down a knot, suddenly paranoid he might be his next victim.

"Nah…there ain't." He sighed, crinkling his mouth to the side. "So how's that small talk workin' out for ya, ol' man?" he asked him, stood up from the table, walked past him, ready to go to his room. JB took in a deep breath, then frowned confidently, balling a fist of courage…

"You ain't foolin' me, mister!" he said, twisting around to face him again. "Believe it or not, I've talked to…well, rambled to…a lot of men in my plenty years on this god-forsaken earth, and I…I can tell you right now, ya're…ya… ya just ain't like the common kind — the sick kind…

"There's men who've raped women and children, more often than not who were their own flesh and blood. There's folk pretending to be your friend, then stab ya in the back like ya'd never expect in a million years. Bloodthirsty liars, greedy sons of bitches who create useless wars, wiping out entire countries — and it ain't never enough.

"There's a lot worse in this goddamn world, Mr. Kinnon. Yes…indeed; ya're a cold-blooded killer, so they say, but I bet ya there's a story behind those scars." He finally paused, as he surprisingly noticed that he had grabbed his attention for the very first time. He blinked with the fact, and continued.

"There lies kindness within your heart, Mac Kinnon. Ya just don't know it yet." JB stared solemnly, then he too stood up to leave.

Mac paused in his tracks, repeated his words in his head. A sudden wave of sadness washed over him, one he rarely recognized. Memories flashed before him, as he thought of Mickey; how he always urged him to "crack a smile more often", or "to talk freely" — express what he felt within his leaden heart, so the pain would not consume him. He knew he was tormented, he knew he was carrying unbearable weight on his young shoulders, slowly shaping him into a man he was never meant to be. But Mickey would always tell him he was a good person — the best he had ever known, and Mac refused to believe so, for the worm that preached the verses, drilled the conception of sin within him, the conception of his own self.

Yet that all was before he murdered for the first time; before he tasted the pleasure of revenge. Before he found the creeping dark side within him — that was the only thing keeping him company, giving him closure, when he was locked up in that cellar. He did not have a "kind heart" — he was made a sinner; a monster whom everyone feared and loathed — he was never a legend, rather a ghost with a name that nobody could capture. A ghost, that haunted its very own self.

CHAPTER 48

Compliance

I

DISMOUNTING THEIR HORSES CAUTIOUSLY, after following the bloody trail that led them into the thicker woodlands of Red Giants where it was impossible for the horses to pass through, Sheriff Dorman and his deputies untied their lanterns from their saddles, held them out to light up the mossy path before them.

"Keep your eyes open; Kinnon might be lurkin' here too. Load them guns boys, and keep 'em handy." Dorman ordered them, whispering, for he could sense an eerie wind brush against them, almost able to hear a foreboding sough through the trees.

He climbed slowly over a small hill, barely able to lift his arthritic leg over the log before it and the rest followed loyally after him. The night air felt crisp and chilly; gushing swiftly against the dark green sword ferns layered across the ground, swirling around the thick redwood tree trunks — making their silhouettes dance hopelessly, lit by the brightly burning lanterns. The whole army of deputies, glowing like gigantic fireflies throughout the forest, marching cautiously and steadily, following the blood-stained grass before them.

"Sh...Sheriff?!" a deputy called for Dorman quietly. There was a wail in his voice, a tremble of a brave man cowering. The sheriff looked back agitatedly as the deputy raised his lantern before him, lighting — what was left of — a man, tied up around a tree.

II

"I HOPE I'M NOT DISTURBING, MISS?" Amara asked Charlotte, then sat down beside her, searching for her face.

"No...no, of course not!" Charlotte stammered, somehow confidently, not able to look at her in the eyes — the same ones that stared at Mac the whole night before. *Same ones Mac most likely stared into during the hunt, as she shot the buck down with her arrow for him,* she thought bitterly, choking again.

"You must be so very exhausted..." Amara sighed with compassion, that motherly instinct kicking in again. "Levi told me about what happened at Ring Lagoon; I'm surprised you all came out of this...shootout, alive!" she expressed genuinely, noticing her nervous fingers fidgeting with her hair.

"To be honest with you, I'm quite surprised myself. I truly thought I'd be dead, and would be, if it wasn't for...the boys." Charlotte corrected herself, not wishing to mention Mac's name to her. *Why to, anyway? It would only fuel their fervent fire further,* she thought.

"Absolutely. I'm surprised Levi even came back for Mac; you know he ain't so fond of...folk like him, being a bounty hunter and all." She sighed, disappointed, and Charlotte swallowed uncomfortably with a dry throat, almost gagging to hear her refer to him by his name, as though to confirm how much closer they had gotten. "But, I think he mostly came back for you." She giggled childishly, elbowed her arm and winked her direction.

"Ha. Right...they...they're quite the pair." she mumbled awkwardly. "Anyway, I heard you went hunting today! That was a very big buck you got for us." she said, in failed attempts to change the subject, to one that probably wasn't any better. *My God, Charlotte...you're a fool!*

"Yes! It was exhilarating! I longed so much to get out of here, without the boy for once." She huffed, fingers squeezing her skirt as though in deep thought. "Don't get me wrong, he is everything I hold dear, but more often than not, this boy can really drive me iiiinsane!" She chuckled, briefly reminiscing Jonathan's daily shenanigans.

"Well, can't say I know the feeling; however my pony, Finn, can be quite a handful sometimes too when his stubbornness kicks in." She grinned awkwardly, as her social skills were failing her completely, realizing she had no clue about children, for that subject never crossed her mind to begin with, other than praying to God every night to not inhale the impregnating fumes of her mother's clients. She blinked tightly, remembering. "But…Jonathan really is quite a sweet boy; you've done well with him." she complimented her, thinking how quietly he was dining with them the other night, or how respectfully he spoke to them with *sir* and *madam* in every sentence; never screaming frantically around, nor throwing any temper tantrums. He was a very well-mannered young man, compared to the little heathens stealing around in Nephilim Cove — all doing an excellent job of convincing her she would never want children in her life.

"That's very kind of you to say, Charlotte. We've had quite a rough ride the last years, losing my beloved husband to the hands of…some awful, awful 'animals'." She tore her gaze away, shook her head. "Jonathan might have been young, but…he remembers everything." She exhaled deeply, and Charlotte bowed her head, embarrassed, for she didn't know how to respond to such deep confessions. "Seeing his daddy murdered in such a horrific way, has been haunting him in his sleep…until recently." she said, cutting her eyes at her. "So, to be honest, you've all been a blessing to us." she added, holding back her tears.

"I'm deeply sorry to hear that, Amara. It seems life doesn't treat anyone fairly; some say God may have a plan for the…unfortunate things that happen, but…I'm starting to fail to see it." she hummed as she looked at the bookshelf, where a Holy Bible was proudly showcased.

"You may be right. However, I prayed for *so long* for someone to appear in my life, for someone to be a good example for Jonathan…and then this man walks in, and…and my son is absolutely infatuated with him!" There was a smile that curved her lips; an upwards, tight curve of utter gleefulness. "He can suddenly sleep with no nightmares; instead, dreaming of his new hero that slays monsters, and dragons, and…he doesn't seem so…sad anymore. It's truly as if God brought him to us."

Charlotte felt a knot in her stomach form again; it was tight, it twisted, coiled around her organs, smothered them too. She knew she was talking about Mac, seeing her eyes sparkle just thinking about him. Her body flushed with heat, trying hard to not express how she really felt about this, how she burned, how she suffocated, how she slowly died within her illusion that turned into reality.

"That's…that's wonderful, I guess." she mumbled shortly, jaw clenched, her blood quickening within her veins. It pumped. It throbbed. She jittered internally.

"It is…but my cousin! Gah! Levi is so stubborn…you can never reason with him; he would never understand." she nagged as she looked out the window, spotting Levi who was cleaning his rifle.

"Understand…what?" Charlotte tentatively asked her.

"I know this is going to sound very strange…because you've only just gotten here, but…" She paused herself as if to make sure no one was behind the door, eavesdropping their conversation. "But I'm quite infatuated with him, myself." she whispered to her, plastering a shy smile across her face.

Charlotte forced a supportive smirk on her lips, yet her heart dropped straight down to the ground. "With…with Mac, you-you mean?" She sucked in an awkward stutter, legs started to tremble from a sudden rush of adrenaline.

"Yes! Oh, my goodness!" She buried her face within her hands, embarrassed of her confession. "I just…it's been so long since a man has touched me, like he did."

"T-touched you??" Her heart leaped wildly in her chest.

Sadness, turned to rage.

"No, not like that! But…he has touched my heart from the moment he stepped into my house, and I simply cannot understand why!" she said and Charlotte's gaze glazed, dozed off into a void deep within her mind. "Ah! Charlotte, help me please!" She begged, grabbing her hands within hers.

"H-help you?" she stuttered again, realizing the real reason why she wanted to talk to her.

"Can you talk to him about me? Can you see if he cares at all?" She looked her in the eyes intensely, like a puppy dog begging for a piece of meat.

"Uhm…" She coughed, cleared her throat, swallowed down a sob to even make a sound. "Amara…he…you know he ain't…"

"Normal? That he is a murderer? I know! Levi was 'kind' enough to remind me of that! But I strongly see a kind soul behind this mask he has created; I truly want to turn his life around, and I believe I can. You would never guess how kind and thoughtful he was, during the hunt. He has a way...a calm way, that just brings peace to my heart. The way he looks at you, with those *perfect* blue eyes..." she rambled, nailing her gaze up the spider-webbed ceiling, reliving the moment with him.

Daggers pierced through her with every word she spoke. A bile of nausea collected at the core of her throat; an insufferable urge to scream out loud, bust the glass, destroy everything around her, leave nothing but her own memory; the only memory built upon the roots of their feeble relationship, back in Hope. Her skin burned from the anger cooped up inside of her; realizing her irrational thoughts were nothing but her gut instinct warning her all this time.

"Charlotte? Will you help me?" she asked her again, noticing she had gone quiet.

"But...he is a wanted man, Amara. What about your boy?" Charlotte questioned her, genuinely concerned about Jonathan's future.

"My boy needs a father!" she answered agitatedly. "And I...I need someone...I need...I'm lonely, Charlotte...I might appear strong, but...deep within, I'm crumbling." she wailed. "My sweet John left us far too soon... Nothing could have ever prepared me for that loss...that grief, that still feasts at my heart!"

Charlotte looked at her blankly. A widowed mother, desperately grasping for pieces to fill up the hollowness her husband's loss created, and yet somehow it felt as though she was carving pieces out of *her* heart, and they could never belong to hers.

"Please, Charlotte..." she pleaded, and Charlotte tore her gaze away.

"I...I will see what I can do..." she whispered, her voice suddenly too weak to raise it.

Amara embraced her tightly, thanking her a million times for her willingness to help. Black hair squished against Charlotte's face, imprinting a heavy smell of smoky firewood. Charlotte glanced out the window, held captive in the noose of her arms — then realized she had forgotten entirely about Levi, who was still awaiting an answer. Upon a gasp, she freed herself, rather rebelliously. "Ex...excuse me, Amara. I, I need to tend to something urgently."

I I I

THE MAN'S HEAD WAS CLOAKED WITH BLOOD; vividly red, pooling the sockets of his eyes. Hair pulled back forcefully, skin scalped aggressively with the intent of torment. Arrows pierced through his body, nailing him to the bark.

"This…this *must* have been Kinnon…" Dorman whispered to his deputies, feeling immensely repulsed.

"What about the redskins?" one asked, gagging at the sight.

"No…they ain't here…that's Kinnon's work…"

He growled, eyes scanning around. A sharp arrow shot right beside them, slashing the ominous air with a wiping sound of a warning, hitting the corpse once more in the head. It held, affixing it even tighter to the tree. The men turned around, panicked, raising guns and lanterns, quivering.

"Who goes there?!?" Dorman yelled in that direction, aiming the revolver into the dark void before him.

Another arrow shot right through them, this time hitting one of his men to the neck, dropping dead before them. His lantern slipped from his grip, slammed to the ground, slowly extinguishing as the light of his life dimmed along with it.

"Shoot!!" Dorman ordered and his men started firing their weapons, hiding behind rocks and trees, chests rising, blood quickening. "DARN YOU, KINNON!!" he yelled with passion, and countless arrows cascaded against them again, injuring more of his men, slashing wind pipes, piercing lungs, hearts, and stomachs.

His eyes flared at the sight, chest swelled in fear; blood rose to his head, pumping relentlessly through his frail veins. Looking around himself, he counted his deputies, noticing them become fewer by the second; darkness soon engulfed them as lanterns kept on falling with them. "C'ME HEEERE, YA BLOODY COWARD!" Dorman screamed from the core of his soul, fearing for the very first time that this might be the end of him.

IV

"LEVI!" CHARLOTTE RUSHED TO HIM, through the dark and the fog, barely able to see him mount his horse, only his enormous shadow slashed through it. Levi jerked his head back in her direction, in great surprise, not expecting to see her — after all, it was already close to midnight, and he assumed she was asleep.

"Hey!" he called back shortly.

"Where…where are you going?" she asked him guiltily, skidding to a halt before him, feeling as though she had let him down. Forgotten, which she did.

"Ah…" He bowed his head, bit his lip, thinking. "Not anywhere far. Just… just to clear my mind for a moment." he stuttered; seeming as if his confidence had suddenly abandoned him.

"Oh…I understand…" She sighed, nodded.

"You aren't asleep yet?" he asked, shifting his weight on the saddle. The leather squeaked in protest.

"No…" She swallowed hard, looking at the runic rings on his fingers, shining every time he twisted his wrists to adjust the reins. "Reckon we might still be going for a walk…tonight?" She bit her lip awkwardly, not knowing if it was her guilt asking or her heart.

"How 'bout a ride, instead?" he offered her, stroking his horse's neck and looking back down at her.

"But…Finn; I…I don't think he's able to carry me, with his leg right now." she muttered, disappointed to decline the tempting offer.

Levi chuckled; his breath filled up the chilled air around them with a twirling wisp of fog. He shifted that weight again, the leather now was quiet, as if it too gained its confidence back. He reached for her hand tentatively, still worried for rejection.

"Oh…you mean…but…are you sure?" She blushed, as his endearing smile clasped her heart again. There it was, that feeling of escape blossoming within her chest, scraping any sense from her mind.

"We've done it before, haven't we?" He winked at her. "Perhaps this time you won't be so wobbly, and…naughty with words." he said and she snorted, grabbing his frosty hands and mounting right behind him.

"Silly man." She giggled excitedly, wrapped her arms around him, and breathed out in contentment, feeling his cold leather coat chill her body.

"Hold on tight! This boy isn't lazy!" he warned her, cued his horse, and it went into a steady lope — now galloping down a grassy hill, towards a large pond that reflected the full moon — Ravenheart Pond.

CHAPTER 49

Choosing Poison

I

HE GRABBED AN OLD BOLT ACTION RIFLE FROM INSIDE THE SHACK; deserted, as he felt too. Dusty, worn down, stock chipped off, dented, yet still a cartridge was in the chamber, still a heart within his. It quivered within his grip, eyes stared frightened down at it, seated on a broken-down bridge overlooking the lake *she* disappeared deep within. Sunk within. Drowned. His whole life, a carrousel of tender and woeful images, passed before him in the blink of an eye, yet his pocket watch still ticked steadily.

Every ripple of water beneath him, a memory engraved, wrinkled deep into his brain; his most cherished present at Christmas Eve — a tightly wrapped book, leather bound — his mother's favorite author, etching his passion for becoming a writer.

"World of Damage", the first book he had ever written, the only one remaining away from the attic, shoved into the bookshelf, a now choppily written letter within page three-hundred, as though he had known.

His first dappled gray pony their parents bought him for his sixth birthday — perfectly trained, well-bred, not stepping a single hoof out of line, inspiring his love for horse ranching as he grew older. He flinched a faint smile, realizing how much he had grown as a horseman the past weeks.

That smile slipped.

Eyes shut again, more ripples emerged.

His first devastating heartache — experiencing intolerable grief when his mother passed away; losing the only rock of stability in his life, forced to stand

547

on two feet without her guidance, forced to endure his father's cruelty until the day he passed too. Realizing, the world wasn't as bright and welcoming as her tender wing around him.

His first kiss. Elizabeth's virgin lips entwined with his, the first feeling of butterflies flying hectically within his stomach — love; not a million pages could be enough to write down this tormenting, yet most beautiful feeling in the whole world that he felt.

Betrayal; heart torn in half in the most brutal way, yanked out, chewed to pieces, as he watched his wife suck another man's lips dry in the back of the barn. Realizing, for the first time, love never came without a cold-served plate of crippling pain. Love never was all butterflies; never was a linear concept.

It too, rippled.

Charlotte; the first feeling just the thought of a name could give him — fooling with his sanity, deranging the mind. A woman so brave in all her youth and inexperience; holding her in bed, kissing her fervently, his heart felt whole.

Until it was ripped apart again.

Murder; the first wicked feeling of death — tasting the last breath of its being; baring to him how fragile life can be, shifting shapes within the heat of a misjudged moment.

II

"I KNOW YOU'RE QUITE THE COWGIRL, but…as your doctor, I feel responsible to take care of your wrists." he said and she cocked a brow, amused. Dismounting, he lent his arms to her. Swinging her leg, she slid right down to them, as hands held her steady, gripping on her coat.

"Thank you…doctor." she said snidely, and he winked at her.

"How are your wrists feeling?" he asked and she chuckled.

"It hasn't even been a day, Levi…but they do feel…let's say, sturdier." she said and he nodded.

"Good…good. That balm does wonders, like I told you…" he said, walking abreast with her towards a small lagoon.

"Yes, and it smells incredible." she said. He halted, turned and clutched her hand gently. Frozen still, she watched him; lifting her hand up to his mouth, it touched his lips, and the faintest whiff of winter blooms came to him.

"Yes, it does. However, I don't think it smells as incredible as you do." he said, cutting his eyes at her. Her chest constricted a little, how could it not.

"Thank you…Dr. Levi…" she said, in attempts to keep it friendly.

"You're welcome…" he said, somehow saddened, and continued to walk; hand released.

"That's quite…beautiful here, Levi." She sighed calmly, twirling around herself, noticing a shallow lagoon embraced by lush green grass that swayed in all directions with every gush of wind, eyes aglow, flickering within a lattice of dark branches.

"Glad you approve!" He smirked, taking out a bottle of liquor from his saddlebag. "This wasn't really how I'd planned it, so forgive me for having to share the bottle like that." he said in earnest, and she snorted internally, briefly recalling the Fiddler lips she kissed. She gagged, shook her head, and clasped the bottle as he offered her the first sip.

"You didn't even try it yet??" Levi asked her, baffled at her repulsed grimace.

"I'm sorry…it wasn't about that."

"Oh…was it about me?" He teased, yet wondered.

"No…no, it wasn't. It could never…I mean…" She bowed her head, cheeks crimsoned. "Anyway, what is it with you men and your whiskey?" She took a hasty gulp that burned more than the strongest whiskey she'd ever had, making her stretch her tongue out — trying hard not to choke.

"Haha. This isn't whiskey, cowgirl. This is 'shine." He chuckled with her dramatic reaction, falling for her a little more.

"This…this is drinkable??" She tittered in shock, handing him the bottle back swiftly, not wishing to have anything to do with it.

"'Course it is! You don't get this stuff easily, so better appreciate it!" He winked playfully, and gulped it down with ease, showing off as he did.

"If you mean to appreciate the experience of almost choking to death, and flaming up my insides, sure!" She snorted, noticing he had trimmed his beard real close tonight, as though he tried to be presentable for her. *He looked good,* she thought, she admired. *Damn good…*

"So, why you men drink so much? It's just poisoning you…same with those filthy cigarettes…it can't be healthy." she asked, pulling herself back to her senses, then noticed him tuck his cigarette pack back in again the moment she said it.

"Hm, I am not sure; perhaps it's the only escape we have in our world." he confessed, knowing he drowned his troubles with the poison, knowing his kin was heavily relying on alcohol; nursing it like an infant nurses its mother's tit.

"I don't blame you…I guess I never really could afford it, to find out." she avowed in return, thinking back to those cans of beans she used to eat for what seemed like an eternity, briefly realizing she had gained some weight with Amara's and JB's cooking. She paused on that thought, and tucked in her belly swiftly.

"Well, maybe better than wasting all your hard-earned money on it." He chuckled and handed her back the bottle, it clinked against his rings. She blinked at it, not much caring about it, yet forced another sip. It went down easier, *still burned like Hell though.* Eyes set back on him, slightly squinting. "Besides, there's so much poison out there, that ain't liquor or tobacco…" he cryptically mumbled, as he glanced back at her.

"Such as?" she asked, feeling her throat swell up from the burn.

"Women." He chuckled. "Dripping full of poison…" he added rather earnestly, and her face fell, set on a straight line as he strode closer to her, burying the moon behind his wall of a back.

Charlotte blushed uncomfortably, lips sealed involuntarily — not able to come up with a snarky remark this time, as his intense presence froze her. Pulse thudded against the crease of her neck.

"But, you know…" His face leaned closer to hers. "I pick my poison…" Head inclined carefully, watching every expression she made. "…and I'll be damned, if I don't pick you." He grabbed her neck, daringly sliding fingers through her wavy hair, planting his lips on hers.

Charlotte pulled back, stared at him, conflicted; wondering, imagining, panting, wanting, craving, yet not with heart; he leaned into her again, lingering before her lips.

"Don't reject me, girl…again…" he whispered, begged, breathed heavily, luring her being into a state of bewilderment, yet fiery desire surged through her, unable to be extinguished in his wave of heat. Daringly in turn, she pressed her lips back to his, sucking the liquor taste out of them, kissing him deep, long, fervently.

He groaned, clasped her waist, moved with her towards a boulder, slamming themselves against it. Cupping her face, they kissed, bruising each others lips; hands slid down to her waist, resting at the swell of her hip; grabbing tight and firm, clasping the cloth. She kissed him back, yet hands remained restrained, tied up by the thought of *him; them, what they could have been, what they will never be.*

He bent down, grabbed her from the legs, lifted her up, pressed himself against her, between thighs, hands clutching her ass, lips locked around hers; groaning, tensed.

She jerked, startled, pulled back swiftly, and leaped off of him, staring at him in shock, quivering. "Levi, I…" She froze as he stepped back, noticing the confusion in her gaze, yet he felt bewildered himself.

"I'm sorry." He sighed, knowing he rushed it, knowing it was too soon, knowing she was different. "I didn't mean to…to force you." he said, tearing his gaze away in shame, for he would never. "Where were we?" Lips folded together, tasting her for the last time.

"I'm sorry, Levi…I'm…I'm…this…" she stammered, and he breathed heavily, crumbling in embarrassment, aching. "I've never…" She swallowed hard and his eyes set upon her, aghast.

"You…you're a virgin?" he asked, baffled.

She bowed her head, nodding in silence.

"Shit…" he grunted, raking a hand through his hair, furious with himself.

"I'm sorry…" she said, as though she needed to apologize for it.

"No…no, Charlotte." he said, clasped her shoulders. "Don't you ever apologize for that." he said, now everything made sense; her rejection towards him. It was *fear,* he thought. "I just…I would have never guessed so…" he said, bewildered, glancing at her from head to toe.

"What? What do you mean?"

"I don't know…you just…don't act the part. Let alone the way you… kiss…" He cleared his throat, still embarrassed, and she tore her gaze away, knowing the influence of her mother was evident.

"I have kissed before, Levi…I just…haven't slept with a man yet." she said sternly and he nodded.

Charlotte didn't know what to say further; her heart still raced from being picked up from the ground by this giant's arms, feeling another man's growing bulge that wasn't Will's. Her heart sunk in guilt, but somehow her self drowned in a journey of discovering her own.

"I have to talk to you…" Her thoughts averted back to the miserable reality that killed off every hope within her. "…Amara…she, she talked to me tonight." she said, taking another throat burning sip, face distorted with all possible expressions.

Levi went quiet for a moment, scratching his disheveled hair nervously, trying to ground himself from the kiss prior.

"Okay…and what about?" he curiously asked, slamming his hat on top of his saddle horn, worried Amara might have talked to her about him, as though it wasn't apparent he yearned for her.

"How to say this…" she huffed anxiously, not wishing to upset him any further, certainly not after pushing him away again. "Mac…she…she wants me to…to talk to him…about her." She exhaled a stubborn deep breath, feeling the weight of her shoulders slowly lessen.

Levi blinked, grunted, flustered; chugging a big gulp — burning down all the words he'd rather not express in front of her.

"I think she…really hopes they can become something…" she added, the liquor loosening her tongue.

Levi bobbed his head in a state of absence, a state of rage, minutes before exploding. "What is it with you women and your odd taste in men?" He snorted earnestly with the irony. Charlotte was silenced guiltily; realizing she too was besotted with Mac, no matter how hard she tried to deny it for her own good, her own morals, even for Will's sake all this time. "I just don't understand why you never settle for the few good men that are left in this damn world. Perhaps we are just boring you, after all…" he complained and sat down on a large rock, disappointed.

"It's not like that, Levi…I think your cousin is just…desperately hoping to find someone." she defended her, for an unknown reason to her.

"My cousin…but how about you?" he asked directly, wishing he could have his answers tonight, to clear his mind once and for all.

"What…what do you mean?" she questioned him.

Suddenly, putting her on the spot. "Come on, Charlotte. I think I deserve to know something…don't keep me wondering no more." He glanced at the storm clouds forming above them, chest deflated upon a leaden sigh.

"To be honest…I really didn't expect to have this conversation with you tonight…" she muttered worriedly, not feeling emotionally prepared for that type of interrogation.

"Don't I deserve to know? Or do you want me to just keep on running after you, like a starved mutt in the rain?" He chuckled caustically, face furrowed with a frown.

"No, Levi. I ain't like that. I always was honest with you." she said, a raindrop brushing against her cheek, as she looked up as well.

"So, why you came? Why you came tonight?" he asked sternly.

"To…to just get out. To be with you. For you asked me, and…" she stuttered and he shook his head, flustered.

"Why did you let me kiss you? Why…why did you kiss me back…for such a long time?" He interrupted her swiftly. The rain now started to fall steadily. "I understand you're…a virgin still and I respect that, and…I was wrong to rush things, but *shit*, Charlotte…it really felt like you wanted me back. For you was…intense. I guess I'm confused…" he said, lowering his head, hoping for honesty.

"I…I didn't…I mean, I don't know!" She hissed, not really knowing why she accepted the kiss, and all the grinding and moaning; was it to revenge Amara and Mac? Or was it genuine? She never could differentiate anymore between her real feelings and her pretend ones.

"Why, Charlotte? Why to be with me, when you clearly have your heart set somewhere else…I just want clarity in my life, not to fool around with mind games. At least give me that." he persisted, his messy hair slowly soaked by the rain, contrasting strongly with his bright green eyes.

"Yes. Yes, Levi! I have feelings for Mac!" she yelled, and it was good to yell it out loud for the first time ever. "I'm sorry! I don't like it either! I've been trying for months to drown this feeling deep inside me, but yet he always appears in my life again! Causing me great havoc, to the point I'm wanted for the first time in my darn life, in every darn state!

"I lost someone very important to me, who probably thinks I abandoned him — someone I can't even write a letter to…to explain my lack of communication, to even apologize! Someone who perhaps has another wife, and decided I don't mean all that much to him anymore, and yet frankly, that don't bother me as much as it should! However, he is still someone who sacrificed his health for me, and now? Look at me! I'm kissing you!! I'm…I'm kissing you…I'm…betraying him…all over again." she cried and he stared at her, speechless. "And he is the last person on this earth that deserves it…and nor do you deserve to be pulled into my web of mess…for I'm just confused, Levi, to the point that I don't know what I want anymore or who I even am! I don't know who I am! All this is new to me! The concept of men, and relationships… is foreign! What am I supposed to do, or feel?? I have not the smallest clue! It's always just been me and Finn. Always." She drew in a deep breath to refill her lungs again, flipping her wet hair back to compose herself.

Not expecting her to ever talk so openly about her feelings or what she went through, he felt embarrassed to have pressured her to speak.

He nodded. Guiltily.

Rain flushed down. Ruthlessly.

"…you want to go home? Rain's pretty rough now." he asked, noticing her shivering.

"That's all you have to say?" She gasped, agitated, since she poured her heart out to him.

"No! No, Charlotte. 'Course not! I just don't want you to freeze to death out here!" he fussed and stepped on the slippery stirrup, mounting his horse — lending her his arm to pull her up.

"I meant it, Levi, right outside the stables of Mon Louis!" she said, staring sternly into his eyes. They were in shadow, but she could still detect the sadness within them. "I meant it to remain friends, for you mean a lot to me too! There has never been someone who made me laugh like this, and forget everything that tormented my mind! And I'm sorry…I'm so terribly sorry, that I…that I gave you false hope." she confessed, and grabbed his hand tightly not to slip.

CHAPTER 50

Regret

I

THE RAINSTORM HIT THEM LIKE A SACK OF ROCKS, still in cover behind the trees; still shooting towards the dark nothingness.

"Boss!! We are losing our men!!!" yelled a deputy, urging him to retreat as arrows pierced one man after another.

Dorman stood in eerie silence, calculating hard how to defend themselves, let alone escape Kinnon's trap. Ego and pride tied his legs to the vines, yet common sense screamed at him to break free.

"Boss!! It's an ambush!!!" another deputy screamed in anguish, spotting dozens of men in bear pelts wrapped around them, running at them, machetes in hands, bows and arrows ready to pierce through more.

Dorman's eyes suddenly flared aghast. *Feasters,* he thought to himself, now confirmed, and his panic only heightened. "RETREAT!!!!" he distraughtly ordered his deputies, screaming from the top of his lungs, a voice of horror, unable to quell the panic within him.

Sprinting, they leaped over logs frantically, squeezed through tight lines of trees, as the wind forcefully blew them back towards their pursuers; sweat flushed them, sticking the clothes to their chests. Shadows crawled over their faces as they lifted their guns back, shooting randomly at them.

A deputy's leg got stuck in a mossy hole in the ground, pulling him in, almost swallowing him the more he struggled against it, yet nobody stopped to rescue him — they left him there, laying helplessly, writhing in panic. An echo of his agonizing screams, a caterwaul in loud, sharp clarity reaching the deputies ears as the Feasters took hold of him, scalping him alive, tearing his own ears off just to taste excitedly in triumph.

Lightning struck — slammed against the ground repeatedly, sending scattered vibrations underneath their fleeing feet. Rushing to their horses, equally anxious, tied up, stomping and neighing in anguish, as the thunder rolled ever heavier above them.

Arrows still flew, ascending and descending swiftly in their direction, piercing through horse hinds and legs as they galloped their riders loyally away into safety.

I I

STICK AFTER STICK, inhaled like slithering cancer into his lungs, counting the time that passed by; fingers impatiently tapping against the windowpane, muffled by the spitting rain.

Booming thunder lit up his face with every stroke against the ground, like a ghost in human form, staring out the window wickedly; his face, a stern mask, in grim shadow. Hearing JB's irregular snores from the guest room — rhythmic slimy gargles, gushing out with every exhale — made Mac realize it was indeed possible for JB to irritate him even further.

He grumbled, shook his head, and tried to muffle the sound, when a soft, angelic voice brushed against his ears. Amara, singing to Jonathan, lulling him to sleep as the storm terrified him; for shadows emanated in the walls, shone by brooding lightning.

> "*The sky is dark and the hills are white*
> *As the storm-king speeds from the north to-night;*
> *And this is the song the storm-king sings,*
> *As over the world his cloak he flings:*
> *Sleep, sleep, little one, sleep;*
> *He rustles his wings and gruffly sings:*
> *Sleep, little one, sleep.*

"On yonder mountain-side a vine
Clings at the foot of a mother pine;
The tree bends over the trembling thing,
And only the vine can hear her sing:
Sleep, sleep, little one, sleep;
What shall you fear when I am here?
Sleep, little one, sleep.

"The king may sing in his bitter flight,
The tree may croon to the vine to-night,
But the little snowflake at my breast
Liketh the song I sing the best
Sleep, sleep, little one, sleep;
Weary thou art, a-next my heart
Sleep, little one, sleep."

Mac listened carefully, side-eyeing the open door; studying Amara's shadow, formed by the candle she held in her hand. Her gentle voice somehow reaching right through him, plucking thorns subtly from his heart; hypnotizing him once again — chest exhaling an anticipatory relief.

A sudden knock on the window startled him; he grabbed his revolver, spinning it around swiftly to an aim at the glass. His squinting eyes flared as he was met with a raven staring right back at him, knocking repeatedly on the glass, banging its head harshly against it, smashing its beak, tearing it apart, breaking the upper one into a million ebony pieces.

His gun lowered, hair stood up, knowing this was unusual behavior for a bird, certainly one of such intelligence. He stared back at it carefully, as though trying to read its thoughts — yet then, her voice emerged behind him; a slow, dreamy voice.

"Mr. Kinnon?" she called for him, surprised to see themselves both alone in this room.

"Hm?" Mac hummed shortly, jerking his head back to the glass, checking on the raven, yet it had completely disappeared, then looked back at her — surprised to see her in her sheer white nightgown.

"Where is everyone?" she asked, then not long after, JB's monstrous snore startled her in response. "Okay! Ha. Well, we know where JB is!" She chuckled and Mac rolled his eyes, for this man could only breathe, and it would annoy him.

"Levi? Charlotte?" she questioned him again, yet she received no answer, as he gazed out the window cryptically instead. She glanced at him as he completely avoided her, lost in his own deep thoughts — bothered by them being gone for so long in the middle of the night; imagining Charlotte's clothes soaking wet, sticking firmly on her body before Levi's eyes.

His grip tightened, feeling the usual urge he felt every night; to mount up, sharpen a knife, slice some throats, stare at death, wondering *what for*. It had been building up for so many days, like the mind of an addict, crawling into circles, suffering in withdrawal — he thought of Levi, and it only heightened his murderous senses.

"I guess it's just the two of us, then…" She smiled gently, looking out the window herself, noticing the storm roar outside. "Would you like a drink?" she asked, pouring one herself.

Subtly warm. Stinging the air.

His eyes cut at her, the swift way she handled the bottle, already pouring two glasses, putting the cork back with ease, jittering hands of anticipation betraying her own bad habit.

"Sure." he then said dryly and she halted, drawing in a deep breath.

"I feel like I need to apologize for…making things awkward between Levi and you today." She sighed, her face remaining in shadow, yet her white gown revealed some light upon her.

"Hm." He raised a brow, surprised to hear her say this.

She walked around the kitchen isle, glass in hand, arm reaching for the candle again. Her face emerged back, warmed sharply by the flame. She approached him, handing him the glass.

"Ain't no big deal." he muttered, taking a big sip; wetting his chapped lips.

A welcoming, tingly burn hit his throat.

"You know…Levi is just very protective of family; he lost his at an early age, so…he cares a lot about who he has left." she said, and Mac side-eyed her beneath the brim of his hat. "I'm sure he doesn't mean it personally towards you, besides, he might just be showing off to your friend, Charlotte." She chuckled, pulled up a chair and sat before him, straddling it with long, toned legs; those of a huntress who spent hours hiking through woods.

"Like I said; it ain't no big deal." he grunted, reeling himself back to the sickening thoughts of them together, still far away from his sight.

"My boy…Jonathan, he…he begged me to ask you something." she said, blushing, pulling Mac's attention back to her.

"Hm…"

"He wanted to know if…if you are married, or…have a significant other." She chuckled nervously and Mac snorted snidely, somehow feeling the whiskey dimming his anger. "But of course, you don't have to answer that. I suppose…my boy is quite curious, at this age…" she said, as though she spoke about herself.

"Hm…" He bobbed his head with suspicion. "No, lass…" he said shortly, taking another sip.

"Oh…" Her mouth curved into a smile, suppressing a cheering laughter. "Well, I sympathize to such concept of loneliness…" she said, slowly spreading her legs open to wrap around the back of the chair better, spreading open her nightgown with them. His eyes cut at them, noticing her legs shift methodically to get his attention.

"How are your sutures?" She changed the subject, glanced at his wounded arm. Mac sighed and twisted his arm as if to see for himself, then stretched it out for her to inspect it further. She clutched his arm and brushed her fingers across the sutures, tapping softly against them. "Yes, it seems to be healing fast." She smiled at him, subtly caressing his arm, feeling a strange tension and thrill to hold the arm of a legendary murderer. "Can I come closer, to see?" she asked with a sultry whisper, already standing up, kneeling before him, clinging onto his vascular arm.

Mac studied her; pale fingers glided over his roughened skin, slowly reaching up his shoulder, climbing over the usual black cotton shirt he wore most of the time.

"You…you have such muscular arms." She gasped softly, jittering hand feeling of the swell of his upper arm, gently squeezing his muscles in her palm, face leaning before his chest. Quivering whole, for she hadn't felt of a man's muscles in too long, years spent in solitude, in a concept of forced celibacy; almost forgetting how different they felt compared to her own — stronger, manlier, harder — she couldn't help but yearn to feel more.

Mac observed her every single move; yet his expression remained cold and emotionless. He knew where this was leading; ironically he knew how women worked, or thought, or behaved around a man they were ready to please…he had seen it before.

Her hands crept up to his brawny chest, clutched it hard, feeling the warmth within him, sweltering her sweaty palms. A shiver rushed down her spine, witnessing such a perfectly shaped, large, and firm pectoral. Fingers slid over his tiny hardened nipples, reaching down to his stomach — joyfully feeling every single shape of his thick, protruding abs.

Mac watched her curiously, in silence, took another sip of whiskey, and glanced out the window to see if they had returned. Staring at the dark meadows down the hill, he felt her hands carefully inspecting his abdomen, gliding harsh and fervently across it, nails raking it, as though unable to control her lust, yet he himself, felt hollow and frozen — as if imaginary threads were holding him still on that bench.

"I'm a widow…but I'm not dead yet…" she said in earnest, leaned back in the chair and slipped a finger through the gown's strap, pulling it down her arm, fronting him with her breasts; her skin was fair, prickled, her nipples stood erect. Mac's eyes set on them, yet lifted them back to face her.

"Please…stay with us…" She sighed, gasped, as her hand slid down to his buttoned-up pants, subtly brushing over his bulge, already surprisingly hard and impressively large underneath her hand.

She looked up at Mac, oddly puzzled by his lack of expression; dull, grim, thinking she needed to stop, but could not. She grabbed him tighter instead, somehow needing it, somehow hungering to feel him throb against the palm of her hand. Squeezing him rhythmically, his cock stiffened, and Mac watched her patiently; benumbed, feeling himself get harder beneath the cloth, yet knew it was nothing but his bare instinct, simply part of being a man — the plain, mechanical nature of getting an erection with no reasoning behind it, the way he knew all too well, for he had never felt real pleasure in his life.

Farmer Grossman ensured to teach him how to associate a man's lust with nothingness; how to rob him from the purest of feeling man could discover, how to evoke the sensation of being raped by him every time a woman touched him. In failed attempts to drown this memory that assailed him, he chose to sleep with a working lady that was foolish enough to risk her life with him, and yet, all he could feel was the urge to escape the torture, but the authoritative voice nailed him to the ground; paralyzing him like a soldier on duty, until the deed was done.

Amara was no different.

III

DISMOUNTING AT THE HOMESTEAD IN THE THUNDER AND RAIN, Levi had her words still repeating in his head; realizing he was no more than a friend to her, and perhaps she had been clear about this from the beginning, yet he was too deaf to hear it, too blind to see it, and too stubborn to believe it.

They led the horse to the barn, a big shack stocked up with piles of square hay bales for the expected heavy winter. She greeted Finn, gave him a pat on the neck, and turned to face Levi.

"Thank you…Levi. It was…refreshing to get out, after these stressful days." she muttered, trying to end the night on a positive note.

"Yup. You're welcome." he said shortly, as he loosened the woolen cinch on his horse — her words still ringing in his ear.

"I'll let you two to it then; I'm quite exhausted…" she said as she glanced over at Finn once more, resting on his side, cocooned in a blanket of warm straw.

Levi looked back at her as she rushed towards the house. He sighed deeply, feeling rejected all over again. "What a damn fool I am…" he fussed to himself, and pulled the saddle swiftly off his steed.

The storm was relentless; blowing its wrath wildly against the windows of the house; slamming countless droplets of rain upon the foggy glass, rattling the timber as though hands had gripped it in rage.

Charlotte snapped the heavy door open, her frozen fingers slid off the round handle, shooting a harrowing ache to her wrists from the sudden abrupt movement. She grunted, flustered, then took off her coat and hung it on the wall in hopes it would dry overnight, for the house felt toasty enough from the ongoing fire. Taking off her boots, she poured out the collected water from within, stretched her ice-cold feet and wiggled her benumbed toes to regain some feeling.

Approaching the stairs to her room, a sudden noise hit her ears, coming from the living area of the house, which made her wonder in fright, figuring everyone would be asleep by now. Another grunt; this time louder, harsher, emerging from inside. She strode slowly, in slyness, merging with the shadows, deep breath held within her, worried it might be deputies lurking around like they did at Will's cabin that time.

She leaned against the wall cautiously and poked her head slowly around the entryway, peeking through the gap. Her eyes flared, aglow, slashing through the darkness, face falling like thunder, clapping against the oaken ground, yet it only echoed in her head. Blanched. Paled. Blinking tightly, forcing her eyes back open, she felt her heart constrict, punctured a million times over by tiny sharp pins; stinging. There was burning in her lungs as she desperately tried to draw in enough air to breathe. There was she, standing in the shadows, bracing at the flimsy cabinet for support, staring, wishing her eyes would go blind. She crumbled, legs felt gone from underneath her, stomach jolted up to her throat.

And there they were; Amara straddling Mac, with her nightgown halfway down; pressing her perky breasts against his chest, kissing him demandingly, possessively, stealing his chapped lips from *her*. Before she could stop herself, a loud gasp of panic escaped her mouth that traveled right to Mac's ears.

He squinted his eyes suspiciously, side-eyed the doorway, spotting a faint, familiar silhouette in the darkness. Charlotte pressed her hand against her mouth and ran back to the pitch-black kitchen; meeting Levi who had just come in.

"Charlotte?" he said loudly, and she slammed her hand across his mouth, instantly silencing him. He gaped at her, winced, as tears started to flow unapologetically across her face, chest expanding swiftly from hyperventilating, sadness and shock clouding her sharp features. "Wh-t h-pp-n-d??" he mumbled beneath her cold hand, frowning suspiciously — his warm breath subtly misting her fingers.

Charlotte swallowed repeatedly for her throat felt swollen, dry, knotty, clogged up, choking her alive — she couldn't find the words to explain what she had just witnessed; all she knew was her heart had never felt such woe and harrow before; pain, tearing her apart. She longed to scream, let out an explosion of emotions that were so foreign to her — clasp them and yank them out of her, out and far away from her pure self, whatever purity was left within her. The image kept on repeating in her head, assailing her ruthlessly, and she cried more tensely and ever louder.

Levi was left speechless; his expression hardened, for he had never seen her in such distress before. He gently took her hand away, and marched confidently to the main area.

Charlotte rushed in front of him, trying to stop him from creating a huge scene — worrying he might murder Mac, if she wouldn't murder him first that was. "Please. Don't. I…I will explain." She sobbed, stammered, clasping his soaking shirt tightly in her fists.

Levi's suspicion only grew; he knew he could push her away without a single effort; he knew she was protecting a certain something, or someone, *and that could only be Mac Kinnon.* "What's going on, Charlotte?" he whispered solemnly, expecting an explanation.

"Let's…let's go…please!" She urged him, trembling fingers tugged on his shirt, face overtaken by terror. Levi's face went blank, studying her painful eyes, feeling great empathy for her obvious state of devastation. Biting his lip agitatedly, he led her shaking self up the stairs to her guest room.

IV

"YOU'VE SINNED, WILLIAM. WORSE THAN YOUR FATHER EVER DID. *You've sinned, and everyone will find out."* a voice warned him, as if a large entity sat heavily upon his shoulders, crawling down his chest, clutching tight, slender fingers slithering through his shirtfront, claws raking his skin, and yet, he was benumbed.

Defeated.

"It...wasn't me..." Will said tentatively, sweaty hands gripped tightly around the rifle; doubting himself once more.

"*But it was, William. Who else could have killed her? Only but you, William. You can still see your reflection in her cold green eyes...a brooding reflection...*" it mocked him further, a shrill voice drilling into his ear, a rotten breath of death exhaling through his mouth, yet it wasn't his.

"It was YOU! Not me!!!" he yelled, devastated. He wailed from the top of his lungs, the echo of his blood-curdling caterwaul vibrating against the trees of the entire forest, yet the voices multiplied, swarming him, muffling every breath that pierced out of his lungs. They laughed tauntingly within his head — torturing him endlessly, louder, deeper, higher pitched in almost a demonic tone.

He tried to make them vanish, could not, realized he was trapped within a cage with no lock. Clenching his teeth, he hooked his nails into his skull and dug deep, squeezing, pressing against the dent. There were shadows fighting in his vision, blinding him, filling him up with darkness, much different than the ebony night, much different than the eyelids that rested.

"*Get out of the forest, traveler...hold your candle high, light up the path with the purity of your heart.*" a gentle voice brushed against him, yet another interjected swiftly, swallowing it whole in darkness.

"*What is wrong, William...you almighty elite...don't you understand you inflicted this upon yourself? You're pathetic...*" The voice was soft, yet deep, yet more human.

"*You're infested...and I pity you; but I'm starved...for too long, I've been starved. And now, I need you...I need the missing piece, William. You shall feel the same suffering now. Enjoy your mind...be deranged, in delight.*"

"Who are you??!" Will screamed, wailed, moaned, clutched the rifle tighter.

"*Who am I...you ask?*" There was a snide chuckle in its voice. There was pain in his head, heart constricting as though it was sliced apart. Pressure in his skull, needles through its dent; he felt the breathing, heard it, quivered beneath its menace.

Eyes swiftly set down at the rifle, once kind eyes flooded with tears; now as dull and lifeless as he longed to be. He put the rusty barrel in his mouth — gently, like he always used to handle anything he touched — tasting the iron of the weapon, tasting his own fear as well. He glanced up at the storm clouds, slowly tearing each other apart, separating into tiny groups, revealing the faded blanket of stars behind them. It appeared rather peaceful, felt it would be still, quiet. He cried and slid his finger through the trigger guard, then cowardly paused himself for a brief, fleeting moment.

"William, my darling…" An intimate, soft voice appeared behind him, his hair stood erect. Will turned his head hesitantly to witness a bright entity walking towards him. Gun still in his mouth, he remained silent — awaiting the entity to reveal itself. A frail woman with long black hair and blue eyes stopped before him, kneeling down, locking her gaze with his.

"M…mother…" he muttered, sliding the barrel out of his mouth, heart warming up in an instant upon recognizing her serene face, lips cracking a smile after drowning in hollowness. His hand reached for her, yet it went right through the cloth.

"Shh…it's alright, my son." She smiled at him endearingly, hand caressing his head gently; it was rotten, decomposed, bleached bone.

"Mother…" He choked. "Are you…are you real? Is it really you?" he asked, trembling.

"Of course, my darling…" She sighed, tears stood in her eyes.

"I'm…so sorry for what I did…I sinned…I…killed…my wife!" he yelled, reeling back into a heartbreaking sob.

"Shhh…it was her time to go, William…" she said and he looked at her, trying to make sense of it.

"I'm…I think it's over…I…I cannot do this any longer."

He sobbed, holding her cold hand pressed against his cheek.

"Nothing is over, William…" She smirked lovingly, stared into his soulful eyes, begging for her tender hug.

"I'm…I'm just afraid. I'm scared, mother…how will it feel…" he cried, lost, looking back down at the weapon.

"Oh, don't be afraid, my son. There is beauty in darkness…there is peace where we wander. Your mother and father are so very proud of you…come to us, to be reunited again. A pile of bones…bare, in blackness. Hearts merging, mine will be yours, and yours will be mine." she pleaded, reaching down to the rifle, leading the barrel back into his mouth.

Will froze, rehearsing her words with the last trace of sense within him; realizing she'd never mutter such — for she cared too much about him to ask for a sacrifice; and his father…*he never was proud of him,* he thought to himself, as she moved her fingers over his; coiled around the trigger.

"No!" he said solemnly, pulling the barrel out again, grinding his teeth abruptly against the metal. "You are not…my mother." He leered into the entity's eyes, courageous and brave, standing tall, standing proud.

Eyes shut. They opened. Aglow. Locking his. Eerily black, painting his reflection across them, sucking it deep within them, sucking his breath, pulling the purest of souls into them.

"GIVE IT TO US!!!"

There was no tender voice in the air around him, there was a clop of thunder in his head, rattling him around, visions that assailed him, a flash of a dead body laying flat against the pebbled shore; blood oozing out of its skull, face, a layer of ashy flakes peeling off from it and blowing in the wind.

The voices screamed louder, suffocating him the more he tried to yell for help. The scent of rotting flesh smothered him, unable to escape from it. He grabbed the rifle, unwillingly, and forced it against the roof of his mouth — scraping it raw from the sudden pressure.

He looked up at the stars, counting one by one.

"One…two…three…four…"

"I am…you."

CHAPTER 51

Heartbroken

I

"CALM DOWN, CHARLOTTE. It's alright. Take deep breaths." Levi instructed, seated beside her on the bed, arm wrapped around her, both drenched in rainwater.

"I…I just…have never felt like this before — so much…pain!!" she screamed a stuttering cry; burying her face in her hands, so as to not make any more loud noises, muffling herself, pressing her fingers into her lips, teeth gnashed and mouth fell open to inhale a wisp of air to breathe. "I never knew how a broken heart felt like, but now…now, I do…it's broken! It's f…damn broken…" she cried, and Levi caressed her back tenderly.

"I understand, cowgirl…" He sighed, swallowed awkwardly, somehow his own felt shattered. "Kinnon again?" he asked, for he still didn't even know why they were up here hiding and sobbing. Charlotte turned her head to him, paused to find the right words to explain what she saw — yet only tears came out of her. "Charlotte…hey…" He tilted her head up, thumb pressed gently underneath her chin. "What did he do this time?" he asked solemnly, loathing to see her like this.

"He…he is down there, Levi. Down there…with *her!*"

Levi's face blanched, green eyes turned cold — moss frozen beneath a layer of hoarfrost. Imagining the worst, instantly realizing she was talking about Amara. "What do you mean, Charlotte?" He pressured her. "Please, tell me!" He grabbed her from the shoulders, forcing her to face him, holding her eyes with his piercing gaze, not letting go.

"They was…they was kissing! And she was…" She sobbed, forced herself into his embrace, and clutched his back tightly.

Levi fumed; breath burned against her neck.

"GGHH!!!" She groaned. "He was my first kiss!!" she yelled, muffled, wailed into his wet shirt. "How could he just…throw everything like that away!! Why would he!! Why would he hurt me like that!!" She balled a fist and hit it against his rock-hard chest. "I guess I'm not brave enough…or hunting good enough…or not…*being enough,* for his stupid taste!" she growled, squeezed her eyes shut, feeling her heart tear apart in the cruelest form possible.

"I'm…I'm sorry, Charlotte…" he soughed, caressed her back sweetly; burying his ego and anger within her cloth.

"Please…don't tell anyone a thing…please." she begged, oddly feeling embarrassed to have walked into them, oddly feeling wrong for her selfish reaction. Oddly feeling too much, too fast.

"I'll do my best…" He delayed his answer, knowing he could never keep his feelings nor thoughts within himself. "Will you be okay tonight?" he asked her, feeling of her trembling body, clutched to him, leaning into him; he held strong.

"No…I won't. I won't ever be…" She wiped her tears with a wet sleeve, only to shed some more. "In fact…I've never been okay." She snorted caustically. "My mother must have cursed me…there's no other explanation for this sorcery…how could I have been so *wrong* about him…" she said and he cocked a brow.

"Cursed you?"

"No…" She tittered beneath her sob. "Heck, I don't know. If it ain't God, it's gotta be her." She joked, pulled back and sniffed.

"Here, cowgirl." He handed her a soaked cigarette out of his pant's pocket, after fishing for it for the past minutes.

"You want to poison me even more? 'Shine wasn't enough?" She forced a smirk on her lips.

"There are times like these…when a cigarette is warranted. You know it's bad for you, but…I'll be damned if love isn't just as bad, if not worse." he stated, and lit up one for himself.

568

"Most definitely worse…" she added, and gladly accepted the cigarette still waiting in between his ring-cloaked fingers. They tittered together, puffed and exhaled the smoke simultaneously — only Charlotte was choking and coughing awkwardly, making herself chuckle even more.

I I

SUCKING ON HIS CRACKED LIPS, her hands worked on his pants — unbuttoning them hastily; anticipating to feel his hard cock that was stubbornly pressing against the fabric, violently bending underneath her, yet Mac suddenly grabbed her neck harshly, and pushed her face away from him.

"Stop." he ordered earnestly, looking at the doorway of her room.

"What?" She gaped at him, still a faint smile lingering on her lips.

"I said stop. It's over." he said, choking himself with an odd feeling of worry.

"But…I'm confused. Everyone is asleep. Are — are you worried?" she stuttered, trying to figure him out, trying to read him, noticing the vein that popped across his forehead, the grim mask he wore.

"It's time for me to leave." he said, pushed her off his lap, stood up himself and made his way to his room.

Amara pulled her nightgown up over her chest, adjusted her disheveled hair — brushing through it with her fingers in sheer bewilderment, raking it all together into a lazy bun. Petrified by his menacing leer as though a switch flipped within him, she gaped at him forming into a shadow, crossing the narrow path, leaving her only with the echo of boots clopping against wood.

Mac hiked up the stairs, pausing near Charlotte's room; noticing the wooden floorboards before it, covered with tiny puddles of water.

He saw her; he saw her see them.

He stood quietly before the door, fingers faintly brushing against it, for no other reason than to cower behind the oaken wall with a knob in the lower left to be left untouched, rehearsing the words he couldn't express, didn't know how to. Hearing a sudden chatter, a laugh here and there, smelling the scent of cigarette slither through the narrow gap of the door, teeth clenched.

He was there.

Fingers retracted into a fist, and yet he felt a sudden shot in the gut — an eerie feeling he could not explain. It shot him through flesh and bone, spiraling a bile of nausea up his throat. The bullet ached every bone in his being; kept shooting through. Rattling the cage of his ribs. Guilt, perhaps, as if he had done something forbidden — something deserving of punishment, something immoral, which felt the height of irony for his entire life had been an immoral one.

Yet this time, it was different.

It felt different.

Hollowness changed, unseen, into a heart throbbing to feel.

I I I

THE SUN ROSE ABOVE THE HOMESTEAD AT RAVENHEART POND, where lay the shallow lagoon, engulfed by a bright wing, slashing through the early haze. Temperature felt low, competing with a sweltering fire still dancing wildly in a gray-slate chimney, reflecting warmly against its rugged stones, soft ash trailing upwards the hollow suction, billowing from it back out into the open air. A shadow painted beneath the cloud, then it left.

JB poked it steadily, paused, drank a hearty sip from his coffee — bitter black, a shot of whiskey twirled in, swearing by it, as though it was the best remedy for his chronic arthritis, as well as any fungus known and unknown to man he'd ever been misfortune enough to have gotten.

Amara walked in with the boy in her arms, a balled tiny fist still rubbing his sleepy eyes — looking around his surroundings curiously to see who was there, disappointed to find Mac wasn't.

"Hey!!" JB enthusiastically greeted her, spilling his coffee as he waved his hands around.

"Good morning, JB." she hummed softly, yet undeniably her wavering voice sounded tired and sorrowful. She put Jonathan down, and he ran to hug JB. In a way, he loved him, he grew up around him — even though JB could talk his ears off, he enjoyed all his made-up stories and his lightheartedness — always making everyone laugh, even unintentionally. Most of the time, unintentionally.

"Slept well, miss?" JB asked her, poured some more remedy into his coffee, squinting to count his dose, only to overdose himself.

"…kind of. It was a long night." She sighed, cast a glimpse at the bench before her, reminiscing every little detail and feeling from last night.

"Ah! That's a pity. I slept like a darn rock! Sometimes I wish I still had my cabin back in Red Giants; I've lost so much sleep and peace and quiet living in them tents over the years. But oh well, oh well…can't have everything in life, right Jonny? We can't get spoiled now! Actually, we are already spoiled, only in a…*different* way. HaHA!" He chuckled on his own, then glanced over at Amara, who stood there, expressionless, dulled. "Eh…well…maybe not." He bowed his head, lip and beard dipping into the cup, and sipped on his coffee quietly.

"Where is everyone, JB?" she asked curiously, poured herself some coffee, mixing in some whiskey herself, needing it more than ever.

"Well! I wasn't the first one awake, surprisingly! The legendary Kinnon was already here poking the fire and sharpening his knife. Boy, that's a mighty Bowie knife if I ever saw one!" He cackled, eyes flared in awe.

"Yes…I reckon it was mighty…" She sighed, flustered.

"That's all who I saw, before I had some serious tummy rumblings — not sure what in tarnation I ate wrong again! But boy! We might need to check on that outhouse again; not sure if it'll survive another round of that!"

"Ewww!" Jonathan interjected, frowning his face in disgust, crinkling his lips with a milk mustache plastered above them.

"Jonny boy, if ya only knew what your poor ma had to witness as ya was growing up! Ha! Luckily, Levi came to me already potty trained!" He winked at Amara, and she started blankly back at him, unable to feel amused.

"Feeeeck…" Jonathan said, and JB burst into laughter, finding it quite amusing now, as Amara scanned the wall for Mac's coat, utterly detached.

"JB, where did Mac…Mr. Kinnon go?" she asked yet again, losing her patience.

"Out and 'bout!" He proudly answered, pointing at the door, cup still clutched in his grip, spilling coffee as his finger waggled with it.

"To do what there? It's freezing cold outside!" She hissed, fearing he might be preparing to leave.

"Ha! Do ya really think I'd dare to ask him that? If I even fart wrong, he looks at me like he'd skin me alive!" He chuckled, then noticed Amara swiftly covering the boy's ears — realizing too late how just the mention of skinning someone was deeply triggering for him.

"...I should *not* have said that..."

"I will go check on him...bring...bring him a cup of coffee." she stuttered, trying to find an excuse so her worry was not too obvious, or rather, her pitiful need for him.

I V

A LOUD NOISE, A FORCEFUL THUD, like a gunshot hitting the window, woke up a very startled Charlotte and Levi, as they lay there, still holding each other, fallen asleep entwined, sometime in the early dawn. An impressive grouping of burnt cigarette butts was spread out across the floor, scattered like the stories they exchanged all night — and their soaking wet clothes had miraculously dried up from their bodies' warmth radiating between each other.

"What was that??" Charlotte gasped, scanning around the room.

Levi glanced at the window to notice a trail of fresh blood dripping down the glass, three lines forked across it. "Something must've hit the window — a bird, possibly." he calmly explained as he looked out, spotting something black and lifeless on the ground.

"But...that sounded far...larger, than just a bird crashing? It sounded like...a gunshot?" She doubted herself, staring at his lips, waiting to hear a confirmation.

"Yes it did...but, a bullet would have busted the glass." he mumbled, confused himself. "What time is it anyway? It sure is bright outside. You want to grab some breakfast together?" he offered, knowing she might be too shy to go downstairs.

"...could you bring it up here, please? Just one slice of bread, and some cheese." She begged him, eyes still bloodshot from all the wailing.

"Charlotte! You can't be hiding up here for an eternity. Always face your fears; that's the only way to grow stronger." He smirked kindly, and encouraged her to come with him.

"Fine…but we both need to change our clothes. We look…we look horrific!" She huffed, realizing her shirt seemed like a horse had stomped aggressively on it, miraculously crumpled without making it dirty.

"Alright. So, which shirt do you recommend for me? The lacy white blouse? The tiny black button-up cotton shirt?" He teased her, going through a pile of her clothes she always kept in her saddle bags.

"Ha-ha. Very funny!" She snorted and he shrugged, dropping the cloth. "Ah, Levi." She walked up to him, and hugged him tightly. "Thank you for staying up with me last night, and for just…being there…after everything…" she said, exhaling deeply in his large, sheltering arms, feeling as though their friendship was bound to last through any hardship, feeling as though they had reached a clear, mutual understanding.

"'Course, cowgirl. Anytime." he soughed, yet his heart wrenched in loneliness, realizing his place in hers. He smelled the smokiness for the first time in her hair, torturing the memory of them huddled close, arms coiling her, hand clutching his knee, making him still yearn for more. Reminiscing the night of laughter spent together — sharing about all the bad experiences he had with women, mocking each other for being so sensitive, so gullible…always ending up hurt and disappointed, his heart ached for more.

V

"I THOUGHT, PERHAPS, YOU WOULD ENJOY A CUP OF COFFEE…" she offered Mac, stepping into the shack to see him saddling up his black stallion.

Mac threw a sharply agitated look at her, then exhaled deeply.

"Not needed." he mumbled shortly and unclear, while his horse drew in a deep breath habitually before he tightened the cinch.

"Oh…I'm sorry." she stuttered nervously, trying to come up with ideas to continue the already dead conversation. She strode tentatively to him, caressing the horse's neck, soft and fuzzy, already preparing for the heavy winter that was promised to come.

"So, you're…"

"Leavin'." He voiced the words she dreaded to hear, flipped the saddlebags over the horse and methodically attached them to the saddle's metal loops — slowly sliding the leather strings through them, pulling them back in, tying them securely in a knot.

"Oh…so soon?" she questioned him with trembling lips, feeling herself get heated by his unfair behavior.

Mac didn't let a word escape his lips; he tightened the cinch one last time, and pulled the reins over Roy's head.

"Mr. Kinnon? Did I do something wrong?" she asked him again, the warm coffee cup burning her hands, yet nothing mattered, nothing could be felt at that moment.

"Not needed." he repeated himself.

"I don't understand…what is not needed?" She swallowed dryly, fuming with his lack of communication skills.

"All that happened." He snatched the hat off the horn and put it on, covering his face with a shadow.

"Why? I thought you were enjoying it…at least that's what it seemed, or… felt like!" She exploded on him, frustrated with his riddles, heartbroken over his lack of affection — treating her like a prostitute he didn't even pay, but only disposed of after he was done. Mac smirked sardonically, about the only time she'd ever seen him crack a smile since she met him. "What is so funny, Kinnon?" she questioned him, as she would her own child.

"What's funny is that ye believe I give a flyin' feck 'bout yesterday." he scowled, locking eyes with her intimidatingly.

Amara couldn't restrain herself, clutched a fist, and slapped him unexpectedly across his face — leaving a red rash on his cheek. "Don't you talk to me like that! Ever again!" she warned, reminding him she wasn't just a regular town girl; but instead grew up in the wilderness of Red Giants, surrounded by countless degenerates that weren't any better than him, only much dumber.

Mac walked slowly towards her — his hooded eyes drilling right through hers. "If ye think for a moment, lass, that I'd ever hesitate to slice yer throat open just 'cause ye showed me a pair of tits I seen already so many damn times before, not by sleepin' 'round like a horny ol' mutt, but by strippin' the lasses of their clothes, for the only purpose of pryin' their goddamn rib-cages apart with me knife…if ye think so, yer greatly mistaken." he warned her back, meaning every demeaning word he said.

Amara blinked, speechless. Her face fell, mouth pried open, aghast. This was the single longest sentence she'd ever heard leave his mouth, and one she certainly would never forget. She took a deep breath, as though she was hunting for a bear in Red Giants — grounding herself; regaining her calm, as a huntress would always strive to do.

"Well, I guess then, what they say about you…was true."

"Never claimed otherwise." he said swiftly and in earnest, before she could insult him any further.

Suddenly JB walked into the shack led by the hand of the boy, smiling widely to report some great news. "Oh! Didn't mean to disturb you two!" He winked at Amara, wiggling those wiry brows to her, realizing they must be having an intimate conversation that was obviously going well — judging by how close they were facing each other.

"Ya ain't." Mac answered swiftly. "Was just leavin', anyway." he added, and led his horse outside.

JB looked at Amara, confused, as she looked back at him — still fuming from their argument, embarrassed to the core to be left standing before Jonathan's innocent eyes.

Jonathan stared at Mac, wiggled his feisty being around, escaping from JB's grip. He ran to him as fast as his little feet would take him, and Amara rushed right after him — suddenly feeling protective over the son her lustful desire had forgotten. The boy wrapped his arms around Mac's leg, bursting into tears, wailing frantically. "Please! Don't go, Mr. Kinnon!! Please!" He sobbed, pleaded, smearing snot over his rugged pants, as Mac kept on walking, barely feeling Jonathan's weight clutched on him.

"Jonathan! Let the man go." she ordered firmly, grabbed him harshly from his arms, unwrapping him from his limb.

"Feck…" He pouted, muttered beneath his breath, slowly realizing the meaning of the word after all.

"Well!" JB interjected the dramatic scene with a fat smile on his face.

"Perhaps you shouldn't be going just yet, Mr. Kinnon!" He popped up swiftly between them, still excited to deliver the news.

"And why's that, ol' man?" Mac turned his head towards him, thinking this would be the last time he'd hear his annoying voice again.

"You like *'shine,* my friend?" JB asked him, brows flickering wildly, eyes protruding and lifting at the same time, brandishing a cocked head and a smirk of confidence, all while a breath smelling of rotten egg and offal reached Mac's nose. Mac, taken aback by the most ridiculous grimace he had ever seen, simply stared at him, left wordless.

"What is this about, JB??" Amara interrupted, for she couldn't stand to be next to Mac anymore, wishing he would be gone already, wishing to crawl back in her nook of loneliness, to play the role of a widow with a child.

"Well, oh well! You know it's Levi's birthday soon, ah?" The brows flickered again, wiry and wild, frizzed by the chilled air.

"Yes?"

"I mean…*real soon*…like, tomorrow soon!" JB giggled with excitement, rubbing the dirty palms of his hands together.

"Yes, JB! I know exactly when it is! Spill the beans already, will you?" she hissed, flustered, as she saw Mac light up a cigarette — polluting the air they all breathed, as he puffed and exhaled the smoke steadily.

"I got…a long-awaited report back! I visited the station this morning, and sure enough…there was mail! My dearest friend will be coming over with a large wagon of moonshine tomorrow evening!" He proudly announced, hopped up and down with joy, knee creaking every time he did. "She'll be bringing her band over too — let me tell ya, them bunch of hillbillies *know* how to tickle a banjo!" He positioned himself, imitating the banjo player with his round sausage fingers and a face of extreme concentration.

Amara's agitated wrinkles disappeared off her forehead the moment she heard the thrilling news. Her heart leaped with a sudden rush of joy, imagining the big celebration tomorrow — being surrounded with delicious food, live folk music, and enough liquor to last Levi for a lifetime.

JB might've been thought of as a clown by many, but he was also one of the most organized and punctual people imaginable. He had been working extra for months on a pile of hides of the highest quality he could possibly manage, simply in order to trade for the wagon full of moonshine. Every year he took Levi's celebration seriously, ever since he took him under his wing. In his older age, it was the only important event in his life that he looked forward to.

"So, Mr. Kinnon, ya understand ya can't be leavin' now! It would be rude! And ya ain't a rude kind of guy, are ya?" He winked at him, and Mac leered back in response. "Well…maybe you are…but not tonight, and certainly not tomorrow!! For we will have a hell of a good time! Let's just get drunk, us fellow gunslingers or…poor bastards, and just enjoy not being chased after for once. Shall we?"

CHAPTER 52

Let it Happen

I

LEVI STEPPED OUTSIDE AFTER SEARCHING THE WHOLE HOUSE, trying to find everyone with no luck. "What's going on!" he yelled, eyes inspecting his surroundings, counting every single one of them — studying the different expressions on their faces — some guilty, others desperately hiding their agitation.

"Levi! Levi, my boy! All is well here with us! Amara and Mac had a little chit-chatty in the shack in this fiiine morning, and Jonathan and I were just learning 'bout different breeds of...of..." He looked around nervously. "of trees!" he added satisfied, as Jonathan looked at him confused.

"Aha. I see." he hummed shortly, giving a warning look to Mac — with an imputation only men could recognize.

"So, where's Charlotte?! Haven't seen her all morning! Is she sick? Feeling okay? Does she need a warm stew? I can start it right now!" he bombarded Levi with relentless questions.

"No, she is fine. Considering." he insinuated, locking eyes with Mac who wondered if he knew too.

"Wonderful! So...did ya two have a good time last night?" JB asked him with a wink, as a father would ask his son excitedly — only not in front of such an awkward audience.

"Yes. We sure did." He smirked, side-eyeing Mac's grim face.

"Excellent! Why don't ya two go hunt us some deer now? We're gonna need 'em!" His eyes suddenly flared, thinking of all the people he had invited for tomorrow's celebration — already stressing out over it, even if it was his own plan all along.

"What?!" Levi frowned, confused, for the last thing he wanted was to be around the man who apparently slept with his cousin.

"C'me on, Levi! We have mouths to feed!" He pushed Levi's tall being with all his strength towards his horse, already saddled up by JB — who had worked on his master plan all morning.

Mac mounted Roy — deep inside, there was a hint of relief for not leaving, for he knew no birthday party in the world would tie him down, certainly not Levi's. As much as he felt the need to cower away in shame, not wishing to be seen by her eyes as someone he was not, the thought of leaving Charlotte behind, again, utterly burned him alive. For the first time, he felt attached to someone, something he had never been before. A lone wolf all his life, yet felt himself oddly dependent on her; feeling like part of him was incomplete without her presence.

He reminisced the way she ran after him during the down-pouring storm at Great Bend; begging him to not leave — yet could not oblige, for she didn't know better, she didn't know what was hidden behind his mask, she never knew his legend, it oddly appeared to him, besides what Dorman had warned her about — a speck of sand in all the information from a whole vast desert.

She didn't fear him all that much, somehow she trusted him instead. *She was naïve,* he thought. A young woman that tasted the lips of a man for the first time, albeit unbeknownst to him. And he was but a man of flesh, sinews, blood, and bone; sewn together from tarnished parts into an incongruous whole, restlessly laying awake at nights, dreading to kill as the urge to find relief crept up on him, ending up slicing the innocence out of people's hearts after all, only to refill himself with a moment's worth of wicked contentment, only to stroke a few scarlet layers upon his canvas of bleak blackness, watch them dissolve into him. He thought about her — denying with every fiber of his being, just how much he missed her. Realizing, her naïvety was but innocence, coloring his darkness in a better light.

I I

SHERIFF DORMAN SIPPED ON HIS WARM BREWED COFFEE, aligning it with its regular old stain on the table as he put it back down. He huffed, disappointed, realizing the blood trail must be gone by now with all the rain they had gotten — making things more complicated, as it seemed to always happen like that.

He cut his eyes over at the deputy, seated in a corner, legs crossed high on top of another chair. Hat tilted over his face, resting like there wasn't anything important to do. He sniffed his coffee-stained mustache, and frustratedly marched to the deputy, kicking the chair swiftly from underneath his feet — dropping his legs abruptly to the ground; boot heels banging loudly against it.

"Sheriff!!" The deputy awoke, gasped, startled to see him above him with arms folded angrily, face contorted.

"I need ya to get Sheriff Faust up in Rockvale, and all his deputies, out here… tonight!" Sheriff Dorman ordered, fuming to the core.

"Yes, boss. What…what should I report the reason is?" he asked worriedly, knowing Dorman's stubbornness would put him in his grave sooner or later.

"Report to him…" Dorman sighed, puffing on his third cigar that morning. "That there's a wife-killin', lyin', no-good son-of-a-bitch that's hidin' in damn Feasters territory!" he yelled, almost choking on his rage.

"Y-yes, sir." he stammered, dithering, realizing he'd be going back into the forest — unsure if he'd be lucky to make it out alive a second time.

"What ya waitin' for, beatin' 'round the bush like that? GIT!!!" he scowled, and the townsfolk halted their peaceful stroll outside, jerking their heads towards the noise. Dorman watched him rush out of the door, and glanced over at the posters still hanging in his office, a new layer of dust cloaking them whole…Mac's, Charlotte's, and Will's. He rubbed his forehead, feeling greatly disoriented; light-headed from the wrathful throb, pounding within him all these years of a drudging ghost hunt, slowly slithering him into a state of madness.

III

CHARLOTTE SAT QUIETLY IN THE FAR CORNER OF THE DINING ROOM — trying hard not to glance over at *that bench,* as she munched on a piece of rye bread, smothered in fresh butter, dressed with a thick slice of cheese — homemade, straight from the farmer's hands down at Holy Ranch. It was delicious, in all its simplicity, yet, a bitter bile remained in the back of her throat.

Amara strode in, refreshed to spot Charlotte, feeling as though she was the only normal one she could possibly vent to. Charlotte almost choked on the bread crumbs the moment Amara sat beside her, wrapping an arm around her — awfully heavy and uncomfortable.

"Ah, Charlotte…" She sighed heavily. "We are surrounded by some big man-children, aren't we?" She forced a chuckle.

Charlotte noted her tone, bewildered, for it screamed disappointment and resentment. "I guess so…" She smirked vaguely.

"How do you like that cheese?" she asked, utterly random.

"It's…it's really remarkable." she said, awkwardly in return.

"Holy Ranch has the greatest variety of fresh produce…and so on…" she said, somehow her voice dozed off; it quietened, turned feeble, as though she fought back a sob. Charlotte's heart sunk.

"Yes…from what I've tasted so far, which I'm…still extremely thankful to you for letting us stay so long, and…"

"Oh, don't mention it…sometimes the house gets too still, even with a boy storming through it…" She snorted. "It's good to have some company sometimes…good company, that is…" Another sigh. Charlotte nodded sheepishly. "We should ride down to Holy Ranch sometime; I would love for you to taste all the different types of cheese they have. I haven't done so with a friend…in…ages." she said, eyes dulling someplace in the past. Blinking nervously, Charlotte stared at the cheese, wondering if Amara forgot she was a wanted woman, with her mug hanging all over the ranch, then she spoke again, as though needing to hear her own voice to fill a void of loneliness, or rather cover the noise of embarrassment within her. "There is a new farm hand back there…now *he* is kinda cute." She giggled like a little girl and Charlotte's brow cocked, bewildered with such behavior, thinking she herself wasn't all that childish after all. "Very shy gentleman…oh well, he's far too young for this widow, anyway." She snorted, then her smile slipped eerily fast.

"I understand…" she managed to say, not understanding much at all.

"I don't know if JB had a chance to tell you yet, but…it's Levi's birthday tomorrow, and we are having a big celebration!" she exclaimed, excited to talk about something positive.

"Oh!" Charlotte jolted from her seat. "I had no idea…wow. Is there anything I can do to help prepare things?" she asked kindly, accidentally glancing down at her blouse, ashamed to know exactly how her breasts were shaped.

"Well, Levi and…Kinnon…are out hunting now to get some meat for tomorrow — of course, Levi doesn't know about the plan…"

"They're what?" Charlotte interrupted her, picking up her face from the floor, shocked to hear Levi was alone with Mac out in the woods again.

"…Hunting?" Amara looked at her, cocked brow and eyes studying her expression, confused to receive such a reaction.

"Right…I'm sorry, I must've misheard…"

"Anyway, there's a dear friend of ours coming to deliver some liquor, and there's actually going to be a band playing for us!" Her smile widened again, barely able to contain herself with the thought of bringing some life back into the house. Somehow it appeared she craved people's company more than Charlotte ever did; perhaps due to the different upbringing, a more nurturing environment scarring her personality with heartwarming memories of them. Charlotte had none of this. She rather craved to escape people. "Jonathan will be ecstatic…he always loves company — the weirder, the better!" The thought cheered her soul, then she noticed Charlotte still in deep thoughts.

"Yes…it will be — I mean, we will have a wonderful time. Just let me know what I can do…" she mumbled, not able to look at her in the eyes anymore; feeling betrayed by a friend she didn't even know.

"Kinnon…he…he wanted to leave this morning." she finally said, unable to remain quiet about her feelings. Charlotte almost choked, the moment she heard *that* god-forsaken name again.

"Did he?" she asked, detached.

"He sure did…you see, we…we had a little bit of a situation…" she said sheepishly, cheeks crimsoned, as Charlotte instantly relived the scene of them kissing and grinding their bodies against each other before her eyes. "Remember when I asked you to talk to him?" she asked, picked a slice of cheese to nibble on.

"…Yes?" She issued a sound.

"Well…apparently, he doesn't need much convincing to…to get to know him, a little closer." She snorted, as though he hadn't just demeaned her, threatened her. Sense flew out of the window, or perhaps it had drowned within her morning drink. Charlotte's heart fell down to her stomach, her lungs got tight, choking her little by little.

"What…what do you mean?"

Amara looked over at the bench; face now completely flushed.

"Ah, Charlotte! He is so, so handsome! His body…otherworldly…so strong, and…ripped." She sighed heavily, sucking out Charlotte's air, as she did. "We actually…we actually kissed!" Her head slammed against Charlotte's shoulder, daydreaming of the memory. It felt like a brick hit her; a shot, large enough to down a bison.

"Ha…wonderful!" she stammered, fingers twitched. "I'm…I'm very happy for you!" She forced a smile on her lips, yet she felt like stabbing her violently with the butter knife.

"Thank you…but…"

"LADIES! LAAADIES!" JB made his loud entry into the house, marching happily towards them. "Charlotte, dearest! Where you been! We have lots to do!!" He clapped his hands, ordering the women to start preparing the house for the guests tomorrow.

She nodded, tampering down her anger, spiraling through her like a twirling flame. "I just need to take care of Finn's foot again real quick…he needs a fresh wrap." she said, realizing she hadn't seen her pony since last evening, realizing her mind had been too occupied with the vexed subject of "men".

"No, ya don't!" JB waggled his brows at her, as per usual. "Mr. Kinnon took care of it this morning; I saw him wrestle with your stubborn stallion — he even fell on his arse, trying to wrap the damn cloth on his hoof. HaHA! Not like I was watching him, or anythin'…" he mumbled, wheezing quietly, sounding like a squeaky train.

"He...he did?" She blinked, baffled in bewildered amazement, as Amara frowned her forehead in irritation.

I V

LEVI AND MAC RODE THEIR STEEDS SLOWLY, over the rolling hills of Freelands; quietly, loping with a steady gait through the tall frosty swaths of grass, faded in color as autumn slowly gave in to winter, decaying within its lethal embrace. At the top of the hill they stood in the cold and abrupt freezing wind, getting their breath. Looking out, as far as they could see, searching for a herd of swishing white tails or tall proud antlers.

"That's as far as I'm goin'." Mac said sternly, spotting Holy Ranch in the distance, feeling an eerie shiver trickle down his spine.

"Right. Forgot I'm riding with a wanted man!" He mocked him, still thinking about Amara and him together, biting his tongue not to say anything further since he'd promised Charlotte.

"Where we huntin'..." Mac disregarded his remark, feeling oddly vulnerable so close to that ranch.

"'Round here. They'll come soon enough. Spread some bait here and there, they'll come." he said confidently, dismounted, and tied up his horse to a tree — grabbing his rifle and some bait out of his saddlebag.

Mac watched him carefully, the sound of liquid swishing within a glass bottle hit his ears, as he fumbled for the bait in the bag — wondering if it was the same one *they* shared last night.

"So, what went on with my cousin?" Levi asked him, spreading the bait across a patch of grass.

"Don't know what yer talkin' 'bout." Mac said, throat swelling up suddenly, that unfamiliar feeling of guilt again.

"In the shack...JB said you two had a talk." He changed his insinuation, messing with his mind.

"Ye know the ol' man lies out of his arse — there was no talk. Nothin' worth mentionin'." Mac defended himself and crouched down, pretending to focus on the hunt.

"'Course. *Nothing* worth mentioning…" Levi fumed within, feeling the strongest urge to expose him, yet remained loyal to his word.

A loud grunt emerged above the hill, followed by another one right after. Mac looked through his half-broken scope to witness a herd of gigantic bison, grazing about, swinging their heads through the frost, uncovering a fresher patch of grass.

"Reckon we hunt one down?" he offered Levi, taking the opportunity to change the subject effortlessly.

"I'm not sure about that. They're becoming extinct; I don't wish to be part of this." he said sternly, and Mac snorted snidely.

"We all becomin' extinct, sooner or later." he said, knowing he would never get to live so long to witness it. "The ol' man requested food; this will feed a whole village — he'll have a week's worth of work to keep him busy… and quiet." he said, pleasantly imagining the peaceful silence he would gain out of all this, and rushed to mount his horse.

"You know, you always do whatever the hell you want, not giving a rat's ass about other folk's feelings." he implied again, yelling over the noise of Mac's horse's hooves clopping hard against the moist soil.

Mac clasped the reins in one hand, and the rifle in the other, galloping towards the herd — picking a robust, healthy-looking bison as his target.

Levi growled, frustrated, and followed right behind him; not wanting to miss the potential show of Mac being trampled down by a bison, yet secretly wishing to study his movements that undeniably had impressed him in the past. Circling around the herd, Levi rushed behind him, not willing to take his rifle out for this hunt, nor planning to shoot one of these sacred animals either.

"What yer waitin' for??" Mac yelled at him, realizing he wasn't cooperating like he expected him to.

"That's your damn hunt! Told you, I am not part of this!" Levi yelled back at him, flustered.

"Feck it." he grunted, raised his rifle and proceeded to aim at the fattest bison with the lushest coat before him, briefly locking eyes with it, before it lurched, darting to the side.

Levi kept a steady lope behind, feeling his lungs halt his breathing — as if he was aiming at the animal himself, observing Mac's legs control Roy with every single change of movement; so effortlessly, so in tune with his body.

Mac sorted the bison out of the herd, eyes hooked upon it, maneuvering through the giants — leaving only him and it in the middle of the vast Freelands. Raising his rifle again, he loped to the side of the animal, carefully watching the pace of the Bison's stride, perfectly matching it with Roy's. Counting as each shoulder moved, knowing that the heavy leg bone would deflect his shot and only cripple the animal instead of reaching his vitals, he let time slow, waiting for the perfect moment.

He gently squeezed the trigger, drilling a single .45-70 bullet through the freshly exposed area just behind his front leg as it moved forward — the powerful round penetrating right through the thick fur, dense rib-cage, hooking into its enormous heart. The animal roared upon its last strides, slammed its head on the ground, took a few last agonizing breaths — wilting beneath the horizon, the heat of its body melting the hoarfrost along the grass, staring heavenwards as it slowly died.

Levi's face fell upon the animal's lethal landing, dismounted in haste, and rushed to the bison, knowing he had only heard one single shot — denying that it was already gone. Yet, it was. Eyes dulled, glazed with eternal serenity.

Mac tucked in his stomach, making Roy skid to a full stop next to Levi. Yanking the lasso from his saddle, he roped the animal's back feet, dallying it tightly around the cantle with a swift movement. "Yer gonna help me drag it? Or yer too holy for that, too?" He mocked Levi, still agitated that he didn't help make this go faster.

"I'm not going to waste the animal." he said in earnest, tying his rope around its front feet, still in shock that he killed this gentle giant riding on his own with a single bullet; a sense of respect and admiration washed over him.

V

My dear Will,

I've thought long and hard on how to write these words, as I am not sure anymore of anything. I'm afraid I've let you down since my last letter; not knowing if you ever sent me one back. I'm afraid I've broken my promise to you, for somehow it seems I am not strong enough to control my feelings, or perhaps not all that experienced to know how. I do not know, and I loathe myself for it.

You see, I'm not in Mon Louis anymore — but you probably figured as much already. I had to leave…I hate to even write this name here, but I cannot lie to you. Mac needed help. And if that wasn't enough, I will add to your disappointment, for I met somebody… Somebody that is helping us stay away from the law. However, I…loathe myself to confess to it, but I kissed this somebody, Will… And I cannot understand what went into me to do so; for I know for certain, love was not the reason for it.

I'm scared I don't recognize myself anymore, and nor would you. I'm a mess in mind. A confused mess, and you don't deserve to be kept in my mess anymore, in the dark… Not when you're the most intelligent and kind gentleman I've ever had the honor to meet, and I mean this with heart.

But, said stubborn heart does not beat for you the way it beats for someone else…and I felt you deserved to know. I am sincerely sorry for wasting your time, for causing you such havoc and pain, when I myself did not understand what I felt or wanted, or perhaps if I'm being completely honest, I denied it all along.

I have since received my fair share of heartbreak, and please don't think I'm confessing because of any life changing event between me and him. There is nothing. There won't ever be. I'm confessing to you for I know now my feelings, and I feel ashamed I didn't realize them sooner.

It's too much to explain through writing, and I'm sure I'm doing a poor enough job already, but I would love nothing more than to have the opportunity to see you and apologize to you in person, for my sudden silence and disappearance, for breaking your heart, for my selfishness and cowardliness. Please know it was never intentional; I would never disappear into thin air like that, I would never hurt and betray you, not after everything you did for me. But, I suppose, I did.

I hope you have found true love in Bisonhorn. I deeply hope you have forgotten me, betrayed me the same and worse. I deserve as much.

I reside in the Freelands area now. If you ever wish to write me back again; I would be very grateful. Please send the mail to Holy Station, if you do.

Will, please forgive me. My heart is filled with shame. I still think of you often; think about what could have been, and wish I wasn't the way I am.

Yours,
Charlotte

SHE FOLDED THE LETTER, HER FINGERS FELT TINGLY AND NUMB; tears stood in her eyes, and yet there was relief clasping her heart. She needed to confess to him, for she had been carrying this burden for too long. She had never met someone that deserved such honesty and respect as Will did, and yet, she simply couldn't fall for him in return, as she was bound to fall for rougher hearts; colder souls.

It was refreshing to have a moment to herself with no distraction from anyone, other than Finn's contented munching in the stall next to her, as she sat there atop a hay bale. In a way, this shack was more private than her own room, and she craved the time alone with Finn to regain her senses. She heard a sudden loud banging noise, and peeking around a pillar, she spotted JB struggling with several huge pots that could each fit a dozen rabbits inside.

"JB!" she called for him, startling him, making the pots drop on his feet.

"Gah!!! Damn toeees!!" he squeaked painfully, hopping on his leg.

"I'm sorry…" Charlotte giggled, suppressed, for she thought he was so comical with everything he did. "Do you need any help?" she kindly offered, standing up from the bale and rushing to him.

"No! I got it!" He huffed, arching his back, cracking it. "Ya figure it's pretty obvious, all this?" he asked her with a furrowed face of worry, scanning around the yard,where he propped up a dozen benches, campfires, lights attached to trees, torches, and pots for stew.

"Eh…maybe a little bit." She winked at him with a playful smile. "But I'm sure Levi will appreciate it, nevertheless." she said, patting him on the back.

"Yeh. Just hard to hide things from this chap!" He chuckled, feeling emotional, suddenly realizing how time had flown by so quickly.

"JB, I need to ask you for a favor…" Her bright eyes begged him, as a little smirk emerged on her lips.

"Oh, Lordy!" His eyes flared, glaring at her sharp brow that cinched alluringly, or that's what he thought. "Listen, miss, I really think you're a fine lady, but can't do my Levi boy dirty like that. He…he is quite fond of you, ya know."

He declined the offer — assuming she wanted to pull him into the shack.

"What? What are you talking about?" She snorted, confused, thinking he might have misunderstood.

"Oh, well, never mind then. Tell me, what's the favor?" he asked embarrassedly, hiding his crimsoned cheeks with the palm of his hand.

"I need you to send this letter off." she said in earnest, fingers crinkling the paper nervously. "I cannot go to town, or else I would myself. This…this is very important to me, even if it's the last thing I write in my life." she pleaded, not wishing to entrust her letter to Amara, let alone Levi.

"Last thing?? Lordy! That does sound important!" He gaped at her in sheer curiosity.

"It is…"

"Well, what is it so important??" he then asked; he couldn't help himself.

"JB…I cannot tell you. It's…confidential." she said sheepishly, and his eyes grew ever bigger.

"What are ya?? An spy for the army, and it's confidential?? HaHA!"

"No, JB…but…"

"'Cause let me tell ya! Back in the army, we…"

"JB, please! I beg you!" She clasped his arm, handing him the letter, feeling an upwards spiral of anxiety reach her chest the longer she held onto it.

"Will-iam Griff-iths?" he slowly and loudly read out the recipient, raising his brow in great curiosity.

"JB! How rude!" She gasped, then chuckled, not realizing he would invade her privacy so unapologetically.

"What? I need to know, don't I? Besides, how many chaps do ya have wrapped around your finger, miss?" He laughed, realizing Levi was in quite a hot mess again.

"JB! It ain't like that! I mean…it…" She halted, drowning in shame.

"I never was…"

"Oh, don't ya worry! I know women! They are confused creatures!" he said and she blinked, for the first time hearing some semblance of sense out of his mouth. "They never know what they want!"

"It ain't like that, JB…I know what I want, I just…" She stared at him, as his brow lifted heavenwards. "Besides, I shouldn't be the *only* one worrying about any morals." She then hissed, thinking of Mac and Amara's filthy little secret together.

"Well, Margaret certainly didn't care about any morals, even if I was the most loyal man she could have found. Then again, nobody could stand my ramblings for long enough…so, I guess she always had a point." He recalled Margaret's complaints and excuses when she ran away with another man, and a pout scarred his lips. "In the end, it don't matter how many folk we encounter in this journey, what matters is who we settle down with; who's gonna wipe your arse, when ya can't do it yourself! HaHA! Now *that* takes some love, let me tell ya!" he said and she gagged a little, somehow the awful image of the way he left the outhouse one morning still assailed her. "You're still a young lady, you have time! How old are ya again?" he asked and she sighed heavily.

"Twenty-six…"

"Lordy! You look thirty!" he said, and her face scrunched up.

"Great…"

"Ya know, I've got quite the remedy…I call it JB's 'anti-aging' miracle balm!" he said in earnest, and she rolled her eyes.

"JB…please." She tapped on the letter, as he had started to drift off.

"Sure. Sure, I'll do it!" he promised her, and she jumped into his arms.

"Thank you soooo much…from the bottom of my heart; this means more than you realize." she said, squeezing him tight.

"But of couuuurse! But, promise me one thing." He pulled back, gripped her shoulders, locked eyes with her, with one eyeball slightly protruding further than the other.

"Anything." she said, already agreeing to it, feeling ecstatic for Will to eventually receive word from her again.

"Please, dance with my boy Levi tomorrow. Just as a couple friends, nothin' more." he said pleadingly. "I just…know he will really appreciate it more than anything I could gift him." he said, hoping she wouldn't decline, recalling Levi's drunken wish one night, laying there in the meadow beneath a sheet of stars, staring mindlessly besotted at them — right after he had met Charlotte.

"JB…sure I would love to, but…I just don't want to give him any further false hope." she said sternly, knowing very well how attached he was to her already.

"Fair enough…but, if the opportunity arises — if he asks you, please, let it happen." he said. "There's gonna be music, booze, all the right ingredients — I guaranteeee he'll wanna shake that god darn sculptured body of his! HaHA!" He chuckled, and threw a harsh pat on her shoulder.

"I promise. But only if he asks." She smiled back to him, then heard a loud dragging noise behind them.

CHAPTER 53

Feck

I

"SHERIFF DORMAN, GOOD TO SEE YOU AGAIN, SIR." Sheriff Faust shook his hand, clutching his hat to his chest.

"Thanks for coming. I know it was…short notice." Dorman mumbled, embarrassed.

"Very." Faust chuckled awkwardly, as he was about to retire for the night when the deputy found him in Rockvale. "So, heard you're after a man that… killed his wife in Red Giants, is that right?" he asked, shifting his weight to one leg, waiting to hear the full story.

"Yes, sir. At least, that's what we assume." He bit his lip, eyes cutting at him. "Coulda been kidnapped as far as we know. However, the poor chap ain't the brightest; left a bloody trail from the cabin where it happened." he informed, adjusting his shirt in his pants with a swift tuck.

"Hm. Sounds like it wasn't planned, whatever he did…" Faust thought out loud. "So how's the fella's name? Do we know even who we're after?" he asked him, hoping this wasn't the wild goose chase Dorman was generally known for.

"William Griffiths." Dorman had the poster ready in his hand, slamming it on the desk before him. "Son of the wealthy son of a bitch, Thomas Griffiths. Don't get me wrong, he was a good man — alcoholic, but always a man of God." He bobbed his head, reminiscing the times they visited at church every Sunday down in Bisonhorn. "Strayed away from his wife, visitin' with the gals in Nephilim Cove…" he added, realizing a familiar pattern was inherited with Will's disloyalty towards his wife.

"Hmm. Yeah…I know who you speak of." He sighed, as the handsome aristocratic man emerged within his mind. "William Griffiths — he came to me, searching for a gal who is wanted for murder down in Marysville. Claimin' she was chased by a grizzly up in the mountains." Faust scratched his mutton chops, trying to recall more details.

"Yeah, that's old news I'm afraid. Lots has happened since that. Anyhow, we should get goin'. Don't know how much time we still have…" Dorman said, snapping his fingers, wondering if Will was still hiding in this state.

"Reckon them Feasters have gotten ahold of him already?" Faust wondered, as he trod out the door to mount his horse.

"Hopefully not…I have a feeling he ain't alone." he slowly introduced his thoughts.

"What ya mean, Owen?" He shot a suspicious gaze at him, collecting his reins into a firm grip.

"There's a reason why I wanted ya to bring your deputies along…" Dorman drew in a deep breath, hoping this wouldn't turn him away.

"Them Feasters?" He cocked his brow, still confused with Dorman's secrecy.

"Worse…*Kinnon.*"

II

THE ANIMATED SILHOUETTES SLASHED THROUGH the afternoon haze, upon Levi and Mac arriving back at the ranch, dragging the enormous bison carcass steadily behind their horses. JB gaped at them in awe, not expecting to see such a massive kill from the hunt; his mouth fell open, and so did Charlotte's.

"Well, well! Boys! I thought ya was gonna hunt some deer! Not a…a livin' Mammoth!" He burst into laughter, as Charlotte avoided any possible eye contact with *him*, instantly feeling the warmth of his presence, and yet also the heartache that now came along with it.

"Yep…Kinnon here insisted on killing near-extinct animals today!" Levi nagged, making sure everyone knew it wasn't his doing.

Mac rolled his eyes in annoyance and slipped out of the stirrups, hopping off swiftly from his horse. "So, ol' man!" he said, and her breath cut in her lungs, as though she had never heard his voice before. "Ya wanted meat, ye got meat." he said, giving him a disingenuous pat on the shoulder.

"Watch your mouth, boy..." Levi growled to him, not tolerating the mockery towards JB, and led his horse past him to unsaddle it at the shack.

Mac snorted with his threat and cautiously glanced over at Charlotte; her back was turned away from him, talking to Jonathan who had just pranced out of the homestead to inspect the glorious animal.

"Jonathan, this is a mighty big bison! I always loved watching them graze as a little girl..."

Mac heard her explain softly; in a motherly tone he'd never recognized.

"Mommy says they can be very dangerous, and I should never go near them when I'm out riding with uncle Levi." Jonathan sighed, eyes still wide from the shock of witnessing a real bison so up-close, hand reaching to touch the blood-stain, a furled finger poking the bullet-hole in great curiosity.

"Your mother is probably right; they can be aggressive, since they protect their herd...like your family protects you, you know?" She shuffled his messy hair with a bright smile on her face, which captivated Mac instantly, as now he found himself staring at her.

"I ain't needing protecting, miss Charlotte! I'm old enough to fight!" He pouted, folded his arms stubbornly and glanced back at Mac, who was still focused on her. "Mr. Kinnon knows I'm a good fighter! Right, Mr. Kinnon?" Jonathan asked him with a wide smile and Mac blinked, jerking his head away in shame, noticing her still focused on the animal's dead body, avoiding his face, his eyes, avoiding *him*.

"Hm...sure, kid." he said.

His coarse voice, a barbed wire strung around her throat.

"Come on, Jonathan." she said abruptly. "Let me introduce you to Finn. I have a fun idea for you!" She took him by the hand gently and walked away in sheepish haste, as his tiny feet tapped excitedly beside her.

Mac exhaled deeply, feeling the coldness that had swallowed her every being reach through him, throb within like a pitiful heartbeat; distant, bitter, unlike anything she'd ever radiated to him before.

He wasn't even worth a look anymore, nor a single word.

He knew exactly the reason why.

III

"THE BLOOD TRAIL STARTED FROM HERE...continuin' between these trees, and after that, we went on foot." Sheriff Dorman explained to Faust, who was getting his lantern ready before it got darker.

"I understand." he mumbled, fiddling with the lantern, chin pressed against his throat in sharp concentration. "Let's check it out then, shall we?" He looked at his line of deputies behind him, and signaled them to follow after him with a swift wave of his hand. Thirty deputies were marching through the woods; shielding each other in divided groups of three.

"Keep your ears and eyes open...this here is where they ambushed us..." Dorman whispered, legs jittering in panic, almost immobilizing him in soil.

Faust and the deputies scanned around cautiously, shotguns already cocked and ready to fire. But the forest was eerily quiet, peaceful; soft winds billowing out around them, branches whining thinly in the refreshing breeze, brushing gently against their faces.

"Boss!" A deputy pointed with his barrel to an opening of the forest, leading up to a shack that overlooked a lagoon with black thick trees stretching away in every direction. Dorman and Faust looked at each other, eyes cutting right back to the shack as they proceeded to march carefully towards it.

"Owen..." Faust called him with a frightened whisper.

Dorman glanced over at him, seeing a piece of bloody clothing stuck on a branch right before his boots. "They must be here. I feel it. Get ready for the worst!" He motioned behind him, signaling for everyone to crouch low and follow after him. Fog suddenly circled around them — cocooning the thick trunks they hid behind every time they passed the previous trees.

"Faust! I see someone on the ground!" Dorman shouted in alarm, spotting a body on the porch of the shack.

"Proceed with caution, Owen...this could very well be a trap..." Faust mumbled with a thick southern accent, feeling his hands dripping sweat from all the heightened suspense. The sheriffs kept on walking towards the shack, realizing there was no light inside, nor any horses tethered to it. It seemed, and felt, oddly vacant.

"What ya think?" Dorman asked him, some feet before the shack.

"I say we go for it, old friend…I'll send the deputies inside the building. We are too many; not even Kinnon can escape us! We have the upper hand, Owen." he reassured him, although Dorman knew better than to just assume an advantage over Mac.

"Fine…" He took cover behind a mossy boulder, drew in a deep breath, clutching to his shotgun, fingers making a cross, waiting for his command.

Sheriff Faust signaled one last time with a firm forward motion of his arm, and the deputies leaped up like pawns in chess, rushing to the shack with their guns pointed in every direction as they circled around it.

"William Griffiths! And mister 'infamous', Mac Kinnon! Time has come for a first-class arrest, unless you prefer dyin' in this pitiful wooden box!" Dorman yelled from the safety of his rock. Yet, there was no answer — no suspicious sound of a creaking board on the floor, or a moving shadow behind the windows. Wicked silence, as everyone waited impatiently. "This is a warning! A chance for ya both to surrender! Nobody needs to get shot tonight! So step forward!!" he yelled again, and everyone waited.

Dorman glanced back at Faust, and Faust nodded to him.

"Get on with it…" Faust ordered, and several deputies broke off from the others and stormed inside the building. A loud scream of terror came out of their mouths, as countless groups of ravens flew and slammed against their heads, startling them more than even Kinnon could with their frantic clopping of wings, beaks that nailed against their hands, chasing them out like a pack of coyotes herding sheep for their kill.

"What in the tarnation?!" Dorman glanced back at Faust as he folded his lips, confused to see his deputies run out from the building with not a single gunshot to be heard.

"Sir! The shack! The shack is…" A deputy panted, bent his body, trying to catch his breath before them. "It's empty!" He exhaled, relieved, as the sheriffs stared at him with immense confusion.

"What you mean, son?! It can't be!!" Dorman interrupted, flustered, as he was so convinced they were hiding there.

"Owen, the body…" Faust reminded him, pointing with his head to it.

Dorman stood up cautiously; slowly walking towards it with the shotgun pointed at it, hands shaking the closer he got.

A single raven emerged through the veil of fog like a small onyx statue, black as midnight, eyes aglow, beak gray-slate tint, razor sharp, seated atop of the man's head, covering his face with its jet-black feathers.

He stared at the bird, taken aback by the ominous sight, recalling verses; death, darkness, decay. Aiming the shotgun towards it, he waved its barrel, trying to scare it off, yet it would not flinch; there it stood, loyal as a soldier.

A sudden gunshot slipped past Dorman, and the bird fell dead atop the man's face. He glanced behind to find Faust with his revolver spinning between his fingers by his side, as he slung it back into the holster.

"Always hated these…goddamn birds." Faust nagged, grabbing the raven from its wing, tossing it into the lagoon before them.

Dorman's eyes flared in shock; shotgun slipped from his hands, landing straight on the ground with a heavy thud. Utterly breathless as he recognized the man lying in the muddy soil — lifeless, ashen skin, peeling off of him like dust, staring with solid black eyes of horror right back into him.

IV

AMARA WAS WASHING THE DISHES, scrubbing them thoroughly in absent thought the moment Mac stepped into the house, startling her to the core with the abrupt slam of the door. She glanced back with a gentle smile, thinking it was Levi for he too tended to yank them open in the same loud and annoying manner as Mac just did — yet her smile slipped when she locked eyes with him instead.

Mac tore his gaze away instantly and hung his black duster coat on the wall, not planning on staying a second longer here.

"Mr. Kinnon, I need to have a talk with you." she called him earnestly, plopping the cloth atop the counter and grabbing her cup of medicine.

"Didn't we already?" he said and stretched his arms behind his back, feeling stiff from the strenuous hunt, the sutures still holding tight.

"No. Not this kind of talk. I need to talk to you about tomorrow." she responded calmly and maturely, and sat down on a chair.

"Sure. Go on." He leaned himself against the wall, throwing his leg over the other, pulling Amara's eyes to his exaggerated bulge involuntarily, for any movement he made was dangerously and hauntingly dazzling to her.

"These…these folks are very important to our family, so I expect you to behave accordingly; if not, I will kindly have ask you to leave the ranch by tomorrow morning." she said, pulling her eyes away, as even she couldn't deny how his presence affected her.

Mac grinned with her statement. "Ye worry I'm gonna murder anyone?"

"No, but I know you're not one to be trusted. Sadly, I know you couldn't care less about Levi, or anyone else but yourself. I'm just asking you to behave, nothing more." She made her point clear again, entwining her fingers, thumbs wiggling nervously for his answer.

"I'll be on me best behavior, me lass." He winked, and tipped his hat to her.

"You're pathetic." She growled behind him, as she observed him walking up the stairs.

"Yer too kind." he teased her back, shut himself in his room, grunted through gnashed teeth, snatched his hat and tossed it across. He didn't wish to belittle her, he didn't wish to behave ungrateful for having a warm bed to sleep in as winter whooshed its way in, yet the poison on his tongue kept dripping out. It wasn't Amara's fault she saw them; *it was his.*

Amara's stomach twisted in a knot, feeling drenched in shame and filth for letting herself get so attached to a murderer. She thought of her deceased husband, and tears flooded her eyes from guilt, wondering if he had witnessed the embarrassment from above, wondering if he would still wait for her when the time came, wondering if he had cursed her to never find another man, another father for their son. She missed him, more than a faithful widow could, and the loss crippled her, pulling her into the dark void of a drunken cesspit. As much as she longed desperately to find a father figure for Jonathan, she realized there were only a few good men left in this world — and Mac was not one of them.

V

"HE IS A BIG BOY!!!" Jonathan giggled blithely as he stood on a stack of square hay bales to reach Finn's neck, hand resting on his withers, the other scratching his neck.

"Yes, indeed he is. He is the sweetest boy, though." Charlotte said.

"Sweet?" Jonathan looked at her with flared eyes, glimmering.

"Yes…we've had quite some adventures together in the past months; not even a book could describe what we experienced!" Charlotte sighed, briefly recalling every little trouble they had to deal with — thinking back on how she almost lost Finn in that iced lake, if it weren't for…*Mac.*

Another sigh, she pressed her lips together.

"Mommy doesn't let me ride yet. Only with uncle Levi." He pouted sadly, brushing Finn's mane gently over and over again in the same spot. "I want to ride my own horse!" he complained, and Finn snorted sweetly, relaxing beneath his soft strokes.

"The time will come sooner than you think, Jonathan. Horses can be quite unpredictable, and truly can injure you badly." she explained.

"That's what mommy says…but uncle Levi *never* gets injured." he said.

"Oh, well…then he is lucky." she said.

"Are you lucky too, Miss Charlotte?" he asked her, intrigued.

"Ha…generally speaking, no…perhaps not. But, when it comes to horses; I am lucky to ride and love such an amazing stallion, but there was one time, when I was galloping through wide open fields across Caledonia Territory, when a snake slithered before him, spooking him into a full stop — sending me flying right over his head." She snorted. "That hurt a bit…a bit much." she said, squinting, as though still able to feel the bruises across her butt.

"Feck…" he said, and her eyes bugged.

"Jonathan…" She chuckled faintly.

"Yes, Miss Charlotte?"

"You…you know what this word means?" she asked him and he blinked, then shrugged.

"No…" He bowed his head, suppressing a giggle.

"Oh…where…where did you hear that?" she asked, already suspecting.

"Mr. Kinnon said it…when I poked him on the nose." He shrugged and she snorted.

"You poked him on the nose?" She tittered and he giggled shyly.

"Yes…"

"And how did he like that?" She cocked a brow at him, a smirk on her lips.

"He didn't…" His cheeks crimsoned, lips folded, eyes of trouble looking up at her. "He pulled out a biiiig knife, but then saw it was me, and…and put it away again." he said and she breathed out in relief.

"Wow…and you're still here to tell the story. Pretty brave young man you are." She winked at him and he smiled widely.

"Miss Charlotte, I really like Mr. Kinnon…but I'm afraid he doesn't like me." he said, his rosy lips curving down into a pout, hands clasping Finn's mane firmly.

"Oh…I don't think so, Jonathan. I'm sure he likes you just as much." She caressed his little back, feeling the feeble path of a juvenile spine down it, briefly wondering if Mac's scars were inflicted at such an early age. Her heart sunk at the thought.

"Uncle Levi said that Mr. Kinnon is…not a good man, Miss Charlotte." he said with a furrowed grimace, and Charlotte blinked.

"That's…that's quite a big word to tell about a fellow man, Jonathan." she said earnestly. "I think…we should trust our own hearts, and instinct, and… decide for ourselves…always give a chance to those that might appear different at first; always give them the benefit of the doubt…" she said, swallowing dryly, and Jonathan stared at her in sharp concentration, eyes blinking as if taking a mental note to tuck in deep within him, ready to unfold it when the right time comes. "But…I probably shouldn't interfere with what your family tells you…" *Probably should stop also talking right about now, Charlotte…*

"I want a horse just like Mac's!" he said, swiftly changing subject, as if he too understood it was deeper than what he was capable to contemplate. "Black, with a white face, and white socks!" he said excitedly, pointing over at Roy.

"Haha. What about one like Finn? You don't like my chestnut pony?" She complained playfully, taking out some delicate leather strings from her saddlebag.

"He is fine too." the boy agreed solemnly, nodding, then focused back on his job to brush him thoroughly, long tiny strokes, yet more precise each time.

"Look, Jonathan." She pulled his curious gaze back to her, showing him the leather strings in the palm of her fair hands. "We will braid his mane now!" she announced and he screeched with excitement. She took a chunk of mane and separated it into three sections of hair, alternating the passing of each one over the other, until it was time to tie the leather string around it. "Can you do that?" She cut her eyes at him, smiling at him with a challenging smirk.

"Yes! Yes!" He leaped up and down on the hay ecstatically, making Finn's eyes widen, not used to such intense energy, nor used to children in general, nor was Charlotte, yet she appeared to enjoy Jonathan's presence immensely.

"What are you two doing in here?" Levi walked in, a smile scarring his lips to see them braid Finn's mane, to see her with Jonathan, making him almost yearn for a future that would never happen.

"Oh! We are just making a stallion pretty!" She turned around to wink at him, sending shivers down his spine.

"Uncle Levi, look!! I'm breading the hair!!" he yelled excitedly again, and Finn's ears waggled back and forth like rowdy antennae.

"Braiding, Jonny." Levi corrected him with a chuckle, as he now stood right behind them, looking over Charlotte's shoulder. Charlotte felt his presence strongly, feeling his tall self forming a shadow over her, his deep voice echoing in her ear. "Charlotte, can you explain to me what JB is up to?" he whispered to her, fully knowing his friend was preparing something quite enormous at a suspicious time of the year.

"Oh...I don't know what you're talking about. Jonathan and I have been quite busy here, grooming Finn." she giggled, as it was quite obvious what JB was working on.

"Haha. Fair enough...I'd better not ask anything further." He smiled, moved by JB's gentle heart, preparing an elaborate celebration in his older age.

"How was the hunt?" she asked him curiously as she braided the lower half of Finn's mane, hoping he didn't snitch on her.

"Fine...nothing was said, if you're worried about that." he said smartly and she exhaled deeply.

"Thank you, Levi...I appreciate you." she said, feeling a heavy weight leave her shoulders.

"Of course. I always keep my word." He leaned closer, whispered against the skin of her neck — his warm breath crawled all over her body, making her mess up the braiding pattern.

Levi lingered beside her to breathe her in…in all her horse and sweat scent, in all her disheveled plait and mucky clothes, wishing for a moment they could have been alone in the shack, longing to wrap her in his arms, kiss her luscious lips just one more time. He starved for them, unable to forget how she kissed him back that night — lighting up the glimmer of hope within him, still clinging onto it.

"So, I need to get going!" he said, pulling back. "How's Finn's foot, by the way?" he asked swiftly, throwing a glance at the fresh cloth wrapped around it.

"Uhm…I believe it's better." She sucked in a stutter, not knowing how it really looked today since she wasn't the one who doctored it.

"Great! Nice job you did on that wrap; much better than I did it!" He winked at her, not realizing it was actually Mac's doing.

"Oh…well…uhm…thank you, Levi." Her lie hid behind her smile, feeling as though that was the best thing to do. "Levi?" she called for him as he was treading out.

"Yes?" he asked, his heart jolting foolishly upon hearing her say his name.

"I promise, when Finn is well, I will be out of your hair. I appreciate your family having us here, but I don't want to be a bother or overstay my welcome." she said genuinely, giving the rest of the leather strings to Jonathan for him to take over.

"Charlotte…" He walked up to her again, grabbing her softly from her shoulders. "I promise you, you don't bother anyone. It's…it won't be easy for you out there, being wanted like this." he mumbled awkwardly, selfishly not wanting her to leave either.

"I know Levi but…I don't belong here, either. I was thinking of going back out west; it's the only place where I believe I'm not wanted yet." she muttered, realizing how terrible her situation sounded.

"West is a long ways to go. At least let me take you." he offered, feeling a knot in his throat just imagining her being gone.

"I can't make you do that, it's a long journey, and besides…I put you into enough trouble already."

"I don't care." he interrupted her. "Every trouble you brought was worth it to me, or else I would have never known you existed, and *that* is a pretty fucked up thought." he whispered to her, eyes cutting back at Jonathan.

Charlotte blushed, briefly thinking of how similar he sounded to Will — only with some more curse words between sentences. Her head was spinning again, trying to find the right words to say, as her heart felt oddly satisfied to be so close to him, as though she needed him, yet knowing she didn't.

"I...I won't force you not to come, of course, but by all means come at your own risk!" She tittered, teasingly.

He wrapped his arms around her waist, and pulled her towards him. Close. Taking her breath with him. He locked eyes with her, stern and genuine.

"I'll take any risk for you, cowgirl..." he whispered, mouth nearing to hers.

Her chest inflated with a sudden burst of happiness and odd feelings of arousal, masking the woe and anger she now carried within her. She felt the confusing urge to plant her lips on his, as though they promised an escape, a release of her heartbreak, a false sticky web of lust to trap herself within; when she heard Amara's voice in the background.

"Jonathan!!!" she yelled, finally relieved to have found him.

Levi, startled, pulled himself back and unwrapped his arms instantly.

Charlotte's crimsoned cheeks turned pale, as she tried to compose herself.

"He's — he's here, Amara! I apologize; I thought he might want to help me groom my horse." she stuttered, with a shy grin on her face as she glanced over at Levi — still staring at her intensely with the most beautiful shades of green.

"Oh! That's alright. Just didn't know where this little kid was again!" She walked up to Jonathan, inspecting the braids his little fingers were working on. "I hope, I hope I didn't disturb you!" She chuckled, ecstatic to see Levi with a potentially new woman.

"No, Amara. Don't worry." Levi hummed. "I was on my way out, actually." he added, somehow not wanting to admit it. "We will talk later." He winked at Charlotte, making her lose her train of thought again.

Somehow, she quivered. Somehow, she worried for their friendship.

CHAPTER 54

White Cloth

I

"IS EVERYONE AWAKE YET?! WAKE UP, LADIES AND GENTS, WAKE UP!!!" JB startled everyone in the house, loudly banging a wooden spoon against a pot — which sounded more like a drum of war, than a peaceful morning awakening.

"Amara! Wake up!" JB banged the pot before her door, then proceeded to Charlotte's to do the same.

Mac woke up alarmed, revolver pulled from underneath his pillow, pointing it around him frantically — when he heard the once again annoying, painfully penetrating voice of JB, banging the pot outside his door. Mac slapped the revolver against the bed covers in frustration and pulled his hair in all directions, trying with all his might to contain himself; to not skin JB alive.

Charlotte's heart almost stopped, hearing the pot bang before her door rhythmically as well, leaving an echo of a rattle in her head. She rushed to get off the bed, only to fall on the ground — cocooned within her covers.

"Gah! JB!" she yelled, flustered, trying desperately to unwrap herself.

"Haha! Come on, sleeping beauty!! We have a special day today! UP, UP!!" he yelled back excitedly, hitting the pot one more time as he awkwardly danced and hopped towards Levi's room.

He opened the door, expecting to find him still asleep — hand raised, clutching the wooden spoon within his fist, pot on the other; large mouth wide open, ready to sing, yet he was met with Levi's bare hairy chest before him instead, reminiscent of a rearing bear. JB looked up at him slowly, only to find him smirking back at him, ready to burst into laughter.

"Yes, JB?" he asked him playfully, breath indicating he had gotten into a glass of whiskey already.

"Ha…happy birthday?" He cackled awkwardly, disappointed he wasn't able to surprise him.

Levi chuckled and gave him a big hug, even though he had a growing headache from all the banging noise. "Thank you, old man. I appreciate you." He smiled widely, feeling like a little boy again, waking up to his one and only special day of the year. He glanced at JB's bloodshot, protruding eyeballs that stared back at him lovingly, realizing he too had aged with him.

Levi couldn't help but hug him again.

"Levi, my boy! Have you grown again?? Or have I shrunken??" He snorted, as he tried to reach Levi's head to give it a good pat. Charlotte strode out of her room, cranky as can be, on her way to splash her face with some cold water to wake up properly, all the while the noise still rang in her ears.

"Ah! At last! The princess is awake!" JB teased her, as Levi suppressed a laughter, glancing at her grimace of irritation only JB could manage to paint with a pot and a spatula.

"Very, very funny, JB! That was *quite* some music you played right there!" She nagged, advancing to them, freezing into place when she suddenly spotted Levi, adorned only in trousers. "Oh!" She gasped, smiled, grinned. "The birthday boy!" she stuttered, not knowing where to look at him — for his square chest was staring rudely right at her, and his ripped abdomen boldly pulled her eyes further down on him. Evidently, undeniably so, he took intense care of his body, for he could never achieve such a physique just by chasing outlaws. "Ha-happy Birthday, Levi!" she hastily wished him, turning her head away respectfully.

"Thank you, lady." He blushed, for he noticed her eyes lurking all over him.

II

CHARLOTTE RUSHED DOWN THE STAIRS, boots clopping against the oaken steps, and yet somehow she floated in absence, still envisioning his godly body in her head. "Darn it, he is *fine*…" She bit her finger, as to not voice it out loud, albeit could not deny it; she lusted over him like a fool, and perhaps that was what made her kiss him back all along. The curiosity of the unknown, the unseen, the not yet unraveled. Somehow able to paint over any gap of deeper emotions, somehow oddly similar to her mother's habit. She found Amara preparing breakfast for everyone, with Jonathan being in her way every second as he hopped around the table — pretending to be riding a horse.

"Charlotte!!" Jonathan rushed to hug her, sweetly and unexpectedly.

"Oh!" She cleared her throat. "Hey, little…little one." she stuttered, as she didn't know how or what to call him.

"All he's been talking about this morning is your stallion, Flinn!" Amara rolled her eyes, still exhausted from JB's pot concert.

"It's Finn…and that's endearing! I'm happy that he left a good impression on him." She said proudly, not doubting for a second that Finn could impress someone.

JB rushed down the stairs behind them, leaping over the last couple steps with great confidence. "Gah! Should *not* have done that, JB! Ya ain't no teenager no more!!" he reminded himself out loud, kneecap cracking in all directions. Then he arched his back dramatically, widened his mouth, inhaled the whole air in the room upon a wheeze and faced them. "Ladies! I need to go! The guests will be arriving in a couple hours!! Oh Lordy, oh Lordy! I am one stressed-out mother…" He glanced swiftly over at Jonathan, who was waiting to hear the rest of his sentence. "Plucker. Gah! Gotta go! Gotta go!!" he added, hobbling his way out of the house.

Levi strode down the stairs slowly, rolling his shirt's sleeves up as he did. Adorned in a black dress shirt, black pants, and his usual cowboy boots underneath, looking devilishly handsome; impeccably striking. Dark clothes striking a layer of contrast to his bright green eyes and messy brown hair — fitting tightly around his muscular body, one which she could never unsee… Charlotte stared at him in awe, as he walked down with a big white smile across his face as per usual, yet this morning he was glowing differently.

Differently, to her.

"Happy Birthday, Levi!!!" Amara and Jonathan yelled together as they had planned to do, giving him a big group hug, which even jointly couldn't quite fill up his large chest and broad shoulders.

"Haha. Thank you, thank you!" He hugged them back tightly.

Yet, the joyful room turned quiet as they heard Mac's careless footsteps coming down the stairs. Mac noticed their loud, celebratory voices hush awkwardly the moment he approached them, and his charred gut twisted in a way. Levi glanced at Amara, who picked up Jonathan in her arms to rush outside rapidly, not giving the boy a chance to greet him. Charlotte's heart sunk heavily as the empath within her felt for Mac, realizing how awful it must feel for everyone to despise him and avoid him so very obviously.

"Good morning." Levi greeted him, trying to act like the bigger person.

"Hm." He nodded, cutting his eyes at her instead. "Mornin', Charlotte." he greeted her for the first time since he's known her, as he passed by her — hitting her with a scented wave of cigarette smoke.

Charlotte's eyes widened in shock, never expecting to hear him spit out these words. Or any kind words, for that matter. "Morning…" she tentatively replied, eyes still avoiding to set at him, avoiding to sit down on *that* bench.

"I hear it's yer day today?" Mac swallowed his pride, trying his best to warm up to Charlotte again — struggling to pretend he cared, yet her silence burned him inside, worse than the sweltering wax the preacher poured over his open wounds.

"…Indeed." Levi hummed, suspicious of his talkativeness.

"Hm. Enjoy…" Mac muttered, as he daringly sat beside Charlotte, pouring himself some boiling hot coffee from the pot, internally quivering.

"Thank you." Levi said cautiously, not taking his eyes away from him.

Charlotte dropped her gaze down to her feet, that were almost touching Mac's weathered boots. She didn't dare to make a sound, nor make a move, flinch, jolt, or jitter, for her arm could so easily bump into him, and her skin had already goosed by the thought. Her heartbeat started racing, feeling his body so close to hers, reminiscing how his presence paralyzed her, yet something felt odd about him; different, unlike himself. For the first time, his feigned kindness petrified her.

Then he cleared his throat, reaching for the pot of coffee. He halted, stared at it, chest inflating, rehearsing the words in his mind repeatedly, obsessing over them to spurt them out correctly.

"Ye want?" he finally said, offering her some coffee.

Charlotte stared at the pot he was holding for her, in sheer bewilderment. She swallowed awkwardly, and started to braid her hair mechanically, not knowing what to do with herself.

"Hm?" Mac swallowed hard, pressuring for an answer, feeling ridiculed like a vulnerable boy right before Levi's eyes — who squinted his way with a faint grin, sensing, feeling his dark amusement — as Charlotte tore him to bits with her harsh silence, churning him mercilessly. He turned his head to face her, realizing she wasn't even blinking.

"No."

The harsh-sounding word escaped her mouth, imbued with hate, leaving Levi speechless before them. Mac's heart dropped, pulse pounded. Loudly. Anger rose in him like a tide, drowning all sense and reason, as his hand traveled habitually down to his knife, unwillingly, uncontrollably.

Levi watched his movements carefully — noticing his hand wander awkwardly underneath the table. Lowering his hand to the side of his gun belt, it hovered subtly over his revolver.

"No, thank you…I…still have coffee…" Charlotte added, feeling his tension, his wave of fury crash through her.

She turned her head to face him, and was met with a cold expression; pupils dilated, lips folded tightly, fighting the chaos of his own. He strained, a vein popped across his neck, chest heaved, teeth clenched together violently, all from trying desperately not to explode. She could feel his pain, as that's how she felt some nights before, and yet she couldn't understand his ache.

Mac stood up hastily, grabbed a cigarette behind his ear, and left the room.

She, astounded, glanced back at Levi — who still kept his eyes on him, and his hand over the gun.

III

"YEAH, SHE'S BROKE TO RIDE, ALRIGHT. Took some time to…anyhow, she's broke, cowpoke. Get her for fifty bucks, or get outta here and don't waste my time." the rancher said to the young man, as he held onto the reins, ready to pass them over to him.

"Sir, this horse has been starved." he said, aghast, feeling the feeble crease of its neck with calloused fingers. "Ain't no way in hell anyone would pay fifty bucks for such, sir. It was advertised as a ranch horse, not a skeleton." the young man complained, kept staring at its dainty neck, for that's all he could see. "Mr. Walston ain't gonna appreciate that, sir." he said, and yet the ranched snorted in his face.

"Boy, the horse just went through sickness from moldy hay — what ya expecting! She's broke as can be. Guaranteed. Take it, or leave." he pressured him again, losing his patience, spitting his chewing tobacco next to his boot.

"Forty dollars." the young man offered, fumbling the money before him.

"Forty-five, and not a cent less." The rancher held his hand out, expecting an agreement and the man stared at him, conflicted; eyes setting back at the gray mare's gaze, as though she begged for him to buy her, shoot her, and end her misery for all she cared.

"Forty-five dollars it is." The man shook his hand and gave him the money, swiftly grabbing the reins from him. Leading the horse away, he studied its droopy eyelids and chin — admiring its calmness and willingness to follow him anywhere.

"Yer gonna be fine…" he said to her, caressed softly across her withers.

Dithering to mount the gray mare, he hopped atop her, landing as softly as he could on her back of spine and bones, and took off with her, feeling her ribs rub against his legs with every single stride she took. He was headed to Holy Ranch, as they were looking for a new ranch horse — and this one was promised to be able to handle the job.

IV

"YA AIN'T SERIOUSLY GONNA WEAR THAT SAME OL' DIRT CLOTH?!" JB called to Mac, gaping at his mucky black shirt from a distance as he spotted him smoking underneath a tree, withdrawn from the others. Mac rolled his eyes, agitated, for JB's presence would be the last straw for him turning mad.

"Ya hear me, Mr. Kinnon??" he waddled towards him.

"Bad business. Don't own nothin' else." He leered at him, taking in a big cigarette puff.

"Well, you're lucky! 'Cause…I planned for that, already! I went to town and picked up a little somethin'-somethin' for you!" JB excitedly reported, making Mac frown in confusion. "Indeed, indeed I did! Follow me!" he demanded, and limped towards his wagon. "Follow me, mister!" he pressured him, noticing Mac still sitting on the ground, dithering to follow, as such words he had never heard.

Mac stood up, brushed the dirt off his pants, and tentatively strode to the wagon, not knowing what to expect.

"Here you go, mister." JB said, rolling out a flawless white dress shirt — which he traded the bison pelt for, in order to be able to afford it. "It ain't much…ya know, it don't have the bib on the shirtfront, nor the high collar like the elites wear! HaHA! But me and you, we're different folk." he said, winking at him kindly. "We don't need all that fluff, do we now?!"

Mac stared at the shirt, for he had never in his life owned a piece of clothing of such value. Noticing the full button up placket and buttons at the cuffs, leaving him speechless, and as much as JB annoyed him, he could not make himself disrespect him this time.

"Take it! It don't bite!" JB insisted, pressing it against his chest — sadly recognizing the innocent look in his eyes; one just like Jonathan would have whenever he received a special gift.

"I…" Mac swallowed repeatedly, not able to make a sound, choking.

"It's alright! Just take it, already! I gotta go! Folks will be here any minute now! Oh, Lordy!" He forced the shirt into his hands, and rushed on to the next thing.

Mac stood still; feeling the smooth fabric between his distressed fingers, stroking gently against it — lifting it up to his face, burying his nose into it. There was an unfamiliar smell of cleanliness, freshness, kindness, selflessness. His hands quivered, knees weakened the more he realized…*it was brand new; never worn and torn by somebody else, never fished out from the trash to gift him after finishing the whole Bible, never stolen from a dead man's body.*

It was new. It was his.

CHAPTER 55

The Siren

I

"WELCOME, WELCOME, DEAR FRIENDS!!!" JB yelled ecstatically in his blue suit; fine hair combed strategically over his baldness, gray wiry beard drenched in pomade, he welcomed wagon after wagon that drove up to the house.

Charlotte peeked from the window of her room, as she still was getting dressed. "My goodness! That's a whole army of people!" She gasped, petrified, mumbling to herself, as the wagons and riders kept on marching in.

She glanced in the mirror, and to her panicked eyes, she noticed her black dress not fitting as it should, aware of her weight gain with all of JB's fatty stews and Holy Ranch's delicious cheese she had gorged down over the past days. "You're kidding me!" She sighed, squeezing a tummy roll that was protruding. "That's just fantastic!! Absolutely incredible…" she nagged, thinking what a lean body Amara had — even after birthing a child. "Probably from all that hunting…or grinding on Mac…" she muttered agitatedly, for she could just not let her rage go, Mac's sickening behavior that morning only adding to her irritation. "Gah!" She huffed, trying to adjust the dress, to make the roll somehow magically disappear, yet it just wouldn't, it stubbornly persisted instead.

She sorted through her saddlebag frantically, and grabbed the only corset she possessed; raven black — slightly faded, contrasting subtly against the ebony dress. She wrapped it around her waist, clasped the velvet strings and pulled as hard as it would go, covering her tummy completely, yet defining her breasts, unintentionally, even more. "Good." She exhaled heavily, barely able to breathe. "Much better." she said, satisfied with her brilliant idea, as she tied the strings neatly behind her back.

She pulled out a thin black ribbon, and tied it around her neck elegantly to finish her attire. "There's no way anyone would let me in that Caddo River Boat looking like that…" She chuckled, as she briefly imagined Victoria's powdered face frowning with disgust at her appearance. "Oh, Will…" She sighed with a leaden heart. "I will always cherish our dance…always cherish you, my dear one…"

I I

THE BAND OF FIVE SCRAWNY LOOK-ALIKES, bearing wide-brimmed slouch hats covering half of their gaunt faces, all had long strawy blonde hair, tangled and greasy, hanging down to their shoulders like rowdy vines. Adorned in denim overalls, huskily scented from their sweaty armpits, unbothered by the chill, as though immune to it. They bobbed their heads as they tuned their guitars and banjos, in a quiet corner underneath a tree. JB had given them precise instructions of when and where to start playing, as well as a list of Levi's favorite songs…or, more accurately, a list of the only songs JB knew.

There were closed barrels with blankets, full of moonshine bottles, as well as other spirits on top of them. Three different stews were slow brewing across the yard, all filled with chunks of sacred bison meat, potatoes and every vegetable JB could find to toss inside, capturing everyone's noses with the alluring scent of herbs. A large fire burned wildly, surrounded by logs and benches in the very middle of the field.

The evening had already fast approached, shadowing over them with a ponderous cloak of darkness; streaks of light slashed through it by the roaring fire, accompanied by the many small lanterns entwined in the branches. The wind blew, brushing a chime against the glass bottles, gusting loose swirls of flames in every direction; a wildly dancing fire warming up the company, all seated and drinking around it.

Levi greeted the guests, thanked them for their best wishes a countless times, as he sorted through them to try to spot Mac protectively. Everyone respected Levi, for he had been hired by the most of them to take care of sensitive business — clearing out moonshine thieves, or other degenerates that they often had to deal with, therefore, most traveled from all across the states to celebrate him, obliged and honored to do so.

Amara was serving everyone bowls of warm bison stew, while Jonathan blabbered their ears off about all the embarrassing stories JB told him not to tell anyone, yelling out the gunslinger's secret word he had recently acquired in his vocabulary, and yet no-one bothered to wrinkle a frown about it. Amara was beautifully adorned, having slipped into a fiery red blouse and a high-waisted black skirt with beautiful asymmetrical accents, laced with red ribbons from the waist to above the knee, flaring out with a striking set of ruffles; there was not one gentleman who didn't shower her with compliments that evening.

Charlotte stood before the door to the outside world of the chatter-ing and laughing mouths, with sweaty palms, trying to find the courage to walk outside. She never was comfortable around people, let alone so many. Somehow it felt different than the ball, somehow it felt more personal, as all of Levi's personal friends and distant cousins were gathered all together. She didn't even know if her wanted status was an issue around them or not, yet she knew JB was not one to keep such details to himself.

Mac walked out from his room, adjusting the white collar around his neck, gently, cautiously, not to wrinkle it. Turning around a corner, he glanced down the stairs to spot Charlotte peeking out of the door. He paused in his tracks, clutching himself against the wall as though to merge with its shadow. He dared to study her outfit for a fleeting moment; noticing, admiring the hourglass figure, strongly intensified even more with her tight corset coiling her waist. He stared. For the first time, he did. Observing her statuesque body, the soft swell in all the right places, realizing why eyes kept setting upon her, craving to undress her, to pierce through the cloth — and yet somehow, his eyes never had ogled her, for his attraction towards her was always far deeper than the fleshy veil around her being.

He leaned deeper against the wall quietly, yet to his surprise, he bumped into the large pot JB had left there that morning. Startled by the sudden noise, Charlotte looked up to find Mac falling over the pot, swiftly giving her the extra push and courage she needed to rush outside.

"Feck!" Mac slammed his fist on the ground, kicked the pot away from him, realizing he missed the rare opportunity to talk to her; or at least try to.

III

"CHARLOTTE!!!" JB CALLED OUT FOR HER EAGERLY, while talking to an older lady. "Charlottttaaaaaaa!" He kept on calling, and she kept on hiding, quivering with the thought of being introduced to someone, yet then chose to face them, and dithering, a few steps at a time, walk towards them.

She felt her stomach twist in a knot, for she was not one for smooth introductions, since she always managed to make a fool out of herself with her shy awkwardness. She paused cautiously before them, noticing one side of the woman's face was terrifically scarred from what appeared to be old burns, ripples of swollen scarlet flesh all across it.

"Finally!! I've been screaming my head off! HaHA!" He cackled and Charlotte blushed, then nodded. "May I introduce you to Charlotte! She's a fine young lady, with the kindest of hearts!" JB smiled as he spread his hands wide open to point at Charlotte.

The lady looked at her, screening her face and body with one sharp glance.

"Pleasure to meet you, Miss Charlotte." she greeted her with a raspy voice — one she could just tell had been through many years of torment.

"Nice to meet you too, Missus..."

"Oh! Right! I forgot! See? It's that fungus I was tellin' y'all about! It gives me memory loss! Should have never eaten that goddamn swampy mushroom!" JB started to ramble, completely forgetting what he was supposed to say.

"Mrs. Marga." the woman introduced herself, and shook Charlotte's hand with a firm grip.

"Mrs...Marga?" Charlotte's sharp jaw dropped to the ground, vividly recalling Will's lips speak out this name.

"Correct, darling." She shifted her weight to her cane, feeling her leg's strength weaken from standing too long.

"Come, Mrs. Marga, we have a glorious fire goin', and the band should be starting here shortly!" JB enthusiastically led her slowly to it, as they both limped in sync with each other.

Charlotte couldn't believe her eyes, nor her ears; this was the closest way she could get to Will — someone who actually knew him, and would be able to contact him directly. Someone who could share her words; be her voice to him. "Thank you, God!" she emotionally hummed, as she felt her prayers were slowly being answered.

I V

"Cheyenne, Cheyenne, I'm a-leavin' Cheyenne
Goodbye, old Paint, I'm a-leavin' Cheyenne

"My foot's in the stirrup, my rein in my hand
I'm a-leavin' Cheyenne, I'm off to Montan'
Goodbye, old Paint, I'm a-leavin' Cheyenne

"My horses ain't hungry, they won't eat your hay
My wagon is loaded and rolling away

"We ride all day 'till the sun's going down
I'm gonna be glad to get out of this town"

"HAHA! BRAVO, BRAVO!!" JB CLAPPED HIS HANDS, interrupting the banjo's ending riff as he did. Levi had his arm resting around JB's shoulder, laughing together with friends, talking about the latest gossip in town.

Charlotte watched Levi's bright smile compete with the stars above them, and felt genuinely happy for him to be finally enjoying himself — taking a break from this awful reality they were all trapped within.

A burly man leaned towards her, as she was seated on a log underneath a tree, slashing her thoughts with his alcohol-smelling breath that filled up her nostrils. "Some fffine music here, ma'am! Fiiine music here!" he said, and she scrunched up her face in repulsion.

"Yes. Yes, sure is…" she awkwardly scooted away from him discreetly, suddenly feeling the urge to escape — as images of the Marysville man assailed her; as scenes from the cave stabbed through her mind; somehow she hadn't figured out how to get rid of this creeping feeling that would emerge upon a trigger, somehow it still lingered within her, as though bound to remain.

"Ya ain't drinkin' nothin', ma'am?!" He cocked his head, surprised to see her empty-handed.

"No… I'd rather not." She scooted further.

"Shame, shame. That's some goooood 'shine! Ya should try it!" He leaned further towards her, pushing her rapidly over the threshold of politeness.

"Thank you, but like I already said — I'd rather not." she said firmly, this time her tone a little sharper, yet there was a jitter in her hands, a numbing in her legs, threatening to collapse into a ball of panic.

"Mr. Compton, I think she's alright." Levi intervened, a little kinder compared to his intervention at that saloon in Mon Louis.

"Thank God…" Charlotte thought out loud as she reached for Levi's hand hastily, which he held out for her.

"I'm sorry about that." He sighed in shame. "He is not a bad man, just a drunk head." He smiled into her eyes, in the hopes of calming her down.

"Yes…seems I attract this kind the most." She snorted snidely, then rolled her eyes, realizing how factual her statement was.

"Not always." He blushed, sipping on his cup of moonshine, cutting his eyes at her. There was a sudden wave of his cologne that swirled in the air between them — fresh, strangely reminding her of the Sea of De Galio right by her hometown, which always had an intense oceanic smell. It dazzled her senses; something about a man smelling of mucky tobacco and refreshing lemony fragrance mixed in together. He had shaved his beard off for the first time since she'd known him, exposing his masculine jaw even more; that too dazzled her.

"You look beautiful tonight…" He chuckled upon the compliment, in attempts to make it sound as friendly as she desired, glancing all over her — all over her elegant dress — all over her corset, pressing her breasts together, squeezing her small waist tightly. *"Damn…"* he added, shooting a flirty wink at her, for he couldn't help it.

"*Ha.* Thank you." She shied away. "You're quite…handsome, yourself."

she mumbled, hoping she wasn't giving him any false hope again.

"*Ha!* A compliment from your pretty mouth? Impossible! I should shave more often, then." He teased her, as he felt of his smooth cheeks, tapping them with his fingers caustically.

"No, no. It ain't just that. I mean…" she let out a stutter, realizing her own awkwardness yet again — realizing something had changed within her, or perhaps it was the evaporating fumes of all the moonshine around.

"What do you mean?" He smirked playfully, noticing her shyness, as she started fiddling with her long brown hair again.

"Levi! Where are you?!!" JB called for him, as he spotted his tall head poking out from the crowd.

"Gah…" He bit his lip, agitated, wondering how JB always knew exactly when the worst possible timing was to jump in and interfere.

Charlotte giggled in relief as she watched JB pushing the people away from his path to reach them faster, with not a care in the world if they spilled their drinks in the process.

"Levi! Amara, Amara — she's gonna sing, here in a little while!" JB leaned over his shaky knees to catch his breath, as his potbelly flopped over his tightly fitted pants.

"Sing?" Charlotte asked curiously, not realizing she could sing as well.

But, of course she could.

"Yes. At every celebration, she has a Norse folk song she always chooses to sing — a family tradition that has been passed on over the years…goes back many a generation." Levi smiled at her proudly. "You might like it! It's unlike anything you've heard!" he added and led Charlotte to the bonfire, seating her atop a bench.

V

"Drøymde mik ein draum i nótt
um silki ok ærlig pell,
um hægindi svá djupt ok mjott,
um rosemd með engan skell.

"Ok i drauminom ek leit
sem gegnom ein groman glugg
þá helo feigo mennsko sveit,
hver sjon ol sin eiginn ugg.

"Talit þeira otta jok
ok leysingar joko enn —
en oft er svar eit þyngra ok,
þó spurning at bera brenn.

"Ek fekk sofa lika vel,
ek truða þat væri best —
at hvila mik á goðu þel´
ok gløyma svá folki flest´.

"Friðinn, ef hann finzt, er hvar
ein firrest þann mennska skell,
fær veggja sik um, drøma þar
um silki ok ærlig pell."

A SOFT, STILL SILENCE FELL OVER THE AUDIENCE; a slow, rolling build that slammed into the sinews of their being, hooked as ears listened to Amara's angelic voice in awe; hypnotized eyes surveying her peaceful face, lit up by the swirling fire for everyone to admire, be bewitched by. Her eyes shut, forehead strained into few wise wrinkles, singing with ethereal beauty from the very depths of her soul — as though summoning the Norse Gods to the realm of Midgard by a dazzling chant; words only Levi and Jonathan could understand.

He was right, Charlotte thought to herself; it was unlike anything she'd heard before. Amara's undeniably alluring voice prickled her skin across, it almost felt haunting. She was enthralled by the blood-curdling sounds such a slender throat could issue, as the song rose and her chest swelled with it. She couldn't understand the sharp, yet beautiful sounding words, but it seemed as though she could feel her woe, somehow causing a cascade of emotions, crashing against her heart like a ruthless wave. Tears stood in her eyes; they misted over, as memories assailed her.

She was gifted in so many ways — it was hard to compete with, she admired sadly, realizing she never had to compete with someone, realizing she shouldn't have to. Amara was her friend, or at least, someone trying to be, someone she was preventing from being with all her sorrow and bitterness. She sighed in shame, then thought of *him,* wishing she hadn't seen her with *him,* wishing she had never told her how she cared for *him,* wishing they could have just remained friends, as deep down she was fond of her.

A white figure emerged in the dark background, blurred by the dancing flames' swirls of hot air that rose up through the colder air above. There was a shine, a flicker of a glass, seeming to hold a bottle of whiskey the closer it approached. Charlotte squinted her eyes to see through the smoke before her; recognizing the long flowing dark blond hair, now touching the shoulders, the confident stride, and the sturdy body frame with the sharpest v-shape she'd ever known, slashing through fog and air.

It was Mac, slowly trudging towards the fire — dithering, as he had never been around so many strangers — that weren't just deputies trying to arrest him, or other drunkard criminals of his kind. *It must have taken him several hours to feel confident enough to come out of the house,* she thought, for she couldn't spot him anywhere before, and she had certainly tried.

His white dress shirt was slightly tight around his broad chest and muscular arms — tucked into his faded black pants, with his usual rugged boots pulled over them. He took her breath away, inhaling with every step he made towards them, in all his odd innocence adorned in disguise, in all his incongruous attire; she had never seen him dressed so proper, it almost puzzled her. The freshly trimmed blond stubble glowed now by the fire's light as he advanced to it, leading to his thick, vascular neck, down to the slightly cracked shirt collar, exposing an inviting trail towards his chest and…below. Charlotte forced her eyes away, for her thoughts strayed away to inappropriate places she swore to never let herself wander again — not with *him.*

Mac leaned against the wagon wheel, boots crossed at the ankles, sipping on the bottle as Amara's voice lured his eyes towards her. He reminisced the times he used to visit Mickey at his bar in Marysville — in the later hours, when nobody would suspect anything nefarious from this man wearing a duster coat and a hat to hide his identity, for they were too drunk to do so anyway; Mickey made extra sure of that.

He sipped on that whiskey, talking to the only person he considered his friend; struggling with the essential fluency of words to keep up a conversation, for he was never taught proper grammar — only Bible verses from an archaic edition, never meant to scrape any knowledge he tried to grasp from a gazette, plastering images of rules and punishment upon him instead.

Yet Mickey knew him well, and always helped to fill in the void with stories or jokes that Mac smirked at. He didn't know how to laugh, nor entertain a story — but he was trying his best to understand why it was supposed to be humorous, and mimicked Mickey's facial expressions like a monkey would mimic a human. They never spoke about what happened in those fields, nor what transpired in the cellar.

He drank on the bottle, drowning that memory — knowing he'd most likely never see him again, almost sensing the solidarity that will engulf him upon his departure tomorrow; for he threatened to leave, and his ego wouldn't let him do otherwise.

He cut his eyes at *her*.

V I

"IS THAT CHAP HIM?" Mrs. Marga pointed with her cane towards Mac as she whispered in JB's ear, who was seated beside her on the log — smoking a cigar and drinking moonshine in between.

"Yes, yes. That's him in flesh and bone. The *legendary* Mac Kinnon." he whispered back a little too loud, for Levi to accidentally hear, not to mention everybody else around them.

"Interesting. Never realized how good lookin' the bastard is! Ha! Perhaps I should find myself an outlaw after all!" Mrs. Marga chuckled out loud, ogling Mac's muscular body struggling to fit the shirt with her weary eyes.

"Handsome devil…"

"Oh, well…I really think it's just the shirt makin' him look more…appealing, you know!" JB proudly said, happily noticing him wearing the white dress shirt he gifted him. "He ain't anythin' quite like I used to look, that's for damn sure!" he added with a chuckle.

"Of course; we both have aged terribly now, my old friend. Those were the days…careless and peaceful young whippersnappers, until the shit hit the fan. HA!" She snorted, reflecting on how life suddenly changed for the worst, as her hand deftly shielded her scars from view with the subconscious movement she'd developed over the years.

"Cheers to that! Haha! Although you still look fabulous, my dear!" JB burst into laughter, almost rolling off the log.

"You're too kind…cheers." She banged her cup against his.

"That 'shine is remarkable, my dearest!" JB said, slurping some more.

"It comes straight from my tavern in Mon Louis…*but shhh*…you're not supposed to know that." She winked at him and he waggled his brows at her.

"I don't know nothin' 'bout no tavern in Mon Louis…" He winked back and she cackled, knowing everyone would soon find out for sure, then she glanced over at Charlotte, still seated on a bench looking lonely and pitiful.

"And the gal?" she asked him curiously, as her quietness intrigued her.

"Charlotte!" he exclaimed. "Ah! She's quite a sweet one. Quite a helpful hand in the kitchen, can't cook to save her life however! Ha! Don't know much 'bout her. She don't talk a lot, just smiles, nods, and is polite! Not too shabby if ya ask me!" He cackled, and Mrs. Marga bobbed her head, studying her in the faint light. "Levi can probably tell ya more!" He winked at her, then choked on the smoke from his cigar he inhaled too hastily right after.

"Oh. They're, they're together?" Her brows cinched in surprise to hear Levi had time to invest in an actual relationship.

"Hell, I don't know what's goin' on in this house lately. Everybody seems so secretive 'bout who is fuckin' who! Haha! In my old days, I was a wild child! Tellin' everyone 'bout my business, whether they wanted to hear 'bout it or not! Ain't nobody got time for such games as they're playin' now! Bunch of prudes, I tell ya!" he nagged, clearly already intoxicated.

"Ha. Never change, JB. Never change." She grinned, entertained with his rambling, then stood up with wobbly legs, making her way over to Charlotte.

CHAPTER 56

Five Finger Fillet

I

"WHO YOU ARE, MISTER?" A drunken gentleman approached Mac, as he wasn't sure he had seen him before.

"Hm?" Mac nodded in confusion, hovering his hand over his knife habitually.

"Guess I've never seen ya before in any of our previous gatherings! Nice to meet you, partner! Ben Davenport!" He held out his hand to shake Mac's, yet Mac just glanced down at it and continued sipping on his whiskey.

"Sure." he mumbled awkwardly.

"What's your name, mister?" he questioned him again, confused as to why he was so unfriendly.

"None of yer concern." Mac growled abruptly, turning his back to him.

"Darn! Feisty one, ah?" he teased him playfully, grabbing Mac's shoulder without thinking.

Mac turned swiftly around and pushed him back, throwing him to the ground effortlessly. "Get lost, ye eejit." he warned him, and the man crawled hastily away, shaking his head as though Mac suddenly formed into a brooding shadow. Mac exhaled deeply, for he felt seconds away from strangling the man, being several feet separated from the crowd — the idea intrigued him, and yet he chose to remain stationed at the wagon wheel, for everyone's sake.

His hands jittered, teleporting in his mind around the man's neck, coiling tightly like lethal wire, sending an all too familiar feeling of dark satisfaction within him. In shame, and in abhorrence, he craved for release. Clenching teeth, locking legs to the ground — trying to compose himself again, he glanced over at Levi, watching him carefully all along.

"Mr. Kinnon!!" JB slammed his hand on Mac's back, startling him again.

"Gah." He nagged, yanking his shoulder away from him, lighting up a cigarette to keep his mouth busy and polite.

"Just wanted to say I'm glad to see ya wearin' this shirt, son!" he accidentally said — accustomed to the way he talked to Levi. Mac looked at him, aghast; lips folding again uncomfortably, then nodded as kindly as he could. "Looks good on ya! Ladies are all askin' who you are! And when I tell 'em, well…they either scream, leave, or faint! HaHA!" he smiled widely and Mac frowned at him, baffled by his talent to find amusement in everything odd. "Don't be shy! Come to the fire!" He pushed his shoulder towards the crowd; encouraging him to follow after him, like father would reassure son to get over his insecurities.

Mac followed him tentatively; blindly, brain tracing feeble circles within him — not from the whiskey, but from the random acts of kindness he'd been receiving all day from the old man.

II

"MISS CHARLOTTE." MRS. MARGA STARTLED HER WITH A RASPY VOICE, as she stared at the fire, watching each branch burn down to ash.

"Oh!" She gasped, surprised. "Mrs. Marga!" She stood up respectfully, offering her own seat.

"Sit down child, there's plenty room for the both of us!" She chuckled, followed by a smoker's rusty cough, then sat down. Tilting her head towards her, she stared at Charlotte, whose fingers fidgeted with her gown — seemingly nervous to sit beside her.

"So, you're a wanted outlaw?" Mrs. Marga asked her, in an interesting way to break the ice.

"I…no…" She sighed, realizing JB told her everything. "I mean…yes, but I ain't no Annie Oakley — far from it, actually…" She snorted snidely, reminiscing the pitiful way she tried to even hunt a rabbit.

"HA! You're funny…so, you killed a man?" she asked straightforward. "Don't blame ya. Too many filthy bastards runnin' free…" She took a big sip from her cup; thinking back on the man who ignited a fire atop of her — causing her the most prominent scars across her face, still sweltering within her mind, still tormenting her every single day with this devastating experience.

"I didn't kill a man…to be honest." Charlotte drew in a deep breath; her hands grew clammy, trying to dig up the memories she tried hard to bury away. "I have killed, but…only out of necessity — it was either me, or him. Yet, this was not the death they blamed me for. I never killed that son of a gun in Marysville, Mrs. Marga…" She defended herself, glancing absently over at Mac, sipping on a bottle quietly before the fire as Jonathan talked his ears off, even when he didn't receive a response back; she could almost read the infamous word on his lips, spurted out in repeat in sheer delight.

"It don't concern me, my dear. I've killed plenty of men in my life, and never regretted a single bullet I put through their skulls." She admitted proudly, and locked eerie eyes with her.

Charlotte stared at her damaged eye; blind and pale, sunken within the permanent swelling of her eyelids, scarlet and raw guarding around it — yet it felt like it was looking right through her soul, unraveling all her secrets, judging all her buried desires. She didn't expect to hear such a confession, however she noticed the crowd around her was a vague mixture of loudmouthed pioneers, drunken moonshiners, and a few more reserved seeming guests.

"I understand. The more I live in this world, the more I can justify certain… atrocities." she mumbled quietly, briefly watching the fire plow through the burning logs, then her gaze lifted up to meet Mac's — noticing him staring right at her, eyes in shadow, yet alive and glimmering.

She jolted, tearing her gaze away swiftly.

"Take care of yourself, dearie. It's a dangerous world out there. Don't trust *anyone.*" she muttered earnestly, standing up slowly with her trembling legs, pressing the cane against the ground harshly.

"Mrs. Marga! I almost forgot!" Charlotte walked after her, realizing she didn't even ask about Will.

"Yes, dear?" she questioned her suspiciously, leaning over her cane to rest her weak leg.

"We...we have a common friend." she stuttered abruptly, as guilt had consumed her for all the ways she betrayed Will.

"That much I know. Ha!" She cackled hoarsely, pointing around at the crowd with a forefinger.

"No...besides Levi, and his family here. His name is..." She swallowed nervously. "...Will...William Griffiths." she said, heart weighing a ton, pulling her down to the soil in shame, as the mention of his name left a bittersweet taste in her mouth.

"Ooooh!!" she exclaimed, baffled. "Oh, my! Now it all makes sense! I *knew* I had heard your name before!" she shouted ecstatically.

"Please explain to me, Mrs. Marga." Charlotte begged her, longing to hear any recent news she might have had from Will.

"Oh, William. What a sweet, sweet young man." she said, shaking her head, and Charlotte's heart swelled up, a smile scaring her lips, for Will was the sweetest man indeed. "He wrote me a letter some time ago; asking if I could have you stay at my moonshine shack! I failed to write back, as...well, to be honest, I wasn't interested in getting into...further trouble." She shrugged and Charlotte nodded.

"I completely understand, ma'am...I would never wish to impose." she said, enthralled to hear Will had indeed kept his word to write her.

"Thank you. I'm not the youngest anymore, and cannot risk opening my door to...strangers. I can't carry their baggage; got plenty of my own." She sighed heavily, feeling her body ache from straining to stand longer than she could. "What's your affiliation with William? For he hinted you was his... lady." she said, cocking a brow of suspicion.

"Ma'am...I...I...it is complicated." she stammered, knowing after her letter, they would be nothing but estranged, hopeless souls.

"Well, it ain't my business, but I do like ya more than that ginger brat..." She snorted, and she didn't understand, though a thought crossed her mind.

"Mrs. Marga...has Will contacted you again, since then?" she asked, her fingers curled into a sweaty fist, released, strained, and curled again. "It's just that...I'm worried about him. I had no way to contact him for quite some weeks, only until recently, but...I'm afraid it might have been too late." Charlotte expressed her feelings to her, then looked around herself to make sure no one heard her.

"No, child. He has not contacted me again. But I can write him back, if you want me to. I'd be happy to do that for you." She smiled kindly to her, noticing her obvious distress.

"That would absolutely be wonderful!" she said, tearing up. "I will never be able to repay you, but please know if you ever need anything, I'm at your service." She politely offered, holding her hand out for a handshake.

"I have a feeling this won't be the last time we meet." Mrs. Marga winked at her, shaking her hand in agreement.

III

"AND YOU KNOW, MA SAID I WASN'T OLD ENOUGH to go hunting with her, yet I shot a squirrel in the yard with my bow!" Jonathan boasted, neglecting to mention the squirrel was one of his own toy pelts he used as a target.

"Hm." Mac hummed for the hundredth time that evening, glancing over at Amara, who was watching her son like a mother puma.

"Yes! Ma said I wasn't old enough to drink either, but I took a sip from the moon...the moon..."

"Shine..." his deep voice added, startling the boy for he did not expect to hear him speak.

"Moonsh...shine." He giggled, holding on to Mac's knife holster, bouncing up and down next to him with joy.

Amara felt a sudden sadness reach her heart, seeing her son so enchanted by Mac — out of all the men around him, he kept on running to him. She couldn't grasp what went wrong that night; why he suddenly changed from this incredibly passionate kisser, to a coldhearted being of apathy and hate.

"Mister, can I write my letter on your hand?" he asked Mac, and Mac blinked at him, refusing to answer. The boy took out a pen and reached for his hand. Mac jerked it away swiftly.

"No." he said sternly, and the boy pouted.

"But...it is my letter..." he said.

"But it ain't mine..."

"I can write yours!!" He smiled widely, leaped again.

"Settle down, lad!" He huffed impatiently, and his eyes quivered in tears. Mac stared at them, bright blues clouding over. "Gahhh…sure." he said, and handing him his arm.

Jonathan screeched joyfully, and started to scribble Mac's name in sharp concentration, pen gripped tightly in his fist. Mac stared at the letters, knowing he himself had no ability to write them, wondering how his life was like as a four year old, for he could not recall. "Mmmmmmaaaaaac…" Jonathan said, stabbing the pen stubbornly for more control.

Mac grabbed his tiny arm and yanked it away from him. "Enough now." he said firmly, and Jonathan bobbed his head in swift compliance.

"You like it, mister?" he then asked with a hopeful smile, and Mac glanced down at it, cocked a brow.

"Hm…" he grumbled, then looked back at him, longing for more enthusiasm. "Sure."

Jonathan screeched again in blithe, giggling into Mac's ears, a laughter like no other, proud to have impressed him somehow. "Mister…" He suddenly turned earnest, bowed his head, cheeks crimsoned. "I don't miss daddy so much with you here, sir." he said boldly, shying away. Mac's eyes flared, benumbing whole. He swallowed down a lump and looked away.

"Bad business." he said after a long pause, and Jonathan blinked at him.

"Are you sad, mister?" he asked him, lips curving down, a curve of empathy felt too strongly in his pure years, a feeble attribute, threatened to tarnish as life unravels.

"Hm?"

"If you are sad…you look sad." He shrugged and Mac tore his gaze away. "But it's alright, mister. Sometimes I am sad too, and mommy makes me warm milk and bakes those delicious oatsies!" he said and Mac side-eyed him.

"Cookies?" he asked, bewildered with himself to even do so.

"Yes! Oat…oatsy cookies." He grinned. "And when I eat them, it makes me happy." He smiled in his eyes. "Do you want? I can bring you oatsies… mommy thinks I don't know about her secret stash…" He chuckled and Mac shook his head, drawing in a deep breath, somehow suffocating in his presence.

"Go play, lad…" He sighed and Jonathan shrugged defeated, as though he knew he did his best.

"Feck." Jonathan said, cool and contented.

Mac snorted as he watched him prance away, then his eyes nailed down to the scribble and a wave of an uneasy feeling washed over him. He had never murdered children, could not. Somehow they reflected the innocence that was robbed from him, somehow he longed for them to keep it.

The boy now ran through the crowd ecstatically, maneuvering between them as if he rode a wild mustang — known from what he proudly described to everyone he passed — stepping on women's dresses and trampling on men's shoes, feeling the effects of moonshine kick into his little body, efficiently spreading the poison into his brain.

"Mr. Kinnon!" JB called after him, seeing him seated on his own again.

Mac turned to look at him, noticed he was sitting around a table, a knife in his hand, two burly men around him.

"Move your arse over here!" He laughed, excited to include him into a five finger fillet match.

Mac spat on the ground and stood up to walk over to him, as though feeling obliged to listen, clutching the shirtfront of his white cloth, squeezing it, feeling it soften the callouses of his fingertips.

"Wanna make some money, boy? HaHA!" JB chuckled as he had already bet on Mac winning against the brawny man before him.

"What ye mean, ol' man…" Mac asked him suspiciously, then cast a glance over at the man waiting patiently, knife clutched in his fist.

"Ya got a knife, my boy?" JB questioned him, slapping his hands atop his knees, standing up swifter than usual, and limping towards him.

"Hm…" Mac nodded, pulled out his Bowie knife, its high carbon steel blade aglow in the darkness, eyes of perished souls imprinted upon it, yet the living were too blind to see them. He gripped the slim full tang handle with his strong fist, slammed the knife into the wood, and sat down to face his opponent.

"Better watch out! Y'all play fair and nice, now!" JB made sure to emphasize, as he wasn't trusting Mac blindly yet.

"Get on with it…" Mac pressed the man to start first, as he stared at Mac, aghast, knowing what he was.

Gathering up his grit, chugging down some more moonshine of courage, he began tapping the knife between his fingers, not missing a single beat — tapping as fast as he could, as JB was counting the time worriedly, realizing it would be hard to beat. Tapping and tapping, over and again, faster and harsher into the worn wood, he flourished, then slammed the knife against the table as he finished his turn. Smirking, satisfied, knowing his timing was nigh unbeatable.

Mac placed his hand on the table — stretching out the calloused fingers, wide palm pressed down. He locked eyes with the man before him, grabbed his knife, yanked it out of the wood, and started stabbing his Bowie knife back and forth between his fingers without breaking eye contact. He stabbed and tapped as fast as he could, feeling the blade subtly caress against his skin; knowing exactly where it would land before it ever hit the table.

JB and the man's faces both fell, slacked jaws tapping the table with every blade thud, watching him in complete shock, bobbing their heads back and forth, following the flawless movement. JB glared beneath the table, making sure there was no otherworldly magnet attached to it, then gaped back at him, both stopping the count as the speed of his knife was abnormally fast.

He spun the knife in the air, flipped it, gripped it with menace, yet contentment, and continued tapping between his fingers, all without messing up his time. He jammed the knife in the middle of the table, and unlocked his deep ocean blue eyes from him.

"Bad business." He smirked, knowing he had won the match.

"MAC!!! MY BOY!!! MY BOY!!!" JB screamed from the top of his lungs, echoing all across Hollenberg; jumping like a monkey on top of Mac as he stood up, patting his head excitedly for the winner was already clear — shuffling and messing up his long hair as he did. "WE ARE RICH TONIGHT!! AHAHAH!!" he celebrated, and Mac pushed him off of himself, reminding him of his boundaries.

"Nooo touchy-touchy! Right! Got it!" JB chuckled as he slammed his hand against his back, then danced around him as he collected the money from all the men who betted against him, and pressed it into Mac's hand.

Everyone seated at the fire turned their heads around to witness JB hopping and limping up and down, grabbing bottles of moonshine to share with the champion. Roaring, dancing, choking as he drank. Levi looked at him agitatedly, not approving of Mac being so close to him — wondering what in the world went on to be worthy of such celebration. Amara stared in awe, halting her chattering with a handsome older man lured into her web, for she never expected to see Mac entertaining himself in any possible way.

Charlotte couldn't believe her eyes; there was a smirk on Mac's lips, perhaps even a rosy tint of shyness on his cheeks. Her heart fluttered, suffused with a sense of happiness for him, deep inside, feeling ecstatic to see him surrounded by people who for once praised him instead of painting him as a monster. Her eyes flooded, for the sudden sentiment was grasping her heart intensely. She felt proud of him, wishing the inviting warmth they radiated towards him would be engraved within him for eternity, lock inside reality's rare maze of kindness, for he refused to trudge through it; he could not.

Mac turned to spot her, locking eyes with her unintentionally, freezing within a dancing crowd. They stared, while the cheering noise of people muffled around them as if time itself was paused. He held her eyes with every vigor his gaze possessed, yet she pulled hers away, as the sudden arising pain was too much to bear.

CHAPTER 57

Woodland Dove

I

THE DEPUTIES HAD LOCATED THE HIDDEN BODY, sunken in the shallow waters of Flat Bow lagoon; later on identified by the Millers to belong to Elizabeth Griffiths. The entire town of Bisonhorn mourned for her loss, as she was loved and admired by many — known for her elegance, beauty, and the vague veneer of kindness she made sure to portray.

> *"Almighty God, as you once called our sister Elizabeth into*
> *this life, so now you have called her into life everlasting. We*
> *therefore commit her remains; her body; her earthly tent to*
> *the elements. In the hope of resurrection unto eternal life,*
> *through the promise of Our Lord Jesus Christ, we faithfully*
> *and victoriously give her over to your blessed care. Amen."*

They buried her at Bisonhorn's cemetery, followed by a short noticed ceremony which the residents attended respectfully. The Millers planted flowers beside her tombstone, visiting her every other day before they prepared to leave for Mon Louis — for Mrs. Miller's health was declining rapidly.

Sheriff Dorman sat quietly in his office, realizing he had lost every single trace again that he had hoped would point to Mac Kinnon. He choked, gagging in repulsion, as the image of finding Elizabeth's decaying body assailed him; giving him horrifying flashbacks of when he found his brother, rotten to death, eaten by rats in the filthiest cellar anyone ever stepped foot in. He yanked down Will's poster, tearing it apart with quivering hands of malice — throwing it to the bin underneath his desk — burying him with the trash.

I I

THE MOONSHINE SUPPLY WAS GETTING LOWER, as guests kept on greedily pouring more and more into their cups. Some had already dozed off inside their wagons, and others laid there on the ground, counting the stars that seemingly multiplied by every second that passed.

"What do you think?" Amara asked Levi, with an endearing smile on her face, hand caressing his back.

"I think JB outdid himself again." Levi smiled back, thinking how blessed he was to still have part of his family intact.

"Yes, he organized everything flawlessly, I must admit." She surprisingly complimented him, and both glanced over at JB — trying his luck with his own dull knife, stabbing his plump fingers after every tap, yet too drunk to care or feel any pain that came along with it, too stubborn and amused to quit.

"What did you think of…Kinnon?" Levi tentatively asked her, as he spotted him smoking, leaned against the wagon wheel again — enveloped in complete darkness and solitude.

"Don't get me started…" She rolled her eyes to him.

"The feeling is mutual…I'm surprised nobody was murdered tonight." He leered, figuring everyone was in danger just by breathing around him.

"Well…the night's still young." She snorted snidely, and Levi followed with a sigh.

"I'm glad to hear you're not chasing after him no more." he said happily yet stern, as he watched the banjo player tune his instrument again.

"What's that supposed to mean?" Amara gasped, offended, cheeks blushing from guilt.

"It don't matter anymore. Just promise me, you won't go near him again." He cut his eyes at her earnestly and she sheepishly nodded.

"You couldn't pay me to go near the bastard." She defended herself, yet her heart still grieved his rejection.

"Levi!" A deep voice rattled behind him, and he jerked his head around to face the man reaching a hand atop his shoulder. "Happy Birthday to you!" he said. Levi laughed, stood up, and patted his shoulder.

"Sam! My old man managed to invite everyone, I see! All the way from Mon Louis!" He shook his head in gratitude, baffled people had traveled so far just to see him.

"Indeed! Now, my wife wasn't able to come, nor my son, however…"

"Sam…" He clasped his shoulders. "I know it wasn't easy for you, brother. I appreciate you bringing yourself!" He smiled into his icy blue eyes and the man nodded to him.

"Feeling older yet?" He chuckled and Levi huffed heavily.

"No. But worn down, surely!" he said. "How is business…" he asked, voice lowered.

"Not good…since…all that happened with the Mayor." he soughed discreetly. Levi nodded, gritting his teeth. "If it wasn't for you, I'd be in a much worse place however. Thank you." he said, clutching his shoulder in turn.

"Don't mention it. That's what brothers are for. Helping each other in tough situations."

"One day, I will repay you. I give you my word." he said earnestly, and Levi smiled.

"Are you struggling, Sam? Are you all hungering?" he asked him and the man bowed his head, conflicted.

"No…no, my friend. We're doing just fine." he smiled with teary eyes and Levi nodded gravely.

"I heard about the deal with Sheriff Jordon…and Mac Kinnon." he said and Levi bobbed his head in shame. "You're a wanted man in Birdsboro, Levi." he said sternly and Levi swallowed dryly.

"I am aware, Sam…but it was for a good reason, after all." he said and Sam took the message.

"I understand…" he said, realizing he didn't wish to speak further about it.

"Excuse me for a moment, Sam." he said, as he glanced over at Charlotte, seated on the bench like a cocooned ball of shyness. "I have a lady waiting on me…" he said and Sam clapped his shoulder encouragingly.

"That's a beautiful woman, Levi." he said kindly, for he had noticed so all evening, and Levi bobbed his head in absence.

"Hopefully, one day we'll be just like you and Beth." he whispered, and slipped away from him, trudging over to her.

III

THE BAND TOOK A BREAK TO EAT SOME STEW, still brewing over several fires, cooking the meat to melt on the tongue, falling apart into juicy shreds. They refreshed their musical memory with some liquor, re-tuned their guitars and banjos — strumming each string repeatedly against their ears, and picked up right where they had left. A cascade of upbeat tunes now echoed across, the crowd jolly dancing around themselves, meanwhile, midnight rolled in unexpectedly fast, like a wave swallowing them all whole.

"Hello…"

Charlotte cut her eyes to the side, finding Levi holding a bottle of whiskey.

"Hey!" She smiled at him, setting her gaze upon the bottle.

"Are you enjoying yourself tonight?" he questioned her worriedly, for he felt he had abandoned her in an ocean full of strangers.

"Y…yes, of course!" she said, plastering a lie on her tongue, not wishing to upset or offend him in any way.

"Please." He offered her the whiskey, hand reaching out to hers. "I figured you'd prefer that over the 'poison' around here." He chuckled, reminding her how she almost choked to death from it.

"Ha! Thank you. I just don't like drinking when around other people…or at all…" she mumbled, embarrassed, as she glanced around herself to notice the crowd had spread throughout the yard into separate small groups; drinking, chattering out loud, bursting into laughter, clearly intoxicated. Mrs. Marga had already left, and Jonathan was tucked into bed hours ago — that's all she had found out, while seated on that log for the whole evening.

"How come?" Levi asked her, and sat beside her.

"You should be the first to know…remember that Bloody Buck Saloon…" She snorted, hiding her face behind her hands, not wanting to talk about it any further.

"Bucket of Blood Saloon?" He corrected her with a big grin, knowing exactly what she was talking about.

"Gah." She blushed vibrantly. "Yes…don't remind me. And don't even remind me of that powdered witch, Victooooria." She mocked her name, agitated just by the mere mention of it.

"Ah yes, I forgot about that! You were quite talkative that night!"

"Just don't…don't remind me, please." she interrupted him, noticing his grin become wider as he recalled the memories.

"Perhaps I'd like to remind myself." he said boldly. "For I'm very thankful for that night we crossed paths." he said, gulping down some whiskey, side-eyeing her expression.

"Gah…" she groaned in response and grabbed the bottle off his hands, knowing she needed some way to relax her nerves.

"Has he bothered you at all tonight…?" he then asked protectively, as this curiosity lingered in his head throughout the whole night.

"Him? No…" she admitted, somehow wishing he had.

"Strange." he muttered shortly, for he had noticed his eyes setting upon her all night long.

"What is strange? He doesn't care about me, Levi…he…he chose your cousin…or, just one night with her…" she rambled, agitated. "Or what-ever their deal was…" She rolled her eyes, not really knowing what went on between them after that.

"Well…let's not worry about him, then…anymore…" he whispered softly, eyes cutting at Mac, still glued to the wheel.

The guitarist changed into a slow-paced melody; both down and up stroking on his strings, strumming several chords before he started to croon.

> *"The birds of the forest are calling for thee*
> *And the shades and the glades are lonely*
> *Summer is there with her blossoms fair*
> *And you are absent only"*

The man's words reached out within Levi's heart, taking a defiant joy in them, unfolding like a bloom as he turned to look at Charlotte, savoring the feeling of contentment as she watched him sing; his heart throbbed, burning with fervent desire, noticing the profile of her face outlined warmly by the flames, and all he could think was how *goddamn beautiful* she was.

> *"No bird that nests in the greenwood tree*
> *But sighs to greet you and kiss you*
> *All the violets yearn, yearn for your safe return*
> *But most of all I miss you"*

"Charlotte?" Levi called her with a whisper, so as to not disturb the singer, or rather his voice succumbed to his nervousness. Charlotte swallowed nervously, swiftly hearing JB's words ring in her head.

"Yes?" She hesitantly looked at him.

"Would you…would you like to dance? With me?" he stuttered for the first time, fearing for the usual rejection she was never too shy to give.

Charlotte thought about her promise to JB, and reminisced Levi's shoulder, whom she cried on the night Mac betrayed her trust and stomped on her feelings. She stared in his begging eyes and cracked her quivering mouth open.

"As…friends, right?" she said and he smiled.

"What else? As strangers?" he said, and she snorted.

"Yes. I would." She took a big gulp of whiskey; bigger than she could comfortably swallow at once — stood up confidently, grabbed his arm and pulled him towards her. She led him to the center of the circle the guests had formed before the fire; placed her arms around his neck lovingly as he wrapped his hands around her waist, feeling the strings of her corset brushing against his fingers.

> *"The fawn that you tamed has a look in its eyes*
> *That doth say 'We are too long parted'*
> *Songs that are trolled by our comrades old*
> *Are not now as they were light hearted"*

The guests noticed them dancing slowly before the band — pausing everything they were doing, talking about, breathing, to curiously admire Levi and

Charlotte — entwined with each other, lost within their own world and magic.

> *"The wild rose fades in the leafy shades*
> *Its ghost will find you and haunt you"*

Mac lowered his cigarette from his face when he realized it wasn't a random girl wrapped in Levi's arms, but Charlotte instead. He stared; calculating every single move they made — noticing Levi's hands pull her waist closer and closer into him, choking him as he did. He noticed her smile widen, her sparkling eyes locking his, fingers caressing the back of his neck, fingers digging into her cloth. He felt the cigarette burn up, wasting on its own — reaching his fingers, burning his skin little by little, until he crushed the cancer stick and let it drop to the ground.

> *"All the friends say come*
> *Come to your woodland home*
> *And most of all I want you"*

Levi smiled at Charlotte, as he couldn't believe they were dancing unapologetically before everyone he knew so well. He felt her slim fingers play with his hair, as her hands still rested behind his muscular neck. He could not deny it any further; he wanted to fall asleep and wake up next to her beautiful face for the rest of his life, for he had searched far and wide for the right woman to settle down with, and that woman was her.

"What do you think…" he soughed to her and she blushed, dazzled by his gaze.

"I think…this goes beyond all etiquette I had once learned…" she joked bittersweet and he snorted.

"Hmm…so…they wouldn't approve of us dancing so close on that boat?" he said, cocking his brow caustically.

"No…"

"Do *you* approve?"

He clasped her firm, staring into her, chest rising as hers swelled.

"Somehow, I do…" She smiled into his eyes.

JB watched from the table, knife still stuck between his fingers. Eyes flooded with emotional tears, drowning in immense happiness to see his boy's expression full of love and joy — such as he'd never seen before.

"Slumber on my little gypsy sweetheart
Wild little woodland dove"

"Charlotte… I've…" he leaned closer to her face, noticing her eyes slowly shut, anticipating what they both were after — her mouth cracked slightly open, already waiting like a question.

Mac swallowed his anger, yet he could not keep it drowned any longer… he felt his heartbeat race like it never had before, burning within, aching, fading, dying. A fuming monster trudging out from its lair, unraveling the deepest rage from the depths of its core, brimming with rancor, its eyes bathed in a cesspit of devilry.

Levi cupped her face gently, and planted his lips on hers fervently — melting in the softness of her mouth, drowning in her whiskey drenched taste, unearthing a greater love than any he'd ever known. Charlotte squeezed him tightly around his neck, pulled his head even closer to hers — brushing her silken lips against his, feeling the warmth blossom in her chest…

Surrendering.

"Can you hear the song that tells you
All my heart's true love"

642

CHAPTER 58

Permission

I

"EASY, GIRL..." THE YOUNG MAN SAID TO THE GRAY MARE, as he opened the gate for her to step into the barn, hand resting along her withers, as though to guide her through the dark.

Temperatures were dropping to the low thirties at night, just below freezing, unusual for that time of the year in Hollenberg. Weather had changed drastically over the last couple years, and it affected every farmer around — especially Holy Ranch, since it was the main farm where town folks were getting their supplies from.

He unsaddled the horse, threw a thick brown blanket over it, and cocooned it in warmth and shelter. "It's alright now! Yer safe." the man spoke softly, petted its under-muscled neck, fuzzy from the patches of winter coat it had grown, yet its eyes were dull, with no vigor within them.

He locked the squeaky stable door behind him, and watched the mare nest in the straw, slowly lay down on the ground — as if her knees were too weak to carry her. The man fiddled with his rugged stubble worriedly, as he thought hard about the rancher's promises — already hearing all the mockery from his boss, Mr. Walston — knowing he wouldn't be pleased with her sickly appearance.

II

THE BAND HAD PACKED UP THEIR STRINGED INSTRUMENTS, safely in their wagon, and pocketed their reward from JB — who was still staying awake to greet everyone as they left.

"Well done, my friend." Levi walked up to him, holding Charlotte's hand beside him. "Thank you." He bowed to him in gratitude and JB's lips quivered.

"Of course, my boy! Of course!!" JB sniffed, wiping his nose with his sleeve. "Hope you two enjoyed it! We all sure did. HaHa!" He then winked at them, almost stumbling over himself as the moonshine moved his feet for him.

Charlotte blushed, thinking how they kissed in front of everyone's eyes, so very inappropriate, so unlike her shy self, yet it felt freeing, liberating, as if breaking away from the shackles that tethered her to Mac, to the concept of *him,* for they never were something other than a freezing kiss in the middle of nowhere. She squeezed his large hand in hers, forcing her heart to explode with joy again.

Levi looked down at her, resting her head gently against his shoulder.

"Hey, beautiful." He caressed her face lovingly with a chilled forefinger, feeling the happiest he'd ever been in his life.

"Hey…" She smiled, inhaling his cologne, the stronger and deeper she buried her face into him.

"Thank you, for the dance…" He blushed, for she gave him a lot more than that.

"My pleasure, cowboy." She winked at him, already feeling rather tipsy, making her brave enough to stand on her toes and kiss him again for a fleeting moment. Pulling back, staring at his lips, swollen and red, an ethanol filled breath fogging her sight.

"Charlotte…" He sighed heavily, almost groaned, and kissed her back boldly, picking her up in his arms, for he noticed everyone had already left — besides JB, who was counting the moonshine bottles, making sure it was precisely as many they had promised to bring.

"Whoa!" Charlotte gasped, suddenly feeling light as a feather in his muscular arms, forgetting about that tummy roll that made her self-conscious before.

"What's wrong?" Levi chuckled, hands hooked underneath her.

"N-nothing. Just…surprised me, is all." She smiled, embarrassed, scanning the area around her as she shivered from the sudden breeze that reached her bones.

"It's warmer inside, you know…" He gave her a naughty smile, feeling Charlotte's heart beat faster against his chest.

"I…I'm not sure, Levi." Her smile slipped into a worried expression, not expecting things to go that fast, uncertain if that was the right moment for it, one she had waited so long for, longer than anyone around her.

"Trust me." He leaned over to steal a kiss from her, and as he did, she spotted a shadow of what appeared to be a bird, lingering on the roof of the shack, staring back at her.

> *"Nobody is ever gonna love you, you spoiled child. Look at you! You think they'll choose your dull, useless self? No! Never, Charlotte! All men want is to FUCK! Where's your father now?! Love? There is no love, you silly gal. You could be making yourself useful and help pay the bills, but apparently your body is too sacred, more than mine!"*

Suddenly her mother's words played subtly in her mind, as she stared into Levi's eyes, still waiting for an answer — *or permission, or did he already take it from her,* she thought, as he carried her into the house.

III

"MR. DAVENPORT…" MAC WALKED FASTER TOWARDS THE MAN who was walking to his horse, tied up in the very back of the homestead's fields.

"Oh! Mister…No-Name!" Ben mocked him as he tripped over himself, still intoxicated from the party.

"Figured I'll introduce meself, after all…" Mac smirked beneath his hat, taking out his knife that had earned him fifty bucks.

"Well, that would be lovely!" He turned around to face him, foot already slipped into one stirrup. "S-sir?" he stuttered, aghast, the moment the blade shined before his face, as Mac knocked him out with the handle of his knife.

"But first, yer comin' with me." he grunted, tying up his legs and hands, throwing him over the man's own horse who had sensed the danger before Mac even appeared.

I V

LEVI KICKED THE DOOR WIDE OPEN with his black square-toed cowboy boot, fitting his large frame and Charlotte's body through, still wrapped in his arms, still carried with no answer, still surrendering to his experienced force.

Laying her down to the bed, he leaned over her, kissing her daringly — lips brushing violently against hers, bruising her, feeling her cold breath turn warm within his. He caressed her whole body eagerly, feeling the unbearable urge to undress her, his excitement spiking the more his fingers felt of her voluptuous shape, the more he anticipated to finally unravel the cloth away from her flesh. To see her, feel her, taste her, hungering for her like a beast, finally unleashed from the chains of self-restraint.

He pulled back upon a gasp, and Charlotte heatedly watched him take his shirt off, exposing his well-built physique she always secretly longed to peek at, again and again. Now standing intimidatingly before her — inches away from hers. He was enormous; a tower of muscle, threatening to collapse upon her.

Quivering, she placed her hands against his chest, almost possessively to feel a man's bareness in such moment of unquenched thirst; letting her fingers trace circles around it, observing curiously how tight his pecs were — sending shivers down her body with every stroke against them; feeling herself get uncomfortably aroused, as he started to unlock her corset from the front, slowly exposing the dress underneath it.

V

"WHAT-WHAT'S HAPPENING?" DAVENPORT STUTTERED, confused, waking up to find himself hanging upside down within a tunnel. "WHERE AM I?!" he screamed, yet all of Hollenberg was asleep, and the tunnel was far away from any houses. Mac marched before him, slowly — spinning his knife in the air as he approached him, eyes in blackness, locking his. "You!!" the man scowled, shaking his body desperately in the hopes of freeing himself.

"Indeed." Mac smirked menacingly, meeting the man's face with his.

"What do you want from me!?!" he cried, blood rose in his head, pulse thumped in his throat.

"What's it with all ye folks, askin' me this same damn question?" Mac raised his brow sardonically as he stared into his helpless eyes, feeling hollow, nothingness.

"I-I have money!! Lots of money!!" he offered — sweat dripping from his forehead in the middle of a cold November night.

"Keep yer money, lad. Yer family's gonna need it for yer burial." He lit up a cigarette, and checked the time from the man's pocket watch hanging out of his vest — swinging like a pendulum every time the wind gushed against it.

V I

HE KISSED AND SUCKED ON HER NECK DEMANDINGLY, forcing himself between her legs, hiking her dress up to her thighs for his hand to travel underneath it. Charlotte breathed faster against his ear, panting, clinging onto his hair, as his fingers reached her pantaloons, gliding up and down her legs — teasing her, both knowing very well his hand was mere inches away from her wetness.

"Levi…" she moaned, grabbing his arm reluctantly, feeling herself slowly sober up. Yet he ignored her firm grip and spread her legs wide open, as his greedy mouth traveled down on her, kneeling right before her warm sensual embrace, her legs now adhering to his muscular shoulders. "Oh, my God…" she whispered, aghast, not knowing if she was ready for what was yet to come. Her body ached with anticipation — trembling all the more, as she felt his warm breath near her silky lips. She didn't dare to glance down; she felt ashamed with her inexperience, vulnerable the more he took over.

VII

"SO TELL ME…MR. DAVENPORT." MAC PUFFED ON HIS CIGARETTE, exhaling the smoke into his eyes, making him squint and grunt from the irritation. "Yer a godly man, as well?" he asked him, as he stared at the crucifix pendant around his neck.

"I reckon you're not?" The man growled back at him, tired and exhausted from Mac's mindless interrogation.

"Hm." He smirked. "How's the Lord helpin' ya tonight, me lad?" He looped his finger around the cross, and leered at it with resentment.

"I am not afraid, mister. My Lord will take care of me — whether I die tonight, or walk home alive." he stuttered in fright, never doubting the reasons behind his savior's plan.

"And who'll be the one who decides that?" Mac grabbed and tore his necklace, clasping it tightly within his fist.

"It's…it's all in God's plan." he muttered nervously, clutching his eyes tight instinctively — expecting to be killed at any moment.

VIII

HER LEGS QUIVERED UNCONTROLLABLY; squeezing Levi's head into her as he sucked on her smooth lips brazenly, sliding his finger within her warmth, pausing, grasping for air, breathing into her, blowing, pressing his mouth back on her.

Her wide hips swayed in all directions, trying to escape from the teasing pressure — yet at the same time hands grabbed his hair, fingers and nails sunk into it, urging him closer — begging him to claim her, rocking into him, as all sense and worry evaporated in the lustful air.

His tongue circled around her swollen clitoris, feeling himself become harder, stiffer the more he tasted her, and she…she was starting to build, to grow, discovering a feeling unknown to her, finding herself in the depths of the sheets, in the heat of his mouth. Her nails hooked into the bed covers, pulling them towards her, feeling a strange wave of ecstasy rush through her whole body — an unfamiliar feeling she'd never experienced before, every muscle drawn taut. He stood up, with his finger still inside her; proudly watching her squirm, as he felt her pussy slowly clench around it.

"Levi! Something…something's wrong!" she exclaimed innocently, as light-headedness surged through her — as she breathed faster — as her legs benumbed — still quivering intensely — body freezing in place, tingling, tightening every pure inch of it.

"You're just fine, girl." he whispered softly, and continued to tease her with his finger — knowing her whole being was about to be blown by him.

"Come on, Charlotte." He thrashed his finger faster and deeper inside her, seeing her eyes shut and her teeth clench tightly, as she tried hard not to make a sound. "Yes. That's it." he cheered her on as her hands slammed against his bare chest, toes curled around him; feeling the tension that was building up for too long suddenly release — letting herself go completely, floating someplace she'd never encountered, bleak and hollow, where all noise and sense volatilized.

He took her sweaty hand and placed it over his hard bulge; she jerked in surprise, taken aback. "You feel this?" He gasped; desperately wanting her to unravel what he hid beneath the cloth.

"Yes…my God, Levi…" she moaned, grabbing his bulge harder, feeling his large shape fill her hand — her fingertips sensing a penis for the very first time in her life. Her curiosity only heightened, for she had never seen one before, other than the gruesome sight of the inbred creature that left a filthy stain in her imagination.

"Come on, cowgirl." He encouraged her, and still light-headedly panting, dithering, anxious, she unbuttoned his pants, pulled out his pulsating cock, or rather, it sprung out on its own before her flared eyes. She stared at it, aghast, not knowing what to do with it, petrified to touch it, yet craving to. The girth and length of his arousal, brutally intimidating. And as she laid there, ogling it like a fool, he grabbed her hand and placed it atop it. She gasped, a leaden breath escaped her, for it felt unexpectedly soft to the touch, silky, and velvety. It was warm, throbbing in her grip, rock hard. He squeezed her fingers around him, and roughly jerked it with the guidance of her hand.

I X

"YE KNOW, MR. DAVENPORT…" HE CIRCLED AROUND HIM with a steady walk. "I ain't much of a believer." he confessed, scraping the blade against his cheek.

"Why are you doing this to me??" he pleaded for an answer, feeling light-headed from hanging for so long; face flushed red as blood thudded through his head, weighing it down.

Mac thought about his question carefully — suddenly reflecting on Levi's lips meeting Charlotte's. "SHUT YER GODDAMN MOUTH!" He turned and slapped his face, unexpectedly with the handle of his knife.

The man screamed from the pain, and burst into devastating tears, praying for his torture to end soon. Mac felt his rage burn up within his body; wishing so badly to have Levi hanging here instead, yet Davenport appeared so conveniently at just the right time and place.

"Sometimes…we must *feel* pain, to learn how to deal with it." he growled, clenched his teeth together — and stabbed the knife through his shoulder; twisting it as the man screamed in tormented agony.

X

"FOR A VIRGIN…YOU STROKE A COCK FINE." HE GROANED, and she rehearsed the words, as though they didn't sound loving, or romantic, or how she would have imagined them, for silence suddenly sounded more tender.

He lifted up her legs and wrapped them around his waist, for he couldn't wait any longer to feel her, and Charlotte's breath cut in her lungs as she watched him carefully, still trying to recover from the sudden burst of lustful emotions. She swallowed hard, her body tensed as he pushed himself against her, chest swelled in crippling worry.

"Levi…let's not…" she hesitantly asked him, not ready to go that far. Levi pumped himself and pressed his moist tip against her opening, feeling the wetness and warmth swiftly embrace him. "Levi, no…please." she begged him, as suddenly her feelings of lust transformed into creeping worry.

Deafened by his own desire, he started to push himself slowly inside her, yet she was too tight; too virgin, to simply slide within her.

"Levi! NO!" she yelled at him, pulling herself up by the covers, crawling back to the wall away from him — suddenly seeing the O'Donnell before her; suddenly shaking in panic, suddenly mistrusting his intentions, suddenly feeling betrayed. Levi gaped at her, head cocked, confused, for she wore an expression of a scared and helpless victim.

"LEVI!" JB's voice startled them before their door and Charlotte felt a wave of relief hit her, longing to run away from him, longing to find shelter in the arms of anyone *but* him.

Levi jumped off the bed and pulled his pants up swiftly, throwing one last bewildered glance at Charlotte — covering herself with her dress, frightened, quiet, frozen still against the cold wall. He shook his head in disappointment and hobbled towards the door, frustrated by Charlotte's sudden change of behavior, and aggravated by JB's disturbance.

"JB?" He cracked the door open, just enough for him to see his face.

"I'm…I'm sorry to…interrupt…" he stuttered, as he recognized Levi's grumpy expression.

"I'm…a little busy right now…" he impatiently informed him, feeling his penis go instantly soft.

"I know…I'm just…I couldn't find…MAC KINNON IS GONE!!!" JB yelled from the top of his lungs, as he had started to care for him like his own son; his elderly voice trembled in harrowing worry, leaving Levi and Charlotte speechless.

XI

CHUFF-CHUFF-CHUFF-CHUFF "OH…WOULD YE LISTEN TO THAT." Mac teased the man, who was falling in and out of consciousness as his blood was gushing out of the wound.

"Who hurt you…so badly…to have…created such…a monster." he stuttered, voice frail and coarse, barely able to put his words together, barely a sound able to be issued. Body shifting by the gust of wind, swaying back and forth, rope twisting, creaking, stretching.

Mac crinkled his lip to the side, wordless, pulled his bandana over his face, remained in silence. The train kept on coming closer, lighting up the tunnel behind them, tracks rattling, smoke billowing from the long void. He stared at the man, who was looking back at him with begging eyes, yet already faded someplace dark and empty — and a slight wrinkle of doubt formed across Mac's forehead, feeling oddly suspicious of the man, as though he had seen him before.

"It's…it's *you*…" His eyes dilated in shock, as everything now made sense. "Mac Kinnon…" he added, and his fear only grew. Mac froze; feeling the train track's vibrations, its roaring engine thrumming in his ears, a shrill in the leaden air, a foreboding scent engulfing him. "You…used to be…such a kind…young man." Davenport sighed sadly, flinching a nostalgic smile as tears drowned it, reminiscing upon the way young Mac delivered farm supplies to Holy Ranch, spurting shy politeness, cloaked in reservedness. Mac swallowed dryly, feeling his throat swell awkwardly as he slowly recognized the hanging man before him.

"What…what in the world…did this man do to you, my dear boy?" he asked him with all his remaining strength, as he'd always suspected farmer Grossman to have lied about Mac's sudden disappearance. "I tried so hard… to…to…get you out of there. But the law…called me a…lunatic…" He gasped heavily, blood still gushing out. "Forgive me…for I failed to…save you…prevent your…downfall." he said, slowly eyes glazing with death.

Mac stared at him, aghast; as the train was now just moments away from them. He stared, confused, for he never expected anyone to have ever believed him — let alone worry about him. Yet now, he recognized the man fully; the one who gifted him fresh meals every time he visited, for he was the only one who noticed his malnourished self hidden beneath oversized coats.

Eyes flared, upon hearing heavy grunts slither out of his mouth, and swiftly, in a rare moment of shock, he rushed to the top of the tunnel, stumbling over rocks as he climbed frantically to free him, hooking nails and palms into the wall. He yanked his knife out to cut the rope tied around his ankles, yet for the first time, his hands were quivering — and no matter how hard he tried, he could not focus on such a simple task.

Gripping as tightly as he could, he pressed the blade into the rope, but as the crisp air filled with the engine's suffocating smoke, blinding and deafening him, the train shot like a bullet right through the tunnel — taking the hanging man with it as well, leaving nothing but his torn up legs behind.

The first flurries of snowflakes wafted down.

XII

"JB, HIS HORSE IS STILL HERE!" LEVI FUSSED, furious, as he saw Roy still standing unsaddled in the shack, munching on the hay unhurriedly.

"Yes! I figured that much! That's why I'm worried, Levi! Maybe he was...he was kidnapped!" JB gasped. "He was Mac-napped!!!" He looked around the shack, trying to find any possible clue that would explain his disappearance.

"Kid-kidnapped??? JB! Have you forgotten who we are dealing with?! Have you lost your mind?!" Levi yelled, flustered — wondering if he was still heavily intoxicated, for he could not believe his words nor erratic behavior.

"He's just a child, Levi!" JB defended him, feeling his heart fill up with worry the longer he thought about it.

"A child?? He is a MURDERER, JB!! A damn killer! One of the worst! What's gotten into you, old friend??" he questioned him, baffled, glancing over at Mac's saddle still laying on top of a hay bale with his rifle still in the holster.

"The boy barely can put two sentences together. Give him some slack! He ain't normal, I know! But he's been livin' amongst us for so long now, and... and he hasn't murdered anyone!" JB yelled, frustrated by still having to explain it to him. "I'm worried, Levi! What if someone captured him?" He looked at him, begging for him to understand.

"Nobody is capturing the freak, but me! He's probably just having a hell of a good time with someone!" Levi ground his teeth with the irony.

"Oh…well, I guess I did not think 'bout that…" JB looked up the ceiling, scratching his head to consider this possibility.

"Yeah. A hell of a good time…" Levi repeated angrily and walked away, for the very first time, feeling betrayed and disappointed by JB.

XIII

CHARLOTTE STARED AT THE DOOR, BLANK. Absently fiddling the blanket with her quivering fingertips. Every ounce of lustful pleasure she just experienced, for the very first time in her life, had utterly vanished within thin air — drowned within the leaden void she felt, replaced with disgust, and resentment; somehow it appeared that's all she was meant to feel. And after all, none of this mattered as much as Mac's disappearance.

Guilt had swallowed her, knowing he had seen her kiss Levi during the dance, knowing part of her longed for him to see her, yearned for him to feel what she felt, if at all possible. Knowing she was naïve to play such a game with him, and yet perhaps, he didn't care after all; *perhaps he decided it was the perfect opportunity for him to leave, to not have to say goodbye,* she thought to herself, fighting the tears back, choking in a muddy pit of sorrow, loathing herself once more.

She stood up from the squeaky, sin-infested bed, and adjusted her corset around herself, tying it back together behind her back hastily, as she wanted nothing more than to escape from this trap that slowly made her feel confined in a tiny box. The smell of sweat and sex filled up the abyss of the room, asphyxiating her — feeling the dirtiest she'd ever felt, for laying down with a man she didn't love.

For letting him get so personal with her, so close to her, after saving herself for when the right one would come along. He was not the one, he never was the one, and she knew that from the very beginning. She knew she should have listened to her gut, screaming at her not to trust him.

She fought hard to understand why she even let herself be dominated by him; was it curiosity? Was it ordinary lust; the biological urge she'd been keeping locked up for ages, suddenly breaking its chains? The enticing manner of his confident movements — making her tremble in pleasure so effortlessly? His chiseled body…surely she wasn't the superficial kind, or was she indeed that shallow?

Just like her mother?

Or, was it her own damn fault — her own prevailing insecurities preventing her from enjoying such an erotic moment. And if so, would she ever be able to let herself relax in the arms of a man again?

She felt her fingers still sticky from his arousal; she wiped them frantically against her dress, feeling the need to jump into a lagoon and soak there for an eternity — *perhaps to drown to death while she was at it,* she embarrassingly thought to herself.

all night, questioning her useless existence.

"Good morning…" Levi sighed, not expecting to have such an awkward morning with her; wishing instead they had woken up together after a long, lustful night, fallen asleep entwined like lovers, yet now everything felt foreign and estranged.

"Well, you both must have really had some fun late last night! Haha! JB's guests stayed longer than I did!" Amara chuckled, glancing over at their pitiful, hungover selves.

Levi and Charlotte locked eyes with each other simultaneously, choosing to remain in inappropriate silence, as nothing could really explain why things ended up so terrible last night; why Levi couldn't respect her boundaries, how JB suddenly rescued Charlotte unbeknownst to him, and why Mac disappeared — leaving his horse and all his belongings behind. Last night was one to be kept buried deep underneath the surface, never to be dug up again.

JB rushed inside the house determinedly, rubbing his benumbed hands together as he was desperately looking for a pair of gloves.

"It has sure gotten colder outside. Might be a good idea to stock up on supplies again." Amara mumbled, as she noticed her pantry half empty.

"No lie! Figured I'd go for a quick ride, yet the reins felt like god damn icicles! Reminds me of that time in the army, where…" JB paused his story, as he noticed everyone was already in a bad mood, completely disregarding his words or presence. "Never mind. I'll be around!" he said under his breath, slipping his frozen hands into a pair of rabbit pelt gloves.

"Where you going in such weather, JB?" Levi interrupted him suspiciously, as JB rarely rode out, let alone in such conditions.

"Ah. I'm…just…goin' for a winter stroll…" He shrugged, lips writhed, trying his best to come up with an innocent enough lie.

"Winter stroll?" Levi cocked a brow in disbelief. "There is no way, old man! What's going on?" he persisted with a subtle leer.

"N-nothin', my boy! I'll just…head to town for a moment. Amara…she, she needs some supplies! Correct, dearest?" JB giggled awkwardly, buttoning up his thick coat — making his short neck disappear behind it.

"You'll need the wagon for that, JB…" Levi called him out, then walked towards him with an intimidating stance he knew would make JB quiver in discomfort — making him squeeze out the truth without a single effort.

"Ah…*wagon*…didn't think 'bout that." he stuttered, and avoided looking Levi in the eyes.

"JB…tell me. What's going on?" He tilted his head to catch his eyes again.

"Oh, Lordy!! I tried!! I trrried my best!!" he cried, instantly catching Charlotte's and Amara's attention. "Mr. Kinnon!" he exclaimed with immense concern. Amara rolled her eyes in annoyance, having to be reminded by this man's name, and Charlotte felt her heart drop to her feet — as it always did, with the mere mention of him.

"What again?!" Levi asked him, flustered, feeling as if this *Kinnon* was ruining his life yet again.

"I am goin' to look for him, Levi. Somethin' ain't right! I can feel it in my breeches!" He sobbed, blowing a bubble of snot with his nose.

"I told you, JB, he is probably still having fun with one of them girls from last night. So many asked you about him, like you said." Levi nagged, loathing having to say this out loud before Charlotte — as if he didn't have to compete with him enough already.

"Wouldn't surprise me." Amara intervened with a snide smirk, clearly still bitter over her rejection. Charlotte glanced back at her, for the first time realizing something bad went on between them, feeling a hint of relief within her; a curiosity, making her wish she had known about it sooner, and yet that relief swiftly got smothered by yet another assumption.

"No, Levi! I…I really need to! To go make sure the boy's alright! It's freezin' out there, he don't even have his coat with him!" He pointed at his duster coat with the rabbit gloved finger, still hanging on the wall.

"Do you realize who you're worrying about??" Levi raised his voice, feeling his frustration intensify — not recognizing JB anymore.

"He'd do the same." JB defended him, knowing very well Mac would rather skin him alive than look for him.

"He wouldn't." he growled, pointing his finger at him, giving him a stern expression and subtle warning for him to remember, before he rushed upstairs.

I I

"HOW IN THE WORLD COULD ANYBODY WITH A BRAIN buy such a poor excuse of an animal — for forty-five fuckin' bucks!!" the rancher yelled, shocked to see what stood underneath the blanket.

"I-I know sir, I…thought perhaps after she's back on her feet…she'd make a good ranch horse for ye." the young man stumbled, as he covered the horse with the blanket again to hide its protruding spine.

"A good ranch horse??!! This?? What are we here? A goddamn sanctuary for the undead!?!" he scowled — feeling his head about to explode from anger. "Follow me!" he ordered him, as he walked determined towards his house, right in front of the stables.

The young man followed after him, wondering if he would still get paid after all, as he had to pay his rent, and food was running low. Yet the man marched through his house, and came out holding a pistol in his hand.

"Here." He pressed it against the man's chest.

"Sir?" the man questioned him worriedly, as he saw the rancher point his finger to the barn.

"Take care of the crone." he ordered him earnestly, leaving him speechless, his jaw dropped down to the virgin snow.

III

"C'ME OOOON, RINOOO! LET'S SEE IF YA CAN LEAD ME TO YOUR RIDER, AH?" JB patted Roy's shoulder as he tied the reins in a knot around his neck, right before slapping his hind to make him run into Freeland's landscape — frosted with an abundance of renewed whiteness. He mounted his horse and followed right behind him, barely able to hold on with his frosty fingers, as his mount galloped swiftly down the steep hills — its hooves scraping the fresh snow off the ground, as the blizzard steadily continued to cover the land back with it.

"Oh, Lordy! Can barely see anythin' out here." JB muttered, trying to see through the heavy snowfall with squinted eyes — whose lashes were frozen together, now matching with his gray wiry beard.

He searched through every hidden pathway known to him; any areas where he could possibly be camping; small caves, deserted shacks, lagoons, little rivers crossing through tight and rocky land formations — yet surprisingly, Mac was nowhere to be found. He glanced over at Roy, whose black coat had become speckled with white, trotting with his head held low as if he was steadily sniffing of the ground. He urged his horse to run faster behind him, when Roy took off again along the train tracks, disappearing through the whiteout before a dark, ominous tunnel.

I V

"LET'S TAKE A LOOK AT THIS, FINNY BOY…" she mentally prepared her stallion, as he had gotten quite traumatized when it came to messing with his feet since dealing with the abscess. Brushing her hand against his leg, she waited for him to offer her his hoof, yet he wouldn't — he'd move his whole body anxiously away from her instead, as he nervously snorted in protest.

"Come on, boy…you know this!" She sighed, not feeling mentally capable herself of chasing after him that moment. Finn fought hard against the pressure of her hand, stomping his leg on the ground, moving in every direction possible to not stand still; his enormous heavy shoulder pushing her body away from him stubbornly. She backed him up against the wall of the shack, and kneeled low to grab his leg — already exhausted from the whole circus act so far. Finn snorted and suddenly reared up high, catching Charlotte off guard and throwing her down to the ground.

"Finn!!" she yelled at him, flustered, standing up to grab him from the halter. "Whoa!" she demanded, jerking his halter repeatedly, making his eyes widen in fright. "You'll give me that leg now, or there ain't gonna be any oats for you, my friend!" she threatened, as she reached down to grab him, but he stood up on his hind legs again — slamming his knee against her head as he raised himself.

"That's it!" she exclaimed and stood up furiously, grabbed the end of the rope and whipped his hind with it over and over again, making him move his feet more and more swiftly — until he would beg to stand still. Finn circled around her nervously, snorting and huffing in distress, until he started to back up hastily away from her.

Charlotte dropped the rope the moment she realized what she was doing; when she noticed his head stretched up high, his frightened eyes staring at her like they were struggling hard to recognize her, just like Roy looked at Mac in that mucky barn in Hope.

"I'm…I'm so sorry, Finn…" she cried, baffled with herself, disgusted and ashamed, knowing she wasn't behaving as herself — knowing this wasn't the way she would ever treat him. She walked slowly towards him, yet he kept on backing up, alarmed and anxious. "Easy, boy…it's okay." she exhaled deeply, placing her hands on his fuzzy white blaze, scratching the side of his muzzle, which he always so loved. "I'm sorry…this will never ever happen again. I *promise* you." she sobbed into his muscular neck, realizing she'd betrayed and mistreated her friend for the very first time.

V

JB BRIEFLY SPOTTED ROY'S SILHOUETTE, through the whiteout again — seeming to have appeared magically, after struggling to follow him the darker it got outside. He was grazing on the snow-covered grass, in total contentment.

Dismounting his palomino draft horse, he slid down to the ground with his round belly off the slick saddle, feeling his knees and back slowly crack painfully. He wasn't apt to ride for so long anymore, since old age had steadily caught up with him. He walked towards Roy as he sighed, disappointed, ready to give up his search for the day, defeated as if he were going in circles in a land that felt endless. He grabbed the reins, and Roy raised up his head in protest — stomping his feet, neighing loudly.

"C'me on, Roni!! He ain't here!" he said, yet Roy kept on persisting. Then he recognized the snow-covered man behind him — Mac, sitting on the ground; barely flinching from all the distressing sounds his horse made.

"Mr. Kinnon!" JB gasped, yelled, before he took a breath in.

Mac was whittling with his knife as he stared, lost, out at the gloomy horizon — hair and back completely cloaked in fresh snow.

"Kinnon? Maccy boy? Are you…alright?" JB ran up to him, noticing his dull expression — eyes eerily frozen into place, like there was no one behind them. "It's…it's cold out here, Maccy. Let's, let's go home?" he stuttered insecurely, not sure how to make him say a word, without forcing his mouth open.

Mac looked up at him — stunned to see him here; bewildered to notice he actually came to find him.

"You…you must be freezin'!" JB looked concerned at the white shirt he was still wearing — wondering how he wasn't even shivering from the cold.

Mac remained silent; his cold breath fogging the air before him.

"Mac, my boy…please, say somethin' — anythin'! Tell me how ya'd love to skin this old man alive! Ah?!" JB rambled, feeling his stomach turn the more he stared at the expressionless figure. "Mac?!" he yelled at him, reached for his shoulder anxiously, yet Mac grabbed him first — tightening his grip around his fragile wrist.

"I murdered a man…" he whispered aggressively, lips trembling, folded, sealed firmly — while his stone-cold eyes pierced through his; alarmed, sinful.

CHAPTER 60

One More Chance

I

"SHERIFF DORMAN!" THE POSTMAN KNOCKED ON HIS DOOR, frantically, as the sheriff had his legs resting upon the cell's iron — watching the prisoner eat his fingernails in boredom, figuring he might as well join him.

Dorman grunted the moment he heard the man disturbing his peace; or loneliness, or mental absence, as his slumped shoulders rested in defeat. No one in town had seen him leave his office since the expedition in Red Giants. He had locked himself away, and delivered a clear message at Elizabeth's funeral for nobody to disturb him.

"Sir?" the postman repeated urgently, squeezing a letter within his grip.

"What is it now??" Dorman finally answered with an agitated tone, startling the prisoner before him whose nails had been chewed off halfway already.

"Sir, it's…it could be something…important." he shouted from outside, in the hopes he could hear him better.

"Doubt it…" Dorman mumbled for he had given up, devastatingly, on ever finding Mac Kinnon.

"Sir! We received mail!" he yelled again, his dainty arm resting against the door.

"Spit it out already, would ya?!" Dorman fumed, watching the clock tick, counting the seconds pass as the man was wasting them.

"It's for William Gr…Griffiths, sir." He let out a stutter, as he read the name out loud — the name that once meant so much to the townsfolk of Bisonhorn. Yet, Will was nothing but history now. Forgotten; as well as all his charitable donations that had helped to make the town a better place.

"From who?!" Dorman inquired aggressively and rushed to the door, struggling to quickly open each extra lock he had installed.

"Ch…Charlotte, sir." the postman stumbled, nervously hearing the keys jiggle, and the locks scrape against the door frantically over and over again.

Dorman yanked the door open hastily and snatched the letter from his clammy hand without warning. He unfolded the envelope like his life depended on it; as if there was the rarest treasure map hiding within it. The postman saw his eyes scan the letter thoroughly; mouth moving without making a sound, as he read every single word to himself. A wicked smile suddenly cracked across his lips, and a spark ignited within his empty eyes, as he folded back the letter and pocketed it in his coat.

"Well done." He patted the man on his shoulder with a big grin, and proudly marched to his desk to grab a new cigar to celebrate the good news. The postman followed him with his tiny black eyes, noticing his desk was covered with different Holy Bibles; each one opened widely on different pages, all marked with little handwritten notes between the verses. Dorman laughed eerily in the face of the prisoner, puffing on his cigar with a vast pleasure he hadn't felt in a very long time.

II

"HEY, YOU…" LEVI STEPPED INTO THE SHACK, finding Charlotte seated on a bale of hay with the piece of cloth still hanging loose in her tiny grip.

"Hey Levi." She sighed, whole body tensing up the moment he walked closer to her.

"How's Finn?" he asked calmly, noticing him munching quietly on some hay, his hind turned towards Charlotte.

"Ah. He is…he is a mess. But, I don't blame him…" she mumbled, realizing trauma could scar anyone mentally, deeper and harsher than the physical.

"I see. You need any help with that?" he kindly offered, chin jutting out to point to the cloth.

"No…thank you…I got it." she said shortly, awkwardly, not wanting him anywhere near Finn, nor herself. Barely able to face him.

"Okay…" he muttered in disappointment, realizing she still acted quite differently towards him. Cold, distant, and eerily quiet.

"Levi…I have decided to head out west soon." she declared earnestly, then looked up at him — clearly noticing his wide, brawny chest move faster. "Probably once the weather clears out." She sighed, as she heard the heavy snowfall hit the roof harshly.

"That weather's only going to get worse, you know…" He teased her with a playful smile, hoping she'd smile too. She didn't, couldn't, didn't care to.

"I mean…on a sunny day…with clear skies. Can't snow forever." she said, wishing it would have already stopped.

"…am I allowed to come with you still, or…was it so terrible you changed your mind?" he inquired caustically, throat swelled up with a well of emotion.

"It…it wasn't terrible, Levi. It just…" She paused, able to feel the tension quickening his blood. "I think…I think it's best if we…if we just part ways…" she stuttered nervously, somehow not wanting to hurt him any further.

"Aha. I see…" He nodded, folding his lips within his mouth — trying hard not to speak out what he felt, as Charlotte's eyes cut sharply at him, studying every expression of his. "You know…I did a thing today; something I thought might make a difference for you — for you to have some sort of quality of life around here, you know…" He clenched his teeth, fighting back the tears, thinking back on how passionately they kissed during their dance and after, not able to contemplate what he did to ruin it for them to the point of her uttering such words.

"What do you mean?" she tentatively asked him, noticing every fiber of his body tense up.

"What I mean…ha." He chuckled with the irony. "I went to town — Holy Ranch, to be specific; and took down all the damn posters that had your face on them. Not that people won't recognize you, but they would be less likely to be reminded…besides, they know me well, and they wouldn't dare to cause any trouble if they saw you by my side." He sniffed — voice raw and raspy, throat swelling up.

"Levi…you…you shouldn't have done that for me."

"Well, but I did." he interrupted her as he shrugged — glancing out from the shack, agitated — looking at how the white snowflakes contrasted heavily with the dark sky above.

"I know you're wanted in Birdsboro, so…I don't wish for you to get into further trouble due to me."

"I don't give a fuck if I do, Charlotte…" he said gravely and she gaped at him, feeling his rage spiral through him. "I'm sorry. I'm sorry if I hurt you in any way! I really just wanted to make you feel special…" He looked back at her with a furrowed face. "Please don't leave, just yet." He begged her, realizing he would most likely never see her again if she did. "I have fallen for you, Charlotte. I have…fallen badly for you. Please, don't leave me like that, not after everything we went through." He walked towards her, grabbing her hands gently. Clutching them lovingly, tight against his chest.

"Please, give me one more chance."

I I I

"WELL…OH WELL…YA KNOW MAC…THIS…I MEAN, ya could've done worse, ya know?" JB spluttered, trying desperately to find the right words to cheer him .

"I killed the man that…" His hand shook around JB's wrist, as childhood memories suddenly assailed him.

"Mac! It's alright. Listen boy, we all kill someone eventually, right?! Haha! It's…it's how nature is! Look around ya, son! Animals kill everyday — we ain't much different from them! If I could get my hands 'round that scrawny neck of Margaret's now-husband…boy, let me tell ya! I'd be wanted across all of America! Imagine how messed up that would be?!" He chuckled as Mac looked at him sternly — reminding him he was, indeed, wanted across the entire nation. "I mean…I mean for me! For ya it's a different story! Ya're a legend, Mac! Ya're…"

"Hobble yer lip." he interrupted him swiftly. "There's nothin' good or legendary 'bout me life. Nothin'." He stood up, suddenly with a confident and determined stance.

"Wh…where you goin' now?" JB questioned him nervously, following right after him like a lost puppy.

"Gotta hide the body." he mumbled, reverting back in his old state of mind, calculated, devoid of any emotion. "Or what's left of it..."

"Oh! Sure! Sure, we go hide the body now." JB agreed instantly with a swift bob of his head, as he looked around himself to see if anyone was following or watching them.

"Don't puke." Mac teased him, as he stepped out of his way for JB to see a pair of frozen legs still swinging in the wind.

"Oh!" He gasped, eyes dilated in odd awe. "Well. That's, that's...quite interesting! Do ya...do ya tend to...just hang 'em like that?" He chuckled awkwardly, avoiding to look any closer.

"Sure." Mac answered him shortly and cut down the rope, grabbing the legs with each hand.

"Oh, Lordy..." JB whispered to himself, imagining how Levi would react to this if he only knew. "So...why don't we just lay them on the tracks? Surely they'll think it was an accident, or somethin'?" he offered, as his worry only grew, seeing Mac take his sweet time to calculate the best way to hide the legs.

"Less talkin'. More thinkin'." Mac commanded him snidely, as he threw the legs into a shallow lagoon. "By the time they find 'em, I'll be gone." he muttered, and mounted his horse.

IV

THERE WAS A SNOWSTORM STRIKING THE RANCH. A complete whiteout. Herds of wild horses stood in groups, coats silvered by snow, trying to warm up for the freezing night that was approaching, beneath branches coated in ice, behind boulders of snow. The storm hit unexpectedly; too early for that time of year, too harsh for the region.

"You reckon JB is alright?" Amara asked Levi, who was laying before the warm fire — with Charlotte closely seated on a stool by his side, clinging onto her faint promise to consider his words.

"If he don't return anytime soon, I'll go look for him." He sighed worriedly.

"It's getting dark already though, Levi." Amara persisted, as her maternal instinct was kicking in again.

"Gah…alright, alright." he grumbled and stood up, right before the door slammed wide open.

"Heeeeello!" JB made his loud entrance, swinging his hips as he tried to take off his gloves that were stuck on his frosty hands. "I've got a special guest!" He chuckled, thrilled to have brought Mac safe and sound back with him.

"Let it be, ol' man." Mac whispered as he awkwardly stepped inside the house, wearing JB's coat to cover up the bloody evidence, passing JB who was still fighting with the rabbit pelt glove. His deep voice reached Charlotte's ears instantly, and relief embraced her. A shiver crawled down her spine the moment she saw his face again, realizing peace would be to see his face and feel nothing anymore, yet she found herself in a never ending war of emotions.

"Ha. He found you, after all!" Levi folded his arms together, instantly showing their enormous size to him. Mac ignored his statement and looked back at JB, making sure he wouldn't say anything wrong — like they talked about on their ride back here.

"I did! Fella was indeed havin' a good time, *if ya know what I mean.* HaHA." JB tittered out a lie, imagination failing him to come up with a better excuse.

Charlotte glanced over at Mac to catch his reaction, praying he'd dismiss such assumptions, feeling her stomach turn uneasily. She didn't expect for this to be the reason he was gone, yet after all, she'd certainly witnessed him enjoying himself with Amara's breasts in his face — so she was no longer in a place to doubt him, as he was nothing like a shy one, *and who was she to judge him now?* Suddenly, the glimpse of hope and relief she felt before turned into a staggering feeling of nausea.

Mac swallowed awkwardly as he looked at Charlotte, jerking her head away from him. Then at Amara, who was frowning agitatedly, and last, at Levi — who had quickly stopped talking; entirely frustrated by Mac's apparent success with women.

"So, Mac here needs a bath! Urgently! Cause…things got quite messy…*if ya know what I mean.* HaHA!" JB continued his joke pleasantly — perfectly covering for his need to be cleaned up.

"Ew! JB!" Amara screamed in revulsion; covering her ears with her hands, making JB chuckle only harder as she shuddered her shoulders.

Levi stared at them suspiciously; wondering when they managed to get so close to the point of discussing such private matters. Yet, knowing JB —— nothing would surprise him.

"Alright, alright! Mac, my boy, the bathtub is upstairs on your left. Ya've got any fresh cloooothes?" he questioned him, with a raised brow of judgement, now both brows flickering. Mac rolled his eyes at him, and proceeded to walk up the stairs — feeling his head ache with every step he took, limbs benumbed from the ruthless bite of cold, feeling eyes stab him in the back.

V

JB SAT DOWN TO READ THE DAY'S NEWSPAPER, as he poured himself a glass of leftover moonshine to warm up his frosty body.

"So, where was he?" Levi asked him, still suspicious of the whole story.

"Oh…he…he was at that abandoned cabin a ways from here." he stuttered, licking his scarred thumb to turn the page.

"Is that what women like nowadays? A filthy shack?" He needled, still not able to believe any of the ladies that came would settle for that.

"Oh, yes…back in my day! Gals begged me to get all dirty and rowdy anywhere we could find! Don't matter if it was the actual outhouse!! Lordy, that outhouse down by Mrs. Acker was horrifying! Her poor bastard of a husband always managed to fill it up every morning, before he went off to work — and before I came to visit. HaHA!" He chuckled, making Charlotte flinch a faint smirk with his silly rambling.

"Who was the mystery lady, anyway?" Levi questioned him curiously, and Charlotte certainly eavesdropped, devoted.

"What?" JB asked, as he had forgotten what they were talking about.

"The lady!" Levi sighed, agitated.

"What lady?" JB raised his brows, as though to remind himself again.

"That you found Mac with!" Levi raked his messy hair with a hand in frustration, while Charlotte almost fell over her chair trying to hear the woman's name.

"Oooooh!! That lady! That…*that* lady!" he repeated, trying to come up with a guest that Levi didn't know.

"Yes, yes…" Levi pressured him, thinking he caught him in a lie again.

"Well to be honest with ya, I do not remember the lady's name." he mumbled, steering his eyes back to the paper discreetly.

Levi clenched his teeth and cut his eyes over at Charlotte, who stared at the fire as it burned wildly, roaring a lullaby to calm the soul, while Mac was laying in a tub full of warm water — soaking the man's dried-up blood from his body.

V I

HE LAID, CHEST FLOATING, STARING AT THE WOODEN CEILING — veins bulging at the neck and forehead as he felt his heart rate steadily slow down, hypnotized by the water's rippling movements against his skin. Pulling his gaze away from the ceiling, he glanced at the window; there was snow and wind beating in, and all he envisioned was the frozen legs swinging back and forth, as he buried deeper into the snowfall.

He thought of the man's words repeatedly; letting them sink deep into his mind, as his aching legs sunk lower into the rusty tub. The man knew he was starved, and he knew he was abused, and he knew he didn't disappear just like that — but was kept imprisoned instead.

Someone…*knew.*

Someone knew, and this meant something to him — something he couldn't quite comprehend, nor was he able to describe, but it meant he wasn't alone. He laid, stretching his head back with a heavy, raspy grunt and deep blue eyes shut, relieved. Releasing the shadow of tension within him.

His dark blond hair rested over the tub, droplets of soapy water dripping to the ground, the sickening stench of cigarette smoke floating from them. Face lit up by the feeble candle beside him — furrowed in exhaustion, exposing every scar forever carved upon it; some smaller, some wider — each with an untold story behind.

VII

"THE POOR CHAP!" JB MUMBLED OUT LOUD, bulging his eyes the more he read the shocking article in the paper.

"What happened?" Levi asked curiously as he washed his face, ready to go and rest for the night.

"Ah. Just some fella shot his brains off, after killin' his wife." He shrugged, trying hard to contemplate the logic behind this.

"Why would someone even do that?" Charlotte wondered, rubbing her neck absently — thinking it wasn't making any sense.

"Probably to not have to deal with the consequences." Levi intervened, as he drummed his fingers against his thigh.

"Yeah, most likely Levi is right. Some men can have everything, yet never have enough." He sighed, as he studied the wife's picture on the paper — admiring her elegant beauty. "Oh! Happened in your neck of the woods, son!" JB informed him excitedly, as Levi had already one foot on the steps.

"Red Giants? Don't surprise me. All the crazy folk end up there. Well, outside of Petit Jean, that is…" Levi complained and turned his body away, indicating a desire to leave the room — which shortly after, he did.

"Guess it's just the two of us, Char!" JB mumbled as he continued reading.

"Char?" She chuckled, as she never had a nickname in her life — besides "useless", and "spoiled brat", or "Little Lottie" which she abhorred to the core.

They heard footsteps return at top of the stairs — this time lighter, yet sturdier and more precise, as though hiking down in slyness. She felt a flutter in the pit of her stomach when she saw Mac striding down them, eyes setting upon his hair, straight, still wet, with the tiniest hint of curls at the ends — dripping against his wide shoulders, wetting his black shirt bit by bit. The scent of lavender soap drifting through the air — making her almost feel his smooth, fresh skin underneath her fingertips. He captivated her within his haunting silence; torturing each other, as their eyes spoke instead.

"Mac! Feelin' frrrreshhh and cleeeean? Ah?" JB winked at him secretly — discreetly questioning him if all the blood was washed out.

"Hm." Mac nodded as he walked to his duster coat, and pulled out his canister of whiskey — taking a big sip, wetting his sore throat.

"So, my dearest!" JB jerked his head towards Charlotte. "Levi said ya was leavin' west soon, ah?" he questioned her curiously, cracking his neck left and right, feeling his stiffness slowly loosen up. Mac side-eyed Charlotte, hooded eyes trying to grasp any information she might give.

"Yes." She swallowed dryly. "I…I am. Once the weather clears out a bit…" she mumbled, cutting her eyes over at Mac discreetly.

"You know the weather's only gonna get worse, ah?" JB stretched his arms, cracking his numb fingers in the hopes of feeling them again.

"That's what he said too…" She sighed. "Yes. I'm aware, but…I just really need to." She fiddled with her hair — braiding, and unbraiding it again.

"Well, oh well…we're gonna miss ya, sweetheart! Ya always have a home here with us, whenever needed." JB looked at her with teary eyes — forgetting the fact that this wasn't even his house to decide welcomes upon.

"Thank you, JB. I'm going to miss you too…" She felt her throat dry and lumpy, thinking about sweet Jonathan not running around frantically anymore, not sharing his childhood stories with her — or Amara not preparing breakfast for everyone in the morning, that warm motherly gesture she never grew up around. JB's awful jokes and rambling, yet his kind heart plastering a smile on anyone's face. Levi; she hadn't decided yet about him, and she was scared to death to travel alone — now as a wanted woman, especially, yet she could never take advantage of him. His genuine words back in the shack clasped her heart and terrified her at the same time, as though she felt obligated to love him back, as though she felt she owed him. And yet, there was no longer a point of interest felt towards him, for any sentiment was now a shattered wisp of the past, a morsel of an experience she longed to carve out of her heart. He was a blemish, stubbornly engraved in her being. And Mac… Mac would forever remain the ghost she was always haunted by.

Charlotte sniffed and hung her head down — avoiding to look at *him*.

"Well, my little whippersnappers! This old man needs some rest! Whew! That was quite an adventure today, Mr. Kinnon! HaHA!" JB chuckled, thinking it was his first time hiding a body with a legendary murderer, oddly amused by it. JB left, headed to his room — wobbling his way out of the kitchen, leaving Charlotte and Mac alone before the fire.

VIII

"SHE'S SOMEWHERE IN THE FREELANDS...not many ranches or houses out there. It will be so, so easy to track them bastards down." Dorman exposed his neck as he stretched his back — feeling the most confident he'd ever been; the most prepared, as he now had clear directions of their whereabouts.

The deputies listened carefully to the plan, this time feeling hopeful themselves, as nothing sounded illogical, and they weren't relying on rumors or assumptions but Charlotte's actual handwritten words.

"We will separate into groups...Timmy, ya're gonna search the southern part of Hollenberg." He pointed with his finger on the map.

"Josiah, take your group to the eastern side." He drew a thick line on the map, scarring a satisfactory grin on his face. "And us, we'll start up north." He circled around Ravenheart Pond, feeling the thrill of the hunt blossom inside him. "We ride at dawn. Everyone understood the plan?!" he shouted for confirmation, studying the deputies' refreshed faces.

"Yes, sir!" they all yelled simultaneously.

"Fantastic..." he soughed enthralled, taking his pen and circling around Charlotte's face, his determined eyes locking hers. "You're next, princess..." he snidely growled — for the first time, loathing a woman with every fiber of his being.

IX

YOU COULD FEEL THE TENSION RUN ITS NAILS along the cedar boards across the ceiling; lingering in every corner of the room, holding shadows of unspoken words and confessions. The fire hissed, sparking before them, as though fueled by their menacing gazes. Quietly seated across from each other, warming up themselves before the burning charred logs — yet the coldness between them remained like a stubborn thorn, dripping poison.

Charlotte had successfully double braided her hair from her anxiousness; feeling his presence suffocate her, yet in the most beautiful way one could experience. She could feel his silent, subtle gazes without having to catch them with her own eyes. Every move he made, she felt against her skin — every slow breath he took, meeting hers. Her heart raced like a herd of wild mustangs; clopping within her steadily, torturing her whole body from the immense exhaustion of not being able to express her pain to him. The harrowing ache she felt ever since she saw *them* together; the rage churning within her, growing, finding out there was even more.

Mac felt her irregular heartbeat reach his chest; trained by now to notice such fine details, for victims' hearts were always about to leap out from their bodies right before he sliced them open. He reflected on the way she kissed Levi that evening — that awful image in his head assailing him, beating at his heart, unable to quit torturing him — making him wonder why she didn't go upstairs with him tonight, why she still could stand to sit beside him.

A gentle, raspy voice distracted his thoughts, or rather answered them.

"Goodnight." Charlotte muttered to him; standing up to leave, not able to handle the tension any longer, not trusting herself to remain quiet and polite — not confident in herself to not get lost in her feelings towards him, to not wilt, get hurt, break all over again.

Mac watched her as she neared the stairs, somehow the time halted and it sped up again. Clenching his teeth, raking his hair with his fingers — struggling to put the words together he so desperately wanted to tell her, he cracked his lips open, yet he had lost his voice. No sound would come out, not a single noise would be issued; he mouthed the words in darkness, yet all of a sudden, he felt himself go mute, and Charlotte had already vanished up the stairs.

CHAPTER 61

Not My Will

I

"GOOD MORNING, COWGIRL!" LEVI KNOCKED on Charlotte's door, all excited, hoping to be able to mend fences with her; a fresh new beginning.

"Mhm…" Charlotte grunted, displeased, exhausted from not sleeping all night; and the last thing she needed now was an exuberant Levi knocking frantically on her door.

"Wake up, beautiful! We have somewhere to go!" he urged her and stepped into her room, pulling the covers off her body.

"Levi!" she yelled, annoyed, grabbing the covers back with tiny fists of fury.

"What?! It's not time for sleeping now!" He chuckled, then kneeled down before her face — studying her eyes shut beguilingly, and the endearing way her full bottom lip pouted slightly further than the upper — as the sun rays glistened over her, revealing the reddish freckles on her nose. "Charlotte…" he whispered in her ear, making her squint agitatedly, staring right into his playful eyes.

"What is it?" she mumbled, covering half her face with the blanket, as if that would make him go away.

"I would like for us to go to town. Amara wants me to pick up some supplies, and…I figured you might enjoy coming with me." he said thoughtfully, cocking his head to see if she was awake.

"Hm. What town?" she muttered with a grumpy voice.

"Holy Ranch. Nothing's gonna happen to you — you have my word." he promised her and caressed her face with his fingers, his cold rings subtly waking her up.

"Do we really have to experiment now?" she nagged, and stretched her arms in the air.

"Yes. I think it would be nice. Just the two of us." He swallowed nervously, as she arched her back before him — catching his full attention, with the way the covers stretched taut across her chest.

"I suppose…" she mumbled, meditatively stroking one finger down the bridge of her nose.

"Great! I'll be downstairs, waiting on you." He leaned over and kissed her forehead. She flinched away, startled, and yet somehow he didn't notice.

I I

"HEY THERE, PARTNER!" JB GREETED MAC, who was leaning on the porch rail, smoking his tenth cigarette that morning. Mac glanced back at him, tilting his hat to him, then stretched his vascular neck up to exhale the smoke.

"Tell me mister, ever hunted in a blizzard? Ha!" he questioned him with a chuckle, realizing the weather had only gotten worse.

"Sure." he answered gravely, staring through the whiteout, already knowing what JB was wanting from him.

"Well! Wonderful! So, I'm gonna be your huntin' partner today, Mr. Kinnon! Don't worry! I won't talk your ears off! I won't bother ya one bit!" he promised, knowing Mac would be holding a rifle, and there was no way he would risk getting on his nerves this time.

"Hm." he grunted, puffing one last time before smothering the cigarette with his boot. "Ain't stayin', ol' man…I'm leavin' in a couple hours." he said and JB rolled his eyes.

"Come oooon! Weather ain't for travelin' now! Especially for young fellas like yourself!" he said sternly. "We'll be hunting a little south from here. I hear there's more deer grazing there. We shall see, ah?!" He slammed his hand against Mac's shoulder, building him up for the hunt. "I'd send Levi with ya instead, but…he and Charlotte will be going to town, so…ya stuck with this old man! HaHA!" He chuckled, slamming his hand on him once more.

"Town?" He frowned swiftly.

"Holy Ranch! Amara needed some supplies." he explained, as he counted the cartridges on his gun belt.

"What 'bout the lass?" he asked with a leer, as he watched JB's stubby fingers struggling to pull out the ammo.

"The lassie Charlotte? What 'bout her?" he asked Mac, bewildered.

"She's wanted…" Mac fumed, fearing Levi was risking her life.

"Oh! Right. Well! I'm sure Levi knows what he's doin' — everyone has some illegal business goin' on there." He shrugged. "There's actually a whole damn fence, yet the sheriff down in Marysville don't even know it. Can you believe that?! Ha!" He laughed, as a bullet accidentally slipped from his grip and rolled underneath the porch. "Gah! Darn it!"

Mac's face fell, lost in deep thoughts; fearing this would only expose Charlotte to an environment where deputies would be plowing through towns to interrogate its people. He spotted Levi inside the kitchen, and marched through the door to meet him, as a fresh swell of rage rose stronger within his smoke-infested chest.

Meanwhile, JB was now halfway stuck under the porch, trying to reach for the missing round — legs wiggling in the air, as he forced his belly deeper and deeper into the opening.

III

"What ye think yer doin'?!" Mac approached Levi in a storm of fury, who was putting on his thick coat.

"What are you talking about?" He instantly straightened his back, making himself a couple inches taller.

"Talkin' 'bout takin' the wanted lass to the feckin' town!" Mac fumed, his spread-out hands shaking beside him, balling a fist.

"Why is it any of *your* concern?" Levi leered, anger reaching his tongue.

"Yer playin', boy…dangerously!" Mac warned him, as he only could do; since it indeed was none of his business — not after she saw *them*, not after he saw her kiss *him*. For this time it wasn't an O'Donnell, it was someone she gave permission to.

"Starting with threats again, I see? Haha. Deal with it, loudmouth. You had your chance…before you fucked it up." He teased him, letting him know that he too was aware of what happened with Amara.

Mac pushed him on his chest with all his strength, dropping him down to the ground — slamming his back on top of the bench as he fell. "Don't ye feckin' dare to laugh at me, *ever again,* ye goddamn eejit. Charlotte's NOT goin'!" Mac insisted, shooting a threatening leer at him.

"Going where?" Charlotte emerged behind him, shocked to see Levi on the ground, boots softly stroking the floor the closer she strode towards them.

Mac, startled, jerked his head to her — feeling oddly vulnerable before her disappointed gaze. Levi stood up swiftly and reached for his revolver, as Mac heard the all too familiar scraping sound against his holster, and pulled out his own revolver even faster; spinning it a full circle before him.

The men now stood in the room, with their guns pointed at each other.

"I'd be more than happy to drill one into that thick skull of yers. Don't tempt me." Mac warned him again, cocking his gun.

"Would you just stop, please, with this childishness??" Charlotte begged them, trying still to figure out what in the world happened again.

"You see, Charlotte. This fella right here don't want you to go nowhere no more. He likes to have control over you. To isolate you from everyone, and everything." Levi growled out loud, eyes not leaving Mac's.

"That ain't true…" Mac muttered angrily — his hand sturdy as a rock, still gripping his gun with perfect aim at his adversary.

"Oh, but it is. I'm surprised Amara hasn't kicked you out yet — such a filthy…*maggot* you are." He spat his chewing tobacco beside his boot, yet hand shook nervously.

"Enough!!" Charlotte yelled with tears in her eyes. "Drop the damn guns already! Just stop!! Isn't life already challenging enough?! Why does someone need to die?! Over what?!" She shouted at them; her writhing, coarse voice reaching JB, who had gotten himself ever further trapped underneath the porch, helplessly, all this time.

Charlotte positioned herself between them; reached out with her trembling arms for their barrels — grabbing and slowly lowering them both down to the floor. "Please…" she begged them, feeling her heart rip in two pieces.

"Don't worry. I wouldn't have wasted a bullet…" Levi muttered, as he always had to have the last word.

Mac's gaze was fixated at Charlotte, noticing the obvious distress clouding her face — seeing her body shake uncontrollably with adrenaline — feeling his heart drop steeply to his stomach, just like the moment he saw her panicked face in Marysville. *If only she understood why he didn't want her to go*, he thought to himself, retrieving his gun.

I V

"JB?" MRS. MARGA POKED AT JB'S EXPOSED HIND WITH HER CANE, making sure he was still alive.

"Oh!!" He screeched. "Lordy!! Finally! I've been screaming my arse off out here in the freezin' cold!!" JB yelled, relieved, with the lost cartridge held tightly in his fist.

"What in the world are you doin' out here, and…*under there…*" She tried hard not to laugh, for the view of him was quite comical.

"Oh! I lost a goddamn bullet! Back in the army, those things were priceless! Ya needed every single one of them bastards!" he rambled, as Mrs. Marga was trying to hook the cane around his leg as a way to pull him out.

"Oh Lord, JB. This ain't working." she groaned, her frail body shaking with exhaustion, making her misstep on the frosty ground.

"No, it ain't! Can ya get the Kinnon chap, or Levi, or a damn wagon with draft horses to pull me outta here!!! Just, get anyone — please!" He urged her, suddenly feeling claustrophobic.

"Alright, old friend. Hold your horses…" She chuckled and slapped his hind with the cane and limped towards the door as fast as she could, hand clinging onto the frosty rail — carefully planning every step she took.

Turning the handle to find Levi and Mac still standing opposite each other with guns tensely pointed down beside them, and Charlotte still between them, waiting for things to cool down. "Ha! That's quite an unusual orgy!" She snorted snidely, knowing very well they must have been quarreling prior.

"Mrs. Marga!" Charlotte greeted her excitedly — ecstatic to see her again.

"Hello, dear child." She hobbled towards them, feeling each limb of her body ache with every step. "Levi and Mr. Kinnon, would you please go help an old fella out of a predicament? JB has wedged himself underneath the porch…"

She rolled her eyes and sat down on a chair, rubbing her aching knees.

"Wedged under…" Levi mumbled in disbelief.

"Indeed. So please, if you would be so kind? Mr. Kinnon, that goes for you too. I need to talk to Charlotte." she commanded them, with not a single care in the world if they'd decide to point a gun at her.

V

"WHAT IN THE WORLD DID YA NOT UNDERSTAND!!!" the rancher screamed at the young man, finding the emaciated mare hidden in a different stall.

"Sir…I didn't think it was a…wise decision." he stuttered, stepping before the horse protectively.

"Not a wise decision?? Who are ya to decide 'wisdom' over me?! Are ya payin' to feed her?! Winter's here, and it's a bad one, boy! She'll need twice as much food as the rest! Ya reckon I'm rich?!" he continued screaming, and the mare pinned her ears to him — slowly behaving like herself again.

"No, sir. But…sir, I rode her all the way from Cottonmouth State with not a single issue!" he defended, adjusting his hat on his head. "She rides real smooth, and don't have a single spook within her, sir!"

The farmer paused his wrath, then looked into the mare's eyes. He had seen a lot of scrawny horses in his life that were right at death's door, just like her — yet, she still had a strange light shining in her sunken eyes; a will to live that others had all lost.

"Ya've got two weeks to get her back on her feet, and show me what she can do. Two weeks, no more." He pointed his finger at him, warning him for the last time, setting him up for failure, for with two weeks under such weather conditions, it would be a challenge to put an ounce of fat on her ribs.

The man watched him march away and turned to pet the gray mare's face, fingers brushing against the velvet muzzle, the frosty whiskers — relieved and emotional that he didn't have to shoot her down.

"It'll be okay. We just gotta prove to him who ye really are. Help me do that." he whispered in her ear, and the mare rested her head against his chest, as though comforted to have found herself in his care, as though able to feel the benignity within his soul.

V I

"PULL!! PULL ME OUTTA HERE, GODDAMMIT!!!" JB SCREAMED, wiggling, squirming like a worm, suddenly letting out a massive burp from straining too hard.

Levi pulled on one leg, Mac pulled on the other, while completely avoiding any cooperation with each other — which resulted in zig-zagging JB's legs, ripping a huge tear across his pants.

"How the hell did you do that, JB?!" Levi asked after he accidentally pulled his boot off, trying to recover from the overwhelming aroma of the most putrid cheese he'd ever encountered.

"I don't know! I guess! I suppose, I ain't as thin as I used to be, back in the army…" He briefly reminisced the two protruding tummy rolls he would try to pass off as abdominal muscles, *to the ladies,* of course. "Gah, never mind! Just pull already!" he ordered them, feeling the crisp cold air reach deep within his freshly exposed rear end.

"It ain't workin'. Gotta dig him out." Mac pointed out, with considerable asperity.

"Right. You *should* know about that the best." Levi mocked with a growl, grabbing a shovel from the shack behind them, thinking how his whole day with Charlotte was ruined again.

"Careful of me!!" JB wiggled his legs anxiously, as he heard the shovel slam right beside his belly.

"Ye'll be alright, ol' man." Mac grinned, taking out a cigarette, staring at Levi with amusement as he shoveled in the snow; for once, grateful to JB for the timely distraction.

VII

"MRS. MARGA, THANK YOU SO MUCH FOR COMING!" She sighed heavily, in relief.

"Of course, dearie…" Mrs. Marga nodded, yet her gaze had dulled.

"I didn't expect to see you anytime soon, to be honest, ma'am, but…I suppose you must have some news for me? Hopefully?" Charlotte inquired excitedly, not able to contain her thrilled self as she imagined Will's response to her. Picturing his beautiful handwriting — his lovely, articulate words that were so different from anyone she'd ever met, somehow needing the comfort of his civilized manner, *in contrast to those nincompoops at gun-point,* she thought, agitated. She felt her heart warm up, just by thinking of the possibility of seeing him again, realizing she would be able to apologize to him in person, and part of her heart would selfishly be mended. *Perhaps he was already on his way over here, as now he knew exactly where she was staying,* she wishfully hoped and prayed.

"I do. Indeed, I do…" Mrs. Marga sighed, when she met Charlotte's face, aglow in glimmering blithe. "Sit down, my child." she said and pulled a chair towards her with her cane, glancing at the corner of the house as if to collect her thoughts.

"Mrs. Marga…?" Charlotte tentatively questioned her, noticing subtle tears stand in her eyes.

"William…he…" She paused herself and swallowed down an uncomfortable knot, formed the moment she saw Charlotte again. "He murdered his wife…Elizabeth." she said bluntly, stretching her neck, adjusting her locked up jaw — trying hard to retain her composure.

Charlotte's face fell. It landed somewhere in the memory of the elite witches spurting out that name on the dance floor. It got trampled. Her chest swelled up, flared from a breath taken too deep, for she never expected to hear these words. She never expected Will to hurt a fly, *let alone kill someone.*

Someone who was his very own wife.

"That can't be, Mrs. Marga…he'd never." she said sternly, defending him, reminiscing his sweet gestures, endearing words, the gentle melody of his voice lulling her to sleep in his arms; the shy smiles, the genuine titters, the reservedness in the name of etiquette, the tender strokes of his fingers against her face, the quivering lips pressed against her in the stables, in fear of offending the passing eyes.

"He would never murder someone — not my Will — not him." she growled with heart, for Will always spoke kindly about everyone, even those who did not deserve it. Even rescuing Mac without knowing how to fend himself properly with a gun, yet he was brave enough to attempt to do so, for her. "This is absurd, Mrs. Marga…" she added, after rambling in her head for a freezing moment of silence.

"That's what we all thought, dearie…that's what we all thought." she reassured, then glanced down at her custom-made cane, which Will had imported just for her.

"So…is he…captured now? Or…what is going on? Is he wanted? Does he need to hide here too? What, what's going on?" her words shot out of her mouth like gunshots; still doubting the claims in her head — feeling flustered at the unfairness for anyone to accuse Will of murder.

Mrs. Marga sucked in a deep breath and reached out to grab Charlotte's soft hand. Charlotte swallowed down her thoughts, as she noticed the old woman's cheeks now coursed by tears, trapping within the gaunt lines and charred burns. "He has passed." she hummed sternly, looking straight into her innocent eyes.

"What…what do you mean?" she asked, hoping — praying she misunderstood her. An absent chuckle escaped her, as though it were a bad joke.

"William Griffiths died, Charlotte…" She breathed out heavily, the article flashing before her eyes. A scorching silence in a damp air, a reach of emotions, stark and gray, swirling between them, raw, alive, crawling down their spines, waltzing around them eerily.

"How? How is this…how is this even possible?" she soughed, legs numbing, falling, dragging beneath her, as though her whole world was falling apart.

"He shot himself with a rifle…nobody knows why. No letter or note left behind; nothing." She glanced over at the window, watching the snowstorm bear in, bold and reckless. Heavy snowflakes wafting down like rocks, cloaking the whole glass white, cracking it with a line of frost.

"No…not Will…" Charlotte's eyes burst into tears, feeling a well of emotions suddenly overflow from her core — spurting, one after the other, drumming, knocking, throbbing at the chamber of her ribs.

"I'm sorry, child. He was one of a kind...a good man. No matter how they try to paint him now." she stated, gnashing down her teeth. Charlotte sobbed unrestrained; she couldn't find the words to speak, nor the thoughts allowing this to make sense. "I just thought I should let you know...it was clear to me you cared about him, and I'm sure he knew you did too." She caressed her hand, letting her shield down for a brief moment.

"I...I betrayed him...it's all my fault..." she stammered, shivered, slumping into a pit of darkness, convulsing in guilt, turning into her worst enemy.

Herself.

VIII

"Mrs. Marga! My dearest!" JB marched through the door, with a muddy coat torn in multiple places, pants ripped up the entire length of his hind.

"JB...glad to see you...out of there." she whispered calmly, trying not to take her attention away from Charlotte, seeing as though she was slipping into the unknown, someplace where hearts pile up, indistinguishable from each other, meant to crash and bleed out.

"Oh, let me tell ya! I feel a hundred pounds lighter now! HaHA! The boys did good! Just don't know if I can hunt, after all this...strenuous exercise!" he mumbled as he walked towards her, noticing Charlotte in heavy tears, halting in his tracks. "Oh! Oh! I'm, I'm sorry to interrupt?" he stuttered, not expecting to find anyone crying.

Levi and Mac followed right after, instantly feeling the thickly asphyxiating air in the room. "What happened??" Levi asked Charlotte, the moment he saw her a wailing mess.

"Can't you just leave me alone?!" she exploded on him, then rushed, sobbing, up the stairs.

"What in the tarnation...?" JB muttered under his breath. "Mrs. Marga? What happened?" he said, realizing something deathly serious must have occurred. Mac observed the old lady carefully, feeling his heart oddly wrench for Charlotte.

"Oh well...long story short, we had a mutual friend — perhaps he was more for her; or certainly so. Anyhow, he was found dead in Red Giants... after killing his wife." she explained, as she composed herself again.

"Ya mean that poor chap in the newspaper today?! What's his name now, Wil...Wilbur?"

"William. William Griffiths." she interrupted him swiftly, not wanting to hear his name be disrespectfully confused with someone else's.

Mac's eyes flared, not expecting to ever hear this name again — and certainly not in this way.

"Damn. That's the chap she wrote the letter to." JB gasped, remembering the choppy handwriting behind the letter.

"Poor thing...she will need some time after that shock. Be kind. Don't fool around with guns no more." She gave a stern look at both Levi and Mac — making sure to insinuate they'd get in trouble with her own connections, and she certainly had them.

CHAPTER 62

A Good Man

I

SHERIFF DORMAN AND HIS DEPUTIES REACHED MARYSVILLE. Tethering their horses before the saloon, they strode inside to grab a drink to warm themselves up. "Mr. Mickey Longley! Serve us some drinks, will ya?" Dorman commanded tauntingly, and sat on a stool before him — stretching his benumbed legs underneath the table.

"Of course, Sheriff." he murmured, displeased to see him again.

"How's life been for ya?!" Dorman asked him teasingly, knowing very well he was a poor man, desperately trying to make ends meet.

"Very well, sheriff. Thank ya for your concern." he responded snidely, pouring a dozen glasses of whiskey for them.

"Well, tell ya what, Mr. Longley." he said, cutting his eyes at him. "Grab yourself a glass, and I'll pay ya the drink. *Today* is a reason to celebrate!" He excitedly lifted his glass in the air, ready to toast with the whole world, the living and the dead.

"How come?" Mickey folded his arms, suspecting there was only one reason to see Dorman so ecstatic.

"We're gonna catch him, Mr. Longley. We are close. *Very* close this time." he soughed, leaned over the counter with a wicked grin on his face. His mustache twitched, eyes stared, groping him.

"Oh. Exciting…" He cleared his throat. "So, where's he hiding at now?" he asked, cautiously.

"Haha…" Dorman chuckled and took a big sip of his drink. "I'd be a fool to tell ya…" He winked at him, feeling as if he was the smartest man on earth.

Mickey looked at him with a stiffened jaw, feeling the urge to stab his nauseating face with his knife; to pluck the snide grin out of his grimace.

"But I'll tell ya one thing, Mickey…" He flicked a finger in the air before him. "God *always* has a plan. God led him right back to where his biggest ever atrocity took place — where everything started." He chugged down his whiskey, eyes locking back at him.

"And there, it shall end."

II

THE TORRENT OF HER TEARS SOAKED THROUGH THE COVERS, as she laid there, lifelessly clinging onto a feeble thread of sangfroid — gently clutching the orchid flower Will had left, somehow its petals had sunk, wilted, bent, as if to portray her own fragility. Each gasp she took tore down her raw throat, and her mind raced as she lost herself within the sounds of the blizzard banging against the window pane, as though threatening its entrance. Lungs desperately rummaged for wisps of oxygen, as she felt her own weeping forcefully drown her little by little. "Why, oh why…why did you have to leave like that, Will? Why…" she sobbed into the pillow, feeling the smooth flower petals caress her fingertips in return. "I am so…so sorry…so sorry…" she wailed, choked, screamed into the cloth.

Mac sat on the ground of his room, back leaned against the freezing cold wall. He could hear her muffled cries, reaching through the barrier between them, making him feel odd himself, as though longing to offer comfort, yet not knowing how. His thoughts wandered to Will; the way he came searching for him in the middle of the night — within a heavy snowstorm reminiscing the one outside, rescuing him with jittering hands and a blanched face. How he was generously selfless to offer for him to stay at his place; knowing the risks that would follow with it. *He was an awkward man, soft, weak, but respectfully knowledgable, regarding history and the world around him, yet gunslinging was not his forte* — Mac thought to himself as he clutched his eyes shut, head pressed against the wall, fist squeezed, hearing her more clearly.

III

DEPUTIES HAD REACHED THE FREELANDS AT THE BREATH OF DAWN; the snow-storm swayed away in a flurry of wings, occasionally calming down, allowing them an opportunity to ride and move faster through the meadows of frost.

They had started plowing through houses, investigating room after room. Interrogating ranchers and townsfolk alike — anyone they would come across; not leaving a single shack unchecked, snapping sealed mouths open with the menace of a weapon. Anything that appeared like a potential hideout, they investigated it thoroughly, like maggots piling up into a corpse, feasting upon every sinew from the inside out of it.

This time they seemed to work much smarter, much faster, and interestingly, much more calculated. Perhaps the reason behind it was Sheriff Dorman's sudden change of attitude, comporting himself as a confident leader — rather than a lost and angry fool, chasing frantically after Mac with irrational and misjudged measures.

They rode their way through the snow-covered hills, seeing Holy Ranch in the distance. Dorman squinted through the snow to glance over at the farmhouse to his left — the Grossman's farm — still abandoned, still infested with ravens hovering over the ashen crops. Heart fell heavily; sudden bilious nausea reaching the back of his throat, as he recalled *his* torn-up face — the burnt Holy Bible stuck deep inside *his* sliced-open mouth, eyes carved out of their sockets — placed sarcastically in the palms of *his* tied-up hands.

"When I get my hands around ya…" he whispered out loud, as a wicked tear of wrath scarred his face.

IV

"HOW YA HOLDIN' UP THIS MORNING?" JB ASKED HIM as he was secretly, as discreetly as he could, rereading *the* article in the newspaper.

"Hm." Mac nodded absently, adjusting his suspenders over his back.

"Ya…gettin' ready for somethin'?" he questioned him curiously, as he watched him fill up canister after canister with water.

"Sure." He sighed, as his fingers sealed the full canister back again.

"Well, will ya tell me already, or do I need to beg for more information? HaHA!" He chuckled, sipping on his coffee, wondering if he was going on a killing spree again.

"I'm leavin', ol' man." Mac said dryly as he stretched his back, making all his muscles protrude in subtle waves. "Don't know why I didn't already..." he soughed to himself, instantly answering his own question as Charlotte's face emerged before his eyes.

"Oh! Lordy!" He gasped. "In such weather??" JB yelled worriedly, waking up Amara in the next room.

"No. Waitin' for it to get dark." He pulled out his knife to test the sharpness of its blade, almost in a state of trance, as though to delay his departure from her.

"But...then the blizzard will hit ya?" he stuttered with concern, still holding the coffee cup — spilling drops on top of the article as he moved his hand around swiftly.

"Exactly." He tilted the tip of his knife towards him in agreement. "Less risk to be seen." he added, then slipped the knife back into its worn-down sheath around his hip.

"More risk to freeze your balls off!" JB chuckled, yet his eyes started to swell, and lips trembled in sadness. "Mac, my boy...if ya allow me to call ya by your name..." he muttered calmly and Mac cut his eyes at him, cocking a brow. "I want ya to know I've had a lot of fun, getting to know ya the last few days." He bowed his head and looked down at his coffee, realizing it had spilled all over him.

Mac listened carefully, as he was loading his revolver with fresh cartridges.

"I know ya probably loathed every minute to be around people here, and especially me, but ah...please know you'll always have a special place in this man's old stinkin' heart." He silently sobbed, feeling as if he was losing his own son.

Mac stared at his gun — a Smith & Wesson Model 3 Schofield — and all the history that implied. He repeated his words inside his head, reminiscing the brand new white shirt he gifted to him, still cherished, folded carefully within his saddle bag.

"Just…just wanted ya to know that." He stood up, slowly drowning from swallowing down a sob. He walked up to Mac and clasped his shoulder with heart. "You're a good man, son. A little crazy sometimes, but good. It's been an honor."

Mac stared into his red-streaked eyes, aghast, feeling an unfamiliar heavy fist punch him in the gut as his loving words echoed within him. "Sure." he hummed, for any other word seemed too exhausting for his brain to process.

JB chuckled tenderly, and limped to the kitchen, ready to prepare the rabbit for today's stew.

V

THE DOOR SNARLED, STARTLING CHARLOTTE, who had finally fallen asleep not too long before — with the flower still cradled protectively in her hand.

"Charlotte?" Amara's soft voice reached her ears, borne by the chilled wind.

"Great…" Charlotte muttered under her breath. "Come in!" She propped herself up hastily on the bed, adjusting her only good shirt, which she had accidentally slept in.

"Hey, sweet lady." Amara greeted her as she sauntered through the room.

"Hey, Amara…is everything okay?" she asked her, wondering what else could have happened to bring her here.

"Oh, yes. I just wanted to check on you…I heard about your friend…"

"JB?" she interrupted her, fearing JB might have notified the whole state about it already.

"Yes…" She nodded with a grin, knowing exactly JB couldn't keep secrets to himself, not even if his life depended on it. "I'm very sorry. I know how it feels to have…someone taken from you." she hummed, trying hard not to recall her husband's skinned body.

"Thank you. And I'm deeply sorry, too…I guess I've never felt something quite like that. It…kind of hit me in unexpected ways." she confessed, as even her mother's death didn't really affect her like this.

"He sounded like a wonderful man…based on what Mrs. Marga told us after…" she said, brushing her lips with a forefinger nervously, as she noticed Charlotte's puffy eyes straining to look at her.

"He was remarkable…and I was too blind — too dumb, to see it." She clenched her teeth agitatedly, realizing how lost her mind was; how undeniably focused her heart was on Mac, all that time.

"I can relate to that. I always choose the wrong men, and ignore the ones worthy…" She tittered awkwardly, thinking of how Mac dropped her like a sack of potatoes.

Charlotte's sudden silence was evident — aware exactly of who she was referring to, and the guilt arose within her; as she too chose Mac over Will, even if unbeknownst to her at the time. "I understand completely…" she muttered, drumming her thumb repeatedly against her leg, hoping for the conversation to be over soon.

"I also heard Kinnon was leaving tonight. Probably for the best." Amara exhaled deeply, feeling relieved not to ever have to see this man's being again.

"Oh…he is?" She choked, bowed her head, fingers clutching the cloth of her pants.

"Yes. So I heard…" She uttered with slight excitement, shrugging, utterly detached from any prior sentiments towards him.

"And how does that make you feel, Amara? I know…you had…wished otherwise." she said, wondering if she was still sad over him, as though her feelings mattered more than her own.

"Couldn't make me feel better. I'm ready to have him out of here." she confessed happily, and glanced out the window.

"But…I thought…"

"No. There's nothing between us. It was my mistake to think there ever was…" she said, snorting snidely. "But he's just a typical pig of a man." she fussed and stood up, ready to leave.

"I'm sorry…" Charlotte sighed.

Yet, her mind instantly painted a picture of Levi.

VI

"WHERE YOU GOING, UNCLE LEVI?" Jonathan ran up to him hastily, as he was putting on his boots.

"To town, son. Your mother needs some supplies." he answered and picked him up in his burly arms.

"In the snowstorm?" His eyes widened in surprise, since Amara forbade him to go out under such weather conditions.

"In the snowstorm." He gave a big smile, before putting him down again.

"Uncle Levi? Is miss Charlotte sick?" Jonathan pouted, wondering why he hadn't seen her for breakfast that morning.

"No, Jonny." He sighed. "She's just...tired, I suppose." He stretched his neck tensely, reminding himself of how she went between him and Mac, infuriating him.

"Oh...I'm *never* so tired!" he pointed out, as he always was a bundle of energy from the moment he woke up.

"Haha. Trust me, we know. We all know!" He chuckled and patted his tiny shoulders with gigantic hands.

"JB said Mr. Kinnon was going on an adventure tonight. He also said I couldn't go with him when I asked him." He pouted again with rosy cheeks of sadness, feeling as if Mac was avoiding him.

"I'm sure it won't be the adventure you're imagining...but tell you what! Next fall, why don't we go camping in the Rockies? I think you'd be ready by then." He winked at him, giving him a promise he knew he couldn't keep.

VII

MOUNTING HIS HORSE, HE GALLOPED HIS WAY OUT of the mudtown, Marysville. The Freelands were half a day's ride away, yet with the relentless blizzard blocking the view on the horizon, and the frosty roads risking the horse to slip — the travel would be delayed immensely. Road signs were completely cloaked with snow, and there were no Mon Louis road-clearing services for them to be uncovered again. He'd be a fool, or a brave fool — to rush a journey like this on a horse that was not accustomed to such harsh conditions. *Yet if ever there was a time for foolish bravery, it was this one,* he thought to himself as he kicked the sides of his horse to gallop faster.

CHAPTER 63

Running Away

I

MAC PACKED UP HIS LEATHER SADDLEBAGS, as he trudged across his room — throwing in his few pairs of woolen socks and a couple of worn-down shirts he'd been carrying with him for ages, trapping his fingers into the holes that had engraved within them as he did.

He paused his tracks before the mirror, stood there, dithering, then looked up, eyes setting upon fogged-up glass — noticing the rugged dirty blond beard that engulfed his jaw, forgotten to be shaved for some time. His gaze lifted, now staring at his own eyes, noticing the ominous misery portrayed within them, somehow different than before. There was a color of emotion merging with his blues, a wave of sadness, for last he looked, there was just a dark void; devoid of any sentiment. His eyes trailed off down to his hands, reminiscing how many times they were stained in innocent blood — how the sin they manifested could never be repented. He stared at his chest, as he felt his heart thud violently against it.

"Gah…" he grunted, agitated, picked up the saddlebags and headed to the shack. He pried the barn doors widely, frozen wind pushing them back towards him. He squeezed himself along with the bags through it — feeling his patience run low, mentally drained.

"Crap!" Charlotte yelled, as Finn got spooked by the sudden banging sound of the doors — bolting into a nervous circle around her. She turned around to detect Mac, standing there, bags thrown over his shoulder, black duster coat swaying from the wintry squall prior, spooking Finn even further.

"Hm." he muttered, as he stared into her alarmed eyes — not making a step further — not *able* to make a step further, feet suddenly frozen to the ground, staring at her as if she was the breath, the heart, the life of his.

Charlotte broke off the tense eye contact, and continued in her failed attempt to calm Finn down, still needing to wrap his foot for the day, still protesting with all his stubbornness. Yet her heart leaped instantly, beating harder against her rib cage, knowing this was the last time she'd ever see him.

I I

HOLY RANCH SEEMED HECTIC; all the workers rushed to collect their cattle and horses, locking them up in their stalls and barns. Goats and sheep were warming up each other in their cozy shelter, while their paddock was covered in six feet of snow.

"Young man, could you help me please." Levi grabbed the man's attention, who was busy blanketing a horse.

"Yes, sir. What do ye need?" he asked him, as he secured the blanket around its neck. Levi glanced at the emaciated horse before him, wondering what such a mistreated animal would be doing in a ranch like this. "Sir?" The young man pulled Levi's attention back to him.

"Right. I'm needing to grab an order made by my cousin, Amara Strom. You probably know her already." he said, rubbing his hands to warm them up, as his fingers felt frozen together beneath the gloves.

"Yes, sir. I believe she had ordered eight quarts of milk." The young man jumped up in an instant, rushing to grab the box with the bottles within it — leaping over fences, fit as a fiddle — making Levi's knees ache just by watching.

III

"COME ON, BOY. WE CAN'T BE DOING THIS EVERY TIME!" She grunted, exasperated, not wishing to make a fool out of herself right before Mac's eyes, *as she was already known to be a useless huntress,* or...a useless anything.

Finn snorted and stomped his feet down, bolting yet again away from her. Charlotte clenched her teeth, covered her face with the palm of her hand, letting out a deep breath, calculating all the carrots she wouldn't be feeding him for the evening.

"Need help?"

His voice reached her, rattled her, erected her hair, goosed her skin, sent the coldest shiver down her spine, benumbing her for a fleeting moment. Mac was peeking over the saddlebags he was adjusting on Roy's saddle, studying all the mistakes she was making.

"No." she said shortly — acting like she meant it.

"Hm."

There it was again; *the hum,* she thought, biting her lip, knowing she had burned the bridge of communication. Then he spoke again, startling her.

"Got a trick for such situations…" he said with a bowed head, somehow, hiding behind Roy made it easier for him to find the words.

"Oh, yes?" She swallowed hard, tempering down the beating of her heart. "That's great! But, it won't work with this…this stubborn…carrot-head!" she hissed, devastated, feeling herself sweat from all the wrestling, or rather from the sudden conversation they were leading. Finn snorted, offended by his new nickname, and looked around as the mere mention of carrots — a word he knew all too well — gave him a sudden appetite.

"Let me see." His deep calm voice hit her ears from behind, accelerating the already rampant pounding of her heart. Now standing quietly beside her, with his rope tangled in his roughened hands. He stretched the hawser out, looped it around his foot with a swift throw, then gently pulled it upwards to its body; releasing the pressure every time Finn gave the slightest try. Finn hesitated at first, yet his ears flicked behind him — paying full attention to Mac's every movement. He lifted his leg reluctantly, following the pressure of the rope more and more.

"Eeeasy, lad…shh…" His voice only deepened; a harsh sounding melody that meditatively reassured Finn, all the while torturing *her,* reeling her back into a pit of fire, burning within it, burning for him, burning for what they weren't, burning for what they had become; charred wood, splitting apart, ready to turn to ash, evaporate in the past. He wrapped the cloth around his heavy hoof — with his calm energy radiating across the room, reminding her of how much she missed this aura of serenity, soothing the soul, sheltering her light with his veil of tranquil darkness.

I V

"HERE YOU GO, SIR. THAT'LL BE FIFTY-SIX CENTS." the man said, as he placed the milk bottles inside the pack bags of Levi's horse.

"You new around here?" Levi questioned him suspiciously, as his face reminded him of someone.

"Yes, sir. Just started work here a few months ago." he mumbled, and adjusted his slouched hat nervously.

"How old are you, boy?" He leaned over his saddle horn, noticing his youthful face — embraced by his shoulder-length blond hair.

"Twenty, sir." he confessed, wondering the reason for his asking.

"I see." He bobbed his head and eased himself back into the seat. "Well, you're doing a great job here. Keep at it, kid." he encouraged him, and trotted down the pathways of the ranch, still wondering who he reminded him of.

"Mr. Krog!"

Levi halted and turned around, confused by the unfamiliar voice — noticing a bright gray mustache shining underneath a black hat.

V

"HE CARED 'BOUT YE." MAC MUMBLED, letting Finn's hoof down gently, taking care for it not to slam the ground. "I'm sorry." he added bravely, as he glanced over at her startled self.

Charlotte blinked blankly at him. Her heart crashed against her ribs — his words echoing in her head. "...excuse me?" she soughed, aghast, for she couldn't believe her ears; perceiving him talk so empathetically.

"Will." He broke off eye contact abruptly, jerking his head away, embarrassed, intimidated to finally be speaking to her.

Her throat swelled up, as she studied his awkward gaze fixate on the floor. His sharp lipped mouth went mute, sealed, folded like a loser's game of cards — a deep ache settled in his jaw, realizing he was clenching it nervously.

Charlotte couldn't help but notice his sunken cheeks, sharpening his bearded jawline as he swallowed repeatedly. She clutched her eyes, blinding herself from his sight, yet she still could see him. He was still there, groping into the memories of them, dragging them to the light, reeling her eyes back open, as though to convince her of something; something neither of them understood. Her fingernails bit into her palms — feeling his suffocating silence haunting her all over again. Feeling as though she had kept pouring to him, while he kept leaving her empty, thirsting for an answer.

She sliced the thick air with her hand as she threw Finn's halter to the stall before her. "I…I'm sorry, but I have…I have to get out of here." she said, almost cried, feeling her legs go suddenly numb, her whole body shaking in panic, the ground vibrating underneath her, now rushing towards the door. Trying desperately to leave this man behind; his presence that compelled her to feel so powerless, so vulnerable. So lost in his subtle, flawless movements, in his bewitching gaze, his alluring scent of fire and smoke — so lost within *him*.

"Charlotte!" Mac called out. Her heart constricted, fell, dropped. He strode after her without having to convince himself twice, as he watched his last chance escape before his eyes. She hastened towards the door, as his footsteps reached her ears — crashing through the vehement thudding in her heart, and yet there was no trace of fear within her by being chased after, for she knew the sound of his boots evinced shielding, and the shadow they carried, a safe haven to fade within. Suddenly the clops of heels and the jiggle of spurs halted, and as she paused her legs, her breath, and her thought, an oddly soothing relief slithered down her spine when she glanced behind to notice his face before hers, mere breaths away.

V I

"I'M AFRAID I DON'T RECOGNIZE YOU, MISTER." Levi confessed politely, his eyes traveling to the man's badge.

"Oh, but of course. How *rude* of me." he mumbled snidely. "Let me introduce myself. Sheriff Dorman, all the way from Bisonhorn." he flicked his hat to him, exposing a big grin on his face.

"Levi Krog…" He nodded to him. "Good to meet you, sir." He remained polite, yet his gut was on high alert.

"It's aaaall my pleasure. I've heard lots about ya, Mr. Krog. Loooots about ya…" He dismounted, nearing him closer.

"Did you?" He cocked a brow, suspicious, collecting his horse's reins discreetly.

"Yes. Yes indeed. Ya see…" He snatched his felted cowboy hat off his head to look at him better. "Ya don't know me, but ya *did* know my associate up in Birdsboro." he insinuated, and grabbed Levi's reins from the horse's mouth.

"What you want?" Levi fumed, realizing deputies had circled him already.

"Justice." He gawked, expecting a smooth confession. "I want justice…"

"That makes two of us, sir. But I'm afraid you've got the wrong one." Levi kicked his horse, urging it to go — yet the sheriff just clasped the reins tighter.

"Not so fast, mister. Ya see…I know what ya did up in Birdsboro, as well as at Ring Lagoon…" He grinned with sarcasm. "Many innocent lives was taken unfairly…" he said, cutting his eyes at Levi, whose sin was painted across his face. "I know who you're hidin'. Do ya really wish for a lifetime of regret? A lifetime of hidin', and chasin', and runnin' away like a madman?" he whispered to him, ready to offer him a proposition. "You're a wanted man, Mr. Krog…all over Birdsboro, very close to Mon Louis…the town of opportunities. The town, with the well of money…ya don't wish to lose that, hm?"

He winked at him tauntingly. Levi tore his gaze away, a breath of guilt slashing through the silver frost of air. He had already risked his entire career for a man whom he loathed; for a woman, that seemed to loathe him.

"Come on, Mr. Krog…do the right thing. Your father would want you to."

VII

"WHY YER RUNNIN' AWAY FROM ME ALL THE DAMN...TIME, LASS?" his raspy voice whispered before her face, feet awkwardly waltzed in reverse until they stumbled against the cold wall.

"I'm not..." She breathed out heavily, choking her words, as his troubled eyes followed hers intimidatingly. "Be-besides, I have, I have...nothing to say to you no more." she stuttered, lost in his sharp gaze, back now pressed against the wood planks — his broad shoulders blocking the view before her, towering over her, and yet there was no threat.

"Why, Charlotte?" he grunted, glancing briefly down to their boots, lifting his chin up to face her again with a question across his cracked mouth — chapped lips begging desperately to be felt. "Why are yer eyes...avoidin' me?"

"I..." Her throat felt tight; making it hard to swallow, to talk, to breathe. "...what do you want from me, Mac?" she growled defensively, squinting her eyes back at him with anger.

Mac stared in her threatening eyes, captivated by their every shade of brown and green — *so innocent, yet bold; daring, and beautiful,* he thought briefly; feeling his weary chest glued to hers as he slammed his hand against the wall in anguish, leaning right over her. "Don't ye understand...?!" he muttered under his breath, feeling his rage burn within him, frustration building up — slithering through his veins, reaching his tormented heart, ready to burst out of its cage.

"No...I'm afraid I don't understand anything, anymore." she whispered heavily, studying his harrowing expression — his thick brows frowning, shadowing those blue eyes — *those damn blue eyes,* the eyes she could never stand to gaze at long enough to read, yet drowned within, as though blind.

Mac dropped his head to her shoulder vulnerably, burying his furrowed face in the softness of her neck — the earthy scent of her hair filling up his lungs, the deeper he breathed it in, veiling the coldness of his being.

"Mac...what..." She gasped quietly, uncertain, eyes shutting for her — feeling the harshness of his lips glide tormentingly against her skin.

VIII

"INDEED. YOUR FATHER WAS A MAN OF RIGHTEOUSNESS, as ya already know, I'm sure." Dorman mumbled as the snow hit his mustache, slowly forming streaks of ice atop of it.

"He was…" Levi agreed in an instant, watching the deputies carefully as they clasped their rifles in their hands.

"Twenty-five thousand bucks — all yours, as well as your freedom — if ya just lead us to him." he offered, hand reached out to him.

"And the girl?" Levi questioned, knowing they were after Charlotte as well.

"Haha…" Dorman chuckled, his sarcastic breath slashing the cold air. "Ya really think the gal is what we're after? Keep 'er and enjoy her, for all I care." he said, hand still stretched out to seal the agreement.

Levi stared at his wrinkled fingers — perfectly unscarred. He stared with confusion, feeling his sense betray his heart. The storm gushed its snow against them; covering their coats and hats, blinding them for a fleeting moment, as though to reconsider. The fading sun had started to set behind them, sinking deep into the hoarfrost, into the pale meadows; fresh virgin snow descending, swaying, as the temperatures lowered below freezing — a sudden handshake of that moment, the only sound within the void.

"Follow me."

IX

"WHY…WHY DO YOU DO THIS TO ME, MAC…" She exhaled deeply, as his mouth brushed against her skin — shocking her neck with his cold, wicked breath.

"…Charlotte, I…" He pulled back to face her, cupping her jaw with his calloused hands. "I feel weak…" he growled, in earnest, his upset eyes locked with hers. Wondering himself, *why he felt so damn much in her presence.*

"Yer…me only thought. Me only feelin'."

Tears stood in her eyes, flooding them, as though his words were thrown like daggers into her heart, as though this was the moment she begged and hungered for before the turquoise rippled waters of the lagoon.

"Why…?" Her shaky hands clutched his face, and before he could answer, before he could breathe — her lips laid possessively on his.

She kissed him. Unforgivingly.

A moment she'd craved for too long; a desire she hopelessly denied she felt.

He wrapped his arms around her waist and pulled her close; with hands clutching her shirt, feeling the warmth of her body reach through him, feeling the wetness of her lips heal his dryness. They breathed into each other; kissing and exhaling deeply in between — a lustful haze forming before their mouths — swiftly vanishing as they met again. He unlocked his lips briefly, just to glimpse her face once more; letting his fingers travel across her cheek, making sure all this was real.

"I don't know…I don't know what's happenin' to me, lass…" He kissed her again, and again, long, deep, fervently, breaking it off to face her again, claiming the beauty of her being. "Nothin' makes sense no more, only…yer being." He picked her up in his muscular arms — pressed her hastily against the wall, fingers digging through her sensual thighs, not out of lust; out of desperation to merge with her as one, as though he was incomplete. She wrapped her legs around him, nails hooked into his back, pulled him as close to her as she could.

Kissing, soul to soul, lips to lips, heart to heart.

"Don't go, Mac…please." she sobbed as her lips slid effortlessly off of his, gliding down his rugged chin, mouth feeling the scars beneath his beard — falling in love with every single one of them — falling in love with every imperfection of his. "Not without me…" she cried in a sigh, hands sliding down his muscular back — lips cravingly locking his once again.

Mac grunted deeply, as her words sunk down into his chest — choking the breath from his lungs, realizing they *couldn't*, they *shouldn't*, this *had* to come to an end. "Charlotte…" He chocked, unwrapped her legs, and placed them down gently — his trembling fingers running through her hair to forever capture that texture in his memory.

"No…don't even go there." she wailed, knowing what he was about to say, as she saw him hesitate, and the lines on his face deepen. "I don't want to hear it, Mac. Not again. Not this time!" Her seething torrent of tears ran down her face, hands clutching his chest tightly — intending to never let go.

"One of these days, they'll catch up…and…when they do, Charlotte…" He sighed with a knot in his throat, halted, grunted furiously, leaned over to steal another kiss from her lips for he couldn't resist anymore; feeling the softness of them crush his heart — shattering it into million shards, kissing her in ways he'd never thought possible. "I cannot risk yer life, me lass…" he growled softly, forehead rested against hers. "I can't, could never forgive meself if…"

"Let me decide that!" She leered, noticing his eyes red, swollen, for the very first time.

"No…" he said gravely, tearing his gaze away.

"You don't get to decide that, Mac…you don't!" she hissed, clutching his jaw, pulling it back towards her, facing him, not letting go.

"Ye've got yer whole life ahead of ye…I'm…I ain't…"

"Life's not worth living in loneliness!" she cried, not wishing to hear it. "And Mac…it's fucking lonely without you!" She pressed her lips against his — feeling the sudden burst of pain consume her, crying into him, wilting and tensing up at the same time, shivering for his lips felt like nobody else's. They felt like home; a home she never had, a home that was threatened be lost.

"I give ye me word…if there's ever such a chance again — I'll come back for ye when ye need me, like I've always have when I could…I give ye me word, Charlotte." He squeezed his grip around her arm, sliding off, clutching her hand, fingers entwined. Rough against soft. Sin against purity. Dark against light.

He brushed his mouth against hers for one last time, clutching her face as softly as he could, breathing her in, letting his grip loosen around her cheek — as he pulled his body reluctantly away from hers — wishing he could freeze the time forever.

"No…no, Mac. NO! Please!" She grabbed frantically for his shoulder, yet he started walking away. "Don't do this, goddammit!!" she yelled in despair, feeling her world crumble to dust once more — feeling her pain intensify so much, she no longer knew where or who she was.

"PLEASE!!!" she cried. "Don't do this to us again! Don't…break me!! Don't…leave. Don't ruin this…" She strode after him, yet he paced faster.

"I love you, Mac!!" she yelled the words out loud for the first time — words she had kept locked inside herself all these months, words that tormented her heart no matter who she laid with — words that had no meaning, before she met him. "I love you, you fool!" She crashed down on her knees, unable to feel her legs anymore; chest, heavier than ever — heart incapable of feeling any further pain, as it had long passed her threshold. She hid her face within her hands, not to see him leave once more, weeping, crumbling within.

Mac froze his tracks in utter shock, a stab hitting him in the chest, a shot in the gut, as her powerful words echoed in his head — losing any connection to the world around him, since he'd never heard these before. All the emotions that gushed out of his heart, rolled into one, swirling round like sand in a storm, pebbles tumbling in the river. Unable to grasp that this human being, unscarred, virtuous, felt safe and secure enough to spurt out their innermost feelings towards him; a sinner — begging to become two against the whole menacing world. Realizing, her beauty stemmed from being able to love a thorn, as roses flaunted their grace around her, promising a garden.

"I love you…" she soughed, wilting in sorrow, and he turned swiftly to face her, tentatively cracking his mouth open…yet the clicking of a gun through the door behind him spoke first.

CHAPTER 64

Welcome Home

I

THE ICE COLD WIND TUGGED AT HIS HAIR; feeling his face freeze by the second as the night rolled in, blocking the slightest hint of direction on the horizon. The deep snow-covered ground rushed by him, and the only sound in the Freelands was the vigorous pounding of his horse's hooves, as they continued galloping to the east — mirroring the runaway's path from many years ago.

He was hurtling forward, faster than he'd ever gone before, feeling himself slip sideways off the saddle, squeezing his thighs frantically in an effort to stay on. The horse picked up the pace, leveling out even faster…taking him within just a few hills of Holy Ranch.

II

"SO, WE FINALLY MEET…MR. KINNON." the voice said, from behind the gun.

Mac stared at Charlotte, whose eyes were flared in fear and distress, feeling the gun come closer to his head — sensing the footsteps sneak up behind him.

Dorman walked around him, scarring an eerily pleasant smile on his face that only the capture of Mac Kinnon could give him, almost salivating, pulsating whole as though he had just met his savior; and yet, meeting God himself would not inspire such feelings. Dumbfounded, he stared at him, scanning him from head to toe, in flesh and blood.

He quivered, for he could not grasp the rare sight, as rage simmered within him, roaring like a storm to have him stand at the end of his barrel, one trigger away from his death. Mac locked eyes with him for the first time since he'd been a wanted man, wondering why his face seemed so familiar.

"The legendary Kinnon…my, my…" He shook his head, aghast, gun still pointed at his head.

"Leave him alone!!" Charlotte screamed, her leering eyes boring into him.

"Oh! Miss Charlotte!" He cocked his head, as though surprised. "So good to see ya again, miss." he said snidely, as he motioned for the deputies to enter the shack. "Ya see, Mr. Kinnon…we've known each other for quite some time now; Charlotte and I." He walked closer to him — hesitantly, as Mac's cold stare intimidated him to the core.

The deputies all pointed their rifles to his head, as if one wouldn't be enough to control him. Mac remained quiet; gaze switching from Dorman to Charlotte repeatedly. His mind burning as he calculated all the ways he could escape, yet for the first time, he couldn't. He glanced back at her and she gaped at him with a furrowed face, as though expecting him to do some magic, for he was the ghost, after all, that everyone spoke of. And yet, he was a mortal man in the end. One of bone, flesh, and sinew. A man of shape and mass.

He couldn't escape, he shook his head to her subtly.

"We met in Bisonhorn, Mr. Kinnon. Ya reckon how? Or would miss Charlotte like to explain herself?" He glanced over at her, an evil grin planted underneath his mustache. Charlotte swallowed awkwardly, fearing for Mac to hear the truth she had forgotten herself. Yet Mac did not care to dwell in the past, for her heart confessed more than Dorman's mind game could. He frowned, agitated; wondering how they found them here.

"I suppose she is a little shy." Dorman chuckled. "She was so kind to let me know ya legendary self was seen in Boomtown. Not only that, but she offered to chase after ya. Twenty-five thousand bucks ain't little for a whore's daughter."

"This isn't true! I *never* offered this! You came to me! You filthy scum!" she growled and stood up swiftly to grapple him, as the false accusations infuriated her immensely — yet deputies surrounded her in an instant. Mac's jaw clenched tightly; the obnoxious remarks of the sheriff greatly repulsing him.

He was there. In the shadows of the trees. Looming, as her guard along the way, somehow knowing she would get assaulted in a town.

"And, if that wasn't bad enough — she *already had* a lover!" He laughed caustically, glancing between them, amused and satisfied by their uneasy expressions.

"No…this isn't true, Mac. Don't believe anything this snake says!" She warned him, feeling the sudden urge to strangle his lying throat.

"Oh, so the name William Griffiths don't ring a bell to anyone of ya lot?" He scratched his chin theatrically — pretending he didn't know. Charlotte and Mac glanced at each other; his eyes calm and collected, for he trusted her.

"Poor bastard, shot his brains off after all." He teased them, as he noticed Charlotte's eyes burst into tears again, bending and breaking by his verbal abuse. "I suppose he felt betrayed, in the end; betrayed by love, and forgotten by the one he risked so much for…"

"Stop!!!" Charlotte screamed, feeling the guilt creep up on her; crying, she dropped her head to the ground — cowardly, as not to face him. Mac clenched his fists, for seeing her in anguish was more torturous than being trapped within a circle of rifles, realizing what would happen next to him.

They had caught up. He had risked her life, by daring to get too close.

"My apologies, miss. I just figured nobody ever told ya why he killed himself." He leered at her, making sure his tongue's thorns would sting her one more time. "Well, we should be gettin' on." he announced, when Levi strode through the doors.

III

HIS HORSE CAME TO A FULL STOP, right before the wiry fences, the muddy paddocks, and snowed in fields of Holy Ranch. His legs quivered from the relentless galloping through the freezing cold, after trying so desperately to hold on for what seemed an eternity. Dismounting hastily, he spotted the young man moving hay bales to the barn, one after the other, step by step, shuffling through mountains of snow.

"Sir!" he shouted at him, with a break in his voice.

"Yes, sir!" The young man jerked his head around to face him. "What can I do for ye?" he asked — willing to help out anyone that came across him, no matter how busy his tasks were keeping him.

"Tell me, if ya can…" He paused, grasping for a lungful of air. "Did ya… did ya see any deputies or a sheriff come through here?" He panted and leaned himself on the fence next to them, his jacket tangling up in barbed wire.

"Yes…" the young man hummed with suspicion, placing the bale of hay on the ground. "Yes, sir." he said cautiously. "They talked to a lad, and headed up north together." he informed him, taking off his glove to scratch his neck that was itching from the hay, and locked back eyes with him.

"How recently?" he asked him anxiously, shivering beneath his coat.

"Not too long ago, sir. But…I'd be careful; there was a dozen of 'em." he warned him, somehow sensing to do so.

"I appreciate that…" He bobbed his head, and kept staring at him. "Have we…have we met before, by any chance?" He froze in his tracks, as he could have sworn he recognized the man's face.

"No, sir. I doubt it — I would have remembered ye." the young man muttered, picked up the bale again with muscular arms and proceeded on with his chore.

"Boy, ya don't happen to have any…*special* ammunition layin' 'round here?" he questioned discreetly, knowing the fence sold a wide variety of explosives.

IV

"LEVI!!" CHARLOTTE YELLED, RELIEVED, yet his expression seemed unfazed; eerily composed. "Levi?! Do something! Please!" she begged him, then noticed none of the deputies pointing their guns at him.

Mac grinned snidely, able to smell Levi's guilt the moment he passed by him, staring straight at his eyes; eyes that wouldn't dare to look back at him. "Ye snake…" Mac growled, and Charlotte's breath crushed within her lungs — finally realizing what had happened.

"We had a deal, Kinnon. And I heard you was leaving tonight." He stepped back to face him as he chewed on his tobacco, as though to keep himself composed. "I always told you, the moment you leave — it's on." He shrugged derisively, giving him the only excuse he could find.

"Levi!" Charlotte gasped, aghast, and he cut his eyes at her. "Why?! Why did you do this?!" she cried, fumed, feeling the anger coil around her stomach, surging rapidly through her; trust, betrayed, infringed — everyone's trust, that took so long to build up all these weeks.

"I'm sorry, Charlotte, but I would not let such a freak of nature run free no more. I hope you understand." he said earnestly, then glanced at Dorman's face; the only one he felt wouldn't judge him.

"He ain't a freak of nature, Levi!!" She leered, fury only spiking within her chest.

"Get him out of here!" Dorman commanded the deputies, as Charlotte tried to escape and run to him — only for them to grip her arms even tighter and restrain her completely.

"Don't feckin' touch her!" Mac yelled, growled, feeling his wrath come alive again, heating his blood. "If ye touch one strand of hair of hers…"

"Move, loudmouth!" Levi interjected, pointed the revolver to his head — wishing he could put a bullet through his skull.

"LEVI!!!" She scowled, screaming with all her soul.

"It's over." He smirked, pleased. Mac stared at him, then nodded snidely.

The deputies tied up his hands tentatively, as if Mac was something other-worldly; the legendary ghost, finally taking shape and form before their eyes, after decades of being haunted by him.

"No!!!" Charlotte wrestled with all her strength, pulling her shoulders away from the deputies, yet there was only so much she could do.

"It's alright, Charlotte. Don't worry 'bout me. It'll be alright…like we said." Mac reassured her with a confident voice, nodding to her as he turned to face her for the last time.

"No!!! You bastards!!!" she sobbed, screamed, her shrill voice reaching the ranch house — alerting JB and Amara, who were building a fire and cook-ing a stew for the rest.

V

THEY GLIMPSED OUT THE WINDOW TO SEE AN ARMY OF DEPUTIES, pushing Mac with their rifles against his back. Eyes flared in shock, and before Amara could say a word, JB rushed outside. "Hey!" he yelled at them, grabbing their attention in an instant. "What in tarnation ya think you're doin' on my property, ya damn peasants?!" he shouted, feeling his heart drop to the ground seeing Mac nearing the sheriff's wagon.

"Who are you, ya fat slob?" A deputy chuckled with JB's pear-shaped body and short stubby legs, as he pointed his rifle to him.

"Who ya callin' a slob, ya son of a bitch, lookin' like a damn snake on stilts?!" JB started marching towards them, with not a single fear or worry within his body.

"Careful, old man! One step closer, and you'll meet your savior!" he warned him, cocked his gun, ready to fire.

"Spare me your little threats, ya ugly bastard — wearin' a ten-dollar Stetson on a five-cent head, my hairy arse." He fussed, and hobbled down the stairs hastily to get his hands around his scrawny neck.

"JB!" Levi rushed to him, as Dorman followed after him with Charlotte still confined by the deputies behind them.

"Levi! What in the world is going on here!" he asked him, baffled, furious.

"I suppose the day came." Levi mumbled cowardly, as he rubbed his neck.

"What's that supposed to mean, boy? What day?" he asked, watching the deputies open the wagon hastily, with Mac behaving oddly calm.

"The day that innocent folk all over have been waiting for. The monster has been captured, at last." he said, smiled at him with an expression of awe, feeling proud of his accomplishment — hoping he would be, too.

"Monster…?" JB gaped at him, pausing to catch a breath. "Levi, my son. He ain't no monster, he…he needs us more than ever, now!" he said, lips trembling by seeing Mac climb into the wagon; or rather, being forced into it.

"No, mister. This man's a sinner…" Dorman intervened as he walked leisurely towards the wagon, staring at Mac's expressionless face. "And you… are lucky to not have been cuffed as well, just for protecting this sinner…"

he said, cutting his eyes at JB.

"All sins are innocent endeavors, to fill voids…" Charlotte spoke up, suddenly becoming aware of why Mac attempted to go down that road, as she felt herself now nearing it as well.

"Oh, don't ya worry — we will fill the void of so many innocent lives lost…when he swings." He spat on the ground before the wagon, getting ready to depart.

"You're an awful man!!! You're…you…" She choked, losing Mac behind the gridiron, within the shadows, yet these shadows did not belong to him.

"Mr. Krog, please be so kind and make sure the lady doesn't do anything… regrettable." He chuckled, as he got on the wagon with a shotgun waiting by his side. Levi trudged to her, and Charlotte stared at him, dumbfounded, unable to grasp a single thought. She jerked herself from within the deputies' arms, until Levi restrained her as gently as he could — still expecting she would forgive him, expecting her to magically forget about everything.

JB stared at him, with tearful eyes set in utter disappointment.

V I

THE BLIZZARD BLEW WITHIN THE WAGON'S GRIDIRON WINDOW — freezing Mac's face as he glimpsed outside. The area was familiar to his eyes, even if completely covered in snow; the rolling hills shone to him, engulfing the shallow lagoon where cattle would quench their thirst on their sunny grazing days. Yet now they were gray and stark, cloaked in a veil that could bury them whole. He recognized the line of those tiny oak trees that for some reason never fully grew; *how many times did he have to collect the sheep that had escaped from their pens, that went to rest underneath them,* he wondered — too many, he smirked snidely.

Breathing deeply, he eased himself against the wall; each breath, a distinct smell of snow from the north, winter blooms of honeysuckle, somehow reminiscing *her* scent. Charlotte's words still lingered deeply in his mind; loathing himself more than ever for being a wanted man — realizing he was so close to grasping something so beautiful and pure, for the first time in his life; experiencing *love,* as she called it.

Laying pensive in the shadows, his shaggy head held in his hands, as he rehearsed every single word she bravely screamed at him — every haunting emotion it conveyed within him. Yet, how could someone love a stolid monster...*the haunting reflection of himself he captured today,* he thought, and his jaw locked tight in shame.

The wagon drove down the white glen in a rough, hastened manner, undulating over a dirt road now cloaked in silver frost. The wheels trapped pebbles and chucks of snow, the horses heaved, sinking deep, whole wagon shaking as the road turned into a rocky path, barely able to plow through the density — a path that hadn't been taken for a very long time. The wheels finally came to rest; the sudden gasp of silence hitting his ears. Crawling swiftly to the tiny window, he glanced through the gridiron to notice the barn — the barn where stolen liquor and poker cards were hidden in a weathered chest, beneath the moldy straw — the barn where he lit up cigarette after cigarette, with the boy who was just as lost as him. He glanced further away to notice the shacks where the hay was stored, now brutally worn down and deserted, snowed in.

Heartbeat hastened, sweat formed in rugged hands, breath shortened to shallow whispers in lungs — vanishing, suffocating him, as he dared to cut his eyes at *the* house before him. The smell of the mold in his room reached his crooked nose — the bug-infested bed he had to sleep in sent shivers down his spine — bugs, reborn, crawling all over him. The leather belt choked him anew around his neck, and the breath of evil blew into his face. Suddenly, the leaden wind of terror was tangible, and a foreboding air of fear rose. His sharp blue eyes flared in shock and vulnerability, as Dorman opened the wagon with a face of pure menace.

"Welcome home." He winked at him, and bashed the butt of his shotgun against the top of Mac's head — blacking him out at Grossman's Farm.

CHAPTER 65

Vulnerability

I

"I WILL NEVER FORGIVE YOU...NEVER..." Charlotte muttered under her shallow breath, as Levi watched her every move carefully after letting her free in the shack.

"I'm aware...believe me." He sighed in shame. "I never expected you to stop...caring about him." he said, stretching his stiffened back — fixating his envious stare back towards her.

"So? What's your plan? Keep me locked up in here? What is it, Levi?" She snorted snidely, swallowing down a sob, feeling as if her purpose in life was already over.

"No...of course not." He paused to think, realizing that's precisely what he was doing. "You're free to go...I suppose." he grumbled.

"Where are they takin' him, Levi?" she swiftly asked — not caring to hear any useless words out of his mouth anymore.

"Why would I tell you?" He snorted, straightened his shoulders defensively.

"Oh, are you worried I will free him from so many goddamn deputies??" she yelled at him and her throat started to swell again.

He walked towards her. She stood still, yet tall and brave.

"To be honest, Charlotte...I couldn't give a damn where he will be hanged. All I know is that he will, and that's...that's what matters to me. For all the varmints in this world to become less and less, until there's no goddamn more left." He growled, as his tall frame towered over her — hoping to make her feel even smaller, succumb to his threatening stance like a fragile bloom, weighed down by a weed.

"You're delusional…we are all varmints in this cruel world, and perhaps that's how it should be." she hissed, clutching a fist. "Look what you did! You betrayed someone who trusted you!! Tell me, how does this not make you a monster as well?! You led him to his death, you did!!" she cried in anguish, jerking herself away from him, marching to grab Finn and leave.

"Where you going??" He shouted, striding right after her.

"Leave me alone. I'm done here. I'm done with all you traitors!" she yelled, as she threw the saddle over Finn — who was feeling her tension to his bones.

"No! Charlotte! Hear me out! Please!"

"You've said too much already…" She aimed her eyes at him — eyes shrieking in pain, still reaching for someone she thought was within him; a friend, willing to save another. But there was only ashy hollowness in the pit of his chest; carved by odious pride and dark amusement.

Levi watched her mount Finn, and felt his legs crumble underneath him. He strode swiftly towards her, standing beside them, yet eyes avoided his existence. "What…what did you expect, Charlotte? For you and him to live happily ever after??" he exclaimed fervently. "You would have gotten yourself killed by his side, if he wouldn't have killed you first…" he stuttered nervously, clutching the reins firmly — hoping she would change her mind.

"And that's just the thing, Levi…something you seem to not quite understand." She looked down at him with a hopeful smirk. "I'd gladly be killed by his side, if that meant to die next to the man I loved." She kicked Finn's sides and shot out of the shack, burning the tips of his fingers as the reins yanked through them.

II

"WAKEY-WAKEY!" DORMAN STOOD BEFORE HIS SQUINTING EYES, as blood trickled down from his forehead, where a scarlet welt had formed. The blurred vision started to clear, bit by bit, slowly identifying the man kneeling before him. He felt of his hands, tied in chains against a wall — a wall so familiar in shape and size, scent, feel; the brutal coldness groped his spine through his flesh — yet he knew this sensation all too well. Suddenly, he could sense iron and blood, pervading the air with shades and echoes of vivid memories; images assailing him raw, jarring him.

Mac snapped his startled eyes open, to find himself confined in the dark cellar…the same cellar he spent years of his childhood locked within. Years of ongoing starvation — years of rape and abuse — years of making him forget who he ever was; where he even came from. Years of torment, taunting him, beating him, training him, shaping him into the man he is now, years of lessons on how to handle pain, as though his body couldn't feel it. Years of methods to benumb his emotions; to bury them so deep, no one could ever capture them. The breath collapsed within his defeated lungs, and his heart fell below the floor, licked by its filth, tasted by the reanimated carcasses of rats, buried deep within the void of memories.

He instinctively pulled on the chains so hard his wrists cracked, and bled.

"Not so hasty now, Mr. Kinnon…what's wrong? Ya don't like this place?" Dorman pouted snidely, cocking his head.

Quivering, wilting back into a young boy again, Mac couldn't talk for words were tangled up in the blank space of his mind, caught inside his throat, throttling him; he couldn't breathe, for his breath was cut in his lungs, couldn't fixate his gaze on anything around him — he could only feel every single scar across his back and chest sear through his flesh as if though new, raw, and alive. Mystically set ablaze, to remind him what pain really felt like.

He yanked and pulled on the chains in the body and mind of that young boy again, the scrawny figure, a shadow in a gaze. The lifeless mass of flesh, still breathing, still gripping onto life as though there was a purpose, for suicide was sin as well, and fear prevailed misery. He saw them. He saw all the buried memories, suddenly surfacing boldly, sending his body into a state of panic. Shaking. Convulsing, shrinking into that woeful ball of being. He saw *him*. Towering over him, leaning close; the scent, the breathing, the slobbering lips of ominous lust, eyes unholy.

"Yes…yes, yes. Terrible ordeal, ain't it? To be chained up like that…help-less, vulnerable, and alone in such a dark, hollow cellar…" Dorman soughed upon a foreboding leer — anger festering within him, rage seizing him all the more, as the vivid images of his brother's corpse flashed before his eyes.

"G-get…get me out of here!!!" Mac growled in anguish, whole body arched desperately to escape, mind devoid of any sense, for suddenly all there was left was bleakness; a spark of the past drawing him out of his hardened shell, shattering it, smothering it.

"Oh." Dorman chuckled in dark amusement, seeing this legendary killer squirm within his control. "But we're just now getting started…" He pulled out a black Bible book from his coat, waving it snidely before his eyes; studying Mac's expression only languish in utter desperation, feeding him more.

III

"WHAT HAPPENED WITH CHARLOTTE?" JB hobbled his way hastily to Levi, who was standing lost before the shack, fingers still stinging from the harsh rope-burn of leather reins.

"What happened, old man?" He snorted bitterly, cutting his eyes at JB. "She left! She left — she wants nothing to do with us no more." he said, taking in a deep breath to tamp down his anger.

"Ya blame her? This wasn't right what ya did, Levi…not after all we been through. He was part of the family now." he said, shaking his head in disbelief.

"Part of the family?? What the hell are you talking about? He barely said two words to me the whole time he was here!" he growled, poking chew tobacco in his mouth.

"Levi…this man has probably been through some kinda shit we know nothin' 'bout. He's feral, couldn't ya tell?" he fussed, exhaling in regret for the unfairness of it all. "…but I be damned if he don't have a good heart within him, 'cause that's what I saw, Levi!"

"We've all been through some shit, JB! We've all! But we don't go out on killing sprees at the expense of innocent folk! Have you forgotten everything?? Everything he's done? All the articles over the years — all the lost bodies, strangled — drowned — decapitated — hanged — sliced open — dismembered, do I need to go on?! This man has no remorse!" He trudged back to the shack to grab his horse.

"That ain't true, son. He does have remorse… I've seen it with my own eyes! He just…doesn't understand it yet, goddammit!" he squeaked from the core of his heart, then drew in a breath. "Those cold eyes of his don't lie, my boy! There's pain behind them — pain we both can't imagine!" He paced, recalling how lost in his thoughts he was when he found him, after he killed Davenport; how he had never seen such hollow and regretful expression on a man's face before. Levi mounted his horse and strode outside the shack, completely disregarding JB's attempts to convince him about Mac.

"Where ya headed, Levi?" he asked, with the slightest hope he might try to retrieve Mac.

"I'm bringing Charlotte back." he said through a lopsidedly cracked open mouth, still chewing on the tobacco agitatedly.

"You're talkin' mad, son!" JB's eyes flared, petrified of his ominous words. "Levi… don't do nothin' your old self wouldn't do!!" JB warned him, as he saw his eyes disappear within a shield of wrath — barely recognizing the kind-hearted young boy he raised.

I V

"TELL ME, MR. KINNON, HOW DOES IT FEEL TO SEE THIS BOOK AGAIN?" Dorman questioned him, a taunting smile scarring his elderly lips.

Mac breathed heavily — the frozen gush of wind slithered through the cracks in the brick wall above him, touching him, benumbing his whole face with its lashing caress. He recognized the book all too well; the one he was raised with — the one he had to study every single evening, seated on the farmer's perverted lap. The one he was tortured with, having it hammered down his protruding spine; carrying the monster's weight as he stepped on top of it — crushing his frail body as he did. He recognized it as the book he stuffed in farmer Grossman's mouth, after he sliced it revengefully open. Yet, silence paralyzed Mac's mouth, for he didn't have the strength to talk nor defend himself, as though all vigor was sucked out by the jaundiced pages, as though big fat fingers grabbed him with crushing strength, choking the words that attempted to spring from his throat.

"My brother always said ya was a good student…" He chuckled tauntingly, and paced before him back and forth. "He also said ya was a sinner, and no matter how hard he tried to lead ya to the right path — ya kept on choosin' sin." He bit his lower lip, feeling the unbearable urge to stab Mac's body a dozen times — yet he was not permitted to do so, for the government expected him locked up in Rike's penitentiary.

"Yer *brother*…" Mac's eyes snapped open, realizing what this was all about.

"Yes, my brother…a man of God, helping the poor and lost souls like yours, and for what?" He halted, lingering before him, hand squeezing the book. "Do ya remember what your youthful hands did to him?!" He slammed the Bible across Mac's face — his vengeful spit spreading in the air as he yelled at him. Mac spat out droplets of blood, his nose denting once more. A red vein stood out across his forehead as he cut his eyes at Dorman, the book, still with Grossman's blood engraved within it. Somehow, it spoke to him; he heard a croaking voice, slowly amplifying within his head, reminiscing the sounds that would echo in the past, upon every turn of page, unheard by Grossman, yet intensely heard by him.

There was no sound of the friction or the fibers snapping, there was a mellow voice that prevailed instead, and it was at that very last moment of vulnerability, when the subtle lulling reminded him of who he was. That forsaken voice snapped out from the book again, as Dorman held it open, reminding him *who* he had become, *why* everyone feared him.

He leveraged against the ground with the palms of his tied hands, arched his muscular back, and lifted his legs — delivering a brutal kick to Dorman's arrogant face — making him drop to the floor before him.

"Yer brother was a child rapist, abuser, pathetic liar — the most filthy animal I've ever had the pleasure to kill!" He scowled, veins bulging across his neck. "Oh…oh how I enjoyed stranglin' the slobbery bastard alive…how I enjoyed feelin' his pulse, throbbin' underneath me broken nails — feeling his greasy skin slowly give way to flesh, the harder I forced me fingers through it!"

"Shut your forsaken mouth!!" Dorman screamed, yet couldn't dare to face him, stand before him — for suddenly an irrational fear consumed his entire being.

"How I enjoyed tyin' his slimy hands, in those same chains that confined me for years! How I enjoyed carvin' his beloved cross deep into his fat, disgustin' stomach; busting him open like an overripe peach. How I enjoyed drillin' the knife into his eyeballs, while he could still hear them…POP." Mac grinned, as he relived the moment with emphasis — he grinned seeing Dorman crawling away from him, as if he were the Devil incarnate. "Yer brother screamed, Sheriff…he screamed like no other victim ever did, in all them years after. And ye know what I did 'bout it?" He smirked, as the deputies around him pointed their rifles on his head, ready to silence him, yet they quivered.

"I sliced his goddamn mouth open, so he could scream louder."

"SHOOT HIM!!!" Dorman yelled, Mac's haunting laughter intensifying in his head.

"Shoot me already, ye bastards! Do as yer boss says! Shoot already, ye sons of bitches!!" he threatened them, as terrified arms shook the barrels before him. "Shoot me ye damn fools, give me that last thrill…of hearing me own blood spurt out of me thick skull." He laughed at them, and Dorman stood up swiftly, pointing his revolver to his head.

"As ya wish…" he whispered with a writhing voice, eyes locked with his, daring each other.

The trigger was pulled.

CHAPTER 66

Dead in the Meadows

I

TREE BRANCHES BRUSHED AGAINST FINN'S BODY, stretching into them as they trotted deeper into the secluded woods. A path that once was known and clear, suddenly an eerie maze covered in thick layers of snow.

"Finn...I don't know where we're going...I don't know if it even matters..." she cried, unable to get Mac's distressed face out of her head.

Finn listened carefully; ears pinned back to hear every breath she took, watching out carefully for any cues she might give him. Legs sinking deep into the snow — cooling his abscessed hoof, making it easier to bear the ride.

"They're gonna hang him, Finn... they're gonna hang him just like that... and I...I can't do nothing about it." She sobbed tensely, feeling her body stiffen from panic; limbs benumbing, pain and despair overwhelming her senses. "Remember how he pulled you out of that iced water, my sweet boy? He rescued you too. Without him, you wouldn't be here, Finn." She swallowed down a torrent of tears, lungs expanding instinctively to be able to breathe.

"He saved me more times than I can count; yet he didn't have to. He didn't have to risk his life for me, yet he did...he selflessly did..." her eyes swelled up, as she'd wept relentlessly for the last hour. "...and now, he's gonna be hanged...murdered...and I didn't even say goodbye." She gasped, grasping for air, then looked up at the sky, spotting a group of ravens fly above — steadily, as if they were taking the same path together, shadowing over her. Her head bowed back down, eyes absently nailing at the cantle.

"All I said was...that I loved him..." She leaned over Finn's neck and embraced him tightly, burying her face into his winter fuzz — exploding into tears — screaming, as she couldn't silence the agonizing pain she felt tormenting her.

"Charlotte?" His voice, a blade in her windpipe. Levi emerged wickedly behind them, for he had followed Finn's hoofprints in the snow — laid out like a red carpet before him.

I I

A TWELVE GAUGE DOUBLE-AUGHT BUCKSHOT SHELL blasted through Dorman's body; dropping him to the ground as a torrent of blood gushed out from his stomach. Mac locked eyes with the dying man, as he kneeled before him — Bible pressed upon his abdomen, clutched as though upon a prayer, barely covering the wound — slowly soaking all his blood into the weathered pages, gurgling through his last breaths in an agonizing death.

Yet before Mac had any chance to identify the shooter, smoke rapidly filled up the cellar. To their panicked eyes, the deputies rushed to find their way out, fearing there was an explosion about to happen. Suddenly, cold fingers awkwardly clasped the chained hands — freeing them from their restraint. Mac listened carefully to the man's movements, trying to identify the sound of his walk. "Mickey?" he questioned with a grin, recognizing his shallow, nervous breathing — the trembling fingers he always got under pressure.

"We need to get out of here, Mac! Smoke's gonna clear soon!" Mickey urged him, as he helped him stand on his feet.

"How did ya…how did ye know?" he asked him in awe, feeling his heart oddly warm up to see his face again.

"It don't matter now, my friend. We gotta leave! Deputies are surrounding the building — do ya know a way out, without being seen?" He glanced around himself, seeing for the first time the cellar Mac always spoke about; feeling his skin stand erect in terror at the sight of it.

"No. There ain't…" He shook his head, and grabbed Dorman's revolver from his blood-stained hand. "…but we can make our own path out of here." He smirked, and spun the gun between his fingers.

III

"YOU RECKON SHE'LL COME BACK WITH HIM?" Amara asked JB, as she was cleaning the glass window nervously.

"Oh, Lordy. I think the gal don't want to come back — for good reason. But...I'm really worried 'bout Levi." He sighed, observing Amara's hand scrub the same spot over and over again.

"How you mean?" She turned her face to look at him with concern.

"Oh...well...I don't know. He just had this...expression I hadn't seen before. Not since his father died, anyway." he muttered, as he snatched his hat off to scratch his bald head.

"I'm sure Levi won't do anything he would regret later on. He is very level headed — more than anyone of us. Besides, it's Charlotte's loss for not giving him a chance, and running after a degenerate instead." she growled, feeling pleased for Mac to have been captured after all.

JB brushed his beard, agitated. "My lady, if there's one thing I learned in my life — and it was a very expensive lesson, let me tell ya." He spread his hand open, peeking at his ring still shining around his finger. "Ya cannot force love." he mumbled, as tears formed in his elderly eyes. "And it takes some damn powerful feelings to chase after someone like Mac." he said in earnest, swallowing dryly and repeatedly, as the lump in his throat only swelled. "The gal loved him — it was clear as night and day, and he loved her back..." He sighed, bowed his head and shook it, then side-eyed Mac's leather hat still hanging on the wall.

He reminisced the way he always stared at Charlotte at the dining table, around the fire; how he always watched Levi protectively when he got too close. How he murdered Davenport instead of him, after they danced and kissed before his eyes — how he chose to remain by her all this time, until that very instance. He thought her heart belonged to Levi, and he loved her too much to fight him over her.

"This animal don't know about love..." Amara murmured, flustered, not willing to accept that he could fall in love with anyone but her.

"Even the wildest of beasts, can have their heart be tamed."

IV

"LEAVE ME ALONE, LEVI." SHE ORDERED HIM STERNLY, and kept on trotting away.

"No. I can't!" he grunted. "What happened to *us,* Charlotte?" He trotted his horse next to her — squeezing them onto a tiny path between slender lines of trees.

"To us? This was just one night, Levi! And…to be honest, I wasn't so sure about it either!" she hissed, reflecting on how forceful he was with every gesture; deaf to her pleadings, blind to her struggle.

"Oh really? That's why you enjoyed it so much?!" He growled with the unfairness and blatant lies she spoke out.

"No, Levi!" She turned Finn's face towards him, blocking the way of the path. "No! I wasn't planning for this to happen! But I let it, you're right! If you really care to know — I am not good at standing my ground, because that's how I was raised to be. Being a whore, who accepts any filthy behavior from men, is all I've seen in my life! So aside from that, no. This didn't mean anything more to me than…just what it was. A pleasure of the moment. It didn't mean more to me; you didn't mean anything deeper to me! And you never will!" She leered at him, feeling the satisfaction refresh her soul, being able to finally speak her thoughts and cooped up feelings.

Levi stared at her in awe; shocked to hear these words leave her luscious lips; the ones he always fixated on, and craved to feel all over his body. "You… you haven't given me a chance, cowgirl!" His voice weakened and broke, as he saw her trot away into darkness.

"There is no chance." she mumbled, then heard his horse trot faster. She squeezed Finn's sides, urging him to lope — as Levi was right behind her.

"You really think you can just leave like that now??" he yelled, as Finn's legs struggled tensely to lope through the deep snow.

Charlotte's heart raced, slamming against her ribs, realizing this wasn't the same Levi she had met. His voice suddenly sounded different; ominous, and oddly similar to the O'Donnell. "Finn…come on…run, boy. Run!" she whispered urgently to him, and he pinned his ears forward with utmost concentration to navigate through the snow, leaping over it faster.

Levi galloped right behind her, with a grin of dark satisfaction plastered on his face as his horse was trained to maneuver through such terrain, and intuitively knew when there was a target before them he had to reach. Its hooves' clopping sounds against the hardened snow reached her ears, closer and closer by the second.

"Finn!! Come on!!" she yelled, and he snorted — bolting as fast as he could.

"We can play this game all night, cowgirl! There's no point in resisting no more!" He took out his bolas, clasping them tightly in his enraged fist.

Charlotte took a sharp turn, making them leap down a hill — trusting Finn's sure-footed legs to land safely down. Levi followed right after, sliding down, leaning his body weight back to balance, swinging the bolas in his hand. The sound of the air whirling around hit her ears, making her turn her head behind worriedly — seeing the shadow of bolas flying right at her, as Finn kept on galloping into the blanket of pure white snow.

V

"STAY BEHIND ME, YE HEAR?" MAC ORDERED HIM, knowing Mickey wasn't used to any gunslinging.

"Mac...I...I don't know if I can do that..." he stuttered nervously, thinking of his family waiting patiently for him back home.

"Ye can. Just stay behind me, and in cover at all times. It ain't that many. We can do this, Mickey." He shook his shoulders, reassuring his worried face.

"Alright...alright..." He swallowed nervously, then cocked the shotgun in his hands.

"Yer brave, Mickey. Always was." He patted his shoulder, realizing he'd saved him once more. He kicked the cellar's door wide open, sliding into cover against the walls of the house. "Stay low." he ordered as he sneaked across the open room, heading to the row of fogged-up windows, with Mickey loyally following right behind him. He peeked through the glass, to notice the deputies aiming their rifles at the building. "Bastards..." He scowled.

"Ya reckon we can take 'em?" Mickey questioned with a shaky voice, as he studied Mac's blue eyes — not betraying any hint of worry.

"Sure." He smirked at him. "Got any of those smoke grenades left?" He faced him with a cinched brow — impressed to find he carried such a thing.

"Well…I got one left…a fella at Holy Ranch gave them to me." He pointed, as he thought back on the young man helping him out.

"Did he? Holy Ranch?" He wondered suspiciously, as he didn't expect anyone there to be smarter than their flocks of sheep.

"Yeah. Very odd fella. Kind, but odd." He shrugged and Mac bobbed his head; gaze darting away.

"Mickey…I want to ask somethin' of ye." He sighed, before he raised his gun to the window pane.

"What's that, Mac?" Mickey mimicked the same motion with his shotgun.

"Her name's Charlotte." he said, then looked through the revolver's sights. "Brown hair, hazel eyes — she's a wanted woman…" He swallowed nervously, as Mickey suddenly realized who he was talking about — the lady at his very own saloon. "If ye come across her, Mickey…would ye tell her that I…" He clenched his jaw tightly, eyes glistered. "That I uhm…" His aim started to quiver, for he couldn't speak out the words no matter how hard his brain repeated them in his head, blocked by a mental barrier, welded by menacing hands.

"I understand, my friend. I will." He placed his hand on his shoulder with an endearing smile. Mac nodded his head, a smile peacefully carved upon his dried-up lips — finally able to give his full focus to the task at hand.

> *"Come out ya Ol' Grossman*
> *come out and let's fight like men*
> *Show yer God how ya sinned*
> *behind yer filthy bibles"*

Mac started to hum softly, with eyes aimed at the deputies.

> *"Tell him how we drank whiskey*
> *and toast the Devil's health*
> *As yer fat slob self*
> *chased us in the meadows"*

Mickey continued, knowing the shanty all too well. Only this time, the boys' voices were deeper and weathered.

> *"The time is comin' fast*
> *and the day we think is near*
> *When Ol' Grossman won't*
> *make us run like hell away"*

Mac took the smoke grenade off Mickey's hand.

> *"As we sharpen up our blades*
> *and we tighten up our grips*
> *That nasty Ol' Grossman*
> *will lay dead in the meadows"*

Mickey raised his shotgun again, feeling the sudden boost of confidence within him.

> *"Will lay dead in the meadows…"*

Mac hummed, slammed the window, and threw the smoke grenade at the deputies — with his flurry of gunfire following right after.

CHAPTER 67

Black Feathers

I

A SUDDEN CHOKE TOOK THE BREATH OUT OF HER LUNGS; the bolas wrapped tightly around her neck, like a spider tangling prey within its web, making her fall off the galloping horse beneath her. Finn bolted; taking off into unknown paths before him — limping heavily, as the strenuous ride through the hard snow destabilized the abscess again.

Levi's heavy footsteps slowly approached until they hit Charlotte's ears, as she struggled to take the shallowest of breaths — gripping the bolas tightly; trying desperately to untangle them from her dainty neck.

"I told you, Charlotte. We can play this game all night, or…" He kneeled right before her with a cocked head, as though grasping for a sense of regret. "…we can start to behave ourselves a little, ah?" He spat his chewing tobacco to her side, as its bitter taste suddenly became overpowering. Charlotte felt herself become light-headed, as the bolas kept on squeezing her the more she resisted. "I would help you out there, but…I'm afraid you would just run away again." he said, took out his rope, and reached to tie her hands together.

Charlotte started kicking at him with all the strength that remained in her benumbed legs — crawled away from him, bare hands sinking deeper into the snow. Yet his anger amplified, making him grab her legs hastily — binding them together in an instant — realizing she was the lightest victim yet; realizing the restraint required of an innocent body.

"W-why…" she sobbed, panicked, barely making a sound as the dizziness consumed her, breathing only with the top of her lungs.

"Shut up!" He slapped her leg, and reached for her shaking hands. "I'll get the bolas off of you, when you stop resisting!" he offered with a grimace, tying her hands together with the rope — biting the corner of his mouth in total concentration. He loosened the bolas; and she gasped, drawing in a deep breath of the fresh cold air. Filling her tortured lungs, after struggling so long for a hint of oxygen. "I'm sorry, Charlotte. I'm sorry…" he uttered words that only hurt her even further with their irony, and sat down beside her tied-up self. Charlotte kept quiet; not wishing to risk getting her voice muted — her only last defense. Suddenly a stranger like O'Donnell seemed more inviting than her own once-friend. Suddenly Levi seemed miles away, and yet too close.

"Talk to me, Charlotte. Talk to me." he begged her — eyes starting to water, hand clasping her leg, for he himself couldn't understand what he was doing. She avoided turning her head towards him, for sudden repulsion and hatred overwhelmed her — skin crawled with the unfairness, skin burned by his touch — scorned to realize she once trusted this man, giving herself to him. "I am not a bad man, Charlotte. That I am not. My heart's…I suppose, my heart's broken." he muttered, and sipped down on his bottle of moonshine.

"So you're wanting to break mine…" she whispered subtly, as she thought of Mac being captured; tortured, hanged to his death — as she thought of Finn being gone; for the first time ever, not striding right back to her.

"No…I'd never, Charlotte. I'd never." He sobbed, while the moonshine kept on running lower and lower, disappearing into his slurred mouth — drowning all his common sense and inhibition.

II

MICKEY'S SHOTGUN PAINTED A HOLE INTO A DEPUTY'S BODY, and he took cover swiftly — cocking his gun, ready for the next one.

"Breathe. Slow." Mac instructed, head shooting two men already through the glass. Mickey nodded, yet his hands had started to shake uncontrollably — frightened, for he had never killed a man before; he wasn't the kind to settle disagreements at gunpoint, nor even create ones, he was a family man — he longed for the invaluable peace and quiet.

"Easy, son." he muttered softly and glimpsed down at Dorman's gun belt, strapped loosely around his waist, counting the remaining bullets — calculating how to make them last.

"Mac…I've, I've…I've only got one shell left in the—the chamber…" he stuttered in panic; realizing he didn't come prepared after all.

"Keep it. Use it in a tight spot — for yerself only. Ye hear?" he ordered him, peeked over the window, noticing the deputies still shooting at them — covered behind deserted wagons and shacks. He aimed the revolver at the wagon, waiting for the man's head to appear again — patiently anticipating, as the bullets brushed near him.

"Kinnon, I'd advise you to get your arse out of there pretty soon! Things won't end pretty, otherwise!" A deputy threatened, then saw his partner suffer a bullet in his skull.

"What's he talkin' about, Mac?" Mickey questioned him — feeling the threats clutch his stomach, as he glimpsed at the deputy's hand holding a stick of dynamite. Mac glanced over at him, noticing the unbearable distress in his friend's eyes.

"Mickey, stay here. I'll go out and take care of 'em." he mumbled with great confidence, as though he could handle all the deputies on his own.

"Mac!! They'll kill ya!! There's too many!! Don't be talkin' crazy now, brother!!" He reached for his shoulder, as he saw his eyes fixate on the door.

"I've lost more important things than me life, Mickey. The least I can do is make sure ye get out of here safe." He glanced over at Mickey's shocked self, knowing he had a family waiting on him — knowing he himself had no one, *no one other than her,* who he shouldn't have anyway. "So, do me a favor and stay the hell behind cover!" he commanded, and Mickey's hand slid off his shoulder the moment he stood up and ran out the door.

III

"I JUST NEVER THOUGHT I'D BE…TIED UP, by someone I trusted — hunted down by you, Levi. I *never* thought…" She paused to take a breath, as fear and anger consumed every fiber of her being — making her tremble from the rush of adrenaline that still remained. "I never thought you'd do such a thing, not after everything you pretended to be." she growled, feeling Levi's drunk presence pollute the air she breathed.

"I'm — I'm just, the s—same." His slurred words came out of the liquor bottle, as he wrapped his arm around her shoulder unapologetically.

"Please…please, Levi! I need to…I need to find Finn." She begged him, his poisoned smell hitting her nose — not much different than the one in Marysville; only this time it stung far deeper — far more personal.

"I…I don't think so, cowgirl. He can t-take care…of his own arse." He chuckled, and leaned towards her face — grabbing her jaw abruptly, planting his dehydrated lips on hers, bruising her.

Charlotte could hardly move; there was no point in resisting anymore. The feeling of despair and defeat lingered within her stomach — screaming internally, clenching teeth, paralyzing herself for she knew any squirming would only satisfy him more.

"Isn't that…b…better?" He smiled into her eyes, even as tears betrayed her emotions. He forcefully laid her flat to the ground and continued kissing her lustfully. She wept — keeping her frosty lips locked as hard as they could press against each other.

"Don't…don't worry. I'll — I'll take you home…" He soughed, took out his knife to cut through the rope around her legs. "Won't need this now, will we?" he added; an ominous smirk hollowing his heart furthermore, as the sudden harsh sound of a rip freed her feet. He picked up the pace. Hastened. Breath turned into a pant, restless, he groped her again.

Charlotte watched him carefully, as he forcefully wrapped her legs around his waist. Sensing his thoughts and sickening desire, she remained still, waiting patiently for the right moment to attack. She studied his eyes, circling in all directions — so apparent how the liquor got into his covetous mind. She glimpsed back at the shine of his knife, mistakenly placed on top of the hard snow, right next to her hip — begging to be picked up, yet her hands were tied.

"I just…just want…want you so much, Charlotte." he stuttered, as he unbuttoned her pants possessively.

IV

"COME AT ME, YE HOPELESS BASTARDS!" MAC SCOWLED, shooting down a deputy off his mount — his badge exploding off his chest, as the bullet drilled through it. The deputies peeked out at him, intimidated as he stood before them, anticipating the next man to kill. "Lazy lot yer sheriff hired…or just feckin' dumb."

He laughed, for no heads dared to poke out from their hiding spots anymore. "Eejits…" he leered upon a whisper, lifting his gun with a steady grip and a lustful aim to kill; pointing at each silhouette the guiding moon above him illuminated — counting men, matching them with the few bullets remaining in the cylinder.

"Give it up already, Kinnon! It's over, and so is your cursed legacy!" one of the men yelled over a tower of barrels.

"Nothin's over, boy…ye can kill me all ye want, but bigger monsters will come after ya in yer time." he growled and shot through the wagon, piercing a man's skull. "Four." he soughed to himself and loaded another bullet, spinning the cylinder, cocking that golden Remington Model 1875 again.

V

HE PULLED OFF HER WEATHERED BOOTS, baring her cold feet in the freezing snow, and yanked off her pants obsessively — unbuttoning his own too, for *his own* discomfort was too much to bear. Jittering.

"Why, Levi? Why…" she asked him calmly, as calm as she could compose herself, as calm as she could hide her tears and the agony she felt; looking at the man she once trusted and cared about.

"Why?" He snorted, almost wailed.

"This isn't the Levi I met…" she cried, muffled, muscles constricting.

"No." He pouted, quivering. "You don't *deserve* the Levi you met, cowgirl." he growled and she hunted for his eyes, hoping to pull some sense out of them.

"Why are you doing this…why…" she repeated, yet was met by a blank wall of creeping lust.

"'Cause you owe me, since…since last time." he uttered urgently, feeling himself get stiffer. "Last time you left me hanging, Charlotte." He gasped, taking out his junk. "You left me hanging, girl." he grunted, the warmth between her legs reaching him, luring him in.

"Owe you?" She drew in a big gasp of air, fear intensifying the moment he lifted her legs on his shoulders. She jolted, yet he clutched her firm. Her mind raced, breath cut in her lungs, panic sat atop her, chest constricted, heaved, choking her — fingers benumbed from being dug into the snow for too long. She glanced at the knife, still with its blade gleaming brightly, as her innocence's light slowly dimmed. Petrified, she glanced back at him, unable to grasp the infringement of their friendship.

"Levi…no…NO…please!!" She panted, as he pulled her close.

"Shut up…" he muttered, as though in sharp concentration, fighting against the blur of his poisoned senses.

"Please don't do this…don't do this!! I trusted you!!"

Quivering, cramping up, she wailed, begged.

"And I trusted you, Charlotte…"

"I thought you were my friend, Levi!!" She screamed, as she felt *him* push against *her*. "Monster!!!" she cried, yanking away her legs, pushing against his chest violently — freeing herself from his evil for a split moment, long enough to grasp a lungful of air, long enough to shift away.

"Shut the fuck up, you whore!" He scowled and leaned towards her, trying to grab her again — yet she started crawling away like an injured dog — desperately searching for the ground to step on.

"Leave me alone!!! I warn you!!" she screamed, yet the despair cracked her voice — betraying her fright, her vulnerability, feeding his ego all the more, pumping vicious blood within his veins. She screamed, yet her echo muffled in the somber woods of frost. Groping her feet, he pulled on her, wrapping her legs around him again — quickly shutting her mouth with a harsh hand, pressing hard against her lips.

"I know you fucked Mac. You filthy thing!" he yelled, and forced himself inside her; raw, alive, crawling within her like a maggot, feasting at her last ounce of purity — breaking the only thing that hadn't been broken before — tearing through her, like a soulless piece of meat.

Charlotte screamed beneath his wicked hand, writhing in anguish and woeful harrow — relentless pain; a pain she'd never felt before, pain that was supposed to be overpowered by tender, guiding eyes from the one she loved. Eyes that she would long to lock with, for the rest of her life — yet this, this wasn't what she envisioned, what she waited for, for so long — it wasn't *him,* it wasn't *Mac.*

V I

"TWO." HE SOUGHED, SPINNING THE WHEEL AGAIN. "I can see yer shadows shiverin'…what happened? Ya need a damn sheriff to encourage ye bastards?" He smirked and leaned against a wagon, anticipating the next one to threaten him.

"Yer sheriff's dead — just like his goddamn brother."

"You're sick in the head, Kinnon!! You're goddamn sick!!" the deputy screamed, rifle shaking between his hands.

"Oh, I'm a lot more than that, me lad. A *lot* more." He strode slowly towards the wagon where the deputy's voice betrayed him, spinning the empty wheel once more. His confident steps reached the man's ears — feeling his heartbeat pulse up his throat, freezing him into place.

Suddenly, the ghost of a man emerged before him, dropping his jaw to the ground. Mac grabbed him from his neck without a second thought, and slammed the revolver against his face — grabbing his rifle before it hit the ground. He shot the man in his chest, and a pool of blood gushed over him.

"Sufferin' ain't for the weak…" he muttered, setting his eyes upon his tormented gaze for a fleeting moment. His face furrowed; suddenly his body froze in place, noticing the torture the man's eyes expelled; noticing his own heart drop to his stomach — feelings of guilt and empathy surging through him, as the man struggled futilely to breathe before him.

"One." the last deputy spoke behind him, his rifle touching Mac's head.

Yet that last shell drilled through him, making him drop to his knees like a stone in a puddle of water. Mac turned around to face Mickey, standing with his shotgun still pointed, as the shock paralyzed his hands in place.

"Mickey…" he said, barely audible, locking eyes with him.

"I…I…I shot him for ya, Mac." He quivered in shock.

"Ye did…" He nodded calmly, watching his finger still kissing the trigger. "Put down that weapon now, me lad." Mac urged him calmly, as he looked around himself to notice the pile of corpses spread out across the yard.

"Put it down, Mickey…" he repeated and Mickey bobbed his head.

Feeling his feet planted like ancient roots deep into the ground, he lowered his shotgun, breaking into tears. Mac nodded to him, walked towards him and pointed the gun's barrel away from Mickey's boots.

"Good lad…" he said, then grabbed a deputy's mount and turned it into circles to calm it down, facing him again. "Ye did good there, Mickey." he said, hopped, and threw his leg over the saddle. "I owe ya…again." His fist struck gratefully against his chest, locking eyes, he nodded earnestly to him.

"I'd do it anytime again, Mac. Ya don't owe me nothin', brother." He gave him a wide smile — reminiscing how this quiet young boy brought life into his meaningless childhood. How he always admired him as the greatest role model; *and here he was now, gunslinging by his side,* he thought to himself, making his smile crack even wider. "Mac…need to go back to my family; told them I'd be there by dawn." he then said.

"'Course." He nodded down at him, clutching the reins in his hand.

"Was…good seeing ya again, my friend. Perhaps you'll join me one day for a drink? Now we won't be worried 'bout that ol' lunkhead." He chuckled, making Mac smirk in shadow.

"Sure. Sure, me lad." he muttered, glancing over the crop fields — feeling a sense of serene victory within him.

"Won't keep you longer. I…" He paused awkwardly, then drew in a big breath of courage. "Mac…you…you was always like a brother to me." He tilted his gaze down at his boots, shying away, for he'd longed to mutter these words for decades.

Mac swallowed down a lump, as he glanced at Mickey fiddling his thumbs nervously. "Ye was too." He smiled at him, and kicked the sides of the horse — vanishing steadily through the field, trampling down the dried-up crops with immense satisfaction, merging within the hoarfrost of an ebony night.

VII

THERE WAS EMPTINESS BURIED WITHIN HER; shattered remains, faced by the jealousy and greed above her. Screeches of pain, now but a faint whisper of hopelessness. Blossoms, stained with rage. Deflowered in vain. Heart covered with thorns entangled. Suddenly, there was no place lonelier than what she felt within. Woe froze her mind.

Her strained neck, now resting benumbed on earth's coldest pillow — freezing and deafening the ears to sounds of the eeriest grunts. Bloodshot misty gaze, now hollow — counting the ravens circling atop, through snow-capped branches; closer, and closer.

Half shut and defeated eyes, now wide open with a question, as the black feathers brushed tenderly over the humiliating face. Throaty and hoarse gurgling croaks — suddenly, emerging screams of distress.

Charlotte propped herself up, alarmed, as she witnessed ravens' claws tearing into Levi's face — drilling their beaks into his wasted eyes, time and time again; rending his eyeballs violently apart within their own sockets — while he struggled to defend himself, wobbling his giant body over her.

She stared in awe at the creatures before her; creatures displaying more empathy than a man with ethical reasoning and a soul. She unfroze her feet and rushed to crawl away, as he kept on yelling in agony — grabbing the birds, squeezing them to their death between the palms of his monstrous hands.

"CHARLOTTE!!!" His angered voice reached her ears, as he felt her captured body vanish from underneath him. Hyperventilating, she hobbled, pants down, trying hastily to lift them up with tied-up hands behind her back.

Fresh blood. Leaking between her inner thighs. Sinfully.

She ran as fast as her panicked feet could take her across the hardpack snow, maneuvering through the maze of trees — her loud, anxious breath betraying her location as Levi pursued her.

Blinded by the ravens' gruesome attack, yet intoxicated enough to not feel the excruciating pain; he ran, and ran, after her — crashing forcefully into trees and stumbling over boulders, yet still not slowing down as his ears faithfully led him to the sound of her footsteps.

Words Kept

I

THE YOUNG MAN RODE THROUGH THE SNOW-COVERED FREELANDS; after a hard day of shoveling manure and stacking hay bale after hay bale in the large barn for the winter — he longed to reach his cabin, warm up his frozen feet.

The path was secluded; guarded by endless lines of bare trees leading up to the highest hill of Hollenberg. The solitude was sacred to him; in a way he despised being surrounded by the townsfolk in Holy Ranch, yet the pay was decent, and he was saving up to upgrade his revolver.

"Ol' Tucker! What a night, ain't it?" he mumbled to his horse, feeling the chilled snow land all over his stubble. "Winter's gonna be harsh, ol' man. For everyone…" he hummed to himself, worrying about his elderly horse pulling through another winter.

Tucker froze in place suddenly.

"Did ye just read me mind, Ol' Tucker?" He snorted, yet Tucker's ears stood alert, eyes flared open; he snorted as though he smelled a threat, or rather the familiar scent of his own. The man leaned over the saddle, squinting through the heavy snowfall, hand gliding down to his revolver.

He heard the sound of hard tapping against the snow — repeating steadily.

"Who goes there?!" He threatened, pulling his gun out swiftly, aiming at the thick haze before him. A loud, impatient snort hit his ears, and dithering for a brief moment, he urged Ol' Tucker to go closer. His eyes widened in shock, a saddled chestnut horse with a wide blaze on its face emerged through the darkness — pawing relentlessly at the ground.

Dismounting his horse, he approached the enormous stallion calmly — yet with every step he took, he'd snort louder. "Easy, lad…" he whispered softly, hands reaching for his distressed face. The horse pawed aggressively, wheezing. The man advanced closer, hand clasping his mane, now patting his neck — noticing the sweat that had formed into icicles all over its coat.

"Ye've been runnin'…from somethin', haven't ye?" he hummed, caressing it. Eyes scanned over the saddle, hands trailed their way to the saddlebags; searching through them discreetly, not wishing to upset the stallion any further. Fingers fiddled through clothes, canned food — pulling out a leather pouch excitedly, hoping to hear the clinking sound of coins. Yet the pouch was light as a feather, and within it, only a single orchid flower.

I I

"WHERE IS SHE?!" MAC STORMED INSIDE AMARA'S HOUSE, finding her and JB still seated around the fireplace — staying up all evening, waiting for someone to come back. Yet their faces turned pale, blanched, as though they'd seen a ghost. Seeing Mac stand before them after being hauled off by an army of deputies; suddenly confirming to them why he's been a legend for decades.

"Where did she go, JB!" he insisted, glancing around the room to find any signs from her.

"Oh Lordy, oh Lordy!" JB gasped, shaking his head alert. "Mac! How? How did ya?" He looked at him, in awe — as Amara tried to pick up her jaw back up from the ground.

"Where is she, ol' man!" he persisted, snatching his duster coat from the wall — motioning for him to follow him outside. JB wobbled after him enthusiastically, as the previous silence and lack of action had been torturing him the whole evening.

"Mac! My boy! How the hell did ya escape??" JB bombarded him with questions, watching him take Roy out of the shack.

"Tell me where she went! Did they take her??" He mounted hastily, noticing his rifle still holstered onto the saddle.

"No. No, no." He bit his lip, unable to find the right words.

"Speak!!" he growled and JB bobbed his head.

"I reckon, I reckon she is with Levi…by now…" he stuttered, reflecting on Levi's wicked obsessiveness to find her — fearing what Mac would do to him, were he to find them. Mac's eyes squinted upon a leer, anger rose in him like a tide, for he suspected as much. "But…but son, please…don't, don't harm him. He…he don't know any better right now." Mac clenched his teeth in frustration; trying desperately to pull himself together. "Where?" He scowled, as he glanced around himself — detecting horse hoof prints in the snow.

"Never mind." he grunted, kicking Roy's sides to lope away.

"Mac!! Mac!!! I need to tell ya…tell ya somethin'!" JB strode after him worriedly, knee cracking in all directions possible as he did.

"What??" he yelled urgently, squinting through the darkness, noticing JB's pear-shaped silhouette hobbling after him.

"Levi! He…he ain't being himself…" he stammered hesitantly, as though he was betraying him. "Be careful…" He sighed, bowing his head in shame.

"Perhaps, he is just that." Mac noted with sarcasm, then rode into the void, leaving JB's words on the edge of his quivering lips.

III

"WITCH!!!" HE SCREAMED FROM THE TOP OF HIS LUNGS, filled up with anger and desperation, the more her swift movements echoed in his head — slowly comprehending how completely his vision was impaired. "You bewitched me!! Blinded me!!" he yelled, tripping over himself, nails hooking onto bark, halting, breathing, recalling how strongly she always stared into his bright green eyes; pretending to be enticed by them, making him believe she wanted him, as much as he wanted her — yet she only used him, and his power, to save and hide a murderer — one she betrayed him with.

Charlotte hid behind trees, trying to abrade the rope against the trunks, yet she couldn't stay long enough to finish the task as Levi was steadily following behind her. Blood rose up to her head, making it throb in unbearable fright. Jittering in panic, caught in an iced cage, she longed desperately to call for her trusty steed, yet was too scared to make a sound — lips too frozen and tightly sealed.

"Why, Charlotte, WHY?!" Levi sobbed loudly, his trembling fingers traveled over his sockets — feeling of their hollowness, the pieces of gelatinous flesh still hanging loosely by nerves and tendons. He recoiled in shock as the effects of moonshine had started to wear off, yet resentment only intensified, the more his irrational thoughts assailed him raw. "I'll kill you when I get my hands around you!! You betrayed me!!!" he threatened, as he heard her startled footsteps pattern her location on the ground.

Charlotte scrambled away, upon noticing his enormous shadow emerge behind her. Her lungs burned hot as fire from running as hard as she could, his gut-wrenching shriek echoing within the forest; so much so that she couldn't tell if he was further away now, or again right behind her. Lost in this labyrinth of identical-looking, yet so foreign feeling woods — ragged trees confining her as the blizzard had started its midnight ride, blowing its frozen dust over the path — covering their footprints, for them to never be found again; muffling the sounds of the unwavering strides of a hunter.

I V

"WHERE'S YER RIDER, LAD?" THE MAN STROKED FINN'S NECK, as he glanced down to his pawing foot — held up from the immense pain that had spread through it. He noticed the swollen leg, and instantly realized something wretched must have happened. He thought of the clothes he discovered in the saddlebags; woman's attire; a scrunched up letter from a loved one — and felt his heart drop to his stomach, knowing that in this weather nobody stranded would make it through the night.

"Yer a smart son of a gun." he mumbled, realizing Finn had stopped running away when he'd reached the man's cabin a few feet below the hill; instinctively knowing he might find help here. The man took his hawser off his weathered saddle, looped it around Finn's neck, tying it up to his saddle horn, then mounted Ol' Tucker again.

Unlike with most strangers, Finn trusted the young man's calm energy; a familiar confidence and serenity he radiated, a well-known scent that lingered within him — and so, he followed him without a fuss. He was exhausted from the relentless running and rushing through the snow, freezing, as the temperature dropped rapidly from his sweaty body. Coughing and wheezing with every step he took, he limped slowly over the hill towards the man's cabin. Steadily led by the man's elderly horse, listening to its arthritic legs crack the steeper they climbed.

"Ye'll be alright. I ain't got no fancy barn, but…a shack will give ye break enough from this weather." he hummed softly, as he glanced worriedly into Finn's defeated eyes — desperately longing to rest for the night. "Don't know what happened to ye, or yer lady, but…we'll — we'll find out somehow." he soughed to himself, leaning forward to support his horse over the hill.

V

ROY LEAPED THROUGH THE HILLS OF SNOW — a task that felt so effortless, compared to conditions up in the Rockies. "Find her, Roy." He loosened the reins, laid them over his neck, as he hunted down the scents of the snow-covered footprints. His mount's blue bright eyes fixated through the hazy darkness, scanning tree after tree — feeling for a sudden, fleeting heartbeat across the woodlands. Fear, the air was laced with; reaching Roy's enlarged nostrils, making his determined strides rapidly elongate. Mac reached for his rifle, recognizing the way his mount arched its neck; meaning they were close to danger.

Charlotte's toes were frozen; starting to turn blue underneath her woolen socks — she ran herself mad going into circles, praying he would just disappear. Praying the snow would swallow him whole, and she'd wake up in the morning realizing it was all just a horrible nightmare. Her body ached, her insides burned, stung, as though he was still slashing her with a knife.

She couldn't hear his distraught voice or obsessive stomping any more, as the blizzard was roaring like an awakened elemental beast through the trees. She couldn't spot his unholy shadow on the ground, for the snowfall suffocated the guiding light that had been warning her all this time. She drew in a deep, courageous breath, and dared to look behind — snatching fleeting blurred glimpses around, to notice if he was still there — yet the silhouettes of trees doubled and tripled the more she stared, the more her hazel eyes squinted through the whiteout. She cowered in the darkness as her heart hammered loudly in her ears, taking some steps back tentatively — carefully feeling the earth dissolve beneath her feet — lungs catching a fleeting breath, as her body suddenly crashed against his.

She let out a screech of cooped up terror, and he covered her mouth swiftly — one that made the snow fall off the branches around them; one that would echo into the woodlands — alerting any predator close by. Her confined shoulders, struggling to escape his vascular arm around her stomach — teeth gnawing into his hand unforgivingly, kicking at him repeatedly.

"Shh, shh…" He kept his hand over her mouth, now bleeding from her ferocious bites. "Lass, it's me!" he whispered urgently in her ear — feeling her strained, wrestling body slowly unfurl into his arms.

Charlotte recognized the deep, sedating voice; making her break into tears of disbelief, wilting into his arms in blind trust. She turned around cautiously, locking eyes with those dark ocean blues she knew so well. Her heart wrung within her. "No…it, it can't be!!" She gasped, sobbed with a harsh voice, throat burned by the relentless cold. "This is not real…this is not real, it…it can't."

She buried her face in his neck, heartbeat ripped out of her chest.

"I told ye I'd come back…" He caressed her face with trembling fingers, longing nothing more than to be close to her, for the viscerally refreshed image of the cellar still lingered in his mind.

He grabbed her and pulled her in for a crushing embrace — freezing the moment for a split second, where no guns were firing, no people were struggling to survive — just them; their exhausted bodies entwined with each other, chest to chest, heart to heart, falling snow enveloping them in a veil of haze.

"Take me out of here!!" she whispered against his cloth, wailing in an upwards spiral of panic, still able to hear his wicked grunts, still able to feel him tearing her apart. "Please! Take me, take me out of here! He's coming! He's here! Somewhere! Anywhere!" she yelled frantically, quivering within his arms.

He pulled back and took out his knife swiftly to cut the rope from her hands. "Stay still." he ordered calmly, and freed her hands — feeling the growing, revengeful urge to hunt him down and slice his chest open in ways he himself could not even imagine yet.

Charlotte wrapped her arms around him tightly — collapsing into him, feeling his heart beat against hers, cradling each other tenderly. "I'm so afraid, Mac. I'm so afraid!!" She clutched his coat in her fist, squeezing tight, shaking from the rush of adrenaline that was keeping her alert on this ongoing chase; letting out a huge exhale of suppressed breath.

Mac took off his coat, and wrapped it around her.

"…He'll pay for it." He leered, enraged, as he noticed her pants — torn.

"No! No, Mac! You don't understand, he…he is different! He is ungodly! He is…" She paused briefly, recalling the ravens feasting on his eyes. "We have to leave!!" She grabbed his hand and started striding through the snow; legs sinking deeply into it — making her lose her balance at last. Mac scooped her up, held her in his arms, and rushed through the woods — feeling her tears of distress brush against his face. "He…he's, he's gonna kill us!!" she stuttered, petrified, fingers hooked onto his shirt, eyes scanning in hysteria behind every single tree they passed.

"He won't." he muttered confidently, glancing behind him, cutting his eyes left and right, making sure they weren't being followed.

"Mac…" She gasped, clasping him tighter. "Thank you. Thank you! Thank you so much!!" She sobbed uncontrollably, feeling the first hint of relief slither through her, unable to grasp how he escaped, unable to ask him how he did.

"Don't." he hummed calmly as he reached Roy, who was patiently waiting for him to return.

"No. Don't leave me!" she cried, distraught, wrapping her legs around his waist, refusing to let go.

"I ain't, lass." he said in confusion, clutching her legs, unwrapping them.

"I ain't…" he said, trying to raise her up to the saddle.

"Don't leave me again, Mac. Please. Never again!" she repeated, panicked, quivering with the thought of never seeing him again.

"Woman, we gotta go." he said sternly, sensing a sudden danger lurking in the woods close by.

"Just don't leave me…" Her eyes shut as she spoke, feeling the exhaustion finally take over her. Mac watched her struggle to stay alert, fearing she was hit by hypothermia, lips a bluish tint, face pale as snow.

"I won't leave, Charlotte. Not this time." He grabbed her shoulders, shaking her awake again. "But ye gotta stay with me. Lean on me!" he ordered, and lifted her leg over the saddle.

CHAPTER 69

Good Shot

I

"YER A BIG OL' LAD, AREN'T YE?" THE MAN SMILED in awe after unsaddling Finn in the shack, glancing over at his pronounced muscles and powerful hip. "Sure must be thirsty." he said, offering him a bucket of warm water, yet Finn refused, and kneeled down to lay in the chilled straw instead. Hacking and rasping, he stretched his neck for some comfort.

"Weather ain't being nice to no one…heard some folks lost their cattle overnight. Froze to death…" he hummed to him, listening to the keening wind outside — slamming against the doors, spitting flurries of snow through their cracks. "There's no tellin' what's awaitin' us all." he huffed and covered Finn's body with a blanket, noticing his shivering being. "Won't be easy for us poor bastards, I do know that." He shut the stable door behind him — leaning on it, dithering upon his next move.

"Suppose I'll head back out. Someone must be lookin' for ye, worried sick, or…well." He put his slouched hat back on, snatching a cigarette from behind his ear — studying how well cared for Finn's physique appeared. "Perhaps I'll get paid a good amount for the deed." He sniffed his runny nose, and lit up the cigarette.

11

HE GRABBED THE REINS AND SLID HIS STONE-HARD FROZEN BOOT through the stirrup, yet a sharp knife pierced him violently through the shoulder. "Gahh…" he grunted, groping for the hand that held the knife.

"Mac!!!" she screamed one second too late, eyes flared in shock when she recognized Levi leaping onto Mac through the blizzard. Mac growled loudly, feeling the knife scrape against his shoulder blade — slashing his flesh wide open on the way back out again.

"You son of a bitch!! How many times do I need to warn you to get your hands off of her?!" Levi yelled at him, and Mac turned around to grab his arm swiftly — blocking him from slicing at him again.

"Charlotte! Leave!! NOW!" Mac commanded with a strained voice, fixating his gaze upon the wall of shadow, squinting, noticing Levi's damaged eye sockets — reminiscing farmer Grossman's face before him, so eerily familiar in the way they were carved and destroyed.

Dismounting as fast as she could, she tackled Levi from behind; arms coiled around his masculine neck, trying desperately to choke him with all her strength. "Leave him, you monster!!" She bit his ear and pressed her fist against his throat, as Levi continued to force his knife down upon Mac's face.

"Charlotte, no!! Leave!!" he yelled at her earnestly, for he wasn't able to shoot Levi with her hanging over his back.

"You're fucked, Kinnon. And so is your little whore."

"Shut yer mouth…" he growled, keeping a firm grip around his arm. "Charlotte, leave!!!" he growled, and yet Charlotte kept on squeezing her benumbed arms around him.

"I fucked her, in fact, I did. She is no virgin no more, Kinnon…and I thought you had her first." He punched his elbow onto Charlotte's ribs, making her fall onto the hard icy ground — taking the breath out of her lungs, upon landing harshly against it.

"Ye feckin' bastard…" He kicked Levi away from him, and swiftly pulled out his revolver — yet as he shot at his chest, he realized he still carried Dorman's spent revolver.

"Haha…" He snorted snidely, a sickening sound issued from his throat. "I might be blind as a damn dog, but I know when I hear an empty cylinder. You're in deep shit, you lunatic!" He warned him, reaching for his own gun.

"Mac, run!!" she screamed, launched to him, leaping to dig her nails into Levi's arm the moment he pulled the gun out — shooting at the ground before Mac's boots.

Mac rushed across the snow — tackling Levi to the ground. He confined his body between his legs, punching his macabre face, as the gun slid next to them. "Get the gun, Charlotte." Mac ordered, thumbs pressed into his hollow sockets, while Levi's hands pulled desperately on his arms — the agonizing pain awakening his senses.

Charlotte grabbed the gun with trembling hands, as her adrenaline was pumping profusely again. She aimed at Levi's head, yet the barrel was shaking in all directions. "I…I, I can't!!" she screamed, unable to even see the sights of the gun — fearing she might shoot Mac instead.

Levi slammed his fist across Mac's face, bloodying his nose and cracking his jaw — yet Mac wouldn't stop forcing deep into his sockets' interior walls and pressing them forcefully, until he heard them break. Levi screamed in harrowing anguish, back arched, overwhelmed by pure survival instinct to escape; he punched Mac's wounded shoulder over and over again — making it dislocate, further and further, with every hit.

Mac clenched his teeth and groaned heavily, as he'd never felt such excruciating pain before. He reached to block his fist, yet Levi threw him off, while Charlotte's body froze shocked into place.

Levi climbed up on top of him — taking the knife out again; aiming for his chest, yet Mac's hands swiftly pressed against it — hearing his shoulder crack with every strain, feeling the pain shoot right through him, half of it disconnected already as he pushed past his body's own limits.

"This…will be…the happiest…moment of my life." Levi whispered ominously calm, as all his strength was concentrated on his kill.

"Then yer whole life…was but a waste." Mac scowled, feeling his entire arm benumbing — losing what strength it had left, watching the knife get closer and closer under all of his sheer weight.

POW!

A powerful round shot suddenly into the air, and borne upon it was a sentiment of horror. Charlotte fired the gun into Levi's skull; piercing the bullet through it at point-blank range, instantly dropping him dead atop of Mac. Time froze still as she watched gravity take hold of Levi, pulling him down; hearing her pulse vibrate in her throat, witnessing her fleeting breath escape her mouth — spreading like nothing but fine mist through the void.

I I I

"M...MAC...MAC!" SHE GASPED, QUIVERING WHOLE, STAMMERING. "We...we did it! We did it!!" she exclaimed excitedly; feeling a sense of thrill she'd never felt before; an eerie thrill, after killing a man with a single shot to the head — a man that dared to steal her innocence, infringing any sense of trust within her — now dead, before her doubtful eyes.

She rushed to help pull Mac out from underneath him, for he struggled to throw the heavy body off of him. Levi landed beside him — his expression, still scarring a haunting smirk — a chuckle, painted across his mouth, as he always used to carry, yet eyes were bleak, mirroring the last veneer of soul he died within.

"Good...shot..." Mac soughed with a faint, strenuous breath, coughing.

Charlotte kneeled beside him, helping him sit up against a boulder, jittering hands clasping his chest in great relief. "I can't believe I shot him..." She gasped and he nodded.

"Ye did...me lass." He smiled in her eyes, yet his face was oddly furrowed.

"I couldn't have done it without you, Mac...I would have died here..." She smiled back to him, caressing his face, yet his eyes betrayed a worry.

"Yer safe now..." he said, struggled to say. Smiled.

Charlotte cocked her head in suspicion, studying his expression, as though too serene; she paused her thoughts in shock, as her victorious eyes glided down to Mac's stomach.

He snorted snidely.

Her eyes flooded, lips emulated words they couldn't speak out, the more she looked at the knife's handle sticking out of his puncture wound — blood dripping out — freezing, as it hit the ground. They sat awkwardly in silence for a brief, fleeting moment in time; locking eyes.

Shy; as if they'd never met before.

Worried; as they both knew.

Scared; as they could never be prepared enough.

"Don't. Charlotte…" he mumbled with a wet cough, wiping her tears away with a quivering hand. She tore her gaze away, choking. "Yer a strong lass. I…always knew." He smirked, eyes squinted in pain. "Ye know how to shoot now…" he teased, as though finding themselves back at the shooting range of Hope.

"Mac…don't you dare." She locked eyes with him again, in earnest. "Don't you dare die on me." she cried. "We've…we've been through so much…don't you die on me now…"

"Shh…" His fingers brushed against her cheek, feeling its softness once more. "It was…bound…to happen." He clenched his jaw, as he felt the blade radiate a searing pain through his organs.

"I will…I will ride down to Marysville, and, and…get the doctor, and…"

"I'd rather ye stay…"

Blue eyes flickered in the dark, staring tenderly into hers.

"I can't…I can't lose you, Mac! You're all I have. You're all I ever cared about! My life never meant anything until…until you came along. You promised, you promised to never leave again…" She grabbed his hand — pressing it desperately against her face.

"Look at me. Look…at me, lass." His breathing decelerated within his lungs, as he pulled her face towards his. "Yer…so beautiful…" He frowned, shivering.

"Mac…please. Please don't do this to me…" she wailed, knowing he was running out of time, feeling the sun rise beside them, warming them in the peak of irony. "Don't die on me…not like that! Not so soon!!" she cried, as the pain she felt was intolerable, pulsing up within her chest.

"What ye say…" He chuckled. "I couldn't have…wished for a better way…" He wheezed, lungs struggling to breathe, forcing the words out of his mouth. "…than to die beside ye."

"You're not going to!" she insisted, yet his eyes were losing their witty spark.

"I lied to ye, Charlotte." he said earnestly, gaze not escaping her eyes, holding on to them for dear life, ensuring he wouldn't go without avowing first.

"What...? What do you mean..."

"I...I do *feel*." He cracked a smile on his lips, as though proud of himself to not go completely hollow. There was a scarlet swell to his eyes, glaring at her.

Charlotte felt her heart shatter within herself. She couldn't find the words to speak, as staying composed took all the strength she had. She leaned into him, dropped, wilted in all her tension.

"I love you so much, Mac...I love you so very much..." She pressed her face next to his — feeling his temperature drop by the second. "I love you..." she whispered in his ear, throat swelled up, tears burst from her eyes, heart bled, dying little by little.

He grabbed her hand, placed it gently against his thudding heart. "I...I..." he stuttered awkwardly, as so many heartfelt emotions exploded within him.

"I know..." She caressed his face lovingly, feeling his jaw strain, and lips struggle to let out a sound.

"Kiss me?" he asked worriedly; feeling himself slowly drift away into a dark path with no return.

"Mac...I...I can ride down, and..."

"Charlotte..." He sighed, cupped her face and pulled her close. "I want to shut me eyes, leave this world with this memory...for I ain't got one purer... than yers." he soughed and she nodded, choking, leaning closer.

Her lips brushed softly against his. A cascade of tears coursed down her face, chest heaved, pain throbbed within her. He pulled her closer, breathing her in, letting her light slash through his darkness, as lips locked, and hearts beat as one.

Hand rested on her cheek, taking in the moment — forever to bury it within himself. "Don't...stop..." he begged, a sudden sense of fear brushing by him — longing for her to guide him across.

They kissed; as the mellow sun lit up their faces. As their breaths merged into one. They kissed passionately — in the purest form of love — knowing it would be their last.

They kissed, as his hand slid off her face.

Dropping to the ground.

IV

THEY LAID TOGETHER, SUN MELTING THE SNOW OFF THE BRANCHES; irritating sounds of drops hitting the soil didn't faze her, could not, for benumbed, she wilted within him. Face buried within his, begging for the cold to take her too, arms still wrapped around his neck; pulling herself closer to him — longing for a macabre sleep to suffocate her — never to wake again.

"You saved me...once more..." she hummed softly, staring at his peaceful face — so hauntingly beautiful; brushing his blond hair tenderly with her fingertips. "But nothing will ever save me from this..." she cried, searching to hear her own heartbeat — wishing it would die off already, yet all she could find was a being of woe crawling within her, with knifes for claws scraping at the sinews of her flesh.

The sound of guns squeaking within their holsters hit her ears unexpectedly. Snapping her eyes open, she spotted a dozen deputies searching the woods before her, awakening the wrath within her once again, as she watched them in silence — contemplating what to do with herself, and with Mac's body. She knew she couldn't carry him; she had tried that already, yet the thought of leaving him behind tore her apart.

She started covering him frantically with the fresh snow; burying him as fast as her frozen hands could shovel, as though that would be more dignifying than their eyes setting upon him. She didn't wish for them to know. She didn't wish for anyone to know his legend had dimmed; that his ghost had taken form, only to die the agonizing death of a mortal man.

"I will see you again..." She clasped his hand, cold, frozen. "I promise, Mac." she whispered in his ear, looked at his face — prayed this wouldn't be the last time.

"I love you..." she cried, muffled by her lips kissing his, burying his face within a blanket of snow.

She rushed to mount Roy, tentatively taking a glance back, not wishing to leave, yet knowing Mac wouldn't wish for her to be captured if she stayed next to him. *He died for her to live;* she thought to herself, as she spotted the deputies nearing closer.

V

"TAKE ME...WHERE HE'D TAKE YOU..." She dropped the reins over Roy's neck; feeling defeat and exhaustion consume her entire being. She rested herself over him, his smooth and steady strides underneath her rocking her to a state of trance — counting them, as she started to drift off to sleep.

Roy carried her weight across the woodlands; a familiar, heavy burden he had borne before. He knew who she was; more than anyone else, perhaps. He reminisced his rider's heartbeat intensify every time he thought of her, during their long and strenuous journeys. A heartbeat that once was dull and muffled, suddenly turn vibrantly strong; a burst of colors that could paint the darkest of hearts. For it did his. Roy trusted her; therefore felt bound to care for her, yet as hard as he tried to keep her safe with slow and calculated moves, Charlotte slipped off the saddle — falling unconscious into the snow.

EPILOGUE

GLOVED HANDS CLASPED THE EDGES OF THE DUSTER COAT; pulling her out from the white-covered ground. Dark ocean blues squinted through the snow-fall, as the face of a pale beauty emerged before him. The lantern lit her up, faintly awakening her, as hands held onto her shoulders. Clutching tight, yet grip gentle. Hazel eyes flared in doubtful shock, upon locking with his — as the surrounding darkness of the cold night froze the moment between them.

"M…Mac?" her lips painted the question with a glimmer of hope, as his familiar face cleared before her — noticing the chiseled jawline, the intensely staring hooded eyes, and the long blond hair resting beside his face.

"No…no, ma'am."

ABOUT CHRISTINA MARAZIOTIS

Christina was twenty-seven years old at the time she began writing *Loveletting*. Born and raised in Greece, she has always had an affinity for language; fluently speaking Greek, German, and English. After years of experimenting with different professions, suddenly it dawned on her: writing was the only thing that actually made sense. It all started with a simple prologue in the notes of her phone, and since then, she hasn't missed a single day of writing and working on her very first novel series — breathing life into it, as it breathes life back into her. The primary goal as a writer is to strike certain melancholic chords in the heart while reading, pulling from deeply haunting personal experiences to create books that linger in the mind long after the story is finished. Her stories combine gothic romance, intense adventure with nerve-wracking suspense, entwined with vague and unsettling horror subplots — and a myriad of controversial subjects to challenge any reader's views — all taking place in the historical setting of late 19th century Victorian west. Focus lays heavily on character development, as it is crucial to her and her story; for the reader to bond with the characters, and feel like they're reading about an old friend. Her purpose is for the reader to be transported to another world, escaping from reality, and finding an eerie comfort within a haunting experience.

Printed in Great Britain
by Amazon

19740007R00442